The TYRANNY of the NIGHT

Book One
of the Instrumentalities of the Night

GLEN COOK

TOR®
fantasy

A TOM DOHERTY ASSOCIATES BOOK
NEW YORK

This is a work of fiction. All the characters and events portrayed in this novel are either fictitious or are used fictitiously.

THE TYRANNY OF THE NIGHT: BOOK ONE OF THE INSTRUMENTALITIES OF THE NIGHT

Copyright © 2005 by Glen Cook

A Tor Book
Published by Tom Doherty Associates, LLC
175 Fifth Avenue
New York, NY 10010

www.tor.com

Tor® is a registered trademark of Tom Doherty Associates, LLC.

ISBN-13: 978-0-765-34596-7
ISBN-10: 0-765-34596-X

First Edition: June 2005
First Mass Market Edition: November 2006

Printed in the United States of America

0 9 8 7 6 5 4 3 2 1

For my wife, Carol, for thirty-five wonderful years

The TYRANNY of the NIGHT

It is an age lurching along the lip of a dark precipice, peeking fearfully into chaos's empty eyes, enrapt, like a giddy rat trying to stare down a hungry cobra. The gods are restless, tossing and turning and wakening in snippets to conspire at mischief. Their bastard offspring, the hundred million spirits of rock and brook and tree, of place and time and emotion, find old constraints are rotting. The Postern of Fate stands ajar. The world faces an age of fear, of conflict, of grand sorcery, of great change, and of greater despair amongst mortal men. And the cliffs of ice creep forward.

Great kings walk the earth. They cannot help but collide. Great ideas sweep back and forth across the face of a habitable world that is shrinking. Those cannot help but fire hatred and fear amongst adherents of dogmas and doctrines under increasing pressure.

As always, those who do the world's work most dearly pay the price of the world's pain.

CHAOS SCRIBBLES WITH NO REGARD TO LINEAR OR NARRATIVE thought. Events in Andoray, in the twilight of the sturlanger era, when the ice walls are still a distant curiosity, precede those in Firaldia, Calzir, Dreanger, the Holy Lands, and the End of Connec by two centuries.

Events among the Wells of Ihrian seldom seem connected to anything else, early on. That region is in permanent ferment. There are as many sides to a question as there are city-states capable of raising militias.

The just cause, always, is rooted in religion. The private motivation might be greed, power hunger, the lure of loot, or revenge for last year's holy mission by some old enemy. But the squabbling princes and primates are, in general, true believers.

The feud between the Grail Emperor and the Patriarch is nothing new. The penchant of the Patriarch to preach holy war is nothing new. The fratricidal mischief between Santerin and Arnhand is heating up again. Their great families have feudal obligations to both monarchies. Confused feudal ties generate absurdities. Father can face son across the bloody field.

The divine conspiracy is no great engine with goose-greased parts turning over smoothly. It is a drunken tarantella in a cosmic town square where the dancers frequently forget what they are doing and wander off drunkenly, bumping into things, before purpose is recollected.

And, like ants at their labors in the town common, those who do the world's work will, too frequently, enjoy the sudden, unpredictable strike of an inebriant's flashing hoof.

1. Skogafjordur, Andoray

Drums muttered like a clutch of old ladies gossiping. Their job in the ritual was to keep the children out from under foot while their parents watched the old folks manage the funeral. Night gathered. Torches came to life. Old Trygg thrust his brand into the bonfires. Starting from the left end of the line. Flames rose in defiance of the night. Horns called from the heights overlooking either shore of the Skogafjord. Horns called back from watchtowers inland.

A great man was about to go to sea for the last time.

Singer Briga stood at the cold water's edge, singing his song to the sea, reminding the tide that it was time to ebb.

The sea knew its part. Each wavelet fell a little farther short of Briga's bare toes.

Pulla the Priest waved to young men knee-deep in the chill water.

The drums shifted their beat. Erief Erealsson's own long-ship crew, last of the great sturlanger, pushed the ship out onto the dark tide.

A breeze caught the simple red-and-white-striped sail. A breathless silence overcame the celebrants. There could have been no better omen than that breeze, which would carry the ship down the fjord on the breast of the tide.

The horns resumed mourning. The drums took up their dialogue with the night. Erief's crewmen sped burning arrows toward the ship. Which now drifted into a fog that had not existed only moments before.

A kelpie surfaced, long green hair glowing in the firelight.

The fire arrows seemed to have been loosed by the most inept archers ever. Only a handful reached the ship with the screaming bear's head prow. They failed to start a fire—despite kegs of oil having been splashed everywhere. Despite Erief's corpse being surrounded by tinder.

Not good.

A dozen sea people surrounded the ship. Was their sorcery

stifling the fire? It had to be sorcery that kept the arrows missing the kelpies.

"Stop!" Pulla roared. "Do you want to waken the Curse of the Sea Kings?"

The archers desisted.

The ship drifted. Erief Erealsson would be missed. His genius in war and diplomacy had gathered the fractious families, clans, and tribes of the Andorayan fjords and islands under one banner for the first time since Neche's Reach.

"Everyone sing!" Briga shouted. "The Priga Keda! With heart!" He sounded frightened. The people picked up the song. It was the only one they knew that begged the Instrumentalities of the Night to overlook Skogafjordur when they chose to meddle in the lives of men.

The Old Gods, the gods of the forests and the sky and the north, were not the sort who responded to the prayers of men. They existed. They ruled. They were indifferent to mortal suffering and tribulation. Unlike some gods away down south, they made few demands. But they did know what went on in the world. They did notice those who lived their lives well. And those who did not. Sometimes they sent luck or misfortune where those seemed particularly appropriate.

Times change, though. Even for the Old Ones.

The First Among Them, the All-Father, the One Who Harkens to the Sound, sometimes called the Walker or Gray Walker, was aware of the murder of Erief Erealsson.

The people of the sea screamed suddenly and plunged into the deeps.

Then the people of Snaefells and Skogafjordur fell silent again. This time in anticipation and awe. A huge presence began to fill the night. *Something* of great power, *something* terrible, was approaching.

Two shrieking streaks of darkness arrowed down at the longship. They circled like fluttering cloaks of darkness, defined by the bonfires.

A murmur of fear and awe: "Choosers of the Slain! Choosers of the Slain!" Everyone knew about those insane demigoddesses, but only ancient Trygg had seen them, when he was a boy of fourteen, off Mognhagn, during the thousand-ship battle of Neche's Reach.

"There're only two," someone muttered. "Where's the other one?"

"Maybe it's true, the story about Arlensul." One of the mad daughters of the Walker had been exiled for loving a mortal.

The air grew as cold as the land of ice farther north. The blankets of darkness squabbled like sparrows aboard the longship. Then they soared up and away.

The fire spread rapidly now, growing so enthusiastic it roared.

The people watched till the fire began to fade. The longship was far down the fjord, then, again accompanied by the people of the sea.

Pulla summoned the elders of Skogafjordur. "Now we deal with Erief's murderers."

There were several schools of thought about who had struck Erief so treacherously.

The law insisted that the fallen be seen into the next world before any trial or revenge or ruling of justification. Tempers needed time to cool.

Briga said, "The Choosers of the Slain." He could not get over that. "The Choosers of the Slain. They came. Here."

Trygg nodded. Harl and Kel did the same.

Briga completed the thought. "There wasn't a battle. He was murdered."

"Frieslanders," Pulla said. Everyone knew there would have been a war with Friesland if Erief had had another summer to finish uniting all of Andoray. The Kings of Friesland claimed Andoray too, despite Neche's Reach.

The old men stared at Pulla. The old women, Borbjorg and Vidgis, too. None agreed with the godspeaker.

Pulla shook his head. "Maybe I'm wrong. But that's what I think."

Trygg observed, "Erief was a great one." Speaking no ill of the dead. "Maybe so great the Walker himself wanted him. Who else would send the Choosers? Did anybody see His ravens? No?"

Pulla said, "I'll throw the bones and consult the runes. There may be something the Night wants us to know. But first, we have to decide what to do with the outlanders."

The law had been observed. But tempers were no cooler than when the murder had been discovered.

* * *

PULLA SENSED A WRONGNESS BEFORE THE TORCHLIGHT RE-
vealed the prison pit. He barked, "Stop! Something *huldrin* has
been here." *Huldrin* literally meant "hidden." In this instance
huldrin meant a creature of Faerie, spawn of the Instrumentalities of the Night and the Hidden Realms. *Huldre* people, the
Hidden Folk, while seldom seen, were part of everyday life.
You disdained the Hidden Folk only at great peril.

The priest stopped. He shook his bag of bones overhead.
Their clatter would intimidate the things of the night.

Still rattling the bones, Pulla moved forward. He stumbled
after a dozen steps. He asked Briga to lower his torch.

He had slipped on a stick as thick as his wrist. Had he fallen
forward he would have plunged into the empty prison pit.

"They're gone." Briga was a master at stating the obvious.

The outlanders had come to Snaefells and Skogafjordur
three weeks earlier, peddling some absurd religion from the far
south, where the sun burned so hot it addled men's brains. They
seemed harmless enough at first. Their stories were so ridiculous they were entertaining. No grown man with the smarts to
scratch his own lice would buy that nonsense. Physically, they
were bad jokes. A half-grown girl could thrash them. Except
that they refused to get that close to anyone female.

But sometime during the night last night somebody drove a
dagger into Erief's heart while he slept. The dagger got stuck
between the hero's ribs. The assassin abandoned it.

That blade was foreign, like none known in the north. Not
even Trygg had seen its like. And Trygg had visited many far
lands in his youth.

The foreigners went into the pit, protesting their innocence,
minutes after the crime was discovered.

Trygg thought them innocent. His view, however, constituted a minority. The missionaries were awfully convenient.

Pulla gathered the old folks close. "These foreigners must
be powerful sorcerers. They scattered the stick hut over the pit,
then flew away."

Trygg snorted derisively. "Someone helped them climb out.
The someone who really murdered Erief. Someone *huldrin.*"

That started a ferocious argument over whether the foreigners had been beaten badly enough before being dumped into the pit. They should not have been able to climb, even with help.

Herva, a crone so ancient she made Trygg seem young, snapped, "You waste your breath. None of that matters. They have escaped. They must be brought back. There must be a trial. Find Shagot the Bastard and his brother."

The people of Snaefells heard her. They approved. Shagot and his brother had been Erief's lieutenants. They were hardened, cruel men who made their own people nervous. Especially now that there was no Erief to rein them in. So why not get them out of the village and exploit their experience at the same time?

Something screamed on the mountainside. Nearer, something laughed in the dark.

The hidden folk were never far away.

2. Esther's Wood, in the Holy Lands

Else wakened instantly. Someone was approaching his tent stealthily. He grasped the hilt of a dagger. A silhouette formed at the tent's entrance, limned by the campfires beyond.

"Else! Captain! We need you." A hand parted the flaps beyond Else's toes. The firelight leapt inside.

"Bone?"

"Aye. We have a situation shaping up, sir."

The blazing campfires had told him that. "What kind of trouble?" It was nighttime. The fires were up. That was all the answer he needed, really.

"Supernatural."

Of course. Here in the wilds of the Holy Lands, amongst the Wells of Irhian, the most supernaturally infested corner of the earth, human danger seldom prowled the Realm of Night.

Else dressed quickly, slid out of his tent like a big cat, six feet tall, lithe and hard, with striking blond hair and blue eyes, at his physical prime.

"Where?" A glance at the horses told him they were not yet troubled.

"There."

Else jogged. Bone could not keep up. Bone was too old to be in the field. He should have stayed home to teach the youngsters coming up. But Bone knew the Holy Lands better than any other Sha-lug. He had fought the Rhûn here for two decades, long ago.

Else joined al-Azer er-Selim, the band's Master of Ghosts. Az stared fixedly into the darkness.

"What have we got? I don't see anything."

"Right there. The darkness that hides the trees behind it."

He saw it now. "What is it?" He saw more as his eyes adapted. Vague black wolf shapes prowled beyond the fringes of the light.

"It's a bogon. The master spirit of the countryside. In a more settled land it would be a local deity, probably confined inside an idol in a town temple. To limit the amount of evil it could do. Out here, where no one lives, it would remain diffused. Normally."

"Normally." The darkness now had a vaguely manlike shape, but doublewide and fourteen feet tall. "It's manifesting? Why?"

"Somebody compelled it. Somebody—or something—conjured it, commanded it, and here it is. Once it manifests completely, it'll attack us. And slaughter us. Our charms can't repel that much brute power."

The wolf shapes were there in anticipation of the collapse of the mystic barriers protecting the camp.

"I thought things were going way too smooth. What do we do?"

"Right now we can only get ready to do whatever we'll try to do. We can't hurt it while it's still pulling itself together. Once it manifests, though, we'll have a few seconds before its intellect catches up with its body. That's when you'll have to act. So you'll have to be ready."

"I will, eh?"

"You're the captain."

"How much time do I have?"

"About five minutes."

Else turned. The men were all awake, now. Some seemed frightened, some resigned. In this foreign land, the Realm of War, their confidence in their own god was less than complete.

Other gods stalked this land. This was the land where gods were born. And devils, as well.

They stared at those restless wolf things, growing more defined and bold.

"Mohkam. Akir. Bring the falcon."

"What're you going to do, Captain?"

"I'm going to save your sorry asses. Unless you'd rather stand around asking me questions. Heged. Agban. Bring the money chest. Bone. I need a pail of gravel. Norts. Get a keg of firepowder. Az. Get a reliable torch going. All of you, do it on the run. Because if you don't you'll all be dead in about five minutes." Else ignored his own racing pulse. He did not look at the wolves directly. They looked like the real thing, now, impatient, snapping at one another. But they were half the size of real wolves, which had been exterminated in this region ages ago. They did not fear men. They were amongst the most common terrors generated by the Instrumentalities of the Night, known wherever men sat round campfires and looked out at the eyes of the Night. They were more dangerous in number than as individuals. Any semicompetent hedge wizard could run a singleton off or keep a pack from breaking into the circle of light. Even a normal, unskilled man could handle a singleton if he kept his wits about him. Powdered wolfbane would chase those spawn of Night.

Mohkam and Akir came running with the falcon, pushing the carriage. The little brass cannon could be as dangerous to its operators as to its target. It had not been fired since its test shots at the foundry where it had been cast. Falcons were new, secret weapons meant to be used only in desperate circumstances.

"Firepowder!" Else thundered. "Get moving! Bone! You lazy old fart, let's go! Heged! Agban! Where are you? Move it! Come on. Come on. Get that firepowder loaded. Charge and a half."

They looked at him warily but did as they were told. Bone arrived with the gravel. "This shit is everywhere when you're trying to sleep on the ground. But try to find a gallon when you need it."

"Get the chest open. Just silver. Fast. Mix it with the gravel."

"Captain! You can't . . ."

"Bitch about it later. Akir. Prime it. Heged. Agban. Load the shot. Move. Move." The bogon would not wait.

Seconds later, Agban jumped back. "It's ready."

"Get the ram out."

"Oh. Yeah."

Else said, "Good. Done with time to spare. Az. Get your ass over here. *With* the torch."

The wizard sputtered. He was no common soldier. He was a Master of Ghosts.

"You're the one who knows when to touch the fire. Get in here and do it."

The wolf shapes dared the light, testing the encampment's wards. The bogon towered eighteen feet high and eight wide, hunched forward like an ape. Its eyes had gained definition.

"Az!"

The wizard shook as he stepped up beside the falcon.

"The rest of you, get down. Get behind something. Or go calm the horses and oxen." He was pleased that the bogon had chosen to manifest on the side away from the animals. And wondered if there was any significance to that.

In an eye's blink the bogon finished manifesting.

Al-Azer er-Selim set torch to match hole.

The falcon gouted flame, thunder, and a vast cloud of sulfurous smoke. Else understood instantly that he had been right to overcharge. The firepowder had been damp. It had burned slow. It created so much smoke that, for half a minute, it was impossible to discover the effect of the shot.

Ah! That part had gone perfectly. The bogon was down, full of holes, with darkness evaporating off it like little streamers of black steam. Shredded wolf lay scattered around the monster. Beyond, brush had been leveled and trees stripped of their bark. Several small fires burned out there, already dying. And then there was the quiet, a silence as profound as that in the Void before God created Heaven and Earth.

Awed swearing began to leak from the nearest raiders.

"Bone. Mohkam. Akir. Have you checked the falcon for cracks? Have you swabbed the embers out? Are we ready if that thing gets up off the ground?"

The Master of Ghosts said, "The bogon won't bother us, Captain. It won't bother anyone ever again."

"Then the bogon is no concern anymore, Az. Now we worry about the man who raised it. It isn't him that we just killed."

"Worth remembering. He'll know that he failed. And awareness of the bogon's destruction will spread fast. Though not how or why. A secret to be kept for sure. A lot of folk will think that some terrible feat of sorcery did it. We should get out of here fast. Before people come to investigate. We aren't supposed to be here."

"We can't move now. Not with our cargo. And I need to collect up as much of the silver as I can."

"This isn't our territory, Captain, whatever Gordimer and the Kaif say. The Rhûn, the Arnhander princes, and the Kaif of Qasr al-Zed claim it, too. Their presence is more concrete. We have several unfriendly fortresses within a half day's travel. Even those mad Unbelievers from the west have their Masters of Ghosts. Anyone who owns a horse is going to head this way. The destruction of a bogon is a major event. You don't dare ignore it."

"You're right, Az. Every word true. And every faction in the Holy Lands has heard that a band of foreigners is skulking around." You could evade men's eyes but only the most powerful sorcerers could avoid being noticed by the Instrumentalities of the Night. Else had no means of keeping his force concealed. His tools were speed and deception.

His band had drawn little attention so far. They had collected what they had gone after. They were well on their way home again.

Az continued, "There might even be wild tribesmen around."

"There might be. They'd have to be stupid to think that we're an easy chance."

That could not be denied. Particularly if Else ordered the Sha-lug standard revealed. The wild tribes showed the slave soldiers great respect. Gordimer the Lion, the warrior slave so great that he mastered the mighty and ancient kingdom of Dreanger, would have it no other way. That lesson had been bloodily taught several times.

Else did not want to reveal the band's allegiance. Too many questions would be asked. Once those started it would not be long before someone unfriendly put answers together. Who knew what evil would come of that?

Else asked, "Do we have any reason to worry again tonight? Will there be another monster?"

"I think not."

"Then let's stand down. Get some rest. Bone. I want to be ready to move out as soon as we have enough light. Even if we don't go right away. Az, have you checked our cargo?"

"I haven't, personally. The job is being done. Falaq!"

Of course the job was being done. Else's companions were the best of the Sha-lug. He did not need to mother them.

AS SOON AS THERE WAS LIGHT SUFFICIENT TO INTIMIDATE THE Night, Else sent scouts out, posted sentries at the wood's edge, and had men start collecting the coins that had killed the bogon. He did not expect to recover many. There would be no time. Az was right. Soldiers from the Arnhander city-states, and everyone else interested in the Wells of Ihrian, would head for Esther's Wood the moment their Masters of Ghosts told them it was safe.

Else observed, "This land could see some blood spilled before the Tyranny of the Night reclaims it."

Someone suggested, "Suppose we check in with God? We could ask Him to make sure we don't do any of the bleeding."

ELSE STARED AT THE SPOT WHERE THE BOGON HAD FALLEN. The earth was burned barren, the soil cooked to dust, across a fifteen-foot circle. That formed a shallow bowl a foot deep in the middle. What looked like an obsidian egg six inches on its longer axis lay there. It still radiated heat. Likewise, occasional streamers of mist curled away. You could see into the egg. Which, Else decided, was more kidney-shaped than egg-shaped. Silver coins remained trapped there. The coin nearest the egg's surface had melted around its rim. The inscriptions upon it were illegible.

Else asked, "The bogon can't pull itself back together here, can it, Az? It can't hatch out of this egg? It isn't some kind of phoenix?"

"No. A bogon is really strong. It's a king of spirits. But it's as simple as it's strong. Easy to kill in its manifest form, apparently. If you have a falcon, forewarning, and some silver shot. Not to mention the assistance of a Master of Ghosts who doesn't get rattled." The unshakable Master of Ghosts collected the egg using a pair of heavy sticks. He wrapped it in rags, being careful not to touch it.

"I see. Good to know." Else was not reassured. Sorcerers, sorcery, and the Tyranny of the Night were beyond his simple understanding. He did not believe them capable of being straightforward or positive, whether they were on his side or opposed. Nor had he ever encountered any evidence to suggest that his attitudes were overly pessimistic.

"Captain!" One of the coin hunters beckoned.

"What have you got?" The man was quite wide of eye.

"A dead man. And not that long gone, either."

The corpse was charred. What remained of clothing and jewelry was foreign. Likewise, his weapons, though his sword was a horseman's blade. Around him lay what looked like foreign tools of sorcery.

Al-Azer said, "There should be horses around here somewhere. They'll tell us a lot."

"He what I think he is, Az?"

"Probably. Long way from home."

"Find those horses. You think he was spying on us and got part of the falcon's load?"

"Looks that way. He had no idea what the falcon was."

"Interesting. Is he the one who raised the bogon?"

"No. He was too young. But he might've worked for the man who did. As an eyewitness. On the other hand, he might have been following us because he knew about the mummies."

"Too many might haves, Az. What I'd like to know is how one of his kind can be down here, south of Lucidia. Bone! Are you ready to travel?"

"Just give the order, Captain."

Al-Azer said, "We'll know more after we look at his horses."

"You're sure there'll be more than one?"

"If he's really what he looks like he'll have had at least three."

A SOFT TONE FROM A RAM'S HORN SOUNDED AN ALERT. THAT horn's voice did not carry far. Else and al-Azer hastened toward the source of the sound.

A youngster named Hagid—not to be confused with Heged the cannoneer—crouched just inside the northeast edge of Esther's Wood. Hagid was remarkable because he was second-generation Sha-lug. His father was an intimate of Gordimer the Lion. Hagid had been sent with Else for tempering. With the courtier expecting that the boy would return alive, with his parts all still attached. But Else knew the Lion. He understood that the mission meant more than the survival of any privileged boy.

Hagid pointed. A cloud of dust shone brown-orange in the light of the rising sun. The men raising that dust were not moving in a tight column. They were scattered. Later in the day, when the sun stood higher, that dust would be much less obvious.

"Over there," Az said. "More of them."

The second cloud, due east instead of north-northeast and emerging from the desert, owned a more yellow cast and was much more obvious.

Else grumbled, "Bone! Where's Bone? Az. Who's likely to be coming at us out of the east?" That was all desert in that direction. The little principalities of the Holy Lands lay all tangled up with one another nearer the coast, to the north and west.

Az said, "It's time to go, Captain. One of those parties will be responsible for our spy. I'd guess the other would include the people who raised the bogon. Which is probably somebody who has something to do with the Kaif of Qasr al-Zed."

Bone finally turned up. "We found the dead man's horses. Three of them. We brought the stuff that was on them."

Else examined bridles, blankets, a saddle, saddlebags containing little but dried food, and things Az said a wizard might carry on a trip. One closed case contained arrows. Another contained a fine recurved bow made of laminated horn. Else said, "This stuff didn't belong to any Lucidian. Az, check this stuff over with your third eye."

"Captain . . ."

"I know. Don't get technical. Do what needs doing. Just be careful. He was out spying while your monster king was hunting. Hagid. Tell Agban to move out now. Due west, toward the coast road." The sea was less than thirty miles away.

The wood would mask the dust the company raised. And those hunters out there would have to worry about one another. They would not be friends.

Else examined the bow. "This is horse people work. They must be sending scouts out to see what comes after Lucidia."

"They've never been defeated, Captain," Bone said. "Not in twenty years."

"They haven't met the Sha-lug." That might be an interesting encounter. The horse barbarians of the steppe were cruel, fearless, and disciplined. Their numbers were supposed to be inexhaustible but that could not be true. They made the best of what they had. They were, first and foremost, nomadic herdsmen.

The Sha-lug knew no life but war and preparation for war. They purchased boy children in slave markets everywhere, though mainly in Qasr al-Zed. Those boys grew up with weapons in their hands. The best and strongest became Sha-lug, the slaves who were masters of the sprawling, wealthy kingdom of Dreanger, the heart of the Kaifate of al-Minphet.

The Kaif of al-Minphet was Karim Kaseem al-Bakr, puppet of Gordimer the Lion, the Supreme Marshal of All Sha-lug, before whom the Enemies of God Wet Themselves in Terror, and so forth, and so forth.

Unlike most Sha-lug, Else was not impressed by Gordimer. He suspected the Lion was less noble than he pretended. Gordimer kept handing him these deadly chores, verging on the impossible. Like Gordimer hoped Else would not return.

In minutes the company was moving toward the coast, where friendly ships would be sure to see them.

Else, al-Azer, and Bone stayed behind.

Bone asked, "You know we're looking at the Plain of Judgment?"

Else grunted noncommittally. He knew without knowing the significance. Everything in the Holy Lands had historical and religious meaning to someone. Every crag, every dry wash, every wood, and most of all, every mystic well was a thread in a vast and ancient tapestry. Bone or Az would explain. Whether Else was interested or not.

Bone resumed. "Battles have been fought here since before men began recording history. Eleven major battles have been fought between the Well of Calamity south of us and the Well of Atonement to our north. A distance of nine miles. There've been scores of skirmishes."

"Indeed," al-Azer said. "The Written itself says this is where God and the Adversary will come together in final battle. Some sages, both ancient and modern, say that history began here and that it'll end here."

Else was no more religious than he needed to get by. He had not connected this place with the Plain of Judgment in the Written.

The scattered riders in the north drew near enough now for individuals to be discerned. They failed to notice the cloud in the east. They were near enough for the combined effect of their hoofbeats to be sensed, more on the edge of feeling than hearing.

The Master of Ghosts said, "Time to leave. Those are the buddies of the guy who got killed last night."

Else usually listened to his Master of Ghosts. It seemed the safest way to deal with the Tyranny of the Night. So, he was not there to witness a clash between steppe horsemen and cavalry from the northern Kaifate. The Lucidians were led by the famous Indala al-Sul Halaladin.

Not much happened. Neither force got the other to do anything stupid. Arhanders from Vantrad arrived in the afternoon. The earlier forces faded away as twilight gathered.

After dark supernatural forces got busy.

The Sha-lug made camp on the seaward side of the coastal road. Their carts had suffered badly, traveling cross country. Else doubted that the band would survive the journey south to Dreanger.

Bone was concerned. "What'll we do if a ship don't come?" Gordimer had vowed that warships would patrol the coast as far north as the roads of Vantrad until Else and his band were safely home.

"If no ship shows up I'll strap a mummy on your back. And like some black crow of an old woman, you can lug your baby around while you work."

Bone was no more religious than Else. That was characteristic of Sha-lug. They had seen too much to be unquestioning in their conviction of God's Mercy. The old man made a sign warding the evil eye. He followed that with a gesture meant to invoke God's favor—if He so willed.

Bone did not like the dead. He bore a particular prejudice against those dead who had practiced their trade a long time. Of the ancient dead of Andesqueluz, the Demon Kingdom, whose sorcerer kings' accursed relicts Else's Company had pilfered from their tombs, Bone's opinion consisted of irrational hatred deeply awash in stark terror. These days the Demon Kingdom was lost in the backwaters of history, known intimately only to scholars, but echoes of the terrible truth lived on in myth and fairy tale.

But Bone was a good soldier.

Sha-lug was synonymous with Good Soldier.

There were no incidents that night. Nevertheless, Else did not sleep well. He could not help anticipating further deviltry from the night.

Al-Azer claimed that the supernatural reverberations of the bogon's destruction had not damped out yet. Anything might be attempted by sorcerers who wanted to spy on their neighbors during such unsettled times.

ELSE DID NOT POSSESS AN IMAGINATION ADEQUATE TO ENCOMPASS the magnitude of his one cannon blast. None of the company but al-Azer er-Selim realized that the blast had changed the world forever.

Al-Azer would never speak the words. He would not write them down. Few mortals would realize the truth, even within the supernatural trades. But that one inspired blast had proclaimed the imminent end of Mankind's long subjugation to the Tyranny of the Night. Mankind now had a means to contest with the gods themselves, did Man but realize it, for even the greatest gods were nothing more than bogons on a mightier scale, some with a dollop of intellect.

The Wells of Irhian vented concentrated magical power, the fertilizer in which the things of night flourished. The Holy Lands seethed with supernatural beings. The region was as critical to the Instrumentalities of the Night as it was to the religions that considered the Wells of Ihrian the Holy Lands.

There were dozens of other wells of magic scattered around

the world but none were as potent as those found in the Holy Lands. Nor as concentrated. And all the wells, everywhere, were in a weakening cycle. Which meant a more difficult existence for the Instrumentalities of the Night, much harder work for sorcerers, and a lot more cold along the bounds of the inhabited world.

The greatest, least recognized power of the wells was that their magic kept the ice at bay.

Nothing about the wells was common knowledge. Changes in their flow were never obvious. Nor was the advance or retreat of the ice along the bounds of the world.

Both the Written and secular historical documents mentioned lions, apes, and wolves in lands around the Mother Sea. In antiquity. The lions had been hunted out by classical times. Apes survived only in the extreme west, in small numbers. Wolves could be found in the forests of the north and the mountains beyond the Kaifate of Qasr-al-Zed. Even the forests around the Mother Sea were, mostly, gone now.

And now a way had been found to tame the Instrumentalities of the Night.

Now a man like Else, with no mystical talent whatsoever, with not one of those delicate skills a sorcerer honed for decades so as to manipulate a few minor spirits, could butcher a count of the night as easily as he could exterminate his own kind.

Understanding left Az filled with stark terror. The falcon's blast might catch the eyes of the gods themselves.

The gods—pressed, al-Azer would admit that there *were* more gods than the One God, the True God, There Is No Other—were not known for indulging mortal behaviors offensive enough to be noticed. In particular, they would resent the threat to their own dominion.

Else did not know what he had done. A threat revealed itself. He did what he was supposed to do. He dealt with it based on hearsay and the tools at hand.

Al-Azer rested more poorly than did his captain.

A SMALL WARSHIP SHOWING THE BANNER OF AL-MINPHET appeared early next morning. The vessel brought a letter from Gordimer, meant for Else if the ship happened upon him.

Else gathered his men. "The Lion has ordered me to report to him immediately, with the mummies and their accoutrements. He has another job for me. Already. Bone, that leaves you to take the company home. The galley only has space for maybe ten more men. One has to be Hagid. Bone, pick the others. There're other patrol ships out. I'll send them to cover you."

Bone named nine names immediately. Each belonged to an injured or sick soldier.

Else nodded. Those men were likely to be more burden than asset. He said, "It should be under a hundred miles to the Shidaun naval fortress. Abandon the carts. You'll make better time."

Else hoped he was not whistling in the dark. The fortified harbor at Shidaun was at least a hundred twenty miles away. Probably more. And while the Kaif's enemies might not be fast enough to catch the Sha-lug from behind, their sorcerers had ways of reaching out to potential allies between here and Shidaun. Once the night returned.

Al-Azer looked grim. He would be the last man in the band allowed to board a ship and scurry away to safety. The Master of Ghosts was the company's most important protector.

Else made the ship's master put in at Shidaun. There he used his authority to compel the garrison commander to send marines north to meet Bone.

That was all that he could do for his men.

3. St. Jeules ande Neuis, in the End of Connec

Brother Candle reached St. Jeules ande Neuis after noon prayers, on the third day of Mantans, in the third year of the Patriarchy of Sublime V in Brothe. Man and boy, adult and child, the villagers should have been getting ready for the bitter long hours of spring planting.

They had been preparing, naturally. But with little enthusiasm. Word had come that a Perfect Master was headed their way. The peasants were eager to see a famous holy man, even if few of them were believers themselves. The people were eager to hear and debate the message the Perfect Master would bring.

Even poor farmers in the Connec enjoyed an active intellectual life. Many minds still could not understand the Maysalean divergences from Episcopal creed—but most Connectens were willing to argue.

The Maysalean Heresy had been around for decades but only lately had it begun to catch on. Though there was as much nationalistic fervor in that as philosophical conviction. The Heresy's growth was a response to the incessant outrages practiced by the illegitimate Patriarchs of Brothe.

ONE HUNDRED AND FIFTY-SIX YEARS HAD PASSED SINCE THE election of the Connecten Ornis of Cedelete to the Patriarchal throne. Within hours the unheroic Ornis fled the Holy City, harried by a mob whipped into a frenzy by agents of the Brothen Five Families. Who considered the western religious Patriarchy a part of their birthright.

Legitimate Patriarch Ornis, taking the reign name Worthy VI, established himself in the Palace of Kings at Viscesment. Though legitimate in canon law, Worthy's Patriarchy in exile was impotent. His own countrymen in the End of Connec did not take him seriously. His successors made up a parade of ineffective, craven, and often quickly murdered Patriarchs. Meanwhile, the illegitimate line of Usurper Patriarchs in Brothe came to be recognized by most of the Episcopal bishops, archbishops, and Principatés. The Five Families of Brothe could pay much bigger bribes. Only lukewarm support from the Grail Emperors kept the Viscesment anti-Patriarchy breathing.

Barely, now known as the Pretender Patriarchy.

The current Pretender Patriarch, Guy ande Scars, styling himself Immaculate II, sputtered and fussed at the Episcopal world from his family estate outside Viscesment. His entire Patriarchal establishment, horizontally and vertically, consisted of fewer than a hundred persons, the majority of them extremely competent Braunsknechts Guards from the Grail Emperor Johannes' own Kretien Electorate. Their presence assured Immaculate a definite, though modest, level of respect.

For fifty years the usurpers in Brothe had been strong men. Principality by principality, by persuasion or by bribe, they had gained the allegiances of the lords of the Church and the Lords Temporal, so disdained by the Collegium.

The Maysalean Heresy renounced all things worldly, power and property and the pleasures of the flesh in particular.

Long ago Brother Candle wore the name Charde ande Clairs and was a wealthy merchant of Khaurene. Once his children were grown and married and had established their own lives, the merchant foreswore the world of trade. As a simple mendicant brother he set out in search of Perfect Enlightenment. His wife, Margete, entered the Maysalean nunnery at Fleaumont, where she attained Perfect status herself. Around Fleaumont Sister Probity was better known than her former husband.

The folk of St. Jeules ande Neuis welcomed the missionary heartily. His arrival guaranteed a break from boredom. Even devout Brothen Episcopals embraced the Perfect. The mendicant brothers were the news bringers of the back country. At a time when the world was quickening with fears and alarums. In rumor of late, it seemed every far land was boiling with conflicts.

Almost out to the edge of imagination, a fanatic styling himself Indala al-Sul Halaladin had overrun much of the Holy Lands, the region known as the Wells of Ihrian. Al-Sul Halaladin served the Kaif of Qasr al-Zed, a man something like a western Patriarch. With much more temporal power. He headed the al-Zhun Path of al-Prama, the Faith. Al-Prama made no distinction between religious and mundane leadership. Every ruler was responsible for both the secular and spiritual welfare of his people.

A few Praman rulers took that charge seriously.

The Kaif of Qasr al-Zed was determined to remove all westerners from the Holy Lands. His successes of a decade ago so disturbed the now-dead Usurper Patriarch Clemency III that the false Patriarch called for a new crusade to recover the holy places and strengthen up the small kingdoms and city states created by crusaders in ages past.

All this and much more Brother Candle explained to St. Jeules the first evening of his stay. Most of it they had heard already, in garbled form. News traversed the rural world slowly but it did travel. Those who were Viscesment Episcopals were intimately familiar with the wickedness of the Brothen Usurper Patriarch Clemency III and his successor, Sublime V. Bishop Serifs of nearby Antieux, sent out by Clemency III to wean the peoples of the eastern Connec from their allegiance to Immaculate II, and confirmed in his mission by Sublime V, was hated with immense vigor by Maysaleans, all subspecies of Episcopals, Devedians, Dainshaus, and the Connec's remaining handful of Pramans, of every station and faction. Because the Bishop seemed to have decided that his main mission was to deprive anyone who defied him of any hint of wealth. Wealth that, somehow, always found its way into his personal control.

Brother Candle was but one of numerous Perfect wandering the byways of the End of Connec, gently witnessing their creed without speaking ill of either Patriarch or anything Episcopal.

He failed to mention, right away, that most of the Perfect would come to St. Jeules after him.

Brother Candle went on to talk about the sharp religious fighting beyond the Verses Mountains, in Direcia, orchestrated by Peter of Navaya, who had married Isabeth, younger sister of Duke Tormond IV of Khaurene, the overlord of the End of Connec.

Brother Candle also predicted a resumption of hostilities between Santerin and Arnhand, partly because of dynastic disputes complicated by confused feudal obligations, but also because Santerin was not satisfied with the disaster their forces had visited upon Arnhand's at Themes in Tramaine last summer.

Connectens cared little about the squabble between Santerin and Arnhand except that it did keep Arnhand from taking an interest in the Connec. Connectens were more concerned about events to the east. It was in that direction that the big predators prowled.

"Tell us what Hansel is doing," Pere Alain insisted. Pere Alain meant the Grail Emperor Johannes III Blackboots, Hansel the Ferocious, supreme warlord of the New Brothen

Empire, the Anointed Fist of God. The Usurper Patriarch Sublime's bitterest foe and abiding nightmare. Little Hans was a fierce critic of ecclesiastical corruption, which ran deep and was almost universal in the Episcopal Church. Johannes blamed all that on the Patriarchy, which defended the priesthood, however heinous or egregious its crimes. He hated Sublime V and held today's Patriarchy in deep contempt.

The Emperor was almost always at war with the Patriarchy somewhere but only desultorily because the Grail Empire could not finance a more vigorous campaign.

Sublime V had been Patriarch for barely two years. In that time he had issued numerous thunderous bulls excommunicating Johannes Blackboots and his captains, frequently to the dismay of those nobles who worried that God might be standing behind Sublime V instead of Immaculate II.

Hansel tirelessly belabored the point that Sublime was illegitimate and his decrees therefore no more momentous than those of other thieves and perjurers. Only the Patriarch in Viscesment could issue Writs of Anathema and Excommunication.

Unfortunately, even patriotic Connectens admitted that Immaculate II was a feeble joke who would fade faster than morning dew without Johannes behind him.

Pere Alain asked, "Master, will you stay long?"

"Call me Brother. Maysaleans consider all men equal. All men are brothers. We suffer nothing from hierarchy." Hierarchy caused more trouble amongst Episcopals than did any point of dogma. The Church and churchmen were hierarchical in the extreme. And jealous of every little perquisite. Which offended a great many layfolk, who retained the ancient values.

"Will you stay and teach?"

"Of course. That's my work. I teach, I witness, I perform acts of charity. And I'm tired of traveling." Brother Candle grinned his winsome grin but did not mention that other Perfects planned to gather in the village.

They put him up in the chapel. St. Jeules did not have its own priest. It was a time of prosperity. Few Episcopals were taking orders. The smaller livings went begging.

The people of St. Jeules trekked four miles to St. Aldrain's for weekly service. Once a month, old Father Epoine made the difficult climb to St. Jeules to deal with baptisms, confirma-

tions, marriages, and funerals. When extreme unction was
needed a boy ran down and one of the donkeys of St. Aldrain's
fetched Father Epoine up as fast as might be.

If good Episcopals were involved.

A quarter of the folk of St. Jeules belonged in that category,
supporting Viscesment. A third were Maysaleans. The rest
were largely indifferent, though a handful, all connected to the
Ashar family, still favored the ancient ways, bending to the
Will of the Night.

By day Brother Candle taught basic ciphering and the most
rudimentary fundamentals of reading, more Maysalean habits
that scandalized the Church. After supper he sat with those
who were interested and helped them explore new ways of
thinking about the Creator, his handiwork, and the place the
thinking animal occupied in the worldly pit.

One young man, who had been all the way to Antieux and
was considered an adventurer, said, "They say the wells of
power are weakening. That snow keeps piling deeper and
deeper in lands where it's always winter."

"I don't know. That could be. Maysaleans are more concerned with the ice inside."

Their vision mirrored the traditional. To a Maysalean Perfect this world was not the handiwork of a kind and loving Creator. This world was an artifact torn violently from the womb
of the void by the Adversary, to become a weapon in His great
war with Heaven. Souls caught up in mortal existence were
separated from the Light, subject to the Tyranny of the Night.
Some would cling to the Wheel of Life forever, never attaining
Perfection, never rejoining the One.

The End of Connec had been tamed for fifteen hundred
years. Yet minor spirits of wood and field and stream
abounded, lurking, abetted by the Ashars and their like, doing
mischief where they dared. Maysaleans considered all the Instrumentalities of the Night, great or small, to be concrete evidence of their creed's first principle.

The Heresy was a gentle creed. Traditionalists found its social notions more disturbing than its religious absurdities. In a
time when senior churchmen lived more grandly than princes,
the Maysaleans preached—and lived—lives of poverty and
service. Their property ideals were communal, as had been

those of the Founders of the Church. Their attitudes toward the sacraments were relaxed, particularly as regarded marriage. Though the Perfect abstained from the pleasures of the flesh. If one yielded to their temptation one fell from Perfection.

There were not many young Perfect.

Old Juie Sachs, the carpenter, told Brother Candle, "Sounds like a slow curse upon the world you got there, Master."

Puzzled, the Perfect said, "Please explain."

"It's a mathematical thing. If only the best people become Perfect and escape the world, then, each time one does, the world will get a little darker."

Jhean, the carpenter's son, said, "Maybe that's why the permanent snows get deeper and the winters get longer and colder. Maybe it don't have nothing to do with the wells of power."

Brother Candle was a fine missionary. When he explained the Maysalean Heresy it sounded obvious and inarguable. He had won countless converts. It was a harsh world even in good times. That made it easy to assert that life was a toy of darkness rather than a gift of light.

"We inspire the will to do good works by doing good works. The soul of the newborn does not bring with it the burden of sin accumulated in its previous life. In the beginning we stand equal before the Light, a book not yet written."

That did not answer the question posed, however. And now he was on difficult doctrinal ground. There were several points of view on the clean slate.

"Life starts as a blank tablet," he said. "Character is created and written each day. Meaning that there will always be more good people coming up."

That was an idea difficult to embrace. Common sense said some souls were so black that they could not become better if they went around the Wheel a million times. Even devoted Episcopals offered Sublime and the Bishop of Antieux as examples. The Bishop had taken ecclesiastical corruption into previously unknown realms.

One of the young men announced, "There's another Perfect on the way."

The old men in St. Jeules' little church eyed Brother Candle. It was time for him to tell them why he had come to their village. "All the Perfect who can are going to gather here. They'll come by the most remote and obscure byways."

The announcement caused no stir of excitement.

"We won't presume upon your charity. We'll pay for food and drink. And we'll help in the fields."

Someone asked, "How many Perfect Masters are there?"

"Forty-five," Brother Candle replied, though he had no real idea. "But they won't all come. Most are too far away."

The Maysalean Heresy did well wherever the Church was its most corrupt or oppressive. The ugliest accusations retailed by the Episcopal priesthood convinced no one that the Perfect were evil or out to harvest souls for the Adversary. Nor could the Church obscure the fact that most of the Perfect had been successful men before they donned the white robe.

So the bishops and priests of the Brothen rite peddled tales of devil worship and sexual license in secret, remote places. Credulous folk in cities and foreign places willingly believed anything wicked of anyone different. And neither accusation was an outright lie. Maysaleans did not worship the Adversary but they did believe that it was not the Evil One who had been cast out of Heaven. Nor did they believe in proprietary rights to the flesh of any individual, even in marriage.

Brother Candle said, "No more than twenty Perfect should turn up."

The old men wanted to know why the Perfect were gathering. There had been no Maysalean synod in more than fifty years.

"The Usurper, Sublime, intends to send selected priests to the Connec to destroy our beliefs. Some will belong to the Brotherhood of War. Some will be armed with writs granting them extraordinary powers. Bishop Serifs will be in charge of spiritual affairs throughout the Connec, with permission to use any means necessary to expunge our faith."

Old men spat. Young men cursed Serifs. The women offered prayers for the Bishop's disgrace and ruin.

"He'll be able to get away with anything as long as he claims he's doing it to suppress Those Who Seek the Light."

A key tenet of the Maysalean Heresy was a conviction that its followers were the true Chaldareans. Although that stretch was extreme, in truth, modern Episcopal dogma bore only a lip service resemblance to the gentle, egalitarian, communal doctrines of the Holy Founders.

The Episcopal Church survived on size, inertia, and the staying power of vested interest. It had survived challenges more serious than the Maysalean Heresy. The Borgians of the previous century had been more critical of the establishment and more militant in their defiance and disdain for all temporal power. The Borgians wanted to rid the world of all priests except part-time village clerics, and all nobles, period.

The Borgian dogma was naive. It required an already indifferent God to make sure no new hierarchies established themselves. It counted on that lazy deity to ensure that no savage invaders descended upon the pastoral Borgian realm, that no bandits took advantage.

The fatal flaw of the Borgian fallacy was that it assumed all men to be good and empathetic at heart, endowed with an innate drive to harm no one who would not fight back.

There were no Borgians anymore.

The Maysalean Perfect were pacifist but not blind. A man just had to glance around to find villains willing to eat him alive, then sell his bones.

Maysaleans were worldly enough to distinguish between ideal and real.

The second Perfect was the Grolsacher, Pacific. His speech was heavily accented and strong with dialect. Two more Perfect arrived before sundown. Brother Bell had made his home in Arcgent before he put the world aside. Brother Sales hailed from Cain, in Argony. He was in the Connec on a pilgrimage of personal discovery. His dialect was impenetrable.

That night St. Jeules went to sleep certain that momentous decisions would be made in their shy little village.

THE SYNOD OF THE PERFECT BEGAN FORMALLY MIDWAY through the second week of Mantans. Twenty-four Perfect had gathered. Their presence was a strain on the village. The people grumped about the disruption while pocketing startling amounts of money and taking advantage of the free labor.

The Perfect baffled the Episcopal faction by treating the female Perfect as the equals of men.

Equality had been part of early Chaldarean practice but had fallen to revisionism even before the founding prophets left the world.

The non-Maysaleans of St. Jeules were disappointed by the absence of orgies. Nor did the Perfect hold midnight masses where they celebrated their love for the Night.

The great difficulty for the Brothen Church in the End of Connec was that everyone there had friends or neighbors or cousins who were heretics. Everyone got an occasional glimpse of the truth. Maysaleans truly were Seekers After Light. And their gentle witnessing drew purses away from the established Church.

Sublime and Bishop Serifs were correct.

The Church was losing the Connec.

If the Connec went, the spread of heresy would accelerate. The Grail Emperor might profess it simply to seize a new weapon to wield in his squabble with Brothe.

The Maysalean Heresy was dangerous in ways that only a few of the Perfect understood. Which was one purpose of the gathering at St. Jeules.

The Seekers had good friends in Antieux, close to Bishop Serifs. They had friends in Brothe itself. And Sublime had numerous enemies willing to befriend the Seekers for as long as he survived.

The synod of the Perfect would also decide how Maysaleans should face the coming repression.

4. Andoray, with the Old Folks of Skogafjordur

The old farts, who had not gone sturlanger since the Father was a pup, did not have the stones for busybodying. Shagot the Bastard and his little brother, Svavar, would not suffer that from their mother. They would not tolerate the unflattering nicknames, either.

Their real names were Grimur and Asgrimmur. They had

been bullies all their lives. They never fit in, except in Erief's warrior cult. When Erief died their niche went with him. The old folks decided to send them after the fugitives. Because of those two there would be no more loot, no more rapes, no more wars to unite the clans under one Andorayan king. Nor would the brothers receive honors for their parts in creating this new and remarkable kingdom.

Grimur and Asgrimmur were too thick to understand that their neighbors just wanted them gone.

Pulla, Briga, Trygg, Herva, and Vidris concluded that the missionaries were not guilty of murder. Because those fools really believed the nonsense they preached. Which left them incapable of raising a hand against a fellow human being— even one who needed it.

Shagot, Svavar, and their friends were excited. The brothers appointed shipmates Hallgrim, Finnboga, and twins Sigurdur and Sigurjon Thorkalssons, to join them in their race to kill them some southern lilies.

Vidgis was a great-aunt of the Thorkalsson twins. She spoke to them privately before they departed.

It was not yet dawn when the sturlanger avengers began the long climb around the flank of Mount Hekla. They crossed the ever-expanding Langjokull glacier, then descended to the inland road the fugitives would follow to get back to their own country.

The old folks watched the troublemakers go. There would be peace for a while.

MOST OF THE OLD FOLKS DID NOT CARE WHO HAD KILLED ERIEF Erealsson. Not while the far more intriguing question of why the Choosers of the Slain would appear remained unanswered.

The arguments were heated. The parties separated according to individual attitudes about the unification of Andoray. A lot of people wanted every island and fjord to continue as its own little principality. The religious question languished.

Freedom or unification. It was the question of the age in Andoray. Anyone tall enough to walk had an opinion, almost always informed by ignorance. Opponents called Erief a tool of Gludnir of Friesland, who styled himself King of Andoray,

too. That made no sense. Gludnir and Erief had been bitter
foes forever. And a united Andoray could easily overawe the
Frieslanders. But sense and reason seldom inform political discourse. Particularly when the growth of ice up north tried to
factor itself in. Erief's partisans insisted that only a united Andoray could survive the advance of the ice.

Erief's enemies insisted the ice thing was pure hogwash.

The old folks drank a lot before the women put their heads
together and concluded that Erief's murderer must be Kjarval
Firstar, Eyjolfsdottir, with whom Erief had cohabited, against
her will, since his return from plundering the nether coasts of
Santerin, Scat, and Wole. During which expedition Kjarval's
father, Eyjolf, took a fatal arrow in the eye. And died begging
his captain to take his only daughter as his concubine.

There was a substantial dearth of witnesses to Eyjolf's dying wish. Even Erief's staunchest allies did not believe that
story.

Trygg proposed that Erief's assassin served a certain foreign
king, not to be named, who dwelt in Mognhagn in Friesland.

The debate warmed as the ale flowed. But some people fell
asleep, the ale ran out, and then nobody was interested anymore.

No one cracked the puzzle of the brazen appearance of the
Choosers of the Slain. Dread had had time to mature. That was
mythic stuff. Skogafjordur folk were accustomed to the mythic
staying safely and comfortably tucked away inside the myths.

Singer Briga was last to fade. He stared into the dying fire.
He kept thinking he had become one of those characters
named in passing in a saga, filling some role completely unlike
the real Briga.

He had seen it happen. He was ancient enough to have
known many of the people featured in the more familiar sagas.
He had helped create several larger-than-life reputations. Ex-
aggerate a little here, overlook something there. There was no
absolute Truth or absolute Reality, anyway. Truth was whatever the majority on hand agreed that it was. Real Truth was
egalitarian and democratic and not at all compelled to corre-
spond to the world in any useful way. Truth had no respect
whatsoever for Right, What's Best, or Needs Must. Real Truth
was a dangerous beast in need of caging in even the quietest of
times.

Ask any prince or priest.

Truth was the First Traitor.

Half a step short of discovering Final Truth, Briga tumbled into the realm of alcoholic dream.

5. Antieux, in the End of Connec

Serifs's secretary was too hasty in showing Bronte Doneto into the personal audience of the Bishop of Antieux. The Patriarchal legate saw a long-haired, blond, probable preadolescent hurriedly leave the skirts of the Bishop's robe and run. Doneto noted the tenting in the Bishop's lap. So the rumors were true. The Lord had blessed Serifs in that regard.

The Bishop seemed more angry than embarrassed. He glared at his secretary. He would have glared at Doneto but did not know the legate so did not know his standing in Brothe. But Doneto *was* from Brothe, sent by Sublime himself. That established the pecking order.

Both men pretended that there had been nothing to see. Doneto failed to show Serifs all the courtesies due his station. Which might mean that he was a member of the Collegium and Serifs's senior.

But Serifs considered it deliberate, a sign that Sublime was not satisfied with his progress at extinguishing the Maysalean Heresy.

The legate said so right away. "We serve a straightforward prelate, Bishop. He instructed me to be direct." The legate did not speak the Connecten dialect. He used ecclesiastical Brothen. "He directed you to stamp out this heresy. Instead of positive reports he keeps hearing complaints from Antieux, Khaurene, Castreresone, and so forth, all accusing you of abusing your office for your own enrichment."

The Bishop was not pleased. These stubborn Connectens . . . Sublime V was overconfident of his own security and power.

Serifs answered carefully in the ecclesiastical tongue. "His Holiness is welcome to deal with these people himself. From Count Raymone down to the lowliest shopkeeper they disdain my efforts. They refuse to see a problem. They ignore bulletins posted in the churches. The priests provide sacraments to those heretics who ask. They bury heretics in holy ground. Parish priests, especially in the countryside, will not condemn the heretics. Most tell their parishioners they can ignore anything coming out of Brothe because the true Patriarch is Immaculate II, at Viscesment. If I'm to get anywhere, that man has to be dealt with. And not just by swapping Writs of Anathema and Excommunication."

"His Holiness armed you with the authority to confiscate the properties of heretics. He expected you to show enough vigor to underwrite the Church's efforts here. Yet you send appeal after appeal for more funds."

"Duke Tormond overruled me. He says the Church has no power to confiscate anything. His lieutenant here, Count Raymone—whom I suspect of heretical sympathies—had my men whipped when they tried to execute their duties."

Bishop Serifs hoped to divert Doneto from questions about the disposition of properties that he had seized.

The legate did not visit the matter. "You explained to the Duke that by defying the Patriarch he risks his immortal soul?"

"Of course. And he told me he isn't defying the Patriarch, he's protecting the Connec from the predations of Firaldian thieves. He may be another who questions His Holiness's right to speak for God."

"I'm wondering if a strain of that hasn't insinuated itself here." Accusation edged the legate's voice. His disdainful expression made it clear that he did not approve of the way Serifs lived. Nor did he care about the obstacles life and a stubborn land placed in the Bishop's path.

Results. Sublime was interested only in results.

"I have an idea," Serifs said, congratulating himself on his own cunning. "Go into Antieux yourself and see how things really are. Disguise yourself as a merchant. Visit low places. Listen to what's being said when no one thinks Brothe is listening. Then we'll formulate a strategy based on your new appreciation of the Connecten reality."

The Bishop restrained a smile. The legate was exasperated. Again, Brothe cared only about results.

To his surprise, Doneto agreed. "You may have a point. I'll come back tomorrow. After that there'll be no more excuses."

"Absolutely."

Serifs watched the legate go. The door was not yet fully closed when he snapped his fingers at the shadows to his left.

Armand, pretty Armand, came forth, licking his lips. No words had to be exchanged. Serifs slid down in his seat. Armand crawled up under his robe. In a moment the Bishop felt soft lips nursing and gentle fingers stroking. He closed his eyes and tried to fathom why Sublime was so determined to impose Brothe's control on the End of Connec.

It had to be the revenues. There could be no other answer. Sublime needed money to stave off the Grail Emperor while he sent crusaders to recapture the Wells of Ihrian and to liberate Calzir. The revenues were the only possible answer.

The Connec was the richest land claimed by the Church. It had been two centuries since war had stained it, back when Duke Tormond's ancestor Volsard recaptured Terliaga from Meridian, a Praman kingdom of Direcia and former seat of the western Kaifate. After that triumph the Reconquest proceeded inexorably. A third of Direcia was back in the hands of Chaldareans of the Episcopal rite. Given the ambitions of kings like Peter of Navaya, the entire region would be reclaimed. Then the Reconquest would move on to reclaim the southern shore of the Mother Sea.

All that, Serifs thought dreamily, was Sublime's goal.

The Bishop slipped a hand under his robe to tease Armand's hair, to encourage him in his efforts.

6. Al-Qarn, in Dreanger of the Kaifate of al-Minphet

From the north al-Qarn appeared to stand in the deep desert. Its strange, dirty bistre wall rose from the bitter earth left by Gordimer's paranoia. The barren, unoccupied ground was the same color as the wall. It was a breeding place of flies. Garbage and night soils ended up there every morning. No human habitation, not even a nomad's tent for a night, was allowed within a mile of the wall.

Years ago an astrologer told Gordimer he would be brought low by an enemy from the north. The Lion had taken that to mean an army.

The astrologer could not be faulted. There was no other direction whence such an army could come. For six hundred miles westward the coastal cities owed allegiance to the Kaif of al-Minphet and were content. The nomad tribes of the desert and mountains sometimes acted up, but they were a threat to one another, not to Gordimer or the Kaifate.

South of Dreanger the many petty kingdoms all acknowledged the Kaif—despite the fact that the majority were some variety of Chaldarean who refused to accept the Brothen Patriarch as the head of their Church. They considered him a pompous upstart. Luckily, he was comfortably far away.

Else strode toward the Northern Gate, as alone as a beggar seeking his fortune. He had sent the Andesqueluzan mummies ahead while he dealt with the barge master who had brought him south from the island of Raine. The Lion's own warships were not permitted to proceed upriver from Raine.

Two log booms spanned the Shirne, above and below al-Qarn. Cargos destined for the upper Shirne had to be transshipped several times.

Dust devils danced across the barren. Else worried. Some evil spirits could come out in the daytime. If the Lion feared him enough, he might have er-Rashal al-Dhulquarnen set something diabolic on him.

Else knew that Gordimer feared him but did not know why. Unless another soothsayer had filled the Lion's head with absurd ravings.

Gordimer was addicted to his augurs.

Else knew his life and performance were beyond reproach, back to his earliest days in the Vibrant Sapling school. He did nothing less than what was expected.

He was not perfect. No one is. Perfection is reserved for the God Who Is the One True God.

Else entertained a suspicion that many of the gods of the infidels were real, too, they were just less than the God of gods.

Al-Qarn's North Wall spanned Gordimer's Waste in a line as

straight as a razor's slash. Windmills surmounted it at intervals, which made it unique amongst all the city walls in the world.

The windmills were there to pump water.

The top of the wall was an aqueduct. It carried water from the Shirne to reservoirs in the highest part of the city. Which, at Gordimer's insistence, were kept filled and free of settled mud.

Gordimer's Waste left Else wondering if all Dreanger might not end up barren because of that man.

Right now, a hundred seventy miles south of al-Qarn, the last forest in Dreanger was being clear-cut to provide timber for construction of a vast new war fleet. Gordimer had decreed the expansion because he feared the ambitions of the Patriarch of Brothe, the Emperor of Rhûn, and the fleets of the mercantile republics of Dateon, Aparion, and Sonsa. An invading army would need ships to reach Dreanger.

Else entered the city. Behind the wall differed from Gordimer's Waste like day differed from night. Every inch of al-Qarn was vibrant and busy, humming with life. Some claimed a million souls dwelt in al-Qarn. That was an exaggeration, but it delighted Else.

Al-Qarn was home. To Else and all Sha-lug. Al-Qarn's great mission was to produce the Sha-lug who protected the Kaifate and who were—in their own eyes—the chief defenders of the Realm of Peace and al-Prama, the Faith.

ELSE CLIMBED THE LONG FLIGHTS OF BROAD STEPS THAT TOOK him up to the Palace of the Kings, no longer aptly named because there had been no kings in Dreanger for centuries. The name seemed the more unusual because God did not accept the competition for affection presented by kings. There were no kings anywhere inside the Realm of Peace. Only strongmen who arrogated the powers of kings.

Else's Vibrant Sapling school was one of seven that turned young slaves into polished Sha-lug. Before Gordimer there had been more. Gordimer compelled the surviving schools to watch one another, in a competition that perverted the original competition for excellence between schools.

The midday call to prayer came before Else entered. He

abased himself, going through the motions. In al-Qarn everyone did. Even visiting infidels. There were spies everywhere. Transgressions were punished swiftly and brutally.

Gordimer the Lion had no respect for his Kaif, the captain of the religious ship, and held the man hostage, but he was a fanatic devotee of the Written. Despite the circumstances of his birth.

The record of his purchase survived. The slavers claimed Gordimer was a Cledian from the Promptean coast. But his name, his coloring, and his build suggested Arnhander ancestors. The Lion himself claimed descent from the Holy Family. Which Else thought must be a loyalty test. If you could swallow that obvious untruth, and never dispute it, you could survive in Gordimer's world.

But you never knew who might report to him. It might be someone with a grudge.

Everyone in direct contact with Gordimer spied for him, one way or another. He expected answers when he asked questions. He was feared universally. And respected by many because the culture honored strongmen. Only a strongman kept the dogs of war and civil unrest at heel.

Dreanger was rich. For millennia it exported grains and cotton and imported gold, silver, and luxuries. Its neighbors were less wealthy but the peace provided by the Kaif's suzerainty was treasure enough for most. War profited only the few.

Else rose from stone worn by the tread of a hundred million sandals. He strode into the cool shade behind the structure's immense, square outer pillars. In passing, he noted that artisans were still removing or rewriting inscriptions that had come down from those fabulous ages predating Gordimer's ascension to power.

Posterity would know the tiniest details of Gordimer's life—those he did not keep secret—until the next ego-driven strongman decided to rewrite history. In which case Gordimer the Lion would be remembered only in the annals of his enemies.

"Captain Tage?"

Else paused. His eyes had not completed the transition from intense noon sunlight to interior gloom. "Yes."

"Will you follow me?"

The speaker wore simple clothing of a style recollecting that of the pagan priests of antiquity, a white cotton jacket with skirts that hung to the knee. This was the uniform of Gordimer's court wizards and augurs. This youngster would be a novice, not yet officially apprenticed. He would be a pure-blooded indigene, descended from the priestly caste of pagan times. Some of whom, if rumors could be credited, still followed the old ways in secret.

Though Else was supposed to report to Gordimer the moment he arrived, he could not refuse this summons. Er-Rashal al-Dhulquarnen, called Rashal the Rascal by some, was as dangerous as Gordimer the Lion. Possibly more so. Er-Rashal's connections with the Instrumentalities of the Night made him powerful in his own right.

Er-Rashal was the nearest thing to an actual friend that Gordimer had in this world.

THE COURT SORCERER MET ELSE IN A ROOM NOT FAR FROM Gordimer's private audience. If Else were asked to pick the wizard out of a hundred strangers he would have chosen er-Rashal because the man fit the description of the wicked sorcerer in every old story and fairy tale told in this end of the world. He was a tall, dark man with heavy lips, a hooked nose, and a shaven skull. His eyes were dark and cold. His body was big and powerful. He looked two decades younger than his fifty years.

Er-Rashal chose to look like that specifically because everyone, noble and common, was raised on those stories. He wanted to be feared.

"Lord Rashal," Else said. "The Lion insisted that I see him as soon as I get here."

"He's aware of your arrival." The wizard's voice boomed. "You know him. It will be an hour before he gets around to you. I've told the guards you'll be here with me if they don't find you outside the audience door."

Else did not like this. It reeked of intrigue. This was the side of al-Qarn that he did not love.

He became nervous whenever he came in from the field. Al-Qarn was a political jungle. He was not cut out for its intrigues.

He was a soldier. He did not care who did what to whom in the capital. He had to take care of the men who followed him.

All of which made him a popular field commander. Officers beloved of their troops do not flourish in a dictatorship. Gordimer himself was once a popular commander who came to power by eliminating an elderly, no-longer-effective predecessor.

Else nodded his understanding, waited for the wizard to get to the point.

Er-Rashal said, "You did well with the mummies. I didn't think you'd manage it. Gordimer had more faith. I owe him twenty silver drachmas. Which you shouldn't take to mean that I didn't pray that you'd be successful."

Else nodded again. "Good thing you weren't determined not to lose your money. One miracle survival a mission is all I can manage."

"That's what I want to ask you about. What I've heard so far baffles me."

Else shrugged. "There isn't much to tell, really. We were threatened by something that Az called a bogon. I did the only thing I could think of. Everything came out right."

"Nevertheless . . . Your Master of Ghosts might have failed to notice something."

Else told the story in detail. He was able to recall a lot because he knew he would be questioned repeatedly. Gordimer, in particular, would be interested in inimical supernatural manifestations around Sha-lug in the field. Especially north of al-Qarn.

Er-Rashal asked, "Why did you load your falcon with coins?"

"I can't figure that out. I guess because I heard somewhere that night things don't like silver. I do remember thinking that it wouldn't really work."

"Yet you never showed a doubt to your men."

So er-Rashal had talked to Hagid. "A good leader doesn't betray his doubts and doesn't become confused or flustered. He has to do something, even if it's wrong. When I had the falcon loaded with coins and gravel I was sure it was pointless. But it kept the men calm and occupied. That was the whole point, at the time."

"You were lucky. Silver is a potent poison to some night things, but only a few. Plain iron bothers more. You might consider taking along a sack of iron pellets if you're on a mission where you think you might have that kind of trouble."

"Now I'm wondering if there wasn't iron gravel in the stuff we put in the cannon."

"How did the falcon itself perform?"

"Better than I expected. You finally found the right alloy, or the right cooling process, or something. We couldn't find one flaw in the weapon afterward, although we overcharged it."

The sorcerer indulged in a little preening. He had produced a portable cannon that worked under combat conditions. No one had done that before.

"That's good news. I'll make more, now. I wish there was a practical way to cast an iron tube."

Else observed, "Logically, iron *would* be better than brass."

"Absolutely. And iron is almost immune to the Tyranny of the Night. We're hunting ways to get around the difficulties. It's all trial and error, though."

"The firepowder needs improvement. It draws moisture. The damper it gets the less power it has and the more noxious smoke it makes." Else exulted secretly. He had diverted the thoughts of the smartest, most dangerous man in the Kaifate. "If it ignites at all."

If you got er-Rashal onto one of his obsessions and grunted in the right places you were home free.

Else talked about firepowder weapons until the summons from Gordimer came.

ELSE WAS NOT AFRAID OF GORDIMER THE MAN. GORDIMER, THE grand marshal of the Sha-lug, was another matter. Gordimer knew that. And was not pleased. Gordimer preferred to be feared by everyone. Personally.

Else did not fear the man because he was pushing fifty. Else himself was a hardened warrior in the prime of life.

When Else entered the presence with er-Rashal he accorded the warlord every ounce of respect he was due. He would continue to do so, regardless. While the marshal deserved that respect.

Gordimer the Lion was a tall, strong warrior risen so high he no longer worked to maintain the marvelous attributes that had helped him become famous when he was young. Else noted hints of fat and a sleepy droop of eye that suggested excessive personal indulgence. Further, he noted the flash of a female shape in gauze two steps slow in departing as he and the wizard arrived. Almost certainly on purpose, as a reminder of Gordimer's power.

"Cut the crap," Gordimer told Else while Else was amidst an elaborate ceremonial greeting. "You put him up to this, Rashal? Captain Tage, there's nobody watching and I'm not the Kaif. Let's just talk, soldier to soldier."

Gordimer still had the vast mane of blond hair that had given him his nickname. His nature was suitably ferocious both toward his own enemies and those of God.

Else told his tale simply. "Things just went too smoothly for too long. Something like the bogon was bound to happen."

"Rashal. You invited yourself here. Explain that to me."

"A bogon is a shadow entity of great power, almost never seen anymore. It would equate with a count or baron or even a kaif in the mundane world. But harder to kill." Er-Rashal betrayed a tiny sneer. The Kaif of al-Minphet, through his proxy, Gordimer, had been trying to eliminate his irksomely deviationist rivals in Qasr al-Zed and al-Halambra for years. The main result was a missive from Indala al-Sul Halaladin indicating that he would not be pleased if anything happened to his Kaif.

Gordimer accepted the message at face value. The marshal respected Indala al-Sul Halaladin because of his signal successes in the Holy Lands.

Never having met, the men had been allies in wars against the outlanders. Wars that achieved little because whenever the northern Kaifate became involved in the Holy Lands it developed immediate border problems elsewhere. Inevitably, Rhûn would invade Lucidia's northernmost provinces in an effort to recover lost territory. In the east, the Ghargarlicean Empire would start probing the borders there. The Ghargarliceans were very aggressive under their current emperor. Though now they had their own distractions from the Hu'n-tai At.

The Hu'n-tai At were pressing Lucidia from the northeast,

too. They were like the Wrath of the One God being vented against everyone.

Some Lucidian clerics believed that resisting the Hu'n-tai At meant defying the Will of God. Those clerics argued that Tsistimed the Golden, warlord of the Hu'n-tai At, was the Scourge of God prophesied in the Written, a pagan fury who would punish the Realm of Peace for all the indulgences and sins and lapses of the Faithful.

But there were fundamentalist mullahs who believed that living in fixed houses, dwelling in urban areas, living under any but the harshest conditions, constituted a surrender to the seductions of the Adversary.

Gordimer and his Kaif had not abandoned hope of seeing the end of the Kaif of Qasr al-Zed. That Kaif's champion would soon be too busy to hare off on any mission of vengeance.

Fundamentalist priests were more a nuisance in the Lucidian Kaifate than in the Dreangerean. The Lion was the sort who made certain no one became too critical.

Gordimer listened attentively while er-Rashal analyzed Else's journey into the Idiam, to Andesqueluz, and his return with six mummies.

Er-Rashal praised Else's quick thinking and unswerving determination. Praise from the sorcerer was rare.

The marshal interrupted. "All right. He's a paragon. Nobody else could have pulled it off. But that's why I sent *him*. He doesn't need to stand around listening to a clutch of broad-ass bureaucrats tell him he's wonderful. He needs to know why I wanted him. So he can get to work planning."

Else said, "I did hope to spend some time with my family."

Gordimer scowled. He had no family. Family weighed you down. Family other than the Sha-lug was a weakness. Case in point. Else was distracted. But family were useful as hostages.

Er-Rashal observed, "It wouldn't be good to leap into the flames again, right away, after dancing in the fire as long as the captain has."

Gordimer waved a hand. "It'll be a long mission, anyway. A short delay won't matter."

The Lion relied on er-Rashal's advice but did not always like it. Else thought it might be wise to send his family out of town before he left al-Qarn again.

The horrors he could imagine had happened before, to others.

Gordimer the Lion was a genius on the battlefield but petty and vindictive as a ruler. And extremely selfish. And unable to recall the main reason he had removed his predecessor.

You could not keep pissing people off. They would do something about it eventually.

"My curiosity continues to grow," Else said, as a reminder that he had not yet been told why he had been summoned.

Gordimer said, "I'm sending you to Firaldia, to the Brothen Principalities, to find out what Sublime is up to. Our spies aren't making sense anymore."

Er-Rashal said, "They say Sublime is preaching new crusades. To reverse Indala al-Sul's successes. To drive the Faithful away from the Wells of Ihrian and out of the Holy Lands. To conquer Calzir. The same silly things Patriarchs always preach, but this one may mean it. Though a crusade doesn't make sense. Sublime is on the brink of war with the Grail Emperor. And still has problems with the Viscesment pretenders. In addition to which, he's preoccupied with something known as the Maysalean Heresy, which is strong in an Arnhander province called the Connec. Our spies suggest that the man has no acquaintance with reality. We don't believe anyone of his stature could be that disconnected."

The marshal added, "The only people capable of undertaking a new crusade are the same ones who backboned previous Chaldarean expeditions. The Arnhanders. But they're at war with Santerin. And they'd have to provide any soldiers needed to put down the heretics and anti-Brothen forces in the Connec."

Er-Rashal continued, "Nevertheless, this Patriarch seems convinced that he need only say that something is God's Will and it'll happen."

"Sounds like people should question the Patriarch's sanity."

Er-Rashal agreed. "But those people believe Honario Benedocto became something transcendent when he was elected Patriarch. In an election renown for bribery, blackmail, and at least one murder."

Gordimer growled, "Sublime worships a false god. He worships idols. Naturally, he's mad. But how deep does his madness run? Will crazy talk lead to crazy deeds? We need to know."

That made sense. Gordimer had to guard and preserve his portion of the Realm of Peace. But that could not be the whole story.

Er-Rashal said, "I want to know more about the Collegium. Besides what they're up to politically."

Then Gordimer said, "If Sublime is as crazy as it sounds, there ought to be factions in the Collegium willing to replace him."

"I don't know much . . ." Else cut himself short. No point offering even an appearance of contradiction. "Can I pass in Brothen society?"

Er-Rashal said, "In Brothe, in the Brothen Principalities, in Firaldia as a whole, yes. Easily. Brothe is as cosmopolitan as Hypraxium. I went there, once, years ago. Without knowing the language. I got by. You won't have trouble as long as you don't claim you're anything but what you are, a professional soldier. Be an unemployed mercenary from somewhere far away. If you don't tell anyone where you're from, you'll never have to deal with someone who wants to talk about the good old days back home. Say you don't want to talk about the past because there's a price on your head. Let the story involve the virtue of a woman whose husband you crippled when he caught you with his woman. That's the kind of crime westerners find amusing."

Gordimer said, "Rashal is as excited as a kid about finding out what the Collegium is up to in the catacombs under the Chiaro Palace. Me, I want to know if anybody can be turned against Sublime. And I want to know Sublime's plans. I want to know who his most likely successors are and what their attitudes are toward Dreanger, the Holy Lands, the Arnhander states, and the Realm of Peace. And I want to know everything I can find out about a man named Ferris Renfrow."

That caught Else from the blind side. "Ferris Renfrow? Who is Ferris Renfrow?"

"Exactly."

Er-Rashal had pity. "Ferris Renfrow is a very odd bird. He's visited al-Qarn twice. He represents himself as an agent of the Grail Emperor Johannes. He's slipperier than a freshwater eel. He wanted information without giving anything back."

Gordimer added, "He wouldn't be pinned down but it sounded like he wanted to forge a secret alliance against the Patriarch."

Er-Rashal said, "The Grail Emperors and Patriarchs have quarreled for more than a century over whether the religious hierarchy takes precedence over the secular. Also, there's a question of whether the Patriarch and his bishops have a right to the Episcopal Principalities. Under secular law, no feudal subject can leave his fief to the Church, or anyone else but his sons, without consent of his liege. In most cases the liege-ultimate is the Grail Emperor. Further, in the feudal estate, the Episcopal Principalities all have obligations to the Emperor and the Kings of Favorate, Stiluri, Alameddine, and—God laughed—even Calzir."

Else observed, "We do things more sensibly here."

The sorcerer missed Else's sarcasm. "In theory. Until the Imperial Electors elevated Johannes Blackboots the contest seldom amounted to anything. But now the principals are Johannes and Sublime. And Sublime is willing to use the full power of his office to improve the fortunes of his family, his city, and his Church. There's a real chance of war."

"Which we would like to encourage," Gordimer said. "Without getting pulled in. Better the Unbelievers butcher each other than attack us or the Holy Lands."

"I see," Else replied, careful to sound neutral.

Gordimer asked, "So, can I count on you?"

"Can I take some of my men?"

"Not this time. This time you go alone. A merchantman will take you to Runch on the Isle of Staklirhod. At Runch you can buy passage to Sonsa. Your documents will identify you as a minor Arnhander knight. You've been called home to deal with family matters in LaTriobe, in Tramaine. This is because of the confusion following Santerin's obliteration of the Duke of Harmonachy's army at Themes last summer."

"Sounds like you've done some detailed planning."

Er-Rashal admitted, "Actually, we're improvising on the fly."

Gordimer said, "We captured a Sir Aelford daSkees last week. He was in those exact circumstances. Pretend to be him till you reach Sonsa. It isn't likely that anyone knows him. Talk about changing ship to a Minochan coaster and traveling on to Sheavenalle in the End of Connec. When you reach Sonsa, though, drop the daSkees guise and head south toward Brothe as an unemployed mercenary."

Er-Rashal added, "Once you leave Sonsa you'll be on your own."

Gordimer added, "There'll be a lot more to rehearse before you go. But, for now, relax. Rest. See your people."

Else imagined a sinister tone there. Perhaps inventing the Lion's implication that his family were hostage to his behavior.

Imagination or not, Else needed no reminding. He bowed.

Gordimer said, "A moment more. To show my gratitude for what you accomplished bringing those mummies out of Andesqueluz. Without losing a man. Rashal?"

"Extend your hands, Captain." The sorcerer placed a leather sack in Else's right hand. A generous reward indeed unless the coins within were bronze or copper. Then er-Rashal wrapped Else's left wrist with a strip of worn brown leather. He brought its ends together, muttered something while he drew a finger along the join. The leather closed seamlessly. Else rolled his wrist. A dozen odd stones and metal shapes decorated the leather.

Er-Rashid said, "That will fade from sight. It will shield you from a range of sorcery and most of the things of the night. Not that you should expect trouble. Brothe is almost as old as the temple cities of the Lower Kingdom. It's even more tamed."

"Thank you."

Gordimer told him, "Go. Enjoy yourself."

IN REMOTE ANTIQUITY DREANGER BECAME DIVIDED ADMINIS-tratively into the Lower, Middle, and Upper Kingdoms. The Lower Kingdom consisted of delta country and seacoast. It was prosperous agriculturally and commercially. It was also home to the oldest cities in the world, each of which grew up around the home temple of one of the Ancient Gods of Dreanger. Seven hundred years before Gordimer the Lion, when the Church became the official religion of the Old Brothen Empire—Dreanger was a province of the Empire then—the temples were stormed and torn apart by followers of the fanatic Josephus Alegiant. The priests were murdered.

Josephus was a mad devotee of Aaron of Chaldar. Aaron was one of the Holy Founders of the Church, born in Chaldar in the Holy Lands. Chaldar gave its name to that whole religious movement. Chaldar existed still as a dusty village beside the Well of Peace.

Aaron was the first of the Holy Founders to preach the Chaldarean creed. His great message had been one of universal peace, love, and equality, informed with an abiding loathing of violence in every form.

Two hundred fifty years before Gordimer another wave of murderous apostles of love and peace swept through the Lower Kingdom. It swamped the ruling Chaldareans, destroying both their works and anything pagan that had survived Josephus Alegiant. That consisted of thousands of books. Burned, those took with them the secrets, knowledge, and histories of thousands of years.

The Peqaad warriors of the Conquest were ignorant, superstitious, unbathed desert tribesmen frequently only weeks past their epiphanous moments of conversion. They came to Dreanger knowing a deep terror of books and writing. Literate men always worked evil by taking advantage of their education.

From earliest times the Middle Kingdom was the seat of Dreanger's governments. Even when priests ruled and kings were gods and Dreanger prostrated itself to the Tyranny of the Night whether sun or moon ruled the sky. And al-Qarn, wearing other names before the Conquest, had been the seat of administration since before men had begun to distinguish their rulers from their gods.

These days the Upper Kingdom was wild country, frontier country, snuggled up against the Slang Mountains, that shielded Dreanger from the south. Chaldarean cultists and anchorites, and pagan nomads, still haunted the Upper Kingdom, in company with the ghosts of seven thousand years worth of Dreangerean dead.

Today the Upper Kingdom was commonly called the Kingdom of the Dead. The barren hills on either bank of the Shirne, for as far as thirty miles back, were networked with tunnels that led to the tombs of half a thousand generations. The Instrumentalities of the Night made grave robbers and tomb raiders wish they had chosen more auspicious careers.

The original significance of being buried in the Hills of the Dead had gotten lost centuries before Josephus Alegiant, but even now, amongst those who claimed unalloyed Dreangerean blood, there was a social imperative for having one's corpse laid down underneath the Hills of the Dead.

That part of the Upper Kingdom had accumulated immense reserves of dark magic. Only the Holy Lands boasted a superior supernatural status and more concentrated magical power.

The Wells of Ihrian were the Heart of the Soul of the World.

GORDIMER ASKED, "WHAT DO YOU THINK OF CAPTAIN TAGE, Rashal?"

"I think you're letting your fears get the better of you again, my friend. That man might be your most loyal and valuable follower. He's truly, totally Sha-lug." No man but er-Rashal al-Dhulquarnen would dare speak so directly to Gordimer the Lion.

The marshal was not pleased. But he could do nothing. Much as he hated it, he was at er-Rashal's mercy.

Gordimer had great difficulty grasping the fact that not everyone thought the way he did, that every man was not a slave to bloody ambition.

Captain Tage was a competent man. How could he not . . . ?

Er-Rashal said, "Huge events will overtake us in coming years. If you go on the way you have been, those events will devour you, me, Dreanger, and the Kaifate of al-Minphet. Because you, driven by baseless fears, will have eliminated everyone with enough nerve, strength, and ability to lift a sword."

Gordimer rose. He stamped around. He cursed. He threatened. He appealed to God. He told his only friend, "You have to help me, Rashal. I can't control my thoughts. But they can control me."

"I'll do what I can. For Dreanger's sake as well as yours. But my best efforts won't do any good if you don't make an effort yourself. Remind yourself, whenever you think you smell a plot, that there's an excellent chance that it's imaginary. Talk to me *before* you start killing people. Sit down with me and we'll study the evidence. And let me question the suspects before you kill them. We don't want to waste good people. Abad did that. Abad wasted too many good people. Which was why you gained enough support to remove him."

Er-Rashal did not mention that he had been chief wizard to Gordimer's predecessor. No need to give Gordimer anything else to brood about.

"I try, Rashal. I really try. But it's a disease."

"Just let me question your suspects. Don't do anything yourself. Don't draw the lightning."

Gordimer grunted agreement. But he did so with secret reservations.

7. The Andorayan Travelers

Shagot rested his palms on his knees. He panted. He had stopped only seconds before he started puking from the exertion. He had done way too much drinking and loafing lately. Though he would never admit it, particularly to Sigurdur and Sigurjon, whose parents must have lost a riddling contest to a boulder to come up with names as unimaginative as those. Not that he and his brother had fared much better.

"Shit," Shagot gasped. He fought for air. "How the hell . . . can we still . . . be this far . . . behind . . . those assholes?"

Shagot and his companions stood in a saddle on a ridge in the Jottendyngjan Mountains, fighting for wind while studying the road south. The fire in Shagot's lungs was less a problem than his incredulity at the fact that those pussy missionaries were still safely ahead. But, there they were, looking like ants scaling the flank of the next line of mountains.

Svavar said, "I don't like this. We should've taken a ship down and waited for them at the Ormo crossing."

Shagot grunted. He did not waste breath reminding Svavar that the Ormo Strait was not friendly territory. Any ship from Andoray appearing there was inviting a ferocious disaster.

The Southron villains had to be overhauled from behind. On dry land.

Sigurdur asked, "What're we gonna do when it gets dark, Grim? They's trolls and dwarfs an' shit up here."

"Yeah. Not to mention ghosts and haunts left over from the god times," Sigurjon added. By the god times he meant prehistory. The gods were marginally active even today—witness the Choosers who took Erief away—but not much had been heard from them since those legendary times when the early Andorayans drove the wild, mystic, primitive Seatts north beyond the cliffs of ice, into the lands of always-snow.

"The old folks gave me all the wards and charms we'll need to get through the night. For as long as it takes to catch those girls."

"*Who* gave them to you?" Svavar wanted to know. "Not Vidgis, I hope. Because if it was Vidgis we're dead already and we're just too boneheaded to lay down and stop kicking."

Vidgis had gotten Svavar to top her once, in a drunken hour. He insisted that it would not have happened if she was not some terrible witch who had enchanted him.

Chuckling, Shagot agreed. "Oh, yeah. She's a witch." The way all women are witches. She just had a few extra years on her. "Pulla, Trygg, and that bunch gave them to me. They're tribal charms. Charms they wouldn't have given us if Snaefells and the Skogafjordur hadn't witnessed those marvels."

"Huh?" Sigurdur said. Not the brightest man, Sigurdur. "What marvels?"

"Sigurdur, you think the murder of a king is something that happens every day?" Erief would have become king if he had lived, Shagot knew. "You think the Choosers of the Slain just drop in?"

"Oh. No. I get you. But I do reckon they picked us six mainly so they could get us out of town."

So Sigurdur was blind in one eye but could see out the other. Shagot had not realized that the old folks might have chosen this group so he and the others would not be hanging around causing trouble.

Those assholes Trygg and Pulla would pull that kind of shit, too. Old people did not like chaos, confusion, tumult, or excitement. They wanted life calm, quiet, and predictable.

Shagot thought he must be getting old himself since he had no trouble understanding why the old people wanted him out of the way.

"Let's just catch these guys, then get our asses on home." Of a sudden, Shagot found himself able to consider Snaefells special. Found that he could think of the village as home.

He was amazed.

* * *

SHAGOT THE BASTARD WAS NOT ABLE TO CATCH THOSE MIS-
sionaries. Those ferocious southerners who did not believe in
raising a hand against their fellow man. Day by day, hour by
hour, he and his companions gained ground, but never, ever,
did they actually catch up.

Shagot's band was a scant thirty yards behind when they
reached the shore of the Ormo Strait, at a village called Ara.
Hallgrim and Finnboga both wasted arrows. Naturally, they
missed. Shagot barked, "Quit it! You might hit the ferryman in
the fog."

The boat the fugitives had chartered was small, manned by a
single oarsman who must be a true man's man, for the strait
was fourteen miles wide here. Ara was not the customary jump
off for those who wanted to cross. That was Grynd, thirty
miles southeastward along the coast. Commercial ferries ran
there, making the four-mile journey through treacherous currents to Skola on the tip of Friesland.

Grynd and Skola were too civilized. Shagot could not go
there. Erief's enemies and King Gludnir's friends were much
too common there.

Unstringing his bow, taciturn Finnboga observed, "If we
need proof that those two are villains, this is it."

"Because they chose a smugglers' crossing?"

The boatman would conduct his passengers to Orland, a
swampy, sparsely inhabited, totally impoverished island off
the west coast of Friesland. The fugitives would have to tra-
verse Orland on foot, then cross to the mainland from Orfland's nether end—without ever attracting the attention of
anyone who mattered in Friesland.

Sigurdur said, "I'm not comfortable leaving Andoray on
foot."

That was such a dumb thing to say that Shagot just nodded.
"You guys go scare up another boatman."

There was no boatman to be found. There was no one in the
village. Not a soul. But the evidence said Ara had been a busy
little town until a few hours ago.

Sigurjon said, "I don't like this, Grim. Something weird is
going on."

"I think you're right. Let's wait here. When that boat comes back we'll go across. Keep your bows strung. Just in case." He made sure his sword was loose in its scabbard. It was a fine old blade that had come from a monastery in Santerin, probably left there by some noble trying to bribe the local god.

Hallgrim asked, "What do you make of this fog? Fog usually burns off by this time."

"We're at the mouth of the Ormo Strait. There're strange currents and tides and fogs here all the time."

Hallgrim did not talk much. Shagot wished he would give up the vice altogether. When he did speak he always brought up something disgusting. Often he belabored the obvious when everyone else did not want to be reminded.

He did not shut up. "Will we all fit in that boat? It didn't look that big."

Shagot grunted. His brother Svavar asked, "You want me to hit him on the head?"

"He might not notice. Besides, it's a good question. And I think we will fit. What I'm wondering is, how long will we have to wait? I didn't see a mast or a sail. And at the wrong time of day the current is going to be vicious."

The Ormo Strait joined the landlocked Shallow Sea with the Andorayan Sea, to the west. The Shallow Sea was so called because at dead low tide a tenth of its bottom lay exposed and a third of the remainder did not rise above a tall man's head. Ships on the Shallow Sea were broad of beam and drew very little water. And had to be guided by very knowledgeable pilots. There were just two small areas in all of the Shallow Sea where, at high tide, the water was over a hundred feet deep.

Navigation in the Ormo Strait was particularly harrowing. Immense volumes of water raced back and forth as the tides turned.

People like the smugglers and fishermen of Ara knew their waters better than they knew their wives. They started learning the waters when they were toddlers.

Svavar sighed. "Yeah. We'll be lucky to get out of here today."

Sigurdur said, "The moon is almost full. We could manage a night crossing."

Finnboga mused, "We should liberate some horses after we get to the mainland. Then we could catch up fast."

Except, Shagot thought, that would make it impossible for
them to come north again—assuming they stayed ahead of the
pursuit after they stole the horses.

Svavar said, "It looks like the fog is thinning out."

But visibility remained less than a bowshot.

Shagot said, "You guys that went sneaking around, poking
into stuff. Did you find anything that explains why nobody is
home? Or where they went?" The absence of Ara's villagers
bothered him. That likely meant an intercession by the Instrumentalities of the Night.

Those nights on the road, coming down from Skogafjordur,
had produced only the feeblest of troubles. Even considering
the charms the band carried, the supernatural weather had been
unnaturally mild.

Shagot shuddered. He did not like thinking too much. But he
was captain of the band. And it never hurt to be paranoid about
the dark.

The Huldre Folk had followed them. The hidden people
were of more than passing interest to them. Maybe they were
responsible for all those little delays that kept the band from
catching the foreigners before they escaped from Andoray.
Why? If the foreigners' god became established here he would
chase the hidden folk away.

"Hey!" Finnboga shouted. "There's a boat out there. It's
coming in."

Shagot saw it, too. It was not the boat that had taken the missionaries away. This was a regular fishing boat, the kind that
spent every clement hour at sea, fishing. It was shorter and
wider than the war craft Shagot and his companions knew. But
it seemed too well kempt to be your usual fisherman.

Shagot pulled his band together. "As far as these people are
concerned, we don't know starboard from larboard. We're
landlubbers. Understand? And let me do the talking." The
fisher looked like it would require a minimum crew of three,
though he could see only one man on deck. And there was a
deck. So the boat had a hold. Which made sense for a
fisherman—or smuggler—who wanted to keep his cargo from
washing overboard in heavy seas.

The closer the fisherman approached, the more perfect she

seemed. They could pile aboard her and run all the way down the western coast of Orland, to put themselves into position to ambush the missionaries after they completed their grueling passage through the island's bogs. They would not have to slay the crew of the boat, even. If the fishermen were cooperative.

"NAME'S RED HAMMER," THE BOAT'S MASTER SAID. "AND YOU men look like you need to get somewhere in a hurry, without being noticed." Before Shagot could respond, he added, "And this's my cousin, Smith."

"Smith?"

Red shrugged. "He just wants to be known by his nickname."

Shagot grunted, confused. He could not get his thoughts to follow. "What about the old man?"

"That's Walker. My father. He's getting old and slowing down. He isn't much use anymore. But he don't want to quit the game. So we take him along when we go out."

Shagot said, "We do need to get across the strait. And down the west coast of Orland, to Tyrvo, or even to Grodnir's Point on the Friesland shore. That would be particularly useful."

Red Hammer nodded. "We can do that. So we just need to agree on a price. And to unload our catch." The stench of fish filled the air.

"We'll help you unload," Shagot promised. "So let's talk cost."

Initially, Red Hammer asked if what they wanted was worth thirty-five gold pieces.

Shagot laughed. "No. How stupid do we look? We don't have that kind of money, anyway. We look like kings? You won't find one piece of gold between us. You lunatic. Be happy that we'll give you five Santerin silver pennies."

The bargaining did not last long. Shagot was in a hurry. The fishermen were impatient to unload their cargo.

The tide was turning.

Svavar worried aloud as he stumbled along under a heavy sack of fish, some of which still wiggled. "We're getting too good a deal, Grim. They'll try to rob us."

"There's six of us. They may be big and dumb but they

aren't that dumb. What do you want to bet they've got some illegal cargo that we'll help protect in order to get where we're going?"

Shagot understood such thinking. He had done things like that himself when he was not off with Erief.

"They have them a devilish look in their eyes, Grim."

"And I don't blame them. This is as lucky a day as poor people ever get."

Svavar went right on worrying about treachery and betrayal. Red Hammer might sell them to Gludnir.

Whenever Shagot met the eye of Red or Smith they seemed amused. As though they knew his worries and found them entertaining.

Shagot was sure he had the angles covered. These men were just fishermen and smugglers with no reason to turn treacherous.

It had been a hard go for Shagot, lately. Weariness hung on his bones like tattered cloth. He told the Thorkalssons, "Don't wake me up unless the ship is going under and the water is up to my nuts."

He found a place out of the way, on deck. He wanted nothing to do with the hold. The stink of fish was bad enough where he was.

The fog was closing in again.

He thought he dreamed.

He was sound asleep but saw his surroundings as though he was wide awake. The fog grew weaker. The sea became calmer. The people of the sea came up to frolic round the boat. Beautiful maidens from the deep, indistinguishable from human girls except for their beauty, sang to the fishermen. Walker seemed to bless them. He seemed to get younger as the boat moved out to sea, too.

The sea itself changed. The water darkened. A growing chop came running in on the bow. The people of the sea stopped following.

Soon the fisherman was battering its way into the teeth of a rising storm. Its crew remained unperturbed, even after waves started leaping over the bow, hurling white spume. Then it was green water, pounding the foredeck with the fists of giants.

Indifferent, the crew forged on.

The three were no longer amiable or chatty. They worked ship—when they did anything at all—with very little talk. Shagot could not understand how they managed to cope.

Fierce lightning began dueling inside the storm. Several bolts stabbed the sea near the fishing craft. A bolt hit Red Hammer.

Shagot understood, then, that these mad fishermen had sailed them all to their deaths.

His eyes recovered from the glare. He saw the lunatic redhead standing with his arms upraised, his roaring laughter competing with the thunder. He welcomed the caress of the storm.

Shagot finally realized that he was not at the mercy of insane fishermen at all. He became more frightened than ever he had been, even in the deeps of the night, far from any friendly shore.

Walker sensed his shift of being the instant the fear took hold. He turned away from the storm and looked Shagot directly in the eye.

Shagot almost cried for his mother.

Walker was old but not nearly as old as before. He had become someone of strength and substance. But what pierced Shagot with terror was the fact that Walker had only one eye.

Shagot scarcely had a chance to whimper before darkness collapsed upon him.

THE BOAT, NOW A GOLDEN BARGE, EMERGED FROM THE STORM onto an emerald sea like none ever seen by the traders and raiders of Andoray. The barge, invisibly propelled, moved in alongside a quay of polished rose granite. Officious, chattering dwarves with vast beards tied the barge up, then hustled aboard. They collected the sleeping warriors and took them ashore, carried them up a long road that led to a vast sprawl of a castle barely discernable atop a tall, sheer-flanked mountain.

Barge, sea, dwarves, mountain, and castle all appeared exactly as portrayed in legend and song.

Somewhere along the upward road there would be a bridge woven together from rainbows.

* * *

THE PEOPLE OF ARA, ALL SHAKING THEIR HEADS, BEWILDERED, stumbled back into their village. A whole day had slipped off into eternity unnoticed.

Someone—or something—had come to Ara during their absence. Nothing was missing and no damage had been done. But someone had gone through Ara, poking into everything.

A cry came from the icehouse. The villagers all rushed over. And discovered that Ara had been blessed with the biggest catch of fish anyone had ever seen.

Folk scattered to collect gutting and scaling knives. The work began. The traditional malcontents grumbled because all this found wealth forced them to gut and bone and fillet and capture roe like never before in their experience.

For some people there is a cloud inside anything silver.

8. Antieux, in the End of Connec

The Patriarchal legate to the Bishop of Antieux, Bronte Doneto, was a bishop without a see. Which was an indirect way of saying that he was a member of the Collegium. One of those quiet, frightening members little known to anyone outside. Bishop Serifs, although a creature of the Patriarch, did not know the man. Had he done so he would have been less sanguine while awaiting his next meeting with the emissary.

Bronte Doneto was a close ally of Sublime V because they were cousins. Doneto expected that they would go far together. They were young. They were strong. They dreamed big dreams. But the path to fulfillment of those dreams was strewn with obstacles like Bishop Serifs, men venal enough to be used but without drive enough to do anything useful on their own. They were content to secrete themselves in their grand palaces, playing with their concubines and catamites while stealing the wherewithal to keep themselves in style.

Doneto was a cynic. He expected the worst of everyone and bragged that they seldom disappointed him. But he was a true believer, too—in his conviction that the Church ought to be the be-all and end-all of the Chaldarean world. He was not as deeply engaged by Church dogma.

Doneto chose to accept Bishop Serifs' challenge. He would sample the mood of the people. What the rabble had to say would tell him what needed doing to cleanse the Connec of heresy.

BRONTE DONETO DID NOT SHIFT ROLES EASILY. HE WAS NOT A prince who could disguise himself as a pauper and pass. He was not an actor with any range. This trip into the Connec was the farthest afield he had traveled, ever. Only once before had he ventured outside the safety of the Episcopal States, in an unsuccessful attempt to convince the families of Aparion that they should donate ships to transport an army that Sublime's predecessor wanted to send to invade the Firaldian Praman kingdom of Calzir.

Calzir was a more suitable target for a crusade, Doneto believed. It was not powerful. It had no friends. It just had those great natural defenses, the Vaillarentiglia Mountains. Expunge Calzir and you would clear Firaldia of the last vestiges of the Praman in the heartland of the Old Brothen Empire. That would encourage Chaldareans everywhere.

But Bronte's cousin wanted to be a Patriarch whose name echoed down the ages. He wanted to be remembered as the Patriarch who triumphed over the Pramans and the rest of the Church's enemies while uniting all Chaldareans under the Patriarchal banner and recovering the Holy Lands.

Doneto did not believe that they would live that long. It was too huge a task.

Bronte Doneto thought it would be easy to pass as lower class. All you had to do was talk crudely and smell bad. Never mind that your clothing was foreign and too rich. Never mind that bodyguards followed you around. Never mind that disdain rolled off you like steam even when you kept your mouth shut.

The folk of Antieux did not recognize him as a Patriarchal legate, though. So he did get an earful of Connecten attitude toward Sublime and his shit-eating, thieving running dog, Bishop Serifs.

Vries Yunker was the legate's chief bodyguard. Doneto found nothing to recommend the man other than the fact that no blade had yet found the episcopal throat. Yunker could have been a mastiff as far as Doneto was concerned.

Yunker suggested, "We should return to our quarters, sir. We're tempting fate." This after Doneto's passage through a farmer's market, as safe a venture as could be arranged.

Yunker knew the people who frequented the places that Doneto wanted to visit. He was that kind of people himself. They understood that something was going on immediately.

Doneto refused to listen. He was having too much fun feeling superior.

Yunkers' pessimism was not unfounded. In fact, when trouble came it was far worse than Yunker anticipated. There was a sudden rush of bodies, right there in the twilight street, in front of a hundred witnesses. Pain exploded in his side.

All three bodyguards died. Bronte Doneto suffered numerous stab wounds before he dragged an earthenware ball out of a pocket. He smashed that against the nearest building.

The world vanished in a torrent of light. Voices screamed, "Sorcery!"

Bronte Doneto plunged into unconsciousness.

THE ATTENDING BROTHER SEEMED LESS THAN THRILLED WHEN Doneto opened his eyes. The look vanished instantly.

The legate gasped, "Do I need supreme unction?"

"Sir? Ah. No, sir. I'm a healing brother. Don't try to get up. You'll open your wounds."

Doneto recalled the sudden, brilliant pain of blades probing his flesh. He felt no pain now. But he did feel numerous bandages. He did feel the pull of stitches in a half-dozen places. "How bad am I hurt?"

"Only God's Grace saved you, sir. Or incredible luck. You were stabbed six times. Two of your wounds are so deep they must have been made by a sword. You lost a lot of blood."

When Bronte expressed no interest the healing brother volunteered, "Your companions weren't as lucky as you. All three perished."

Which they deserved for their failure. But Doneto did not vent his sentiments aloud. "Who was responsible? And why?"

The priest shrugged. "Robbers, I suppose."

Those were not robbers. Those were assassins. Those men were serious about their work. Those men were not novices. Bronte Doneto was supposed to be dead.

"You suppose? What did they have to say?"

The healing brother seemed baffled by the question.

"They were captured, weren't they?"

"No."

Of course not, Doneto thought. He insisted that the rest of his guards investigate. Obviously, the local authorities were incompetent.

It took his men almost no time to determine that no one would tell them anything. Mica Troendel told Doneto, "Nobody actually said so, Your Grace, but I got the distinct impression that your survival was a popular disappointment."

Doneto assumed that meant the assassins were locals able to intimidate the populace. Only later did he entertain the possibility that the populace might wish the assassins well without knowing who they were.

Lying there, unable to move, Doneto had a lot of time to reflect on the situation in the Connec as seen by ordinary folk. And he was not pleased. Not at all. But maybe the truth could be a useful tool, too.

"Maysalean heretics tried to murder me," Doneto told Serifs when the Bishop found time to get away from his indulgences.

Serifs disagreed. "No. They're pacifists. They wouldn't murder anybody."

"Not even a Patriarchal legate who's their sworn enemy?"

"Especially not a legate. They want no trouble with Brothe. They want Brothe to leave them alone. That's all the people of the Connec want. For Brothe to leave them alone."

"Put the accusation out there anyway."

"Nobody will believe it. The likely result is, they'll decide that you staged the whole thing so you'd have an excuse to make accusations." Serifs sounded mildly accusing himself. That suspicion had found a comfortable home in his mind.

Doneto realized he faced a no-win situation. His time

amongst the unwashed had shown him how little they respected Brothe and the Church and how much suspicion they directed that way. Worse, the Connecten Episcopals were more critical than their heretical Maysalean cousins.

The fearful lesson of the night of the knives was that Connectens were convinced all social evil and moral depravity originated in Brothe and Krois, the Patriarchal Palace there.

"Then lay it at the feet of that syphilitic at Viscesment."

"As you wish. But the people won't believe that, either."

"What will they believe?" Doneto had to force himself to relax. He felt stitches tearing.

"Anything negative about the Patriarch and the Collegium, however absurd."

"So who tried to murder me? Really."

Bishop Serifs shrugged. "It might have been robbers." Then, as Doneto was about to explode, "Probably supporters of Immaculate who acted without approval from Viscesment. Or it might have been someone whose property we took."

"How would anyone from any faction know about me? This was *supposed* to be a secret mission. Even you don't know much about me."

Serifs shrugged again. "I told no one anything. So, once again, maybe they were robbers. Or, maybe, somebody in Brothe thought it might be convenient to kill you out here where it wouldn't cause much excitement."

Robbers? Bull. Robbers did not attack armed bands.

Murder as a political instrument was not common. Not this way, at least. When it did happen it involved poison or a skillfully placed dagger, usually after the fact of a coup or the unwinding of a skein of extreme duplicity. It did not happen in front of hundreds of witnesses. Unless . . . unless someone wanted to send a powerful message. As, for example, to Sublime himself.

Suddenly, Doneto trusted no one. Maybe Serifs himself was the villain. Or Duke Tormond. Tormond commanded soldiers. Those men might have been soldiers. But how would the Duke know? "I want to see my man Troendel." Mica Troendel was his senior surviving bodyguard. Doneto wanted to be ready to travel as soon as he could. And he wanted to feel safe until he was able.

He would deal with the problem of the Connec after he was safely away from it. Harshly.

This mission was a disaster. And he suspected that things would get no better.

Doneto wanted to flee Antieux but the healing brothers insisted that he needed a lot of recuperation. In the end, they let him travel as far as Bishop Serifs's manor in the vineyard-strewn hills overlooking the city. It should be easier for his remaining bodyguards to protect him there.

That move did exactly what the healing brothers warned it might. It opened his wounds. He began a battle with infection that lasted for months.

9. Travels on the Mother Sea

The merchant ship was too small. It bounced on the water like a cork. It creaked and groaned of imminent disintegration even when the waters were calm. It stank. There was nothing for a passenger to do but hang on desperately when a blow came up. Its one saving grace was that it let Else keep his boots dry by not having to walk to Staklirhod.

The Sha-lug sprawled on something that might have contained cotton in the process of being smuggled. It was against Dreangerean law to sell cotton to Chaldareans. Merchants, though, did not let themselves get caught up in religious dogma or political faith. Gulls drifted around the ship, hoping for scraps but snapping up small fish churned to the surface in the wake. The sky was almost cloudless and of a blue so intense that it felt like he could fall in.

From where he lay Else could see the loom of several islands and the sails of a half-dozen ships.

An Antast Chaldarean seaman named Mallin sprawled close by, also feasting on the lack of tension. He hailed from the Neret Mountains, which faced the coast in both Lucidia and the southernmost province of the Eastern Empire. The region shifted between Rhûn and the eastern Kaifate frequently.

The Antasts harkened back to the Founders. They argued

that their vision was identical to the one set forth by Aaron, Eis, Kelam, and the others.

"Don't you worry about pirates?" Else asked. "All these islands, seems like pirates' heaven."

"Maybe in ancient times. Before the Old Empire. And a couple of times afterward. But not today. The Brotherhood of War doesn't tolerate piracy. When piracy happens, a lot of people die. Most of them in bad ways. Wives, children, anyone fool enough to live in the same town. And if the Brotherhood don't get them, the Firaldian republics will. If the fleet of the Eastern Empire don't get there first. Nah. The problem we're likely to have is official harassment. See that island, looks like a saddle? We pass that, you'll see Cape Jen straight ahead. That's the eastern tip of Staklirhod. We should make port on the morning tide."

"I thought we'd need another day."

"We made good time. Nahlik says you're a good luck charm. We didn't have to pay bribes to get out of Shartelle and our cargo was ready when we got there. And there's been no bad weather."

"No bad weather? You're mad."

"Landlubber. We've seen nothing but mild breezes and light seas."

"So it is true. It does take a streak of insanity to be a sailor. A wide streak."

"No point denying that. What's your excuse for being out here?"

"I just like running around on water filled with things that want to eat me." Mallin was fishing. All the crew did. They were loyal to Dreanger but they were curious. They thought he might be Sha-lug, not some ransomed Arnhander knight.

Mallin grunted.

"It's family trouble," Else said, sticking to the official story though the whole crew knew he would not be on their ship if he really was an Arnhander knight headed home.

A whistle sounded up forward. "Warship off the port bow."

Else and Mallin sat up. Mallin asked, "What colors?"

"Still too far off to tell. But she's a big fucker."

Mallin told Else, "In these waters it'll be the Brotherhood of

War. Or maybe the Sonsans. They do most of the trading in these islands."

The Brotherhood of War was an order of Chaldarean knights and soldiers who dedicated themselves to war against the enemies of their God. Their mission was to wrest the Wells of Ihrian from Praman control. They were fine warriors, often victorious, never daunted by unfavorable odds. The Sha-lug had learned never to engage them on their choice of ground.

The crewman forward announced, "They're not headed our way. She's a fast fucker. Three decker."

The galley loomed larger and larger. It was long and lean and dark, quiet and astonishingly fast. It shifted course slightly, toward the little merchantman without bearing down directly. Then it was right there, sliding past a hundred feet away, silent but for the hiss of the water along its hull and the muted creak, squeak, splash of its oars.

"Well, I'm baffled all to shit," Mallin said as the galley rushed away. "That was like a fucking ghost ship, or something. New fucker, too. Never saw it before."

Else had not, either, but he knew whose ship it was. It belonged to Gordimer the Lion. Among the gawkers at the galley's midships rail, staring at the sailors staring back, had been one er-Rashel al-Dhulquarnen from the Dreangerean court.

Two hours later a second galley appeared, smaller, older, shabbier, and much noisier. It belonged to the Brotherhood of War. It was looking for a strange warship roaming the archipelago.

Else remained unperturbed when Nahlik indicated the direction the other warship had gone. Er-Rashal could take care of himself.

"That would be an interesting fight," Mallin said. "Those two ships."

"It sure would."

THE SUN WAS BARELY UP WHEN THE SHIP TIED UP AT RUNCH. Else hired a boy off the dock to help move his knightly gear. He followed the boy to a great stone building that housed the local factors of the Three Families of the Sonsan Republic. He presented himself as Aelford daSkees and explained his needs to a clerk who looked like a gnome left over from some creation myth.

The gnome said, "We don't have anything going out today or tomorrow. Should've gotten here yesterday. We sent a full cargo out then. Times are slow. The Dreangereans are cracking down on cotton smuggling and there isn't much *kuf* coming out of Lucidia." *Kuf* being Lucidian for narcotic hemp leaves. "We have wars and rumors of wars. Wars are always bad for business."

Else was surprised to hear a Sonsan say that. He thought merchants always prospered when there was fighting. "They're a little hard on families, too."

"I suppose." The gnome did not apologize to the daSkees dead. He listened to no one but himself. "Yes. Here. *Vivia Infanti* expects to be fully loaded by the day after tomorrow. Would you want a private cabin, shared quarters, or just to sleep on deck?"

"On deck. The Holy Lands didn't make me rich."

"They never do. Not the fighters. Will you take your own food? Or will you share the sailors' mess?"

"Which would be cheaper? I still have a long way to travel after I get to Sonsa."

"Bringing your own food appears marginally cheaper up front. But then you have to manage your own cooking. Or you have to hire the ship's cook to do it for you."

"I'll eat with the crew."

"Are you bringing the boy?"

"I'm traveling alone. I hired the boy to help with my gear."

The gnome glanced at the pile. "Hardly worth dragging around, is it? You're looking at fourteen Sonsan silver scutti. Or any equivalent weight in other mintages."

Else suspected he was being overcharged. He glared at the old man. Which was water off a duck's back.

The gnome said, "Or you can walk. Though you would've been better off doing that while you were still on the mainland."

Else produced his sack of miscellaneous coinage, struck at a dozen different mints in as many lands. Near as he could tell, the gnome made no effort to cheat him. Unless he lied when he said Gordimer had begun debasing Dreanger's coinage recently.

Debasing the coinage was in character for the Lion.

The gnome asked, "Do you want to stay here while you wait for *Infanti*? Or will you room somewhere else? Any seaman's flop will be cheaper but they won't provide meals and you'll probably be robbed in your sleep."

"How much will staying here hurt me?"

The gnome named a figure that Else found reasonable.

The gnome explained, "Our charter from the Brotherhood of War obliges us to house and feed crusaders at at-cost rates."

"Oh. Of course I'll stay here." Else had nighted over in sailors' hostels before. He would do so again if he had to. But he was willing to forgo the pleasure.

The gnome retreated into the shadows. His employers did not seem inclined to invest much in lighting. He returned with a great man-brute trailing behind. "Goydar will show you where to bunk."

Else gave the boy his pay, then followed the huge man, who carried everything. The big fellow never said a word. He carried a little extra soft weight, like a eunuch. Might he be a fugitive from some eastern court with tongue and testicles removed?

ELSE HAD A ROOM TO HIMSELF, THOUGH IT WAS ONLY FOUR FEET wide and not tall enough for him to stand up. He stowed his gear under the narrow cot.

Seldom in his life had he enjoyed this much personal luxury. As a boy and single man he had been crowded into a barracks or tent. As a married man he shared a one-room hovel with a woman and two children, both daughters. It was part of being Sha-lug. You were never alone.

Alone actually made him uncomfortable.

He was going to be alone a lot from now on.

He searched the room for spy holes, then decided to skip his religious obeisances anyway. Who knew what sorcery might be at work in this foreign place? Every shadow might conceal some wicked spirit of the night.

He began rehearsing his recollections of Chaldarean religious rituals.

He was bound to get something wrong. He hoped the excuse of having spent years overseas, in the company of rough, impious men, would get him by when he moved farther west. He did think that westerners were more casual than Pramans.

His first trial came at dinner, which he took in a communal hall resembling a military mess but with food placed on the tables. It was not a meal taken on a set schedule. Sonsan workers came and went as they liked, as did guests. Quite a few men awaited transport eastward or west. At Else's table was a Direcian veteran, Enio Scolora, headed home after two decades spent fighting the Unbeliever. He wanted to share every incident with fellow warrior daSkees. Scolora would sail aboard *Vivia Infanti*, too. Else dreaded the moment when he would have to talk about some personality they should both know. However, it did not take long to discover that keeping his own mouth shut while grunting occasionally would keep Scolora chattering indefinitely.

The real danger proved to be the meal itself. The main course was a massive roast. The diners all agreed that it was a huge treat. Mutton and more mutton garnished with mutton was the customary fare. Which would have been perfectly acceptable to Else.

Enio Scolora carved himself a chunk big enough to choke a tiger. "Ha! Confusion to our enemies. What kind of menace can they be if they can't stuff themselves with a good roast piggie once in a while?"

Another old soldier said, "This is where we separate out the Joskers and the Deves, all right." He snickered. Which blew snot onto the table. He wiped that away, smearing it on his leg.

Else knew what he meant by Deves. Devedians belonged to an old minority religion that had arisen in the Holy Lands before the modern contenders. Devedian dietary law resembled that of al-Prama. The Devedian prophets had schismed away from the ancestral Dainshaukin creed three centuries before the Chaldarean Founders—all of whom had considered themselves devout Deves—first discovered their voice. Deves were less numerous than Chaldareans and al-Pramans but remained influential.

"Not to mention the Dainshaus who started everything,"

Else said. "Joskers? I must've been living in a hole like some anchorite. I don't know that one."

"That's what we called the Kaif's men. It sounds a little like the Peqaad for 'Freaks from Qasr.'"

Arnhanders tended to drop the al-Zed when they talked about the eastern Kaifate. Which they called by the name of its older core kingdom, Lucidia, most of the time.

Else took a piece of pork. There was no choice. And he had a dispensation from the Kaif of al-Minphet personally, set forth because it had been clear from the beginning that he would have to break religious laws if he was going to pass as one of the enemy.

"This isn't bad." Eyes turned his way. "After the gruel and crud you get served in Triamolin." The real Aelford daSkees had served that minor coastal city-state before being summoned home.

"Good old maggoty hardtack straight out of the barrel, with meat so foul a vulture wouldn't touch it," Scolora said. "It's the romantic soldier's life for me."

The exigencies of life in the field were universal. Else said, "You have to keep your livestock on the hoof until you need it."

"You guys never did that. I never saw such a piss-poor excuse for a bunch of soldiers as you guys when you came in before the Battle of the Well of Days."

Else pretended to look around for eavesdroppers. "You didn't hear this from me. Prince Aderble is an idiot. Literally. He doesn't care about anything but his own vices. The priests use him as a figurehead while they line their purses. Your real reaction should be amazement that we got there in time for the fight."

He was retailing nothing that was not common knowledge. Triamolin's company had been devoured by Indala al-Sul Halaladin. The rest of the crusader force had not fared much better. Which led to the inevitable question.

"How did you survive the Well of Days?"

"I was clever enough to be laid up recovering from a poisoned arrow I took in a skirmish with bandits from Dreanger." He had a scar he could show if necessary.

"There is a God."

"You wouldn't think much of Him if you ever took one of those arrows. They stings a bit."

"Where you from?" Scolora asked. "Originally."

"LaTriobe. In Tramaine. I know. You never heard of it. I've been in the Holy Lands since I was fifteen. Why?"

"You've got a funny accent."

"I talk Peqaad or Melhaic most of the time."

The old soldier made a sudden warning gesture. The table fell silent. The rest of the hall had done so already.

Two members of the Brotherhood of War had entered the mess. One was a grizzled, scarred fellow in his fifties. The other was under thirty. Both were lean, hard men, very clean and well-groomed. They looked enough alike to be family, though the Brothers took vows of chastity when they took orders.

The older man said, "Continue your conversation." He took a seat at Else's table. The younger man did the same.

Both wore Brotherhood black with a red hourglass and crossed white swords embroidered over their hearts, on their overshirts. The same symbol was repeated on their backs, much larger.

"Are you traveling?" Else asked. No one else seemed inclined to speak, let alone make introductions.

Most crusaders did not like the Brothers. They were fanatics, much too humorless, grim, and in a hurry to get to Heaven. Good to have on your side when you were in deep shit and needed somebody to save your ass, though.

Trenchers arrived for the newcomers. The older man said, "We're bound for Dateon. Sometime tonight." His stare was piercing. It reminded Else of Gordimer at his most intense. "You were talking about your adventures in the Holy Lands."

"I didn't have many. My father sent my uncle and me to Triamolin because *his* uncle told him that young men could make their names and fortunes there. He didn't understand the reality."

The younger Brother grunted, swallowed a chunk of pork he had not yet chewed. "The Carpets are a waste of flesh as warriors or nobles."

The elder said, "Except for Ansel, who founded the Triamolin state."

"A pity the Patriarch back then didn't check the Carpet offspring out before he put a crown on the old man's head."

The elder Brother let that slide. He addressed Else. "So you finally had enough, eh? You could become part of something with real meaning, here. The Brotherhood of War always has room for men who want to do the Lord's work."

Else did not observe that, to his recollection, the Chaldarean god was a pacifist. "That isn't it. I've been called home. I'm the last daSkees. The rest died when the Duke of Harmonachy invaded Tramaine. His Grolsacher mercenaries killed anybody who got in their way when they were running away from Themes."

"You said an uncle went east with you?"

"Reafer. Yes. Dysentery got him."

"It's a harsh world. Disease claims more good men than the efforts of any enemy."

That was true on the other side, too, where the medical and surgical arts were more advanced and ideas about prevention and containment of disease were more practical. Else grunted agreement. He continued to down bites of pork mechanically.

The younger brother observed, "You aren't afraid of us. The rest of these are."

"No. Should I be? Are you demons wearing the skins of men?"

"They all think we're sorcerers."

This was news to Else. He knew of the Brotherhood of War only as a band of ferocious warriors. "And? Have you turned on your own kind?"

Gentle gasps told him that a few of his companions did harbor some such suspicion.

"There are weeds in the gardens of the Lord. We face an age of renewed crusade. The steel must be tempered. We face formidable enemies in Indala al-Sul Halaladin and Gordimer the Lion. The battalions of the Lord will have no place in them for doubters or the faint of heart."

Some things *were* the same on both sides, Else reflected. "How about the worn out and exhausted who don't have anything left to give to kings and warlords who care more about their own glory and fortunes than they do about reclaiming the Wells of Ihrian?"

"God and the Patriarch willing, that won't be a problem, next crusade."

"Enough," the old brother said. "He hasn't seen the Holy Lands yet," he told Else.

Apparently, the younger man had said something he should not have. Would extraordinary measures be taken to arm a new crusade with competent, motivated, true-believer commanders? That was not good. Arnhanders were formidable fighters. Only the pettiness and incompetence of their captains assured the failure of their efforts.

ELSE STARED AT THE CEILING IN THE DARK. THE PORK CHURNED in his guts. Somewhere nearby someone used a woman with great vigor, with her enthusiastic participation. He paid little attention.

He had collected important intelligence already. The next crusade might be better organized and led. And the new Brothen Patriarch expected to pick and choose his commanders.

Else's thoughts drifted to the company he had taken to Andesqueluz. They should be home, now. He hoped they had been well rewarded.

He drifted on to the puzzle of the slain bogon.

Who conjured it? No friend, certainly. Someone who did not want the mummies to reach er-Rashal? That made sense. Assuming those brittle old sticks could be put to major sorcerous use.

In theory, the mysterious enemy could be any sorcerer aware of what er-Rashal was planning. Which, certainly, was nothing urgent. Or he would not be cruising the Mother Sea just to check on one spy's progress.

That deserved reflection, too.

There was a soft tap at his door. He did not respond. That would be another house whore offering her services. Or maybe a boy, since he had refused two women already.

NAHLIK SAT DRINKING WINE ACROSS FROM ELSE. ELSE CONfined himself to coffee. It would take him a while to wean himself from dietary law.

Nahlik had succeed a long time ago.

Two more men shared their table in a sailors' dive known as the Rusted Lantern. Mallin had come in with Nahlik. The other man was a stranger. He had been there when Else arrived, unconscious in a pool of his own vomit. Customers took what seats they could, though that settled them in the company of strangers.

Mallin said, "We'd better talk before they throw this one out so they can fill the seat with a paying customer."

Else grunted. "Nahlik, you were on the mark when you said don't take anything embarrassing ashore. Somebody went through my stuff last night. While I was at supper."

"Probably just looking for something to steal," Mallin said. "But you'd a' heard about it if you had anything that didn't fit."

Nahlik said, "You were followed here. By that scrawny, stringy-haired character bellying up over there. He's too busy getting himself on the outside of a few quarts of wine to keep a close watch on you."

Else quickly related what he had heard last night and what that might mean in terms of the character of the new Patriarch.

Mallin opined, "He's just coming in overconfident. They all are at first. Then they find out how powerless they really are."

"This one has a different feel, even from here."

Nahlik said, "We don't know you anymore."

A big, sturdily built brute was talking to the stringy-haired character. Neither looked at Else but he knew they were talking about him.

Turning so it looked like he was talking to Mallin, Nahlik asked, "You know what ship you're taking?"

"*Vivia Infanti.*"

"We'll get your stuff aboard. Mallin, take hold of the drunk. We'll walk him out like he's our friend."

They barely got the drunk off his stool before a boy materialized, armed with a filthy rag and a bowl of dirty water. He made a dispirited effort to clean up the vomit.

"Do a good job I'll give you a copper for your own," Else whispered.

The boy discovered reserves of enthusiasm. Else slipped him a coin. "I need more coffee. No! I don't want your sister, your mother, or you. I just want more coffee."

A newcomer started to settle opposite Else. The big man who had been talking to the skinny one pushed him aside. "Go away," he said. He took the stool himself.

Else studied his coffee and waited for another cup to arrive. He felt the big man staring at him.

He appeared to be alone. His behavior had attracted no attention despite its rude and provocative nature.

Else said, "That was inexcusably rude."

It was clear the big man meant to become violent. Else trumped him.

The man started to speak but gasped in surprise instead.

"Don't pick a fight with a man who has one hand under the table. If you take a breath I don't like I'll ruin your knee. If you move at all I'll ruin your kneecap. Nod if you understand."

The man nodded. He showed no fear, just pain and confusion. He was not accustomed to being on the downhill end of the pain/terror equation.

Else's fresh coffee arrived. He paid using one hand. Then he told his new friend, "You were going to explain what you're doing. And why. You were going to do that because you don't want to live the rest of your life with only one good leg."

The big man was careful not to move.

"Speak to me," Else said. He pushed the long dagger's razor-sharp tip a quarter inch deeper into the space beneath the man's right kneecap. Nothing. "There'll be no help. Your long-haired friend left." Still nothing. "If you have the brains God gave a toad . . ." The Sha-lug had a saying, You can't fix stupid, said of crusader captains who fell for a trick more than once. This looked like it might be a major case of stupid. "You're bothering me for a reason. I want to know what it is." He probed a little deeper with the dagger.

Else saw the moment when the shock cleared enough for realization to strike home. The moment when understanding arrived.

The big man ground his teeth. "There is nothing I can tell you." He spoke mechanically. "I was told to find Carpio. He would point you out. I would kill you in a brawl that Carpio would swear you started."

"But Carpio took off right after he talked to you. Where do

you suppose he went? Who told you to kill the man he marked?"

"Starkden. The order came from Starkden."

"Is that a man's name?"

"Starkden is a woman. They say."

Volunteered information. A good sign. A watershed in this relationship. "Be that as it may, Starkden sent you. Why?"

"Because she wanted you dead, I guess."

"Why?"

Shrug.

"Tell me about this woman. Including where I can find her."

The big man knew nothing. He'd never met Starkden. He'd heard that she was an older woman, in her forties or even her fifties. If you did what she said she paid well. She supposedly had no political or religious axes to grind. Not that he cared about that stuff himself.

Else questioned the man for another ten minutes and learned nothing more. "All right, Ben." The big fellow's name was Benatar Piola. "I want you to sit right there till your knee stops hurting. If you put any strain on it right away it'll fold up, you'll wreck the joint, and they'll probably have to cut off your leg." You could not fix stupid but you could use it.

Else called for wine for Ben, paid and left.

Once back at the factor house he told his story to anyone who would listen. He thought a legitimate traveler would do that. And he hoped somebody would have an idea about what really had happened. He got nothing for his trouble but insincere sympathy. He should have had sense enough not to frequent waterfront dives. Nobody seemed willing to guess who Starkden might be.

The morning he was supposed to board *Vivia Infanti* for Sonsa he received a summons through a house messenger. He followed nervously. Something must have gone wrong. Then he was sure it had when he found himself in a room with four older members of the Brotherhood of War.

"You're Sir Aelford daSkees, homeward bound after service in the Holy Lands?" one asked.

"I am."

"I'm Parthen Lorica. From the Special Office. We're interested in your encounter in the sailors' tavern."

"Why?"

"Excuse me?"

"I complained myself gray around here and the only thing anybody cared about was whether I owed anybody any money. Somebody's out to kill daSkees? Better not let him have anything on credit."

"Sound business practice."

Else grimaced but kept his mouth shut.

"Someone passed the story on to us. And here we are. Interested."

Else responded with a grudging, "All right."

"Tell us what happened. Try not to leave anything out. Any little detail might help. This might give us a chance to do something we've wanted for a long time."

"Which would be?"

"To get a line on a witch and spy who calls herself Starkden."

Else was tempted by the notion that any enemy of the Brotherhood of War was a friend of Else Tage. Only this particular enemy of the Brotherhood had paid to have Else Tage murdered.

Else told his story almost exactly as it had happened—discounting some creative editing on behalf of Nahlik and Mallin.

"Those sailors you were sitting with. You didn't know them?"

"No. The soberest two knew each other but not the unconscious drunk, I'm pretty sure, even though they carried him away. He was there when I sat down. Those two didn't show up until a few minutes later."

"And their names were Ren and Doy?"

"That's what they said. I didn't really care about them. I was in there because the Lantern has Peqaad coffee and I developed a taste for that . . . I was trying to relax some before I travel again. I hate sea voyages. I get seasick. Bad."

"Carpio and Benatar Piola were the other men?"

"Yes."

"We know Carpio," the oldest Brother said, speaking for the first time.

Lorica said, "Only a moron would trust Carpio with any secrets. But someone must have hired him. So he's a thread we can tug at. Piola shouldn't be that hard to find, either."

"Can you tell me anything about this woman who wanted me killed?"

"No. But only because we know so little ourselves. We're hoping to change that. Why would she want to kill you?"

"Please don't start that. I've already got my brain twisted into knots trying to figure that out. The only thing that makes any sense to me is, somebody picked the wrong target. That Carpio. If he was following me around, maybe he followed me from here. Maybe he was supposed to follow somebody else who was staying here."

"Possible, I suppose. Or Starkden might think you're someone else in disguise. Who could she mistake you for?"

Else shrugged. "I've spent my whole adult life fighting for Triamolin. I don't own anything worth stealing, in the Holy Lands or back home in Tramaine. I'm carrying my whole fortune with me. Who would this woman be spying for?"

"Rumors have linked her to the Patriarch, to the Eastern Emperor, and to Hansel Blackboots. Do any of them have any reason to kill you?"

"Hardly."

Lorica added, "Starkden has been associated with the Unbeliever, too. With Lucidia in particular."

"I never had much to do with them. We mostly dealt with tribal raiders that Dreanger bribed to harass us. Except for the battle at the Well of Days. Which I missed because I was laid up with a wound from a poisoned arrow."

Parthen Lorica told him, "We've been forthcoming with you. We hope you have with us. You're leaving aboard *Infanti*? If anything turns up before she sails we'll send a message."

"I appreciate that." It was a generous gesture. These men respected what they believed him to be. But he hoped they would have no success. Success could mean them finding out that Starkden really was after a Sha-lug chieftain pretending to be Aelford daSkees.

He devoted himself to mental exercises meant to conquer stress. Success eluded him. He envisioned a pretty little blonde girl, a toddler grinning wildly as she tried to walk toward him.

He puzzled that until he realized that she must be his sister.
And that left him with the icy chills.

Normally, he failed miserably when he tried to remember
his family. Which was surprising. The boys of the Vibrant
Spring, while they were still little, remembered their families.
Their mothers, especially. And spent a lot of silent tears in the
darkness, when their instructors could not see.

ELSE BOARDED *VIVIA INFANTI* SHORTLY AFTER NOON, HAVING
eaten nothing all morning. The ship was still taking on cargo
when he arrived. He spied both Mallin and Nahlik on the quay.

A Sonsan seaman checked his name off a list. Another man,
wearing a pipe on a chain around his neck, drew him aside.
"Sir Aelford, the stuff you sent ahead is in your personal
locker, up forward. I'll show you."

Vivia Infanti did not resemble the long, lean sharks of war
that Else had seen while approaching Staklirhod. She was a
huge wooden bathtub with exaggerated castles on either end, a
hundred and thirty feet from stem to stern and fifty-five wide at
the beam. A monster of a merchant ship, probably originally
meant to transport soldiers eastward on the crusader routes.

There were stowage lockers below the rails up forward, obviously installed as an afterthought. The seaman opened a
hatch on what proved to be a cubicle slightly more than two
feet in each dimension.

"This will keep your stuff from sliding around. Or washing
overboard in bad weather. It won't keep anything from getting
stolen. It won't keep anything dry if we do run into any
weather. Use it accordingly."

"Thank you." Else considered the small oilskin bundle lying
inside. The bundle contained written instructions from
Gordimer. He was not allowed to open them until he was on his
way to Sonsa.

Else stowed his gear, shut the locker, and joined Enio Scolora at the landward rail. Scolora said, "I heard the Witchfinders
had you in."

"Who? The Brothers I talked to this morning? They wanted
to know what happened at the Rusted Lantern. What nobody
else cared about."

"I heard it was Parthen Lorica and Bugo Armiena."

"One said his name was Lorica."

"That's them. They're from the Special Office. They hunt down ghosts and demons and sorcerers and whatnot. You don't want to get noticed by them."

"What? Tell me about this Special Office."

"You didn't have the Brotherhood underfoot in Triamolin, I take it."

"Triamolin is the back end of beyond. We're still there only because it isn't worth the trouble of kicking us out."

Scolora related a long tale about fanatics hidden inside the already fanatic Brotherhood. Men with strong sorcerous talents who wanted nothing less than the extinction of the tyranny of the night.

Else did not understand. The things of the night were no more evil than lions or hyenas. They did what God made them do, like dogs and flies and rainbows. They might be dangerous and deadly but so might any other part of the natural order. The tyranny of the night was part of the world and life.

Scolora shrugged. "They got it made. They can afford to be fanatic. They live out here where the night ain't part of their life every minute of every single day." Which it was amongst the Wells of Ihrian, more so than anywhere else in the world.

"How do they manage when they visit the Holy Lands?"

"They grumble a lot. And take it out on the Pramans. Word is, though, something happened over there that's got them all stirred up."

"Uhm?"

"I think somebody skragged some kind of big deal spook thing. Just a regular guy, not a wizard. They want to know how he did it."

Sailors asked Else and Scolora to move away from the rail. They began singling up the mooring lines. Boats gathered to nudge the vessel away from the quay and toward the channel. *Vivia Infanti* depended entirely on sail power. Eliminating oarsmen offered huge labor savings.

There was a ghost of a breeze directly on the ship's beam, pushing her toward the quay. The oarsmen in the boats earned their pay.

The deck force did not take in the fenders until *Infanti* was thirty feet out from the quay and her bow was swinging toward the channel.

The first small sails broke. *Infanti* soon held her heading on her own, and crept forward, though without adequate steerage way. More sails spread.

Else said, "The master of this tub is good."

"He wasn't, he wouldn't be her master. Sonsans are practical and pragmatic in the extreme. You all right?"

"I'm never all right when there's water under me instead of dirt. Big things with lots of teeth live down there. And they all want to eat me."

Scolora chuckled. "You get seasick, eh?"

The merchantman put more way on. She eased into the channel and ranged the lighthouse that marked the mouth of the harbor. Once *Vivia Infanti* passed that two-hundred-foot-tall brick structure she would be on open seas and Else would feel more and more like he had fallen off the edge of the world. "Yes."

Infanti's master lined her on the range markers. Signalmen exchanged messages with the harbormaster ashore and the traffic watchers in the lighthouse. There was a lot of traffic at Runch.

Excitement broke out on the stern castle. One of the signalmen called for the ship's master. Else said, "Something's up."

"They can't get anything past you, can they?"

The ship's master, first officer, and several others closed in on the signalmen. After two minutes of wigwags the chief boatswain shouted orders to the deck crew to get the sails taken in. The helmsman took the ship to starboard, out of the channel. She lost way. Shortly, the anchor chain squealed and rattled.

"Bet that there is the reason why," Scolora said, indicating a longboat putting out from the small quay at the foot of Mount Calen, which was crowned by the Castella Anjela dolla Picolina, headquarters of the Brotherhood of War. "Somebody wants a ride."

Else hoped that was all.

The ship's master barked. The deck hands began herding passengers belowdecks. Demands to know what was going on received no answer.

The working crew followed the passengers, no more pleased about their situation. The ratings and officers followed them, until no one remained above decks but the ship's master himself.

Else heard a boat come alongside and scrape against the hull. People clambered aboard. There was a muffled, heated exchange on deck. That faded away.

Crew and passengers alike virtually exploded onto the open deck when permission came down.

There was nothing to be seen now but a longboat headed toward the quay below Castella Anjela dolla Picolina. The ship's master resumed issuing orders. The crew prepared to get under way again.

An hour later no one knew more than what was obvious immediately. Scolora was of the opinion that, "It's somebody from the Special Office. A big-time sorcerer. Something's going on, Alf. This is history in the making. And we're right here in the middle of it." That excited him.

Else was not excited. He feared that he was why *Vivia Infanti* had stopped.

No sign was seen of any Brotherhood passenger. If such a creature existed he did his own cooking. The ship's cook was not fixing anything for any secret traveler. No one had been evicted from his quarters.

THE WEST COAST OF FIRALDIA, APPROACHING SONSA FROM THE south, was the most heavily settled rural land Else had ever seen. Every headland boasted some kind of fortress or watchtower. The land sloped down steeply to the Mother Sea.

Sea traffic was heavy. Any boat that came within hailing distance tried to sell something.

"They're all out because the weather is so nice," Scolora said. "You have to take advantage of the good days."

"Sounds like words to live by." Else had grown comfortable with Scolora. Enio talked constantly but asked few questions. Enio did not mind the silent veteran type. A lot of old soldiers were that way.

Several other passengers were headed home from the Holy Lands. The lot formed a clique. The remaining passengers were pilgrims who had gone to visit the Wells of Ihrian. Else, Scolora, and two others from farther west had agreed to continue on from Sonsa together. Else wondered how he could get shut of Scolora long enough to disappear.

He had not managed enough privacy to look at his sealed orders. Gordimer's packet contained a dozen letters, each to be opened only after he reached a prescribed point in his mission. There were three letters he was supposed to read before he reached Sonsa. They remained unopened. He worried. There might be some critical detail that needed handling . . . though he doubted that. Gordimer fussed worse than a clutch of old women.

"Looking forward to getting home?" Scolora asked.

"Not really. It won't be anything like what I remember. Everybody I knew will be old or dead."

Scolora made a sour face. "You sure as fuck take the fun out, Alf. Now you got me thinking I'm heading for a foreign country."

"There was an old Deve in Triamolin who used to say that."

"Huh? What?"

"That the past is a foreign country. I keep thinking I'm dreaming and pretty soon I'll wake up on my own cot back in Triamolin."

"Yeah? Dream about that. That's the outer lightship." Enio had visited Sonsa before.

Sonsa proper was a riverine city eight miles inland. *Vivia Infanti* would travel from lightship to lightship until regular river buoys became visible. A pilot waiting on this first lightship would take control for the rest of the journey.

That pilot came aboard. Hours passed. The ship proceeded slowly. Else grumbled, "We're going to spend a whole day just covering the last few miles."

"Bet you they'll let you get out and walk."

"Probably would," he admitted. "I'll be a new man once I get some dirt under my feet." He knew his companions were tired of his complaints.

"We're looking forward to it, pal."

It did take almost all day to climb the Sawn River to Sonsa's great waterfront. Else marveled at the strange, busy buildings, all so tall, so ornate, so gaily painted. Al-Qarn was a dun city of mud brick, low, square buildings, the only color the awnings merchants used to identify their trade. The Kaif did not like color.

Vivia Infanti passed berth after open berth. Else asked one of the sailors why.

"Those don't belong to us. They're Red or Blue. *Infanti* is a Durandanti ship. The Durandanti are Greens."

Color was a facet of Chaldarean culture that baffled Else. In the Eastern Empire, in the Firaldian kingdoms and republics, in the principalities along the Promptean coast, anywhere that the Old Brothen Empire had had an enduring impact, the populace divided into two or more Colors. These days those usually identified political factions. Colors had begun, in antiquity, as wagering societies and fan groups of team events at the circus and hippodrome.

Sonsa claimed it was the most important mercantile force on the Mother Sea. Aparion and Dateon disagreed. Platadura, over in Praman Direcia, offered a nay-say of its own. Sonsa showed a unified, determined face to the world but the squabbles of the factions at home were worse than those of spoiled children. Without rational basis in the eyes of outsiders.

There were no doctrinal or ideological conflicts. Just a perpetual, intractable contest for control of the state. As in local politics everywhere in Firaldia, it all came down to families.

The Durandanti had the largest merchant fleet. They were of the fixed opinion that that made them the foremost Sonsan family.

The Scoviletti and the Fermi did not concur.

The Scoviletti possessed the smallest fleet but the mercenary army they managed, and rented out, mainly in Chaldarean Direcia, gave them a big edge in crude sword power.

And the Fermi, of course, always had a cousin who married the brother of the Patriarch, a daughter who married into a great family of Dateon or Aparion, or made loans to the princes of the city states on the northern plain, or in some other way forged alliances that sheltered them from the envy of the Durandanti and the Scoviletti.

Else grumbled, "Somewhere in Sonsa I'm supposed to find

a solicitor who represents most of the families of Tramaine. The letter I got in Triamolin told me to find him. He'd know the latest."

"Makes sense," Scolora said. "So you do need to find him. But will he put you up?"

Yes, probably. There were Dreangerean agents in Sonsa. He was expected to make contact. "I'll hunt him down. If we ever get ashore. Here's my plan. You and Tonto and Adrano go get us set at the factor house and see about our passage to Sheavenalle. I'll find my man, then catch up with you there."

"Good plan. Except for one angle."

"And that would be?"

"I want to find out who's been hiding in the captain's cabin since we left Staklirhod. We can hide on the dock and watch until whoever it is sneaks ashore." Scolora's tone left no doubt of his conviction.

"You sure you want to take that chance?"

"Don't you?"

"I think it's a waste of time." But he did want to know if some Brotherhood of War sorcerer had followed him across the Mother Sea. "But, all right. Let's just be careful."

"Must be a holiday," Scolora said. "Hardly anybody seems to be working." He dragged everybody behind a cluster of fat cotton bales a hundred yards from the ship.

Else was appalled. This much cotton had been smuggled out of Dreanger? By just this one Firaldian house to just this one Firaldian port?

Scolora had chosen a good spot. It offered an excellent view of *Vivia Infanti* without the watchers being exposed to the curiosities of the few men working the docks.

"Can you understand these people?" Scolora asked. The Sonsan dialect was almost impenetrable. Else shook his head. He had trouble understanding Scolora.

Tonto whispered, "Something's happening. Shit. You cocksucker, Enio. I didn't believe you. Nobody believed you. But you were right."

They all found places to peek over or around the bales.

Sure enough, there was a stir aboard *Vivia Infanti*. Only moments earlier the ship had seemed dead, the crew having gone ashore right after the passengers.

"That isn't a Brother," Else said. Two men were leaving the ship. The first was tall and arrogant in bearing, looking around as though daring the universe to try something. The other was older, bent, and struggling with an unreasonable amount of luggage. The tall man did not help. Neither had been seen during the voyage.

"You think they'd run around in their black and red yelling, 'Hey! Here I am?' Whatever they're up to, we already know it's supposed to be secret."

A closed coach drawn by a two-horse team clopped to the foot of the gangway.

"There's what I call timing."

The older man began wrestling baggage aboard the coach. The driver helped. The tall man examined his surroundings intently.

"I don't like this," Tonto said. "Something's wrong. I'm out of here." He slid away into shadows, fast and silent.

"Damn!" Scolora said. "What was that all about?"

Adrano had known Tonto in the Holy Lands. He said, "I don't know. But him and me are still alive because his instincts were always right around the Wells of Ihrian."

"Then we'd better listen," Else said. He was accustomed to crediting the undirected misgivings of Bone and al-Azer er-Selim.

"Coach is moving," Scolora said. "Coming our way."

"Damn! Get down, then. Get invisible."

Scolora protested, "There're other people around."

The coach, moving fast, drew abreast of their hiding place. Else glimpsed its polished ash flank through a gap between bales. Then all the darkness went out of the world.

A god's fist smashed into his chest and flung him against a warehouse wall. As he flew he heard shredded screams from his companions. Cotton fountained, some of it on fire.

Unconsciousness came.

It did not last long. A few numb-looking dock wallopers were just starting to get in amongst the bales, chattering too fast to be understood. Else picked out the word for sorcery, though.

He became aware of pain in his left wrist.

"God is merciful," he murmured. His wrist had been burned. Blisters were rising already. His amulet had protected him.

He staggered to his feet, covered in cotton, startling the Sonsans. "What happened? Where are my friends?"

In an exchange made difficult by language problems Else explained that he and his friends had thought that they could save money by sleeping amongst the cotton bales. Then there had been an explosion.

That was all the Sonsans knew. Just, *Boom!* and the quay was covered by tons of smoldering cotton. They thought it might have something to do with the squabbles between the great families.

They found Scolora right away. The Direcian was dead. Thoroughly and gruesomely so. He had been torn into four pieces loosely connected by strings of skin and flesh. And Adrano was scattered almost as extensively as the cotton.

At that point the dock wallopers really caught on. They had used the word *sorcery* before. Now they saw the proof. They scattered immediately.

The quay was a complete ghost town, now. Where were the workers? The crews from the ships? Where were the curious, drawn by the explosion? Did bad news spread that fast here?

Else considered Scolora and Adrano. He could do nothing for them now. He felt guilt and anger.

He collected their gear and helped himself. Then he eased out onto the quay. No one was watching. All was still. Darkness was falling. He had to disappear into the city.

He could not turn up at that factor house now.

A light shown through the leaded glass stern lights of *Vivia Infanti*. From the captain's quarters.

ELSE MOVED QUIETLY INTO THE STERN CASTLE. NO LIFE HAD yet returned to the quay. But that would not last.

Someone in the master's quarters played a lute, a dolorous tune that Else did not recognize. It was a sad song of unrequited love. Like most of its kind, it originated in the End of Connec, where such things had been invented.

Else pulled the latch string slowly, swung the door inward without a sound.

The ship's master sat in a plush chair, beyond a chart table, staring out the stern lights at stars coming to life as indigo skies gave way to true night. His back was to Else.

He ceased playing his sad song. "I didn't think you'd keep your word, sorcerer." The seaman made that final word a curse and an expression of boundless contempt.

He turned. And was startled. "Who the hell are you?"

"An unhappy man. Your secret passenger just killed two friends of mine. You're going to tell me about him."

"You're kidding, right?"

"He's bad. But I'm here. And I'm angry enough to make you wish you were carrying a lamp, to light the road to Hell for my friends."

The ship's master struggled but was past his prime and never had been a fighter. Else was in his prime, a fighter, and he knew how to get prisoners to talk.

Once the inevitable was obvious, the ship's master said, "The man was a stupid, arrogant, bigoted pig. I'll actually wish you luck if you go after him."

That was not Else's plan. It was not his mission. He just wanted to know what was going on in case it affected future planning.

The ship's master talked. Else prowled. He considered relics that said this man's whole life was right here aboard this ship. That there was nowhere else he would rather be. He had collected exotic souvenirs in interesting places, including swords with unusual blades; a composite bow of the type used by the steppe horse peoples; a Ghargarlicean infantry bow six feet long, of a type that had gone out of use centuries ago; and a Lucidian crossbow of a sort mass-produced for use by local militias tasked with defending city walls. It did not have much power but any idiot could use it at close range. This one had been painted, then decorated with sutras from the Written and given a quality string. None of which had done its user any good, obviously, or the weapon would not be in a Chaldarean sea captain's weapons collection.

"Be careful with that," the Sonsan pleaded. "It has a hair trigger." There was, of course, a bolt in the mechanism.

"It isn't a good idea to leave the bow bent all the time. Takes the spring out." From questions about the Brotherhood sorcerer Else moved on to broader questions. What were the attitudes of Sonsans toward the Church? Toward Sublime V? Toward the Patriarch's apparent determination to launch a new crusade?

"Crusades are good for Sonsa," the ship's master replied. "The Patriarch is a raving lunatic, but we don't mind as long as his gold pours into our coffers."

Else settled into the master's chair. The master himself was strapped down on his own chart table. Else finally broke out his letters from Gordimer.

Those letters did not contain much that he could not figure out for himself. Keep low. Keep his eyes and ears open. Learn whatever he could, even if it did not appear relevant. Try to discover why Arnhanders thought the way they did. Sow seeds of conflict between Dreanger's potential enemies so they would have no attention to spare for overseas adventures. Work his way closer to Sublime and the Collegium when he could. And so on and so forth, with not one word about what to do when attacked by murderous spies. Or sorcerers from the Brotherhood of War.

He did find out how to contact two Dreangerean agents in Sonsa, neither of whom knew about the other. He was to keep it that way.

"Idiot crusader," the ship's master barked, harshly enough to recapture Else's attention. "Wake up. Somebody just came aboard."

Else did not ask how the man knew. It was his ship. Else collected his letters and the Lucidian crossbow and faded into a shadowed corner.

The latch on the cabin door rose. The door swung inward. A shape in black stepped inside, saw the ship's master laid out, blurted, "What the hell?"

Else triggered the crossbow. "Give my regards to Enio and Adrano."

The invader moved like a cat but not fast enough. He grunted in pain, pierced through the right arm and shoulder.

Else discarded the crossbow and moved in, hoping to strike before the man could use his sorcery.

But the Brother met him with a short sword. He showed no

lack of confidence despite being wounded and having to fight left-handed. Until he realized that he faced a skilled opponent.

He lunged, pressed Else back a step, fled through the doorway. Else thought better of charging into whatever awaited him out there. It was nighttime now. And a major sorcerer was afoot.

He found another quarrel for the Lucidian weapon, made sure his letters were safely stowed inside his shirt, then extinguished the one lamp burning and opened the leaded-glass stern light.

He clambered outside, grabbed a mooring line and spidered down to the quay. He was crouched behind a big wooden bollard, catching his breath, when the wounded Brother clumping down the gangway looked over his shoulder.

Why had he not used his sorcery?

Else loosed his second bolt.

He heard it strike but it did not hamper the man's flight. Maybe he was wearing something under his Brotherhood clothing.

THE DREANGEREAN AGENT WHO ACCEPTED ELSE INTO HIS SHOP at an impolite hour was a dwarf, a twisted little Devedian scarcely four feet high. He was not pleased. "I knew this day would come. I tried to pretend it wouldn't. I told myself it would just be a few pieces of silver now and then in exchange for the occasional letter. But this is what it was all about, isn't it?"

Else examined his surroundings by the weak light of the tiny lamp the dwarf carried. The place was a miniscule silversmith's shop. The dwarf's clients would be mostly Devedian. Almost everything Else saw looked like Devedian religious paraphernalia. Which seemed likely, the shop being located in the heart of Sonsa's Devedian quarter. "Yes. You're right. This is what you've waited for. What you've been paid to wait for. I need to disappear. And to stay disappeared. I have a letter for you from al-Qarn."

The dwarf's name was Gledius Stewpo. "That's how they say it here and that's good enough to get by." Stewpo might not be pleased about developments but he was prepared to deal with them. He had a secret room underneath his house. It pretended to be a hidden workshop, in case somebody stumbled in. A man could hide there in relative comfort. "They won't find you here without using some heavyweight sorcery."

Stewpo had several ticks that Else found distracting. First, his head was in constant motion, nodding or shaking. And he ended every other sentence with a strained laugh, as though he was enjoying a joke he had just told himself.

Else did not find a single thing the dwarf said even vaguely amusing.

Worse, when the dwarf sat down, he rocked. Forward and back, forward and back, quickly and incessantly. And he was unaware of his ticks.

Stewpo read the letter from al-Qarn. "All right. Here we go. I'm ready to help any way that I can."

Else told him everything. Anything less seemed pointless. "I rigged Adrano's remains so it would look like it was me that got blown apart, then I went through everybody's stuff and took whatever might come in handy."

"That's good. What about the Brotherhood assassin who got away?"

"I don't know if that's what he really was. I know they're not rational people. But they must realize that murdering people like that ship's master, after all he did to help, is counterproductive. People don't pitch in if you kill them for their trouble."

"I was thinking more about what became of him."

"He got away."

"And never smacked you around with any sorcery?"

"That's right."

"They snookered you. The one you assumed was the servant was the sorcerer. The other one was his bodyguard and assistant."

"You could be right. How safe are we from the night here?"

"Quite. This country was civilized before the Old Brothen Empire rose up. The spirits have been winnowed a thousand times. Only the benign ones are still around. The malignant ones have all been driven away or bound into stones and trees and streams. There isn't much left that a sorcerer can use. Sonsans want it that way. They want a world shaped by the laws of economics, not those of pain and chaos."

"The laws of chaos?"

"Even disorder is orderly if you look close enough."

"Suppose this sorcerer brought his own spirits?"

The dwarf had wild white hair not well acquainted with a comb. He ran his fingers through that when not indulging another tick. "That's a possibility. But you said he's from the Special Office of the Brotherhood of War. Those people want to end the tyranny of the night. They don't drag it around."

"Will they employ the tools of evil in order to conquer evil?" A common human failing, even in the Realm of Peace.

"They'd say not. Whatever, they won't find you. If you stay in this room. Rest. In the morning I'll find out what they're saying in the streets."

"Don't change your routine. And I really could use a snack. I haven't eaten since this morning."

"I could be your grandfather, Sha-lug. Don't teach me my craft."

"I wasn't . . . I see."

GLEDIUS STEWPO BROUGHT SUPPER NEXT EVENING. "SHA-LUG, you don't want to be out there now. I assume you didn't lie to me. Yet your story is nothing like what the Brotherhood says happened. They say they were chasing a foreigner who wants to spy on the Church."

"Really? That sounds a little silly. Do they say who? Or why?"

"No. Around here nobody believes anything the Brothers say, anyway. Unless you're a Blue and beholden to the Fermi."

"So there's a lot of excitement. And Color politics is trying to take it over?"

"There're other theories out there. The point is, *you* don't want to be seen. Having blond hair will get you dragged in for questioning, guaranteed."

Else nodded. Typical luck. All he was supposed to do in Sonsa was get off the boat and go somewhere else.

"If you hadn't interrogated *Vivia Infanti*'s master you could've gotten away without anybody suspecting anything. But you tried to kill a member of the Brotherhood."

Else grunted. "I wasn't thinking strategically. Tactically, I thought I needed to find out what was going on."

"You're in luck. They don't know who they're looking for. But they are looking hard. Word from inside is, the wizard is in a tizzy because nobody should have lived through that explosion."

"Didn't you tell me that Sonsa is supernaturally pacified?"

"Obviously, I was jabbering out the wrong orifice."

"What do Sonsans think?"

The dwarf chuckled. "I don't know many people who'd be upset if a few Brothers from the local barracks got themselves dead. They don't have much power here, and little influence except with the Fermi, but they do make themselves thoroughly obnoxious to Devedians and Dainschaus."

"Do they have the kind of power that lets them grab people off the streets? Without Sonsa blowing up?"

"The Durandanti and Scoviletti don't want to alienate them. Because then the Brotherhood might line up with the other family."

"And the Brotherhood squeezes every ounce of advantage out of that, right?"

"Of course. They're not stupid. They don't understand how much they're disliked, though."

"Uhm?"

"They're too powerful. But they're powerful only because the situation here is repeated in every city in Firaldia. There's no unifying national nobility. There's just the Church. And the Empire meddling from outside. In Brothe there are five families dancing the power dance, with the Patriarchy itself the big prize. Without the Brotherhood of War behind him, particularly the Special Office, Sublime never would've gotten elected. He's beholden to them. His aggressive policies are their policies. I've kept telling al-Qarn. But al-Qarn won't listen."

"Gordimer is a great warrior. But as a ruler and planner he has shortcomings. Unfortunately, if Dreanger's fortunes were left to Kaif Karim Kaseem al-Bakr, we'd all do nothing but say prayers while crusaders harvest us like hay. You know Sonsa. How long before the novelty wears off?"

"Most people will forget by tomorrow night. The rest will give up before the weekend. Unless the Brothers offer a big reward. That would bring the sharks out."

"So I'll just wait them out. Do they have sheep here? Or cattle? Or anything that isn't a pig? I ate salt pork all the way from Runch. Despite an indulgence from the kaif, I feel unclean."

Stewpo was no fool. "You think I'm an idiot, Sha-lug? You want to test my loyalty by studying my diet? You've been here twenty-some hours. You're not on a Brotherhood rack yet. In addition, you need to know that you've been badly misled. The Founding Family of al-Prama were self-deluded maniacs addicted to narcotics. But religion isn't the issue. Not for me. For me, it's what the crusaders have done to Suriet."

Suriet was the Melhaic name for the region everyone else called the Holy Lands.

The early crusader armies plundered the temples and towns of non-Chaldareans. As well as those of those Chaldareans who failed to acknowledge the ascendancy of the Brothen Patriarchy. Those were the times when the Brotherhood made its name and wealth.

In olden times, before the Praman Conquest, the Wells of Ihrian belonged to the Eastern Empire, where a less virulent strain of the Chaldarean faith held sway. It was tolerant. Followers of other religions were not molested as long as they met their legal obligations to the Emperor. That did not change much after the Conquest except that several Chaldarean subcults became part of the minority mix.

When westerners arrived to liberate the holy wells they considered even their religious cousins as subhuman resources there to be squeezed for wealth.

Else said, "Trust is the first casualty of our trade. My apologies. Though I'd still love to get next to a leg of lamb."

"I understand. I'm not entirely comfortable with you, either. Satisfy my curiosity. How did you survive an attack that shredded your companions?"

Else chuckled. "Now who's testing who?"

Stewpo shared a mutton roast with Else. Afterward, he sipped a dark wine from the coastal vineyards. "Another interesting day." His ticks were less prominent tonight.

"Tell me. Anything. They didn't do well when they taught me patience."

"I found a source of Ambonypsgan beans."

"Excellent. I assume they reach Sonsa by the same routes and hands that bring the cotton across."

Ambonypsga was a black highland kingdom south and east of Dreanger, the former separated from the latter by an inhospitable stony waste. Ambonypsga was strongly proto-Arianist Chaldarean with a minor admixture of pagan and Devedian tribes. Ambonypsga produced the finest coffee beans grown.

Else raised his left hand. "In answer to your question the other night, I'm alive because I wear an amulet that shields me from sorcery and the things of the night. You can't see it. But you can see some burns. It got hot when it turned that killing spell."

"I see. I do wish you'd try this wine. It's a fine vintage."

Else shook his head.

A bell tinkled softly. The dwarf jumped. He muttered, "At this time of night? There aren't any more of you coming over, are there?"

"Not that I know of."

The bell continued to demand a response.

"Go." Else presumed there was no danger. The people looking for him would not ring bells, they would kick down doors.

STEWPO RETURNED LOOKING WORRIED. HE WAS ALL FIDGET and tick, now.

"What is it?" Else asked.

"There have been developments. They found your friend who fled before the attack. They think they know who they're looking for, now, too. Someone named Sir Aelford daSkees. Because he's the only passenger off *Vivia Infanti* who hasn't been accounted for. Because you named names before you didn't kill that Brother on the ship."

"The kid can't help it. He was born stupid."

"There's more. It's more interesting."

"I'm listening."

"*Vivia Infanti*'s master complained publicly about the bad behavior and murderous intentions of the Special Office wizard he was forced to bring over from Runch. Here's an interesting piece of trivia. Your captain is the brother of Don Aleano Durandanti."

"Who would be a big name in that family. Right?"

"The top dog. And the way the Brotherhood started acting after this sorcerer showed up has everybody pissed off at them." The dwarf rocked double time. "Even the Fermi are grumbling."

"What happened?" Else scarcely noticed Stewpo's ticks, now.

"The Durandanti foreclosed on the Brotherhood barracks. The Brotherhood took a major loan against it a while back. And they weren't making payments."

"You don't seem disheartened."

"The Brotherhood of War are the worst predators in Suriet. Their order is built on stolen wealth and the sale of slaves."

Most Deves outside the Holy Lands, these days, were the descendants of peoples who had been sold around the shores of the Mother Sea.

"I understand," Else said.

"Can you keep information from those who sent you, Sha-lug?"

"I shouldn't. My reports are supposed to include anything al-Qarn might find interesting."

"There are things that I'd rather al-Qarn didn't know. Not Gordimer, particularly. But the other one. The wizard."

"Er-Rashal? Why?"

"He's a sorcerer. And we hear rumors about him. As a Deve-dian there are things I don't want him to know. If you feel obligated to report everything you observe, then I won't always be willing to help you."

"I can fail to see those small matters that don't pose any threat to my family, my people, my country, or my God." This one dwarf could not be a threat to Dreanger.

"Good. Very good. So I'll take a huge risk and assume that a Sha-lug's word is as precious as the Sha-lug want the world to believe."

Else growled a soft imprecation. Hell. The dwarf was making fun. And the truth was, al-Prama saw nothing wrong with deceiving unbelievers.

"You need to remember that Gledius Stewpo is no Sha-lug.

Gledius Stewpo is a Devedian patriot helping his people by assisting the enemies of their enemies."

"I understand that."

The Deves of the diaspora kept quiet but those who survived in the Holy Lands professed it publicly. They wanted all invaders evicted from Suriet. Their Suriet.

Their dogma ignored the historical truth that they had been invaders themselves, in their time.

"I want you clear on the point. Before I show you what I'm considering showing you."

The history of the Holy Lands was one of war and invasion again and again as one people after another tried to get control of the Wells of Ihrian.

Why had there been no empire, ever, based in the Holy Lands?

Else said, "We're clear on where we stand. If you think that something needs to be kept between just us two, I'll honor your wish."

"Good. Because I'm afraid we Sonsan Devedians are going to need the assistance of a real warrior soon."

Else grunted an interrogative.

"The Brotherhood aren't accepting the inevitable. They aren't walking away. They *believe* God is on their side. They won't leave their barracks. They're willing to fight. One Durandanti retainer has been killed already."

"And this ties in with me keeping secrets from al-Qarn?"

"The inevitable next stage—while the Brotherhood is temporizing and hoping for help from somewhere else—will be to lay off blame for the crisis on foreigners and unbelievers.

"They always attack the Devedian quarter when they riot. In the republics the ruling families discourage bigotry because it's bad for business. They depend on Devedian artisans and clerks. But the intolerance is still there in the mob."

Devedians were important in many Praman cities, too. In Praman Direcia the Devedian minority formed a bureaucratic class that supported its Praman rulers enthusiastically.

Stewpo added, "This new Patriarch, though . . . He has no tolerance at all. He preaches against everyone. Even his own people when they fail to agree that he's the Infallible Voice of God."

"You think something is going to happen?"

"I think the Sonsan mob will try to run the Brotherhood out. The Three Families will sit on their hands. People will get hurt. The Brotherhood will claim that it's all our fault. So the mob will turn on the easy victims. Meanwhile, the Brotherhood will work out an accommodation with the Three Families and nothing will change."

"And you want what from me?"

"Professional advice. On how to defend ourselves. Preferably in a way that keeps the casualties down so the mob doesn't get outraged because we did defend ourselves."

"Good luck with that." Else knew of no way to fight people without making them angrier than they already were. All you could do was hurt them until they were in so much pain that they let the anger go.

"So what's the point of asking me not to pass information on to al-Qarn?" He had seen nothing unusual yet.

"Oh. I thought you understood. We'll fight if we're attacked."

"Again, how does that concern al-Qarn?"

"Our methods might be of interest to the sorcerer."

"Fighting back might not be the smartest thing to do."

The dwarf shrugged. "So be it. Come with me."

THE DEVEDIAN QUARTER WAS QUIET AND DARK. ELSE NOTICED pairs of armed men in its shadows. There was a racket in the direction of the Sawn. At least one large fire illuminated the underbellies of dense, low clouds.

"Looks like rain," Else told Stewpo.

"That would be good. It'd cool tempers."

They traveled barely a quarter mile, which was a large fraction of the width of the Devedian quarter. The quarter was densely populated. It occupied very little ground. Deves had to bury their dead outside the wall, in unhallowed ground set aside by the Church.

The dwarf muttered, "There are spies everywhere."

Two determined-looking youths challenged the dwarf quietly. Stewpo responded. One youth hurried ahead to open the door of what looked like a rich man's home. It had no shops at street level.

The door opened on a narrow hallway illuminated by a single candle. The floor was worn hardwood. Four doors opened off on that central hallway. Each was shut.

At the end of the hall a door opened on a steep cellar stairway. The dwarf needed no guide.

Stewpo stopped at the bottom, said nothing until their guide climbed back up the narrow stairs. Then he opened what appeared to be a derelict clothes cupboard stuffed with castoffs, reached through the clothing, pushed sideways. The back panel moved slightly, then swung away to reveal a darkness behind the cupboard.

Stewpo said, "There isn't anything lurking in this darkness."

"I'll be right behind you," Else said. And, "Have you visited Suriet yourself?"

"No. Have you?"

"Yes. Nowhere is the night so dark as it is there."

The dwarf pushed into the darkness. Which proved to be hanging strips of black felt.

There was no light on the other side of the felt, though. Until Stewpo said something that must have been a password.

An ancient Deve in traditional costume, wearing a huge beard, appeared behind a tiny candle. He said nothing while Stewpo and Else eased past and pushed through another set of felt hangings into a large underground room.

Else suspected the whole neighborhood was rife with tunnels and underground rooms, escape routes and places to hide. He wondered what the Deves had done with the surplus earth.

These Deves had been getting ready for trouble for a long time.

The underground room contained an arsenal and seven wizened, shrunken old men. Stewpo said, "These are the Devedian Elders of Sonsa."

Else noted forests of gray facial fur. These old men might not have seen the real world in a generation. One old man looked like he might have been around, criticizing and complaining, when the Creator was putting together his great, flawed clockwork piece of art.

Else considered them, pigeonholed them, shifted attention to the arsenal.

He was impressed. "There must be a lot of money in the Devedian quarter." He saw fire-throwing weapons from the

Eastern Empire and Lucidian crossbows of the sort any fool could use with almost no training. He saw weapons meant for use by specialist troops like grenadiers. He saw amphorae marked as containing deadly poisons suitable for use on arrowheads, spearheads, crossbow bolts, swords, and knives.

It all suggested a ferocious determination.

The Devedians of Sonsa had suffered all they were going to take.

"I'm here," he said. "And I see that you're serious. What do you expect me to do?"

"Nothing if we're not attacked," Stewpo said. "Everything if we are. You'll be our general. You'll be our hope. But no one who isn't in this room now will ever know that a foreign soldier was involved."

Else felt his arm being twisted figuratively.

"Let's see what we have to work with." They did have him at their mercy.

Five minutes later, Else told the elders, "What'll happen is, you'll get yourselves massacred. First time they roll a wizard in on you." Sorcery, even in the hands of its masters, seldom operated on a large scale. In a large battle a single sorcerer was almost irrelevant because he could impact only a tiny fraction of the struggle at a time. But on the close, intimate battleground of a house-to-house struggle, the ability of a sorcerer to crush resistance systematically could be terrifying.

Else asked, "Why do Chaldareans want to attack Devedians?"

One old gray shrub with eyes said, "They say we're a worldwide conspiracy to bring on a permanent darkness."

"I guess that explains why Devedians are everywhere. Never mind that you arrived as slaves. You don't want to confuse true believers with facts." Also, there had been two earlier Devedian diasporas, before the most recent, brought about by the crusades. Those came during the age of the Old Empire.

Stewpo demanded, "What are you driving at?"

"A mob breaks into the Devedian quarter. It runs into military weapons used by determined fighters. What happens next?"

"A lot of people get killed."

"Confirming the universal suspicion that the Deves are up to no good and need to be wiped out before they overthrow the Church and corrupt every Chaldarean virgin."

There was no point reasoning. These people wanted a fight. They did not intend to let good sense get in the way. "What's this?" he asked, having just discovered an instrument of destruction that had no business existing outside Dreanger.

It was a firepowder weapon of smaller bore and longer tube than the falcon that had gone to Andesqueluz. A craftsman had been working on it only moments ago. The smell of hot iron still tainted the air.

The tube had been created by wrapping iron wire around a steel rod, then heating the metal and hammering it. "Is a sword smith doing this?" It was a stretch but a similar concept underlay the making of the best swords. And the best sword smiths in Praman Direcia were Devedian.

Would this be something he was supposed to report? The existence of the weapon? Or the fact that there were Deve agents inside er-Rashal's secret workshops? Firepowder weapons had seen field use only rarely. Until the incident of the bogon they had attracted no attention because of their freedom from success.

Stewpo finally confessed, "It's an experimental weapon. I don't pretend to understand it. I'm told it'll give us a way to deal with unfriendly sorcerers."

So. The elders were not blind to reality after all. Their chances would be improved if they could protect themselves against sorcery. Particularly if they were a quarter as wicked as the Church accused them of being.

Else said, "If you really want to fight back and live you'll get that toy finished fast."

How could the concept behind it have gotten to Sonsa so fast?

Silver-tipped arrows and poisoned iron daggers were the stuff of legend. However, any marginally competent sorcerer could surround himself with spells that would weaken or destroy the wood, feathers, bone, cotton or flax, and animal-glue parts of any missile, leaving nothing but a tumbling silver point that would cause harm only by chance.

A man with a dagger was easily frustrated, too, if the sorcerer was not napping.

Else realized that the Deves had trapped him neatly. Their most insidious lure was his need to find out what they were doing and the true depth of their resources. They betrayed themselves a little so he would feel compelled to find out more.

His discovery of the firepowder weapon was no accident.

That left him more convinced that there were Devedian spies close to er-Rashal al-Dhulquarnen and, perhaps, even Gordimer the Lion.

CONFLICT AROSE PREDICTABLY, FOLLOWING A TEDIOUSLY UN-surprising escalation. A band of adolescents got into the Devedian quarter and threw rocks at Devedian youths, tried to break into a shop, attempted to assault a Devedian girl—then found themselves surrounded by unsmiling men who were not amused by their gentle ethnic jests. They beat the invaders senseless, then flung them into the filth of a midstreet gutter.

The fathers and brothers and cousins of the injured boys took umbrage. That led to confrontations that escalated into the use of weapons. A dozen Chaldareans perished.

In time, a too bold mob of drunks started a battle during which overly enthusiastic Devedian crossbowmen slaughtered scores of raiders.

Every confrontation occurred inside the Devedian quarter. For what little value that was as an arguing point before the city's masters.

Escalation took eight days. Else played the restraining general where no general was necessary and no restraint was possible. On the eighth evening the ruling families felt compelled to take notice because the rioters, turning to Color politics, began starting fires on the Chaldarean side of the Devedian quarter wall. They directed their household troops to restore order. But those forces were besieging the barracks filled with Brotherhood of War squatters.

Knowing success might doom Sonsa's Devedians, Else nevertheless organized an ambush that embarrassed the household forces.

The outrage of Sonsa's Chaldareans, naturally, knew no bounds.

Else told the elders, "Now they'll make war on you. You

won't like the way it turns out. There are a hundred of them for every one of you."

"There always have been," Gledius Stewpo said. The Deves were drunk on success. To this point they had suffered no dead at all.

One of the beards said, "The weapon is ready."

Another said, "The business of Sonsa is business. That business can't go on without us. The Three Families have to let this run its course."

SONSA BECAME QUIET. ORDER RETURNED OUTSIDE THE DEVEdian quarter. The ruling families *did* try to let emotions cool. But too many people preferred otherwise. Especially the Brotherhood of War, guided by the unidentified sorcerer off *Vivia Infanti*.

A rumor said foreign mercenaries were behind the uprising. One description of a Ferris Renfrow was good enough to get Else lynched.

Circumstances were changing. Else began to consider risking trying to get out of Sonsa.

He would be of no use to Dreanger if he got killed in a local uprising.

News of the uprising reached Brothe. The Patriarch had, already, issued a bull insisting on complete obliteration of the unbelievers. He ordered the Three Families to place all their armed men at the disposal of the Brotherhood of War.

Because the Devedian community had friends and spies, because the Brotherhood had enemies determined to see it embarrassed, those who schemed against the Deves had few secrets.

The Brothers were no fools. They would not believe that they could surprise the Deves. And because they numbered fewer than two score they would not be eager to lead an assault.

"Isn't that always the way? Those most eager get behind somebody who doesn't want to be there and push," Else said.

Bad timing. Right now the old men were solidly behind the young men but had no pushing to do. The youngsters were more eager than the old folks. Their situation had not yet grown grim.

Else asked, "What do you expect to do when the Brotherhood comes? They won't run from a few missiles. They'll bring their sorcerers. And they'll kill anybody who isn't one of them. I've seen it before."

Blank looks. Cold stares. The old men did not want to listen. And Else was trapped in their nightmare.

Not once since his first visit to the armory had he been alone. But he was sure he could shed his Deve shadows if he wanted.

THE BROTHERHOOD'S ATTACK CAME AT NIGHT, AS EXPECTED. Sorcerers felt more comfortable working in the dark. The family household forces, more afraid of the Brothers behind them than the Deves ahead, broke through the barricade barring entry to the Devedian quarter. Others climbed over the wall, which was slight and less than ten feet high. Its purpose was not defensive, it was intended to contain.

They met no resistance. Nervously, they moved ahead, cautious to a fault, anticipating some deadly trap.

It was dark, after all. And Deves were agents of the Will of the Night. Everybody knew that.

The invaders found the Deve buildings boarded up. They were empty when broken into. Not only were the occupants gone, so were their valuables.

The Three Families had told their soldiers to hurt as few people as possible. Deves were critical to Sonsa's prosperity.

The Brotherhood of War moved in as soon as they heard that there was no resistance, determined to plunder.

The household troops grew ever more unsettled.

Any minute now, those Deve sorcerers would unleash all the hounds of darkness.

ELSE OBSERVED THE INVASION THROUGH A CRACK IN AN unglazed cellar window. As he had anticipated, the invaders had worked themselves up immensely in anticipation of a desperate fight. Many were drunk. They did not know what to do if there was nobody to fight. They were standing around scaring one another, not even looking for something to steal. Else whispered to Stewpo, "You see? Discipline is failing. They're drunk enough to forget why they came. They'll get a notion to start looking for secret Deve treasure in a minute. Then we'll have them."

The families and their most precious possessions had moved into the tunnels and cellars undermining the quarter. If complete disaster befell, there was an evacuation tunnel running under Sonsa's south wall. Though Else was not supposed to know about that, or several other tunnels leading out of the quarter. The younger Deves often forgot to speak Melhaic when he was around.

Else had done his best on behalf of the resistance because any success might inspire Devedians elsewhere. If Sublime was busy suppressing minorities at home he might not have time to look to the east.

"Here's the man we're waiting for."

A tall man well-wrapped in black appeared. This was the taller of the two who had come over aboard *Vivia Infanti*. The one Else had attacked. He seemed in surprisingly good health.

"Stand by," Else cautioned. "He'll use his powers to see what became of the people who should be here."

There was some truth to the rumor that old Deves were sorcerers. Not all of them, just a few. About as many as in any similarly sized group of old people. Those with that dollop of talent had been tasked with masking the hiding places of the women and children.

A number of obvious hiding places had been singled out for the opposite effect.

The tall Brother moved toward Else's hiding place suddenly, swiftly, sensing something. "Match! Now!" Else said. He held the firepowder weapon on target. The sorcerer broke into a sprint.

The match man did his job.

There was a thunderous boom and a great cloud of sulfurous smoke. When the smoke cleared the Brother was sprawled on the cobbled street, ten feet back of where he had been when the weapon discharged, pierced through the heart by a silver ball, dead before he hit the ground.

The explosion was the signal hidden Devedian fighters were awaiting.

They made themselves known from the roofs, with a surprise rain of death directed mainly at the Brotherhood of War.

Men shouted orders to put all torches out.

Men shouted orders to belay those orders.

Devedian fighters emerged from the narrow byways, struck, faded away. Snipers up high continued to deliver misery to the intruders.

Else barked and swore at the men working the firepowder weapon. He wanted the weapon ready in case the older Brotherhood witchman turned up. But, even with three men working, it took five minutes to swab the fire tube and repack it with powder, wads, primer, iron pellets, and the silver scrap that was all skinflint Stewpo was willing to provide for a second firing.

It grew quiet outside. The Deve fighters faded away, taking their injured. They let the raiders remove their own casualties. Hope remained that it might be possible to get through this without alienating the Three Families.

"Outlander!" one of Else's team barked. "Here comes the other one."

Else elbowed his way to the window slit.

The mystery man from *Vivia Infanti* arrived shouting. Like whipped dogs the Household troops returned and began to creep off into the tight alleys and streets of the Devedian quarter.

The Brotherhood sorcerer spotted his fallen henchman. He studied the surrounding night as he edged toward the dead man. But he became so distressed that he failed to remain sufficiently alert.

One of the crossbow bolts whizzing around caught a nip of flesh.

He let out a roar driven more by emotional pain than the sting of his wound. Then he began to cast a spell that had been prepared in advance.

That would be something meant to blind or disarm the snipers. Otherwise, he would suffer an endless shower of missiles. The spell would effect his own men, too. But he would not be worried about them.

"This isn't good," Else said as soon as he recognized what was happening. "Not good at all. Do we have any cold water handy? Do we have rags we can soak?"

His assistants wanted to know why that mattered.

"Because we've got a ferromage on our hands. This tube is going to get too hot to handle. Maybe even hot enough to set off the firepowder inside. If that happens, the weapon is useless. And we'll be dead."

The sorcerer did them a favor, though.

While his magic was still growing, while his surviving Brotherhood henchmen were bringing out weapons made of wood or glass, he seemed to sense the source of, if not the cause of, his apprentice's misfortune.

He uttered another thunderous cry and headed toward Else and his team.

Else aimed desperately, the tube not yet too hot to rest atop his shoulder. "Match man! Match man!"

He heard the firepowder hiss in the primer pan. The Brotherhood sorcerer seemed to hear it, too, because he made a sudden, violent effort to stop.

The firepowder exploded. Silver scrap and iron sand spewed into the night. Impact laid the Brotherhood sorcerer out in the air and flung him backward.

Something hit Else from behind, violently.

ELSE WAS OUT ONLY MOMENTARILY. HE RECOVERED CONsciousness, found the cellar filled with smoke. It stank of spent firepowder, with a taint of smoldering timber.

The firepowder tube had exploded. He was still alive only because the match man had absorbed the blast. The Deve's blood was all over him now.

Else tried to look outside again. The view was inadequate. The target was down but did not seem mortally injured. The surviving Brotherhood soldiers were dragging him away.

The smell of wood smoke grew stronger.

It was time to find somewhere else to be. There was a whole cask of firepowder somewhere in the darkened cellar, along with all the brave, dead young Deves.

HIS EVERY BREATH NO LONGER MONITORED, ELSE SEIZED THE opportunity to serve his God, Dreanger, and the Sha-lug elsewhere. He abandoned the Devedian quarter by means of a deep, wet tunnel that led not to the country outside the city wall—that one would be crowded and well-guarded—but to a crypt in a mausoleum in the cathedral cemetery a hundred yards northeast of the Devedian quarter wall.

The existence of the tunnel was one of those secrets Else picked up when young fighters had not paid attention to what they were saying.

Despite the tumult in the Devedian quarter the rest of Sonsa was enjoying a quiet summer night. No moon interfered with the view of the sea of stars. A few belated fireflies still sparked among the tombstones and memorials. Neither the dead nor the living nor the Instrumentalities of the Night seemed interested in the progress of one filthy fugitive armed with a long knife and a short iron bar he had picked up during his flight.

Smoke and firelight rose above the Devedian quarter. The keg of firepowder had gone up while Else was in the tunnel. Household troops and Devedian fighters now worked shoulder to shoulder to stifle the flames.

Else took advantage of the opportunity offered by Fate's indifference. He looked for his other Sonsan contact, wishing he had sought this one first. He could have avoided all that Devedian unpleasantness. By now he could be in Brothe, employed in the Patriarch's armies. All unaware of the fact that Deve spies had penetrated the Palace of the Kings.

Rumor said the Patriarch was assembling an army to conquer Calzir. Or it might be the Emperor. Whichever, evidently, there were few takers. The campaign, if ever it materialized, would be extremely arduous while offering private soldiers little hope of plunder. Calzir was poor, agricultural, a bitter place to live. For two thousand years not much had changed there but the names of the masters.

An old joke said that Chaldareans and Pramans fought a war with Calzir at stake and the Pramans lost.

Calzir, though, did have considerable strategic significance. It bestrode the horn of Firaldia and the huge island of Shippen, gazing out at the slim waist of the Mother Sea. And it provided a Praman bridgehead on the Firaldian peninsula.

Else passed by four times before he discovered the cast

bronze leopard that identified the home he sought. The leopard was no bigger than a house cat. It did not stand out. He had anticipated something more dramatic.

He slipped up to the door and knocked the prescribed series, unsure that anyone would respond at this hour. He ran through the series a second time, then a third, shrinking into shadow in order to be less noticeable. He leaned out once to consider the progress of the fire in the Devedian quarter.

They seemed to have gotten that under control.

His fourth effort was rewarded by appropriate counter-knocks from inside. He offered the counter countersign.

The narrow door opened a crack. Else saw nothing but heard a whispered query. He offered the proper response.

The door opened another inch. It was as dark as the Patriarch's heart in there. He did not move. He would not until he was invited or refused. There would be some sort of protection set up for the householder.

"Come forward."

He moved carefully, keeping his hands in plain sight, doing nothing that might be considered suspicious. The agent would be nervous, what with the Brotherhood raving on about foreign agitators stirring up the Deves.

"Turn to your right."

He could not see the speaker in the dark. The whispers came from a low altitude.

Not another dwarf?

No, it developed. Not another dwarf. A woman. Which he discovered once they entered a small room where a single weak candle burned. "I thought . . ."

"You were expecting my husband. He passed away last winter."

"I don't believe they know that at home." He did not mention al-Qarn because, he recalled, this agent believed he served the Eastern Emperor.

"It hasn't been reported. I need the money. Pledga left me no other income when he went."

Else did not ask how or why. He did not care. And knowing would change nothing. He considered the woman. She was small in stature and frame, about forty, graying, obviously proud, still striking and still betraying traces of the beauty she had been not so long ago. "I understand. Are you alone, then?"

The woman studied him as intently as he studied her. Each considered his or her life to be in the hands of the other.

"Yes. As long as the stipend keeps coming, I can afford that."

"Your husband let you know what he was doing?"

"We had no secrets. He told me a story he believed. But he was a bit gullible. What do you need?"

"A place to hide."

"You're the foreign spy they're warning everyone about." Her large, dark eyes came alive with humor.

"I'm *a* spy. The one they're talking about is one they made up to scare people. A boogeyman to make people behave the way they want."

"They described you pretty well. We need to do something about your hair."

Else sighed. "Maybe so."

"Right now you need to get clean."

ELSE REMAINED INVISIBLE FOR THREE WEEKS. HE RETREATED to an attic room whenever Anna Mozilla had company. Which was often. The widow was a gregarious woman with numerous friends and relations who enjoyed gossiping. She had no children.

She was energetic and positive and must have been the driving force in her marriage. She gathered regular news of events in the city.

The Three Families fell out with the Brotherhood of War because the badly wounded Brotherhood sorcerer tried to order the Devedian population exterminated after he escaped the fighting in the Devedian quarter. That was a presumption of such epic arrogance that the Three Families all refused to allow it.

Brotherhood casualties that night included twelve dead and nineteen seriously injured. The uninjured survivors were unable to resist when the Durandanti evicted them from their barracks.

"They chartered a ship to take them to Brothe," Anna Mozilla reported. "But they'll be back." A large Brotherhood establishment, Castella dollas Pontellas, the Fortress of the Little Bridges, existed just a few hundred yards from the Chiaro Palace, and even closer to Krois, the island stronghold of the Patriarch. And the current Patriarch had that sweetheart relationship with the Brotherhood.

Anna continued, "The dons aren't pleased. The sorcerer threatened them with writs of anathema. Bishop Indigo threatened right back, banning the Brotherhood from the Son-san See forever. He was never their friend. He preached against letting them set up here in the first place, back when I was a girl."

"The sorcerer did survive?"

"Yes. But they say he was hurt so bad he'll be crippled from now on. And he'll never perform major sorceries again."

"Uhm?"

"I heard he lost part of his left arm and the rest is useless. And that side of his face was destroyed. There's so much silver embedded in him, his own body will ruin whatever spells he tries." She sounded pleased.

"I really wish he was dead," Else said. "But I'll settle for second best. You say he left Sonsa?"

"Almost two weeks ago, now. He offended Don Bonaventura Scoviletti so badly that the Scovilettis say they won't support the Patriarch in anything that involves the Brotherhood in any way. Bishop Indigo is Don Bonaventura's uncle, by the way."

"Interesting. That must've taken guts. So. We had a nasty, major black-hearted villain here and even now we don't have any idea who he was."

"One of the top sorcerers from the Castella Anjela dolla Picolina. They say he came here because the augurs predicted that a huge threat to the Church would materialize in Sonsa."

"Be an ironic twist if his attempts to prevent that actually caused it."

"A lot of people are saying that."

"The trouble with the Deves should fade away, now. For a while. Without the Brotherhood to keep everybody angry."

"That's the talk. But things will never get back to normal."

"I should slip out of Sonsa, now."

"Not yet." Anna Mozilla sounded reluctant to see that happen, though what she said was, "The dons are still looking for somebody who sounds like the man I found at my door one night a while back. The Devedian elders insist they were duped by a provocateur from Dreanger who died in the explosion that started the fire in their quarter. You don't look like a Dreangerean."

"Goes to show you, you can't believe everything you hear."

Anna Mozilla gave him a look. He was fooling nobody but himself.

FOURTEEN DAYS LATER, IN THE VILLAGE OF ALICEA, TWENTY-two miles east of Sonsa, Else chanced on a dozen men out of Grolsach, Rence, Reste, and several other small political entities in the confusion of Ormienden and Dromedan. They were mostly very young and very tired. Else was tired himself. But he was on the road to Brothe at last.

He had killed a hare with a slung stone earlier in the day. The rabbit bought him a place at the fire. The dozen were headed for Brothe, too, with ambitions toward finding work as soldiers. They were mostly strangers who had come together on the road.

The Grolsacher brothers Pico and Justi Mussa and their friend Gofit Aspel had deserted the men who held their apprentice indentures. They had picked up Rafi Corona and shifty-eyed old Bo Biogna while drifting through Dromedan, in Ormienden. The rest had accumulated since. Except for Biogna and a very large and slow-witted fellow who insisted on being called Just Plain Joe—whose traveling companion was a moth-eaten mule named Pig Iron—the men had no military experience. This was a first adventure for everyone. Even Bo Biogna and Just Plain Joe did their military stints in their home territories. When they heard Else was a traveled veteran they insisted he tell them all about the glory of war.

He told them the truth. They were not happy. That was not what they wanted to hear. But they had seen enough of the world to suspect that reality refused to bow to wishful thinking.

10. Khaurene, in the End of Connec

Word spread throughout the End of Connec. The synod of the Perfect had ruled that true Maysaleans *must* resist evil when evil became oppressive. So the Bishop of Antieux could be ignored if he confined himself to his cathedral or just lurked in his country manor, ranting about heresy. If he sent men to harm Maysaleans they would not be expected to turn the other cheek.

Brother Candle expected that most would, even so. Seekers After Light were gentle folk who longed for a world free of greed and hatred and all the evils Man practiced upon his fellows.

Brother Candle had argued against *any* surrender to the venom of the flesh. But he would not contest the will of the synod. God would be acknowledged His role as final arbiter. In any event, the targets of the Brothen interlopers were more often Connecten Episcopals than Maysaleans.

Bishop Serifs had kept his head down since the attack on the Patriarchal legate, though the Patriarch kept demanding a more aggressive campaign against heresy.

The legate was slow to recover from his wounds.

Antieux was quiet. Count Raymone Garete, young and quick of temper, remained in Khaurene, Duke Tormond's seat, held there by Tormond so he would not provoke the Church.

Brother Candle made his way through the crowded morning streets of Khaurene for the first time in two decades. No retinue accompanied him but he received more attention and respect than he had when he was Charde ande Clairs.

Episcopal and Maysalean alike, people saluted him or bowed or even hailed him in the ancient imperial manner. Becoming Perfect was considered a great accomplishment by Connectens of all faiths. Even Deves and Dainshaus, who could be found in all the larger towns and cities of the Connec, respected a holy spirit when they encountered one.

The old fortress called Metrelieux stood on an eminence overlooking a bend in the fat, slow, brown Vierses River. Metrelieux had been the seat of the Connecten dukes since time immemorial. The present fortress had been erected using dressed limestone from local quarries four centuries ago, on the foundations of an Old Brothen fortress that had served the identical purpose in imperial times. The original structure had been looted for building stone during the two centuries following the collapse of the Old Brothen Empire.

The stone of the modern fortress was soft. It was dirty. It showed severe weathering. Brother Candle doubted that it would last another hundred years.

Metrelieux reflected the nature of the man who occupied it. So the folk of Khaurene said, who knew him as the Great Vacillator.

Tormond IV just never seemed to get around to doing the big things.

Tormond was loved by the people of the Connec, as much for what he did not get around to as for what he did.

Tormond did not involve himself in the lives of his people. The people of the Connec found that an endearing trait in a ruling duke.

Tormond's father and grandfather had set the precedent. Though the grandfather (also Tormond, the third duke of that name) had gone crusading as a young man. *His* grandfather had been one of the founders of the crusader states of Kagure and Groves, which, in forms much diminished by Indala al-Sul Halaladin, survived today. Ruled by princes, nominated by the Brotherhood of War, and confirmed by all the more recent Patriarchs.

Brother Candle came up to the barbican gate of Metrelieux. Two sleepy, overweight, and elderly guards were all that stood between the fortress and invasion. They observed sporadic foot traffic from beneath a portcullis that, in all probability, would not come down in an emergency.

No one living could recall the last time the fortress had closed its gates.

There was fear in the streets today, though. The folk of Khaurene sensed that centuries of peace and prosperity were in peril. The people were troubled by a failed attempt on the life of Immaculate II, the anti-Patriarch.

Rumors in the street said that, through great good fortune

and the grace of God, assassins intent on murdering the prelate had been overwhelmed by Immaculate's Braunsknechts Guards. There was talk of miracles and divine intervention. The killers should not have failed.

Sublime V, was, of course, the chief candidate for villain behind the crime. Though, naturally, Sublime would deny all responsibility.

The guards at the gate asked him what he wanted.

"I'm Brother Candle. The Duke . . ."

"Eh. Ye're late, sair. Himself pro'ly guv up on ye comin'." The heavier guard spoke a dialect used way out west, possibly from beyond the River Payme in Tramaine. "Come wi' me, sair."

Brother Candle asked, "What brought you to Khaurene?"

"Khaurene were where I was when I figured out I were ta ald ta be an adventurer anymore." Adventurer being the common euphemism for mercenary soldier. "An' I shoulda done 'er twen'y years sooner. The Duke, he bees a good man ta work far."

"I hear that everywhere." Brother Candle eventually left the guard with a blessing, at his request.

The Patriarch was right. They were everywhere.

Brother Candle passed through dusty halls where, it seemed, no effort had been made to keep house since the current reign began.

Tormond had unusual priorities, it seemed.

Tormond of Khaurene was a balding, graying, gaunt man in his early fifties. Handsome and vain in his youth, Tormond had lost interest in his appearance when he lost Artesia, his Duchess, in childbirth at the age of forty-four, four years past. The child was both deformed and stillborn. Every Connecten who put words into the mouth of God had something to say about that.

Tormond disdained them all.

The Duke had aged terribly. His gray eyes were haunted.

"Charde ande Clairs," Tormond said, leaving a clutch of nobles to greet the Perfect.

"Just Brother Candle these days, Your Lordship."

"It must be true, what they say about you people drinking the blood of virgins. You don't look a year older."

"You flatter me, Your Lordship. My bones feel like the bones of an octogenarian. My joints creak and groan any time I bend over. My best years are behind me, alas."

Duke Tormond continued his own thought. "I, on the other hand, have aged for both of us. I'm so tired, Charde. Since I lost Artesia I wake up already weary of the world and its trials."

Had this been anyone other than Tormond, Brother Candle would now witness the peace to be found amongst the Seekers After Light. But this was Tormond IV, beloved by his people, whose only male child had been stillborn. Whose most likely successor was Count Raymone Garete of Antieux, a friend of the Seekers but barely out of his teens and a ferocious hothead. Count Raymone suffered from the unfortunate delusion of an independent Connec allied with and protected by King Peter of Navaya in nearby Direcia.

Brother Candle said, "Send a courier to Fleaumont. The nuns can provide you an herbal remedy that will have you stamping the earth like a young stallion again in three months."

"Ah. Your wife is there these days, isn't she?"

"That's where she took her orders."

"I'll do that. You chose the perfect moment to arrive. I suppose that's why they call you Perfect Master." Tormond's sense of humor was not entirely dead. When Brother Candle did not correct him, he went on. "My sister is here." He indicated the group he had departed. Among them was a handsome woman in her early thirties.

"Pardon my brash observation, Your Lordship, but she's become quite a striking woman."

Isabeth was twenty-one years younger than Tormond. She was more like an indulged daughter than a little sister.

"I didn't know she was visiting."

"Officially, she's not. Officially, she's in Oranja, running the state while Peter besieges Camarghara. Please don't tell anyone that you saw her."

"Of course. If that's what you want."

"It is. Come over and sit with us."

Brother Candle followed the Duke to a table where the Queen of Navaya had just settled with six older men. One was a Dainshau. Two were Devedians. Of those two, one's dress suggested that he had come from Direcia, perhaps accompanying Isabeth. The other, named Michael Carhart, was a Devedian religious scholar of considerable substance and Khaurene's senior Devedian.

Of the remaining men, two were Episcopal priests and one looked like a professional soldier. Brother Candle recognized none of them.

Once Brother Candle and the Duke seated themselves, there were no empty chairs. Brother Candle said, "I presume that I'm the last to arrive. So what's the occasion for such a distinguished assembly?"

Tormond said, "A communication from the Patriarch. Sublime, not Immaculate."

Brother Candle surveyed the others. How had Isabeth gotten here so fast?

"Isabeth was here when the letter arrived. She came because King Peter had heard from the Patriarch earlier, on a related matter."

"I see."

"Sublime has commanded me, as Duke of the End of Connec, to rid the province of all heretics and unbelievers. He's done that before, but never backed by the threat of force. As always, he didn't specify who the offenders might be."

One Episcopal priest muttered, "The man is an idiot."

The other priest glared.

The first said, "Does he suppose Johannes would let him get away with that?"

The man who looked like a soldier said, "The message seems timed to arrive right after Immaculate's assassination. That failed. So the threat has no substance."

Queen Isabeth said, "Sublime presumes too much. He believes his own propaganda. His grasp on reality has become suspect."

Brother Candle turned to Duke Tormond for further explanation.

Tormond said, "The fool *ordered* Peter to ready his forces for an invasion of the Connec."

"Peter of Navaya?" That *did* indicate a serious disconnect with reality. Why would Sublime think that Peter would abandon the Reconquest to attack his wife's brother? Also, while Peter was a devout Chaldarean, he was tolerant. He did not persecute the minorities within his own kingdom. Not even Pramans, so long as his own suzerainty remained unchallenged. Hell, rumor had it that Peter's queen was a Maysalean heretic herself. And there were more Maysaleans there than anywhere outside the Connec, except the rump Praman mercantile republic of Platadura, a port on the Direcian coast of the Mother Sea just beyond the eastern coastal end of the Verses Mountains.

Brother Candle suggested, "King Peter now regrets that his father shifted his allegiance from Viscesment to Brothe."

Queen Isabeth confessed, "He did that only because a few important vassals insisted. And they still do."

The military man asked, "Will they make war on fellow Chaldareans?"

"No, Sir Eardale. Our lords are of one mind militarily. The Reconquest. They won't respond to Sublime's call. They all have ties with our Connecten families. But someone else certainly will respond if called."

"Who?" Tormond asked.

"Arnhand, brother. Those people are all thieves."

"Arnhand has its hands full with Santerin."

"No one else has the manpower and moral flexibility. Consider helping make sure the conflict with Santerin stays hot."

"Why are we here?" Brother Candle asked.

"Because your peoples are the ones it's going to happen to if Sublime forces the issue. Father Clayto, here, has condemned Brothe though he's an adherent of the Brothen Patriarchy. Bishop LeCroes, though, is teetering."

Absurd. Brother Candle did not know the man but knew the name. LeCroes was Immaculate's bishop in Khaurene, where the Episcopal population favored the anti-Patriarch.

Father Clayto was critical of Brothe and what Brothe wanted to do in the Connec. For that he had received severe reprimands. Sublime had demoted him to assistant pastor in one of Khaurene's poorest parishes.

The righteous never go unpunished.

Tormond said, "I want to know where each of you will stand if Sublime does try to make war."

Michael Carhart said, "That man doesn't care about heresy or dissent. Greed drives him. He means to plunder the Connec to finance a war against Calzir and another crusade into Suriet. The Holy Lands." Suriet being the name of the Holy Lands in Melhaic, a language spoken amongst the Wells of Ihrian and by the Devedians of the latest diaspora. "He's been trying to make forced loans from us in the Episcopal States. In Sonsa the Brotherhood of War tried to destroy and plunder the entire Devedian community."

In truth, whenever the Brothen Church gained power, laws controlling the activities of non-Chaldareans soon took effect. And those, invariably, worked to the detriment of the larger community.

The more educated people in most communities were non-Chaldareans because most Chaldareans of standing disdained literacy. If the Episcopal nobility wanted something written or read, or if they needed accounts kept, they hired some slinking, greedy, hand-wringing Deve to do the job.

Brother Candle said, "You've heard rumors of the synod of the Perfect this spring?"

Several people nodded. The military man shook his head.

Brother Candle continued, "The consensus was that all who follow the Path are *required* to resist evil actively, even to the extent of countering force with force. If the Patriarch—or anyone else—directly attacks any Seeker After Light for nothing more than the fact that his feet are on the Path, then the Seeker will be absolved of the taint of sin acquired by resisting evil."

Father Clayto asked, "Are you declaring war on the Church?"

"Don't be willfully ridiculous, Father. I said the synod believes that we're morally obligated to fight back if we're attacked. Nobody will be given a dispensation to go to Brothe to root Sublime out and hang him."

Michael Carhart said, "That's an entirely reasonable attitude. The Devedian community will assume the same posture."

Father Clayto snipped, "I suspect the Deves of Sonsa made a similar claim before committing their atrocities there."

Gently, Michael Carhart asked, "How many of those atrocities occurred outside Sonsa's Devedian quarter, Father? How many? Tell me, how many Chaldareans had their homes burned? Explain to me how it is that you people always find your way to the argument that us resisting rape, robbery, and murder is a crime against your god."

Duke Tormond stepped in. "Enough. I just want to know if your peoples will lie down should Sublime actually do something besides talk." Before anyone responded, he continued, "I've sent a deputation to Brothe. Another deputation. Though the first had no impact on Bishop Serifs's bad behavior and the second did nothing but bring back absurd demands. Sir Eardale was part of that mission. He had a good look at Firaldia, the Episcopal States, and Brothe." He pronounced the soldier's name Eh-ahr-dah-lay. "Brothe itself has been demilitarized."

Brother Candle knew the name, if not the man. Sir Eardale Dunn hailed from Santerin, a minor noble banished for reasons known only to himself, his king, and presumably, Duke Tormond. He had been Tormond's leading soldier for two decades, never having had to fight a war. He was not well known outside Metrelieux.

Sir Eardale said, "Sublime's ability to undertake a significant military operation exists entirely inside his own imagination. He believes his own propaganda. God is on his side because he's the Patriarch."

Sir Eardale continued, "Sublime has no troops he could send out on a foreign adventure. Every man he can afford to keep is waiting for Johannes Blackboots to attack. Most of them keeping their boots on at night so they don't have to waste time getting started running if Hansel does strike.

"Meantime, I'd be remiss if I didn't tell you that the Emperor is interested in Calzir. Vondera Koterba, his puppet in Alameddine, is recruiting mercenaries, possibly with an eye to annexing Calzir."

Brother Candle took a moment to consider what he knew of Firaldia. Alameddine would be the Chaldarean kingdom that bordered Praman Calzir, on the north side of the Vaillarentiglia Mountains.

Sir Eardale stopped talking. He devoted himself to one of the large cups of coffee that Tormond himself had prepared while his marshal spoke. The Duke offered the drink all round. No one refused. Not even Brother Candle, who had not taken coffee for decades. "Oh, that's good," he confessed. "I'd forgotten. More than the pleasures of the flesh, the Adversary could use coffee to seduce mortal man."

The Duke asked, "Are we exercising ourselves about nothing? Is the Patriarch just a blowhard?"

Sir Eardale said, "He is, in great part. The problem and danger is that he doesn't know he is. He really thinks that all devout Chaldreans are spoiling for a war against everything non-Chaldarean. But he's wrong. Even the most devout Chaldareans just want to get on with their lives. In peace."

"What about us?" Tormond asked. "Is he likely to carry out his threats against the End of Connec? Can he?"

No one could answer that. Only Sir Eardale had seen what was happening in Brothe. His observation was, "You can't predict what a madman will do."

Father Clayto asked, "Does it matter if Sublime can carry out his threats? A better question is, will he try? I'm afraid that, unfortunately, the answer to that one might be yes."

The Duke asked, "Do you find all this amusing, Charde?"

"Yes. In an irreverent fashion. Though no less frightening, for all that." He explained how a Maysalean could see God as a cruel practical joker in this. Once he finished explaining, he asked, "How will the Emperor react if Sublime launches a crusade against the Connec?"

"Excellent question," Sir Eardale said. "We expect to take that up with the Emperor himself. He'll certainly be interested now that his soldiers have disposed of those assassins who wanted to kill Immaculate."

Brother Candle was intrigued by the incident at Viscesment. Immaculate's defenders must have been forewarned.

Dainshaukin were notoriously quiet and sternly withdrawn from everyday life. Within their own dwindling communities they considered themselves an elder race, the first masters of the transition between the Age of the Gods and the Age of Man. The Dainshau at the table showed a palm.

The Duke identified him. "Tember Remak wishes to speak."

The Dainshau said, "Tember Remak has a question. Where does the Collegium stand in this? Does the Patriarch have their support?"

"They elected him," Father Clayto said.

"That would be a function of bribery and political persuasion. That would mean nothing in the time of the Festival of Hungry Ghosts. We have seen no evidence that Sublime fronts for the Tyranny of the Night. He is a great blusterer living in Bad Dog Village, not the sweet lord of Once Glance Great Fortune."

Though couched in unfamiliar terms from Dainshaukin parable, the questions were important. If the sorcerers of the Church did not support Sublime his ambitions would be curbed. In particular his intelligence efforts would suffer. Espionage was one area where an alliance with the Instrumentalities of the Night could be very profitable.

"Is there any way to know?" Tormond asked. He peered at Brother Candle.

Brother Candle replied, "Our familiarity with the night is considerably exaggerated, Your Lordship. The fact is, Seekers After Light reject the night when we pledge to follow the Path. That's why we're called Seekers After Light. Some of my colleagues here, though . . . They probably do roast Chaldarean babies and run naked under the full moon with demons from the Pit." He could not keep a straight face. Father Clayto had denounced the Seekers After Light for those very things.

One by one, each religious leader denied any involvement with the Instrumentalities of the Night. Mostly with good humor.

"So we're blind," Tormond said. "So we have no choice but to sit here and take whatever Fate hands out."

That earned him a clutch of scowls. There was no "fate" involved in the Will of God.

Brother Candle said, "Isn't it always that way in the Connec? Time and fortune have been generous. Never compelling us to bend the knee to the tyranny of the night."

Brother Candle received scowls himself. There was no "fortune" in the Will of God, either.

It was a strange convocation. No one demanded war. Almost everyone pled for peace—while making it plain that there would be no acquiescence if Sublime chose to make war.

The gathering broke up before Brother Candle fully understood what was happening. He suspected that Tormond and Isabeth wanted it that way. The religious leadership was prepared to fight the agents of darkness and forces of oppression. Without Tormond himself having committed passionately to any particular course.

Vacillation and procrastination were Tormond's best-known traits. In the slow-moving world of the Connec doing nothing often proved to be the best way of handling problems.

Brother Candle was sure today's troubles would not fade away. Unless God chose to introduce Sublime to heaven's reward early.

11. Great Sky Fortress, Realm of the Gods

There was no time in the Hall of the Heroes. There was only horror without end.

Shagot wakened and slept, wakened and slept, ten thousand times, or less, or more. Each time he wakened he found himself in the same place in the same black-and-white world filled with the same silently screaming dead.

This was not the Heroes' Hall of legend. There was no roistering. The Daughters of the All-Father, when they could be seen, looked more like Eaters of the Dead than Choosers of the Slain. They walked but looked more like crones who had starved to death than the voluptuous maidens of myth.

Shagot never expected much of the Choosers of the Slain. Not even to see them, ever, fair or foul. Even so, he was disappointed in the Hall of the Heroes.

The dead heroes were heaped in there as though just dropped. Not even stacked. As they had died, faces contorted in agony, limbs missing, guts spilling, wounds open.

But there was no decay. There were no carrion bugs or birds. No worms. And no odor of death.

Shagot sensed nothing to convince him that he had died and gone to heaven.

Shagot did not spend much time awake but after a few decades of tiny slivers of consciousness, he concluded that a different destination had claimed him. Perhaps something as bleak and terrible as that burning pit those Southron girlie mis-

sionaries had insisted would be the destination of the wicked
and those who did not believe in their weird god.

Not once did his view change. He saw nothing of his companions on the road, nor anything of the fake fishermen who
had brought them here and then abandoned them. The
Choosers of the Slain turned up once in a while, evidently
bringing in new clients.

Only sleep kept insanity at bay. Vast sleep and the fact that
he was not an imaginative man.

Then, on his ten-thousandth, or twenty-thousandth, or
thirty-thousandth day of imprisonment in Paradise, Shagot
wakened from eternal fog to find his view of heaven changing.

He was being moved by the Choosers of the Slain. He
caught glimpses of their shrunken-head shriveled faces as they
carried him by supporting him under the armpits. His feet
dragged. He tried to help. Feet and legs would not cooperate.
They just slipped and flopped.

Feeling began to return. He felt his heart try to beat, something he could not recall happening at any time since the boat.
The Choosers' bony, hard fingers dug into his flesh. He felt the
numbness and pain that spring up in muscles long unused.

He tried to speak.

Nothing but a gurgle emerged. But, at least, he was breathing again.

It was a long journey to wherever those horrid women
dragged him.

His vision expanded and improved. He was able to lift his
head for seconds at a time. He found himself being hauled
into a part of the Great Sky Fortress that, despite vast empti-
ness, seemed more humanly comfortable. Not in the sense
that it was anything like anywhere he had been before but because what he saw now fit in with what he had heard about the
Eastern Emperor's palace at Hypraxium, from old-timers who
had followed the amber route south to serve in the Emperor's
lifeguard. That was something the old adventurers always
mentioned. The unoccupied vastnesses of the Emperor's
house.

Shagot's hearing began to return. He wished it had not. The
Choosers of the Slain argued bitterly in a tongue that sounded

a lot like Andorayan. Shagot understood about a third of what they said.

Ah! They used an ancient form of Andorayan.

Language had been a gift of the gods a long time ago. It stood to reason that that language would have been their own and that men would have corrupted it over time.

The Choosers of the Slain proved to be extremely negative minor goddesses. They were not happy about anything. They did not like Shagot and his band, other members of which were being resurrected as well. They did not like their Father's plan. They did not like the Hall of Heroes. They did not like the dead. They did not like their lives. They were especially put out with their sister Arlensul. Her selfish behavior had gotten her exiled and her share of the work dumped onto her long-suffering sisters.

The Choosers were just plain not happy with anything.

They got to wherever they were going. They dropped Shagot and went away. Shagot found himself resting on what appeared to be a vast plain of an empty floor. He saw no bounds, no walls, just a gradual fading into foggy darkness starting an arrow's flight away. There were no columns to support the ceiling. If one existed. It was too far above to be seen.

Distant movement caught his eye.

The hideous pair dragged Svavar his way.

Shagot heard something behind him. He found the strength to roll over.

His face was less than a foot from polished black granite. Polished black granite that had not been there just minutes ago.

Tiers of black granite went up and up and up almost forever.

Somewhere, at the very edge of hearing, singing went on, funereal choral stuff that made Shagot's spine shudder with cold chills. What the hell was wrong with those people?

Shagot levered himself onto his hands and knees. That gave him a better view all around. The granite rose in one-yard steps and setbacks, only about twenty times. There were what might be thrones way up top.

Svavar groaned beside Shagot.

There followed a time of no time, when time must have passed because Shagot discovered that dramatic changes had taken place between one moment and the next.

Finnboga, Hellgrim, and the Thorlakssons were there. They remained disoriented. Beyond them was Erief Erealsson. Erief looked exactly like what he was, a dead man erect only by virtue of some supernatural power. Hundreds of equally color-drained dead men formed behind him, rank upon rank, as far as the eye could see.

Shagot did not greet his former captain. Erief exuded the same bleak creepiness Shagot felt whenever he neared one of the ancient burial mounds found throughout Andoray. The haunted mounds. Mounds said to be filled with blood-starved undead who, if they broke their bonds and caught one of the living to drain, could reclaim life. For a short while.

Shagot was a skeptic. He knew no one who had had a genuine encounter with a draug. He wanted to remain skeptical, too. But the Choosers of the Slain had been equally unreal. And these dead men had a hungry look in their eyes. Those that still had eyes.

One by one, his companions climbed to their feet. No one spoke. They were not brilliant but they understood that this was a place where any word spoken might be the wrong word.

The Choosers of the Slain came forward. They were nightmares now. They looked more like the harpies of southern myth than the beautiful daughters of the great god of the north.

The chamber crackled. Shagot's hair stood out. Lightning flashed. Thunder bellowed. Shagot screamed. He recovered to find himself clinging to the top of the first granite tier, trying to remain upright. His equilibrium was gone.

The Choosers of the Slain were up top now, with a dozen more sublime beings. They were not ugly anymore. The gods all looked like they had just stepped out of the old stories. Each was good-looking. Each shed a golden glow of youth.

Excepting the one wearing the dark gray, with the eye-patch, the staff, and the long white hair. The one with the wicked, winged night thing riding his shoulder, unlike any raven that ever flew the skies of Shagot's earth. That one god was not in a cheerful, playful, or youthful mood.

The Gray One spoke to one of his companions, a small, bent god who looked like he might be part dwarf. The small god nodded, floated down toward the heroes. Shagot paid little attention, other than noting a vulpine calculation in the god's expression as he approached. Shagot was far more interested in the several goddesses.

The bent god came to rest on the bottom step, in front of Shagot. "Hi there, Hero. Ready to go to work? Hell. Who gives a peck of rat shit if you are or you aren't? My half-idiot brother wants you. So he can tell you what your future is going to be."

Shagot knew whom he faced, now. His name, in modern Andorayan, could be rendered several ways. Trickster. Liar. Deceiver. And, in a stretch, Traitor. Shagot's analytical side always wondered why the other gods did not exterminate him. Maybe by drowning him in a peck of rat shit.

The bent god made a couple of gestures. Shagot lost his allegiance to the floor. He tried to grab on to nothing. Trickster laughed but made sure Shagot drifted up toward the First Among Them, Whose Name Is Never Spoken. The One Who Harkens to the Sound.

Shagot knew the name, as did every Andorayan and everyone else who accepted the northern pantheon, but he did not know how he knew it, since it was not supposed to be spoken.

The agony of standing in the glory of a god drove Shagot to his knees. He was afraid, which was a rare sensation. He stared at the granite beneath him and awaited the will of the god.

These gods were old. These gods were tired. These gods were supported by a dwindling number of believers. The Chaldarean insanity was a thousand-tentacled monstrosity creeping in everywhere. It converted kings and princes and chieftains by political persuasion and bribery. They then converted their peoples at sword's point. These gods might not have many centuries left before they began to fade away to lesser spirits.

Sometimes, for a flickering instant, they failed to reflect the expectations of mortals. In those moments the All-Father and his spouse, his sons and daughters, his nephews and nieces and half-brother, looked no more appetizing than the Choosers of the Slain. Many became something to raise the human gorge.

But even that was because the human mind insisted on imposing form upon the formless.

The All-Father addressed Grimur Grimmsson, known to the

world as Shagot the Bastard. His voice sounded only inside the sturlanger's mind. *Hero, we stand in the Postern of Fate, facing the end of time. Facing what could become the Twilight of the Gods. You have been chosen to accomplish great things.*

That was like a scream deep inside Shagot's brain. The voice of the god was far too loud. Shagot smashed his forehead against the floor, trying to fight the pain.

The All-Father understood that mortal flesh had limitations. The volume went down. So did the level of divine sententiousness. The god chose to speak out loud, like an ordinary man.

"Grimur Grimmsson, we have chosen you to be our champion in the world of men. We're approaching a critical age. The gods themselves are threatened. Not just your gods but all gods. The Heroes will go forth from the Hall to fight once more. And Grimur Grimmsson will show the way."

"As you command." Shagot could not stop shaking. Nor could he concentrate enough to listen closely. Nevertheless, he understood what the gods wanted done.

Despite his lack of mental acuity, Shagot did wonder why the gods needed mere men to affect their will in the mortal world. They were gods, weren't they?

Shagot and his companions were going to visit the south, where other gods reigned. Once they found what the gods wanted found they would perform rites that would summon the Heroes of the Hall. All of them. The Heroes would execute the will of the gods. The full extent of which those gods did not see fit to reveal to Shagot the Bastard at the moment.

12. Firaldia, Ormienden, and the End of Connec at Antieux

By the second afternoon, after Else fell in with the youngsters, they were deferring to his leadership. He did not want that. But it fell out that way.

That evening the band reached Ralli, where the main industry was wresting white marble from the flank of a nearby mountain. Ralli marble was renown for its lack of flaws and its almost translucent quality. Quarrying had gone on there for two thousand years. Ralli marble could be found in palaces and memorials all around the Mother Sea.

The townspeople eyed the travelers warily, which was understandable. They might be brigands or criminal fugitives. Soldiers commonly were.

A fellow who might have been a constable came and told them, "If you're looking for quarry work you need to go up to the quarry head in the morning. If you're looking for the man hiring soldiers, he's set up on the barren south of town."

The constable wanted them to keep on moving.

Else grunted. His ragged bunch would generate confidence in no one.

"The recruiters are offering a hot meal to everybody who'll listen to their pitch."

Else asked, "Any of you boys interested in the quarrying trade? I recommend that over taking up the profession of arms."

Nobody volunteered. The youngsters were all sad and homesick and going on mainly because they did not want to reveal their humanity to their companions.

Two dozen tents stood in the waste ground mentioned by the constable. Else did not like the camp's look. It was too orderly. Too professional. He observed, "It looks like we're in time for supper." In the twilight a line of men received food from a pair of squat, wide cooks who might be brothers. "Anybody see any banners or shields?" It would be nice to know who was hiring.

A voice asked, "Does that matter?" An armed sentry materialized from brush beside the road. Else was startled. Professional indeed.

"Of course it does." Else assessed the man as best he could in the failing light. The sentry did the same with him. Each saw a professional soldier. Else said, "Some people I won't follow. Maybe because of who they are. But, mostly, because they have reputations for failing to pay their men."

The light was not so weak that Else failed to catch the sentry's contempt. He was not a mercenary himself so did not think well of mercenaries.

Else did not think well of them himself but he had to play that part.

The sentry shouted, "Post number three! I have thirteen and a mule, coming in."

Else asked, "Are you expecting an attack, or something? Here?"

"You let your guard down because you think you should be safe, you'll end up prematurely cold."

Else grunted. That confirmed his suspicion. Professionals, indeed. He had fallen in with the Brotherhood of War again. Not so good.

On the other hand, maybe not so bad, supposing they were putting together a gang to assist the Patriarch in some of his mischief.

But knowing who these men were made Else uneasy. He was marching a little too close to the Brotherhood lately.

Someone jogged up. He was not one of the fighting brothers. He was too small and too young but, obviously, had been around them long enough to have picked up a military patina. "Come with me, please."

Bo Biogna grumbled, "I got a feeling they's gonna be way to much spit an' polish horseshit aroun' here for me, Pipe."

Else was using the name Piper Hecht.

"There's honest work in the quarries, Bo."

"Then why not trot your ass back up there and sign on?"

"Not my kind of thing. I'm not made to stay in one place."

"So how's it different for me?"

It was different. Bo Biogna was not good at what he wanted to do. Else suspected Biogna never was much good at anything, but he was mostly honest and he tried as long as somebody was watching. "It's your life, Bo. I'm just reminding you that you have options."

Their guide took them directly to the tail of the chow line, where he said of Just Plain Joe's mule, "Hey, you can't take this critter with you."

"How come?" Just Plain Joe's friends wanted to know. Pig Iron was the most popular member of the company. He was like no other mule that ever lived. He was friendly and mostly cooperative. And Just Plain Joe insisted that Pig Iron wanted to join the cavalry. "This here horse is a born destrier."

The guide had no sense of humor. Which might have been why he had been assigned his particular job. He led the future cavalry steed away.

Else was impressed. This was a well-organized camp. And some thought had been invested in this recruiting scheme. Hot food, and plenty of it, was guaranteed to get potential recruits thinking kindly of you. Severe hunger was commonplace for the poor.

Else asked the nearest unfamiliar face, "Whose camp is this? What kind of campaign are they getting ready for?"

The guide showed up in time to hear the question, without Pig Iron. "This camp is commanded by Captain Veld Arn- volker. He hasn't told us what we're going to do, only that we'll have the Patriarch's blessing and there'll be plenty of booty. Talk is, it might have something to do with what's been going on in Sonsa."

"Where's Pig Iron? He doesn't usually like to be away from Joe."

"He's hobbled beside the tent you'll be sharing. He has hay and a ration of oats."

"He's turned traitor that cheap?" Joe grumbled.

"Plenty of booty?" Else queried. "I'll tell you, that doesn't sound promising. Not in Firaldia." Unless this was the Broth- erhood preparing to punish Sonsa for having run it out by en- gineering the sacking of Sonsa and the Three Families. He found the possibility that he might go back to Sonsa in Broth- erhood employ ironic.

"Then you're in for something new and marvelous, aren't you?"

Else had to restrain powerful urges springing from a lifetime of Sha-lug training. He understood the western approach to war- fare philosophically but could not make a connection in his heart.

When westerners decided to make war they swept up the dregs and leavings of their societies, handed out old and poor quality weapons, added a few hereditary warriors as leaders, then turned the mob loose. Such armies were as dangerous to friend as foe. Either they would indulge in outrageous slaugh- ter or they would break at the first threat of combat. But they were cheap during peacetime. It was not necessary to feed, house, clothe, or train them. And they were never the threat always presented by a standing army.

The evanescent loyalties of its frontier armies had been one cause of the breakdown of the Old Brothen Empire.

Else would have been willing to bet gold. And he would have won. The meat being served so generously, to the members of the company and prospective recruits, was pork. Else was beginning to develop a taste for the unclean flesh.

"You guys sure picked your time," the one-armed cook in charge told Else. The other, who, up close, looked enough like him to be a twin, still had both of his arms.

"Eh?"

"Pranced in here just late enough so you'll get you a free breakfast, too, didn't you?" He did not seem to mind, though.

All of Else's band were baffled.

The one-armed cook said, "The wizard does him a whole show on why you should praise God and sign up to the serve the Brotherhood. It's mostly a crock a shit but you get yourself a meal for sitting through it. Two meals, if you're just clever enough to wander in here too late for him to do his buck and wing tonight. For a wizard he sure likes to hit the sack early." The implication being that any wizard would be on intimate and extended terms with the Instrumentalities of the Night.

"Wizard?" Else had another bad feeling.

"I didn't stutter. Move along. It's time for the changing of the guard. And those assholes don't like to be kept waiting at chow time."

"And who could blame them?"

The youngster assigned as guide showed them where they were supposed to eat, then where they were supposed to clean up the wooden plates and cups and utensils they had been issued at the head of the line. That much order could not last, Else was confident.

They were shown to a large tent where they were supposed to bed down with another half-dozen potential recruits. Pig Iron was hobbled alongside, outside. The mule seemed to think that he had elevated to mule heaven. Else had spent much of his life in worse quarters than that tent. He told Bo Biogna, "They're sure trying to seduce us here."

Biogna grunted. "You seen, they got an actual, real shit-house?"

Else had not overlooked that fact. It was an improvement on the traditional Praman field latrine. Which, Else felt, proved that the Brotherhood of War *was* in charge here. *And* it proved that the warrior monks were not so narrow of vision as to remain incapable of learning from their enemies.

Traditionally, more crusaders perished of dysentery, cholera, and typhoid than they did of the most violent efforts of Indala al-Sul Halaladin and other defenders of the Holy Lands. And the main reason that diseases got them was because they failed to recognize any possibility of a connection between illness and the presence of their own ordure.

Even here, though, there was a problem with the by-product of the animal population, especially horses and dogs.

"THIS ALL SEEMS NICE SO FAR," GOFIT ASPEL OBSERVED AS THE band ate breakfast.

Else agreed. "They're doing everything they can to make us want to sign on. Things won't be nearly as nice once we take an oath."

Bo Biogna grumbled, "Let's hope that don't mean they figure it will all to go to shit whenever they get to wherever they're going."

"You fibbed. You've done this before."

"No. Only stands to reason that it might."

"So just keep expecting the worst. Then you'll be ready for it."

Their guide materialized. "You need to hurry. They want to get started early. Something important happened somewhere."

That something was all over camp in fifteen minutes, a secret out strutting its stuff in a dozen different dresses, none of them more than one quarter accurate.

"Somebody tried to kill the anti-Patriarch!"

"The killers were all wiped out by his guards!"

"I heard the assassins were ambushed!"

Before it was over Else could have put together a version where God himself had sent down an archangel with a warning while, in Viscesment, an army of elite Patriarchal troops was destroyed to the last man by invulnerable shadow knights magically whisked in from Hansel's capital in the New Brothen Empire. Which was a sufficiently delicious rumor that everyone played it up despite it being common knowledge that Johannes Blackboots and his daughters had taken up permanent residence at the Dimmel Palace in Plemenza, declaring an end to any interest in Firaldia, with the Emperor saying he was taking a vacation from politics.

Rumor and speculation simmered all morning. Else found the camp command's reaction to the news interesting. He told his group, "I think the Brotherhood is recruiting for a foray into the Connec, not Sonsa."

"They're starting to pack up," Just Plain Joe observed.

He was right. Men were striking tents, breaking down the kitchen facility, loading all that into wagons. Horses were being gotten into harness. Dogs were running around, being confused. The only thing missing was a train of women and children.

A grizzled old Brother named Redfearn arrived to take the potential recruits in hand. In addition to Else's group, four more would-be soldiers had come in since the last recruiting speech. Redfearn did not have much to say. "We're moving out." He had a strong accent that suggested an origin somewhere deep inside the New Brothen Empire. "You have until we begin movement to decide if you're with us. Pay will be regular. It will be on time. Food will be provided. It will be the best our quartermasters can obtain. Your enlistment will be for a period not to exceed one year. Weapons will be provided. You'll have to pay for any weapons or equipment you lose or throw away. If we have the opportunity to acquire it, uniform clothing will be provided. In return for all this generosity you'll be expected to train hard, behave well at all times, observe all religious obligations, and submit to Brotherhood discipline. Punishments will be harsh. But fair. Oh. You'll be expected to fight like hell in the name of heaven if we do get involved in a battle."

Else studied the veteran closely. The man had characteristics that were almost Sha-lug. He would be the Brotherhood's equivalent of Bone.

"What're you gonna do, Pipe?" Just Plain Joe asked. Bo and Gofit and the others all looked at him, too.

"Hey, you all thought you were grown-up enough to leave home." He softened his pushing away by asking the old soldier, "Who are we signing on with? We've heard talk about a sorcerer."

The Brother frowned, having trouble grasping the fact that mercenaries might have intellectual difficulties with their services. The man came closer, where he could whisper, all talk lost in the increasing bang and clatter of an armed camp preparing to move. "Are you serious?"

"Of course I am. I assume you're a religious man. Which would mean there are things you won't do because they're just not right."

"This is the Brotherhood of War! The Sword of Heaven!" The old soldier could not imagine the rectitude of the Brotherhood being questioned.

"But there was talk about a sorcerer."

"You're not one of those fundamentalists who believes that any sorcerer, by definition, has to be an agent of evil, are you?"

"No. But I don't like getting close to anybody with ties to the Instrumentalities of the Night."

"Oh. I don't think you'll find a straighter arrow than Grade Drocker. He came all the way from the Special Office headquarters at Runch."

"A witchfinder!" one of the boys blurted, suddenly frightened.

Bo Biogna asked aloud what Else had wondered in private. "How come, if they want to fight sorcery an' all that shit, an' get rid of the invisible people, an' all that shit, too, how come they're all big-time sorcerers an' necromancers, an' all that shit?"

The question did not bother the old man a bit. "You don't send a pacifist priest to duel an enemy champion. Not if you want to come out on top."

For just an instant Else caught a glimpse of a man leaving the one tent still standing. He was dressed in worn Brotherhood field apparel but Else was sure he was the sorcerer from Sonsa.

"The witchfinder's name is Grade Drocker?"

"That's not his real name. Look, we need to move out. You have to make a decision."

"Rate of pay?" Else asked.

"Raw recruits, three and a half silver scutti monthly, with a boost to five when training is complete. That's the good Sonsan scutti, too. Food, weapons, and clothing provided. We don't have mail or protective clothing available. Experienced soldiers will start at five scutti, be expected to lead and teach the greenhorns, and will get a kick up to six scutti when the training period is complete."

"What about guys what's been officers an' shit?" Just Plain Joe asked. Just Plain Joe seemed to get smarter when he was in touching distance of Pig Iron.

"You mean you?"

"Shit. No. Piper. Lookit. Pipe don' say shit 'bout what he done 'fore he hooked up wit' us, but even a dummy like me can see that he musta been some kin' a officer or a sergeant at least, once upon a time. He always knows what ta do an' the best way ta do it."

The old soldier turned to Else. "What do you have to say?"

"Joe is letting his imagination get away from him."

The Brother started to question Else more closely. Else was evasive, offering vague remarks about, "the fighting east of the Shurstula," "pagan savages," "the Grand Marshes," and whatnot. The more specific his story became the more likely it would be that someone would trip him up on a detail.

He was saved a harsher grilling by the fact that the real Brotherhood soldiers started moving out. Their recruits followed.

Pico Mussi said, "Nuts. I'm going. We won't get a better deal anywhere else." He and his brother and their friend Gofit started getting ready to travel. Bo Biogna joined them. Then a few more did the same.

Else was unsure why he joined the others. Did he feel responsible for the kids? Was it because the man now calling himself Grade Drocker had done so much evil during his brief sojourn in Sonsa? He was sure Drocker and that monster were one and the same.

"All right. I had my heart set on finding something cushy in Brothe. But there's nothing all that nasty going on around here."

The old soldier said, "Right, then. If you're coming, get moving."

Else tried not to notice that his companions seemed relieved because he was joining them. He did not want to become responsible for them.

THE STORY WAS, SUBLIME HAD SENT A MEMBER OF HIS OWN family into the Connec to see to the details of ensuring that the True Church did not suffer any more outrages at the hands of the heretics so common in that province. The heretics had responded by slaughtering the legate's bodyguards and leaving the legate himself sprawled upon death's stoop.

Soon afterward a team of assassins invaded the Palace at Viscesment with the intention of murdering the anti-Patriarch, Immaculate II. By the grace of God and the competence of Immaculate's company of Braunsknecht lifeguards the assassins all died before Immaculate knew that he was in danger.

Sublime was, naturally, suspect. And was, naturally, expected to denounce such behavior as soon as news of the failure got back to Brothe. Sublime was as blatantly hypocritical in serving his God as his deadliest enemies could imagine.

ELSE DEVELOPED MORE RESPECT FOR THE ANCIENT ENEMY. THE warriors he had faced in the Holy Lands were created from men like these youngsters, never short on courage and hardiness.

There was little hardship in the Brotherhood camp. The survivors of the embarrassment in Sonsa seemed to have everything they could possibly need.

Following his ejection from Sonsa, the sorcerer sailed to Brothe, where he gained an immediate audience with the Patriarch. He was on the road north the next day, with reinforcements out of Castella dollas Pontellas. He began recruiting immediately. Money was not a problem.

After weeks spent crossing the confusion of principalities forming Ormienden, the Brotherhood force went into camp on the lands of a monastery in the wine country of Dromedan, a tiny Episcopal state tucked into a corner where the Connec, Grohlsach, the Firaldian dependency Seliné, and the Sorvine Principiate snuggled up to one another. There were no clearly defined boundaries. The End of Connec was not alone in its near independence. Ormienden was equally on its own, although carved up into numerous smaller feudalities that had obligations in many directions, including to Hansel Blackboots.

"It's worse up north, in the Empire," a career mercenary named Pinkus Ghort told Else. Ghort was a fellow enlistee who had betrayed his military experience, though with considerably less reluctance. He and Else had charge of companies of inexperienced recruits the majority of their training hours. The members of the Brotherhood were too few to manage everything in a camp that kept growing by the hour. "Even one solitary little town in the middle of one lonely little county can owe its allegiance to somebody who really ought to be the ancient enemy. But up there the problem is because of dowries, not confused inheritance rules."

"The Grail Emperor will straighten it all out."

"Sure, he will."

"You fail to impress me with your passion."

"Hansel can't do much. Almost anything he does try has to have the approval of the Electors."

"Uhm." Else tried to sound like he understood what Ghort was talking about. The west was far less monolithic and much more complex than had seemed plausible, viewed from al-Qarn.

"You got any guess what these lunatics are up to?" Pinkus Ghort was willing to take Brotherhood silver but did not think much of their divine ideology.

"I think we're just for show. The Patriarch wants to bully the Connec. The Connec keeps disdaining him. So he ups the ante by sending this crackpate Grade Drocker to conjure up a make-believe army as a boogerman to scare the Connec into line."

"Boogermen are real where I come from."

"Nobody could seriously expect this mob to actually do anything useful militarily."

"Where have you been working? I've seen a lot worse. Not that long ago, either. These guys are trying hard because they're actually getting paid good and fed well and the Brothers keep whipping them up with those rah-rah speeches." There Ghort went being sarcastic again. "You should've seen what we had to work with when we went out to Themes."

"You were part of that?"

"And on the Duke of Harmonechy's side, too."

"You were lucky, then."

"I was fast on my feet. Also, I saw it coming. I was ready for it. My point, though, is that the men who followed the Duke out there were the worst scum you can imagine. The Duke made no effort to train them and very little to arm them. Or to control them. It was ugly. Santerin did the world a favor by exterminating seventeen thousand of its worst two-legged beasts."

"And their leaders? The nobles?"

"They had horses, don't you know? Only a handful didn't get away. Those ended up getting ransomed."

The sorcerer remained invisible. But Else felt his presence constantly. Like the man was always right behind him, making his wrist itch. If he could just spin around fast enough . . . "Have you worked for the Brotherhood before?"

"No. Nobody has that I know of. This is a big old first. And it wouldn't have happened now if we didn't have Sublime for a Patriarch."

"You know if we're going to get that weapons delivery any time soon? I don't have enough to go around, even for training."

"They don't tell me anything they don't tell you. I'm more concerned about food." Summer would be over soon. "We can't sit here sucking up the area's surplus forever." The force had been in place below the Dencité Monastery for more than a month, so long that whores, cheats, and sutlers had begun to build their own village just outside the bounds of the religious estate. "Here comes Bechter."

Redfearn Bechter was the Brother-sergeant responsible for the mercenaries. That was a huge load. He was willing to share it with Else, Pinkus Ghort, and several others. Else found him reminiscent of old Bone. He had seen it all. Only something truly unusual could shake him.

He seemed shaken now. His accent thickened. "Gentlemen, this cluster fuck is about to turn into the real thing. The wizard just got word that the heretics and their running dogs have the Bishop of Antieux treed in his manor house outside Antieux. The Patriarch himself says we have to do something about that."

"What?" Else asked in disbelief. "That's sheer lunacy."

Ghort said, "A local bishop has a manor house? In the wine

country?" Ghort appreciated wine. He talked about it a lot. And experimented with it a lot because the Ormienden region was famous for its fine vintages. "Since when do priests . . . ?"

"Never mind," Bechter said. "Thinking isn't in your job description. Or mine. Anyway, I'm not saying we *are* going to go. I'm saying there's a chance we *might* go. It isn't official yet. Call it a warning order. So you can look like you know what you're doing if movement orders do come down."

Ghort said, "I beg your pardon. My excitement overcame me for a moment." Pinkus Ghort was long on sarcasm and irony.

Else asked, "So what's the word on the arms? I've still got men practicing with sticks."

The great Patriarchal army now numbered almost eight hundred men. Each day ten, twenty, even thirty more men arrived. Else was surprised that there were so many. Ghort took the opposite view, being astonished that they were so few, particularly with the Brotherhood being so generous. Perhaps rumors recalling the Battle of Themes discouraged the more thoughtful potential volunteer.

Bechter shrugged, "On the way. So they keep telling me."

Else said, "We'd better tell our poor children that they now have some real motivation for learning their trade."

THE NEWS REMAINED RESOLUTELY UNPLEASANT. BISHOP SERIFS kept screaming for help. Else observed, "If this man whines any louder he won't need to use messengers."

Bo Biogna agreed, "If he was as bad off as he says he'd a been dead before he started hollerin'."

Two Brotherhood members sent to reconnoiter failed to return. Orders came from the sorcerer's tent: Prepare for movement. Those were rescinded almost immediately, after Else, Ghort, and several others reminded Redfearn Bechter that a third of the troops had no weapons and the rest, in general, were armed very poorly. Then came word that the Grolsacher mercenary chieftain Adolf Black was going to join them. He would arrive within a week with five hundred veterans.

The possibility of real fighting had an impact. Those who

had signed on just for the meals became invisible. Those who stuck around paid much more attention to learning lessons that might keep them alive.

The arms shipment arrived. Adolf Black did not. The Grolsacher had caught wind of the changed situation. He wanted more money.

THE LITTLE ARMY CROSSED OVER INTO THE CONNEC. THE Brothers made sure there was no plundering, nor any behavior the locals would find objectionable. There was no resistance, though the force was not welcomed anywhere. Even those few Episcopal priests oriented toward Brothe observed them with an abiding suspicion.

The Connec as a whole was deeply xenophobic.

Firm and absolute discipline had begun at the moment of first enlistment. The Brotherhood knew men. Amongst the low, crude sort who joined it was inevitable that there would be predators. The Brotherhood did not tolerate behaviors common in other camps. Bullying earned ten lashes in the first instance, followed by a severe caning and dismissal without pay if the bully did not learn right away. The one man caught forcing himself on one of the youngsters found himself face-to-face with the sorcerer before he could get his pants pulled up. Which interview proved fatal for the buggery enthusiast. Although his final breath followed pronunciation of his sentence by fully ten days.

A minor theft generated a severe caning.

The troops got the message, at least for the time being.

The column reached the Dechear River, below Mount Milaue. They spent a day crossing on the ferry there. The west fork of the main Inland Road from the north ran down the west bank of the Dechear. To the north and east that same Old Brothen military road marked the boundary between the New Brothen Empire and the states where some version of Arnhander was spoken. Farther north still, a branch of the road ran northeastward to Salpeno, seat of the Arnhander kings.

In the Connec, one branch of the ancient road ran westward, past most of the main cities of the Connec. Eventually it reached the Vierses River at Parliers. The Vierses, navigable

from that point, ran northwestward, past Khaurene and on to
the ocean.

Two days later the Patriarchal force left the road and turned
south into rolling hills covered with vineyards. Before long,
the little army settled on the estate of Bishop Serifs, overlooking Antieux.

The Bishop's manor was a vast sprawl resembling the old-
time latifundia, mostly given over to vineyards. The manor
house had a fine view of the tall walls of Antieux. That city
clung to the flank of an ocher hillside within a loop of the
River Job. Its fortifications were strong and in good repair and
appeared to justify the confidence of its defenders, which the
invaders had begun hearing about days ago.

Count Raymone Garete and the folk of Antieux, contemptu-
ously disloyal to their bishop, openly told the invaders' scouts
that they had stores enough put by to withstand a siege that
would last all winter. They would be eating well, still, when the
enemies of reason and sense outside their city were stewing
their boots and eating mud because all the dogs, cats, and rats
had been devoured.

Bishop Serifs came out of the manor while the invading force
was setting up camp. He was livid over the damage to his vines.

Else was not far away when the bishop encountered Grade
Drocker. He was not close enough to overhear their exchange.
But the sorcerer had an immediate impact. The bishop gulped
air, became pale, sputtered. The sorcerer stalked away. The
bishop gradually regained his breath and went red again. He
stormed back into the manor house.

Grade Drocker must have some real power behind him. The
bishop was supposed to be one of the Patriarch's favorites.

Else settled his bunch where he could see the sorcerer's tent,
the manor house, and still had a good view of Antieux. Else
considered the city and concluded that its denizens were justified in their confidence. Those tall walls could withstand the at-
tentions of this incompetent mob forever. Even if Grade
Drocker chose to invest the full extent of his remaining sorcery.

THE PATRIARCHAL FORCE HAD BEEN IN PLACE FOUR DAYS.
Those who had besieged the bishop were a problem no longer.

The force's only intercourse with Antieux was a regular exchange of insults. The Patriarchal soldiers were young and intemperate and would have gotten themselves badly hurt had anyone inside the city had the sense and smarts to exploit the fact that the besiegers were so inexperienced they still could not yet stay in step.

Of course, the folk of Antieux had no need. They could sit back and let winter drive the besiegers away. Count Raymone Garete, in fact, issued proclamations to that effect, confident that it would be possible to end the siege with the only casualties being the bishop's vineyards and the Brothers' pride.

GRADE DROCKER ASSEMBLED HIS OFFICERS. HE WANTED THEIR opinions before making any decisions. At Else's level no one saw the point. The man would do what he wanted. Why waste time on voices that would not be heard?

Else was now a brevet officer who held his position only because none of the Brotherhood soldiers wanted it. He did not rate a chair in the room Bishop Serifs provided so the meeting could be held safe from the drizzle outside. That room had been stripped of everything crude men might steal or sully. Else leaned against a cold, damp wall, out of the way in the rear, beside Pinkus Ghort. It was ironic. He had slipped right into the same role that he had played at home. He was God's company commander.

Ghort murmured, "Brother Drocker seems a tad disgruntled, don't you think?"

"I'd say." And almost completely incapacitated, too.

Rumor was right. That blast of silver shot had left Drocker damaged dramatically and permanently. Spots of raw bone could be seen on the left side of his face.

Ghort observed, "Man, he's totally fucked up. He looks like he spent about four hours on the wrong end of a toothless tiger."

Else had heard Drocker wore a mask most of the time. He wondered why the sorcerer had not done so today.

Drocker needed assistance seating himself at the high table. And he was angry. His voice was not weak when he said, in breathy, three-word bursts, "Bechter. Find Bishop . . . Serifs.

And Principaté . . . Doneto. They were . . . told to be here."

Ghort murmured, "I hope Drocker reams them two a new set of assholes. Them fuckers got us up to our tits in the shit and think they're too fucking good to show up when we're going to fix it?"

Else kept his expression blank. Ghort must have had wine for breakfast. He had stated his opinion loudly.

Ghort was not so tipsy that he failed to recognize his gaffe. He shut up. He stayed shut up. For a while.

The bishop arrived. Else saw a sizable man showing obvious signs of prolonged and diligent dissolution. His fat face was florid, suggesting an old, long-term acquaintance with drink and a current case of apoplexy. There was somewhere else he would rather be.

He arrived full of bluster. That vanished under the force of one cold, grim look from Grade Drocker.

It had to be hard to whine while face-to-face with Drocker, soldiering on despite his injuries.

Drocker said, "There's a chair for you on the end, Bishop. Where is Principaté Doneto?"

The legate arrived shortly, aboard a litter carried by his guards and a borrowed member of the bishop's household. The rest of Doneto's bodyguards had deserted him. Which did not bode well for Doneto if he got into another unfriendly situation.

Else feared Ghort might say something about the Principaté, too. But it was obvious immediately that the legate was getting around the only way he could.

That ambush had injured him much worse than had been made public.

The bishop began to vent his displeasure, suggesting that Sublime himself would get an earful.

Drocker said, "You have attracted the attention of the Special Office, Serifs. Don't compel that office to take official notice. We're beholden to no one. Not even His Holiness. Do you understand?"

The bishop subsided into a bitter silence. Life, fate, and the universe itself were completely unfair.

"Excellent. Now, let us see what can be done about the problem of heresy in the Connec. Bishop, I require you to deliver straightforward answers. No whining. No self-serving. No excuse-making. You will respond in simple, declarative sentences. If you fail to comply you will suffer the displeasure of the Special Office. Is this clear?"

Evidently not. Serifs rambled angrily.

Then he shrieked.

"Must not have been listening," Pinkus Ghort observed, unable to keep quiet. He chuckled. He had conceived a strong dislike for the bishop based on hearsay.

According to Connecten witnesses, only two people alive had any use for the bishop, the Patriarch and Serifs's pretty blond catamite.

Nevertheless, Serifs did have allies within the Church and the nobility, wherever there was concern about the Maysalean Heresy.

Else tried hard to hear the sorcerer's questions. Drocker had no energy, now. The bishop's answers were louder. Questions could be inferred from his responses.

Questioned closely, prodded judiciously, the bishop made it evident that the main reason the Connec was in critical spiritual straits was because its Brothen Episcopal spiritual shepherd was a bad character.

No surprise to anyone paying attention. The core of that problem was the Church's intransigent insistence that its people could do no wrong.

Drocker passed the questioning to one of the Brothers. He had reached his limits.

Else studied Drocker. The man should not be able to do much in the way of sorcery, crippled up and saturated with silver as he was.

Pinkus Ghort whispered, "There's something wrong with that Doneto guy. He's using opium, or something."

It did look that way. "Maybe he got addicted. He doesn't look like the sort who thrives on pain."

The meeting grew less interesting by the minute. Bishop Serifs enumerated steps already taken to combat the Maysalean Heresy. Ideas about what to try next consisted mainly of, "Let's kill them and steal all their stuff." Which view enjoyed considerable support. Potential perpetrators stood to profit.

Drocker returned to the discussion, "That approach will profit the Church, the Brotherhood, and us, only briefly. Meanwhile, Brothe informs me that Arnhand will be sending an army to assist us. That news, by the way, doesn't leave this room."

Enforce that, Else thought. That news would sweep the Connec. Because somebody here would *have* to pass it on to one special friend. Who would have to . . . And so forth.

Drocker could not be that dim. He wanted the news to get out.

PINKUS GHORT PINCHED ELSE'S ELBOW. "SHOW'S OVER. TIME to wake up."

Else grunted, embarrassed. He and Ghort were nearest the door so were first to leave. Ten steps down the hall Ghort walked into Else, who had stopped suddenly. "What?" Ghort barked.

"Nothing. I had a thought."

"Sounds dangerous. Maybe even potentially lethal if it had anything to do with the Church."

"No." No. It had not been a thought at all. It had been a vision. A sighting. A pretty blond boy observing the exodus from behind a tapestry that masked a doorway. Bishop Serifs's catamite, no doubt. And a ringer for someone Else had known in another place and time. But probably not a ringer at all because the boy's reaction to seeing him had been shock followed by outright terror.

Else shook his head. It was impossible. The boy he remembered would be twenty years old by now.

ELSE ON THE HILLSIDE, AMONGST THE VINES. HE STARED DOWN at Antieux but did not see it. He was thinking about that boy. That boy complicated matters.

Antlike comings and goings marked a postern gate on the river side of the city. People went down to the water, then climbed back to the gate. They had been doing so for generations. The path was paved.

Kids from the city were out swimming, in defiance of the besiegers. Else paid them no mind, though something told him he ought to.

What was the catamite's name? He had heard it mentioned. Serifs's relationship with the boy was another reason Connectens loathed their bishop.

A dozen men under a flag of truce left the main gate of Antieux.

Else returned to his company.

It took an hour for the deputation to reach the manor house. By then speculation and rumor were rife. The more thoughtful soldiers, having considered the height and thickness of Antieux's walls, hoped that those men meant to bend their knees to the Church. So there would be no need for fighting.

The lord whose demesne centered upon Antieux was Count Raymone Garete. Count Raymone was a stranger in his own land. He preferred the Duke's court at Khaurene. At Khaurene there were a thousand intrigues to entice a handsome young nobleman. Nevertheless, perchance, Count Raymone was home for the siege and now headed this delegation. He carried no weapons. His head was bare.

From confrontations in the east, Else understood this to mean that the Count intended to submit. Later, it came out that the leading men of Antieux had decided to yield to most of the Patriarch's demands. They would submit to the will of the Brothen Patriarchs. They would ban the Maysalean heresy and exile any Seekers After Light who refused to renounce their false doctrine. They would expel those Episcopal priests determined to maintain their allegiance to Immaculate II.

Bishop Serifs, stinking of brandy, rudely interrupted the Count before he could say more than a few words. "Just close your mouth, boy. I'll tell you what you're going to do." He produced a scroll. "These persons are to be arrested immediately and bound over for trial before a tribunal of Holy Father Church."

Coldly, Count Raymone responded, "The Church does not try laypersons. That is the logical and obvious corollary to the Church's insistence that secular courts have no right to try ecclesiastical persons."

That remark shattered Serifs's civility and self-control. He began raging about grievances so petty that everyone forced to witness his outburst was appalled.

Count Raymone interjected, "What does that have to do with the works of the Church? Or with its rights?"

Four of the men accompanying the Count were Episcopal priests. Three of those were supporters of Sublime V. Until today they had remained unswerving in their support of Serifs simply because Sublime had assigned him.

One priest said, "It isn't the peoples' responsibility to harvest your grapes, Bishop."

A second suggested, "Perhaps if you sent the boy to a proper orphanage those things wouldn't be written on the cathedral walls."

The people of Antieux put on airs about their main church. It was large and grand but not a true cathedral, yet they applauded that bit of Serifs's hubris. Even if most people who lived in Antieux were Seekers After Light or Episcopals who recognized Immaculate II as the True Patriarch.

Grade Drocker appeared at the peak of the bishop's diatribe. He was angry but did not interfere. He consulted Brotherhood henchmen who had seen the whole show. He sighed, glared, shook his head, but did not intervene.

He was content to let Sublime's pet idiot make a complete ass of himself. And Serifs piled up the reasons why he ought to be reduced to itinerant brother status and sent to convert the pagans of the Grand Marshes, such a mission being a common fate for truly bad priests.

Count Raymone said, "We came here to submit, in the name of peace, despite our experience of the Brothen Church and its people. Our efforts have been rejected and reviled. Hear me, all of you who serve the Adversary, and especially the usurper Honario Benedocto: Antieux rejects you completely and utterly. Let the Lord Our God look down upon this abomination of a bishop and understand why. Let him examine each of our hearts. Then let Him proclaim where the right of the matter lies."

Obliquely, Count Raymone had declared war. And had placed the outcome in the hands of God.

As Raymone and his companions returned to Antieux, a hundred minds were hard at work already trying to determine how best to guide the hand of God toward a favorable conclu-

sion. Even Bishop Serifs himself did not fail to notice that all
three pro-Brothen priests returned to the city.

Else Tage thought that God must spend a lot of time being
amazed by the words men put into His mouth.

"THEY DIDN'T MEAN IT WHEN THEY MADE THEIR OFFER," ELSE
told his troops. "They were pretending in hopes that we would
go away. Raymone Garete's family are almost all heretics." He
regurgitated the official position recently articulated by Grade
Drocker. He intended to parrot the sorcerer as long as he remained caught in his current role.

He needed time to digest what the folk of Antieux had just
tried to do.

No Sha-lug would have yielded an inch, religiously, in similar circumstances. But you would not expect unbelievers to do
the same, simply because they were wrong.

Bo Biogna expressed a common sentiment. "Sounds like the
smart thing to do, you ask me."

"Oh?"

"There ain't twenty guys in this crowd who give a fuck if
they worship rocks or snakes down there, Cap. An' most of
them is probably thieves like that fuckin' buzzard bishop."

Else nodded. What Bo said was, largely, true.

He glimpsed the pretty blond boy in a second-story window,
watching Garete's party withdraw. Else studied him until he
realized he was being watched.

"The idiot bishop's play toy," Pinkus Ghort said, following
Else's gaze.

"Yeah."

"You up for some close-order training? My guys against
yours?"

"If you keep your rat-face Berger away from my Pico and
Justi."

"You afraid he'll hurt them?"

"No. I worry about what Just Plain Joe might do if he figures
Berger is bullying them."

"Good point. I've never seen nobody as strong as that Joe.
Now what the fuck is going on down there?"

A big clatter and uproar was developing beside the river.

"Ah, damn!" Else swore. "I knew this was going to happen. This is why I make my guys get their water on this side of the hill."

Water for the camp came up from the river. The manor's cisterns could not sustain an army. Not even a pathetic little mob like this.

Water carriers from the camp had gotten into it with city youths who were swimming. There were more of the latter than of the former. The situation was a nightmare that found a way to be born.

Younger soldiers camped farther downhill whooped and ran to help the water carriers. Ghort said, "Ah, shit. Here we go."

Else said, "Bo, go tell our guys I want them to fall in here, right now."

Ghort asked, "You're not going to get into this, are you?"

"No. I'll take them on a march so they *don't* get into it."

"I'd better get mine going, too. Or half of them will end up dead due to their own stupidity."

The situation developed too fast, and with a mad inevitability. More mercenaries raced downhill. More young men came out of the city. Their meeting became a big street brawl beneath the city wall. Count Raymone Garete was still on the far side of Antieux so was unable to stanch the stupidity of his city's youngsters. In the vineyards overlooking the town the Patriarch's authorized Brotherhood officers failed to take notice. They were all inside the manor house, pouting and avoiding the weather.

Else finally figured out what he had missed about the situation down there. While the town boys frolicked in the river and traded insults with the besiegers, hundreds of people were carrying water into the city.

Antieux's cisterns were not ready for a siege.

Initially, neither side brought weapons to the fray. But it was not long before the mercenaries seized that advantage.

It took only a few killings to panic the people of Antieux.

The mercenaries pressed forward. A seething mob fought around the postern gate, trying to get inside. People inside did not shut the gate. They put up no resistance when the mercenaries began pouring in. Archers on the walls sent a few shafts down, to no effect. The flood would not be stemmed.

Else could not stop his own company from rushing down there

once talk of plunder started. Only Bo Biogna, Just Plain Joe, and Pig Iron, of course, controlled themselves and stayed back.

Of Ghort's company only Ghort himself failed to surrender to the reek of blood on the wind.

Redfearn Bechter finally came charging out of the manor house, demanding, "What the hell is going on? Where did everybody go?" There were not thirty men left in camp.

"Our boys have gotten into Antieux," Else told him. "I imagine they're murdering everyone in sight."

"Who told them to do that?"

"The Patriarch and Bishop Serifs seemed pretty clear on the no mercy stuff."

"How long has this been going on? Why didn't somebody come tell us?"

Ghort observed, "Us riffraff aren't allowed in the house. Unless somebody comes out and invites us. I assume because we might track mud and pig shit all over the parquetry."

The city was not far enough away for the screaming to go unheard.

"You don't need to be a wiseass, Ghort." Bechter hurried back into the house. Soon all the Brothers came outside. Then the bishop materialized. And flew into a rage that worsened dramatically when no one paid any attention to his orders. He knocked one of the Brotherhood soldiers down. Before he could do anything more obnoxious, Grade Drocker arrived.

The sorcerer's fell stare calmed the bishop. In a moment Serifs announced his intention of finding a horse so he could get over to his city in a hurry. He had properties in Antieux. Somebody had to protect them.

Drocker spotted Else and Ghort. "You. With the attitude. What happened?"

Ghort did as he was told. He explained.

Drocker asked, "Why are you still here?"

"I was told to make war on enemies of the Church, not to murder no women and children. Whether I'm there or here won't make no difference. You've seen this stuff before. These things are like fires that have to burn themselves out. If I stay here—and I ain't got orders to go nowhere else—I won't stain my soul with no more sins than it's got on it already."

"And you? Hecht?"

"I agree with Pinkus."

Drocker grunted. "From what I see, you who stayed are men who have seen this beast before. As have I. But I must show my face over there, even so." That face was in such a state that no expression could be read there. He did seem to be inviting comment, however.

Else did nothing to attract any more attention.

Drocker said, "You men stay here. Protect the Principaté. And the bishop's property. If that's your inclination. I'll try to salvage Antieux. But I fear that God has turned His back."

The moment Drocker was out of earshot, Ghort asked, "Where you figure on heading when we're done here, Pipe?"

"Uh? I don't know. I haven't thought about it. Why?"

"I'm thinking there's a good chance we might be out of work tomorrow morning. We might even be running for our lives."

"What?"

"There's a big slaughter going on over there right now. Because them people did something really stupid. And then they panicked. But there's a lot more of them than there are of our guys. Who are just overgrown kids who don't really know what the fuck they're doing."

"You think they'll get themselves killed?"

"I think there's a good chance. I also think that, no matter how it turns out, what's happening is going to decide how the Patriarchy and the Connec get along from now on. Meantime, let's go protect Doneto."

"When did he get promoted? First I heard of him, he was just a bishop who had one foot in the Collegium door. But the sorcerer keeps calling him Principaté." Which was the top title in the Church, after Patriarch. It came from an Old Brothen word meaning prince.

"Drocker came from Brothe. My guess is, Sublime gave him the title figuring it was a freebie because Doneto was going to croak in a few days, anyway."

"You're a cynical bastard."

"Absolutely."

DROCKER WENT TO ANTIEUX'S MAIN GATE FIRST. HIS PARTY were refused entry. The city's defenders were active there.

Pesky archers compelled the Brotherhood soldiers to work their way around to the open postern. They followed the path Bishop Serifs had been forced to take a short while earlier.

Horror reigned inside the city. The invaders suffered wherever they encountered serious resistance. But the defenders were equally inexperienced, were scattered, panicky, and without credible leadership where the actual bloodletting was happening.

Hundreds of dead and dying littered the streets. The butchery was worthy of a historical epic. One of those where the gutters ran swollen with torrents of blood.

The greatest horror occurred in Bishop Serifs's own cathedral, where more than a thousand of Antieux's population, Episcopal and Maysalean alike, tried to find sanctuary.

The invaders broke down the cathedral doors and brought the slaughter into the house of the God whose work they were supposed to be doing.

The madness continued elsewhere as well, growing instead of subsiding. The invaders broke up into small bands and raced through the streets in search of easy victims and loot.

Bishop Serifs reached the cathedral while the killing there was still in progress. He made himself beloved of the people of the Connec, of all faiths, everywhere, when he broke down in a foaming-mouth rage over the damage being done to "his" property.

THERE WERE FEW LIVING PEOPLE INSIDE THE CATHEDRAL when Grade Drocker arrived. Bishop Serifs was among them, though his fat body bore witness that he had been punished severely by someone. His survival was a miracle. Maybe his God did love him.

Fighting continued but began to run out of impetus. The invaders were tending their wounds, looting, or were just too exhausted to go on.

Grade Drocker chose to exercise his right as commander. He sent Brotherhood soldiers out to remind the mercenaries that the distribution of booty was entirely at the discretion of the army commander.

Not the brightest move. He was surrounded by a city inundated in lawlessness. His only protection was a handful of men who did not think highly of him or the Special Office.

Several messengers were assaulted. But the truly awful response of the mercenaries was, in places, a decision to destroy everything if they could not take what they wanted for themselves. They started setting fires.

THE LEGATE DID NOT SEEM SURPRISED TO SEE ELSE, GHORT, and their companions when they bullied their way past his remaining two bodyguards. He murmured something.

"Drocker told us to guard you," Ghort said. "The way things are going, it looks like you might need some protecting."

Doneto mumbled a question. He was drugged, obviously. Even so, his mind was working. He wanted to know what was going on.

Else said, "You explain it, Pinkus. I'm going to look the place over, see if we can defend it."

He knew the answer already. Thirty men, a mule, two nervous bodyguards, and a smattering of terrified servants who were disappearing fast would not be able to hold out. This house had not been built with defense in mind.

He wanted to find that boy. The catamite should be a treasure trove of information.

The house was vast. And richly appointed. And falling apart. And empty.

Empty. That struck home. A place this big needed a staff of dozens. But Else saw no one at all above the ground floor. Serifs was too miserly to employ an adequate staff.

Else found the bishop's personal quarters. The concentration of comfort and wealth there was astonishing.

Candles burned there already, though it was not yet dark. They were beeswax candles, too. The most expensive kind. They did not dispel the darkness completely. There were curious little twitchings in the corners that revealed an uncomfortable truth. Bishop Serifs had some small communion with the Instrumentalities of the Night.

They were not big enough or powerful enough to be threatening, but they were there. The Instrumentalities of the Night were always there. The wise man never forgot that, not for a moment.

Else made no noise as he drifted through the apartment until he found a room where a small, slim form stood framed by a window, watching Antieux burn.

"Osa."

The boy jumped as though slapped. He spun, looked for somewhere to run.

"There's no way out."

The boy eyed him more closely. "Captain Tage."

"Piper Hecht is the name."

"What're you doing here in the Connec?"

"The Lion sent me to spy on the Chaldareans. What's your story? You were eleven and top boy in the Vibrant Spring school last time I saw you. That was eight years ago. But you're still eleven."

"The Lion sent me, too. After I spent half a year in er-Rashal's hands. My body won't ever look any older than it does now."

Else nodded. The Osa Stile he remembered was extremely bright and totally fearless, though he did not know the boy well and did not give it a second thought when he disappeared from the Vibrant Spring barracks. That happened.

"And you're supposed to do what?"

"Create chaos and dissension so the Chaldareans can't put together another crusade. I've been doing pretty well."

"You've been poisoning Doneto, haven't you?"

The boy nodded. "I set him up to be assassinated, too, but it didn't take. Now having him alive but not recovering is more useful than having him dead. He keeps the Patriarch looking this way."

"How could you arrange an assassination? We don't have anyone else here."

"I'm an agent of the Grail Emperor, too. He sent me here. He knew Bishop Serifs was a pederast."

"You're the reason the Patriarch's assassins didn't get Immaculate. You warned him."

Osa smiled wickedly. "I make life difficult for the enemies of al-Prama. And of the Empire, when that's convenient."

"You may not have your bishop much longer."

"I know. I've been trying to decide what to do if he doesn't survive."

"He's over there. The sorcerer is over there. Doneto is at my mercy downstairs. If all three of them die . . ."

"That can't happen. If the disaster is complete Sublime might forget the Connec and focus on an eastern crusade."

True. Yet Sublime could not be allowed to succeed here, either. Conquest of the End of Connec would give him the wealth to finance other adventures. If the Connec ceased to distract Sublime, only Calzir and the Grail Emperor would remain as brakes on his ambitions in the east.

"Explain your business with the Grail Emperor."

"Gordimer gave me to Johannes. As a gift. As a weapon to use as he saw fit. At the Emperor's request. A man came to al-Qarn. He spoke to the Lion but he really was talking to er-Rashal. He wanted to acquire a special slave."

"Ah. So they trained you and put spells on you before they sold you. Was someone named Ferris Renfrow involved?"

"He was the go-between who arranged everything."

"You actually met him?"

"Yes. I still see him sometimes. When there's going to be a change in the way things are set up. Why?"

"Gordimer and er-Rashal told me to find out anything I can about Ferris Renfrow. They're worried about him."

"He's devious and clever but he's devoted to the Emperor. They don't need to worry about him. The Emperor isn't interested in anything but thwarting the Patriarchs and widening the influence of the New Brothen Empire. He couldn't care less if the rest of the world vanishes under the ice."

Else decided to let that rest. Osa had some emotion invested in Johannes Blackboots. "Does the name Starkden mean anything?" He had not forgotten the incident in Runch.

"Starkden? I've heard it. It's the name of a smuggler, I think. Is it important?"

"It is to me. Starkden tried to kill me. In Runch. The Special Office was particularly interested." Else still wondered if there was a connection with Grade Drocker's emergency passage to Sonsa.

"I can ask Ferris Renfrow. He knows everybody on the underside of the world."

"You do that. Without mentioning me."

Else had a feeling that Renfrow would be in touch soon.

Osa asked, "How long before they come looking for you?"

"You're right. I didn't find you. You don't know me. I'll talk to you again, if I can. If Bishop Serifs gets himself killed, maybe you can catch on with Doneto."

"Maybe. But it wouldn't be the same way. That man has no sexual side at all."

PINKUS GHORT ASKED, "WHERE'VE YOU BEEN? I WAS ABOUT to send out a search party."

"Lost, sort of. This dump is a warren upstairs. And totally indefensible. If the people of Antieux come after us, we're dead. I say we fill our pockets and run."

"A couple of faint hearts came back. I guessed right. Antieux is going to wipe out those idiots who charged in there. But I took care of us."

"Uhm?"

"We're fixed. We're Principaté Doneto's new bodyguards. And our new boss wants us to take him home to Brothe. Now."

Else was stunned. "You're a genius, Pinkus. An evil genius."

Ghort shrugged modestly. "It was the obvious thing to do. You'd rather be in Brothe. I want to go to Brothe. The Principaté doesn't want to stay here. He claims he'd rather die on the road than stay. He's worked up a real strong dislike for the End of Connec. It might go real bad for the Connec if he does make it back and starts blowing in his cousin's ear."

"Good. Excellent. And I don't see how we could be held accountable by the Brotherhood."

"That's a real, big-time cluster fuck going on over there, Pipe. And we *were* ordered to protect Doneto."

"I'm in. All right. What about the rest of these guys?"

"Some of them want to sit right here and see what happens. They smell plunder. But the smart ones know it's time to go. Even if our guys come out on top. Because everything has changed. Because now these people, these peaceful fools, these Connectens, will *know* that the Brothen Church considers them resources that it can exploit. There's going to be a

backlash against all things Brothen. So we need to be somewhere else."

"You're probably right. When were you figuring on leaving?
And can Doneto handle the stress?"

"I'm thinking we should move out as soon as there's light
enough to see. Unless that mess over there looks like it's
headed this way before that. As for Doneto handling it, we can
baby him along for a while. But it don't matter much if he
makes it, I figure. As long as we show up in Brothe with his
body, looking like we tried real hard."

JUST PLAIN JOE AND PIG IRON HELPED ELSE STARE AT THE
burning city. Else said, "I wish there was some way to fish
those idiot kids out of there. If they haven't gotten themselves
killed already."

"Don't beat yourself up 'cause you couldn't keep them from
being stupid, Pipe."

"Easier said than done, Joe. You seen Bo?"

"Him and Ghort was seeing if they couldn't find the Brotherhood's war chest."

"Of course. I'll find them. You be sure you're ready if we
need to take off in a hurry."

13. Near Rhecale, on Arnhand's Southern Border

Finnboga was first to waken. He was terrified. His mind remained engulfed in the nightmare. It took him a while to
realize that he and his companions lay tumbled in a grove of
trees in a land unlike any he had seen before. The sun was too
bright. The hillsides were covered with tawny brown grass.
The trees all seemed old, gnarled, and not evergreen. There
was no sign of human habitation. But a paved road slithered
through the valley below. An arched aqueduct spanned that
valley, three tiers high, in the distance.

Finnboga did not know that it was an aqueduct, never having seen or heard of such a thing.

The twins recovered next. Finnboga watched their horror fade. Sigurdur asked, "Where are we?"

Finnboga responded, "I don't know. In the realm of the living. Maybe Grim knows. They talked to him." The horrors of the Hall of Heroes were fading from memory already, leaving only chills and a vague recollection that heaven was not what it was supposed to be.

Svavar and Hallgrim also awakened before Shagot. All five tried to figure out where they were, why, and, most of all, what had happened to them.

Finnboga muttered, "Surrender to the Will of the Night."

"What?" Sigurjon asked.

Finnboga frowned, baffled by his own remark. "I don't know."

They concluded that they must have been out of the world for months. Possibly even for years.

Shagot took much longer to recover. The sun reached its zenith, then sank halfway to the ridgeline behind the band before Shagot was upright and sufficiently in touch to answer questions.

Finnboga asked, "How about it, Grim? You got any idea where we're at? Or when? Or why?"

Shagot could not see well. He felt like he was stinking drunk. But he was the captain. He was the one the gods had entrusted with the mission.

He was the one who would retain every memory of every horror of their sojourn in the Great Sky Fortress.

Shagot spent a while longer collecting himself. "We should be in the country of the Arnhanders, near a city called Rhecale, in some hills that are still fat with old magic from a time when tribes who worshiped our gods ambushed a big Brothen army. In that valley down there. In those days this country was all forest. There was an altar here. Which is why the gods put us here. This was the closest they could send us to where we need to go."

"Which would be where?" Svavar wanted to know.

"We have to figure that out. We're looking for a man. We'll

know him when we find him." Shagot felt bad. He was lying. But the Old Ones compelled him.

"We have to wait here. An army is coming. We'll join it and stay with it till we find our man. He's with another army this one will be joining."

Hallgrim asked, "How come this guy is so high on the god's shit list that they snatched us to kill him for them?"

That was not quite the mission. "He might've found a way to fight them. They want to get rid of him before he figures that out." Shagot frowned. There must be more to it than that. "Meantime, while we're waiting, we have to dig up some holy relics. We'll need them later."

Weapons, tools, armor, foodstuffs, anything the gods thought might prove useful, remained scattered all over the slope. Shagot said, "Get all that shit together. Turn this into a fucking camp." He glanced northward. There was a chill in the air. There was a hint of rain as well. "There should be some kind of tent in that mess. Get it set up. Unless you like sleeping in the rain."

They did have a fire burning. He did not need to think of that.

Shagot ambled around the hillside, muttering. His meanderings made no sense to the others. They made little sense to him, either, except that he knew the pattern he was supposed to walk. He kept rehearsing it under his breath. Each time he paused, visions of another time filled his mind. He saw strange, wildly hairy men in wolf and bear skins fighting and drinking and sacrificing Brothen captives to their gods. At first, Shagot did not understand their speech, though it shared some sounds and rhythms with his own. They were angry, bitter men, as content to butcher one another in brawls and blood feuds as to massacre the enemy for whom they were waiting.

The ancient language gradually assumed meaning. And Shagot began to understand why these men, dead fifteen hundred years, had gathered to battle the legions of Brothe.

Where Brothens went Brothen culture followed, along with Brothen ideals and Brothen prosperity. Brothens welcomed all gods into their community of deities. Brothens were at peace with the Instrumentalities of the Night. Where Brothens went the old ways and the Old Gods became diminished and softened and, too often, subsumed or, at best, paled into extreme obscurity, recalled only as demons or night gaunts.

Shagot did not understand that this battle had happened centuries before the births of the founding apostles of the Chaldarean creed. He did know that his gods believed that only their meddling in the middle realm kept them strong.

All Shagot knew of the ancient battle were snippets the gods had given him. There were things he did not see. Such as the fact that the tribal priests saw him as clearly as he saw them. He would never know that the biggest factor in the barbarians' victory was their conviction that one of their gods walked among them.

Svavar brought Shagot out of his reverie. "Come on, Grim. Get something to eat."

As he gnawed dried meat, Shagot muttered, "The trouble was, there was always another Brothen army."

Svavar said, "I'm worried, Grim. It ain't like you to do so much thinking."

Hallgrim wanted to know, "What was all that stalking around, mumbling and staring at nothing, Grim?"

"I was figuring out where we were going to have to dig. We'll take care of that tomorrow. Build the fire up. I'm cold to the bone."

The others eyed him strangely but Finnboga tossed more brush on the fire.

Once he finished eating, Shagot crawled into the tent and began snoring almost immediately. The others worried a while but, as twilight gathered, they retreated into the tent themselves. They felt the power of the night. It was strong here. This was a place where ghosts would walk and might even talk if a man was fool enough to put himself at risk of having to listen.

Shagot slept a sleep close to sleep of death. He would not remember it in the morning but his spirit returned to the Great Sky Fortress. His companions did not rest well. Strange lights moved around outside. Weird shadows played on the walls of the tent. No one had the nerve to go look.

You did not prosper by tempting the Instrumentalities of the Night.

* * *

SHAGOT KNEW EVERYTHING THAT NEEDED KNOWING. IT TOOK just half a day to recover the necessary treasures from the graves of ancient priests. Despite the fact that Shagot had slept in. Despite the icy drizzle that fell all day.

"Hang that stuff where the rain can wash the mud off. Good. There's one more grave that we have to find. The most important one."

Shagot knew where to dig. The work went fast—until the others saw what lay under the earth.

Time had shrunk and shriveled it but it had not decayed.

"What is that thing?" Finnboga asked.

"It ain't human," Svavar declared.

"It looks like a giant dwarf without a beard," Sigurjon said.

It was as tall as a man and shaped like a man but it was wider and much more muscular.

Shagot said, "Get the grave goods out. I need to go through them." As the others did that, Shagot jumped into the grave and took the corpse's head.

Svavar asked, "Grim, what the hell is that thing?"

"I don't know what he was. Something like a man but not a man. A powerful mage. The last of his kind." Shagot mounted the head on the tip of a spear taken from the creature's grave, so the drizzle could wash the dirt away. "We'll need him in order to complete our mission."

"What mission, Grim? The old folks told us to catch those pansy priests that murdered Erief."

"Those priests didn't kill Erief."

"What?"

"I have that from the gods themselves."

"Who did, then?"

Shagot found that he could not say. And it was not that important, anyway. That had nothing to do with their mission.

Shagot retired early, again, and slept for an abnormally long time.

SHAGOT INDICATED A TURN IN THE ROAD ONTO A STONE bridge over a nameless creek. "We'll wait there."

The band moved to the point indicated, weighted down by the stuff that had arrived with them and the relics they had recovered. Shagot carried the head in a sack. An hour later an old man on a donkey appeared, coming from the south. He spied them as he was about to cross the bridge, which did not speak well for his eyes. He halted. He stared. His mouth fell open. He stared some more. Then he headed back south, spanking his donkey.

Hallgrim said, "He must've thought we were robbers."

Svavar said, "We might ought to keep an eye out for bandits. There's been almost no traffic the last two days."

One reason was that, though modern maps labeled the area the White Hills, those who lived in their shadow called them the Haunted Hills. The tyranny of the night remained in full sway in the Haunted Hills. And, lately, travelers reported that the hills had become more active.

There were, as well, rumors of war, coming out of Arnhand, as did the road itself.

Another hour passed. A pair of riders appeared, coming down from the north. Two more pairs trailed them by a hundred yards, out on either side of the road. The lead riders stopped. They gawked.

The Andorayans gawked back. Those soldiers were like none they had ever seen.

The outriders eased closer carefully.

The Andorayans had placed themselves beside the road rather than in it. Shagot thought that should make it clear they were waiting, not blocking the way. Even Arnhanders ought to be able to figure that out.

At which point Shagot began to wonder how he would communicate with these men. In the past when he dealt with people unable to speak Andorayan he was in a position to bluster and threaten and make himself understood by hurting people who did not do what he wanted. That option would not be available here.

The riders talked it over. One rode back the way they had come. The rest remained where they were, distinctly uncomfortable.

"Are they afraid of us?" Finnboga asked.

"I don't know," Shagot replied. He did not think his bunch looked threatening, if only because they were weighted down with so much clutter. The gods should have sent a few slaves or pack animals along.

An hour passed. The Andorayans ate bad cheese and dried meat. The Arnhanders watched. They did dismount, loosen their saddles, and let their animals graze.

"Hey, Grim. There's people coming."

Shagot had fallen asleep. There was no time when he could not use a little more sleep.

Twenty-five or thirty riders approached in a hurry. Shagot wondered, "Does everybody in this country carry his own flag?" The riders all carried long spears with pennons attached. Except for a handful in black, riding among them.

Sigurjon swore. "It's those damned crows who killed Erief!"

Shagot had better eyes. "No. They're priests but they aren't those priests. Even if they were, this isn't the time to close that account. Erief can take care of that himself."

The band all stared at him.

"No, I don't know why I said that."

"You're getting spooky, Grim."

Somebody who had to be of superior rank moved closer, accompanied by bodyguards. And the priests. There were four of those. One of them was of exalted rank, too.

Shagot leaned on the shaft of a spear, cheek to cheek with the dead ogre's head. His brother and the others eyed him nervously because that dead monster bothered him not at all.

With those memories that he did retain it seemed unlikely that he would be squeamish about anything ever again.

The senior priest and senior soldier halted eighty feet away. Shagot began to feel impatient. He could not fathom why those people acted so strangely.

The priests came forward without the soldiers. They stopped ten yards away. They were unnaturally pale. Two shook so badly they could barely keep hold of their reins.

"By the thunder!" Finnboga said. "These guys are shitting themselves just looking at us."

"Yeah," Shagot said. "So what are they seeing that we can't? Why are they scared of us? Hey! Assholes in the slave smocks. What's your fucking problem? We just want to join up with your army."

The priests chattered among themselves in a nasal, whining tongue unlike any Shagot had heard before. He asked his companions, "Any of you guys understand them?"

The priests began trying different languages. Probably their best course, Shagot thought. His bunch, between them, might stumble through in two languages beside their own. And one of those would be Seatt because Finnboga's family used to trade with the witch people of the extreme north, up on the permanent ice.

"Ha!" Svavar said. "That fat, scared asshole just said something that sounded like it might be in Santerin."

"Hallgrim," Shagot said. "You were a prisoner in Santerin for a while. Talk to him." Shagot had a little Santerin himself, but only enough to ask where the treasure was hidden.

Hallgrim said, "It's Santerin, all right. But it ain't like any variety I ever heard before. I only get about a third of what he's saying. They seem to think that we're demons."

"Keep him talking," Shagot said. He was starting to pull it together. He began to catch up with Hallgrim. But that was only good enough to leave him puzzled.

Why would these idiots pick them out as demons? Because he and his bunch did not understand their bizarre religion?

"Start beating on the point that we're just the opposite. The gods have sent us to join their army."

"They won't believe that. Not even if you've got a signed letter of introduction from the All-Father."

"Just keep them talking. Keep telling them we're here to join their army."

THE ANDORAYANS WERE ALLOWED TO ACCOMPANY THE ARN-hander force, which was commanded by the Baron Martex Algres, a cousin of the king of Arnhand. His second in command was Archbishop Beré of Source, the foremost cleric of Arnhand, an *in absentia* member of the Collegium. The army numbered about fifteen hundred, plus camp followers. Many noble Arnhander families were represented in the force. Its mood was optimistic in the extreme. The army would join up with Adolf Black's Grolsacher mercenaries in a few days, on the border of the Connec. Then they would sweep through that province, destroying its heretics root and branch. The Duke of Khaurene would himself join them somewhere near Castreresone, after they settled up with Antieux for what it had done to the Patriarchal force sent to stifle the unholy rebellion of its people.

Shagot and the Andorayan band trudged along, always spied upon by several priests, never able to understand what moved these people. Always, at least one of the monitors was something called a witchfinder.

Shagot spent all of his time with the Arnhanders, confused. Their reasons for war made no sense. People were going to die over differences in doctrines between Episcopals and Maysaleans? When anyone old enough and smart enough to tie their own bootlaces could not possibly believe any of the crap put out by either bunch?

The most disturbing aspect of the situation for Shagot, though, was the universal conviction of the Arnhanders that the murder of Erief Erealsson had taken place two centuries ago. Today Andoray, Friesland, Weldence, and far Iceland were united under a single crown. And the official religion there was Chaldarean.

Were the gods mad to send him into such a mad world?

14. The Connec, Antieux, and Beyond

The rape of Antieux saw almost seven thousand of that city's people slaughtered. The majority were women, children, and the old. As shock and despair faded, the survivors became ever more animated by anger, horror, and deepening hatred.

People who wanted to help straggled in from the ends of the Connec and beyond. Count Raymone Garete burned bridges by publicly vowing a vendetta against Sublime V and the Brotherhood of War. That was a bold pledge. Not even Johannes Blackboots dared go that far. The Count's vow was so intemperate that Duke Tormond showered him with letters demanding that he recant.

Now a new army approached Antieux. This one was stronger than the last, better equipped, and consisted of veteran soldiers. It included members of many of the noble families of Arnhand. It was commanded by experienced men determined to make Raymone Garete eat his words one at a time, without condiments, chewing carefully.

Count Raymone was not dismayed. The previous mistake would not be repeated.

It was late in the season. The Arnhander troops were feudal levies on short terms of obligation. They would head home before many weeks passed.

Bishop Serifs paid for his perfidy. The people of Antieux vented their anger on his properties and on those of the Church.

Everywhere priests who supported Sublime suffered. At Gadge, previously a devout Episcopal town, an angry mob exhumed Bishop Maryl Ponté, Serifs's predecessor, tried him for crimes against God and humanity, then reburied his bones in an unmarked grave in unhallowed ground.

MESSENGERS SCURRIED EVERYWHERE AS KINGS AND PRINCES and the Grail Emperor himself made their opinions known.

Sublime V received no congratulatory letters.

THE ARNHANDERS AND ADOLF BLACK'S GROLSACHER MERCENARIES took up positions around Antieux. Their Brotherhood predecessors had not been numerous enough for a complete encirclement so they had not wasted any effort trying.

This time there would be no accidental invasion caused by the stupidity of adolescents. The stupid kids were all dead. And, this time, every possible cistern, barrel, and container had been filled with water beforehand. This time Antieux was prepared. This time Antieux truly understood the stakes. And this time those caught inside the wall remained calm under pressure.

Archbishop Beré himself demanded that Antieux open its gates, swear allegiance to the Brothen Patriarch, and turn out the heretics dwelling there. He presented a list of people the Church wanted arrested and bound over for trial.

Count Raymone Garete responded by evicting that handful

of Episcopal priests who refused to denounce Sublime V. They took with them the relics of St. Erude the Wayfarer.

Count Raymone was a hard, bright youngster who feared nothing and believed that he had nothing to lose anymore. He was determined to remain Brothe's most terrible enemy while he lived.

THE SIEGE OF ANTIEUX PROCEEDED FOR THIRTY-ONE DAYS. THE weather turned colder. The Arnhander soldiers became increasingly disgruntled. Where was the easy plunder they had been promised? Their enemies were getting fat, staying warm inside the ruins of burned houses while out here the soldiers starved, amidst fields and hills stripped of edibles and combustibles. And now there were reports of incursions from Argony and Tramaine, as Santerin captured castles and villages long in dispute between Santerin and Arnhand.

News that reached the besiegers' camp also found its way into Antieux. The siege lines did not extend across the River Job. The folk of Antieux came and went as they pleased, in that direction, under cover of darkness.

COUNT RAYMONE GARETE TOOK ADVANTAGE OF THE BE-siegers' failure to finish surrounding Antieux on the other side of the river. He slipped away and joined a group of hotheaded young nobles eager to take more aggressive action against the invaders.

BARON ALGRES AND ARCHBISHOP BERÉ ENJOYED AN ANGRY confrontation in the Baron's quarters in the ruin of Bishop Serifs's manor house. The Archbishop refused to understand why the troops would abandon the siege when God's work remained incomplete.

The Baron had a reputation for being undiplomatic. "Go out there and find me one private soldier who gives a shit about God's work. You go look, you'll find a whole lot of men who figure God is big enough to take care of himself. And I can't say I don't agree with them."

"But . . ."

"You knew the situation when you bullied my cousin into sending me down here to help the Church rob these people. Sixty days is all we can demand of the soldiers. That's been the goddamned law since our ancestors were savages in hide tents. If Sublime wants to war on these Connecten fools all year round, let him put together his own army and leave us to protect ourselves from Santerin. Oh. Wait. Sublime already sent his own army. It got wiped out."

As always, in all times and in all places, despite the scale of the stakes, personalities gave definition to history. These two had loathed one another for half a century. The Archbishop was the less articulate of the two. But he was determined to execute the will of the Patriarch and his God.

SNOWFLAKES WERE IN THE AIR. ON THE WALLS OF ANTIEUX the city's defenders jeered and taunted. The Arnhanders were on the move, headed home. This time they would use the westward route because the one they had taken coming south had been foraged already. Baron Algres and his captains were uncomfortable with the situation. They were not accustomed to being in the field this late in the season, this far from home. Even Archbishop Beré now wondered aloud about the wisdom of those who had decreed this folly.

Adolf Black and his Grolsacher veterans stuck with the Arnhander army. Their commission was about to expire but they had been offered employment on the frontiers of Tramaine. More telling than that offer, though, was news that angry Connectens were gathering to intercept them if they withdrew directly toward Grolsach.

A thousand rumors plagued the army. Lately, there was a cycle of stories about the Grail Emperor asserting his rights in the Episcopal States of northern Firaldia and in Ormienden. And he had begun to revisit Imperial claims to several towns in Arnhand's eastern marches.

Atop everything else, the Arnhander-founded crusader states in the east kept shrieking for help. The Lucidians were pressing them hard.

Worse still, the King of Arnhand was extremely ill. His only surviving son was eleven, a will-less extension of his ambitious mother, a woman detested by everyone. She, like her failing husband, seemed incapable of understanding that just wishing would not make something happen. An example: soldiers had a regrettable tendency to demand regular pay, on time, for the risks they took. The money needed to pay and maintain them refused to be conjured out of thin air.

A lot of time and treasure had gone down a rat hole so Baron Algres and Archbishop Beré could visit Antieux, be embarrassed, and leave two hundred Arnhander subjects in graves beneath Bishop Serifs's vineyards. To a man, they had perished from disease rather than enemy action.

Starvation made it difficult to resist diseases.

Dysentery remained widespread as the army made its stumbling retreat.

TO THE RIGHT OF THE ANCIENT MILITARY ROAD, TWO HUNDRED feet back, stood a dense growth of gray-barked trees of a species common along the verges of high-altitude wetlands. The ground was soft but not soggy. To the left of the road lay two hundred yards of increasingly boggy ground, then a narrow, slow, shallow stream. Beyond the stream stood a thin curtain of trees, then rocks that had fallen off sheer cliffs that rose for hundreds of feet. The morning sunlight crept down the dull face of the cliff. The stone was a dark gray but had a pinkish tinge wherever it was freshly bruised or broken.

This was near the summit of the pass through the Black Mountains, still on the eastern side. Soon the road would swoop downhill and the worst would be over.

A small breeze stirred the mist. The brightness of the light waned as the sun elevated itself above the trailing edge of those clouds that continued to shed the occasional desultory handful of snowflakes.

The Arnhanders and their Grolsacher hirelings, traipsing along the ancient road, were cold, bitterly hungry, and thoroughly demoralized. They had invested three months of misery for no return. And their prospects were completely bleak.

Worse than bleak.

Connecten trumpets sounded.
Far worse than bleak.

COUNT RAYMONE GARETE'S AVENGING ARMY WAS OUTNUM-
bered. Despite the rage sweeping the Connec, not that many
men were willing to defy Duke Tormond. Raymone's initial
plan had been to launch a surprise attack on the invaders' column, in a place and at a time when they would be least alert.
He wanted to punish the Arnhanders, then fade away, going
more for an emotional and moral victory than a physical one.
But the stunned Arnhanders made little effort to defend themselves. Instead of fighting they fled toward the marshy ground
at the base of the cliffs.

Adolf Black's Grolsachers gave a better accounting of
themselves but with the same ultimate result.

The slaughter continued until the Connectens had sated
their bloodlust. That paid little attention to rank or station. The
Arnhander leadership perished because the armored Connecten knights could not ride out onto the wet ground. The
men on foot, possessed of no class commonality with the nobility they slaughtered, took no prisoners.

15. Ormienden, the Ownvidian Knot, and Plemenza

Principaté Bronte Doneto could not travel with any vigor.
There were days when he could not endure more than an
hour on the road. Two weeks passed. The party covered no
more ground than a normal band might have spanned in four
days. Fortunately, no one seemed interested in interfering.
And, Else noted, the Principaté's color and health improved
steadily as he put distance between himself and Antieux.

Once back in Ormienden, at the Dencité Monastery, the
Principaté decided to convalesce.

*   *   *

"HEY, PIPE. WANT TO HEAR SOME NEWS?" PINKUS GHORT asked one morning.

"If it's the real thing. I'm not looking for any more of the same old thing."

"Guess I can't help you, after all."

"Groan. So rain on me."

"Just Plain Joe came in from his lookout down by the bridge. He says people are headed this way. Eight or nine of them. He thinks one might be Bishop Serifs."

"Well. Makes you wonder what kind of sense of humor God really has, doesn't it?"

"Makes me wonder if the Maysaleans maybe don't have it right when they say it was the Adversary who won the war in heaven."

"Good thing our boss can't hear you. He'd have you burned."

The Principaté had been making those kinds of noises lately. The Church was bleeding and Bronte Doneto was determined to cauterize its wounds.

Ghort was cynical about the whole thing. "Doneto is posturing. He doesn't believe the shit he's putting out. It's excuse crap he tosses around so he can do cruel shit and claim he's got a good reason."

Else observed, "You're awfully critical of the guy who's paying you to protect him."

"He ain't paying me to lie about him, only to keep his ass alive."

Else shrugged. "I don't think I'd have the moral flexibility to protect somebody like Serifs. Somebody wanted to cut his throat, I'd probably hand him a knife and hold his coat while he's working."

Ghort got a laugh out of that.

Bishop Serifs went straight into the monastery. He was not seen again for days. Else noted that Osa Stile became invisible when the bishop did so.

Several days later a message arrived from Brothe. It included news that Grade Drocker had made his way successfully to the Castella dollas Pontellas in the capital city.

Which news caused Pinkus Ghort to declare, "My heart is all aflutter. The world can go on. Old Ugly lives."

"I was kind of thinking that way myself."

More interesting news washed the thrill of the sorcerer's survival away. A substantial Arnhander force had rushed into the Connec. It was besieging Antieux. Else observed, "That won't do the Patriarch's cause any good. Those people won't be simple twice."

"Fine by me," Ghort said. "Let them sit there freezing their asses off and starving. They ought to put all Arnhanders through that. And double for that asshole, Adolf Black."

"Every day I spend around you I find out about somebody else that you don't like."

Ghort laughed. "He's got me figured."

Bo Biogna had just wandered in. "What've I been missin'? What's so funny?"

"Life itself," Else replied. "Sit down and look at where you're at. Then remember where you hoped you'd be now, say, twelve years ago."

Biogna shook his head. "Pipe, I got a notion you're a good guy to have in charge when the shit comes down but the rest of the time you're too fuckin' serious."

Ghort sneered. "Now Bo's got you nailed."

"Blame it on my upbringing." Which was a truth that revealed nothing.

The time spent loafing around at the monastery, waiting for Principaté Doneto to heal up, passed into Else Tage's personal history as close to halcyon. Not once before in his life had he had a month where he had so little to do.

Then snippets of news about the Arnhander disaster in the Connec began to arrive. At first Else was sure the reports were exaggerated. But next day a courier arrived from Brothe. He brought orders from the Patriarch himself. The Collegium would convene to formulate the Church's response to the massacre. Not only had the Connecten heretics spit in the face of all good Chaldareans, they had raped away the lives of numerous members of the most important families of Arnhand.

Bronte Doneto assembled his band. "We're not ready to travel. But travel we must. The Instrumentalities of the Night walk the earth unopposed. The Holy Father has summoned me. He plans to charge me with managing the Church's response once a course is decided."

Odd choice of words, Else thought. The messenger said Sublime wanted Doneto back in Brothe because he needed the Principaté's voice and vote in the Collegium. The Collegium frustrated Sublime's ambitions too often, thwarting him just to remind him that even the Voice of God on Earth was subject to checks.

Else told Ghort, "Doneto must have sensed something that wasn't in the literal text of the summons."

"He saw what he wanted to see."

Bo wanted to know, "What happens after we get him home, Pipe? To us, I mean."

"I don't know. I'm not sure I care. I'll be in Brothe, which was where I was headed when I ran into you guys originally."

His path had taken several unexpected turns but he was not dissatisfied, overall. He had learned a great deal about the west. He had become a tick in its fur. And now he was headed toward the center of the web again.

"I like that," Ghort said. "I was headed for Brothe myself when I let me get distracted by a chance to get rich."

Else said, "Well, let's all go get rich in the heart of the old empire."

DONETO BEGAN TRAVELING THE NEXT DAY. BY THEN MORE rumors had reached the monastery, painting the Arnhander defeat in darker, bloodier colors. There had been few survivors, even amongst the nobles and clergy, who usually bought their ways out of the consequences of military disasters.

This would rock the world. This would define the future. After this, surely, Sublime would abandon all overseas ambitions and focus completely on the Connec.

BRONTE DONETO WAS IN BETTER HEALTH BUT COULD NOT travel with any speed. A week after leaving the Dencité Monastery his party still had not departed Ormienden.

The travelers were nervous. Things of the night had been active throughout the hours of darkness, though with no obvious purpose. When they were restless, then so must be the creatures of the day.

Grumbling softly, Else walked with Just Plain Joe and Pig Iron. Bo Biogna tagged along behind. They made up the rear guard. With the mule being the most useful of the bunch.

Pinkus Ghort was out front, as vanguard and point, shouting back alarms about ghosts in the mist.

It was cold. Colder than Else had encountered, ever, in Dreanger. The wet weather did not help. It hid night things that were not false alarms.

Just Plain Joe teased Else about how he had gotten soft since he had come south.

Winters in the land whence Piper Hecht purportedly hailed were renown for their savagery. Each summer the ice did not retreat as far as it had the summer before.

Else did not keep up his end of the banter. He watched Bishop Serifs and Osa, examining the depth of his own devotion to his god and country. He could not imagine enduring what Osa had.

Else suspected that Serifs's awful behavior had come about because of Osa's bedroom manipulations.

The weather was miserable. A cold, fine mist kept falling. That wore a man down, made it hard to concentrate. The resentment and controlled hostility of the local populace did not help, nor did the constant presence of night things in the mist, even by day, just beyond the range of vision.

A psychotic depression brought to life, Else thought. This was what he had expected the west to be like all the time.

The mist crawled with shadows and whispers.

Ormienden was not as tame as most would claim.

That was probably true everywhere. In some places things of the night concealed themselves better.

Some sort of excitement broke out at the head of the column.

In moments Else found himself being disarmed by soldiers in unfamiliar livery.

The Instrumentalities of the Night had been active because some wizard had used them to help conceal the presence of the soldiers.

Resistance was pointless.

Only Bishop Serifs was dim enough to try to make demands, to boom orders at people who did not give a damn what he said.

The soldiers beat Serifs. And laid on with renewed enthusiasm every time the bishop opened his mouth. Nor did they help him once the beatings took their toll. A noncom told Serifs he would be killed if he did not keep up.

Else made sure his companions did nothing to trigger their captors. Their easiest way of dealing with prisoners would be to kill them.

Else said a silent prayer and placed himself in the hands of God. "Ghort, you have any idea who these men are?"

"They're the Emperor's men. From his own guard. The Braunsknechts. Maybe from Viscesment."

On political maps Ormienden lay within the New Brothen Empire, despite its constituent counties and principalities sometimes owing their first allegiance elsewhere. Viscesment sat on the border between Ormienden and the Connec, on the Ormienden side of the Dechear River. Although the folk of Viscesment spoke the Connecten dialect of Arnhander and everyone in the region considered the city Connecten.

Viscesment lay ninety miles northwest of the ambush site.

The Braunsknechts were not in a bloodthirsty mood. Their captain had orders to avoid making the incident more irksome to Brothe than the actual kidnapping of a Principaté of the Collegium would cause.

"But we're not headed toward Viscesment," Else pointed out. "Viscesment would be back that way."

"Look at the bright side, Pipe," Ghort said. "We might get to meet the Emperor himself, if we keep on headed this way."

Bo Biogna grumbled, "Pipe, this guy is so contrary I bet he was born feetfirst."

"How's that?" Else asked. He was still trying to make sense of what had happened. Why did God keep turning his path away from Brothe?

"Shit, Pipe. When things is goin' good Ghort don' do nothin' but bitch. And when we're standin' on our heads in liquid shit, he goes to hummin' an' singin' like he just got laid."

Ghort said, "That's because I know all is right with the world, Bo. It's normal, everyday situation is, throw the dick to Pinkus Ghort. I'm used to that. I'm comfortable with that. I can deal with that. Slip me the pork pole and I strut around grinning."

Misty rain continued. Else grew nervous for no discernable reason. The nervousness was a state, an intuition, not connected to his current situation. Which, while better than it could have been, did not seem promising. The Braunsknechts tolerated their prisoners, excepting Bronte Doneto. It was clear that Bronte Doneto was what this was all about.

Not keeping up with Doneto really might turn fatal.

But the mist itself was most troubling. Else still felt presences out there more numerous now than before the ambush.

Curious. The Braunsknechts were uncomfortable, too.

This was the kind of day when the things of the night stayed out and caused mischief.

The west was too tame. Its major shades, all bound into the features of the land now, slept a deep sleep.

In the Holy Lands, the Wells of Ihrian either generated or attracted all the Instrumentalities of the Night. In the Holy Lands you were inundated.

"Hey, Pipe! What the fuck's the matter with you?"

"Uh? Eh? Oh. Bo. Just lost in my thoughts. We're not in a good place, here."

Ghort looked him askance. "Just stay calm, don't give them no shit, and you'll be all right. They'll probably ask us to sign on with Hansel. Where've you been working, Pipe?"

Else sighed. He had forgotten to think western. Even in the Holy Lands the Arnhanders employed turncoats recruited from amongst their prisoners. And the Rhûn were even worse. The Rhûn recruited whole tribes to patrol their frontiers.

"The north country isn't nearly as friendly, Pinkus. They like to sacrifice you to their gods. They burn you or drown you or hang you, or whatever, depending on which god they're bribing."

"Bribing?"

"Yes. Their whole way of praying, worshiping, and sacrificing is meant to distract their gods, so they'll leave the people alone."

"Sounds primitive."

"It is. But the Grand Marshes are more intimate with the Instrumentalities of the Night than these tame old lands down here."

"Whistling past the graveyard, eh?"

Ghort was aware of the shades in the mist around them.

Else remained confused. This business made no sense. Yet.

Ghort told him, "You'll catch on. In about a hundred years. It's all politics."

Else was baffled by politics back home, where the players were fewer and their motives more transparent.

The Emperor's men were typical professional soldiers. They worked with calm, quiet efficiency, and no passion. Workaday work. If they had to kill somebody, they would, dispassionately, without regrets. Ghort was right. Given no stress, no provocation, no excuse, they would not behave badly.

The rain stopped in the afternoon. The sky rose.

The Imperials left the main road. They followed a winding track upward into harsh, precipitous, ice-capped limestone mountains. Those were like nothing Else had seen before. Vegetation was scrubby and the road seldom more than a wide animal track.

Ghort murmured, "I know where we're at, Pipe. This is the Ownvidian Knot. They're taking a shortcut. Twenty miles of this and we'll come out in the Duchy of Plemenza."

Else reviewed what he knew of northern Firaldia. Ghort could be right. But his estimate of distance sounded optimistic. Forty miles sounded more like it.

Bishop Serifs did not like heights. He balked when he saw what lay ahead. The Imperial troops pushed him, showing no respect.

Day had begun to fade. The bishop demanded, "When are we going to stop?"

A soldier replied, "We would've been there already if you didn't keep stalling and whining. But you do keep on. So we still have three miles to go."

That set the bishop off. He stopped. He refused to move. The captain of the band told his men, "Keep going. There's still enough light. I'll reason with the priest, then catch you up."

"Not good," Ghort whispered to Else. "If you happen to be an asshole bishop."

Else grunted.

"He's about to get spanked."

Else noted that Principaté Doneto started to argue with the

captain, fell silent at a look, then developed a smug little smile. Almost as if he saw a serendipitous answer to an old prayer.

The bishop's boy whore would not be separated from his patron.

Sometime later, after a mile or so, Else heard a distant cry, short and sharp. It might have been the scream of an eagle. It might have been something else.

The captain did not have the bishop in tow when he caught up. Armand preceded him on foot, running, looking grim and frightened.

"How about that?" Pinkus Ghort mused. "The brat weaseled out."

Bo Biogna observed, "You got to figure a kid like that is gonna be a survivor."

Ghort whispered. "We might want to set our own watch and keep ready for anything, Pipe. I didn't think they'd go this far. That captain must be damned sure Hansel will back him up."

By morning everyone had heard the catamite explain that the bishop, stubbornly refusing to go any further into the mountains, had tried to escape back the way he had come. His horse had lost its footing on a patch of ice. Bishop and beast had gone down the side of the mountain, mostly with the horse on top of its rider.

The Imperial soldiers noted that ice had been spreading throughout the Ownvidian Knot for half a century, never fading during the summers.

"This guy is slick," Ghort said of the Braunsknecht captain, whose name they had not been able to discover. "Getting somebody else to tell his story for him."

Else wondered. Osa claimed to be an agent of the Emperor. Maybe he thought that his association with Bishop Serifs had outlived its usefulness.

Breakfast was thin. The Imperials had consumed most of their own rations while waiting to spring their trap. The Principaté's party had expected to reach another Episcopal stronghold late that afternoon.

Else asked, "What'll happen when we don't turn up at Dominagua tonight?"

"They'll send somebody out to look around. When they

don't find us, they'll go back and panic. What's the matter? You're shaking."

"I'm cold. I hope I'm just cold, not coming down with something." He had been lucky so far. His only brush with illness, this mission, had been seasickness aboard *Vivia Infanti*.

After repeating his story several times, Osa Stile joined the rest of the prisoners. Else managed a slow, cautious, conversation. "What really happened out there?"

"Almost what I said. Though the bishop's horse might have had help wandering onto the ice. We weren't alone, just the three of us. There were things you couldn't see. They're all around us now. The Night is very interested in us."

The Ownvidian Knot was wild and uninhabited and not much visited since the ice began to creep down from the highest peaks. It was the kind of country where the creatures of night fled when civilization pressed. The road had markers each hundred paces, every one charmed, but those spells were old and limited in how much protection they could extend.

Else continued to suffer bouts of the chills. He was relieved when he heard they would stop early. He contributed his share of labor, then bundled up and crowded as close to the prisoners' fire as he could.

Supper was spare again.

Just Plain Joe did not take kindly to a suggestion that Pig Iron volunteer to become the main ingredient in a mule goulash.

"That's enough," Else said when tempers started to heat. "Bo, you're a hill country boy." So Biogna had claimed, when he was not telling one of several other tall tales about his origins. "Suppose you ask our hosts to join you in a nighttime goat hunt?" Else had seen wild goats during the day. "The moon should rise early tonight."

"Hate to disappoint you, Pipe," Biogna replied. "But my ass is gonna starve before I go out there in the dark. Anyways, by the time moonrise comes, it's gonna be snowin'."

"I see. And, no doubt, those goats would be too tough to eat, anyway."

"Hell, no. They's probably tastier 'n shit. But it's a fact. It's gonna be as dark and cold as a whore's heart and this ain't

country where you wanna be wanderin' away from camp after
the sun goes down."

"You're probably right." He stroked the invisible thing on
his wrist and wondered if its presence had dulled his thinking.

"In that case, make noises like a nanny in heat and wait for
some stupid billy to come running."

"That wouldn't work, Pipe." Sometimes Bo's thinking was
too literal.

Else studied his captors. They were a little larger, a little
healthier, and a lot more professional than the mob he had accompanied to Antieux. Still, they joked and grumbled and
bitched around their own fire, and generally agreed that the
natural order was all wrong because, obviously, the farther you
had your head up your own ass the higher you soared in the
chain of command.

Another bout of shivering took Else. He wriggled closer to
the fire.

ELSE DID NOT DREAM OFTEN. NOT THAT HE REMEMBERED. BUT
that night he did. And remembered.

He dreamed that trouble was coming. Major trouble, down
from the ice, out of the night so cold. The Instrumentalities of
the Night had become focused upon the Ownvidian Knot.
Something old was awakening out there. And its attention was
focused on the Braunsknechts' camp.

Else awakened. His wrist ached. His amulet felt hot. He felt
terribly cold himself. Everyone else was asleep. His own sentry, the Braunsknechts sentries, all were sound asleep. The
fires had burned low. The warding posts put out to protect the
encampment leaned drunkenly or had fallen.

Even Pig Iron snored like a mule.

Not good. Not good at all.

Ignoring his pain, Else crept across a dusting of snow to
shake Principaté Doneto. He could not imagine anyone else
who offered any hope against what was coming. This night resembled the one in Esther's Wood, amongst the Wells of Ihrian.
But now he had no falcon, no treasure chest, and no inspiration.

Bronte Doneto did not want to wake up. Else shook and
shook. His wrist hurt worse and worse. The Principaté groaned

but remained asleep. And now he began to sense a second something, possibly even more terrible than the darkness close at hand.

Else pinched Doneto vigorously, in tender places, still to no effect. Grinding his thumb into the sensitive spot between left hand middle and ring finger finally got results.

The Principaté leapt to his feet, instantly awake and immediately sensing wrongness. "Go away."

Else stole away, found a place where snow had collected. He crushed that against his wrist, hugged his stomach, folded up around the pain. Which became the center of his being. Then, gradually, it began to go away. Reason crept back into his mind.

Still clutching his wrist, Else got up onto his knees and looked around. Little had changed. The snow was falling more heavily. Doneto was on his hands and knees, but staggering anyway, heaving his guts up like a man who had tried to chug a gallon of cheap wine.

The sense of a great dread gathering had begun to fade away. Reluctantly. Powerfully angry at having been thwarted. And behind and beyond, afar, something faintly smug and satisfied.

As was often the case in encounters with the things of the night, at no time was there ever anything to be seen.

The nameless Braunsknecht captain was first to waken. He discovered his sentries snoring and his protective charms down, saw the state of Doneto and Else. Groggily, he kicked his men awake.

The sense of presence beyond the rim of firelight continued to fade.

Vaguely, Else heard the captain muttering, "What happened to our wards? There shouldn't be anything strong enough to overcome our wards. Not in this part of the world."

Soldiers and prisoners all had suffered nightmares like Else's, consisting of an overpowering impression of approaching menace, with an added certainty that escape was impossible.

"But you woke up," Pinkus Ghort said. Ghort remained disoriented.

Struggling to reclaim his dignity, Bronte Doneto leaned on Just Plain Joe and said, "You woke up, Hecht. In time. How did you manage that?"

"I don't know. It was the stomach cramps, I guess. The pain . . . It was instinct, mostly. Once I was awake enough I knew something supernatural was going on and I didn't know what to do. So I woke you up. How did you make it go away?"

"I prayed." Doneto's tone suggested that he did not expect to be taken seriously. The fact that he belonged to the Collegium was no secret. Many members of the Collegium were accomplished sorcerers.

The Braunsknecht captain invited himself into the conversation. "Principaté. Can you explain what just happened?"

"Something from the dawn of time woke up. Something that must have been put to sleep before the old empire came in. But why would it wake up tonight? Did someone wake it up on purpose? Because of us? What's special about us? Or about you?"

"That will be the question, won't it?"

Else held his aching wrist to his stomach and grimaced. He did not need to become part of any investigation. His amulet could not possibly evade notice during a close examination. He did not mention sensing a second supernatural presence.

Ghort suggested, "Maybe it was the bishop."

"What?" That from half a dozen mouths.

"I was just thinking, maybe whatever was coming after us was one of those old-time gods that wanted human sacrifices. It was almost dark when the bishop fell down and killed himself. Maybe that woke it up."

"That's as good a hypothesis as any," Doneto said. "But suppose we just let ourselves recover? Let's fuss about it later. Hecht. Will you be all right?"

"I passed some gas. The pain isn't as bad now."

Ghort snorted. "Swamp Boy passes gas. The rest of us fart or cut the cheese."

DESPITE GOOD INTENTIONS AND A UNIVERSAL LUST TO GET THE hell out of the Knot, movement did not commence until noon.

Everyone needed to recuperate. Else felt drained of will and strength.

Last night had been no simple brush with a mischievous sprite or malign minor shade. That presence was the dreadful equal of the thing in Esther's Wood. And it had not been vanquished.

Darkness threatened again before they exited the Ownvidian Knot on its northeastern side. Prisoners and captors had redefined their relationship, somewhat, though, as Ghort observed, "I don't hear nobody making wedding plans."

Plemenza maintained a small garrison in a watchtower on the Knot side of a village named Tampas. A dozen Imperial soldiers waited there, guarding supplies.

The Braunsknecht captain disappeared immediately. Professional to his core, he would prepare a report for his superiors. His own needs he would see to later.

After an enthusiastic meal, Bronte Doneto bellowed, "Hecht! Ghort! Come here."

Else and Ghort joined Doneto away from the others. Doneto said, "Something remarkable happened last night. A thing called a bogon came after us. Luck or God's favor saw us through. Which doesn't matter. What does is, the Instrumentalities of the Night fear one Episcopal Principaté enough to raise something ancient to attack him. Which doesn't happen in modern times. I'm astounded to see it anywhere outside of Scripture."

Else was pleased. Let Doneto think that whatever happened had to be about him. And that just might be.

He asked, "You sure the darkness did that on its own?"

"What do you mean, Hecht?"

"I was wondering if some unfriendly sorcerer was behind it."

Doneto took time to consider. "That's plausible. But I don't see how it could be managed. I don't know of anyone powerful enough to do it."

Ghort volunteered, "Maybe you pissed off one of the gods."

Doneto's face darkened. He was a prince of the Church. That Church acknowledged the existence of only one God.

"Excuse me," Ghort said. "Amend that to say some devil or demon."

Else nodded. "Slick, Pinkus." His own coreligionists handled the matter that way. There was the One God, the Merciful, the True God, There Is No Other, and everything else out there belonged to that vast host of lesser supernatural beings sworn to serve the Adversary.

Bronte Doneto relaxed. "You could be right, Ghort. Having endured the impossible already, we shouldn't discount any possibility."

"An open mind is a mind that has a chance to see the one path leading through darkness to tomorrow's safety."

"Of course. A child's lesson."

Else tried not to look baffled but failed.

Ghort told him, "It's from Kelam. *Letters to the Toscans*."

"I missed that, I guess."

"Most people do who don't spend some time in the seminary."

Else did not have a clue, now.

Doneto chuckled. "I suspect that Brother Hecht had very little opportunity to acquire a solid religious foundation growing up on the verges of the Grand Marshes."

Else grabbed that straw. "My family was never particularly devout. So don't expect me to have anything memorized."

Doneto said, "That is of no consequence. Survival and the work of the Lord is."

"Sir?"

"God has given me a calling. I didn't see that at first. I went to the Connec full of arrogance. Those assassins failed to waken me. Our Lord was forbearing. He sent you. He brought me out of the Connec. He saw me through the Ownvidian Knot. And now I'm ready to hear Him. I'm prepared to do His work." Doneto was intense. He continued, "All right. I didn't expect you would experience the same epiphany. But I do want to talk about what our situation means."

"It means we're out of work," Ghort said. "We can't protect you here. They chunk you in the dungeon, you don't need us anymore. Even if they don't, you couldn't pay us."

"Possibly. Johannes wouldn't be that bold, though. He'll just put me under house arrest until Sublime ransoms me by acknowledging the Emperor's claims somewhere. It'll all be handled quietly. Then I'll be on my way to Brothe again, with a need for lifeguards."

Else considered Doneto. He had arrived too late to experience the old Doneto but he had heard plenty from survivors of Doneto's original bodyguard. He did not believe that men changed their basic nature. They just pretended for tactical reasons.

"I'm trying to tell you that I want you to stay with me, despite this setback."

Else grunted. There could not be a more advantageous position than that of officer in the lifeguard of a member of the Collegium. "I'll stay."

Doneto nodded. "We'll see how onerous the Emperor makes our captivity. You may not miss a payday."

PLEMENZA WAS ONE OF THE WEALTHIER CITIES OF FIRALDIA. Nominally, it was a republic. An independent city-state. In truth, as with most Firaldian cities, the real rulers were a handful of families. Here, however, those had less influence than elsewhere because here there was a bigger dog.

The Grail Emperor had ancestral ties with the House of Truncella, the noble family whose firstborn sons were the Counts of Plemenza but who no longer much mattered locally. Johannes had been a minor noble himself when the Electors chose him Emperor as a compromise candidate who could be manipulated easily and pushed aside shortly. But Johannes Ege revealed a potent personality, was passionate in his convictions and persuasive in his arguments. The grasping cupidity of recent Patriarchs made Johannes particularly appealing to Firaldian nobles eager to slip the squeeze of the Church.

The Grail Emperor was staying in the Dimmel Palace with his son and two daughters. The Dimmel Palace had been the seat of the Truncella Counts for centuries. His stay had no stated date of termination.

Johannes's presence underscored his abiding interest in Firaldia. His expansionist interest, his enemies would say. Though Hansel himself insisted that he had come to Plemenza only to establish his daughters there, in a city where they could avail themselves of cultural and educational opportunities absent in the bleak agricultural lowlands of the Kretien Electorate.

The daughters were of interest for their political value. No match had been made for either, yet. Johannes's reluctance to entertain suits was causing strain amongst the Electors—some of whom secretly hoped to become Hansel's successor.

Johannes was looking for sons-in-law—if he had to tolerate such beasts at all—who would bring him treasure and soldiers and, most of all, enthusiasm for his struggle with the Patriarchy. There were few suitors of sufficient stature who shared his abiding loathing of the Patriarchy. And those matches all wanted bequest of the Empire itself. Because Johannes had only the one sickly son, Lothar.

Lothar's sisters and nurses doted on him, mainly because he was not expected to survive to succeed his father.

Hansel himself loved Lothar with an unreasonable fervor but could not deceive himself about the boy's prospects.

Else learned most of that from Doneto on the road to Plemenza.

Pinkus Ghort fell in beside Else. "Pipe, do we *really* want to stick with this weasel?"

Else chuckled. "I can be a weasel, too. I plan to gouge him for a better deal."

Ghort snickered but nodded. "When you make decisions, don't forget you're making them for more than just you."

"Excuse me?"

"Wherever you go now, for reasons they couldn't explain themselves, Bo, Joe, and Pig Iron are likely going to follow. You're just one of those kind of guys. That Pig Iron is a good soldier. But the rest . . ."

Pig Iron *was* a good soldier. The mule did more than his share of the work. He never complained, unlike Joe and Bo. Pig Iron was content just to go where Joe went.

Else had no trouble imagining schemers like er-Rashal al-Dhulquarnen trying to breed a race of warriors as placid and pliable as Joe's favorite mule.

Ah. The Sha-lug were not that way? The ideal Sha-lug. Not those Sha-lug like Else Tage, with a regrettable tendency to think for himself.

"Pinkus, here's an original notion. Instead of worrying about that stuff, how about we concentrate on getting out of this alive?"

"Shit, we got no worries, Pipe. Things are so ugly right now that I guarantee you everything's going to turn out all right. That's the way the Pinkus Ghort story gets told."

16. Andorayans and the
Black Mountain Massacre

Blood and murder swirled around the Andorayans. The Connecten attack had caught them off guard. But they were shambling along through an alien time, unready for much of anything but being amazed.

The Andorayans could no longer refuse to believe that they had fallen into a world where the grandsons of the men they had pursued were long dead of old age. That truth hammered them constantly.

They were never a part of that army. Their presence was tolerated but to the Arnhanders they were less than remoras to sharks. Unpleasantnesses had hounded them since that day at the bridge in the Haunted Hills.

In the matter of the murder of Erief Erealsson Shagot grew ever more suspicious of the gods themselves. The murder served them too well. He did not share his suspicions. Words spoken were words sure to be overheard by the Instrumentalities of the Night.

Shagot had no idea what they wanted him doing now. He knew only that he was supposed to recognize the moment when it arrived.

Shagot was doubtful of any convictions he discovered when he explored his own inner landscape. Or was amazed at the depth of his own cynicism.

The rest of the band were deeper in the dark. All they could do was stick, protect him, and hope that a time would come when everyone would understand what they had to do. But there was no enthusiasm for the task.

When the Arnhander army entered the pass below the Black Mountain of the Steigfeit Range, Shagot's companions were beyond complaining. They no longer talked to their leader much, either. They just trudged along, bent to the Will of the Gods, indifferent to a world that betrayed no interest in them.

Thus, because of their self-involvement, they responded slowly when the attack came.

Shagot said, "They don't see us."

Indeed. The attackers paid them no heed at all. Until they began to run toward those same trees whence the attack had come. Then a couple of infantrymen came at them. Svavar and Finnboga dispatched the two almost casually.

"Don't anybody move," Shagot said. More attackers were headed their way.

The Connectens lost interest.

"Like old Trygg," Hallgrim said. "He was always forgetting what he was going to do."

Shagot said, "Let's move. They aren't looking, now."

They covered maybe eighty feet before a lone horseman in heavy armor charged them. Sigurjon flung an axe. While the rider fended it Shagot dropped his mount with a two-handed sword stroke to its forelegs. The others murdered the rider before he hit the ground.

Trial and error showed them that short bursts, a dozen yards at a time, followed by a minute of inactivity, let them travel without attracting attackers.

"Pretty damned feeble magic if you ask me, Grim," Svavar said.

"It's keeping your stinky ass alive, ain't it? Once we get to them rocks over there we'll lay up until this shit is over and the survivors go away."

It was clear who the victors would be. Already it was all over but the butchery.

THE BATTLEFIELD WAS QUIET. THE CONNECTENS HAD GIVEN UP looting the dead and murdering the wounded. Now they were coping with the enormity of what they had done. It was more difficult for them than for men of Shagot's land and time. The Connec's only acquaintance with war was through those few adventurous sons who went to fight in the Holy Lands.

Svavar asked, "What do we do next, Grim?"

Shagot had no idea. This disaster was nothing that the gods had foreseen. "I need to sleep on it. I'll let you know in the morning."

The others did not question that.

They were all weird men.

They had been to heaven and back.

Or maybe they had gone somewhere else.

But in this world all beliefs were true. In this world the gods came first, then men re-created them in images they preferred.

In time the victors went away. The surviving Arnhanders and Grolsachers were long gone by then. Shagot and his friends took the opportunity to scavenge what they could.

They did not find much.

"SO WHERE ARE WE HEADED, GRIM?"

"Back the way we came. Staying away from people."

After Shagot explained what he had learned in his dreams, Hallgrim wanted to know, "Who is this Godslayer?"

"I don't know."

"So how're we supposed to recognize him when we find him?"

"I don't know."

"This whole thing is turning into a cluster fuck, Grim."

"I know."

"And the answers are all in this place called Brothe?"

"Unless the Old Ones change their minds. Now shut the fuck up. We've got a long walk ahead. And most of the time we'll need to stay out of sight of the natives."

"Why?"

"The Old Ones don't want us noticed. They didn't say why. Same old shit. We're supposed to be thrilled to be used like a pack of dogs."

Each hour left the six less sympathetic toward their gods.

THE GODS OF THE ANDORAYANS REFLECTED THE NORTHERN folk themselves. Which meant that they were rowdy, drunken, not too bright, drunken, violent, drunken, and short-sighted. While often drunk.

Those were values their culture had accreted over the ages.

They were not the values of anyone in the world where the Andorayans found themselves now.

"We'll find the man."

The others scowled but readied themselves for travel. With less enthusiasm than ever.

The serious grumbling started a week later, as Shagot tried to sneak past Antieux unnoticed. Finnboga snapped, "What the fuck are we doing, Grim? We were supposed to catch some assholes that killed Erief. But I ain't heard Erief's name come up in a month."

Sigurdur grumbled, "I'm ready to go home."

Shagot reminded him, "Home ain't there anymore."

"Whatever is there, it'll be a lot more like home than this is."

Even Asgrimmur was restive. "I'm thinking maybe it's time the gods looked out for themselves."

Shagot drew a deep breath, released it. He did not know how to fight this creeping defeatism. He had trouble enough motivating himself.

He slept longer now than he had while they were part of the Arnhander army. He could not help it. He *wanted* to pursue a normal waking cycle. He wanted his band out of this country where they could be held accountable for the bad behavior of their former Arnhander companions.

That was the worst. The sneaking. The creeping along, trying to get by unnoticed.

Hallgrim wanted to know, "Why the hell are we doing this, Grim? These people don't know who we are. We should get down on the regular road. Just be some guys headed east."

Hallgrim's argument made sense. But the god voices inside Shagot would not let him acquiesce.

"This is bullshit," Finnboga insisted. "I'm about ready to take off on my own."

"It'll get easier once we get to the country they call Ormienden."

It seemed to take forever to get there, though, because Shagot spent so much time asleep. And, after they reached Ormienden, Shagot still refused to travel normally.

Svavar, Hallgrim, and the others became increasingly mutinous. While Shagot became more and more unable to be anything but "a huldrin mouthpiece for a gang of lunatic gods who ain't relevant no more," according to Shagot's own brother, Svavar.

A week into Ormienden, Shagot wakened to find himself alone except for his brother. The way Svavar hunched as he cooked told Shagot that something was seriously wrong.

Horses were missing.

"They left, Grim. They couldn't take it no more. But they left all the stuff."

Shagot could not get an emotional handle on what had happened. "I don't understand."

"You won't listen, will you? They been telling you and telling you."

"You're still here."

"I'm your brother. But if I thought you could keep yourself alive on your own for a week, I'd be gone, too."

Shagot did not resume traveling that day or the next, sure the others would recover their senses and return.

Svavar did not push. Svavar no longer believed in any mission from the gods. But Shagot was family.

Svavar had concluded, after all he had been through since Erief's murder, that it might not be a bad thing if a few gods died, too.

In time, Shagot pulled himself together enough to get up on his hind legs and start traveling again.

"Where are we headed, big brother?" Svavar wanted to know.

"For now, the Old City. Brothe. I don't know why. That's where they want us to go."

Shagot was puzzled with himself. He had no drive left. But for the nagging of the god voices in the back of his brain he would have headed home himself.

Asgrimmur, for his part, began to see his brother as a holy madman. Those were rare in northern tradition but the notion of the insane having been touched by the gods was entrenched. In Shagot's case there was no doubt.

THE GODS OF THE NORTH WERE SPITEFUL, CHILDISH, AND PETTY. A great many gods, across the earth, went way long on the famine, pestilence, and war, but came up short on characteristics their worshipers would find congenial.

Finnboga and Hallgrim, Sigurdur and Sigurjon, encountered the malice of the Instrumentalities of the Night just two evenings after abandoning Shagot and Svavar.

They were sheltering for the night beneath an old stone bridge spanning a stream less than six yards wide. The river was low because of the season. It had snowed that afternoon. Now a brisk and bitter wind muttered around the old bridge. Gusts whipped their little fire, threatening to kill it.

This shelter had served travelers for centuries. Numerous fires had burned on the same spot, surrounded by the same blackened stones. Another fire burned on the north side of the stream, where half a dozen southbound travelers huddled against the cold.

Hallgrim grumbled, "I'm getting old. Ten years ago this would've been a spring breeze. Now I'm thinking about emigrating to Iceland."

His companions grunted. None had visited Iceland but they had heard about the geysers and hot springs and magical vents that defeated the most ferocious winters. When the cliffs of ice crossed the Ormo Strait to begin devouring the New Brothen Empire, Iceland would still be warm.

Sigurjon observed, "Things could be different out there, though. If it's part of one big kingdom and those black crow priests run things."

Finnboga inquired, "How hard could it be to kill a few priests?"

"How hard?" Sigurdur snapped. "Look at us."

Sigurjon said, "It must be harder than it looks. Otherwise, why would those lilies be in power?"

Sigurdur said, "You're right. They are in charge in these parts. And it don't look like there's much chance of that changing. Shit!"

"What?"

"I've got to crap again." It was the sixth time that day. Sigurdur had begun to worry. A man who lost control of his bowels could end up shitting himself to death.

Sigurjon told him, "Well, take it downwind. That last load was so foul the flies dropped dead."

Stomach cramping, Sigurdur stumbled away, headed for a spot he had scouted before darkness fell, anticipating this emergency.

He located the twin stones, fumbled with his trousers, urgently willing them out of the way before the explosion came while dreading the crude bite of the wind on his buttocks.

He managed in time, voided the first nasty charge. He indulged in a little self-congratulation even as he bent over a fresh, more ferocious set of cramps.

As that departed in a rumbling gush Sigurdur realized that he was not alone. And that whoever was there was not one of his traveling companions. He could see his brother, Hallgrim, and Finnboga huddling close to the fire, making jokes at his expense.

He eased a hand toward his knife.

A shadow drifted nearer. The campfires cast just enough light to show him a woman wearing a hooded black cloak. The cloak's hem dragged the ground.

He could see nothing but her face. It was a beautiful face, much like his mother's must have looked when she was young.

Sigurdur thought, you heard about this sort of thing all your life but you were never ready when it happened. You never believed *you* would attract the interest of the Instrumentalities of the Night.

The woman opened her cloak. She wore nothing beneath. Her body was perfection. It exuded warmth. It could not be resisted.

It was too late even for the wary.

SIGURJON BEGAN TO WORRY. "WHAT'S TAKING HIM SO LONG? He's always been full of shit, but . . . gods."

"Maybe he's trying to get it all worked out in one granddaddy load."

"He'll get frostbite on his ass if he fools around too long." Sigurjon rose. He yelled. His twin did not respond. He sat back down, sure that if there was any real trouble he would sense it through their twin bond.

Half an hour later Finnboga and Hallgrim were troubled enough to go out searching, shouting, leaving Sigurjon by the fire.

They found nothing.

"We'll look again after it's light. We can't find anything now. Let's cast lots for first watch." That would have been Sigurdur's job.

THEY FOUND THE PLACE WHERE SIGURDUR HAD EMPTIED HIS bowels. Then, despite the tracks they had left all over while searching in the dark, they discovered the trail Sigurdur had left when he headed upstream, beside the river. They found Sigurdur himself half a mile from camp, half in and half out of the river, naked from the waist down. They never found his trousers.

"He died happy," Hallgrim said.

But Sigurdur's skin was as pale as the snow, not because he was dead but because all the blood had been drained from his body.

The frozen mud retained footprints made by a woman's small, bare feet.

The tale was not hard to read, just hard to believe. You heard the stories but you never really believed.

But the things of the night were as real as cruel death. And every bit as wicked as the stories claimed.

The survivors made no immediate connection between Sigurdur's misfortune and their having turned their backs on their gods.

When they returned to camp they discovered that they had been plundered by their neighbors. The villains had left them with little more than what they wore and the weapons they carried. Which they had come near ruining while hacking out a shallow grave for Sigurdur.

Sigurjon was the smartest survivor. He began to suspect divine mischief when something got Hallgrim a week later. This death in the dark did not leave its victim smiling. It did not leave its victim with a face at all.

Neither Sigurjon nor Finnboga ever heard a sound.

17. The Connec, After the Blood

Brother Candle's captors let several days pass before he was allowed to see Count Raymone Garete. No one accused him of anything. He was known and respected throughout the End of Connec. To be deemed a traitor he would have to indict himself out of his own mouth.

"Well?" the Count asked. "What do you have to say for yourself?"

"I was on the road. Trying to overtake you. The Arnhanders captured me. At the moment you attacked the Archbishop was offering me the opportunity to be the central character in a heresy trial."

"I can see why he'd think that way. Why were you trying to catch me?"

"In hopes that I could talk you out of attacking the Arnhanders. This war can only end in disaster for the End of Connec."

The Count's henchmen laughed, mocked Brother Candle, made chicken-clucking noises. Few were older than the Count. One said, "Looks to me like the disaster boot is on the other foot, Brother. Twice, now."

Brother Candle shook his head. "I have no hope of selling sanity, now. The die is cast. You arrogant young men. Listen! Don't rest on your laurels. Next summer, or the summer after, or the summer after that, the armies of Arnhand and the Brothen Patriarch will return. And they'll descend like the Wrath of God Himself."

That was not what they wanted to hear. They wanted to be told that Santerin would never stop feuding with Arnhand. They wanted to hear about dynastic troubles that would cripple Arnhand. They wanted to be told that the Patriarch was a bucket full of wind, with the Grail Emperor hard on its flank, poised to strike the instant Sublime overextended himself.

Brother Candle had enjoyed success in his worldly life. His success as a Perfect was more limited, because he was now a holy man. A holy man who lacked the advantage enjoyed by Sublime: an army to *make* dimwits listen.

He did not remain with the Count. He got back on the road. He would rejoin Duke Tormond and try to subdue the future from Khaurene.

There was no way to stop the coming war. Arnhand's leading families would all demand it. What he had to do now was keep emotion from gaining complete control. The more the emotions could be blunted the gentler the future would be.

He would try to convince the high and the mighty—Tormond in particular—that they *must* prepare for the worst.

He did not want war. But if war could not be avoided, then the Connec should be prepared to respond with a ferocity and vigor that would overawe anyone interested only in fattening his fortune.

Brother Candle walked the ancient, cold highway to Khaurene uncomfortably aware that the one last thing he had to do in this world, and had to do better than he had done anything before, was a work that he loathed. He had to nurture and guide the Seekers After Light through an age of horror and violence that would determine whether their faith persevered or vanished from the earth forever.

The Maysalean Heresy would not go meekly, however gentle its hopes. Ironically, though, those Connectens who would bear the brunt of the expense and fighting would be devout Chaldareans defending themselves from men who claimed to be the champions of their own faith.

18. Plemenza: The Dimmel Palace

Plemenza was a bright and colorful city but the captives got no chance to enjoy it. The troops who brought them in made sure they had no contact with the locals. As far as Else could tell, the locals were not curious.

The party passed through the gates of the Dimmel Palace. And that was that, for a long time.

Nothing cruel happened. Nothing happened at all. The captives entered a section of palace where the windows and all but one door had been bricked up. Then they were ignored. Though meals did arrive regularly. Initially, Bronte Doneto raged and demanded to see someone, anyone, even the Emperor himself. The only servant they ever saw never responded in any way.

Doneto was outraged but not concerned for his safety. "This is just a logical escalation in the Emperor's squabble with Sublime. If Johannes keeps me away from the Collegium, the Patriarch will have a lot of trouble getting their backing."

Else listened closely. If removing one man could paralyze the enemy's center of power . . . A little work with some sharpened steel and . . .

Much better, more clever, to make a key vote disappear somewhere away from Brothe. Keeping the survival of the voter a mystery.

The Collegium could not replace Bronte Doneto unless they knew he was no longer healthy enough to assist in the glorification of the Church. And then they would need the Patriarch's blessing.

Doneto was positive. He wakened every morning sure that this would be the last day of his captivity. And every night he fell asleep on a thin mattress, confused and alone except for his despair.

SOME EVIL GENIUS HAD INVESTED DEEPLY IN THE PREPARATION of their prison. The captives had no contact whatsoever with the world, no way of knowing if it were night or day, or even the season—though it must be winter. The Palace was frigid. There was no privacy whatsoever. The Principaté had to share facilities and space with his men. And with Pig Iron, because the Braunsknechts did not want the mule in their stables, where he might inspire uncomfortable questions. The mule's presence was a statement, too. Someone wanted Doneto to know that in the eyes of the Grail Emperor a Principaté of the Episcopal Collegium was of the same significance as a clever mule.

Not true, of course. But the Emperor's clear contempt ground away at the Principaté.

Yet there was iron behind Doneto's arrogance and self-admiration. And some humanity as well. Doneto adapted to his company. Thirty sleeps into their confinement even Bo Biogna and Just Plain Joe could sit down with him and talk.

In the middle of his days, when his optimism was strongest, Doneto returned to his beginnings as a priest. So he said. Though everyone knew that members of the Collegium bought their positions. Few ever endured the workaday cares of the priesthood.

"He was born a bishop," Pinkus Ghort said, making the point. "If you're a Brothen from the right family and a second son, you start life as a bishop. He probably got his miter when he was fourteen."

Else was amused. Here was Ghort being Ghort. Ghort spent more time with the Principaté, toadying up, than did any three other captives. But he would not surrender his right to criticize.

Ghort said, "You need to work on Doneto more, Pipe. You're never gonna get another chance like this. Remember, we could be out of here tomorrow. They won't give us any warning."

This *was* a unique opportunity to position himself. Doneto had offered him work in Brothe already.

Doneto's notion was to pretend to keep Else at a distance, then ease him into a position where he could keep an eye on Bronte Doneto's enemies.

Ghort had snapped up the plum, commanding Doneto's lifeguard, already.

Else told him, "Don't let it go to your head, Pinkus. You're the third one this year. A whole lot of people don't like this guy."

"Oh, I'll be careful. This is the kind of job I've been angling for all my life. This is Easy Street. No way I'm not gonna do the best job anybody ever did. And if we can get you set up in the right place, you can warn me whenever some shit is about to happen."

"I've been thinking about that."

"I don't like your tone, Pipe. It means I'm probably not gonna want to hear what you're gonna say."

"That wouldn't surprise me. What I'm thinking is, if we do find ourselves in the situation the Principaté wants to set up, then the information has to go both ways."

"Meaning?"

"Meaning that if I'm going to be your guy on the inside, you're going to be my guy on the inside. I'll need to look good sometimes, too. Unless you think you have to be one way about the whole thing."

"Not me. God forbid. I'm just trying to set myself up with a comfortable life."

"If we do it right, we can write both of us letters of marque."

Ghort chuckled. "You ain't as simple as you let on, are you, Pipe?"

* * *

BEFORE THEIR QUARTERS WERE CONVERTED THEY HAD EN-
joyed an incarnation at the palace lumber rooms. There were
heaps of tattered old books and records left over from the last
century. Many dealt with the Truncella family, histories of
generations long gone. They were of little use to anyone but
Else, who used them to study western manuscript styles.

There were a few actual books mixed into the mess. Else
found those educational. In a professional development sort
of way.

Those written in the modern vernacular were not interesting. Mainly, they delved into the lives of Chaldarean saints, of
which there were hosts. Information useful if you wanted to fit
in, but of no practical value otherwise.

The majority of the real books were in Old Brothen, meticu-
lously copied from texts first set down in classical times and
interesting now because they opened marvelous windows into
pasts never rewritten by the prejudices and ambitions of inter-
vening ages.

Else got help from Bronte Doneto, who enjoyed teaching
when he could find no loftier target for his energies. Doneto
told Else, "These are copies of texts set down before the Chaldarean Confirmation. They're in the formal Brothen of their
time. Which is lucky for us. The formal language didn't change
as fast as the vulgate. But these are treatises on technical things.
How to manage vineyards and wineries. How to manage latifundia, which were large commercial agricultural enterprises
that included fig, olive, and citrus orchards, along with grain
and vegetable crops. They weren't big on meat in those days,
except for seafood. This one is a treatise on how to construct
various engines, from wine and olive presses to artillery and
siege machines. This one concerns the conduct of war. These
are about the lives of the emperors and key personalities of
their times."

Doneto taught Else a smattering of classical Brothen. Else
then spent most of his waking hours puzzling his way through
the old books.

He set a precedent. He started a fad. Captivity was so dull
that even Bo Biogna and Just Plain Joe were ready to do anything to stave off the boredom. Even if that meant learning,
with the Principaté doing most of the teaching.

"Pig Iron will be next," Else predicted. "And he'll learn faster than the rest of us." He told an old Dreangerean story about teaching a camel to whistle, though he made it a mule instead of a camel.

Armed with what he was learning, Else would be able to spy on the mail of Dreanger's enemies.

Gradually, as time passed, Else allowed himself to be drawn into the Principaté's plans, but according to his own goals.

THE CAPTIVES HAD NO CLEAR NOTION OF THE LENGTH OF THEIR captivity. At least three months, everyone agreed. Some thought it might be as much as five. Else was surprised that they managed to survive without becoming violent. That, likely, was due to how much space was available. And because despair never set in. Bronte Doneto never stopped believing that rescue or ransom was imminent.

Just Plain Joe was content. He told Else, "I never lived this good in my whole life. Look at this. I'm warm. I got plenny a food. I got frien's. I got Pig Iron. An' I'm even learnin' how ta read an' talk right."

Joe's dream did not end anytime soon. Inevitably, eventually, Bronte Doneto began to lose his confidence. Else wondered if there had not been a complete collapse of human nature in Plemenza.

It was impossible that news of Bronte Doneto's whereabouts would not have reached people who cared.

Ghort suggested, "Maybe our boss has a big head. He's a hundred eighty miles from home. Why would anybody recognize him?"

"I'll buy that," Else replied. "Tell you the truth, I don't think most of those Braunknechts knew who he was. Rounding us up was just a job."

That notion did nothing to improve anyone's mood.

Ghort said, "You'd think the Emperor would want a few people to know. He can't profit just by having Doneto locked up."

He could, though. But that was not obvious from inside a prison.

Else said, "Maybe it's what we were talking about, way back. If Hansel has the Principaté, the Collegium is locked up.

If the Collegium is locked up, Sublime can't do the crazy stuff he keeps ranting about. Including making life miserable for the Emperor."

"You're probably right, Pipe. But I don't like it. That means Hansel told the world he's got Sublime's boy. And Sublime thinks he can out-stubborn him. Or flat don't care what happens to his cousin."

Bo Biogna organized a pool. Whoever came closest to guessing the exact length of their captivity would collect. Even Bronte Doneto bought in.

Else often wondered why the Doneto he knew was so unlike the Doneto who had been sent into the End of Connec to help Bishop Serifs and enforce Sublime V's will.

"Why not ask?" Ghort queried when Else posed the question. "What I'm wondering is, whatever happened to the bishop's pretty boy?"

Yes. Osa Stile vanished the day they reached Plemenza. Perhaps the Grail Emperor had found new work for him.

Else gathered his daring and, during a card game, did ask Principaté Doneto why his character seemed to have changed dramatically.

"You aren't even a little slow, are you, Hecht? You notice things."

"I'm a professional soldier, sir. I like to understand the people I work for. These days you aren't anything like the legate we heard about when we first got to Antieux."

"You're right, Hecht. But remember, the job isn't the man. I was fulfilling a role on behalf of the Patriarch. A role hung on me by Bishop Serifs, may that fat, corrupt moron roast in Hell for the harm he did the Church."

ONE DAY SOMEONE CAME WHO WAS NOT THE ONE SILENT SERvant they always saw. The newcomer scanned the nineteen prisoners. The seventeen who were not too sick crowded toward him. He indicated a man. "You. Come with me."

He had chosen Bo Biogna. Bo did not want to go. But the new face had not come alone. Three armed men surrounded Bo. They did not look reluctant to employ the tools of their trade.

"Go on, Bo," Else said. "If they intended to do anything awful they would've already done it to save on feeding us."

Else told Ghort, "I hope I'm right," once Bo left.

"Made sense to me. You know they plan to use us somehow."

Bo Biogna was gone less than fifteen minutes. The men who returned him took another captive away.

"Well?" Ghort asked Biogna. Everyone able crowded around. Even Bronte Doneto positioned himself to hear Biogna's report.

"I don't know. They took me down the hall to this room with nothin' in it but this long table wit' four guys who asked me questions. That they didn't seem to give a shit about the answers."

"What sort of questions?" Else asked.

"Who was I, what was my job, how did I hook up wit' the Patriarch's army."

"Why would they want to know that instead of something more operational?"

"Yeah, well, they asked a bunch of questions about all kinds of shit. Especially about that Brotherhood sorcerer. That Grade Drocker. An' about what happened in the Connec. Only like not about what, exactly, but more like why an' how. An' who really stirred things up. I think they gave up on me pretty quick on account of they realized that I'm a nobody who don't know nothin' about nothin'."

The second man said much the same. Likewise, the third, though by now Else had the impression that the interrogations were tailored to their objects. Which suggested that the interrogators had a good idea who they were questioning before they started.

Pinkus Ghort was the fourth man taken. He was absent more than an hour. He returned unhurt but drained. He flopped onto his pallet. "That was rough. In a nonphysical way. It's hard to keep everything straight when they ask you the same thing fifty different times fifty different ways."

Bronte Doneto was curious. And worried. His turn would come. He was right there listening when Else countered, "How so?"

"It was like Bo and the others said. Only there was more of

it. They was infatuated with the notion that I know all of the Patriarch's personal secrets on account of I was like a pick-up captain in a half-ass gang of robbers that Sublime sent out. So what if I've never been any closer to the old boy than I am right now?"

"Did they threaten you? Did they try to bribe you?"

"No. And that was weird, too. I don't think they really cared what I answered. They just wanted to ask the questions."

That bothered Bronte Doneto. Else asked, "Sir? Have we missed something?"

"They may be using lie-detecting spells. If they have specialist adepts, our answers won't matter. What were the questioners like?"

Ghort replied, "They didn't look like no kind of wizards. They was just soldiers. Guys used to getting their hands dirty. I recognized one of them from somewhere. The guy on the end, on their right, was somebody that I should ought to remember. But I don't know where from."

More men went through the process, some for longer, some not so long. Just Plain Joe was away only eight minutes.

When Joe came back the soldiers beckoned Pinkus. Ghort protested, "I've already been."

"Then you know the way. Let's go."

Ghort was gone a long time.

The soldiers wanted Principaté Doneto next. Things got tense. Ghort said, "Take it easy, Chief. It ain't that big a deal."

"Why did they call you back?" Else asked after the door slammed behind the Principaté.

"Maybe they didn't understand me the first time. They asked all the same questions. I'm thinking maybe Doneto is right. Something is going on besides them asking questions."

"It took them over an hour to get the same old answers you already gave them?"

"Oh, no. That part added up to only maybe twenty minutes. In the middle of it they all just got up and left. Like they went out for dinner or something. And didn't need to worry about me."

"So you just sat there?"

"Well, I got up and wandered around some. I didn't go far. They locked the door."

Bronte Doneto was gone for hours. He was exhausted when he returned. He had little to say. He sucked down a bowl of lentil soup, curled up in his blanket and slept.

His was the last interview of the day.

THE INTERVIEWS RESUMED NEXT MORNING. THE FIRST MAN taken had gone before. He reported, "They're up to something different. It was about religion this time."

Else went third. He was not nervous. He could handle basic religious questions. He had been paying attention.

The room was exactly as described, featureless and brightly lighted. The smell of tallow was strong. Four men sat behind a table, their backs to a wall. One straight-backed, hard chair faced the table. The men did not look like professional inquisitors. The man farthest to Else's right might be a priest. He pegged two more as soldiers. The man between the priest and soldiers, though, was someone important.

The man to that man's right asked, "Piper Hecht?"

"Yes."

"Religion?"

"Yes."

"Excuse me?"

"Yes. I'm religious."

"What religion?"

"Why?"

The man Else suspected of being in control said, "Stop that. Sit down, Hecht. Answer the questions put to you."

"Why?"

A flicker of anger. Nobody else had been difficult.

His left wrist began to itch. He scratched. His fingertips tripped over the invisible amulet, which had begun to get warm.

Sorcery. Of course.

Else said, "I don't understand why you would expect me to cooperate. Why would I help my employer's enemies?"

The man farthest to Else's left said, "Tell us about your life before you joined the force the Patriarch sent to rescue the Bishop of Antieux."

Else suppressed an urge to remain argumentative. Maybe he

was not supposed to be able. Maybe that was the nature of the sorcery at work here.

Else spoke vaguely of growing up in Duarnenia, a minor crusader principality on the southeastern coast of the Shallow Sea, on a small estate near Tusnet, well inland, just inside the marches where Chaldarean crusaders of the Grail Order remained constantly at war with the Sheard heathen of the Grand Marshes. He mentioned running away at fifteen, banging around from one minor employer to another, drifting southward. He offered no specifics. Mercenaries seldom did.

He included more detail about his service since joining the Brotherhood-sponsored force. The four probably knew all that already.

The man in charge told the others, "Step outside, please. I want to talk to this one alone."

The room cleared so quickly Else suspected that it must have been planned.

He kept his baffled face on. Just another dumb soldier, he had no clue. Though that would not work for long. His own men tried it on him, regularly, with limited success.

The man who stayed behind considered Else. Else studied the man back. This must be Ferris Renfrow. No one else would fit in just here, just now, would they?

He was about fifty, looked more Firaldian than northern. He had all of his hair. That was black, lightly salted with gray. It had no luster left, though. His eyes were small, brown, squinted, permanently suspicious. His lips were frozen into a pout, suggesting that he thought everyone was lying to him all the time. His nose was completely unremarkable. His chin was strong. His face was rectangular and weathered. He had excellent teeth, which was uncommon in Chaldarean lands.

"Tell me what happened in the Knot. The night your company fell foul of the bogon."

"Sir? The what?"

"The attack. By the night monster. The thing is called a bogon."

"There isn't anything to tell. We survived."

"You saved the band."

Else shrugged. "That was Principaté Doneto. All I did was, I had a nightmare. It woke me up. It felt like something bad was happening so I woke the Principaté. That's all I did. He belongs to the Collegium. After that I was tied up with bad stomach cramps. He took care of the monster."

"This wasn't your first time, though. Did it go the same at Esther's Wood? And Runch?"

Shaken, Else managed better than he expected. And even tucked away a curiosity about the mention of Runch. No bogon manifested there. He did not reply.

Renfrow said, "There's a connecting thread. I don't know what, yet, but the more recent attacks must have followed because the first one failed."

"Huh?"

"I know who you are, Captain Tage. I've been waiting for you for months. You haven't done anything you were expected to do. That ruction in Sonsa, that was a masterpiece."

"Sir, you've lost me completely. You're not making any sense." Else suspected, though, that the man was not just fishing. "Who are you, sir?"

The inquisitor shook his head.

Osa Stile. That little bastard had not been able to keep his mouth shut.

Renfrow must be the man Pinkus Ghort remembered from somewhere else.

"It's possible you may not know what's going on. If I was to send you into enemy territory I wouldn't tell you everything. I'd let the touchiest parts wait till you'd survived making all your contacts."

This felt more dangerous by the minute.

"Yes. That's it. They just flung you in, like throwing a snake into a campfire. Either they figured you could handle the heat or they wanted you to burn. Which was it? What did they tell you to do?"

Else kept his mouth shut, stared at the inquisitor like the man was raving in tongues, the way the al-Kobean dervishes did.

Else would not surrender his identity as Piper Hecht. They had no means of proving that he was not Piper Hecht.

"Lest you think you can bluff your way past me, I remind you that we've met before."

"No, sir. Even if I was who you say I am. I'd remember you if we'd met." Else spoke with complete conviction. It was true.

"I get the impression you really believe what you just said."

"I don't just believe it, it's true. Who are you? Where are we supposed to have met? I doubt that you're the sort who volunteers to serve in the Grand Marshes."

"Ah, no. No. I have to rethink this. There's a page missing." For a moment he listened to something only he could hear.

Else concentrated on ignoring his left wrist. He itched terribly.

There was sorcery at work here . . . So many candles. They made it warm. He had begun to sweat. And the odor of candle smoke . . . There was another odor there, behind the burnt tallow. An incense sort of smell. Which would be why he felt light-headed. These naughty people were doing something to make him more pliable.

The inquisitor could not understand why Else was not more suggestible. He would be wondering if he had not made some grotesque mistake.

"Ah. I recall the circumstances. You're right. We haven't met. You were pointed out by a gentleman named er-Rashal al-Dhulquarnen, in the Palace of the Kings in al-Qarn two years ago. The wizard said you were leaving on a mission that could impact the balance of power in the east. If you were successful. Were you successful?"

Else tried to recall all he had heard about Ferris Renfrow. While mulling the fact that the Grail Emperor's people might have known that he was coming. Was that Osa's doing? Or had there been word from al-Qarn?

Why would Osa have been told?

"I have no idea what you're talking about. But I'm at your mercy. I won't argue."

"We're at loggerheads, then, Captain. And if you won't be Else Tage from Dreanger, then I can't help Else Tage accomplish his mission. Nor will Else Tage be able to help me with mine."

"What would you do for me if I agree to be this Else guy?" He mispronounced his own name. "What would I have to do? On account of, if it'll get me out of here, I'll be the Patriarch's favorite daughter. Or any saint you want to name."

Renfrow showed signs of exasperation. Nothing was working.

"There's something wrong here," Renfrow said. "Even if you aren't the man I think, you shouldn't be able to reason or argue." He waved a hand. Smoke swirled around his fingers.

Else grunted an interrogative.

"Sit still." Renfrow left the room.

The smoke and whatever else was in the air dragged Else down into unconsciousness.

ELSE WAKENED BACK IN THE LOCKUP. HE HAD THE SHAKES and a headache. Pinkus Ghort and Just Plain Joe were there to nurse him. Joe had cold water. Ghort had a cold, wet rag and was mopping his face, soothing his fever.

Ghort asked, "What the hell happened, Pipe?"

"They tried to get me to confess that I'm a spy. They used some kind of drug on me. It was in the air, like incense."

Just Plain Joe asked, "How could you be a spy? You weren't never been in these parts before. An' the only reason you ever was was on account of they brought you."

Else finished a pint of cold water. "Joe, I don't have any idea. Maybe you could ask them. All I know is, they want me to be a spy. And they drugged me to get me there. And, before I passed out, I was thinking that it didn't matter whether I was a spy so long as I told them I was a spy. I think I volunteered to be the spy if they'd just let me out. What time is it?"

It was noon of the day following Else's last clear memory. The inquisitors had interviewed prisoners all morning. The tenor of the interviews had changed. The Imperials wanted the prisoners to talk about their comrades.

Ghort said, "I just had my third round. My head's still fuzzy. You're right about that smoke. They asked me about everything but Pig Iron. They're definitely looking for something."

Just Plain Joe said, "They've got the Principaté in there, now. You better eat somethin' while you can, Pipe. In case they jump your ass when they find out you're awake."

Ghort agreed. "Sound advice. The way they worked on you yesterday, they'll be right back at you. What's that all about, anyway?"

"I told you. They want me to be a spy."

"Eat," Joe said.

"And suck down some more water," Ghort told him. "A lot of water."

"Did they drug you guys?" Else asked.

Joe shrugged.

Ghort replied, "I told you. They're putting something in the air."

Else described the man who had interrogated him alone. "You know who I'm talking about? Is he the one you said you thought you'd seen before?"

"The very one. *And* I remember where, now. It was six years ago. I was new at this stuff. I was working for the Duke of Clearenza. That's up north, in the foothills. They call it a Duchy but you can throw a rock across it. Johannes was just getting going. He kept his people distracted by pushing the Empire's claims in Firaldia. Clearenza owed allegiance to the Grail Empire but that wasn't being enforced. The Dukes were related to the two Patriarchs before Sublime. They thought that would protect them."

Else chuckled. "Evidently it didn't. So what does that mean to us?"

"When Hansel's troops showed up Clemency III didn't do anything. He was about a hundred years old and too busy croaking. The Duke decided to shut the gates and sit tight. Then this guy who'd been with us about two months went down to the gatehouse in the middle of the night, killed the guard on duty, and opened up. They say it didn't look intentional. That he just wanted to choke the old man until he passed out. But he broke the old man's windpipe.

"It turned out the killer was the Grail Emperor's man. He called himself Lester Temagat but his real name was Ferris Renfrow. They say he pulls tricks like that all the time."

"And you put him on your grudge list?"

"The guard in that gatehouse was my old man. My father."

Just Plain Joe shoved food into Else's hands, "You got to eat, Pipe. Come on. Don't be a dope. They're going to nab you again."

Else ate. And reflected on Ghort's story. It was interesting. But was any of it true?

The Imperial interrogators sent for him half an hour later.

* * *

OSA STILE WAS IN THE INTERROGATION ROOM. ELSE ACK-nowledged the boy with a glance. He took the seat that Ren-frow indicated, facing the table.

"Captain, I think you know this young man."

"He was Bishop Serif's boy whore. Armand. I expect he's found himself a new bed to bounce in. He disappeared when we got to Plemenza."

"Osa is an agent of the Grail Empire. One of our finest. He was a gift to us from your master, Gordimer the Lion. But you know that already."

Else said nothing. He maintained his baffled expression and waited for the situation to show him the way to go.

"You'll remain stubborn to the end, won't you?"

"No. I told you already. I'll be anyone you want me to be. If I can just get out of here. Tell me about this Captain Tage and I'll do my best. As long as you don't put me anywhere where there's somebody that already knows him."

Rage flared behind Renfrow's eyes. For some reason he had a lot of emotion invested in getting Else to confess his true identity.

Osa Stile smiled thinly. Renfrow did not see him do so.

So. The boy might belong to Renfrow but he did not love the man. Good to know.

Renfrow turned. "Tell me, boy. Is this the man you knew as Captain Else Tage of the Sha-lug?"

"He looks a little like Tage. But with an awful lot of wear and age on him. If he is, I don't how you'd prove it. Anyway, I think he's too tall."

Amusing. Osa was giving Renfrow nothing.

Ferris Renfrow stared at Osa Stile for half a minute. The boy did not flinch. He was Sha-lug on the inside.

Renfrow rose and patrolled the circumference of the room, as though hunting the little night things rumored to be used as spies by sorcerers and such. He completed two full, careful circuits before he resumed his seat.

"All right. We'll do it your way. You'll be Else Tage, Dreangerean spy, for me, because that'll help get you out of confinement."

Else sat quietly. He waited.

"But from now on you're going to be an agent of the Grail Empire, too. It shouldn't be long before the Emperor releases Principaté Doneto. It looks like the Patriarch will give up trying to wait us out. Things aren't going well for him. He needs Doneto's support in the Collegium.

"I understand that the Principaté plans to keep all of you as part of his lifeguard. With you near him the Emperor could have someone close to one of the men closest to the Patriarch."

Else said nothing.

"Well?"

"And if I decline?"

"Then you'll never leave the Dimmel Palace. You'll never do your Dreangerean masters a lick of good."

Else grunted, unsurprised.

"So you won't forget us as soon as you get out of here, we'll have you sign a contract. We'll give it to the Principaté if you fail us."

Else grunted again. "Tell me about the pay. I won't do it just because you twist my arm."

"You want to get out of here?"

"I told you I'd be your foreigner so I can get out. Once I'm out, I need to make a living."

"The Principaté will be . . ."

"He'll pay me for working for him. There has to be balance. The workman must be given his due." Was he being too clever? Although common to most religions, that notion was a pronounced favorite of the Maysalean Heresy.

Osa Stile said, "Don't be such a damned skinflint, Renfrow. It isn't your money."

They argued. Was that for show? Was Osa Stile diverting Renfrow from thoughts of Dreanger, Gordimer, and the Sha-lug?

Had he been able, Else would have slipped away. He muttered, "Being a prisoner does limit one's choices."

Ferris Renfrow turned to Else. "Tage. I'm finished with you. For now. You know where we stand. I'll see you again. Be prepared to sign on with the Grail Emperor. You'll be paid well." Renfrow rang a bell.

* * *

ELSE MADE SURE NO ONE COULD EAVESDROP. HE TOLD PRINCI-paté Doneto, "They're trying to force me to spy for them against you and the Church."

"Tell me."

Else left out little but Renfrow's insistence that he be Else Tage.

"Here's what we'll do. You go ahead and agree. I'll get you a job outside my own household. Cooperate. Build their trust. And someday we'll use that."

"Of course." That was his own plan. Better to let Doneto verbalize it, though. Part of that development of trust thing.

Doneto said, "Go tell tales. I'm sure the others have had of-fers from that devil Renfrow, too. And service to the Emperor would be attractive to a certain sort."

"Renfrow?" Else asked.

"Ferris Renfrow is the man trying to enlist you. He's one of Johannes's favorites. Baseborn but one of the most powerful men in the Grail Empire despite that."

Else joined Pinkus Ghort, Just Plain Joe, and Bo Biogna. They were working on a cheese and a salami and did not have much mouth to spare. Biogna did ask, "You feeling better now, Pipe?"

"Some. I don't think they drugged me this time. I'm hungry. Give me some of that cheese." In the nature of things, the salami would be mostly pork. "And give me one of those sausages you're trying to hide, Pinkus." That would be pork, too. But it would be juicy and tasty and about the only thing he would miss when this captivity came to an end.

Scowling, Ghort asked, "What was all that with the Princi-paté?"

"I was holding him up. The Imperials want to recruit me for a campaign to establish the Emperor's rights in cities that are supposed to belong to him. Bo. Joe. Did you guys tell them something to make me look good? They seem to think they can trust me with my own battalion."

"Shit." Ghort did not sound happy. "And I was thinking about giving you another sausage."

"What?"

"I'm jealous. They didn't offer me nothing that good. And I did every bit as good a job as you did."

"Better. I've only got three of my guys still in one piece. And the only one of them worth two dead flies is a mule."

"But a real special mule," Bo Biogna said.

"Hey!" Joe growled. "Don't go making fun."

Ghort said, "Calm down, Joe. We all know that Pig Iron is the best man."

Else asked, "So what did they want from you, Pinkus?" He wondered if Ghort would tell the same story twice.

"Mainly, to stick with the Principaté and report back what the Church is up to. Same thing they probably asked everybody to do."

"They didn't ask me," Joe said. "They never asked me much of anything, neither time."

"Me, neither," Biogna grumbled. "Story of my life. I'd a done it. Double pay. An' I got no use for neither side, so let me get fuckin' rich sellin' them both out to each other."

Else told him, "They probably realized that, Bo. You were probably too eager."

"Yeah. I ain't so bright sometimes."

During the day all of the captives enjoyed a few minutes with the inquisitors. Six of the first twelve men to go did not return. Imperial people came for their possessions. As always, those refused to talk.

"Something's going on," Ghort declared, compelled to state the obvious.

Else grunted. "And they haven't pulled in you, me, Bo, Joe, or the Principaté yet."

"Don't forget Pig Iron."

"I haven't. But they have. You notice, they never question him."

"We ought to complain."

"You go first."

Just Plain Joe was the next soldier taken. He was back ten minutes later, grinning from ear to ear. "I done it, Pipe. I guv 'em nine kinds a hell on account of they don't respect Pig Iron the way they do the rest of the troops."

"Good for you, Joe," Ghort said. "I'm gonna do that myself. Pipe, I figure we're about to get out of here. That's the only way all this makes sense. The guys not coming back are the ones going over to Johannes."

Only Bronte Doneto himself remained to be called again when Else was taken for the last time.

ELSE TWITCHED AND SHRUGGED, UNCOMFORTABLE AND ITCHY in badly fitted formal clothing. He wore it in order to escort Bronte Doneto to an audience with the Grail Emperor.

Pinkus Ghort kept reminding him, "I told you so."

Principaté Doneto was not pleased. Ghort and Else were his only supporting cast. He felt he deserved an entourage. He was a Prince of the Church. He was a cousin of the Patriarch. He had Patriarchs among his ancestors, despite Church policies concerning clerical celibacy.

"We should've brought Pig Iron," Ghort said. "We could've dressed him as ugly as us, no problem."

Else scratched and fidgeted. "Pig Iron would've been more comfortable than I am. And wouldn't feel half as ridiculous."

Doneto grinned, but that flash of polished teeth vanished immediately. The Prince of the Church took over. The Principaté scowled, impatient with this familiar humor.

The Counts of Plemenza had been wealthy. Recollections of that wealth remained, though the Truncella themselves were out of the Dimmel Palace and lived on only in circumstances so reduced that they could afford staffs of fewer than forty servants.

The antechamber where the three waited boasted silk-upholstered furniture, oil portraits of past Truncella greats, busts that appeared to have survived from antiquity, and a tapestry from the last century portraying a confrontation between Chaldarean crusaders and Praman warriors.

Noting Else's interest, the Principaté reported, "That would be the Battle of the Well of Remembrance. I had an ancestor die in that battle."

"Ah!" A closer examination of the banners portrayed helped.

Sha-lug remembered it as the Battle of the Four Armies, an abomination in which Praman fought Praman, with the Arnhanders aiding the weaker side. At the time the Kaifate of Qasr al-Zed and the Kaifate of al-Minphet were struggling for control of the eastern approaches to the Wells of Ihrian. The Lucidians had help from the Crusader states. The Sha-lug were supported by swarms of Ishoti tribal auxiliaries out of Peqaa.

The battle did not take place near the Well of Remembrance. The westerners named it for the Well because both sides were hurrying to grab it before the other could get there. An unplanned encounter battle took place on the eastern edge of the Plain of Judgment. Thanks to the insanely fanatic Ishoti the situation devolved into chaos. Each side brought more and more swords up to support those already engaged. The epic slaughter swept back and forth until the mercurial Ishoti suddenly lost their taste for blood and ran away.

The battle, by whatever name, was the bloodiest of the long contest for control of the Holy Lands. And the least decisive. It changed nothing.

A year later the Sha-lug and crusaders joined forces to evict the Lucidians from those few territories they had captured after the Battle of the Four Armies.

In the Holy Lands alliances were as fluid as imagination, treachery, and shortsightedness could write them.

Pinkus Ghort said, "Pipe's folks were still pagan when that cluster fuck went down."

A majordomo type materialized. "His Imperial Majesty will see you now." He bowed slightly to the Principaté.

"Show time." Ghort began to adjust his clothing. He and Else followed the Principaté, two steps behind, flanked out to either side.

The audience hall was unimpressive. It was a room fifteen feet by twenty-something. The only furniture was one heavy wooden chair. That was occupied by a dark, ugly little man. He was dressed as though he planned to ride to the hunt once he got this unpleasant chore out of the way. This was Hansel, Johannes Blackboots, the Grail Emperor, Elector of Kretien, and terror of Sublime V's cohorts.

The Emperor wore black boots. Of course.

Else pegged him immediately as a man determined to live up to the reputation awarded him by rumor. He liked being the Ferocious Little Hans.

At least twenty people crowded the room, mostly men with shields and spears. They lined the walls. A handful of unarmed people surrounded the Emperor. Three of those appeared to be Johannes's children. Two were attractive young women. The third was a thin, pallid boy. The men posed nearest Johannes would be his closest advisers.

Those deserved close study. Particularly the one who was not Ferris Renfrow. But Else could not concentrate. His attention had been arrested by the woman who must be the Emperor's younger daughter, Helspeth.

Strangely, the impact seemed mutual and electric.

Else forced himself to focus. Critical things could happen. A prince of the Church was engaged with the most powerful lord in the west. The future might be shaped here. That ugly little man, Johannes Ege, troubled men as self-confident as Sublime V. Else's next few years would find him—he hoped—intimately involved in the affairs of the Church and all these men.

His attention stole back to Helspeth.

Helspeth was young enough to get away with considering him frankly.

Helspeth Ege was taller than her father by a hand. She was thin by prevailing standards, in Firaldia and Dreanger both. The most desirable women were expected to be more substantial, more rounded. Helspeth was too slight even by the standards of her own people. In the Grail Empire, particularly in the north, women were supposed to have hips and muscles, possibly so they could give birth while pulling a plow.

Helspeth's features suggested exotic ancestry. Her eyes were large and dark. Her hair was almost an oriental black. It fell straight, in a single heavy braid that hung down past her waist. Her mouth was wide and her lips prominent, almost puffy. Her nose, though, was small and pointed. She looked like she might have freckles. The light was not good enough to say for sure, nor to reveal the exact color of her eyes.

Except for the ugly, she seemed very much her father's daughter. Which meant that her older sister Katrin must take after her mother.

Other than being tall and slim, the sisters shared little in appearance. Katrin's hair was blond almost to the point of being white. Her eyes were small, narrow, and appeared to be an icy blue. That hinted at a mean streak. Her mouth was a severe slash, almost lipless and definitely colorless. At a glance, Else guessed that Katrin Ege did not like the world very much and suspected that on close acquaintance that feeling might be reflected right back. Katrin's clothing suggested an austere, inflexible personality. It was of a quality consistent with her station but plain, white, and a very pale, washed-out, misty sort of bluish-green. She could pass as one of the more exotic strains of Episcopal nuns.

Katrin's gaze swept across Else once, like a moving beam of winter. Then it went away. And stayed away.

Not so Helspeth's interest. Helspeth kept trying to concentrate on her father but her gaze refused to shun Else for long.

He noted, further, that the younger sister was more blessed with breasts. Seemed to be, anyway. Imperial style did not contrive to flatter women in that arena.

Else could not work out why the girl had such an impact. And she was, really, just a girl. And he was a married man with familial obligations.

And Helspeth Ege was the daughter of an emperor.

The atmosphere in this realm of Unbelievers must have stricken him with a brain fever. He had no business even noticing the woman except as an accoutrement of the Grail Emperor's court.

Bronte Doneto's interview with Emperor Johannes went as those things could be expected to. Platitudes were exchanged. Not one forthright word was spoken.

Doneto nearly lost control when he learned that the Patriarch had not yet committed to his ransom. "Sublime agrees in principal," Johannes said. "But he just doesn't want to turn loose any money. If he does, his effort to force the Connec to bend the knee will be crippled. Which is the point of the exercise from where I sit."

Hansel ended the diplomatic hot air just that simply. He continued, "I had you brought up from the underworld because my agents tell me Sublime is ready to face reality. That he's pulling the ransom together. Which isn't going as well as he hoped. Most Devedian moneylenders won't do business with a man who says he wants to exterminate them. Odd. Plus, a lot of people in Brothe aren't eager to have you back."

Else concentrated. Personalities and conflicts were of paramount interest. If Collegium members could be bribed, say, it might be possible to avoid war altogether.

The Sha-lug sang the glories of war and worked hard at preparing themselves for it, but, because they knew it intimately, they were not at all averse to pursuing alternatives.

Bronte Doneto said, "Any man who achieves any stature through his own efforts accumulates enemies. Envy is the most common human failing. You must be familiar with this yourself."

"Indeed I am. You could say that the envy of the Church is at the root of my conflict with the Patriarch."

The Grail Emperor was having fun. He had Sublime V by the short hairs. "So I'm bringing you upstairs, as my guest, until those who love you buy your vote back."

Doneto held his tongue. With obvious difficulty.

Else studied Johannes and his advisers. The Emperor was more than just short and ugly. His frame was twisted slightly. He had a small hump. It was easy to see why someone might not take him seriously. Possibly the other Imperial Electors had counted on his deformities to get him out of the way sooner than later.

Hansel's features were more pronouncedly oriental that Helspeth's. One of the invading tribes that pulled the Old Empire down must have camped near the Ege family tree.

Johannes had made himself the most powerful Grail Emperor yet. If an equally powerful personality had not resided in Brothe, the Empire might have engulfed the hundred states of Firaldia. The Patriarchy might have become an extension of the Grail Emperor's power.

Interesting times. Two mighty men. Both wanted to be lord of the world, king of kings. Excellent for the sons of al-Prama—until one subdued the other. While they fought, men like Indala al-Sul Halaladin and Gordimer the Lion might purge the Holy Lands of crusader states.

Which would fire the contest between the kaifates of Qasr al-Zed and al-Minphet. And waken the inscrutable ambitions of the Rhûn emperors. And, at a remove, there was Tsistimed the Golden and the Hu'n-tai At, the doom now breaking against the far borders of the Ghargarlicean Empire.

The man with Johannes who was not Ferris Renfrow was unfamiliar. Else studied him. The man might have been decoration for all the interest he showed.

Helspeth was eyeballing him again, her interest so frank that Else suspected Ferris Renfrow had rehearsed her as a distraction.

Pinkus Ghort's sudden touch startled Else. "Wake up! We're leaving."

What? Had he become that distracted?

Apparently so. And the Principaté was not pleased.

BRONTE DONETO MOVED TO AN APARTMENT ON THE FOURTH floor of the Dimmel Palace. His imprisonment was no less real, however. He was given three servants, all of whom could be trusted to report to Ferris Renfrow. He was allowed to keep Pinkus Ghort and Else as bodyguards, though they remained unarmed. They could not leave the apartment except for religious services in a small secondary chapel. Where they saw only the same people they had seen every day since the ambush.

Of those who came to Plemenza with Doneto, nine took service with the Grail Emperor. Two succumbed to ill health. So, besides Ghort, Else, Bo, and Joe, only three men chose to stick with the Principaté. Two were the last survivors of Doneto's original lifeguard. The other, Gitto Boratto, a Vangelin, was obviously a spy.

The Patriarch continued to procrastinate. His reluctance to pay had no limit. Crucial tasks of the Church remained untended because of deadlocks in the Collegium.

"WAKE UP, PIPE!" GHORT SHOUTED ONE MORNING, LONG BEfore Else's shift with the Principaté. "We're moving out. The ransom money finally showed up."

"Really?"

"Really. Himself says so."

And well past time. It was spring outside. Else grumbled, "At least we got through the winter without freezing."

Ghort chuckled. He knew perfectly well that Else was sick of Bronte Doneto and even more sick of Pinkus Ghort.

Ghort prophesied, "You may not have to strangle me after all."

Else suspected that, for all he complained about everyone he ever met, Pinkus Ghort had no nerves to be rubbed raw by interminable proximity.

"Maybe. But don't push your luck. What happened? Why the sudden turnaround?"

"Pirates."

"What? You want me to brain you? What's with the cryptic answer?"

"I mean it. Pirates from Calzir are all over the place, suddenly. Raiding both coasts. I'm sure there's a story. But all I've heard is, the raiders are picking on the Church and the Benedocto family holdings."

Piracy was an old-time favorite sport of Calzir's Pramans. At times buccaneering offered better prospects than any more mundane career. At least until the appearance of the Firaldian mercantile republics. Those ferocious capitalists were less forgiving than feeble counts and dukes and kings. The men they sent to scour out the pirates' home villages and harbors were deadly, cruel, and thorough.

Else said as much. "They couldn't be that stupid. Could they?"

"Why ask me? All I know is, we're getting out of here. You want to argue about it, take it up with the Principaté. Or the Patriarch next time you see him. Or those lunatic Calzirans."

"All right. All right. I'm just amazed at humanity's boundless capacity for making stupid choices." How could the Calzirans have grown so contemptuous of reality? Sublime was looking for excuses to preach a crusade. Did they believe that Sonsa, Dateon, and Aparion would look away? Hell. Maybe they did. The Devedian uprisings, fomented by the Brotherhood of War and Patriarchal agitators, might have made the republics withdraw protection from areas not their direct dependents.

Else asked, "Do you know where the raids were? Only Patriarchal States got hit?"

Ghort shrugged. "They didn't call me into any councils, Pipe. They told me to wake your ass up and get ready to hike. And hike for real, because we ain't getting our horses back. So, if you don't mind, get shaking. I'll get Pig Iron and the boys stirring."

THEY MADE A PATHETIC LITTLE BAND LEAVING PLEMENZA. The anonymous Braunsknechts captain watched from the gateway, as though to make sure they really went away.

There were seven of them. The Principaté, Else, and Ghort. Bo Biogna and Just Plain Joe. Plus Bergos Delmareal and Gadjeu Tifft. The spy who had intended to stick with Doneto, Gitto Boratto, was too sick to travel. Which was a genuine coincidence. Boratto came down with the runs the afternoon before the ransom arrived. Bo thought Boratto's troubles were due to a rich diet that was his reward for spying.

So Delmareal and Tifft were reliable. Delmareal was an exile from one of the smaller Chaldarean kingdoms in Direcia, absorbed by Navaya shortly after Peter became king. Delmareal had no inclination to go home.

Gadjeu Tifft hailed from Croizat, a tiny state on the Creveldian coast across the narrow Vieran Sea, east of Firaldia. The details of his story were protean. Men did stupid, impulsive things when they were young.

Tifft did not seem bright enough to be an agent of the Rhûn, though Croizat and all of Creveldia belonged to the Eastern Empire.

No matter. The shores of the Mother Sea crawled with displaced men who, often in some way that they did not comprehend, found themselves far from anyone or anything they knew. They survived by signing on with some warlord.

The Bronte Donetos were always there.

Doneto was in good health now and eager to get home. He pushed as hard as Pig Iron allowed. And Pig Iron was in a mood to put Plemenza behind him.

Pinkus Ghort started grumbling before the first day was halfway done. "Good thing we spent so much time staying in shape, eh? That's paying dividends now." Else was one of few prisoners who had made an effort to stay fit. Ghort was not.

Even the Principaté had to walk. Possibly, Hansel thought, that might inspire him to rein in his natural arrogance.

Only a brace of ancient donkeys had been given the privilege of becoming Pig Iron's associates in the transport department.

Doneto wanted to plot against the future. He told Else, "As soon as we get to Brothe, before anybody even sees you, I'm going to set you up with Draco Arniena. He'll take you on because, although he opposes Sublime publicly, in secret he's our ally."

Doneto bubbled with eagerness to plunge into Brothe's ferocious political dialogue.

19. Andorayans in Brothe

Shagot and Svavar survived by theft and violence while they learned enough Firaldian to get by. Then they worked their way up the ranks of strong-arm men. They started as bouncers in one of Brothe's more riotous waterfront dives, then became wholesale butchers on behalf of an association of shopkeepers grown weary of paying protection to gangs who did not protect them from other gangs demanding protection money.

They had a miraculous knack for surviving. Their cold-bloodedness intimidated the most hardened Brothen criminals. It took just months to convince a superstitious underworld that they could not be touched but would happily obliterate anyone who even *thought* about getting in their way.

Shagot learned that producing the monster head while using weapons from the old battlefield in the White Hills left him and Svavar invulnerable. He did not understand why. He did not care. It was sufficient that he was doing the work of the gods.

The brothers had no trouble being coldly murderous because they were so far out of their own time that they did not see people of the present as entirely human.

This was like butchering chickens. When Shagot could stay awake. Shagot slept up to sixteen hours a day.

Their work came to the attention of Father Syvlie Obilade, who had a special place in the household of the Bruglioni family. The Bruglioni were one of the Five Families of Brothe. They were long-time enemies of the Benedocto. Father Obilade told the brothers they would enjoy an easier, more profitable life if they put their talents on retainer to the Bruglioni.

Shagot had nothing but contempt for Father Obilade. "They're all oil and slime, these Chaldarean priests," he told Svavar. "I'd love to see them delivered to the mercies of the Old Ones. Especially these shit-for-brains Brothen priests. All they're interested in is getting hold of power. Their screams would be sweet music."

Svavar did not reply. He seldom spoke anymore. He did what Shagot required of him, however bloody, insane, or cruel, while abiding his release from his obligations to his gods.

The biggest handicap endured by the brothers was Shagot's sleep compulsion. That worsened almost daily.

SYLVIE OBILADE WAS NOT A BLOOD MEMBER OF THE Bruglioni. He was a boyhood friend of Soneral Bruglioni, who would be the Bruglioni chieftain today if he had not somehow managed to swallow a fatal dose of poison during the maneuvering prior to the election of Honario Benedocto. The priest's apparent loyalty now lay with Soneral's brother, Paludan.

Paludan Bruglioni overflowed with rage and hatred. Paludan Bruglioni's whole being revolved around those. All Brothe believed Father Obilade did nothing to soften Paludan's dark obsessions. Indeed, perhaps, he nurtured Paludan's abhorrence of those who favored the Benedocto Patriarchy.

Sylvie Obilade tried to be a good priest. But he had wrestled with his own faith for years.

Shagot and Svavar entered Father Obilade's small, dank room. The stench of mold and mildew beset them. Discarded clothing lay in the corners, damp and decaying, gifts never worn.

The priest never changed his filthy, tattered smock. His personal odors were powerful, too. "Thank you for coming." His voice was raspy, damaged permanently by the mold in the air.

Shagot exchanged glances with his brother. This ragged old skeleton was one of the more powerful men in Brothe. Which was why Shagot had listened when the priest recruited him.

The view is always better from a high place. From a high enough vantage Shagot thought he could see all the way to the man he was supposed to find.

Father Obilade teetered on the brink of his fiftieth year but a lifetime of self-abuse had him looking seventy. He ate only unleavened bread and drank nothing but water. On holy days he rewarded himself by fasting.

Shagot considered him a madman. He rumbled, "You said your boss would pay well. So we came."

Svavar asked, "Have you found out anything about the man we're seeking?"

The priest was puzzled momentarily. Then, "Oh. The mystery man from the orient. No. Not yet. No one knows anything. But Brothe is big and the search is of no urgency to anyone but you. And the hunt has only just begun."

Shagot grunted, tormented by the alien urgency coiled within him. He forced it down. "You have work for us or not?"

The smelly old man twitched. He had moral qualms about what he had been told to engineer.

The Grimmssons did not yet realize that they had been retained only because the Bruglioni family could deny them. And because they could be used up in some scheme down the road, where deniability would be particularly appetizing.

Father Obilade had spent a lifetime deluding himself. But he was not stupid. He knew Paludan Bruglioni did not intend to exploit these foreigners for the glory of God. But it might be possible that what served the Bruglioni could benefit God as well. This was the mission Sylvie Obilade set himself daily, to weave his day into the grand tapestry of God's master plan.

It is an easy intellectual step to the conviction that whatever you do must be part of God's plan. Justification for villainy knows no intellectual constraint.

Shagot said, "It reeks in here, old man. Why don't you clean this shit out?" And, before Father Obilade could respond, "What *do* you want? You woke me up. So get to the point."

"The Patriarch plans to rectify his weakness in the Collegium by creating new Principaté positions disguised as the presentation of honors to stalwart defenders of the faith."

Shagot snorted. He did not understand Episcopal politics.

"Sublime will nominate three men of three apparently diverse viewpoints: one enemy of Sublime, one ally, and one disinterested outlander unlikely to assume his seat. These seats won't be permanent." Most Principatés served only in their own names, for life. But the Five Families colluded to make sure each clan held at least one seat at all times. You had to be a Principaté to be elected Patriarch. "They'll pass away when these individuals go to their heavenly rewards."

Again, Shagot snorted. "Why should I care about that shit?"

"Rodrigo Cologni has made a secret agreement with Sublime. After his confirmation he'll change sides and vote with Sublime's party in return for castles and estates he can distribute to his children."

The purportedly celibate fathers of the Church could be fathers in the literal sense. They failed to admit the hypocrisy.

"Once these nominations go through and Bronte Doneto returns, Sublime will have a three-vote advantage in the Collegium. But Sublime's plans aren't in the best interest of God's Church. Therefore . . ."

Shagot suspected that the Chadarean god was old enough to look out for himself. "You want somebody killed."

"Crudely put, but, yes. Though it isn't as simple as that. There'll be a clamor if Rodrigo Cologni is murdered. That can't be connected with the Bruglioni."

Shagot was not brilliant but he was a cunning villain. Things fell into place instantly.

He and Svavar would kill this Rodrigo Cologni and, somehow, before they could be arrested and questioned, brave Bruglioni household fighters who arrived too late would kill them while supposedly trying to save Cologni. Or some variant on such a scheme.

"How much time do we have to get ready?"

"It needs to happen within the next twenty days. Before Bronte Doneto returns."

"I'll sleep on it. I'll see what the physical situation is. Do you have somebody inside the Cologni household?" Shagot thought it likely that the Five Families all had spies inside the others' houses.

Father Obilade was exasperated. These outlanders were too clever, by half. But he had to use the tools at hand.

"Why is that of concern?" the priest asked.

"Because we need to know the target's movements. His plans. We can't just march into the Cologni compound to get him."

"Access won't be a problem. Rodrigo Cologni is a whoremaster. He's determined to enjoy as many women as he can before it's too late to futter another. He goes looking for new whores at least three nights a week."

"Good. Good. That'll make it easier." Rodrigo did not sound

bright. Far safer to have women brought to him. "How big a mob follows him around?"

"There haven't been any family wars for a generation. The Five Families want to avoid the excesses of the past. So Rodrigo only needs to worry about robbers. He'll have four body-guards. And maybe a few friends. None of those have to die. But the Cologni bodyguards may be a challenge."

"Uh. Like I said. Let me sleep on it. Let me look it over. Find out whatever you can about Rodrigo Cologni. Be ready to say yes when I name our price."

Once they left the crazy priest, Svavar observed, "They plan to use us up."

"They mean to try. But they don't understand our luck. Let's have a little fun with them." Clever evil was Shagot's sole remaining pleasure.

The Walker himself strode through Shagot's dreams that night.

FATHER OBILADE, OF COURSE, WANTED SHAGOT TO WAIT TILL after the job to get paid. Shagot laughed. That after Svavar spent dozens of hours studying Rodrigo Cologni and the Cologni compound. Which, like the homes of all of the Five Families, was a fortress. Literally.

Shagot replied, "I'm inclined to go along, old man. I mean, why would a priest try to cheat me? But my brother Asgrimmur, he says he didn't just fall off the turnip cart. He's naturally suspicious. Especially of anybody who chooses to live in these southern cities, where honor and the value of a man's word are considered trivial. Well, he's my brother. I've got to keep him happy. So what we're gonna do is, we're gonna take a third for each of us right now, then we'll pick up the rest afterward."

Father Obilade had not yet recovered from hearing Shagot's price for Rodrigo Cologni's life, six hundred gold Patriarchal ducats.

Nor did he like the demand for two-thirds payment up front. He could not make that deal, anyway. Paludan Bruglioni had not put that much specie at his disposal.

Paludan had a powerful desire to turn loose as little money as possible because he might not get it back.

Paludan had a reputation for squeezing a ducat till the Patriarch thereon squealed like a eunuch undergoing his signature procedure.

Father Obilade confessed, "I can't go with that. I wasn't given the power. Your fee is . . . I suppose *excessive* isn't the right word. You pay the most when you buy the best. Meet me here same time, night after tomorrow night. I'll warn Caniglia that you're coming."

"We'll be here," Shagot promised cheerfully. "I'm looking forward to taking your money." And he was. He had found a Deve who would invest it at an excellent rate of return. He had no idea what he would do with his wealth, but that did not concern him. He was enjoying life as much as he ever had.

He did not sit around. He sent Svavar out to dog Rodrigo.

Father Obilade wanted the attack to take place in the Madhur Plaza, as near Basbanes's Fountain as could be managed. In response to questions about why, the priest shrugged and said the location had personal meaning for Paludan.

Shagot examined the plaza personally, and had Svavar do so repeatedly, by day and by night. The site seemed ideal for what the priest wanted done. There were numerous excellent lurking places where heroic rescuers could wait to charge out and, to their eternal sorrow, be just moments too late to save Rodrigo Cologni.

Rodrigo Cologni was an assassination begging to happen. He was predictable in the extreme. He left the Cologni compound at the same time every time. And he followed the same route to the same whorehouses.

FATHER OBILADE YIELDED TO SHAGOT'S FINANCIAL DEMANDS. He turned over four hundred of the six hundred ducats two days before Rodrigo's scheduled early elevation to Heaven. Shagot told the priest, "We'll follow your script if we can, but we'll change shit around if anything comes up."

The old priest scowled. "Just get it done."

SVAVAR AND SHAGOT MOVED INTO THE MADHUR PLAZA hours ahead of time. They brought all their trophies and fetishes. Even Svavar felt optimistic. "Going to be some real surprised assholes, Grim. Going to be some real surprised assholes."

Shagot chuckled. "Yeah. Going to be some good laughs on Father Obilade and Paludan fucking Bruglioni and his butt boy, Gervase. So. Let's fade into the fucking background and let the drama begin."

They did not stand out. Brothe drew countless pilgrims from everywhere. Basbanes's Fountain was a sight the foreigners all wanted to see. It had a history almost as long as that of the Old Empire itself.

Rodrigo Cologni passed through the plaza, outward bound, escorted only by his bodyguards. Shagot and Svavar felt even more confident.

A city watchman reminded them, "No sleeping in the plaza, gents."

"Not to worry," Shagot replied in credible Firaldian. "We've got a place to stay. We work for Paludan Bruglioni." He grinned and chuckled. The sergeant would remember that later.

Svavar laughed softly, too. He was having a good time. For the first time since they had come out of the Great Sky Fortress, he was happy to be alive, partly because he thought they were putting one over on the gods themselves.

"Hey," Shagot said, "we need to get out of sight. The Bruglioni gang should turn up pretty soon."

They slipped into the deep shadows between two buildings. Svavar asked, "You think the Bruglioni guys will do the job if we just sit on our hands?"

Treachery was in the works. Shagot's dreams had confirmed that. But he had dreamed much more. Some of which he had not yet unraveled. What Svavar suggested fit.

"Excellent thinking, little brother. I don't know what they'd do. How about we give them the opportunity? We can always tag Rodrigo somewhere else, later."

The wait seemed both long and short. One of those things relative to the moment. Svavar had trouble controlling the giggles. That was when time fled its swiftest. Time dragged when he grew somber and thought about everything that could go wrong.

"Quiet," Svavar whispered. "Here's the boss's boys."

Six Firaldians stole past, visible briefly in the light of a rising sliver of moon. They went into hiding scarcely a dozen yards from where Shagot and Svavar had holed up.

"Did you recognize any of them?" Shagot asked in a whisper that could not be heard five feet away.

"This isn't going to be a happy night for the Bruglioni. I saw Gildeo and Acato Bruglioni for sure. One of the others looked like Saldi Serena." That put both sons and a nephew of Paludan Bruglioni among the condemned.

In the middle of the plaza the complex menagerie of Basbanes's Fountain kept spitting and peeing and pouring. The falling waters generated a soporific noise that Shagot found hard to fight.

The moon moved on to where its light would no longer betray someone who snaked out of the thin gap where Shagot and Svavar waited. Shagot murmured, "Hang on. I'm going to see if I can hear anything." Carrying the head from the Haunted Hills. Shagot stole toward where his would-be assassins waited. Soon he lay on his stomach inches from the mouth of the gap where the Bruglioni boys had gone to ground.

A heated argument was underway. Somebody wanted to know why the idiot foreigners had not shown. Someone told that one to shut the fuck up. It was not time, yet. Fifteen minutes from now, *then* they could start worrying.

One of the lesser Bruglioni insisted, "I could go a long way, for a long time, on four hundred ducats."

"Your whores would pick your bones within a week."

Shagot could be as patient as stone when he knew there was a point. He remained frozen, listening, as minutes, then tens of minutes slipped by. He listened as the Bruglioni gang grew ever more uneasy.

Their cat's-paws were supposed to have arrived by now. They had not shown. Had Paludan flung four hundred ducats into a great big black sack of nothing?

Soon it was way past time for Shagot and Svavar to be out there hanging around the fountain, a pair of drunken foreigners who looked threatening to no one but themselves. Most of the foreigners infesting the city were too stupid to tie their own bootlaces.

Shagot crept backward. It would not be long before Rodrigo

appeared. Already, it seemed, the Cologni was at the nether edge of the range of his behavior. He was late.

Drunken singing approached.

Rodrigo. And his bodyguards. And some drunks that the Cologni had accumulated during the evening.

This was something that Svavar had not seen before. It was out of character. "I definitely don't think we should do it now, Grim. I don't like the look of this."

Rodrigo's drinking buddies did not seem interested in getting on out of the Madhur Plaza. They stopped at Basbanes's Fountain and stalled around until Rodrigo's bodyguards insisted that Rodrigo get moving.

Shagot muttered, "I think I'll just go pound on that old priest till his balls fall off."

Svavar touched his arm. "There's some excitement starting."

The Bruglioni crew surrendered to the romance of their own stupidity. They rushed the party in the plaza.

As Shagot intuited, the drunken new friends were not drunk at all. But their level of alertness had dropped because no attack had come when expected at the fountain. On the other hand, Rodrigo's guards were sharply alert because of the pretend drunks' obvious stalls.

When the Bruglioni thugs rushed out, the Cologni bodyguards shoved knives into the backs of the pretend drunks.

The rush arrived. Blades flashed. Several men went down, one a Cologni bodyguard.

Then came a surprise second rush consisting of another half-dozen men who swooped in from the far side of the square. A great clangor ensued.

Both Gildeo and Acato Bruglioni thought well of themselves as duelists. They had reputations to support their confidence.

Their confidence was misplaced.

"These guys are fucking professionals," Shagot said. The new bunch were very good, though not good enough to avoid injuries of their own.

The speed and fury of the mess left the Bruglioni thugs and Rodrigo's bodyguards no chance to flee.

Shagot nodded to himself as the winners collected their prize—Rodrigo Cologni—and then their wounded. Those included the backstabbed companion drunks, who were still alive but unlikely to remain that way if they did not get to some skilled care soon. "Four of them are hurt bad. Two more have lesser wounds. As soon as they're out of sight, start tracking them. We need to find out who they are and where they're headed."

Svavar nodded unhappily. He was not feeling particularly bloodthirsty now. Which was, probably, why Grim was giving him this job while he stayed here.

Svavar knew Grim would have no trouble finding him later. Grim always knew where he was.

THE BRUGLIONI WERE TRYING TO PULL THEMSELVES TO-gether, to limp back to the family fortress, when Shagot strolled up. At this point, no one had yet been killed. But none of the Bruglioni or Cologni were in shape to fight on, either. Shagot cut a couple of throats, just to get everybody focused. One of those belonged to Acato Bruglioni, who had not been badly hurt before. His skill as a duelist did him no good what-soever.

Shagot told the rest, "I want to know what this was all about." He asked pointed questions, with a sword's tip encour-aging quick responses. He killed Saldi Serena when that young man tried to run.

Shagot learned that the setup had been what he guessed. He and Svavar were supposed to take the frame for murdering a man expected to support the Patriarch in the Collegium.

"And who stopped you?"

"That's what doesn't make no sense," Gildeo Bruglioni confessed. "Those were the Patriarch's wolves. The Brother-hood of War. They wouldn't have no reason to kidnap Ro-drigo Cologni. He's on their side. But those were the orders they had."

"Really?" Shagot set his undermind to work on that, and the fact that the Brotherhood attackers had been entirely familiar with what was supposed to be happening. "This is what you're going to do. Assuming you want to survive. Finish off those Cologni. Then start hiking. Fast as you can."

Reluctantly, Gildeo Bruglioni turned on Rodrigo's wounded bodyguards, none of whom were able to resist.

Gildeo finished, turned, discovered that Shagot had slain the rest of the Bruglioni crew. His mouth opened but nothing came out.

Shagot killed Gildeo with a single stroke that took the man's head right off. Then Shagot jogged off after his brother. How long would it be before people moved in to loot the dead? Shagot wondered if he ought not to have done so himself.

How big a stink would come from tonight's evils? A huge one, surely, once the evidence was examined.

Shagot grinned. This was fun.

Rodrigo Cologni's captors were headed toward the Teragi River and the Castella dollas Pontellas, which made sense if they were Brotherhood of War.

Shagot stopped trying to overtake his brother. He ranged out in front of his quarry instead.

Those men moved slowly, avoiding notice.

Shagot knew little about the Brotherhood of War. They were some kind of fighting priests, which sounded like a bad joke, considering the Chaldarean priests of his experience.

He ambushed the party from the side, after letting their point man pass the unnaturally impenetrable shadow in which he crouched. A shadow he did not recognize as unusual, only as handy.

Much happened around Shagot that he failed to notice.

He attacked with an ancient bronze sword in one hand and the demon's head in the other. He thought he was jumping in amongst priests like Sylvie Obilade. It seemed he could see in the dark tonight, a talent of considerable utility.

He had no trouble dropping the first four surprised and previously injured kidnappers he encountered. Then the point man returned and Shagot learned the truth about the fighting priests of the Brotherhood of War.

Shagot's opponent was like none he had faced since those far days when he and Erief practiced against one another. Only the fact that the darkness was no handicap gave Shagot any edge.

He kept dancing away, seizing fleeting chances to strike at the others. He had a chop at Rodrigo Cologni's hamstring when he noticed the old man trying to slip away.

Then Shagot found himself with his back to a wall. The best

of three attackers was directly in front of him. Another un-
wounded man came at him from his right while an injured but
capable fighter occupied him on his left, trying to get past the
scowling demon's head. All three were wary, cautious, professionals. Shagot would have been calling for the Choosers of
the Slain had he not seen his brother behind his attackers.

It was not easy, even so. Shagot suffered several wounds, including one that would have been permanently crippling had
he not been touched by the gods.

Svavar fared worse. The Old Ones had placed less of a
blessing on him. He suffered slash wounds to both arms and
stab wounds to his stomach and chest. They were serious but
needed not be fatal if handled quickly.

Shagot performed some hasty first aid, collected the dead—
making sure everyone but his brother belonged to that select
category—in a heap out of sight of passersby, then settled next
to Svavar, shoulder to shoulder, so that his own Great Sky
Fortress blessing would rub off.

Shagot the Bastard might be a festering mold on human
dung but he did love his little brother.

Shagot soon felt sleep trying to take control. He could not
let that happen. He had hours of must-do ahead of him, still.

"Little brother. Can you get up and stumble home now?"

Svavar grunted. He could do that. For Shagot's sake. Thanks
to Shagot. But he could not do much more, if Shagot wanted
something else.

"Good. So do that, then."

Svavar murmured, "We moved our stuff to the backup place."

"That's right! I'm having trouble keeping my eyes open and
my brain working. Go there and lay low. I'll wrap this shit up."

"Grim . . ."

"Go on. Can you carry something? Can you take this totem
stuff for me?"

"What're you going to do?"

"I'm going to go have a friendly chat with that asshole
priest. And make sure we get paid. Take this stuff and get moving." Shagot hugged his brother before the younger man
trudged away, carrying a thirty-pound load and a hundredweight of pain, picking his way through an unfamiliar city in
the dark, his destination a flat he had visited only once before.

*   *   *

THE BRONZE SWORD WAS THE ONLY ITEM OF POWER THAT
Shagot retained. It still cut dead flesh like slicing softened but-
ter. He completed his first task in three minutes. Then he set
about systematically relieving the dead of any coins they had
been carrying when misfortune overtook them.

The Brothers were not rich men but amongst them they did
carry as broad a variety of coin as could be imagined. Shagot
failed to recognize the origins of most.

No matter. Merchants would know them. And would weigh
them, too. They trusted no one. And trusted those with big
names and big reputations least of all.

Plundering done, Shagot slung his sack of heads over one
shoulder, then retraced his route to the Madhur Plaza.

The sack was actually a shirt taken off the largest of the
dead Brothers.

Shagot's wounds ached terribly. He worried about Asgrimmur, hoped the gods had sense enough to protect his brother.
His mission was doomed without Asgrimmur's help.

He returned to the Mahdur Plaza. The massacre in the
square had been discovered. The bodies had been plundered.
Now the righteous folk, with torches and lanterns, were out tut-
tutting and recalling the good old days when there was order in
Brothe and things like this just did not happen where the right
sort of people had to look at it.

Such was human nature.

Shagot headed for the Bruglioni citadel. He might be able to
get there before the bad news arrived.

THE APPOINTED TRADESMEN'S GATE WAS AJAR AND UN-
guarded. Shagot moved through the Bruglioni back court to
Father Obilade's quarters. The priest's door opened instantly.
Sylvie Obilade and another man waited behind it. An unfamiliar voice demanded, "What the hell took you so . . . ?" The
speaker realized that Shagot was alone. And that Shagot was
Shagot. He gawked. Father Obilade gawked. The first man
dropped a hand to the hilt of a dueling sword but did not draw.
Shagot offered him a warning shake of the head.

"You owe me some money, old man." Shagot produced the head of Rodrigo Cologni.

"Sweet Aaron! Blessed Kelam!" Father Obilade made signs meant to ward off the evil eye and the Instrumentalities of the Night. "Did you have to . . . ?"

"You wouldn't just take my word, would you? You're Brothen. Easy there, fellow." The other man, pale as death now, had begun to ease away. "Stand still. I'm not happy tonight."

Shagot dumped his sack.

Both witnesses swore. They looked at one another in horror. The man with the sword gasped, "That's Strauther Arnot! And Junger Trilling! They're two of the top men from the Castella. What have you done? You killed eight of them?" There were eight heads in addition to that of Rodrigo Cologni.

"My brother helped."

"Eight of them. Brotherhood veterans. Just the two of you. What have I conjured?"

Shagot thought this might be Paludan Bruglioni. He said, "We had to kill them. They were taking off with the target."

"What have you done?" the priest whimpered, to himself rather than Shagot.

Shagot sneered. "You've been asking yourselves a question ever since you realized that this was me. You may not like the answer. Let's get comfortable and wait. You. Give me that pig-sticker. You don't want to do something stupid and get yourself killed. You the boss Bruglioni? Not gonna say? It don't matter. Let's you and this smelly old woman go sit by that fig tree. Where I can keep an eye on you."

Shagot drew the ancient sword. It seemed to radiate darkness. With that in hand, Shagot felt renewed. He would not fall asleep while the sword was drawn. He would feel no pain. With that blade in hand he felt as though he could slice through time itself.

The man who might be Paludan Bruglioni considered the old sword with contempt. But Father Obilade's eyes went wide. He whimpered, then commenced a swiftly cadenced, stammering appeal to his god for shelter from the malice of the Instrumentalities of the Night.

It took longer than Shagot expected for news from the Madhur Plaza to arrive. It was almost dawn. Evil, seductive sleep was doing its best to overwhelm the old sword's magic.

Sleep's insidious appeal ended when a small, lean, slightly shaggy man burst in, gasping, "There you are, Paludan! Terrible news! Terrible news! Acato, Gildeo, Faluda, Pygnus, the others . . . they're all gone! Lost! In the Madhur Plaza! Murdered! Along with all of Rodrigo Cologni's bodyguards."

The messenger was so excited that he continued to throw up words until, while straining for breath, he noticed Shagot and the heads. "Shit!"

"Indeed," Shagot said. He felt like a god. They were almost trivial, these southerners. "Slide over there with the others."

The newcomer considered the heads. "Oh, Blessed Kelam and the Fathers of the Church! That's Strauther Arnot! Secretary of the Special Office. What's going on, Paludan?"

Shagot surmised that this must be the deadly clever Gervase Saluda, Paludan Bruglioni's good friend from his youth, from a time when Paludan had slipped away at night to run with a gang of orphans and runaways. That legend was, likely, pure artifice. But Gervase's reputation might be deserved.

Shagot suggested, "Keep your hands where I can see them. Unless you think that set of heads is one short and yours would complete it."

"He's soultaken," Father Obilade whined. "Don't defy him. He can't be defeated. That old sword . . . It was forged back when the tyranny of the night ruled the world complete."

"Thank you," Shagot told him. "What the crone says is true. And this is true, too. The men you sent to murder my brother and me failed. They murdered Rodrigo Cologni's bodyguards instead. These eight showed up while they were at it. They killed everybody but Cologni. They took him away with them. My brother and I pursued them. We had a contract with the Bruglioni. They refused to cooperate. So we took their heads, thinking we might earn a bonus by fulfilling the Bruglioni revenge for you." Shagot used a toe to propel a head toward Paludan Bruglioni. It rolled over on its nose and changed course toward Gervase Saluda.

"What have you done?" Paludan's plea was feeble and rhetorical.

"What demon rules your soul?" Father Obilade asked.

"What ancient horror have you hauled into the modern age, into the heartland of the Episcopal faith?"

Shagot said, "You owe me two hundred gold ducats. Plus a bonus for avenging your dead."

Paludan Bruglioni surrendered to the will of the night. "Obilade. Get the money the man wants. Don't get into any mischief along the way. You understand me?"

The priest bowed. "Yes, sir."

Shagot understood, too. "Excellent. And hurry. Because if that money doesn't get here fast, with no treachery, people will die."

Once Father Obilade was gone, Shagot kicked another head and said, "These Brotherhood people knew exactly what was supposed to happen in the Madhur Plaza. How could that be?"

"What have you done?" Paludan whined again.

I have shaken Brothe's foundation stones, Shagot thought.

Never in all his life had he had so much impact upon others. Not even at the height of the sturlanger raids on the coasts of the Isle of Eights had so many people who had no idea who he was suffered so much because of his actions.

"I'm just trying to make a living," Shagot replied. "I don't think that requires me to be sacrificed to some local half-wit's ambition."

Father Obilade returned. He brought more than three hundred ducats in gold coins bearing the likenesses of dead Patriarchs. Shagot checked a few to make sure they were real. "Good. Good. I hope you gentlemen don't resent the lesson in fair play." He crooked a finger at the old priest. "Closer, Father. Closer."

When the old man was close enough, Shagot leaned in to whisper, "These guys know what really happened, Padre. You'd better hike up your skirt and run." In a voice that carried, he continued, "Thanks, everyone. Try not to be such a bunch of weasels, eh?"

Shagot got out of there before sleep could hammer him down.

Touched by the favor of the night, he managed to rejoin his brother before he collapsed.

Once sleep came, though, it would not withdraw until Svavar neared a state of panic. Could his brother possibly survive?

20. Khaurene, in the End of Connec

Winter in the Connec was a season of worry. For those who tried to come to grips with what Arnhanders called the Black Mountain Massacre. Because the invaders insisted that that disaster was in no way their fault.

Well-meaning pilgrims had entered the Connec to help harried Episcopal coreligionists protect themselves from the predations of heretics who roasted babies and sacrificed virgins. Unless that went the other way around.

"That about sum up your position?" Count Raymone Garete flung at the obnoxious, insulting deformed hunchback of an envoy from Salpeno, Father Austen Rinpoché. "You couldn't invent something more ridiculous? You could've accused us of having sexual congress with goats. Fool. Our intransigent apostasy and heresy is why there's an active Episcopal church on every other corner in Khaurene. It's why there are more real cathedrals in the End of Connec than there are in all of your piss-drinking Pail of Arnhand. We built those cathedrals, of course, so we'd have somewhere to snuggle with our goats."

Duke Tormond tried to restrain the young noble. But Count Raymone was beyond restraint. Following his triumph over Baron Algres, Raymone's voice would be loud in the councils of the Connec. "You're speechless? A priest? Talk to me, priest. Name one Episcopal in the End of Connec who has suffered at the hands of the Seekers After Light."

Gleefully, Father Rinpoché retorted, "Bishop Serifs of Antieux."

Silence.

More silence.

Someone said, "Sweet Aaron on a jackass, the fool is serious."

Count Raymone sneered, "The priest isn't a fool. He's a league beyond. He's a complete idiot."

Even the Great Vacillator, Duke Tormond, stared at Father Rinpoché like he thought the man was a half-wit reveling in his debility. "*Are* you serious, Father? That man was a thief. He abused his office. He was indifferent to the rights of others. He was a perjurer, a pederast, and a sodomite. There's no end to the catalog of his crimes. Absent the protection of Sublime he would've been hung years ago. I did feel some sympathy for your mission until now. But we all know rats who deserve higher honors than Bishop Serifs."

Count Raymone snapped, "Serifs was such a waste that Principaté Bronte Doneto—the Patriarch's own cousin—had him thrown off a cliff after they failed to rob and murder the people of Antieux."

Father Rinpoché clung to his position.

Duke Tormond stood. He clasped his hands but let his arms hang. "I'm a good Episcopal, Father. I attend church every day. I never miss confession. I sent a letter to the Holy Father asking what more can possibly be expected. He hasn't replied. Meantime, we're here and, yet again, we're being subjected to unfounded and trumped-up charges by men whose interest in God's work is secondary to their hopes of plundering the Connec. Hear me, Rinpoché. In this hall, with you, is almost every man of substance in Khaurene. I challenge you to go among them and find one unbeliever."

Not the wisest challenge, in Brother Candle's view. He was there. And not alone in his inability to recognize the infallibility of Sublime V.

The Arnhander priest did not take the challenge. He refused to speak to it, or even to acknowledge it.

Rinpoché could only return to Salpeno and report that the Connec remained recalcitrant, intransigent, and that those agents of the Adversary, the Maysaleans, had gained hidden mastery. The sole practical answer appeared to be the one the Patriarch was pushing privately, a crusade to extinguish the Maysalean Heresy.

The powerful in Salpeno had no trouble accepting Father Rinpoché's arguments. Most hungered for revenge, for plunder, and had little interest in any truth that got in their way. They had, as well, a feeble king unable to execute his royal duties while remaining equally incompetent at dying. Though his death would avail nothing. There was no crown prince.

That looked sweet to a spectrum of ambitious dukes, barons, and relations legitimate and otherwise.

It held an equally powerful appeal to the lords and knights of Santerin's continental possessions, along their frontiers with Arnhand.

There were skirmishes and incursions almost every day, from down south where Tramaine bumped against the Connec all the way to the northernmost villages on the seacoast east of easternmost Argony. Local knights and garrisons did little to make life difficult for the aggressors. Members of the same families lived on both sides of the shifting border. Feudal obligations in the marches changed with every marriage, birth, death, and with the altering fortunes of war.

And a change of rulers made little difference in the lives of local people. Some peasants did not speak the language of either set of masters.

Every Arnhander family of substance had relatives overseas, in the crusader states. They sent their young men east to temper them in the ruthless struggle for control of the Holy Lands.

The young men took servants and foot soldiers and treasure with them.

Usually only the young men themselves returned—no longer young.

With so many strains upon it, it was insanity for Arnhand to listen to Sublime's mad call for help punishing the Chaldareans of the Connec for their recalcitrance and the Connecten Seekers After Light for disrespecting God Himself.

Anne of Menand, mistress of Arnhand's king, had two children by her lover. The eldest was a son, Regard. Regard was just fourteen but of sound mind and body and had a regal air. In normal times no one would consider him a candidate to replace his father. Legitimacy was a huge issue for the Arnhander nobility. But these were abnormal times. Dedicated schemers could get the past restructured to render Regard legitimate.

Anne had presented her favors to a select few outside the royal bedchamber as well, creating a circle of accomplices. The boy's father was amenable to her strident efforts to have Regard designated Crown Prince. But powerful factions were arrayed behind rival candidates.

Anne of Menand was a schemer and manipulator and slut. She bedded men not only to manipulate them but because she was possessed by a huge enthusiasm for night sports. Yet she was a devout Chaldarean with a sincere belief in Patriarchal infallibility. If Sublime asked for troops to punish the apostate Connec, then Arnhand should produce those troops.

It was a measure of Anne's standing that she managed to engineer a crusade of eighty knights and their entourages. The little army never reached the Connec, though. It turned back before the levees completed their obligations. Not once did it engage—or even sight—a heretic. But it did lose three dozen souls to disease and accident.

BROTHER CANDLE TRAVELED THE CONNEC, BRINGING HEART to Seekers After Light who sensed a gathering storm. He visited the nobles of each town. They had to understand that they were obliged to protect everyone from foreign enemies. He reminded them that the jongleurs and poets called the Connec the Peaceful Kingdom. Connectens took pride in their ability to live in harmony.

It was a time of moral posturing. It was a time of absurd justifications, before the fact, of anticipated bad behaviors.

Sublime V issued frequent thunderous bulls denouncing all things Maysalean and most things traditionally Connecten. He seemed driven to alienate his flock.

The people of the Connec began to rally behind Immaculate II, who found sufficient fire to spew a few bulls of his own. Pro-Brothen priests, who had been unpopular before now, faced active hostility.

The sleepy Connec had begun to awaken. And was getting up cranky.

Brother Candle feared Sublime's shortsighted greed would waken the whirlwind. He did not enjoy the increasingly bellicose nationalism churning through the Connec. It grew fat on the fear of bigger and fiercer armies coming to torment the Connec.

Wherever Brother Candle carried his message he saw city walls being heightened and strengthened. He saw castles being readied for siege. He saw local militias receiving instruction in the use of arms from men who were respected because they were veterans of the wars to liberate the Holy Lands. And everywhere he went he found that Tormond's men had preceded him, asking people not to prepare for war. Brothe and Arnhand might find that provocative.

That reasoning left even pacifist Brother Candle bewildered.

No one outside Khaurene paid Duke Tormond any mind. The population plunged into preparations as if expecting Arnhander cannibals in tens of thousands as soon as the first leaves budded.

SPRING EASED INTO EARLY SUMMER. INVADERS PERSISTED IN their failure to appear. Duke Tormond floated the notion of an embassy to Brothe that would work out something with Sublime. Brother Candle was not present for the ferocious debate that followed. He was celebrating his own religion with the Maysalean community of Castreresone. But he heard about the raging arguments. Even Sublime's Connection allies favored not sending anyone to Brothe. Mathe Richeneau, the recently appointed, newly arrived, Arnhand-born Bishop of Antieux, also suggested going slow. Sublime was certain to consider any approach an acknowledgment of his primacy.

Tormond's advisers won that day but never made him understand that he could not just sit down and talk things out with Sublime. Being infallible, the Patriarch knew there was nothing to negotiate.

Tormond did hate committing to anything completely. And there was no arguing the fact that his style of rule, which he shared with his more recent ancestors, had worked for more than a century.

There was no invading army in the spring. There was no invading army during the summer. Preparations for war became less urgent, more relaxed, and, at the farthest removes from the northern frontier they ceased altogether.

Come summer Duke Tormond surrendered to his need to act. He sent an embassy to Salpeno to try to make peace with Arnhand. It failed. Then, as autumn gathered, Tormond surrendered to unreason again. He returned to his notion of opening a dialogue with Sublime.

This time no one could change his mind.

* * *

BROTHER CANDLE RETURNED TO KHAURENE JUST DAYS BE-
fore the news came out. He was staying with a good Maysalean
family, the Archimbaults, who were in the tanning trade.
Raulet Archimbault feared the Duke's decision would hurl the
Connec over the edge of a precipice.

Seekers After Light customarily gathered in discussion
groups in the evening, before the final meal of the day. That
was taken late in the Connec, long after nightfall. A large
group convened at the Archimbaults' because everyone wanted
to hear the Perfect. Familiar with the way Devedian and Dainshaukin minorities were abused by Brothen Episcopals, they
were concerned about their own future. Sublime, clearly, intended to go beyond ranting about heretics and unbelievers.

Brother Candle said, "We've talked about this before,
Raulet, so I understand you. But elucidate for the benefit of
your guests, who may not be familiar with your thinking."

Raulet Archimbault was uncomfortable as the focus of a
group. Haltingly, he explained, "Just by sending an embassy to
Brothe Tormond weakens the standing of the Connec." He
stopped.

Brother Candle encouraged him. "Go on. Tell us why."

"Well, it says Tormond admits the Brothen Patriarch has a
say in our affairs. That sets a bad precedent all by itself. Also,
it diminishes the Patriarch at Viscesment. And he's the legal
Patriarch. Right?"

Brother Candle said, "Diminishing that man isn't hard to
do. How many of you—by show of hands—know who the
anti-Patriarch is? See. Immaculate the Second, Brothers and
Sisters. Those of you who do know most likely do because
somebody tried to kill him last spring."

"Pathetic," Raulet said.

"Yes," Brother Candle agreed. "And he's supposed to be *our*
Patriarch. The Patriarch who represents all Chaldareans. Ari-
anist, Antast, Episcopal, Eastern Rite, Shaker, or Maysalean."
Most Maysaleans did consider themselves good Chaldareans,
in the Antast mode. "He's the Patriarch who's supposed to stop
the Five Families of Brothe from treating the Church as their
own private pot at the end of the rainbow."

"The thing I don't understand," Madame Archimbault said, "is why the Duke would do this despite his advisers. That doesn't make sense." Among Seekers After Light, women stood equal to men, with a full right to speak and question. "They must have explained everything to him."

Brother Candle nodded. "Absolutely. Over and over. I was there once when Tormond heard it all, point by point. He said he understood. But, as all of you who have raised children know, you can't make someone hear what he doesn't want to hear."

Scarre the Baker, asked, "Could he have been stricken mad?"

A little voice piped, "It must be the Night."

Raulet offered, "Or Sublime's god touched him. Maybe the Brothen Episcopal god agrees with Sublime about us." Raulet was trying to make a joke but everybody took him seriously.

Brother Candle said, "I ought to get together with Bishop LeCroes and see what he thinks."

"Unbelievable," someone muttered.

Madame Archimbault inquired, "Will the men around Tormond interfere? Brother, you've said Brothe has no friends in Tormond's court."

"Not many, no. But Tormond's men are loyal and honorable. They'll do what they're told once they know they can't change his mind."

Someone said, "What will Count Raymone do?"

"A critical question," Brother Candle replied. "And one only Raymone Garete can answer. He doesn't hide his disgust."

Madame Archimbault observed, "Raymone is young. The young praise action for its own sake."

The Maysalean Heresy appealed mainly to those who had left youth's distractions behind.

Brother Candle accepted wine from his host's daughter, Kedle, who was thrilled to be auditing the meeting. She was thirteen, a woman by some standards, but would never speak up while a Perfect was present.

Seekers After Light were convinced they were true Chaldareans. They claimed their teachings harkened back to those of Aaron, Eis, Lalitha, and the other Founders, before those became twisted and perverted by the successors of Josephus Alegiant and his clique. The god of the Arianists, and of the

Episcopals who came after them, was actually the Great Adversary reproached by the Founders.

The Great Adversary had wrought a thousand deceptions while hiding amongst the Instrumentalities of the Night. It was impossible to untangle the skein of lies. Because there was always another lie in line.

Brother Candle relaxed and observed as the discussion drifted to reincarnation, which had leaked into the Maysalean Creed despite being an oriental concept.

The group wanted to examine the moral implications of reincarnation. Some thought rebirth gave you an out if you behaved badly. You could do your next incarnation as a makeup.

Brother Candle had not yet worked out where he stood regarding reincarnation. He found the idea comforting. Reincarnation meant a second chance to get life right. It was the Great Wheel of Life.

Someone wanted his attention. "Yes?"

Madame Scarre asked if he believed Seekers After Light were obliged to fight back if attacked.

"Absolutely. It's one more way to resist evil. If we don't fight evil we become accessories to evil."

Nothing but hurried breathing sounded in the Archimbault household. A great Maysalean mind was about to share a thought.

Brother Candle disappointed everyone. "That's it. That's the truth. The lines are never clear. There is no absolute right. There is absolute wrong but it's hard to identify. It manages to adopt a great many disguises."

Scarre the Baker asked, "What do you mean, Brother?"

He began to preach. "We are slaves to reason. Reason exterminates every argument our enemies throw up. Righteousness slides through their fingers like water. All they have left in hand is emotion. Our weakness is, we don't recognize it when dreams and emotion guide us. So we're as much victims of the Instrumentalities of the Night as those we disdain for being less thoughtful."

Brother Candle was afraid he had failed to express himself in a way the others could understand. Not even he was equipped to comprehend the full nature of mankind's relationship with the Instrumentalities of the Night.

Despite a moral code being part of every religion, with innumerable admonitions to do good put into the mouths of the gods, Brother Candle had yet to see any direct evidence that the Instrumentalities of the Night, at any level, demonstrated any innate moral polarity. Like earth, wind, water, and fire, they just *were*. And, like life itself, they *wanted*.

Good and evil were concepts imposed by men, through their perceptions and beliefs, or directly by force of sorcery.

Brother Candle found it difficult to be a spiritual adviser and guide in a world where there were few absolutes to serve as navigational beacons when he charted his own course.

He said, "If we Seekers After Light disappear from the grand pageant of history it won't be because logic and persuasion overwhelmed us. It will be because a superior weight of arms and terror were deployed."

Brother Candle dreaded any future that had roots sunk into the ordure of Duke Tormond's incredible decision to try dealing with Sublime V. The Brothen Patriarch was not a man like him, simple and moved by goodwill toward all.

Perhaps Honario Benedocto was a cosmic prank being played by the Instrumentalities of the Night. Some old religions declared their gods capable of far worse, just for the amusement to be gained by kicking the anthill.

21. Brothe, in the Gathering of the War

Brothe was in a ferment. Neither a Patriarchal nor a Collegium delegation came out to greet Principaté Doneto. Sublime's limited forces were desperately trying to keep order, busy as a three-legged cat in a room full of mice.

The Five Families hurled accusations and pointed fingers. Their young men found excuses to duel. Every duelist who came in second added fuel to the emotional holocaust. The law forbid family forces larger than a personal guard. In the past they had shown themselves unable to refrain from throwing swords at every little problem. Now they sought ways to get around the law.

The Brotherhood of War was mad at everybody.

Word of the troubles, with mystic swiftness, reached the Calziran pirates. A small fleet tried to come up the Teragi River but was driven back by the Collegium.

Then there was the Brothen mob, which had behaved itself for far too long. Riots and looting broke out most every day. Luckily, the civil disorders remained small and localized.

The Devedian and Dainshaukin minorities, working together, resisted the madness. Though they did incense the Episcopal mob by kicking the snot out of would-be looters.

Their situation never grew as bad as had that of the Deves of Sonsa.

The worst was over by the time Bronte Doneto's band reached the city. Today's Brothens couldn't live up to the standards of bad behavior shown by their forbears.

The party's passage through the streets was uncomfortable, though the day itself was clear, cool, and crisp and recent heavy rains had swept away most of the offal usually lending piquancy to the city air. Doneto moved as fast as he could. He wanted to be off the streets before his return became common knowledge.

Everyone who really cared had, of course, been aware of his approach for days.

THE PRINCIPATÉ GAVE HIS PEOPLE JUST TIME ENOUGH TO EAT, clean up, change clothing, and take a few minutes to relax. Then he summoned them to the central hall of his home. That structure was a minor fortress constructed of dirty old limestone less than a bow shot from the larger Benedocto citadel. The Benedocto home was a true castle.

The Five Families all had their true fortresses within the city—despite being denied the forces to defend them. The Benedocto castle was the biggest family stronghold.

Else arrived to discover that Doneto had wasted no time on his own comfort. He wore what he had worn on the road. He was as dirty as he had been when he entered the city. He carried a wooden bowl containing olives, pickled garlic, and onions, plus bite-size chunks of sausage and cheese. He ate as he moved around.

Else presumed that the people he did not recognize—everyone but Doneto and Pinkus Ghort—were Doneto's own people who had stayed behind when their master had gone off to salvage the Connec.

The Principaté's staff had done a superb job of keeping the household ready for its master's return.

"Or somebody warned them that he was on his way home," Ghort said. "Like maybe the guy who paid his ransom. Meantime, it looks like we've lost a friend and gained a boss."

"Must you *always* be cynical?"

That process—the one where Doneto returned to old form—had begun before their exit from Plemenza.

"Look out," Ghort cautioned.

Doneto was headed their way. He said, "Affairs here are tailor-made for us, Hecht. There's so much confusion that nobody really knows what's going on or who is who. Originally, I planned to set you up inside the Arniena family, so we could keep them steering close to the Patriarch's course after they revealed themselves by voting with us in the Collegium. But with Rodrigo Cologni dead there'll be one less vote against Sublime to negate so we won't have to leverage the Arniena into backing him. They can go on pretending to be against us. So we can employ you even more daringly. You are, by the way, in Arniena service now, have been for months, and don't even know me."

Else asked Ghort, "Who is this handsome stranger, Pinkus?"

Doneto showed a flash of irritation, then a moment of amusement.

Else said, "But I do know who you are. Anybody who got out of the Connec will know that. And that includes all those Brotherhood types who ran away to Brothe. And everyone who knows about our stay in Plemenza. Hansel can trip us up anytime he wants. Remember, I'm supposed to be an imperial spy, now."

Doneto scowled. "I suppose you're right. So here's what I'm thinking now. Because of the disaster that hit the Bruglioni they're desperate for competent help. If Inigo Arniena tells Paludan Bruglioni that he can give him a couple of his best men . . ."

Else nodded and smiled but also rolled his eyes. "This is getting hard to follow. I'll be writing reports and sending them to me keeping track of what I've been doing and offering suggestions on how I can influence me to behave in ways that I'll find more useful toward accomplishing my goals where spying on me is concerned."

Doneto smiled thinly. "There's a country folksong about a man who was his own uncle and brother-in-law. Hecht, I want to seize this opportunity before people have time to think. Come with me. There's somebody I need you to meet."

Else went, reluctantly. "You're the boss." He had hoped to ease into the Brothen scene gradually, quietly. But if he could get inside one of the Five Families . . .

Bronte Doneto led him to a shadowed corner. There they found an old man in a wheeled chair, alertly watching the Principaté's guests. Doneto said, "Piper Hecht, this is Salny Sayag. And his son, Rogoz. They represent the Arniena family. You might have run into Rogoz before. He worked in your line for a while, in the north."

Else considered the younger man who stood behind the wheeled chair. "I don't think so. Not that I recall, anyway." He offered his hand. "Have you seen me before, Rogoz?"

"No."

Rogoz was definite. And a man of few words. His grip was firm and confident. His coloring and appearance were not local. He was darker and uglier than was common in Firaldia. Else asked, "You aren't Brothen either, are you?"

"My father came over from Obrizok."

"I don't know Obrizok."

"It's a town in Creveldia. Creveldia is famous for its horses. He was an exile. This isn't the time for personal histories. Collect your possessions."

Else sighed. He was glad he was used to living on his own. The Plemenzan captivity had been his longest settled passage in the past ten years.

"Where're you headed?" Pinkus Ghort wanted to know.

"New job. The Principaté wants me on it right now." He shrugged. "I'll see you on the streets."

"Don't smack me too hard."

"Take care of Bo and Joe. Keep Bo out of the brothels. He'll catch his death."

"Yeah."

Else feared he would miss Pinkus Ghort as much as he did Bone and the others from the Andelesqueluzan adventure. Which now seemed like a story he had heard a long time ago instead of something he had lived himself.

THE SAYAGS EXITED BRONTE DONETO'S ESTABLISHMENT through a tradesmen's postern. Rogoz Sayag pushed his father's chair. A blanket covered the elder Sayag's lower body. It might have concealed tools or weapons. Two armed men joined them outside the gate. Rogoz Sayag explained, "Brothe is a dangerous city. There are a lot of hungry people on the streets."

Else carried everything he wanted to take along. He was accustomed to carrying his whole life and fortune on his back. Like he was some nomadic desert tortoise.

Else talked and pretended not to examine his companions or the surrounding city. It took the efforts of both Sayags and their escorts to generate enough return chin noise to qualify as a conversation.

At one point, Else protested, "I need to know *something* about this city. I've never been here before."

"I understand," Rogoz replied. "But you aren't going to be part of our house. You don't need to know anything about us."

Else understood. Rogoz did not want him picking up anything he might pass along when he moved on to the Bruglioni citadel. "On the other hand, if I don't know anything about the Arniena, after supposedly having been with them for several months, the Bruglioni will wonder why."

Salny Sayag agreed. "Talk to him, Rogoz. All of you, talk to him. Don't hold back. Fill in the details. *Let* him take something with him when he goes. You. Doneto man. The one thing you aren't going to tell anyone is that the Arniena have an understanding with Principaté Doneto."

"Of course not."

ELSE SPENT NINE DAYS WITH THE ARNIENA FAMILY, LEARNING what they were willing to be let known, and about the Mother

City. They gave him work to do. It was not overwhelming. He had several opportunities to go out and get the feel of the city.

The essence of Brothe was elusive. It seemed to be more than one city. In one sense it was almost parochial, with the intense focus of the native-born on family politics, petty feuding, and Colors. On the other hand, Brothe was cosmopolitan in the extreme. It swarmed with foreigners. Else heard dozens of unfamiliar languages. People from all across the world came to immerse themselves in the recollections of what once was the heart of the civilized world.

The glories of yesterday lay in ruins, some looted for building stone, overgrown, haunted by the poor and fugitives or, some said, by a thousand lingering recollections of the Instrumentalities of the Night. There were great sorcerers in Brothe, everybody knew. And not just the tame Principatés of the Collegium.

Foreigners came seeking their fortunes. Many of them had been villains in their own climes. And Brothe boasted a vigorous religion and pilgrim industry. Else found that amazing. Thousands came every month just to see the Church's central physical institutions, and in hopes of glimpsing the Patriarch.

During his stay with the Arniena, Else participated in two minor adventures with Rogoz Sayag and other family retainers. Salny Sayag said the orders came from Don Inigo Arniena himself. Don Inigo was the family chieftain. Neither mission amounted to much. Punishing a servant who had stolen from the Arniena. Avenging an insult flung at one of the don's granddaughters by a gang of street kids who had been stupid enough to open their mouths outside their hideout.

Those jobs did give Else a chance to be seen in the company of other Arniena goons.

"This all you do?" Else asked Rogoz.

"Don Inigo isn't big on squabbling. Unlike everyone else in Brothe."

"Uhm?"

"It seems the more chaotic things get, the more some people use that to cover their own mischief. Which only makes the chaos worse. The don would rather do it the sneaky, sinister way."

Else went along and showed he could be part of the team. He needed only be mildly evasive about his past. Rogoz Sayag

was not eager to reveal his own background. Possibly Rogoz
had not spent much time in the countries where he was supposed to have learned his trade. In lands where he might have
crossed paths with a freelancer from Duarnenia, that little state
on the eastern shore of the Shallow Sea.

Few mercenaries talked about their pasts. Somewhere behind
them, in most cases, were people with grudges. Bad choices
made at an early age were why freelancers left home in the first
place.

While public order in Brothe deteriorated, the broader,
world situation lent the Patriarch no comfort, either. Calziran
pirates grew more numerous and bolder by the day. A sort of
mob madness had taken possession of them. Their worst raids
fell on Church or Benedocto family holdings, always within
the bounds of the Episcopal States. There was hardly a rumor
of piracy along the coasts of Alameddine. That kingdom, beholden to the Grail Empire, lay between Calzir and the Episcopal States. Nor did raiders appear anywhere else protected by
the Grail Emperor or the mercantile republics.

Even dimwits who cared little about distant events began to
think there was a conspiracy. Johannes Blackboots must be behind it all.

In Brothe everything was part of a plot. In Brothe nothing
was what it seemed, or even what it purported to be. Whatever
went wrong did so because of an inimical conspiracy.

Else suspected that any plot involving Praman pirates would
be orchestrated from al-Qarn rather than the Grail Empire.

Anything that distracted Sublime from a crusade into the
Holy Lands would be a good thing, from the Dreangerean
point of view. Any delay moved the man that many weeks,
months, or years closer to his blessed elevation into the Chaldarean heaven. Whereupon the beleaguered and long-suffering
Collegium would, undoubtedly, replace him with someone less
controversial, bellicose, and ambitious.

On Else's ninth day with the Arniena, Rogoz Sayag appeared as he was teaching three Arniena boys exercises that
would improve their stamina against the day they got involved
in a duel. "Remember. When two fighters of equal skill meet,
the one whose strength lasts longest will be the survivor." He
used "survivor" rather than "victor" deliberately.

"Good lesson for them to learn, Hecht." Sayag got it.

"When they're young they think only the other guy is mortal. These boys listen, though. That's good."

Rogoz said, "You've done this before. They do pay attention."

"They're good kids. The main thing I want to get through to them is that half the people who get into duels lose."

"Definitely a difficult lesson. My father wants you. The Don has arranged a meeting with Paludan Bruglioni."

Else grunted. "Soon?"

"Tonight, I think. Not thrilled?"

"Not only am I old enough to know that half the people who get into duels lose, I'm old enough to know that, no matter how good you are, there's always somebody better." Else told the Arniena boys to knock off for the day.

"I'm not sure I follow all of that but I'll take your word for it."

Salny Sayag suggested, "Take a chair, Hecht." Else no longer found that western affectation awkward. The old man said, "I've talked you up to Paludan Bruglioni. He'll put on a show of reluctance but he's eager to take on someone like you. Which should work out well for you. All you have to do is look like you're what he wants you to be."

Else grunted, then said, "There's been a couple things bothering me. One is, why would a family the size of the Bruglioni need to bring in outside help? They lost a couple of important sons but I can't see that weakening them to the point where . . ."

"But it did. You're correct. There're a lot of Bruglionis. And every Bruglioni gets away from Brothe as soon as he can. Paludan is a difficult man. He's consumed by hatred. He keeps it hidden most of the time, though. His brother, and their father, were also miserable souls."

That sounded like a good emotional handle.

Sayag continued, "Last century there was a fad where the Brothen rich considered themselves too good to soil their own hands with war or commerce. The more hirelings a family had, the higher its status. The Bruglioni took that too much to heart. They never really got over it. After a parade of uninspired chieftains, they've pretty much lost their ability to do anything useful themselves."

"I see." He did not.

"The Bruglioni who died in Madhur Plaza were their best young men. Only their reputation for savagery and brutality protects them now. But the wolves smell weakness. The vultures are circling. Paludan's hired swords have all deserted. The Brotherhood of War has him marked. They're convinced that he was behind the killing of their men the night he lost his sons. A Bruglioni servant says he saw the missing heads inside the Bruglioni citadel the next day. And rumor says Paludan himself tortured Father Obilade to death. Sylvie Obilade being the Bruglioni household priest and Paludan's personal confessor, but also a spy. He arranged the ambush in the plaza. Not expecting a bloodbath."

"I see. Convolution in the Brothen tradition. And Paludan Bruglioni isn't a good employer."

"Correct. Don Inigo and I both cautioned him to restrain himself in your case. First, because he needs you desperately. Second, because we consider you more a loan than a pass along, his to do with as he pleases."

"Really?" Now what? He had met Inigo Arniena only in passing. The Don was a wizened little character vain enough to dye his hair black. Yet he enjoyed a joke, even at his own expense. He was less formal and stuffy than Salny Sayag.

Else could see no reason for Don Inigo to extend special protection to a passing rogue he meant to plant on an enemy as part of a larger scheme.

"The Don asked me to see if you won't make that a literal truth."

"You're going to have to be more direct."

"Long ago, when they were boys, Freido Bruglioni, Paludan's father, disrespected Don Draco Arniena in a way that Paludan doesn't know Don Inigo knows about. Don Inigo also knows the Bruglioni consider it a great joke. I'm not privy to the details myself. I do know that Don Draco swore to avenge the insult. Don Inigo promised his father on his deathbed that he would finish it. Last summer, when Don Inigo's heart almost betrayed him, he settled on a scheme where the Arniena vote in the Collegium would undercut the Bruglioni at some critical point. Meantime, publicly, Don Inigo remains Paludan's staunch ally."

"I think I begin to see."

"No doubt already being in a similar position on behalf of the Benedocto."

"Not them. Bronte Doneto."

"Who is an extension of the Patriarch, if you ask most people. No matter. The Don doesn't want much from you that you won't do anyway."

"So. This was why it was so easy for Principaté Doneto to arrange to slide me in through the Bruglioni back door?"

"Yes."

"What do you want?"

"Any information you can acquire that will give the Don a chance to do the Bruglioni a bigger hurt in the public eye."

"Bigger?"

"Bigger than backstabbing them in a vote in the Collegium. Best would be to discover something that would make the mob want to tear them apart."

"What a city. Of course. Since my Principaté tells me that you don't expect to reveal yourselves any time soon. Because until Rodrigo Cologni is replaced the Arniena vote isn't crucial."

"The Patriarch will have to move quickly, just to forestall the idea that *he* might have been behind the murder."

"I thought the murderer was supposed to be a huge blond foreigner. If he wasn't a Bruglioni."

"Either way, somebody killed a whole troop of Brotherhood veterans to get to Rodrigo Cologni. That's a hard sell, Hecht. God Himself wouldn't be interested enough to work that hard."

Else shrugged. "It seems nothing is unlikely here."

"It's just bigger and more complex than what you're used to. I was lost when I first got here. But it's just people being people, only with a lot more enthusiasm. Well, that's settled. Let's get you ready to go."

ELSE WAS AMUSED. HERE HE WAS, ENTERING THE GREAT REARing ugly limestone Bruglioni stronghold through the front gate. Rogoz left him there. "You want me to wait, Hecht?"

"Be a waste of your time, wouldn't it? I can find my way home."

"Take care, then. Some of these Bruglioni are creepy people." Sayag did not mind the Bruglioni sentry overhearing.

"You get used to creepy people."

Rogoz sneered and went away.

Else followed the sentry into the Bruglioni citadel. That man turned him over to a nervous, skinny, short, shaggy little man who told him, "My name is Polo. I'm supposed to assist you as long as you're here. You shouldn't ever forget that I work for Paludan Bruglioni. You'll see him in a minute."

Else considered his surroundings. Seedy described it in one quick, all-encapsulating word. No effort was being made to keep the place up. It felt creepy, as though the last fugitive tendrils of the night had not been harried out of this one corner of Brothe.

"Is the Don a sorcerer?"

Polo squeaked in surprise.

"He's not?"

"No. If you mean Paludan. But that isn't it. Nobody calls him the Don. Much as he'd love that."

"Really? Why not?"

Polo looked around for something lurking in the shadows. "You aren't Brothen, are you?"

"Not even Firaldian. Why?"

"Don is a title of respect. Given only to those who earn it. From here," smacking his chest over his heart. "To the one who leads. By those who follow. Do you understand that?"

"Yes." A similar tradition existed among the tribesmen of Peqaa and other remote regions of the Realm of Truth. Polo meant that the Bruglioni household did not consider Paludan Bruglioni a man who deserved to be called Don. "I do. Do I need to make a special effort with my appearance?"

"Nobody would notice. You're just another tradesman. One who uses a sword instead of a trowel or a hammer."

This half-ghostly Polo was nursing a grudge against his employers.

What Else had learned about the Bruglioni while serving the Arniena had not impressed him. But he had not drawn as bleak a picture as Polo and the Bruglioni headquarters suggested.

Was Polo some sort of provocateur?

This was no life a man ought to live, every waking moment spent wrestling paranoia about the motives of everyone around you. Yet paranoia was bedrock beneath this mission. He could not survive without it.

Later, Else said, "Tell me something, Polo. You said Paludan Bruglioni isn't a sorcerer. Is anyone else? I feel the darkness. Like there's an aspect of the Instrumentalities close to us."

"Others have said the same, sir. Possibly because the Bruglioni are so devoutly determined to have nothing to do with dark powers. They try to ignore their existence. Divino Bruglioni had to leave home when he chose the path that led him to become a member of the Collegium. They say they refuse to surrender to the Will of the Night."

The world could be confusing when the only truth available was the certainty that people would lie to you.

"Time to see the man," Polo announced.

Else narrowed his focus. He became Piper Hecht, wanderer from the farthest marches of the Chaldarean world, an experienced soldier eager to find service in one of the great houses of Brothe.

ELSE MADE A STRONG EFFORT TO SOUND HONEST. "THIS WASN'T my idea. Don Inigo convinced me. He says he owes you, that you've suffered cruel reverses, and he wants to help. Also, he said that I have a better chance of getting ahead with the Bruglioni than with the Arniena." Rogoz Sayag had advised him to appeal to the natural Bruglioni arrogance.

Paludan Bruglioni muttered, "That makes sense."

Paludan Bruglioni was a handsome, darkly complexioned man with a heavy black mustache. He had begun to lose his hair. He was heavy without being fat. His eyes seemed lifeless, though that could be due to the emotional beating he had taken lately. His head was egg-shaped, with the thin end down. His ears lay close. His overall appearance suggested a man in his middle fifties.

Paludan Bruglioni was a decade younger. The lamplight did not betray the floridity caused by prolonged, excessive drinking, or the scars left by the pustules from a disease picked up in Brothe's sporting houses. He had a reputation for vanity and, supposedly, wore a mask when he went out.

By lamplight he was a handsome, wealthy gentleman who was slightly tipsy. He might be in a bad mood for no immediately obvious reason.

"You're saying you want to step into my nephew Saldi's boots as a favor to Inigo Arniena?"

"The Don was good to me. He took me in when my prospects seemed bleak and he couldn't afford to pay what I'm worth. By sending me here he feels he's doing favors for you and me both."

Paludan scowled. Was there any chance that the man was as shallow and dull as he appeared?

Bruglioni glanced at the two men there with him, neither of whom had been introduced. One, though, had to be an uncle or older first cousin. He looked like an older Paludan. The other was pale, had graying ginger hair and a pallid, lantern-jawed death's-head face more ravaged than Paludan's.

Neither man spoke.

Else assumed the death's-head to be Gervase Saluda, Paludan's lifelong friend and reputed right hand.

Else said, "I would've been happy where I was. Don Inigo is the sort of master men in my line dream about. But I had higher ambitions when I left Tusnet. In Duarnenia the future is fixed. Sooner or later, you'll die in the Grand Marshes. Slowly and in great pain if the Sheard get hold of you. The pagans proclaim the tyranny of the night in the daytime. They celebrate their surrender to the will of the night."

Paludan smiled. Death's-head consulted something in front of him. "You were with Grade Drocker and the Brotherhood during the Church's adventure in the Connec last year?"

"Yes. I was on my way to Brothe when I encountered a Brotherhood band recruiting mercenaries near Ralli."

"Where they quarry the marble."

"Yes. A Brotherhood captain named Veld Arnvolker was in charge. I'd accumulated some traveling companions on the road, mostly boys and runaways. They thought they wanted to be soldiers. It would be all romance and adventure. The Brotherhood offered good training, good pay, and what looked like a chance to show them the truth without them having to get killed finding it out. So when the kids wanted to sign on, I went along."

"And it was all too good to be true."

"Yes. Because fate jumped in right away."

"It'll do that. Especially if things start going good."

"We got sent to the Connec. Idiot orders from the Patriarch and a brain-dead local bishop got my kids all killed. Only a few of us got out alive. Mostly Brotherhood guys, of course. You'd figure, wouldn't you? And the bigwigs, naturally."

"That's how life works."

"It does. But it's not right. Anyway, there I was, on my own again. For a whole damned month before I even heard that Grade Drocker, who was supposed to be in charge—You know, I never saw that asshole once. Him and his Brotherhood buddies ran downriver, grabbed a ship and escaped by sea. Leaving the rest of us to look out for ourselves."

The skull-faced man said, "Several survivors of the Connecten adventure were involved the night we lost Gildeo, Acato, Saldi, and the others. Did you know that?"

"No. I don't know much about that. Just rumors. I never knew for sure which Brothers made it back. I don't want anything to do with those people. One exposure was enough."

"Why wouldn't you be interested in the incident? If you wanted to work here?"

"I didn't want to. Not then. And it didn't affect the Arniena until Don Inigo saw the Bruglioni in tough circumstances and decided to show his regard for them."

Paludan asked, "You admit you're a mercenary? That what you're interested in is personal advancement?"

"Sure. Why wouldn't I? The way I'll get ahead is to be dedicated and loyal and do the best job I can. Don Inigo had my complete devotion. The Bruglioni will get it if you hire me. If Don Inigo had released me I might have left Brothe. Vondera Koterba is recruiting in Alameddine. He's offering particularly good terms. But Don Inigo asked me to come here. So here I am. I'll serve you till you release me or send me elsewhere."

What Else said encapsulated the supposed philosophy of the mercenary brotherhood in Firaldia. But it was just talk. Mercenaries and employers alike acknowledged the ideals only when it was convenient.

It was not a time when large, permanent bands, captained by

famous professionals, contracted as units. The last notorious company ended with the destruction of Adolf Black's regiment in the Black Mountain Massacre.

"Why should we trust you?"

"You shouldn't. I'm no different than any other prospective employee. You have to ask yourself, how can I hurt you?" According to Pinkus Ghort and others who had soldiered in Firaldia, Else understood that he had to conduct this interview on the paranoid edge. Firaldians who hired people to fight for them were often naive. Many fighters for hire were naive, too. And no one trusted anyone.

Fortunes, loyalties, allegiances, all shifted quickly in modern Firaldia. Treachery was a fact of life. For some, it was a way of life.

Insofar as Else Tage could see, the Firaldian Peninsula was where insanity went to retire. Nothing there made sense except at the most shallow level.

Paludan Bruglioni said, "Gervase?"

"Inigo Arniena and Salny Sayag recommend him so highly, you'd almost have to suspect them of wanting to get rid of him."

The third man said, "The Arniena have been having trouble meeting financial obligations because of the pirate raids."

Paludan grunted. "Those have hurt everybody."

"Them worse than anybody but the Benedocto. They aren't getting their rents or fees."

"Is that true, Hecht? Are they trying to reduce their expenses?"

"I don't know. There was talk that things aren't going well. But nothing concrete. Oh. There was something about selling an island. In the Vieran Sea. To the Sonsans. The Scoveletti family, I think. There's some kind of marital connection."

That got some attention. "Sogyal?" Paludan asked. "They're considering turning loose of Sogyal? Ha-ha!"

Rogoz had said that a mention of selling that island might seal the deal. Else did not know why. "I don't know. They didn't talk about it when I was around. I overheard by accident. I think it's a big secret that's supposed to stay secret even after the deal is done. There's a lot of worry about Dateon and Aparion finding out too soon."

"Ha! Sogyal. Those fools never have understood how valuable that island is."

Paludan Bruglioni launched a long, rambling tale of treachery, marriages of convenience, more treachery, dowries, and even more treachery, that put a particularly well-located and easily defended island into the hands of the Arniena halfway through the previous century. Sogyal was so strategically located that the Patriarch, both Emperors, all three mercantile republics, and several lesser kings and dukes had tried to buy it. The Arniena would not sell. Their intransigence had led to unsuccessful attempts to take the island by force as Dateon and Aparion strove toward supremacy on the Vieran Sea.

Else just nodded, tried to look wise, and observed, "All Firaldian stories are long on treachery."

"This's wonderful news," Paludan said. "We can profit from knowing this. Gervase, Hecht looks like the man we want. Work out the details and get him set up. Let him have Polo permanently."

ELSE SPENT A DAY ROAMING THE BRUGLIONI CITADEL. NOTHing was off limits. "You don't want to go down there, though," Polo told Else when he considered a descent into the cellars.

"Thought I could go anywhere."

"You can. I'm just hoping you won't."

"Why not? What's down there?"

"Dirt and cobwebs and bad smells. Maybe a haunt or two. Nothing you'd want to find. Then a *long* climb back up."

"You're sure about that, Polo?"

"There're childhood fears, too. The boogerman lives down there."

"The boogerman is real, Polo. If you're in the wrong place, at the wrong time, and you're not ready for the boogerman, you can find yourself in a world of trouble. It happens all the time where I come from."

"This is Brothe, sir. This city exists because the Instrumentalities of the Night are real. You don't have to convince Brothens."

Else did descend the long stair.

The Bruglioni cellars could have come straight out of a spooky story. They had cobwebs, vermin, slime in places, puddles of seepage, and an impressive range of unpleasant odors.

And a few minor, unhappy spirits, hidden in the reservoirs of darkness.

Else soon understood Polo's reluctance to face the return climb.

Polo puffed and told him, "In olden times the whole city had cellars under it. Still does, actually. Some way down deeper than this. Every ten or fifteen years there's a cave-in somewhere when part of the underground collapses because of what all has been piled on top since."

"Bet some interesting antiquities turn up when that happens."

"The antiquities were all looted in antiquity. They never find anything but dead people. Some of them old-timers but mostly ones that haven't been dead long at all."

"Meaning?"

"Meaning there's a class of Brothen who use the old catacombs. For shelter. And to hide bodies they don't want to turn up in the Teragi or an alley somewhere. Any loot down there will be something stolen in the last few days that is cooling off."

First glimpse of another side of the city, Else thought. A side that was always there, in every city, though always more so where the state was weaker. A side that had to exist so that there would be men to condemn to the galleys or the mines.

PALUDAN BRUGLIONI SUMMONED ELSE TO AN EVENING MEETing four days after his arrival. Bruglioni's quarters were austere enough for a monk.

Several Bruglioni youngsters, with bodyguards, were there to meet the new man, whose as yet ill-defined duties included teaching them how not to end up like their kinsmen in the Mahdur Plaza. The bodyguards did not look comfortable. Only a glance was needed to see that they were not what they pretended.

Paludan and Gervase Saluda made no introductions. The senior Bruglioni asked, "Have you been using your time wisely, Hecht?"

"That's a subjective question, but I think so. I've been getting to know this place and the people who make it work."

"I've seem him," one of the young Bruglioni sneered. "Always with the cooks and servants. There's a valuable pastime for a warrior."

"If you'd known your staff you might have recognized Father Obilade's inconsistent behavior beforehand. In which case, those who perished in the Madhur Plaza wouldn't have been there in the first place. The man you discount, overlook, or take for granted will be the man who brings you down."

"Be quiet," Paludan told his youngsters. "You're here to learn, nothing more." The rage that drove him was close to the surface tonight.

The kid who had mouthed off was not yet sixteen. Dugo Bruglioni was a grandson of Soneral Bruglioni and the son of the oldest Bruglioni slain in the Madhur Plaza. Dugo bullied the staff. And did not do much else.

The help dared not fight back. Jobs were scarce and precious.

Paludan continued, "I don't want to hear anybody talk. Hecht. How well do you know the city?"

"Not well at all, sir. The Arniena gave me no chance to explore. My role in their scheme was defense and instruction."

"Learn your way around. Without attracting attention."

"Yes, sir." He was being told to go live his secret dreams, with pay.

"You worked with the Brotherhood in the Connec. Did you develop a passion for their ways?"

"None whatsoever. They're arrogant, self-important fools. They deserved what they got. Though they *were* executing orders from the Patriarch. Which got modified every five minutes by the Bishop of Antieux. Serifs was such an idiot that nobody who didn't know him will believe the truth. I hear Principaté Doneto had him thrown off a cliff because he was such a miserable excuse for a priest."

"I've heard that rumor myself," Gervase said. "But it isn't true. Bishop Serifs did die in a fall, but while trying to escape from a Braunsknechts officer after he'd been captured by the Emperor's men. His death really was an accident."

"Really?" Else said. "That *is* interesting."

"Rumors make everything more exciting."

Paludan asked, "So you have no love for the Brotherhood of War?"

"None. As an organization. There were individuals I found likable. Why?"

"The Brotherhood murdered six Bruglioni. Including my only sons, Acato and Gildeo. And several nephews, one of them the family's hope for the future. If I fall down dead right now, Dugo will take over. And would ignore you and Gervase. And would put the family down the shitter in a year. Unless one of our country cousins has sense enough to cut his throat."

Else said, "It may not fit the Bruglioni way but I have a suggestion."

Paludan brightened dramatically. He did entertain genuine worries about the Bruglioni future. "Tell me."

"Change the rules. Call in the best Bruglioni who've left the city."

Paludan grunted, gave Else a dark look.

Else said, "See who's doing the job out there. Bring them back where their competence can do the most good."

Paludan and Gervase stared at Else like he was a genius talking with the mouth of a fool. Because there was a tacit understanding that Bruglioni who left the city freed themselves from their Brothen obligations.

Paludan said, "That has possibilities, Hecht. I'll consider it." With condescension. "Tell us how to avenge ourselves on the Brotherhood."

"What? Revenge? The men responsible are dead."

Paludan scowled at Else, possibly wondering why he was ignorant one moment and well informed the next. Was he not supposed to know? What about the heads? How about what the priest went through before he fell into the Teragi a half mile upstream from Castella dollas Pontellas? Everyone in the Bruglioni citadel knew all that. Which meant the details would be common knowledge outside the citadel, too.

Else said, "In your place, I'd worry more about protecting myself from the Brotherhood."

"That's a good point, Paludan," Gervase said. "We don't want to get into a war with them."

Else suggested, "Give them the men who did the killing. Say they exceeded their orders."

"That's what they did do. They were just supposed to grab Rodrigo Cologni. So my boys could rescue Rodrigo from them. But the Brotherhood turned up. And Obilade's patsies had minds of their own. They were like supernatural monsters. Anyway, I couldn't give them up if I wanted. Obilade was the only one who knew how to get in touch."

Gervase said, "We're not going to have any choice about bringing family in from the country, Paludan. We need more people here with a stake in keeping family secrets."

Paludan whined, "What happened? Ten minutes ago I was busting with plans. I was going to make Sublime ache. Now I'm facing a potential siege. I'm surrounded by people I can't trust."

Gordimer the Lion's predecessor had used similar words to describe his own situation before his fall. Else said, "Don't change your goals. Just change your plans to reflect your strengths and weaknesses."

Gervase observed, "We have more weaknesses than strengths. We haven't kept our swords sharp."

Else said, "To plan, we need to know what our adversaries might be thinking. We need to know who our potential adversaries are. We need an honest assessment of our own strength. And firmly established goals."

"Meaning?"

"We need to find out what the Brotherhood, the Cologni, the Patriarch, and the Collegium are up to. We need to know how they see the Bruglioni. You have an uncle in the Collegium. He has friends. The Bruglioni have a tradition of being major players on the Brothen stage. You have vast resources. Get them cataloged. Imagine what can be done with them."

Else sensed that Paludan had received no training for the position he held. He was faking it and hoping for the best.

Paludan said, "Gervase, follow up on what Hecht's saying. Real life seems to be closing in. Dugo, boys, come with me." Paludan rose.

Dugo protested, "We were going out to . . ."

"Be quiet. Weren't you listening? People who have a grudge against us are probably planning to do something about it. I don't want you out where they can get you. Come along."

Dugo pouted. It looked like he would have to survive a harsh, close call before he started listening.

*   *   *

GERVASE SALUDA SAID, "IF MY CHIN KEEPS HITTING MY CHEST it's because I just witnessed the longest run of intelligent, responsible thinking ever seen from Paludan Bruglioni."

"Oh?" Else said.

"Until Acato and Gildeo were killed he spouted the same nonsense as Dugo. Which is why Dugo was all confused."

"How did he keep the family going, then?"

"Inertia. And he hasn't. Not well. He never really had to be responsible, growing up. He's always let things ride while he had a good time. He got away with it until the disaster in the Mahdur Plaza."

"The world caught up?"

"It didn't change who he is but it did make him realize that there're challenges beyond just seeing if he can't bed more women than his father did. Even so, he passed the work on to us. He has no faith in himself."

"And?"

"You have to understand. Besides his character shortcomings, Paludan just isn't very bright. He isn't subtle. His preferred solution to any problem is to hit it with a hammer."

"The way Dugo would."

"The way Dugo would. Though now it seems he's started to catch on. He knows that he has to start doing the right thing. For the family's sake. Meantime, his major adviser, which would be me, might not be any smarter or subtler."

"Really?"

"My genius and my gullibility got us into this. Sylvie Obilade manipulated me. I sold Paludan on the priest. Like his ideas were mine. I thought Obilade wanted the best for the Bruglioni."

"Maybe he did."

"Sure, he did. He was a good priest. But he wanted to be something more. He wanted to make the Church all-powerful, temporally as well as spiritually."

"That doesn't sound exciting." Dreanger was not terrible but there were smaller principalities within the Realm of Peace where religious rule smothered everything.

"We need to make peace with the Church over Father Obilade."

"Being a country boy from the far frontiers I'm obviously

missing some critical local angle. Six members of the Bruglioni household were killed. The priest caused that. The men who murdered them were killed themselves."

"So you think the scales are balanced?"

"Yes, actually."

"The Church wouldn't agree. If Church people screw you you're supposed to take it with a smile and beg for more because it feels so good."

"This will take getting used to." It might be the sort of thing he could use to stir confusion and distract the Patriarch from organizing a new crusade. "I need to know Brothe better. Like Paludan said. Even taking into account the natural arrogance of people who believe God speaks with their mouths, there's a lot of flawed thinking in this city."

"Going out there could be dangerous."

"How? Even if word is out that I've been hired nobody knows what I look like except a few Arniena. And they're on our side."

"I don't know."

"Uhm?"

"I'm not sure we should trust anybody out there, right now. I'm not sure why Paludan and I decided Rodrigo Cologni would defect. Father Obilade probably sold us. We know that wasn't true, now. Rodrigo kept faith."

"Treachery is the most popular sport in town. I'll learn what I can, outside. You get Paludan to decide what he wants to accomplish so we can start planning. Find out if he wants to hire real swords. Those bodyguards were make-believe."

"I don't think he'll stand for the extra expense. Right now we're completely clear on who to blame if anything goes wrong."

"I'll do my utmost to ensure that your faith in me is justified."

Else parted with Saluda still unsure of the man. Was he bright or dim? Was he manipulating Paludan Bruglioni? Was he Paludan's dedicated friend?

BROTHE WAS UNIQUE AMONG CITIES ELSE HAD KNOWN. IT showed its age much more than did even the oldest cities of Dreanger. There were ruins everywhere. In Dreanger they cleared the old away in favor of the new. In Dreanger the surviving ruins were not inside cities, they were out in the deserts and mountains and, as it had been from the most archaic times, they were occupied only by the dead.

The priests who had tended them had been massacred by Josephus Alegiant a thousand years ago. Alegiant's successors had been massacred in turn by warriors of the Praman Conquest five hundred years later.

Reminders of the glory days of the Old Empire were everywhere, usually overgrown by creeping vines and brush. Remnants of triumphal arches still spanned the streets. Weeds and brush grew atop them. Else wondered where the soil came from.

Today's Brothe stood on ground ten to twenty feet higher than it had been in antiquity. In places the old low ground lay buried even deeper.

In Brothe the past was as omnipresent and intrusive as the Instrumentalities of the Night in the Holy Lands. It meant more here than elsewhere. Brothe's yesterdays defined its todays.

Sublime enjoyed local popular support because people thought he might resurrect the ancient glories.

In Brothe even the poorest of the native poor worshiped the city's past glories. And seemed indifferent to its present.

Yesterday's toppled memorials loomed large in the lives of squatters and drifters.

Poverty was ubiquitous, too. But that did not touch Else. Poverty and misery were the natural state of humanity wherever he went.

ELSE STROLLED AROUND IN WHAT HE HOPED LOOKED LIKE random rambles. He noticed no obvious tail. Which might mean that someone with superb skills had been assigned to track him. Or someone with a supernatural assist.

He did not count on his new employer not to spy on him. *He* would never allow a stranger deep into his world as easily as he had gotten into that of the Bruglioni.

Else drew dark looks wherever he went. He did not understand. He did note that other foreigners drew equally malignant attention, though.

He had been on his own a long time. Had he forgotten a critical detail of his contact regime? Could life's vicissitudes have claimed Gordimer's local agents? He knew no names, just places to visit. The embassy of the Kaif of al-Minphet was to be approached only in extreme circumstance. A sailor's tavern on the riverfront, as far downstream as you could go and still be inside the wall, was just too far away. The only convenient contact resided inside the Devedian quarter.

Brothe was a vast sprawl south of the Teragi. It seemed to go on forever.

"Hey, Pipe! Piper Hecht! How the hell you doing, asshole?"

Pinkus Ghort jogged across the street, dodging between donkeys and camels, oxcarts, dog carts, and goat carts. Brothe's streets were busier than those of al-Qarn. And twice as ripe. Little effort was made to clean up after the animals. Else had seen some amazing shit drifts.

"Ghort! You been following me?"

"No. Shit. Man. It's pure coincidence. I was just heading over to the . . . How the hell are you doing?"

"As good as could be hoped, I guess."

"They get you in over there yet?"

"In?"

"The Bruglioni thing."

Curious. "They don't keep you in the know?"

"I've been out of town. There was a problem up the road that Doneto needed handled. I got back last night. So are you in?"

"I think. I'm worried about how easy it was, though. I can't believe anybody is as dimwitted as those people let on."

"Believe it. This is the town where dumb comes to stay. Two-thirds of them still think they rule the world. Basically, the whole damn town has their heads up their asses."

"I'll take your word for that."

"We need to work out a way to communicate."

"I know where the Principaté lives."

"How do we get a message to you?"

Else considered briefly. "I can't imagine an instance where you'd need to. Can you?"

"Uh . . . Maybe you're right. But you'll have to make contact sometime. Just so we can keep each other posted."

Ghort had a point. Ghort was supposed to be his eyes inside Doneto's establishment. "That shouldn't be hard. I don't suffer from excessive supervision. My job hasn't been defined yet. Paludan wants to hurt the Brotherhood because he thinks they killed his sons. Gervase is afraid the Brotherhood might come after the Bruglioni because of what happened to their men."

Ghort eyed Else's head. "You going to do something about your hair?"

"What? Why? Like what?"

"Half the nasty folks in Brothe are looking for big foreigners with long blond hair. Two were involved in the debacle you just mentioned. If they get close and bother to think, they'll know you aren't who they're looking for. But suppose you run into idiots?"

"Well. Now I know why I keep getting those evil looks."

"Those are probably just because you're you."

"No doubt. I have work to do. I'll see you sometime."

For a moment Ghort looked hurt. "Yeah. Later."

"Say hi to Bo and Joe. And Pig Iron."

"Yeah."

Else got away before Ghort could delay him. Principaté Doneto was not going to be pleased. He had given Ghort very little about the Bruglioni and nothing about the Arniena.

Let the man stew.

Else wandered aimlessly. Just in case. No point leading Ghort to one of his contacts. He listened to people. He heard little but everyday arguments, whining, complaints and indifference to squabbles on high. The politics that mattered at street level involved next meals. And Colors.

There was a great deal of anticipation of something called the Summer Invitational Games, when chariot racing teams from throughout Chaldarean Firaldia would participate in a huge elimination contest. The Colors would be out in strength, then.

Else's ramble took him to the south bank of the Teragi River, half a mile above the place where Father Obilade had been introduced to the Sacred Flood. In pre-Chaldarean times the river had been considered a goddess in its own right, harboring within her bosom a host of spirits, some quite wicked, all of which had to be appeased. The goddess was gone, now, but not so all of the dark sprites and nymphs and water horses who had attended her.

The Brothen ancients had done well, coming to terms with the Instrumentalities of the Night. The entire waterfront had been built up in a way that revealed ages of complete confidence that the river would not get out of control. Embankments constructed of huge blocks of dressed stone rose high enough that the water level could rise another twenty-five feet before there was a need to worry.

Else strolled downriver, along the top of the embankment, admiring the work of the ancient engineers. He was confident today's Brothens couldn't manage anything like this, if only for lack of will and energy. He had sensed a paucity of those commodities in the modern tribe.

He was impressed by the bridges, both in their number and their engineering. Each was a monument likely to last forever. And there was nowhere one had to walk more than a third of a mile to make a crossing. Above Castella dollas Pontellas, as it turned out.

The whole would have been immensely picturesque. Without the swarms of people and animals and vehicles cluttering the picture.

Else settled himself on a stone block atop the embankment, at a point where he could see Krois on its stone-faced island, the Castella dollas Pontellas and its six little bridges arching over an arm of the Teragi that served as its moat, and, farther left, the immense, massive dignity of the Chiaro Palace, the spiritual heart of the Episcopal strain of Chaldareanism. His was a vantage sought by many. When Else sat down he did so amongst a dozen fellow spectators who were besieged by street vendors selling purported holy souvenirs, hot sausages, and sweet cakes.

Sitting there, those three grand structures so close he could make out the streaks of pigeon droppings down their dun flanks, Else first felt some awe of western civilization. What were these buildings but the greatest ghosts of the glory that had been?

The fortress Krois, out in the midst of the flood, had stood there for twelve centuries. It began construction before the birth of the oldest of the Chaldarean founders. It had been decreed by a Brothen emperor uninterested in becoming a victim of the mob, after that had befallen several of his most immediate predecessors. A later emperor, in the end days of the Old Empire, bequeathed Krois to the Church.

It was the first legacy of the thousands responsible for creating the mad hodgepodge of states constituting today's Firaldia.

Else watched the boats and barges go up and down, enjoying the subtle changes in the view as the sun limped westward and the light altered, growing more golden.

"Piper Hecht?"

Else started, spun toward the unexpected voice, noting that the other sightseers had disappeared.

"Sainted Eis," somebody growled. "This asshole is jumpy."

Else faced four armed men, one of whom he recognized. "Sergeant Bechter? You scared the shit out of me, sneaking up like that. So. You were lucky. You got out with Drocker?"

"I'm a survivor. Evidently, you are, too."

"I got out with Principaté Doneto. Frying pan to the fire kind of thing. We got snapped up by Hansel's men in Ormienden, somewhere up there. They kept us locked up in Plemenza until Sublime decided to ransom his cousin. What's up?"

"Reports came in about a blond foreigner watching the Castella. They sent us to check it out."

"I was just enjoying the view. I mean, look at that. What's going on? Why the paranoia?"

"How long have you been here? In Brothe, not on the rock."

"Ten, twelve days. It kind of runs together. Today was my first chance to get out on my own. I was just relaxing and watching the barges go by and feeling homesick. What's up?"

"Did you hear about the Brothers getting murdered a while back?"

Else lifted himself back up onto the block of stone. "Join me in my parlor, here. Swap lies with me about all the fun we had putting down the heretics in the Connec."

Bechter got the idea. He came and sat. "You do know what's going on, don't you?"

"Not really. Local politics are too twisted. I don't see much that makes sense."

"Here's one for old time's sake, Hecht. Let's don't bullshit each other."

"Ouch! This doesn't sound good at all."

"Oh, it's gooder for you than it would've been if you were the guy we were hoping you'd be."

Else glanced back. "Do they have to hover? Can't we talk, just you and me?"

After consideration, Bechter said, "I'll take a chance on you, Hecht."

ELSE GOT PALUDAN BRUGLIONI AND GERVASE SALUDA TO SEE him when he returned to the Bruglioni citadel. "I think I've managed a coup. I hope you weren't so set on a war that you'll be angry with me."

"Talk to me," Paludan said. He was in a foul mood, his supposed natural state.

"I ran into somebody I knew from the Connecten campaign. He belongs to the Brotherhood of War. We talked. I made him understand what the Bruglioni think happened the night Rodrigo Cologni was kidnapped."

Paludan seemed puzzled, Gervase, amazed. "Go on, miracle worker." Was he sarcastic or serious?

"Here's the thing." Else explained what he had done in boring detail, without mentioning Pinkus Ghort. "Bechter is a good man, despite his affiliation. He's trustworthy. I told him the truth as seen from here. He told me theirs. Turns out the big question troubling his bunch is how to lay hands on some mysterious blond foreigners. They thought the Bruglioni might be hiding the outlanders. I set Becker straight. He believed me because he knew me from the Connec."

Both Paludan and Gervase scowled.

Else told them, "You'll recall that I suggested giving up the men you'd hired."

Gervase snarled, "The point, Hecht."

"The Brotherhood just wants those two men. If you could tell them more about those two, there'd be peace between the Brotherhood and the Bruglioni."

"And the Lord God Himself shall step down from Heaven and kiss each of us upon the lips—before he rolls us over and gives us a good old buttfucking," Gervase said.

"No doubt. But not today. Look. It's a way out."

"Awful convenient, though. Your first walk through the city, you run into an old pal from the wars."

"You religious, Gervase?"

"As religious as I need to be to get by."

"I thought so. Pretty much my attitude, too. But I've found that you can't go wrong by assuming that life is tainted by the Will of the Night."

"You saying supernatural forces are at work?"

"Always. But, in this case, yes, especially. Otherwise, why can't the Brotherhood find those men? Bechter said they get sighting reports all the time but when they check them out there's no further trace. Where I come from we'd think that means they're protected by the Instrumentalities of the Night. The Collegium itself might not be able to ferret them out."

"But the Collegium doesn't care. Not right now. Are you suggesting that we try to reach an accommodation with the Brotherhood?"

Else thought he had made that clear. "You've got nothing to lose."

ELSE FELT GOOD. IT HAD BEEN A PRODUCTIVE DAY. HE HAD MADE himself useful, though Paludan was not yet ready to see that.

In an ideal world he would get everyone thinking he was doing great things. Which would get him established. But an outbreak of peace amongst Brothe's factions would not serve the needs of Dreanger.

Else's quarters consisted of one large room subdivided into three by hanging quilts. He slept in a space no grander than a monk's cell. Polo slept in an even smaller area beyond their common area. That constituted half the total space. The dividers were old and ragged and did little to provide any privacy. They did keep heat from a little charcoal burner confined to the center room.

Else stepped in from the passageway. "Polo? You here?"

Someone groaned behind Polo's quilts. "Yes, sir. What time is it? What do you need?"

"Were you away from here while I was out?"

"I went out to get charcoal, candles, an ink stone, pens, inks, and such. As you instructed. I couldn't find any paper. The papermaker in Naftali Square is out of stock." Polo slipped his head through an overlap between quilts.

"You don't need to get up. I asked because somebody's gone through my things. I don't think anything is missing."

After a noise like a mouse's squeak, Polo joked, "They wasted their time, didn't they?"

"Yes. I'm going to bed."

Else lay back on his rough mattress, a canvas bag filled with wheat and oat husks. He pondered Polo's response.

It did not seem appropriate, assuming the news was a surprise.

PALUDAN AND GERVASE SALUDAN DID NOT KNOW WHAT THEY wanted Else to do. They had felt a need to do something. Hiring him had presented itself. But there was no way he could replace all the hired swords who had deserted.

Else asked to have his duties defined. He was told to protect the house. Without being given specifics. All by his lonesome.

He prowled the citadel, putting on a show. The place was in poor repair and dirty. The staff were slothful and sloppy.

Polo remained close by, most of the time. Else had him pinch paper from the Bruglioni business office. They created a chart of who was responsible for what. Of who was in charge where. Else was an energetic administrator, though he disliked that side of soldiering. He let himself go, now.

The Bruglioni citadel was vast. And poorly designed for its fortress function. Though what could be seen from beyond the perimeter wall was forbidding. Where the gargoyles and whatnot had not fallen off. There were other buildings inside the wall. Stables and tool sheds and so forth. The main structure included one hundred and twenty rooms on four floors. Few, off the ground floor, were of much size or magnificence. The current Bruglioni were not into ostentatious display. The family could no longer afford it.

The family proceeded entirely on past momentum under Paludan. He was not stupid. He lacked drive. He was content to let life slide by. Unless his anger broke through. Then he might do something unwise. Like trying to stage a kidnapping and rescue.

Following two days of review, from which he took time off only to drill the younger Bruglioni in the use of arms, Else summoned the senior household staff to a meeting in the kitchen. Nine deigned to appear, along with a few gawkers.

One of the nine was the chief of the four men who guarded the two gates used to get into and out of the citadel. Else told him, "Mr. Caniglia, you and your men are not to allow Mr. Copria, Mr. Grazia, or Mr. Verga to enter the citadel tomorrow." Only a handful of staff lived on the premises. Paludan did not want to feed and house and pay them, too. "They no longer work here. The rest of you, think about who should take over. Let me know tomorrow. Mr. Natta? You want to volunteer to test the jobs market yourself? No? Mr. Montale. I understand that you find new staff when they're needed."

"Uh . . . Yes, sir. For the household. Not for the people on the business side. Not for anything to do with weapons or body guarding."

"New staff will be needed soon. We're about to shed our nonproducers. How many here now are your relatives? Do any of them actually do anything?"

Montale hemmed and hawed and talked around the edges. Else interrupted. "They won't lose their jobs. If they do them. Would any of you argue that this place isn't a slum? We're going to change that. We have enough people. We start today. Anyone who's been getting a free ride and doesn't want to give it up can take the option pioneered by Mr. Copria, Mr. Grazia, and Mr. Verga. Name a devil. Here's Mr. Grazia."

Grazia was a short, fat man with fat lips and a natural tonsure. The little hair that he did retain was red, lightly touched with gray. Humorists wondered whether his hair would all disappear before the remnants grayed.

Grazia puffed, "Sorry I'm late. There was a crisis."

Some eavesdropper had brought warning.

"Better late than never." The foreigner expected to separate Grazia from his job anyway, in time. "We'll look at your books when we're done here. We haven't been getting the most out of our budget."

Grazia turned a pasty gray.

"Mr. Negrone. Mr. Pagani. General cleaning and upkeep seem to fall within your purview. Brainstorm me some ideas on how to get this place cleaned up, fixed up, and painted, employing a tribe used to taking paid naps and putting in ten-hour shifts playing cards. Madam Ristoti?"

The cook's kitchen was the one bright spot Else had found. She said, "Call me Carina. I have some ideas."

"Excellent, Madam Ristoti. One and all. We're going to be more formal with one another. That will put our work on a businesslike footing. Now. Madam. Your ideas, please."

In the area of managing the backstairs Madam Ristoti possessed a field marshal's mind.

Else gave her three minutes. "Excellent. You're in charge of everything. You *can* manage that and the kitchen both? Mr. Negrone? You want to take issue?"

Else gave Negrone equal time. Then, "In other words, you have no suggestions. You just object to Madam Ristoti's proposals because she's a woman."

"That's putting it baldly . . ."

"There won't be any beating around the bush anymore. Mr. Grazia, I assume you know what everyone gets paid. How much will Mr. Negrone not be taking home if he finds himself unemployed?"

Negrone mumbled something before Grazia could respond.

Else said, "There isn't going to be any debate. If you think there's a better way to do things, tell me. Convince me. If people won't cooperate, tell me. I'll break arms and kick butts. Or instruct Mr. Caniglia not to let them in. So. Let's start. Go figure out how to make this ruin fit for human habitation. Not you, Mr. Grazia. You stay here with me."

Mr. Grazia was not happy.

Later, Else said, "Mr. Grazia, I'm pretty sure you've heard all about Father Obilade."

"Yes."

"You're aware that Paludan Bruglioni tends to overreact when he gets angry?"

"Yes, sir."

"Find a way to put the money back. In the meantime, you'll be my number-one guy around here. Because I have your stones in a vice."

"Yes, sir."

"I hope the others will be as reasonable. Go to work, Mr. Grazia." Else headed for the kitchens. Polo was there, listening to the Ristoti woman.

Caniglia and another man intercepted him. Their expressions were so dark he feared they planned something stupid. But Caniglia said, "A runner left a message for you with Diano."

The other man extended a folded letter. Else said, "I see the seal fell off."

Caniglia grunted.

Else asked, "Why so grim?"

"Some people you told us not to let back in got nasty when I told them. They said they'd be even nastier if I tried to keep them from coming in tomorrow."

"I'll deal with that."

That did not improve Caniglia's mood. That was not the answer he wanted.

"WHO'S THE LETTER FROM?" POLO ASKED. ELSE SAT WITH HIS back against the wall in the common space of their quarters.

"A woman I knew a long time ago. Anna Mozilla. A widow who moved to Brothe a few months ago. She heard I was here. She wants me to know she's here, too. I guess that means she isn't mad at me anymore."

Polo chuckled. "Is this a good story?"

"Not really. She's a widow, but too young to give up the more intimate practices of marriage. At least, she was. And must still be."

"Her turning up mean trouble?"

"I doubt it. Just the opposite, I hope."

"OPEN UP," ELSE TOLD CANIGLIA. "LET'S SEE WHO'S ON TIME for work."

Caniglia opened the servants' postern, which had not been closed and locked for years. Not even after Father Obilade's treason. Paludan was almost willfully blind to anything that he did not want to be true.

Caniglia and young Diano put on a show, allowing the staff in one at a time. Each got a quick visual once-over to see what they were carrying. Which told Else that they had turned a blind eye to that in the past. And, probably, more so when the staff were leaving.

Else wished he understood accounting better. Mr. Grazia's books almost certainly contained more amazing and damning evidence than he could ferret out himself.

What would Paludan's attitude be? He seemed the sort who disdained literacy and ciphering. Though that attitude was less prevalent than Else had expected, based on past encounters with Arnhanders in the Holy Lands. Over there, if you needed something read, written, or calculated, you grabbed a passing Deve.

Where did Gervase Saluda fit? Might he be getting kickbacks? That happened in every palace and large household in Else's end of the world.

"Who is this?" Else asked. A handsome young man carrying a load of tools staggered through the gateway.

Caniglia replied, "Marco Demetrius. A carpenter. Related to the cook. He always turns up when there's carpentry to be done. He's good. And a good worker."

"So Madam Ristoti sent for him." The chief cook seldom left the citadel, though she was not officially a resident.

Copria and Verga tried to get in, one right after the other. Else said, "Mr. Verga, you appear to have forgotten that you don't work here anymore. Don't embarrass yourself. You and Mr. Copria should apologize to the people behind you for holding them up, then leave."

Verga snarled, "Get out of the way. You don't have the authority."

Else hit Verga with a flurry of rib-cracking jabs. Verga fell to his knees, desperately fighting for enough air to remain conscious.

Else told him, "You no longer work here."

Copria was less blustery. He helped Verga get up. They left.

Else hoped that would be lesson enough. He told Caniglia, "I want to know who shows up late. Starting tomorrow, the gate will close ten minutes after starting time. Tardies won't be allowed in and they won't get paid."

ANNA MOZILLA HAD ACQUIRED A SMALL HOME RATHER LIKE the one she had enjoyed in Sonsa. Else climbed the front steps. He used the clapper. Anna responded almost immediately. She looked exactly as she had in Sonsa.

"You were followed."

"Yes. Not competently, either."

"You let them keep track?"

"Yes."

"Why?"

"I explained you as a former mistress. Your letter had been read before it got to me."

She moved up against him, familiarly, as she drew him into her house. "That's why I made the letter general. I thought that would be the best way to explain me."

Though the door was shut and there were now no witnesses, Anna Mozilla did not back off. Nor did Else push her away. It felt good, being close to a woman. Even one who had a decade on him. And who was not his wife.

Anna Mozilla said, "We were completely businesslike before. Completely professional. I teased myself about that afterward. Then they asked me to move down here. It took you so long to get here. That left me too much time to think."

Else did not reply. He knew what he should do but just could not push.

"It wouldn't be a sin, Frain." Else had called himself Frain Dorao in Sonsa. "I'm an unbeliever."

So. She understood that much.

That was an interpretation of Law as stated in The Written. There was no adultery when the woman was not Praman.

Else did not back away. Neither did he take charge, though she had shown him the open gate. He left the initiative entirely in her hands.

Those hands proved capable, if tentative at first.

ELSE TOOK HIS SUPPER IN THE KITCHEN SO HE COULD CONVERSE with Madam Ristoti. "Has there been much obstructionism?"

"Less than I expected. You got them scared. That business at the back gate told them you're serious."

"What do you think?"

"I think you're deadly serious."

"I am."

"Why?"

"Because I want to keep working. I came to Brothe to be near the center of the excitement. I need a job to stay."

"My people have been in service to the great families all the way back to Imperial times. According to family legend. One pearl of wisdom plucked out of all that history is that every house mirrors the interior of its master."

"Meaning this place is falling apart and the staff is slovenly because that's how Paludan Bruglioni is?"

"Yes. Paludan doesn't like the house the way it is. But it's too much trouble to do battle with the night."

"Uh?"

"Oh. I didn't mean that in the supernatural sense. Only spiritually. Like, the night will always be there, no matter how hard you fight it. So why bother? Why suffer all that frustration?"

"I see. Is there anything I can show Paludan and Gervase when they finally decide they have to know what all the racket is about?"

"There will be."

"How do you think this will play with Saluda?"

"What are you asking?"

"Does Saluda have a personal interest in things staying the way they are? Has he been collecting kickbacks? I haven't found any evidence but that's what it feels like."

That notion surprised the cook. "I don't think so. Not that he wouldn't. If he thought of it."

"But he might have an interest?"

"Maybe. But he's also more of a Bruglioni than most of the family who ran off to the country. Who don't want to come back."

Else had heard the same from Polo.

"So it goes. That can be dealt with. Keep on, here. And find me a couple of troublemakers to fire. To remind the others that they can be replaced."

Else found Polo with Mr. Grazia. Polo reported, "There's been some creative accounting here. Paludan Bruglioni is spending thirty thousand ducats a year for half that in results, mostly as payouts to people who don't exist for work that doesn't get done and to vendors for goods that never arrive."

"I see. Mr. Grazia! Did you think nobody would ever notice?"

Grazia shrugged. Like so many caught in his situation, he had no idea why he had not considered possible consequences.

Else asked, "Polo, did you ever get my paper?"

"No. I keep trying the places in Naftali Square. They keep having nothing to sell. I haven't had time to go to the Devedian quarter."

"I'll handle it myself, then. Keep putting Mr. Grazia through his paces." Else patted Grazia's shoulder. "An epic of the imagination, sir. A true epic."

"You won't tell Paludan?"

"Not as long as you're helping me whip this place into shape. You slack off, though, or you dip your beak again, then you can probably count on getting together with Father Obilade."

ELSE TRIED TO SLIP AWAY USING THE SERVANTS' GATE. THAT did not work. He picked up a tail anyway.

He worried who and why for a few minutes, decided that it didn't matter. There were only two of them and they were inept. He shed them near Anna Mozilla's house. Thoughts of Anna distracted him momentarily. But he could reward himself later. He headed for the Devedian quarter.

Brothe's Devedian elders admitted that twenty thousand Deves lived in the city. Rumor suggested there were several times that. If true, then more Deves lived in the seat of the inimical Episcopal faith than in the Holy Lands themselves. But in Suriet the towns could not grow large, except on the coast of the Mother Sea. The coast where western invaders established their crusader principalities and kingdoms.

There were many times more Devedians in their Diaspora than remained resident in the mad country that had given them birth.

Else tried and failed to imagine what it must be like to live in those madlands, in amongst the Wells of Ihrian, where the magic boiled out of the earth incessantly, warping everything around it, birthing malignant new spirits, feeding the Instrumentalities of the Night, and incidentally, unleashing the only power capable of holding the ice at bay.

Even today many Devedian native sons were perfectly willing to leave Suriet and let it become a nesting place of Chaldarean conquerors and Praman liberators alike. Or maybe the reverse.

Let them bash one another's heads amidst the floods from the magical springs. One day He Whose Name Is Legion would cleanse the earth of all but His Chosen.

Aaron, Eis, Kelam, and the other prophets who laid the foundations of Arianism, which evolved into Chaldareanism, departed the Holy Lands themselves as soon as their preaching and witnessing gifted them with donations sufficient to let them travel without having to sleep under bridges. They scattered across the Brothen Empire, carrying their message to those whose lives consisted primarily of despair.

The preaching, the witnessing, the performing of miracles—most of that had taken place far from the Wells of Ihrian, in provinces now part of Lucidia or the Eastern Empire.

As he moved southward Else began to sense a potent electric tension. Something significant had happened. Something bigger was expected to happen. Its threatened scale troubled everyone.

Else could not get an answer when he asked why. There was an immense prejudice against foreigners with blond hair.

His Devedian contact could explain.

There was no threat of rain, but the Deves and Dainshaus scurried about in a jerky hurry, as though trying to get the day's business done before bad weather arrived.

Else entered a tiny papermaker's shop. A sign on the artist's own product proclaimed it the source of the best papers in Brothe. A stereotypical little old Deve, bent, leaning on a cane, his features camouflaged by thickets of wiry gray hair, came from the back in response to the bell that jingled when Else opened the front door. Chemical smells accompanied the shopkeeper.

"How may I be of . . . ?" the little man asked as he forced his head to turn upward. He did not complete his question.

"I'm here to buy paper, not collect heads. I want an inexpensive, working grade. Twenty sheets. Then I want a better grade, suitable for permanent records and letters expected to survive travel over extended distances. Again, twenty standard sheets.

Finally, I want some of that erasable parchment or vellum that students use."

The old man found his tongue. "That's an animal product, not paper, though normally we keep some around. You need a special ink, a treatment sponge, a sanding stone, an ink remover, and Halmas clay. Plus calligraphy brushes."

"I'm in the market for those things, too."

"We don't carry any of that."

"And that isn't a problem. There seems to be a paper shortage in Brothe. I'm prepared to go from shop to shop until I find everything."

"You can pay for all that?"

"Of course. You have a problem with me? You're averse to making a sale?"

"Not at all, sir. This constitutes an excellent sale. My biggest in weeks. It's just that we don't often see men like yourself here in the quarter. Twenty sheets packer grade, twenty choice?"

"Packer?"

The old man shrugged. "Nobody knows why it's called that. Not anymore. It's your working grade. Your most affordable paper."

"I see."

"And how much of the reusable?"

"Six folded to standard-size double exercise sheets. One for me and one for each of my students."

"Students? Uh . . . Never mind. None of my business. I have three of those in stock. I know where to find the rest. And the supplies to go with."

"Good."

"I'll send my grandsons to bring it all here. That'll save you running from shop to shop."

Else scowled.

"Oh. No, sir. I won't add another layer of markup." The bent little man leaned closer to confide, "They'll pay a commission. Because they know I could send the boys to someone else. It's about the extension of goodwill and favor."

"Go ahead, then," Else said. "I've walked enough for today. And I still have to go back home."

The old man shouted in a locally warped exile Melhaic dialect, well spiced with Firaldian derivatives.

Else spoke some Suriet Melhaic and enough of its cousin Peqaad to get by with those tribesmen. He understood half of what he heard. The old man gave orders to collect Else's merchandise, then directed that someone named Pinan Talab be told that a blond stranger was in Luca Farada's paper shop. While the old man jabbered a parade of boys from the rear of the shop snapped quick bows at Else, then headed out the front door. Each brought a burst of chemical smell, a sulfurous cast that Else had associated with papermakers since childhood. The odor stirred memories of the time before time, before his purchase by the Sha-lug. Though those memories were seldom more than a nostalgic mood.

The old man offered plenty of distracting chatter, speaking Firaldian to Else when not instructing his descendents, sometimes changing languages in midsentence. In a puckish moment, Else asked, "Why would Pinan Talab be interested in what kind of paper a Chaldarean buys?"

For an instant it seemed the superannuated papermaker would expire from horror. Then he just stared at Else in silence, disturbed and frightened.

"My paper? Shouldn't you get that ready while you wait to hear from Talab?"

"These are strange times, sir. For example, much of Brothe is obsessing about foreigners with blond hair. It doesn't affect us here, but it's still a concern—if you're the man who caused the excitement."

Else donned a stupid, baffled expression. "I work for the Bruglioni. Uh. You're all lathered about those guys who were supposed to work for us but really worked for the priest who was planted on us by the Brotherhood of War? Pretty funny, huh? Those guys, after the priest turned them loose, went and killed like eight or ten of the bunch that the priest was spying for."

The old man was not amused. His grandsons began to return. As they surrendered their merchandise they hustled on to the rear of the shop. Each passage loosed another puff of chemical-laden air.

Else remained prepared for treachery—though he could not

imagine why these people would bother. But nothing happened. The grandsons came back. The merchandise piled up. Soon everything Else had asked for was ready. "Excellent. I'll recommend you to anyone looking for paper."

"That's kind of you, sir. Tell them to stock up now. Once the fighting starts the soldiers will take all we produce."

"The fighting? What fighting?"

"You haven't heard?"

"Obviously, not. I'm bottled up inside the Bruglioni citadel most of the time. When I do come out people won't talk to me because I have blond hair. What's happened?"

"The pirates. They launched a massive raid yesterday. Against Starplire. They massacred the priests and nuns and scholars and looted everything they could carry off. They even murdered most of the townspeople. A squadron of Imperial cavalry that was headed for Alameddine overran the stragglers. That saved a few people the pirates hadn't yet found." The old man's face darkened as he sketched the disaster.

Starplire, Else thought. Just inland from the coast, south of the mouth of the Teragi. Not fortified. A population in the thousands, mostly monks, nuns, and sacred scholars. Main industries, monasticism and religious education. Starplire boasted Episcopal Chadareanism's principal university. And a tiny Devedian colony, practicing the arts that seemed to come so easily to that race.

"I see."

"They say the Patriarch will convene the Collegium and preach a crusade against Calzir."

"About time, if you ask me." Else accepted his change. The old man put his purchases into a sack that, in a previous incarnation, might have contained rice. "Did you have family there?"

"We're all family."

Else wrestled with mixed emotions as he left. An Episcopal crusade against Calzir would serve Dreanger better than a crusade against the heretics of the Connec. It should occupy Sublime far longer while not profiting him a ducat. Calzir might hold out long enough for nature to catch up with Sublime. Or the crusade might bankrupt him.

But Calzirans were Praman.

And not very bright Pramans. What insanity moved them to do something as stupid as butcher the entire population of Starplire?

Sinister forces were at work.

"Captain."

The soft voice came from a shadow in a foot-wide crack between buildings. Else would not have responded had it not been familiar. A hairy little shape hid in the crack. "Gledius Stewpo? What're you doing here?"

"This is no place to talk. Follow me." Stewpo popped out and hurried along the street, comical in his effort not to appear furtive. What could be more noteworthy than a sneaking dwarf?

Else followed, awash with thoughts and questions. First, war. Now, Gledius Stewpo.

"YOU PEOPLE HAVE AN UNNATURAL PASSION FOR HOLES IN THE ground," Else told Stewpo.

"That's why they talk about a Deve underground."

"Ha! And ha!"

"You're treated like vermin, you adopt vermin's strategies for surviving." Stewpo had led Else down into a warren underneath the Devedian quarter. Which he suggested had been there since early Imperial times. The Deves of those days used to rescue brethren enslaved in the Holy Lands and hide them in the labyrinth. "It isn't just a Devedian thing, though, Captain. Everybody in Brothe has secret cellars and hidden worlds below. The primitive Chaldareans, the Arianists, had a network of tunnels and secret rooms and chapels all over under the city. We know they're still there because they keep caving in."

Four Devedians met them in a hidden place much like the hidden place in Sonsa. Even the odor of the earth was similar. Else recognized two men. Like Gledius Stewpo, they hailed from Sonsa. The others, when introduced, were Pinan Talab and Else's principal contact in Brothe, one Shire Spereo.

Spereo observed, "You've been a hellish long time getting here."

"Such are the mercies of my supposed profession. I got locked up for half a year."

Stewpo said, "Your masters must've been cranky about that."

"They'll feel better when they learn about this war I hear is coming."

"Which will keep the Patriarch preoccupied."

"Are they behind it? What's really going on?"

The Deves exchanged puzzled looks. "What do you mean?" Stewpo asked.

"Somebody has to be putting the Calzirans up to this. They can't possibly be so stupid that they think the Patriarch will tolerate a wholesale plundering of Church property and the Episcopal States."

"Actually, I think they *are* that stupid. They know the mercantile republics are mad at the Patriarch and won't help him. And the first raiders went home in ships nearly foundering with infidel treasure. Gold fever is sweeping Calzir. Anybody with a boat big enough to haul booty is rounding up friends and old weapons to go get rich. Starplire may leave them bold enough to hit a really large, rich target."

Else reflected, "Too much success could make them forget to concentrate on Sublime and the Benodocto. If they bite Hansel or one of the mercantile republics . . ."

"They'll suffer," Talab said. "We understand that. But they don't. Calzir is hip-deep in stupidity these days. Not to suggest that bright is common anywhere, nor ever was welcome in Calzir. That realm's biggest problem is a lack of any real central control."

Stewpo said, "This situation has repeated itself every sixty to eighty years since the Praman conquest. Eventually an allied Chaldarean fleet will scour the Calziran coast. Piracy will stop—until the last old man who remembers how things went dies off."

Another Deve said, "They always think they have God on their side. They always think Firaldians are too soft to put up a fight."

Stewpo observed, "Perhaps if they were a more literate society?"

"Stewpo, I haven't heard why you're here in Brothe."

"Sure, you have. Just not from me. Things went to shit in

Sonsa. The Brotherhood sent another gang of thugs from Castella dollas Pontellas to avenge that wizard."

"This will amuse you. That wizard led the company I joined. He has almost no powers left."

"Good," Stewpo snarled. "Someday . . ." He pulled himself together. "The Dainshaukin and Devedian communities decided to abandon Sonsa. After half the Devedian population died."

Else did not suffer a twinge.

Stewpo said, "Al-Qarn isn't happy with you."

"Anyone there who thinks he can do better is welcome to take over."

"They have no concept of the realities here. But that isn't the point. Part of your job would be to make them understand. I've been reminded, recently, that you haven't reported yet. They know you're alive only through secondary sources."

"I was told to report when I had something to report. I haven't, yet." Ignoring Stewpo's point about the educational aspect of his mission.

"People in power want to know what's going on. They have decisions to make. They need information. They squeal like wounded swine when they don't have it. I'm not interested in making their lives easier, though."

"I understand," Else said. "The enemy of your enemy is your ally."

"But never a friend. Do you understand?"

"Perfectly. Before we worry about the shape of our end of the world we need to rid it of the threat of the west."

Gledius Stewpo said, "You might be too bright for your kind of work."

"No doubt. And here you are, a hound baying at the behest of a false god. Yet you show no shame."

"I hope these aren't the end times where we have to find out which one of us is the deluded devil-worshiper."

Else replied, "None of that matters. Not now. If Sublime preaches a crusade against Calzir . . ."

"The Collegium will approve a punitive expedition against the pirate ports because of Starplire, but that's all. Which is too bad. If Sublime bogged down in Calzir he'd be too busy to do any mischief in the Holy Lands."

"As long as I'm here, why don't I do a report that you can pass along?" Else did not mention that he *had* reported before. "If I can dictate it. It's a long story."

Later, report done, Else said, "I need one more thing. As a Bruglioni henchman. An accountant. A wizard with numbers who can ferret out bookkeeping deceits. The Bruglioni staff have been stealing their masters blind using bookkeeping tricks. I'm trying to make my name with them."

Stewpo nodded. "I'll see what can be done."

POLO SAID, "YOU FOUND PAPER. GOOD."

"In the Deve quarter. But they said, with war possible, the supply won't last. Big price increases are coming."

"War. Yeah. They want to see you about that. Right away."

"Why? They spend all their time hiding out. I can't ever get hold of them when I need something."

"And that's bad? Paludan is happy with you."

"Really? I'm making it up as I go, Polo. They never told me what to do, they just hired me to do something. So I'm doing what obviously needs doing. And wondering why the second richest family in Brothe lives in a dump. How do they stay feared and respected? There's nobody here to respect or fear. Is that a secret? You say they're waiting for me now?"

"Not as such. They're in the private audience. Playing chess."

"What are they up to?"

"Divino was here for a while. It might have to do with the pirate problem."

"Divino? That's the uncle who's in the Collegium?"

"Yes. Principaté Divino Bruglioni. You've probably met him without realizing who he was. He comes around here a lot."

"Take this stuff to our quarters. Then get Madam Ristoti to send me something to eat. In the private audience. I haven't eaten all day."

"You didn't see your lady friend?"

"I was looking for paper. And learning my way around that part of town."

"All business, eh?"

"Always, Polo. That's how you get ahead in the world."

* * *

GERVASE SALUDA HAD HIS BACK TO THE DOOR WHEN ELSE EN-
tered the private audience. The room was twelve feet by sixteen, big by peasant standards but small for a working room in
the Bruglioni citadel. There were few furnishings. One chess
table. Four chairs, two in use already. A fireplace, not lighted.
Paludan Bruglioni sat opposite Gervase, scowling fiercely at
the chessboard.

"Yeah, Hecht. You're here. You were out and around today,
right?"

"I went to the Devedian quarter to get paper. For the boys'
lessons. I took the opportunity to find out more about that part
of the city."

"You heard what happened at Starplire?"

"Only the bare bones of the story. I have blond hair. People
talk to me only as much as they need to, to separate me from
my money. I didn't hear much war talk, though."

"You must not have been listening. There's a lot of war talk.
Uncle Divino says the Patriarch may preach a crusade. And the
Collegium will let him have it."

That startled Else. "Really?"

"Really. Most of them lost family at Starplire. But there're
more pressing problems."

"Yes?"

"The Collegium, according to Divino, began tracking the
Calziran pirates after the news from Starplire. The pirates are
more numerous, more organized, and more centrally controlled
than anybody suspected. The Starplire raid was a rehearsal."

"This is more disturbing by the moment."

Gervase Saluda said, "Indeed. Pull up a chair. Let's talk."

Else did as he was told. "Go ahead."

"The pirates are thinking about attacking Brothe next. They
see no reason to expect much resistance. The only soldiers in
town are the Brotherhood. There aren't a hundred of them,
right now."

"The Calzirans know all that?"

"They do."

"Do they know we know they know? No. I take that back.
Are their captains intimate with the Instrumentalities of the

Night? Would they think that somebody here knows what they're doing?"

"Their leaders . . . might. The Collegium is no secret."

Paludan interrupted. "That's not why we're here. We have to worry about family protection and property preservation."

"By which you mean?"

"We have properties all over the city."

"You won't be able to protect everything. You might not be able to protect anything if you don't know what's likely to be attacked. Consolidate here. Everything you don't want stolen or vandalized and anyone you don't want killed. Better yet, move to the country until the raiders go away."

Gervase said, "That wouldn't be the best option, politically."

Paludan added, "We're Bruglioni. We're obligated to defend the city."

"How? Your army is me. Plus four gatekeepers and some kids who haven't figured out which end of a sword you're supposed to grab."

"Everybody has that problem. The nearest Patriarchal garrison is at Bober, four days away. The nearest soldiers could be here in two, but that would be the Imperial garrison from Gage. Which includes the Empire's best—just in case Hansel decides to swoop down on Brothe."

"So we're afraid Imperials might be more trouble than Calziran pirates?"

Gervase snorted. "No. But Sublime might see it that way."

Paludan agreed. "If the pirates do come, Sublime will just hole up on his island and wait them out."

Else said, "I won't live long enough to understand Brothen politics. That looks like a huge opportunity for Sublime's enemies."

"It is. Uncle Divino and his cronies will take advantage if that happens."

"So both parties might just let the rape happen? One out of cowardice and the other for political gain?"

"I don't know. I do want a soldier's professional opinion of the situation."

"I'll see what I can find out. Ah. Madam Ristoti. Thank you. But I think I'm done here now, so I'll just eat in the kitchen."

He looked to Paludan Bruglioni for permission to leave. After a dark scowl, Bruglioni nodded.

ELSE WENT OUT EARLY. NO ONE FOLLOWED. HE VISITED THE Arniena compound first, where he managed a short audience with Rogoz Sayag and his father. Inigo Arniena joined them briefly.

Else moved on to Bronte Doneto's establishment. Just Plain Joe was on duty at the gate. He whisked Else inside.

"They got some good food here, Pipe," Joe reported. "An' plenty of it. This's the best job I ever had. Except for having Ghort as my boss. He's a real asshole sometimes."

"That's all us officers, Joe. When we have to get some use out of a guy like Bo, every day, after a while it turns you sour."

Joe laughed. "I got you."

"How's Pig Iron?"

"Livin' in hog heaven, Pipe. He's got it twice as better than I do. This's it. Yo! Here's Captain Hecht."

Pinkus Ghort was serious about being Doneto's number-one man. He had six professional soldiers brainstorming responses to a possible Calziran attack.

"Wow!" Else said. "I have a hundred-year-old man named Vigo Caniglia and three other men, none trained and only one young enough to be of any use. Plus some kids, the oldest being sixteen."

"Way I hear, Pipe, these Five Family types are so damned cheap, you're probably better off. Even though the poorest can afford a whole regiment if they want. We were fools when we thought we could make our fortunes here. Though some of us got lucky."

"Any useful news?" Else asked. "What I've got is, the pirates might be coming to Brothe. And nobody thinks there's much we can do about it. I'm supposed to tell the family what to do."

"You know about as much as I do. The Principaté ain't my pal no more. He's all busy with schemes and conspiracies and not giving the guy who has to do the heavy lifting anything to work with."

"He say what his cousin's going to do?"

"No. But I'd put my money on him hunkering down, waiting out the storm, then using it as an excuse to start a crusade. He wants a crusade, bad. He don't much care who against. Come over here. Check this map. If you were a half-ass mob of plunderers used to fishing for a living, where would you make your landing?" Ghort had a nice map of the city laid out.

"I wouldn't come all the way up here. I'd take fire from the bridges and fortified islands."

"But if you unship down here you'll get hung up in the tenements. Where the streets are narrow and tangled and there's nothing worth stealing."

"What's this here? I haven't been downriver from the Castella yet."

"Monuments. Plazas. Memorials. Mostly over a thousand years old. More plazas. Lots of squatters because there isn't anybody to run them off. It's not a good place for fighting."

"How about the north bank? Would they land there first?"

"Then cross the bridges? I might try that if I knew how feeble we are. It would make for an easy debarkation. But not much plunder. The big churches and family holdings are south of the river."

"These Calzirans are mostly fishermen and coastal traders, right? So they'll just be a mob. They could be panicked."

"We're looking at what might be some pretty big numbers, though. Got any ideas?"

"Sure. But we don't have the people. We'd need experienced soldiers. There's nobody out there but the Brotherhood."

"That we can see, Pipe. Or that enemy spies can see. But how about all those squatters out there? A lot of those guys came to Brothe hoping to join the armies the Patriarch hasn't gotten around to putting together."

"Ho! Pinkus, you aren't half as dumb as you put on. Why don't we take a walk? I know somebody over at the Castella."

"Anybody I'd know?"

"Sure. Redfearn Bechter. He made it out of the Connec. I ran into him the other day. He might listen long enough to think you're on to something."

"Grade Drocker is in charge over there, now. He's tight with

Sublime. Sublime might not want the city to be able to defend itself."

"Drocker, eh? I thought Hawley Quirke was number one."

"Sublime got Quirke recalled to Runch. Quirke wouldn't kiss his ass."

"I thought the Brotherhood was big on being its own boss."

"They're big on crusades, too. Sublime says he's gonna give them some. The Special Office is all fired up."

"THERE'S A PLAN IN PLACE, NOW," ELSE TOLD PALUDAN, DIvino Bruglioni, and Gervase Saluda. Divino Bruglioni was the man Else had seen with Gervase and Paludan before. Divino did not seem as old as an uncle ought to be. "I spent all day running hither and yon, seeing men I knew from the Connec. We figured out how to handle a pirate attack. The Bruglioni would have to contribute four thousand, two hundred ducats and any skilled fighters who can work with the Brotherhood. Which would be me. The Madisetti, the Arniena, and Bronte Doneto's subclan of the Benedocto have all agreed already. I'm supposed to enlist the Bruglioni."

Paludan had trouble breathing. The Principaté sat quietly, considering Else. Gervase gasped. "Forty-two-hundred ducats?"

"Forty-two from each of the Five Families. Plus contributions from the Church, the Brotherhood, and the Deves."

"Four thousand two hundred ducats," Paludan murmured. "Tell me the plan."

"That's where it gets a little sticky. Drocker is convinced that the Calzirans have allies and spies here."

Uncle Divino offered, "They do. It was by spying on their spies that we learned that a sorcerer named Masant al-Seyhan controls the pirates. Go ahead, Captain Hecht."

"Because of those spies Drocker doesn't want to discuss his plans. I know you don't like it but that's the way it's got to be. Principaté, he'll explain to you. But only if Paludan isn't willing to take my word that total secrecy is necessary."

Gervase asked, "They don't trust *us*?"

"No. Grade Drocker is the most cynical man I've ever met. He's sure that, fully informed, one of the Five Families would sell out the rest in exchange for not being plundered. Or some abused and underpaid servant might hear something and sell the information. Looking at the historical record, Drocker may be justified."

Uncle Divino opined, "It would be a huge risk just talking to the Collegium."

"I'm sure he has that angle covered. I don't like him. Not even a little. But he's the man to deal with what might be headed our way."

Paludan wriggled and whimpered for days before he financed his share of the Grand Strategy—once pressured sufficiently by his uncle Divino.

Only Sublime refused to contribute to the defense fund. He did not like the master plan. It did not sufficiently aggrandize him or the Patriarchy.

Else felt boyishly pleased when Grade Drocker announced, "His Holiness will receive no protection since he refuses to participate in the common defense. Eis be blessed, even the heathen Deves are contributing."

Else shivered in secret glee. Everything was going perfectly.

THE CALZIRAN PIRATES DID ATTACK UP THE TERAGI, IN NUM-bers far greater than anticipated, a week later than expected. Their sails masked the river for miles.

During the delay week they raided Terea, where the raiders ran into Imperial troops headed south, to take part in whatever adventure Hansel and his local henchmen had afoot in Alameddine.

The Collegium declared the Terea raid a diversion meant to draw defenders away from the city. The Tereans and Imperials were awarded their freedom to twist in the wind.

Rumor said Masant al-Seyhan had secret allies amongst the Five Families. Or the Colors. Or one of Brothe's numerous minorities.

Redfearn Bechter told Else and Pinkus Ghort, "You got to know somebody told them assholes that all we've been doing is trying to fool them into staying away." The occasion was another endless planning meeting where little got decided.

Ghort replied, "I can't believe Drocker counted on them being scared off. I bet he was playing it so maybe he could find out who was friendly with the pirates."

"There's one idea we do need to get spread around," Else said. "The notion that the people in charge know what they're doing."

"This is why I like Hecht," Bechter said. "He's all over fitted up with positive thinking."

Ghort said, "Great idea, Pipe. But a little late." He pointed. A pillar of gray signal smoke leaned southward against the morning sky, way downriver. "Calzirans have entered the river. There's going to be a fight."

This made no sense to Else. How did a mob of fishermen, badly armed peasants, and small-time merchant seamen talk themselves into attacking the seat of an empire in full expectation of looting it? There had to be more to this than was obvious.

Two thousand veterans from amongst the squatters had been recruited and formed into small companies, each commanded by a member of the Brotherhood. Local volunteers and troops the Five Families had brought in from outside added another two thousand men. Else was sure four thousand would not be adequate.

He told Ghort, "These people are insane."

Ghort grunted agreement. "Did you have any idea it would be like this when you decided to come here?"

"No. The stories don't have anything to do with reality."

"No shit. If I'd known what it was really like . . . These Calziran thugs wouldn't have Pinkus Ghort to bang around on. I didn't get into this racket on account of the opportunities for fighting."

Else did not think many soldiers did like the fighting. Mercenaries ended up where they were, doing what they did, because there was nothing else they could do. They were like prostitutes, that way.

If you chose survival you did what you had to do to survive. Morality, ethics, and charity were luxuries enjoyed only by those rich enough to indulge in them.

"Where the hell are you, Pipe?" Ghort demanded. "Pluck your head out of your ass and let's eyeball the situation."

"You know why we get to stop them in the Memorium?" Else asked.

"Shit, yeah. So that anything that goes wrong will be some dumb mercenary's fault. Meaning you and me, boy. We're carrying the sins of the Patriarch and the Five Families on our shoulders. And we'll be in the wrong whatever the fuck we do."

Gervase Saluda eased up beside Else. "Am I catching all the implications, Hecht? You believe the Patriarch is manipulating things so you and this Ghort creature will take the blame for anything that goes wrong?"

Ghort responded, "And wouldn't you try the same stunt if Pipe didn't work for you? Shit. Pipe. Look. Them pricks are at the boom already."

A log and chain boom had been stretched across the Teragi two miles downriver. It was supposed to fix the pirate fleet for artillery on both banks. Unfortunately, demilitarization left Brothe only a handful of war engines. Most were lightweight and held by people unwilling to surrender them to the corporate good. Just six wheeled ballistae had been collected.

A greasy ball of smoke and fire boiled up over the boom.

Else asked, "What do you think, Sergeant Bechter?"

"I think some major sorcery just happened. I think the bad guys have cut the boom. I think that means we're in trouble."

Arriving news soon suggested that Redfearn Bechter was psychic. Except that his sorcery had been an explosion aboard a boat deliberately driven into the boom.

There might be a thousand vessels in the stampede headed upriver.

Before long a messenger announced, "They've started landing on the north bank, just below the Blendine Bridge."

The Blendine was the first bridge encountered by vessels coming up the Teragi. It stood less than two hundred yards downstream from the Castella dollas Pontellas. Its arches rose high enough that ships could pass below if they unstepped their masts and proceeded under oars. They were wide enough to allow the passage of warships headed for the Castella. Militia armed with javelins, cheap crossbows, boulders, and blocks of building stone, were stationed on that bridge.

But the north shore, below the bridge, was undefended. The pirates attacked the bridge from there. They crossed over against resistance that surprised Else, under withering fire from the Castella. Decimated, sometimes stunned by the horror, the Calzirans plunged into the expanse of monuments, fountains, triumphal arches, and little plazas known as the Memorium, where the earliest and most ferocious fighting was expected to occur. Where the success or failure of the raid might be determined.

Brothe's leading defenders had expected the pirates to come ashore on the south bank, at the downstream end of the Memorium, then attack eastward to isolate Krois and the Castella dollas Pontellas while seizing the bridges over the Teragi to keep help from coming from the north. The pirates could then turn to systematic plunder.

By beaching on the north bank and storming the Blendine Bridge the pirates avoided having to fight through 80 percent of the Memorium, where they would have been treated cruelly in ambushes and cross fires designed to exploit their lack of experience and discipline.

Pinkus Ghort observed, "This isn't no mob gone crazy, Pipe. People on the other side knows what's going on. We're about to get slapped around like a couple teenaged whores."

"There's order and planning, anyway. The pirates may just be here for the plunder but I'm thinking somebody is more ambitious."

Redfearn Bechter generally kept his own counsel. He preferred to do God's work quietly. If you asked the Sergeant, he would tell you God was like a tailor. A gentle entity who preferred to carry on the business of the world with minimal fuss. Bechter observed, "We're screwed if we don't decide right now that this is bigger than just some Praman fishermen trying to steal anything that isn't nailed down. There's an evil genius at work."

Else sighed. "What do you think, Pinkus? Stand tough south and up here, but let them do what they want in between?"

Saluda protested, "That would push them into the heavily populated part of the city."

"Which is where they want to go. Right? So, if we let them, without making them kill us first, we stay alive to fight. Where they aren't. Right?"

Ghort snorted. "Their boats! Shit! Eis and Aaron! You're a fucking evil genius yourself, Pipe."

"Only if they're stupid enough to leave them on the north

bank. They do, we only have to fight them on the bridges when they try to get back."

"Heh-heh!" Ghort said. "Let's get the word spread. You know what'll happen, don't you, Pipe? The Brotherhood will harvest the glory."

"That's probably best. They can stand fast against a mob of panicky pirates. Gervase, if you want to make a contribution, how about you run over to Hanbros's Arch, find Gödel Joyce, and tell him not to put up a real fight because we want the bad guys headed toward the ruins of the Senate. Don't tell him anything else. Pinkus. Go see Moglia. Tell him to keep them from turning downriver. That's all he's got to do. It shouldn't be hard. Meanwhile, I'll slide over to the Castella. Bechter?"

"Right behind you, sir. How long before the pirates catch on?"

"Long enough to make it too late, I hope." Else was not optimistic, though. So many boats. Far more boats than anyone had imagined the Calzirans would bring.

Paludan Bruglioni and those few bold servants willing to help a Bruglioni followed Else to the Castella dollas Pontellas.

GRADE DROCKER HIMSELF LED A COMPANY ACROSS THE Rustige Bridge, above Krois, then attacked the beached and moored Calziran boats and ships. Drocker exploited his vestigial powers to confuse and panic the guards protecting the fleet—mostly boats so small they could have carried no more than five men. The guards were the Calziran sick and injured and elderly.

During a lull Else stared across the Teragi. He saw no sign of anything happening there. Closer, the Brotherhood began barricading the Blendine Bridge to fix the returning pirates for archers on the Castella battlements.

Sergeant Bechter observed, "They'll be here soon."

"They should be. Yes."

Drocker had not brought enough men to fortify the bridge and overwhelm the boat guards, both. Not quickly enough. Sheer numbers of boats and raiders slowed the attack. Drocker seemed unable to do anything useful once resistance stiffened. Scarcely a hundred of the smaller, beached vessels had been fired or holed when Drocker approached Else.

"We're already having trouble . . . holding the bridge. I have to go . . . help. Keep after it here. Concentrate on the . . . biggest boats. That will bother them . . . more. They'll do . . . stupid things. Oh. And keep an eye out . . . for a woman."

"Sir? A woman?"

"Somewhere in this mess . . . there's a woman sometimes known . . . as Starkden. A witch. She's here . . . with the fleet . . . amongst the boats. Otherwise, my power . . . would be adequate. Catch her. Take her alive. She has much . . . to answer for to . . . the Brotherhood of War."

"Sir, this isn't a situation I've faced before. How do I catch a witch if she doesn't want to be caught?"

"She will be badly stunned . . . now. I hit her hard. But that won't . . . last. Don't waste time. And don't forget to . . . drag her along if we can't hold . . . the bridge." Drocker had less trouble talking these days. His health had improved over the last year.

"Yes, sir."

"Catch her and . . . we'll win this easily, Hecht. Once they know . . . we control the source of their . . . good fortune. And know that . . . the Collegium will be waking up . . . any minute."

"Yes, sir." Else wondered why the Collegium was not involved already. Had the Calziran sorcerers managed to neutralize them somehow?

Drocker hurried off toward the Blendine Bridge. Else finally relaxed. Although Drocker was unaware that Else was responsible for crippling him, Else never felt comfortable around the man.

Bechter observed, "That ain't a man with much personality, but he's loaded up on willpower."

"Oh, he's got plenty of personality. All snake."

"Hey. That's the Special Office. They recruit people worse than the ones they hunt. So they only sign reptiles."

"Let's find this witch. Anybody know what we're looking for?"

Bechter said, "Amazingly enough, everybody in the Brotherhood does." He described a swarthy woman in her fifties who could have been Paludan Bruglioni's sister or mother—or any fortune-teller on the streets of Brothe.

Else said as much.

"Which explains why she comes and goes as she pleases all around the Mother Sea."

"Who does she work for?" Else was puzzled. He had not heard of Starkden before the events in Runch. She seemed to have a fabulous reputation on this side of the water.

"Interesting question, Captain. She appears to be an independent contractor. Look, we're in the middle of a fight. You want to have a conversation, drop back there with the masked man and his sidekick." Bechter meant Paludan and Gervase, who was back from his mission. They were not inclined to become directly involved in the rough work. "I've got unbelievers to punish."

"And a witch to find." A Praman witch, apparently.

The resistance offered by the boat guards declined as the strongest succumbed. The most easily panicked launched their boats or ran away. Calzirans across the river shrieked at those on the north bank to bring the damned boats over.

Else's wrist began to ache. His amulet had lain dormant for so long that he had forgotten it. Almost.

He dealt with a weak attack by a Calziran trio who appeared to consist of three generations of the same family, all injured in previous fighting. He dispatched them without emotion.

"Good on you," Bechter said. "Now you're getting to work."

"Let's just slash the rigging. I don't think we'll get much chance to start any more fires."

The pirates initiated a spirited effort to clear the Blendine Bridge. Lesser forces rushed the bridges above Krois and the Castella, too.

"We have smoke down there," Bechter said. "Not a good omen in a city."

Else eyed the smoke. Anna Mozilla's house lay in that direction, though farther away.

Else said, "There's a crowd on the towpath by that dhow flying the red pennon." They had damaged the majority of the beached craft now. "Would that mean they think there's something to protect on board?"

"I'd bet. Oh, for a company of Aparionese crossbowmen about now. We could rip that crowd apart without getting close."

The ship with the red pennon was one of a hundred larger

craft that had not been hauled out of the water. Those were tied up downstream from the majority, side by side, in places forming ranks of as many as eight vessels. The shoreward ships were tied up to the flood wall where it ran along the river's edge, making the bank a set of sheer stone faces stepping back from the water at intervals, providing a narrow towpath and landing, whatever the water level. The south bank was built up similarly starting at the foot of the Blendine Bridge and running upriver. The decision to build that way must have had something to do with the curve of the stream.

Else told Bechter, "We can't break through that mob. There're too many of them. You distract them. I'll go around. Gervase. You and Paludan stick with the sergeant." The Bruglioni group had not scurried away, but they did make a point of hanging way back.

"Around, Hecht? How?"

Bechter was talking to the air.

Else dodged between fishing craft. That put him out of sight. He shed mail and clothing, slipped down into the fetid brown river. The water was colder than he expected.

Swimming while carrying weapons was not easy. But you learned how in the Sha-lug schools. A soldier had to be able to take the fight anywhere.

He went under, swam with the current, surfaced behind the outermost ship in the first moored rank, then worked his way toward his target, a dingy coastal trader. One of the biggest Calziran ships, it was small compared to war galleys Else had seen crossing over from Dreanger.

He rested against the dhow's hull briefly, listened, heard only the creak of timbers and groan of strained rope.

Boarding proved difficult. Even amidships, where the vessel had the lowest freeboard, the rail was too high to reach. There were no ready handholds, either.

Else pushed his knife into the caulk and tar between strakes, above his head. He drove it deeper with palm blows, then relaxed, focused, surged. In a violent, one-handed pull-up he launched himself high enough to get his other hand over the gunwale. He let his sword fall, grabbed hold, and continued onward.

He rolled over the rail, recovered his weapons, looked for

opposition. No one came at him. Redfearn Bechter had everyone's attention ashore.

Else dashed aft, severed the after mooring lines, then scampered forward. The dhow's stern began to swing out into the current.

As Else cut a forward mooring line, he realized that he had not thought this out. He would not be able to steer the ship as it turned end for end, descending the Teragi.

His amulet began to irritate him. It had not while he was in the water.

Pirates started yelling. Some began clambering across the ships moored inshore.

One more line to cut.

A Calziran with more courage than brains flung himself across the widening gap between the dhow and its nearest neighbor. He landed on loose rope, fell, broke something. Else heard bone snap. The pirate barked in pain.

Three more heroes followed the first. One leapt and landed successfully. The next came down on the rail and, miraculously, balanced there, arms flailing, for as long as it took the third to fall short and snag his leg as he tried to avoid getting wet.

Sergeant Bechter scattered the distracted pirates on shore. Then he and his men scattered themselves.

The barricade on the Blendine Bridge was leaking desperate pirates.

Else severed that final mooring line, then removed his unwanted shipmates. They were fishermen. They should be able to swim.

The dhow finished its turn end for end. It smashed violently into the flank of a moored ship. Timbers groaned and snapped. Bits of rigging tumbled down. Else hustled around making sure his dhow did not become entangled with the other.

The cycle repeated itself, less violently. Else was no sailor. How was he going to steer this thing? A ship had to have steerage way on in order to be steered. Meaning it had to be moving in relation to the water, not just moving.

There was a more immediate problem, though. The sorceress. Starkden. Who had to know who he was. Because she had tried to kill him in Runch. Which made no sense if she was a true Praman fighter.

The ship was not big enough to have decks and cabins and whatnot, except back aft where there was a platform on which the steersman could ply his trade. There was nothing to cover, anyway. The pirates had brought a lot of empty space they hoped to fill with booty.

There was a sort of hovel under the steersman's platform. Else found the woman hidden there, delirious. He dragged her into the light. She was a stranger. Nevertheless, he thought she seemed familiar.

She was short, stout, unwrinkled, dark, dressed nothing like her pirates. And bald. Her clothing consisted of brightly dyed cotton like clothing favored by fortune-tellers.

Why the shaved head? That had to mean something. He could not recall anyone in the soothsayer racket shaving, then wearing a wig to hide it. For wear a wig she did. Else found it while looking for something to use as a gag and bonds.

It seemed like a good idea to get a sorceress thoroughly restrained while she was too groggy to disagree.

A gaggle of pirates chased the ship along the riverbank. And several boats that had fled earlier had discovered courage enough to join the chase.

Not good. He was alone, cold, and saddled with a dangerous prisoner, with enemies chasing him. Suppose he lured a few in, let them board, disarmed them, and made them work ship?

Daring, yes, but overly optimistic.

His wrist throbbed. The amulet was not responding to Starkden as it had Grade Drocker when the sorcerer tried to kill him. The pain was tolerable. The amulet was responding to presence rather than level of threat. It raised scarcely a tickle around Drocker, nowadays.

The pursuit on shore ended when the pirate rabble collided with a band of militia armed with crossbows they had had little practice rearming. Incompetence battled incompetence. Those able to project their incompetence at longer range seized the advantage by default.

The pursuit on the river never closed in tight. Every Calziran wanted someone else to make the first move.

The ship stopped spinning, drifted broadside to the current, bow indicating the south shore. Else recalled the little cargo and passenger boats he had seen on canals in Sonsa, propelled by one man who waggled a long oar back and forth behind the boat. Maybe the dhow's big, ugly steering oar could be used the same way. After some experimentation he got the bow pointed downstream—within a point or two. The current pushed the dhow toward the north bank.

It ran into a log boom, an accumulation of driftwood piled up against the upstream face of the ruins of some riverside structure harkening back to imperial times.

Else scrounged up an anchor stone, twenty pounds of rock with a hole through where a line could be bent, and was. He heaved the stone onto the driftwood mountain, hauled the line taut, tied it off, grabbed his dusky prize.

Starkden was heavier than she looked, even stripped of jewelry and anything that might harbor some magical tool. Else strained under her weight as he battled treacherous footing. This had better be worth the trouble. He wanted to learn something before he killed her.

He had no choice, there. She knew too much.

22. The Connec, Duke Tormond's Venture

Having recognized that Duke Tormond would not change his mind, the Connecten factions began doing what they could to influence the course of his mission to Brothe.

Yes. Tormond IV, Duke of Khaurene, lord of the Connec, the Great Vacillator, had decided to appeal to the Patriarch in person. So there could be no misunderstanding. So there would be no more random armies wandering into the End of Connec to get themselves massacred.

The popular consensus was that Tormond was willfully naive. A face-to-face with the Patriarch would clarify nothing. Sublime wanted to loot the richest province in the Chaldarean world so he could finance a crusade to recover the Holy Lands.

Brother Candle joined the Duke's train. Also included were Michael Carhart, Bishop LeCroes, Tember Remak's son, Tember Sihrt, and others the Brothen Patriarch was unlikely to welcome. Most tried to travel incognito, a waste of time. The Patriarch's spies knew who was who.

The instrumentalities of the Church could be as insidiously omnipresent as those of the Night. And were more likely to make someone's life miserable. The wickedness of the Night was cruel but seldom personal.

Sir Eardale Dunn declined the opportunity to visit Brothe, not because he opposed the mission—which he did—but because someone trustworthy and capable had to stay behind. Because of Count Raymone Garete. Sir Eardale suspected Count Raymone of intent to commit mischief.

Tormond brought his sister. Isabeth would represent her husband. King Peter was a vigorous supporter of Connecten independence. He found having a buffer between Navaya and the rapacity of Arnhand comforting. And Peter had leverage. His wars of reconquest were important to Sublime. Sublime thought they reflected gloriously on his stewardship.

Peter's skilled professional soldiers were useful in keeping Sublime safe, too. The twenty-four men of the Patriarchal Guard were all Navayan veterans who had received their posts as rewards for service to the Faith.

Then, too, there were powerful Direcian Principatés in the Collegium. Sublime depended on their support. His political fortunes would sink fast if he offended Peter.

BROTHER CANDLE BEGAN TO WONDER. WERE THE INSTRU-mentalities of the Night determined to keep Tormond away from Brothe? The weather remained stubbornly awful. Bitterly cold rain fell for hours every day. Even the old Brothen military roads became difficult.

And then there were sicknesses.

Nothing fatal, of course. Just bouts of dysentery interspersed with flu and bad colds. "The Coughers' Crusade," Michael Carhart dubbed the mission. Brother Candle discharged a nostril load of snot and agreed.

After a month on the road Duke Tormond was two weeks behind schedule. The party had not yet reached Ormienden when Tormond's planners had expected to be in Firaldia, nearing Brothe.

The Duke chose to pause at Viscesment. He would visit Immaculate while his disheartened companions recuperated.

The weather improved dramatically immediately.

Michael Carhart convinced local Devedian physicians to treat the sick. They conquered the ferocious dysentery.

News of Sublime's troubles with pirates reached Viscesment. Reports were confused and contradictory but their theme was clear: the Church, the Benedocto family, and Sublime in particular, were under sustained attack.

Brother Candle joined a deputation put together by Bishop LeCroes. The senior Chaldarean cleric in Khaurene, LeCroes was also related to Tormond. He told the Duke, "I saw Immaculate this morning, Your Lordship. He says Sublime's Calzarin troubles are worse than we're hearing. They might be enough to bring him down."

Brother Candle sensed wishful thinking at work. Though the wishful thinking could be true. It became more clear daily that Sublime, while powerful and driven by a huge dream, was highly unpopular.

Bishop LeCroes went on. "The consensus at the Patriarchal Court—seconded by the Imperial envoy, Graf fon Wistricz—is that Sublime is best left to roast in his own juices. He can't bother us if he's up to his hips in Calzirans."

Brother Candle wondered about Hansel Blackboots's role in all this. Had he provoked the Calzirans?

All the mission's opponents argued for discontinuing the embassy. Sublime had been neutralized. Just let it ride, they said. Let's see how it shakes out before we get in any deeper.

Arguments calculated to appeal to the Great Vacillator. And this situation begged for a hands-off attitude, from a Connecten point of view.

The Duke would not change course.

"He's mad," Michael Carhart insisted. "His mind has gone to rot."

Brother Candle wondered if that might not be true, literally. "You think somebody cast a glamour on his mind?"

LeCroes said, "I've been wondering. Why is he decisive and determined?"

Never mentioned, but recalled by the older men, was the fact that Tormond's father had gone mad when younger than Tormond was now. The Old Duke had lapsed into occasional bouts of sanity, unpredictably, till the day he died. Most of the time his advisers had not been sure which state prevailed.

"Something I noticed on the road," Michael Carhart said. "Besides the fact that it's cold and wet in the countryside. The things of the night are extremely interested in our little band."

Little band? With all the hangers-on and help, the "little band" numbered nearly three hundred. A small army. Or plague of locusts.

Brother Candle had not noticed the night things. But he was insensitive to such. The Instrumentalities of the Night had to indulge in spectacularly blatant behavior before he noticed. Most people were like him. Especially city people. They just did not see what was happening around them.

Michael Carhart, though, lived at the nether end of the scale, in the range reached by some sorcerers. He was aware of every little worm of darkness stirring around him.

Bishop LeCroes asked, "Is that because of our mission? Or just because you're too sensitive?" Chaldareans never ceased to be ambivalent about the Wells of Ihrian and the Instrumentalities of the Night.

Did God create the Wells of Ihrian?

Did the Wells give birth to God?

That philosophical stumbling block—some would say congenital defect—strained both the Praman and Chaldarean faiths to their foundations, in the minds of those who studied the underpinnings of their religion.

No faith seemed capable of withstanding rigorous, rational examination. But they did work down on the everyday level where ordinary men lived. What men believed to be true *was* true, locally.

Belief sculpted the Instrumentalities of the Night. While the Instrumentalities of the Night molded belief. While Firaldia and the Episcopal heartland became ever more tame, remote countries slipped ever more into the sway of the Night.

Michael Carhart said, "No. Not the mission. But worldly things affect the Night. The Instrumentalities want to know what's going on."

"Meaning?" Brother Candle asked.

"They sense the patterns beginning to shape the future."

That sounded like occultist doubletalk. Brother Candle said, "That stuff takes care of itself. And shouldn't be any concern to us."

Bishop LeCroes said, "it better concern you. If Michael Carhart senses a special interest from the Night, the Collegium will, too. And it's your cult that Sublime finds so offensive."

"Every day I find myself compelled to remind me that Man isn't a rational animal. I defer to your wisdom, Bishop."

LeCroes replied, "If there was any wisdom in this crowd we'd all be home cozily closeted with a warm brandy. We wouldn't be traipsing around behind the Mad Duke of the Connec, hoping to keep him from doing any more damage to our cause. We'd still be in Khaurene. We know that nothing Tormond does in Brothe will matter. He's being stubborn because he doesn't like being pushed."

THE PAUSE AT VISCESMENT STRETCHED OUT. A FEW DAYS BEcame a few weeks. No one mentioned the passage of time to the Duke. Tormond seemed content to sit. Unfortunately, Immaculate was not eager to have him keep sitting. He was an expensive guest. Immaculate and his court lived one meal short of destitution, supported more by Johannes Blackboots, for political reasons, than by those whose philosophies he supposedly represented.

The Duke finally got the hint. He assembled his traveling companions and told them they were about to resume traveling. The weather was favorable and everyone's health had been restored. And he remained determined to sit down with Sublime.

News of the massacre at Starplire arrived. "This changes nothing!" Tormond insisted. "Nothing! In fact, it provides a wonderful opportunity!"

Brother Candle, standing with Michael Carhart and Tember Sihrt, murmured, "I can't wait to find out what twist his genius takes now."

Tormond said, "Sublime is lord of a third of Firaldia, a quarter of Ormienden and numerous islands in the Mother Sea. But he has no real armed forces. When he wanted to tame us he hired mercenaries and begged for troops from Arnhand. The few soldiers he does have he has to post where the Emperor might try to assert his rights. His own Guard won't do anything but protect him. They're not numerous enough."

Brother Candle whispered, "The man isn't unaware of the world after all." Even seeing it askew, Tormond was considering the geopolitical situation.

Bishop LeCroes asked, "I don't think I got your point, Your Lordship."

"I haven't made it yet, Bries. Contain your insubordination and sarcasm a moment and I will."

Well. Tormond might not be a semianimate lump after all. He might be a clever actor. Though there was little evidence to support that.

"The point, Bries, is that Sublime is in a bad spot. Calzirans have chosen to make a national popular effort to plunder the Episcopal Church, the Patriarchal Estates, and anything to do with Sublime or his family. And Sublime can't do anything about it. So there he lies, like a naked fat woman on her back, hoping he won't get raped too badly."

It was as though Tormond had, for one incredible instant, come out from under the influence of a drug causing permanent torpor. "We may be looking at an opportunity to avert the fate he wants to visit on the Connec."

Tormond was no longer one of the walking dead. His mind had come to life. He was thinking, calculating, scheming like a true overlord.

Brother Candle suffered the horrified suspicion that everything might work out just because Tormond had stubbornly pursued the wrong course.

"I'm going to offer Sublime the Connec's support in his war with Calzir—if he abandons his designs on us."

That stirred some excitement. Could Sublime be trusted to keep his word? What about the Grail Emperor? What about Immaculate? How could the scheme be managed?

Michael Carhart suggested putting Raymone of Antieux in charge of any force sent to Calzir. That notion won instant support.

Tormond's sister, Isabeth, remained quiet and thoughtful. A

scheme like this would pull her husband in. Peter had veterans able to train and lead. Peter had access to the fleets of Platadura, Direcia's equivalent of Sonsa and Aparion.

A thousand questions flew. Tormond refused to answer them. "We'll complete our journey to Brothe. We'll see Sublime. We'll convince Sublime to put his wickedness aside."

There was no mention of Immaculate whatsoever. Immaculate had no value left, despite recent successes. And Tormond saw that.

No one cared. Not in the Connecten band. Even Bishop LeCroes did not protest.

The Duke's notion inspired his companions. No one raised questions or objections for a week. By then the embassy, enjoying reasonable weather, was just days from Brothe. And those feeble objections vanished when news came that Brothe was under attack by Calziran pirates.

Tormond tried to stir everyone up for a fight.

He was not that sort of leader. His people joked that even he would not follow him into the valley of the shadow.

Brother Candle thought the man looked a little odd again. "I think the crazy is back."

Mad or not, Tormond did not dawdle. He headed toward Brothe like an arrow toward its target.

23. Brothe, Fists of the Gods

Shagot muttered, "Bel's Balls, little brother! How long was I out of it this time?"

"Two and a half days. I've got food warming. And you'd still be snoring if I hadn't started in on you. Here. Drink."

"What's up?" Shagot felt it. Dramatic things were happening.

"Pirates are attacking Brothe."

"*Pirates?* Sturlanger?"

"Not our people. Pirates who belong to that religion that hates the religion they have here. It's hard to explain. I can't get out and talk to people much so I can't understand what it's really all about."

Shagot sometimes doubted that Svavar could understand much of anything, even given his own tutor.

Svavar said, "Grim, we're going to get pulled into it here, ourselves, pretty soon. The raiders are only a few blocks away."

Shagot drank a cup of water and followed that with a huge, long draft of beer. Which he would have to honor his brother for having found in this pussy city infested by cowards, whiners, faggots, and an all-time supply of effete snobs. All of whom did nothing but suck down wine, the preferred libation of boys who thought they ought to be girls.

Shagot said, "We don't have much that they'd think was worth stealing." He had gone to the trouble of ensuring that every spare copper he and Svavar accumulated went into the care of a certain Devedian investment specialist.

Asgrimmur growled, "Grim, get a hold on reality. Right now nobody gives a fuck about investments. Not to mention that these Calziran fish-fuckers could end up stealing our fortune anyway if they end up looting the whole fucking city."

Shagot hauled himself upright. "You got a point, little brother. If they work the way we did, they'll haul away anything they can carry and wreck whatever they can't."

"Now you're listening. So what do we do? They're headed this way. And getting closer while we talk."

"Then I guess we'd better travel on." Shagot shivered, unaccountably nervous.

"You need to eat first. But no screwing around."

Shagot had not been out into the city since the killings. Svavar had, occasionally, after his wounds healed. In disguise, of course. He knew that some powerful men wanted to get hold of them.

Shagot ate, indifferent to what he stuffed down. "How long do we have?"

"I don't know. Let's not tempt fate."

"I guess not. What do we do? Dress me up like your wife?"

"You really are an asshole. How about we just shave, cut our hair, and wear something besides reindeer hides?" Asgrimmur had acquired the tools and clothing. They could not stay denned up. The man they had to destroy would not come to them.

There had been no sign of their quarry. Unless Grim had

dreamed something. But Grim did not talk about his dreams, much.

Grumbling, Shagot let Svavar dress him in local clothing, followed by a trim and a shave. "You been busy, little brother."

"Somebody had to do something. And you're always asleep."

"Good on you. I always figured you could do something. If you really had to."

"Yeah." Grim was full of shit. "You got any idea where to find our target?"

"It's a long reach for the Old Ones down here, little brother. They do know he's in Brothe. They do know that he doesn't know we're after him. They do know that we aren't the only enemies he has. And they insist that we'll know him when we see him. Which they know you've been wondering about."

"Then we shouldn't be hiding out. We should be looking. Like maybe about as soon as you finish gnawing that damned sausage."

The old, familiar sounds of panic came from outside.

"You're always in a hurry. You need to relax. Aren't you done with the hair yet? The killing is getting closer."

Svavar felt it, too. The pirates were moving fast. Meaning they were meeting little resistance.

That did not surprise Svavar. They had no guts, these Brothen girls in their funny pants.

There would be some cherries popped today.

SHAGOT AND SVAVAR WERE STILL EATING WHEN THEY reached the street, each loaded with fetishes from that ancient battleground. Shagot raised a hand to signal a halt. That hand held part of a roasted chicken.

People ran hither and thither around them, not knowing where they were headed but painfully sure they had to get there in a hurry. Svavar had seen this before, in Santerin. Right after he and Shagot and Erief had come roaring over the hill.

Shagot listened for fighting. He said, "This way." He headed away from the excitement.

It was not their fight. They were here to winkle out the Godslayer.

Svavar determined to become more active in that search. It would take forever if they hunted only while Grim was awake.

The brothers rounded a corner and came face-to-face with a band of pirates who were making no noise because no one was resisting them. Shagot and Svavar were carrying stuff. Obviously, they were trying to get that stuff out of the neighborhood. That was all the evidence the pirates needed.

They were swarthy, hungry little men who would not have dared face the Grimmssons one on one. But there were a swarm of them.

"Shit," Shagot swore softly, with no special heat. "The Walker must be thirsty." He discarded the chicken, shed his pack, produced his sword and the head of the dead demon. There was no doubt whatsoever that Shagot was touched by the gods. Svavar even wondered, sometimes, if his brother was still alive, in the generally accepted sense.

Shagot took the fight to the pirates. Perforce, Svavar stayed close, covering his brother's back.

Nineteen pirates were down when the handful still upright broke and ran. None were dead until Shagot removed their heads.

Shagot was in a state of communion with his gods. Svavar felt it. He sensed their attention, too. The Gray One himself was close. There had been blood and slaughter sufficient to span the occult abyss. A little more blood and the Old Ones would be able to enter this alien world and time.

Shagot was possessed. "I feel him, now. Come, brother. This way."

Grim headed north, toward the river. Toward the pirates. He used the latter to provide blood sacrifices in quantity, more than sufficient to assure the continued attention and assistance of the Old Ones.

THEY REACHED THE TERAGI. THEY MUST HAVE SLAIN A HUN-dred Calzirans. Svavar was having trouble keeping up. Grim had been cut several times, too, but was not showing the effects. They were going to need another long convalescence. Unless their luck turned better than he expected and they brought their man down.

Svavar remained alert for the presence of someone—anyone—from the Great Sky Fortress. He was convinced that the slaughter had made it possible for those Instrumentalities of the Night to begin stalking Brothen streets.

However, if one of the Old Ones did slip through, he was not making his presence obvious.

"The Godslayer is on the other side," Shagot said. "There." He pointed vaguely in the direction of some burning ships.

Svavar said, "There's a bridge up there. Half a mile, or so."

Shagot did not care about bridges. A hundred yards directly ahead a dozen pirates were piling plunder aboard a captured rowboat. Shagot killed them and took the boat. Then their heads. Then sat down at the oars.

He pulled like a thing not human. Svavar did not volunteer to take a turn. His wounds bothered him too much. And he did not want to disturb his brother's connection with the gods.

Svavar feared that Grim was so far gone he could turn on anyone. He had become a berserker of the oldest form.

A few Calzirans attacked them when they reached the north bank. And so added their blood to the sacrificial pool. Shagot did not take heads this time. In fact, he abandoned his collection with the boat, retaining only the head of the demon. His wounds had begun to slow and weaken him at last. But that lasted for only a short while.

Shagot healed almost visibly fast. Calzirans overcome, he turned his nose north of northwest and started limping. Svavar had trouble keeping up.

Svavar felt his own wounds healing, though not at the ridiculous rate Grim enjoyed.

In minutes they reached a neighborhood untouched by current events. It was a poor area but not a slum. It was not crowded, horizontally or vertically. Svavar thought he remembered a wall not much farther on. Beyond that the city faded into a typical Firaldian countryside of olive groves, vineyards, truck farms and, farther out, wheat fields. All the ground that could be tamed had been—two thousand years ago.

Shagot began to show an uncharacteristic uncertainty. "We're real close," he said. "Right on top. I can almost smell him. But I can't pinpoint him. Something is getting in the way."

"Any idea how close?" Svavar asked. If he had a distance to

work with he could attack the problem intellectually. Which was a concept almost alien to his brother.

He felt something disorienting, too. Like a mild buzz inside his brain that kept his thoughts mushy at their center. His vision seemed a little wobbly.

"Thirty yards at least. Not more than fifty."

Svavar reasoned the possibilities down to four houses and their outbuildings. He explained, then asked, "Why don't we start with the closest?"

"Let's do it." Shagot hefted his battered blade and hoisted the demon's head.

And Svavar realized that this was not going to go well. Because Shagot was going about it all wrong. And there was something else. . . . Something more . . . A Presence that should not be present . . .

24. Brothe, Besieged

Else dragged his weird burden farther and farther from the river, always with an eye toward a place to go to ground.

Northern Brothe lay silent and empty. A goat cart crossed the street a hundred yards ahead, unaccompanied by any master. He saw several feral dogs. They slunk away. Even the swarms of pigeons seemed subdued and disinclined to pursue normal pigeon business. Remarkable. Nothing kept pigeons down.

The woman did not fight. She stumbled along beside Else, dazed, incompletely aware of her situation. Though she did become more alert and engaged with time. And strove to keep her recovery concealed.

Else's back trail was noisy for a while. The pirates wanted their witch back. Else zigged and zagged, leaving them confused and worried about ambushes as the expanding search forced them to break up into smaller and smaller bands. Now he needed a place where he could hole up and spend some time chatting with Starkden.

He moved more and more slowly. Something was wrong. This silence was not normal. Not in a city being raped. He be-

gan to feel that something dark and dreadful was closing in. He
hit the woman, hard. That changed little but the fact that he had
to carry her again.

That crisp feel that air knows when lightning will soon
strike began to build.

Else kicked in a door. His assault caused vibrant excitement
in a distant part of the house. That faded as terrified residents
fled through a remote exit.

Maybe that was the root of the wrongness. The fear. The fog
of terror that overlay the whole quarter.

His wrist itched. Again. This itch had nothing to do with
Starkden.

Trouble *was* coming.

He got his prisoner fixed in a chair in a room with multiple
doors. Then he awaited her wakening.

She would try to fool him, of course. So he listened closely
and studied the movements of her eyeballs behind her eyelids.
When the moment arrived he cut her arm lightly. She jumped.

"We need to talk, woman. And, because you're stubborn and
think you're tough and I don't have time to be subtle, I won't
ask anything till I'm sure you're ready to cooperate."

This was his first woman. True torturers surely had gender-
specific trade secrets. He was unfamiliar with those. Nor did
he have the specialized utensils a serious interrogator needed.

He improvised. He used the tool at hand, a knife. He started
where she could watch it happen. She would think about the
scars left once he flayed her in a checkerboard pattern.

His work gave him no pleasure. He lacked zeal. Professionals often communicated their pleasure to their subjects. A bond
developed in time. Torturer and tortured entered into a conspiracy, a marriage of pain, wherein each played his role with
passion.

But to Else, for whom torture was distasteful manual labor
and only the information mattered, no relationship was possible. He worked. And waited to hear from Starkden.

She *was* stubborn. Being flayed did not crack her, despite
the pain.

He needed to cut closer to the essential Starkden.

Who was she? He would not know unless she showed him.

What was she? He knew that one. He thought. She was a sorceress. And a pirate.

The witch part would be tied up intimately with *who* she was.

Sorcerers and sorceresses depended heavily on their hands while manipulating elements of the night. Wizards in training spent as much time schooling their fingers as young Sha-lug spent schooling the muscles they would use to wield their weapons.

Else sharpened his knife, then seized the little finger of Starkden's right hand.

Good guess. She grunted. She strained. She indicated that she was ready to cooperate. In some capacity.

"I'll take your tongue, too, if you try anything cute." Generally, people preferred loss of a few fingers to loss of the tongue.

Half from memory, half from impulse, Else brought out every silver coin he possessed. He applied them to the witch wherever magical inhibition might be useful. The woman sagged.

Knife poised, Else removed the woman's gag. "You know who I am. You tried to kill me. Your assassin was incompetent. At the time I was unaware of your existence. That's changed. You caused that. I don't know why. Tell me why."

The witch shrugged, as much as was possible. Else squeezed her hand around his blade. She gasped, whispered, "I don't know why. Somebody wanted it done badly enough to pay for it."

"But you don't know who." Naturally. There would have been a chain of intermediaries so the contractor could remain distanced from the crime.

"It didn't matter. I wanted the money. It wasn't personal."

Else's questions unearthed no hint of why anyone would want his mission to end on an island in the middle of the Mother Sea.

He grew impatient. The woman was not resisting. Neither was she offering up anything useful. Meanwhile, big things were happening to Brothe. He had no idea what. Any scenario wherein the defenders repelled the invaders, while Starkden survived, would not bode well for Else Tage. The woman knew who he was.

He shifted to her involvement with the pirates. Was that just mercenary grasping, too?

The silver was too effective. Starkden could speak coherently no longer. Else removed several coins.

He had been part of several large, mysterious operations lately. Gordimer and er-Rashal had piled them on. He was the best man for the job. And Sha-lug did not question orders. Not even orders to undertake a mad raid into the Idiam in the Lucidian Desert, into haunted Andesqueluz, in search of the accursed mummies of heathen sorcerers of antiquity. He had done the job without asking why.

"I'm getting old," he mused. He had been taught, as a trainee, that the old thought too much. And he was now of an age that had seemed ancient when he was the leading prospect in the Vibrant Spring School.

His wrist went from itch to ache while he was getting little of practical value from Starkden.

"The Brotherhood of War wants you. Badly. And they're better at this than I am."

What might have been amusement and mockery shown back at him. Disdain followed.

His wrist throbbed. He had trouble thinking through the pain.

It was decision time.

The choices were plain.

He drew his sword.

Something hit him from behind, impacting every inch of his body.

He had not been fast enough.

He knew what it was. He knew why he had been itching and hurting. He knew what he had forgotten, because it had not been mentioned for a while. And that was that there was a second sorcerer involved with the pirates. Masant al-Seyhan.

Vaguely, Else heard a man ask, "Can you travel? We have to hurry. It isn't working the way we were promised. It's gone bad already. Oh, damn! What the hell is this?"

Else heard steel strike steel. A second, all-over blow hit him. After that, he heard and felt nothing for a long time.

REDFEARN BECHTER FOUND ELSE SPRAWLED IN THE STREET. Dried blood caked his lips, nostrils, and ears. His skin had turned a nasty, dark shade of pink, with blisters. His nails were cracked. His hair was a ruin. It looked like tiny embers had crawled through it in pursuit of fleas. His face was spotted with little red rings, like the signature of some strange pox.

Else asked, "What happened?" His words were an incoherent drone. "Oh, saints in heaven. I can't hear. Talk slow. I'll read your lips." Assuming he could stay focused. His left eye felt arid. It itched.

His wrist felt like somebody had tried to hack through it with a white-hot iron bar.

"All right. You getting me?"

"Yes. Go ahead."

Bechter grinned. "Just guessing, mind, but I'd say you got your ass kicked."

"Even my gums hurt. What happened? Enunciate carefully. Hey! I'm starting to hear something."

"The neighbors have painted a picture that doesn't make sense."

"And? So?"

"You came running down that street there, dragging a woman. Presumably the witch. A band of pirates weren't far behind."

"I remember that. They wanted her back. I kept trying to lose them before I headed for friendly territory. They wouldn't shake. Every time I turned back toward the Castella, they would get in my way. I decided to hole up until they gave up."

"That would be over there. Where that house used to be." Bechter pointed.

The place no longer stood. Smoke still drifted toward a sky clouding over, promising rain. Most of the afternoon had passed. "Sainted Eis and Heron!"

"No shit."

"Keep it slow and loud. I can hear most of what you're saying now."

"Here's what we have. You broke in there. You were seen. The neighbors didn't do anything because you have blond hair. Later, a band of Calzirans arrived. They seemed to know where they were going. Their leader was a wizard."

"Masant al-Seyhan. I think. That name came up when the piracy started."

"Maybe. He used a couple of spells that must've been real potent."

"Do tell. They knocked a house down on top of me."

"No. That happened later. You'll love this part. Two blond men showed up. It's pretty clear they were the two we've been hunting. They didn't say anything. They just walked up and started killing Calzirans. They were completely savage and totally unstoppable. Eventually, the fight moved inside."

That did not jibe with what Else remembered. But his recollections were kaleidoscopic and vague and incompletely trustworthy. "I can hear pretty good, now. I could use some water."

"Something terrible happened inside that house. But by then the neighbors stopped being curious and went into hiding. We've just started digging into the rubble. We're finding a lot of dead pirates."

"But no witches or wizards, I'll bet."

"Not a one. Nor any blond men, either. Did you get anything out of the witch?"

"She wouldn't even admit she was a witch. Or that she understood me. I kept her unconscious most of the time. Anyway, I was too busy outrunning pirates to have time for questions."

"That's what I figured. Damn it all!"

"I'm sorry."

"Not your fault. You went above and beyond, just making that swim."

"Wait a minute, now. How come you've got time and manpower to waste looking for me?"

"The situation improved. The Collegium weighed in while you were distracting the Calziran talent. Plus, a regiment of Imperial cavalry turned up and took the raiders by surprise."

And everyone else, Else surmised. What was Hansel up to? He had seven or eight hundred regular soldiers handy, deep in Patriarchal territory, just when Brothe's situation was most desperate?

Else said, "I can't get my brain to work. I hurt too much."

"I'll see if I can get you a ride home. But not yet. There's still spots of heavy fighting. Most of the pirates didn't get back to their boats. Those few that were left to be gotten to."

"SO NOW YOU'RE A HERO," PALUDAN SAID, WHEN ELSE appeared before him the next day.

"Not a very successful one." He ached all over, still. His eye and his ears were not yet right. The red circles were worse. They were not restricted to his face, either. He felt old and tired despite ten hours of sleep.

"But one of ours," Gervase Saluda said. "Out there making the Bruglioni name shine."

Paludan scowled. He was not pleased, despite the positive reflection on the Bruglioni name. The whole city would now notice that one of its richest men had sent just a handful of men to help defend Brothe. And that neither Gervase nor Paludan, nor any of their handful of men, had become involved in the fighting. Only the name Piper Hecht would stand out.

Else replied, "I did what I could. I didn't do it well enough. I lost the witch. I never saw the two blond thugs. Or the sorcerer who rescued the witch. Masant al-Seyhan could strut in here right now and I wouldn't know enough to duck."

Saluda sneered. "All that perishes before the fact that you were one of the rare few who actually fought the Calzirans. You were the one who distracted their mages long enough for the Collegium to break the pirates."

"How is that going?" Else asked that rather than why Paludan was determined to be disgruntled by a Brothen success.

"Not good for the pirates. Groups are cut off all over. They just want to leave Brothe, now. But that isn't working for them. There aren't any boats left."

Paludan grumbled, "The Calziran wizards are frantic. They keep trying to salvage their manpower. But that isn't going well, either."

Else asked, "We know that they survived, then?" A concentration on force preservation? Military thinking, that. Which ought to be alien to the pirates.

Paludan grunted. He was ready for a change of subject.

The Bruglioni properties had come through unscathed. Gervase and Paludan wanted to sit back and let someone else clean up. They had little idea of the reality out there in the Mother City. Men with no personal stake in Brothe, the Imperials and those squatters who had enlisted for the pay, had done and were doing most of the fighting. Neither group would take risks. They were disinclined to die for a city that disdained them.

Mr. Caniglia appeared. "Master Paludan, your uncle has arrived. He'll be up in a few minutes."

Saluda told Else, "They may have to carry him. He has trouble with stairs." He did not seem pleased by the visit.

Divino Bruglioni arrived puffing, presumably due to the change of attitude. His footmen seated him in a chair the house maintained exclusively for the Bruglioni Principaté, then withdrew. "Stay, Captain Hecht," Principaté Divino said when Else started to follow.

Paludan's face darkened. But he controlled himself, a habit he had developed since the deaths of his sons.

Principaté Divino told Else, "I hear you did quite well out there."

"I managed to get myself beaten to a pulp."

"You were in the right place at the right time. You distracted our most dangerous enemies at the critical moment."

"I guarantee you, it wasn't part of my grand scheme. I did what I thought needed doing. If those mystery blond men hadn't turned up I'd be just another body to chunk in the river."

"Possibly. Possibly. What can you tell me about those people?"

"The blond men? I never saw them. I just heard about them. I was unconscious when they got there. Sergeant Bechter told me they were there. Bechter from the Brotherhood."

"How about the Calziran sorcerers?"

"I only saw the woman."

"Any idea why they survived?"

"Had to be the timing. The blonds showed up before the Calzirans were done with me."

The Principaté continued asking questions, moving to the Bruglioni household. He demonstrated a close knowledge of Else's efforts. Closer than Paludan or Gervase. Paludan was unaware that some staff had been replaced.

The old man changed course. "Paludan. What are you doing to get family back from the country?"

Paludan looked vaguely bewildered. He had sent letters. Followed by threatening letters. "They're stalling around, Uncle. But they'll respond eventually."

"Good. Good." But Divino did not sound pleased. "Captain

Hecht. I'm going to my chambers, now. Walk with me, please."

Else shrugged at his employer and did as he was told.

Out of earshot, the old priest said, "I left before we got to fiscal matters."

Else waited.

"What are you doing about the books?"

"Bringing in a Deve auditor. To look at everything. Household and business accounts both."

"What do you expect to find?"

"I know what he'll find. That somebody's been looting the Bruglioni treasury. The magnitude of the theft is what I want to determine."

"You have a suspect?"

"I have someone in mind. But he may be too obvious."

"Gervase Saluda. Of course. I think Gervase *is* dipping his beak. In here. We have more to discuss."

"Yes, Your Grace." Else did not conceal his unease.

"Gervase is a true friend to Paludan, Hecht. He's Paludan's only friend. And Paludan is Gervase's only friend. I don't see Gervase putting that friendship at risk by committing a crime too big to forgive."

"The Bruglioni are supposed to have a lot of money."

"The family is wealthy, yes. But not much of it is in the form of actual money. It's mostly agricultural and mining properties. Sit. I have a proposition."

Else remained nervous. Divino Bruglioni was a complete unknown.

"You're bright. You're skilled. You take action when it's needed. Paludan let this place go to hell. His problem is, he doesn't want to be bothered. And he doesn't know how to manage people. He wasn't taught. And hasn't tried to learn."

"I understood Freido never thought anyone but Soneral needed teaching."

"Freido was an older Paludan. My brother wasn't good for the family. He stopped insisting that our brightest youngsters stay here to tend the family fortune. His temper and drunken bad behavior made them all want to leave."

Else sat quietly, wondering what the Principaté had in mind.

"These are difficult times, Hecht. The malaise afflicting the

Bruglioni isn't confined to this family. It afflicts all Brothe. It lies like a fog on the Episcopal world. A crusade might wake us up. But at what cost? The Patriarch is obsessed with making a mark on history. At a time when we have no tools to do the work. And a time when nobody wants to get involved in Patriarchal adventures."

Else nodded. And waited, puzzled.

"Hecht, the whole world seems to be trying to thwart Sublime. These mad Calzirans have distracted him completely from his ambitions in the Connec."

Else considered offering the opinion that a higher power was vetoing Sublime's machinations.

Divino sighed, caught his breath, continued when Else said nothing. "Duke Tormond and a mixed delegation, including the queen of Navaya, who is authorized to speak for King Peter, is approaching Brothe. The Duke is offering the Connec's support in punishing Calzir. Queen Isabeth says Peter would contribute warships to the campaign."

"That's a tit for tat? If the Patriarch leaves the Connec alone the Connec will rescue him from Calzir?"

"It hasn't been said that way, but that's what it amounts to. And Sublime, despite being a prime specimen of Benedocto weasel, can't possibly slime his way around Tormond and Peter this time. Not with the Emperor peeking over everybody's shoulders."

"Which means he'll never raise the money to finance an overseas adventure?"

"True. You do see past the end of your nose. I like that."

"Thank you, Your Grace." Else felt better, suddenly.

"I brought you here so I could get a better look at you. I liked what I heard. And now I like what I see. So. Can I hire you away from my nephew?"

"Your Grace?"

"Not right away. I may be a Prince of the Church but I'm still a Bruglioni. You've only just started whipping this place into shape. I want you to stay after that till Paludan's jealousy, anger, and paranoia crush his good sense and he fires you. Then you come to work for me."

Else gaped.

"What do you think?"

"I think I'm overawed. I think it's too good to be true. It's the hope of finding opportunity like this that brings men from the corners of the world to Brothe. Of course I'll do it." Of course he would do it. It *was* a dream come true. They would sing and dance through the halls of the Palace of the Kings when the news reached al-Qarn. "What would my duties be?"

"We'll reserve that for now. I assure you, though, that you'll be doing what you're best qualified to do."

"Oh?" Else did not press. He would tread carefully now. It would not be his fault if this fell through.

"Meanwhile, keep up the good work. Make the Bruglioni strong again."

"Yes, Your Grace. And what about the current situation, Your Grace?"

"What about it?"

"What's become of the Calziran sorcerers? What became of the blond men? Who are they? They sound like something more than just good fighters."

"They're what we call soultaken. Meaning they're really only halfway alive. Soultaken are the tools of major supernatural entities. Soultaken haven't been seen around here in a millennium. Which makes their behavior more odd. Soultaken are used to commit the highest crimes. Yet these two operate like common thugs."

"You met them, didn't you?"

"Once."

"And?"

"The more I know about the Instrumentalities of the Night, the less I want to talk about them. I think we have reason to be afraid. We can't fathom the motives of the entities using those two. We can't discover their identities. It's probably connected to a strange unrest among the Instrumentalities of the Night that has persisted for months, now."

"I'm confused."

"We all are. It makes no sense. Not in any way we can fathom. We being the Collegium. Our allies among the creatures of the Night, that are normally pliable, won't help us. The Realm of Night is unanimous. . . . You jumped. You had a thought?"

"Not really." It was that Realm of Night remark. Was that an

Episcopal Chaldarean concept? "I suppose time will let you know. When the mood strikes."

"Of course. We'll find those two. Eventually. But they're of no moment to you. Just do your job here. When the time comes, I'll see you well pleased with your rewards."

Else did his best to look like a man whose only interest was exactly that. He promised, "If Paludan doesn't interfere, I can get this place whipped into shape."

"Paludan isn't as stupid as he seems, Hecht. He knows what he's doing, most of the time. I think he intends to let you run your course. Because that will save him having to do all that work himself. In the dark. Because he never learned how himself."

Else grunted.

"My brother served his sons poorly. And now Paludan has no sons of his own. Nor a wife who can give him more. And I have none, even off the sheets. I fear for tomorrow."

"I'm teaching Dugo what I can, Your Grace. But the truth is, that boy isn't fit. And can't be made fit. You Bruglioni need to strain every bone, joint, and muscle to make sure Paludan lives forever. Or finds himself another wife and stays away from Gervase long enough to get an heir or two on her. Dugo could be a disaster big enough to push the family over the brink into extinction. Begging your pardon for stepping out of my place."

Families had been important in Brothe since antiquity. But the Five Families of today did not include among them even one that had been powerful in Imperial times.

"Perhaps the man who isn't as stupid as he looks will develop wisdom, Hecht. Given time. It can happen. A man confronted with powerful responsibilities, knowing there's no one else to handle them, often does grow up. I've seen it happen."

Else coughed. "That's more the case when young people are involved, usually."

"Oh, my! A sense of humor, too? Perhaps we *are* blessed."

That troubled Else. He was not comfortable with the notion that he could be an inimical god's answer to its worshipers' prayers.

* * *

DAYS PASSED. FIGHTING CONTINUED. TRAPPED CALZIRANS RE-
fused to surrender. The pirates shared an abiding conviction
that they would suffer agonizing deaths because of what had
happened at Starplire.

"Call me an old cynic," Else told Pinkus Ghort, slurring because his jaw was still swollen. The red circles and pink skin
were gone, at least. He was down to ugly yellow and purple
bruises. And a short haircut. "But I think I know why the pirates behaved badly at Starplire. They were incited to it. By
Starkden and Masant al-Seyhan. So they'd be scared to surrender later on. The Brothe attack was part of a bigger plan."

"What else could you expect from a bunch of barbarian
Pramans?"

Else did not argue.

"You look like you're coming down with the mumps, Pipe.
You were going to say?"

"That people on our side will behave just as badly, given a
chance. Like, say, Grade Drocker. Note that I express no disrespect by mentioning the Patriarch or the Emperor."

Ghort chuckled. "You hang around with me, you'll end up
as big a realist as I am. Where's your better half?"

"A realist? Is that what you call somebody who sees the
worst in everybody? Gervase?" Saluda had accompanied Else
everywhere the past few days. "He got bored, I guess. Short attention span."

"Tell you what, Pipe. I'm never disappointed by people.
When are you going to move over to the Collegium?"

"I don't know. Not soon. Even assuming Principaté Bruglioni
wasn't blowing smoke. He wants the Bruglioni household
shaped up first."

"And those boys can't do that for themselves?"

"They don't seem inclined to try. Too much like work."

"Principaté Doneto is thrilled with your progress."

"I was sure that he would be."

"Here comes Joe. What's the word, Joe?"

Just Plain Joe rode up on an ambling Pig Iron. Pig Iron
looked bored and put upon. Joe said, "Don't go barking, boss.
This old boy's only got one speed."

Else asked, "What happened to you?"

Joe's left leg was in a splint. It stuck out from the side of the mule at a strange angle.

"Got hit with one a them fish arrows with the barbed heads. The ones they ties ropes on and use to get sharks. Went in and bounced off the bone. Smarted some. They was able to push it on through and got everything fixed up before it festered. Cap'n Ghort, sir, I don't think you're gonna get much cooperation from anybody. Not even the pirates. They ain't giving up. They promise they'll go away, though. If you let them."

"I'd let them if it was my call. But I'm not allowed. The mercenaries and the Imperials won't root them out?"

"Cap, even I ain't dumb enough to get myself killed trying to fix something that's just naturally gonna fix itself if I just sit around and wait."

"And there you have it," Ghort said. "And guess who's fault it'll be if the whole city stays shut down because these idiot fishermen won't lay down and die? I didn't watch my back close enough. Doneto let me set myself up to be the perfect scapegoat."

"I doubt you're perfect at anything."

Just Plain Joe said, "Maybe instead of paying them mercenaries day rates you might oughta pay them piecework. Way it works now, sitting on their hands pays them just as much as fighting."

Ghort said, "The man may have a point. The money from the levy is going fast but there's enough left for some serious bounties."

That would not matter, overall. Those Calzirans who had not yet escaped never would. The Collegium and the Patriarch agreed. Not one Calziran would be there to defend his home when war came to Calzir.

"Let you in on a secret, Pipe," Ghort said, as they strode toward the Castella dollas Pontellas. "This is one I'm not supposed to know. But I happened to be accidentally eavesdropping when I heard."

"Accidentally, Pinkus?"

"That would've been my plea if I'd gotten caught. I know how much you love those guys."

"Uhm?"

"I overheard Doneto talking to his sister's son, Palo. Palo is an aide to the Patriarch."

"The suspense is killing me, Pinkus."

"I doubt it. But here it is, just in case, on account of your ass is too big to haul around if you drop dead on me. That regiment of Imperial cavalry showing up right on time wasn't no coincidence."

"No! You don't say."

"I mean, they weren't headed for Alameddine, after all. They were headed for Brothe from the start. Sublime cut some kind of deal with Hansel. Which explains why I saw Ferris Renfrow sneaking around a while back."

"Our friend the interrogator from Plemenza?"

"The very one. Bo spotted him. On the Embankment, not far from Krois. Bo lost him there. When I heard about Sublime making a deal I knew why. He headed into the Patriarch's hideout."

"I believe you. But I don't understand. Why would the Patriarch and the Emperor get together?"

"Sublime? Because he'd get soldiers. Two ways. Imperial allies on the front end and his own men freed from having to guard against Imperial incursions on the back side."

"What's in it for Hansel?"

"Good question, Pipe."

"What can Sublime give him that he can't get anywhere else?"

"More good questions. And we'll see them all answered. If we're clever enough to stay alive long enough."

"Hey, Pipe! Cap'n Ghort!" Just Plain Joe called. He and Pig Iron were dawdling along ahead of Else and Ghort.

Ghort asked, "What you got, Joe?"

"Crossing the Blendine Bridge."

"Oh. Hey! It's that embassy from the Connec. They want to cut a deal with Sublime, too. I wouldn't want to be Immaculate today. All my pals are fixing to dump me on the shit pile of history."

Two of Sublime's biggest distractions were about to become something else entirely. Meaning the Patriarch might get to preach his crusade to the Holy Lands after all.

Else needed to visit Gledius Stewpo.

Better yet, he needed to visit Anna Mozilla. There was genuine comfort to be found with the widow.

25. Brothe, with the Connecten Embassy

The Mother City awed Brother Candle despite his inclination to remain unimpressed by things of the world. But time lay so much more thickly and obviously on Brothe than elsewhere.

Khaurene and Castreresone were ancient, too, though they had worn different names when Brothen conquerors arrived in the Connec.

Any stroll down a Brothen street provided reminders of the glory that was. Conquerors still remembered had walked these cobblestones. Triumphant armies had paraded along these boulevards. Today the streets carried folk who did not understand that the glory days were gone. Though Brother Candle suspected that for most ancient Brothens the glory had been of little moment. Then and now, what interested the poor would be food and shelter.

They would not be remembered. That honor was reserved for the man who whipped them to the work of empire, who extorted the taxes that financed monuments and legions. Yet, always, the Brothen rabble lived better than the poor of lesser cities. That was a simple, cruel truth, whether or not it suited Brother Candle's ideology.

"What troubles you now, Brother?"

"I was considering the plight of the poor." He looked round to see where the group had gotten while he was preoccupied.

They had reached that scenic overlook used to view the Teragi, its bridges, island fortresses, all the neighboring structures, and the monuments of the Memorium, sprawled in dirty golden splendor.

"Amazing," Brother Candle said.

Michael Carhart remarked, "I've been here before. Twice. I'm still impressed."

Local spectators stared. Brothens were used to segregation of faiths.

Michael Carhart said, "We're here at the perfect time of day, in perfect weather. The lighting . . ."

A far rumble interrupted. A cloud of dust rose against the afternoon sunlight, golden brown. Someone said, "A building just collapsed."

Gently sarcastic, someone remarked, "That would be in one of the areas they told us to avoid because of the fighting."

The struggle with the pirates was winding down.

Brother Candle had seen some captives earlier. They had not been sound enough to understand what was happening. They were hungry and afraid and relieved that it was all over. Brother Candle wondered how they would fare at the hands of the Brotherhood of War.

The Brotherhood was extremely interested in acquiring information about those who had instigated the Calziran adventure. Which was not yet ended. Raids continued along the eastern coast.

The Connecten clerics settled down to watch the afternoon light play amongst the edifices and monuments. Squinting, Brother Candle could just make out soldiers guarding the wrecked ships across the river, valuable as salvage.

Michael Carhart sighed. "I wonder how it's going?" While they roamed idly and gawked at wonders of old renown, Duke Tormond and Queen Isabeth were in audience with the Patriarch. Everyone expected that to go badly. Tormond was too wishy-washy. Isabeth was an unknown. She was just fourteen when she went off to Navaya to be Peter's queen.

Brother Candle said, "Let me become a prophet in my own time. The Queen of Navaya will be more naive than the Duke of Khaurene. Who will become confused and deliver his patrimony to Sublime because that's easier than standing fast and doing the right thing."

"Look there," one of his companions said. "More Patriarchal troops."

Thirty soldiers were crossing the bridge nearest Krois. Sublime was pulling his garrisons in. Prematurely, if he was preparing for a Calziran expedition. It was a huge risk, counting on Johannes Blackboots not to leap at the nakedness of the Patriarchal States.

They knew immediately when Tormond and Isabeth ended their audience. The Duke's party were in plain sight crossing over from Krois to the south bank of the Teragi.

The Duke and his sister and those closest to them were guests of the Cologni family, in a Cologni satellite citadel, the Palazo Bracco. The Palazo Bracco was the seat of Flouroceno Cologni, the Cologni family Principaté. The Principaté, however, had moved to a suite in the Chiaro Palace when the pirates arrived. Most of the Principatés had treated themselves to luxurious security when the enemies of God appeared.

Flouroceno Cologni enjoyed showing off. He was doing so by housing the Connecten embassy. Overall, though, he was a nonentity who, if remembered at all, would lay a claim on history only because he did host Duke Tormond during his unhappy visit to the Mother City.

Members of the embassy began to gather in the central court of the Palazo Bracco. The Duke waited until no one else could crowd in. To his credit, he did feed everyone. On Sublime. "Eat up! We're Sublime's friends, now."

Brother Candle took advantage of the feast, served in every-man-for-himself fashion from tables along the courtyard wall. The horror show lasted for hours. During which Bishop LeCroes cornered Brother Candle. LeCroes, having internalized an admirable quantity of Firaldian wine, had developed a grand despair because he expected the Duke to abandon Immaculate.

"We don't know that," Brother Candle protested. "Tormond is a man of principle. One principle the Dukes of Khaurene never forget is that Worthy VI was legitimately elected Patriarch of the Episcopal Church."

"Of course, he hasn't forgotten. But he won't let what's right get in the way of doing what's expedient."

The Duke signaled a henchman. The man bellowed for silence.

Tormond had imbibed a quantity of wine himself. Eventually, carefully, he announced, "The goal toward which we've worked saw fruition today. There will be peace between the Church and the Connec."

No cheers were heard. Anonymous declarations of disbelief were.

"Isabeth and I spent four hours in converse with the Patriarch." Tormond paused. "I mean, with the pretender to the mantle of the Patriarchs of the Church founded by Saints Eis, Domino, and Arctue. We discussed the Connec's obligation to the Church and the Church's duty to the Connecten people. And the news, my friends, is good."

The Duke wanted to say more but the wine caught up and rendered him inarticulate.

Despite Tormond's incapacity, the facts of the conference took shape and substance. That shape was unappealing. That substance produced an unpleasant odor.

There were witnesses, the nameless, colorless clerks who are always there to write things down.

SIXTY MEN AND A WOMAN LISTENED AS A SLOBBERING, ALmost incoherent Tormond defended the agreement he had made with Sublime, once he spent time having nothing to drink.

The Connec would recognize the Brothen Patriarch. Priests and bishops who refused would be handed over to the new Bishop of Antieux. The bishop would be elevated to the Collegium within five years, guaranteed. His successor, the next Connecten Principaté, would be chosen by the ruling Duke at the time.

Bishop LeCroes flew into a rage. "You've betrayed your own faith, now? For a promise of peace from that feckless Benedocto jackal? You gain nothing, My Lord! Nothing! He can do nothing if you defy him. He's impotent. He'll turn on you as soon as he can. No Connecten Principaté will ever sit in the Collegium."

Tormond let the Bishop rage until his venom was spent. "Second. We must eradicate all heretical cults and beliefs."

The most anticipated of Patriarchal demands, that sparked the most ferocious response. Even pro-Brothen Episcopals were outraged by what seemed an arrogant and inexcusable meddling in matters of no concern to anyone but Connectens.

Brother Candle stood glumly silent, betrayed by a friend.

Tormond's speech became less slurred. That did not make his words any more welcome. "The Connec must provide twenty-eight-hundred armed men to help punish Calzir for the afflictions it visited on the Epsicopal world."

Someone shouted, "You mean on the Benedocto family, don't you?"

Bishop LeCroes said, "In other words, Nephew, you gave the false Patriarch everything we resisted when he invaded our homeland. Then you threw in the lives of our young men as a bonus, so Sublime can work his wickedness on someone else. A true diplomatic triumph, Nephew. There will be jubilation from one end of the Connec to the other. There will be dancing in the streets when the news reaches Khaurene."

The Duke was not so far gone in his cups that he failed to understand. Those dancers might be carrying torches and pitchforks and a notion to shape history by their own hands, by making it necessary to find a new Duke.

Tears flooded Tormond's eyes. Till that moment he had been sure that he had scored a diplomatic coup. Why such bitter anger from his friends and advisers?

"Let me offer a suggestion, Nephew," Bishop LeCroes snarled. "Stay in Brothe until the soldiers you gave away come home. Otherwise, our people might end up doing you personal harm in their wild enthusiasm for the peace that you've won."

Even the drunken Duke heard the soft speculations. How would Raymone Garete react when he heard? Any way he wanted. He would have the support of most Connectens.

Duke Tormond was befuddled. Brother Candle wondered how he could remain so consistently and stubbornly disconnected. Had they done something to his mind inside Krois?

Duke Tormond stumbled away from what he had expected to become a huge celebration. His disappointment, his confusion, were obvious.

His sister put aside her natural shyness, stepped forward to clarify the range of agreements reached. Those were of broad scope and implication and included Navaya, the rest of Direcia, Calzir, and the Empire in addition to the Connec, Firaldia, the Patriachal States, and the Church. Sublime had imposed no hard deadlines except in the matter of the armed men, who were supposed to be available in time for an autumn campaign against Calzir.

Isabeth said her husband would guarantee the independence of the Connec. He would send ships and siege specialists to help with the war.

Brother Candle did not fail to note that a punitive expedition had metamorphosed into a war. A war that would become a crusade, probably. Supported by a king who had no part in putting the thing together.

Isabeth was a sharper negotiator than her brother. In return for King Peter's help in reducing Calzir, Sublime would convey the island of Shippen to Navaya. Along with the smaller islands nearby. Shippen was large enough to have been an independent kingdom at times. It was more vast than Peter's current Direcian territories, though much poorer.

Isabeth also reported Sublime's arrangements with the Grail Empire.

Mainland Calzir, with its coastal islands, would be conveyed to the Empire and Alameddine. Various towns and castles would go to individuals who helped in the reconquest but they would be subject to the Emperor and the King of Alameddine.

Sublime was generous with territories not yet reclaimed.

Peter would do well in a successful war. And Sublime's Firaldian foes would be weakened. While Johannes became stronger.

Brother Candle began to suspect that there was a deeper plan behind Tormond's apparent fecklessness.

If Shippen passed into Navayan control, Platadura would gain immense influence eastward on the Mother Sea, at the expense of Sonsa, Dateon, and Aparion. Of Sonsa in particular. Most of Sonsa's trade passed through the narrow, treacherous Strait of Rhype, which separated Shippen from mainland Calzir.

Brother Candle worked his way close to Isabeth. "I smell a mystery. Where does Johannes figure? What's changed? How can the Grail Emperor suddenly be friends with the Patriarch? They're natural enemies, like cats and dogs."

No one else was much interested, now. Isabeth whispered, "This won't remain secret long. So I suppose I can tell you. Johannes only has one son. Lothar is twelve, sickly, and won't outlive his father. Johannes wants the Grail succession kept in the Ege family. Sublime, as Patriarch, has pledged that the

Church will guarantee the Imperial succession through all of Johannes's children."

Interesting. "Even through the daughters?"

"Absolutely. Katrin, then Helspeth, before anyone else can be considered. The price? Johannes has to help conquer Calzir. You've already heard of the division of spoils."

There would be more to it than that, Brother Candle believed. Sublime would not give his dearest enemy anything that cheaply. Nor would Hansel be subverted that easily.

Later, Michael Carhart wanted to know, "Will any of that really happen? Tormond can tell Sublime anything. What happens if he does try to suppress the Maysaleans, the Devedians, the Dainshaukin, the Pramans of the Terliagan Littoral, or the free-thinking Episcopals of the Connec?"

Seldom spoken Tember Sihrt observed, "He'll find himself in a cold and lonely place."

"Literally," Bishop LeCroes said. "A lot of people will turn their backs if he tries. He needs a lot of cooperation to hold things together."

Michael Carhart observed, "None of you, and no one else since Honario Benedocto's election, has pointed out how few of the world's problems would be problems if Honario Benedocto wasn't Patriarch."

Brother Candle asked, "Are you saying that somebody should do something about that?"

"Oh, no. No! I was stating a fact. Sublime's election has caused a horrible amount of misery and death. And he's just gotten started."

"The man has a point," Brother Purify observed. "Now we're going to blacken our souls further by not keeping the Connec out of this war with Calzir. I know some Pramans. Plenty still live around Terliaga and along the coast there. They're mostly good people. Like most Connectens. Like these Calzirans Sublime wants to butcher."

"Don't mention the Terliagans," Michael Carhart said. "If Sublime finds out that Volsard didn't wipe them out in his war with Meridian, he'll put them on the suppression list with the rest of us. Right up top, probably."

Brother Candle said, "We may be worrying too much. Remember who our Duke is. I'm thinking he'll never get around to doing much. Except to put Count Raymone in charge of the expedition to Calzir so he and his hotheads won't make things worse at home. If Calzir is as obstinate as it's always been, Sublime won't have time to worry about the Connec."

Bishop LeCroes complained, "Sublime is young, though. He could be around for another thirty or forty years."

Tember Sihrt sneered. "In that case, you'd better get in touch with your god. Beg him to nullify that last Patriarchal election."

His attempt at humor fell flat.

THE CONNECTEN EMBASSY TARRIED IN BROTHE NINE MORE days. For eight of them Tormond and Isabeth tried to gain another audience with Sublime, to reexamine those questions causing a furor. Sublime put them off until it became obvious that there would be no further discussion.

The Duke angrily ordered the embassy home following an announcement from Krois that Emperor Johannes would visit Brothe. Some thought that meant Hansel would bend the knee to Sublime in return for a Patriarchal decree that the Imperial succession be fixed in the Ege line. Much was made of the possibilities. Sublime seemed determined to force the future to fit to his personal vision. He had no time for whining bumpkins who refused to understand their role in his grand Episcopal reawakening. He did not fear the antagonism of the Instrumentalities of the Night.

BROTHER CANDLE LOOKED BACK AS THEY CROSSED THE TERagi, knowing he would see nothing like Brothe again. Memories were all he would take with him.

So little gain. So little accomplished. They would go home and try to live as though nothing had changed.

War with the Church had been averted. For the moment.

SQUABBLING AMONGST THE CONNECTENS NEVER CEASED. Brother Candle was tempted to make his way home alone, just to escape the bickering. Yet he did not. As long as his presence was acceptable amongst traditional Chaldareans there was a chance he could speak for peace and reason. He did have some influence but he could not change decisions already made.

The weather was little better than it had been during the eastward journey. Unless the Duke decided to take the day off. Then the weather was fine.

Tormond wasted little time. In the Connec a disgruntled Raymone Garete was assembling the force promised to Sublime. There were fears the hotheaded Count might use the troops to push the Connec in a direction of his own choice.

That fear was not unfounded. Raymone's friends did hope that he would rebel. They tried to delay the embassy's return.

Duke Tormond would not be manipulated. Those who tried to stall he left behind. They always caught up.

Tormond employed dozens of couriers to maintain contact with Sir Eardale Dunn and Count Raymone. Dunn reported no problems in Khaurene. But his news was always stale.

Count Raymone moved from Antieux to Castreresone. That city was more centrally located. His messages all showed proper deference and submission. They lacked the accusation and recrimination so common elsewhere. Raymone seemed wholly engaged with the practical difficulties of assembling twenty-eight-hundred armed men in a province unfamiliar with war.

The nationalist sentiment stirred by the Black Mountain Massacre had evaporated in disappointment and despair once Duke Tormond chose to visit the Mother City.

The people of the Connec had complete confidence in their Duke. He would let the false Patriarch bully him into surrendering their rights and properties. Time proved them clairvoyant. Yet they would not turn on Tormond.

Would they?

Brother Candle feared that answer might depend on choices made by men more animated by pride and ego than national interest.

26. Brothe, the Soultaken

Shagot slept for six days. Svavar slept for the first four of those himself. He was so weak when he wakened that he barely had strength enough to crawl into the kitchen of the home where they had gone to ground.

Pure disaster had befallen them when they tried to get the man the gods wanted destroyed. *Two* powerful sorcerers had gotten in the way. Not one, but *two*. The dispute that ensued should have been lethal. In fact, until Shagot awakened silent and almost insane from thirst and hunger, Svavar suspected that the encounter had, in fact, been fatal.

Svavar dripped water into Shagot's mouth with a rag. He fed his brother by spending hours pushing tiny wads of water-logged bread past Shagot's cracked lips.

Svavar was not in good shape. He had suffered more wounds and brutalities than Shagot. But he had come back faster than his brother, this time.

In moments when he thought beyond immediate survival, Svavar wondered what became of those two sorcerers. He and Grim had not had the power to destroy them. The Old Ones had not been that generous.

Something was out of kilter. Something did not ring right. And had not since the band broke up. This mission should not be this hard.

Svavar had memory problems, too. Reliability problems. Meaning he could conjure up several different but equally convincing memories of what happened after he and Grim had burst into the house that Grim said the Old Ones insisted was the Godslayer's hideout. That resulted in an unexpected battle with sorcerers and Calziran pirates. A ghost, a shadow, a something strolled through that savagery, crafting its outcome. It was in every version of the memory, but Svavar could not compel it to become concrete.

Svavar worried. And was afraid. The Old Ones might not be the only Instrumentalities involved. The Night was no monolith. Other powers might have a different interest in the God-slayer. Though he believed those two wizards were only defending themselves. The Godslayer was incidental.

Had the Godslayer survived? A lot of people had not.

Grim would explain when he awakened. If he awakened.

Shagot was a man on the brink of life's cliff, hanging on with two mangled fingers and a broken thumb.

Svavar's suspected that he and Shagot owed that enigmatic shade their lives. How had they found a place to hide while they were unconscious?

Asgrimmur worried about being discovered before he recovered enough to fight back. These southerners were weak but not stupid. They knew something dark was afoot in Brothe. They were looking for a pair of blond strangers even before this latest dust up.

The hunt would be more serious, now.

Svavar did not know that Brothe remained preoccupied with the pirates. Sublime was not a forgiving man. He had threatened to excommunicate anyone who facilitated the escape of even one crippled old man or terrified teenage boy. The Patriarch, from the safety of Krois, was fierce and vengeful, much like his god in ancient times, before the Holy Founders redefined Him for a new age. So the pirates fought on.

Svavar would have found Sublime's attitude familiar. It was the sort common among the Gray Walker and his kin.

WHEN SHAGOT FINALLY CAME AROUND SVAVAR SAW NO sanity in his eyes. He was not sure what he did see. The mind of a mad god, perhaps. If that was not an oxymoron.

Awareness gradually entered the mind behind Shagot's eyes. Svavar saw the rage fade, noted the exact instant when Grimur Grimmsson returned. Though Grim did not come across as sane himself once he emerged.

"Don't talk," Svavar croaked. He had hardly trouble talking himself. "I don't know how long it's been. A long time. I've been awake, off and on, for two days." In parched snatches he related the little he did know.

Shagot understood the seriousness of his own condition. He did not pursue his usual mad recovery effort. He accepted water and bread mush the best he could, then went back to sleep. Never saying a word.

Shagot slept for two more days.

Svavar slept a lot, too. He felt much better when Grim next awakened, though his strength was still less than half normal. His wounds still hurt badly. His joints ached. As did his soul.

This time Shagot did talk, a few words at a time. "It's been eight days, plus. The city has changed. We have to leave. They'll start looking for us soon. Seriously. House to house. Using the power of the Collegium. We can't take them on. So we'll go away and strike again after they forget us."

"The Godslayer survived?"

"Of course. You doubted that he would?"

"I was pretty sure he had."

"Want a real kick in the ass? We saved the asshole's life by attacking when we did. The way it came together, the Gray One suspects the Trickster's meddling. But I don't think the Trickster has that kind of reach."

"Something weird did happen, Grim. There was another power there, a shade, maybe. Something besides us and them sorcerers. Bigger than us and them put together. I think it would've kept us from killing the Godslayer if we'd tried. It saved us from getting dead, too, though. It even protected the sorcerers from us. No matter how hard I try, though, I can't figure out who or what it was."

"Which is why the Gray One thinks his nephew must be involved, if not directly, then through somebody he conned into doing his dirty work."

"The All-Father doesn't know what's going on?"

"Some things are hidden from the gods themselves. Particularly when other gods are involved."

"What?"

"The presence you sensed must have been somebody who came through from the Great Sky Fortress during the fight. I think somebody seized the power of the blood just when some of the Chosen were going to come help us finish the Godslayer."

Svavar did not understand. "We were supposed to be done with it?"

"Yes. We were that close. But somebody, probably from the

Great Sky Fortress, sabotaged us. Somebody kept me from conjuring the Heroes."

That clarified nothing for Svavar. He did not think the presence of the unknown was something new. He thought they had picked it up as long ago as at that old battlefield in Arnhand. But Shagot's speculation did offer a glimmer of the divine plan as Shagot understood it.

Shagot said, "That somebody is still here, little brother. Out of the Night. On the mortal plane. And not far off. We need to be more careful, at least till we understand what's going on."

THE OWNERS OF THAT HOME MUST HAVE BEEN KILLED IN THE fighting. Nobody reclaimed the place. Nobody tried to loot it, either. People stayed away by the thousands.

Svavar found a razor. He shaved his face and head. He shaved Shagot, too. He appropriated clothing for himself. It did not fit right but he did not need to be a dandy.

"Grim, I can limp around, now. I'm gonna go see what I can find out."

"Be careful, brother. I'm still too weak to tell if you get in trouble."

"You bet, Grim." He *was* careful. Always more so than Grim could imagine being. Grim had complete confidence in the favor of the gods. Everything had to work out when you had the Instrumentalities of the Night behind you.

Svavar, though, was deeply aware that they were in a land with alien gods. In Brothe the Old Ones were rats in the mystic walls. Noisy, malodorous, unpleasant, unwanted supernatural vermin.

SVAVAR FOUND BROTHE LITTLE CHANGED PHYSICALLY, BUT possessed of a new attitude toward the rest of the world, Calzir in particular. Everyone had a hate on for Calzir, now. And those who made decisions intended to take the suffering right back to the pirates' homeland.

Fighting continued in a half-dozen areas where trapped Calzirans battled on. The Brothen strategy urged patience. The pirates were isolated, then ignored. Hunger would bring them out eventually.

There were a thousand rumors afoot. The Patriarch would proclaim a crusade against Calzir. The Grail Emperor would let his subject kingdom Alameddine become a jumping-off platform. He would participate himself.

Of more interest were rumors about the hunt for two blond sorcerers. Proclamations had been posted in public squares and nailed to the doors of churches. Svavar got their gist from literate passersby.

Svavar could ask questions safely as long as he pretended to be one of the immigrant mercenaries fighting the pirates. He returned to Shagot knowing as much as any Brothen in the street.

"We do need to move out, Grim. They're putting together a gang to hunt us down. Two hundred men. They're training right now. They've got a crew of sorcerers coming in, too. From something called the Special Office at the headquarters of the Brotherhood of War. They're going to toss the whole city once they get here."

"We'll need a coach. Or a wagon. Something that can move me. I've got a while to heal yet."

"But you always heal so fast."

"This time, too. But this time I've got to get over death itself."

"What?" Was Grim joking?

No.

"There's no way I should've survived, little brother. Too much happened to me. It took the joined will of the Old Ones to blind death till my flesh recovered."

Shagot sounded deeply disturbed. Maybe he did not understand that they were not wholly alive anyway. But death held no terror for Shagot. Never had. Ah! He did fear life as a cripple.

He had no choice while he remained touched by the gods. He would hunt the Godslayer forever, dragging himself forward with the one finger left on his one remaining hand.

"I'll find out what we can do. I might have to buy something."

"Do what you have to. Fast. We need to get a head start on those Special Office sorcerers."

"You know about them?"

"They hunt and kill people like us. People touched by what

they call the Instrumentalities of the Night. They want to destroy the gods themselves. Every god, every hidden thing, even the least little hulder, except for their own god."

SHAGOT WAS AWAKE WHEN SVAVAR RETURNED FROM TOWN. He looked better. "What's wrong, little brother? You look like you swallowed a bug."

"A big-ass stinkbug, Grim. We don't have any money anymore."

"Huh?"

"That asshole Talab that you picked to take care of it? He fucked us, Grim. He figured out who we are. He reported us to the Collegium. They took our money. Except for twelve percent that he got as a reward."

"And?"

"So I killed him. After I made him tell me about it. I took money he had laying around. He wanted to pay me not to hurt him."

Shagot frowned, worried. "You got away with it?"

"I shook the guys chasing me before I crossed the river."

It had not been easy. He had had help. There had been a woman, put together in the northern style. A woman Svavar was sure he had seen before but could not place. He knew no women here. During his sojourn in Brothe he had been more celibate than any Episcopal priest.

The woman had cast a glamour on the Deves chasing him. First, they lost their emotional edge. Then they became confused and vented their anger on one another.

The woman bewitched him when he tried to approach her. She seemed amazed that he had noticed her.

She was his guardian angel?

He did not tell Shagot. He did not know why. But he was sure Grim would be pissed off when he found out.

Shagot said, "I still have some money in my bag."

"All right. We're out of time. Me killing that Deve asshole will get them stirred up all over again."

"You're right. Did you round up anything to eat? I'm fucking starving."

"Good. I was worried."

* * *

SHAGOT AND SVAVAR DEPARTED BROTHE FOUR DAYS AFTER Svavar gave the Deve money man what he had coming. They left via the gate they had used to enter the city. The guards there were not concerned about people leaving. Particularly people who did not look Calziran. Nor were they alert for three men, a dog, and a mangy mule pulling a wreck of a wagon.

The third man soon stopped being part of the group.

"Get the money back," Shagot said from the wagon.

"As soon as this damned dog . . . Shit. Give me a sword. I'll chop the fucker's head off." Svavar was not afraid of the mongrel, though it was large and still had most of its teeth. After the Great Sky Fortress it would never occur to Svavar to be afraid of any mortal hound.

He was in a foul temper. "Shit! He must've left the money with his woman." He was not kind to the dog.

"Don't sweat it. We can always come up with money. Get shut of the bodies before somebody comes along."

Svavar did so, just in time. They had not traveled another two hundred yards before the vanguard of a cavalry force appeared ahead. Svavar guided the mule off the road in order to be out of the way.

"Recognize those standards?" Shagot asked.

"No. But the one with the keys must have something to do with the Patriarch."

The soldiers were from Maleterra, where their job had been to hold the road to Brothe if the Emperor decided to lash out at Sublime.

Svavar wondered who was poking it to whom in the romance between Johannes and the Patriarch.

The going was slow while the soldiers hogged the road.

The brothers turned east when they reached a road that ran across the Firaldian peninsula. Later, they turned south on the eastern coast road. Vondera Koterba was still hiring in Alameddine. His army would become their hideout.

Shagot remained immersed in his obsession. Shagot was confident that they would encounter the Godslayer again in Calzir. Svavar, no longer in control, lapsed into despair.

Svavar began to see things. Things that may have been

there, following wherever he went—or maybe things that were just in his mind. Things that men who had not passed through the Great Sky Fortress would never notice.

THE WOMAN WAS TALLER THAN ANY OF THE SOLDIERS. SHE was attractive but not in the lush style favored in Firaldia. She was solidly built, well-muscled, without fat. She wore golden hair in braids rolled up at the sides of her head. Her stride was long and businesslike. The troops paid her little heed, which was remarkable for their sort.

The woman left the road. She moved some dead brush. Flies swarmed up, buzzing, angry about being disturbed at work. She considered the corpses of an old man and a headless dog.

The woman scowled. She was disgusted—despite having seen worse ten thousand times before.

Because no one was watching no one noted the fact that, at some point, the woman was no longer there.

27. Brothe, Preparing for a War with Calzir

Polo told Else, "This place is busier than a dog that's been dead for a week."

Else grunted. Polo was right. The Bruglioni citadel was in a ferment. Divino Bruglioni had bullied the rural family into providing funds to hire workmen. And rustic Bruglioni were returning—lest they lose what estate they enjoyed.

Principaté Bruglioni's threats, in Paludan's name, were draconian.

Else went into the countryside twice, leading veterans of the fighting with the pirates. He dispersed parasitic Bruglioni relatives carefully selected by Uncle Divino. That electrified the rest of the family. That and the new wealth and new estates that were sure to fall to the Bruglioni during Sublime's upcoming Calziran adventure.

The Patriarch had proclaimed a crusade. A large majority of the Collegium urged him to do so.

Else expected to take part. Paludan had directed him to raise an infantry company at Bruglioni expense.

Else did not understand Sublime's confidence. It seemed based exclusively on faith.

History was littered with the bones of empires confident of the fearful swift sword of their god. But the scales never fell from men's eyes. They never failed to trust the treacherous Instrumentalities of the Night.

Else attended the planning meetings. His questions generated frowns but weakened no one's confidence.

More time went into divvying Calzir up, all the way down to the parish level, than went into planning the campaign.

Else appealed for instructions from al-Qarn, once through Gledius Stewpo via the Devedian route, once through the Kaifate's embassy. He received no response. He had to make his own choices. Meaning he would always be wrong. If Gordimer chose to see it that way.

Else's borrowed accountant had no trouble penetrating the number thickets of Mr. Grazia's accounts. Else took the evidence to Uncle Divino. The Principaté betrayed a malicious delight. He used the material to bludgeon and blackmail those he wanted to keep in Bruglioni service.

Whenever Else left the citadel, it seemed, he ran into someone who was unhappy about the Bruglioni resurgence.

Principaté Doneto, in particular, complained that Piper Hecht was not sufficiently devoted to the advancement of Bronte Doneto's agenda.

PINKUS GHORT FOUND DONETO'S EXASPERATION AMUSING. "Pipe, I ain't never seen nobody as self-centered as our old jail buddy. Long as he's got pals who'll put up with him pushing them around."

"I'm not surprised. I've had to deal with his type since I was tall enough to toddle. I'll probably turn into his type if I live long enough and rise high enough. So will you."

"Yeah. I can see me wearing Grade Drocker's slippers next time we hit the Connec. Take me along a troupe of them baby whores like Bishop Serifs had, only girls."

"You're disgusting."

"But fun. You got to admit that. You gonna be ready to go when the troops head south?"

"Ready and looking forward to it." Which was a lie. He did not want to war against fellow Pramans. But al-Qarn left him no choice. He had to go on being this character he had created until he did receive instructions.

"That's good. Me, too. How's your lady?"

"Anna?" He and Anna Mozilla had begun to develop a social life. That made him nervous, of course, but Anna was right at home. She drew attention away from him. But if someone decided to study Anna Mozilla they might begin to wonder when Piper Hecht had had an opportunity to develop a relationship with a woman from Sonsa. "She's fine. Had a little scare last week, though."

"When those Calzirans came up out of the underground?"

"Happened right down the street. I hope that's the last bunch."

"Collegium says so."

"That the same Collegium that gave the all-clear a week before that mob popped up?"

"You'd think a gang of sorcerers like them would be a little sharper at their own racket, wouldn't you?"

"Wouldn't you? Can you tell me anything that'll make my job easier?"

"Nope. Well, don't turn your back on nobody. Like I said, the Principaté ain't thrilled about how things are working out. I don't *think* he'd do anything drastic. But he's a little freaky right now. Not much else is going the way he wants, either."

"Why should he be unhappy with me? I'll be moving over to the Collegium any day now. He wouldn't want me to jeopardize that, would he?"

"I'll remind him. He's just anxious for something to go his way so he can get some exercise patting himself on the back for being so clever."

"You ask me, things are going amazingly well. I thought it would take me twenty years to get where I've gotten in just a few months. And you . . ."

"Yeah, shit. I know. I'm lucky to have a job. And Doneto, too. He really screwed the bitch in the Connecten fiasco. But he got promoted anyway."

"They do say nepotism works best when you keep it in the family. Which wasn't what I was going to say, but sometimes the truth just slides out."

"A joke? From you? Damn, Pipe. You're starting to come around. You'll turn into a real human being if you don't watch out."

"I'm trying. How're Bo and Joe?"

"Joe got kicked up to be in charge of the Principaté's stables."

"Good for him."

"Pig Iron lives like a king."

"Good for him, too. I have to go, Pinkus."

"The Castella?"

"Yes. They've brought in a painter who's trying to create a portrait of Starkden based on my memories. I think it's a waste of time. But who argues with the Brotherhood of War?"

"Especially the Special Office. Bechter's all right, though. He's just a soldier. He don't preach at you."

"He is a good man."

"Look out for that asshole Drocker."

"Hey, I'm careful of everybody who hasn't shown me any reason to trust them."

"Ouch."

"I trust you, Pinkus. I trust you to be Pinkus Ghort. I trust you to look out for Pinkus Ghort. And I think I know Pinkus Ghort well enough to know when I need to strap my chastity belt on."

Ghort snorted. "Is it true, what I hear? The Bruglioni are really gonna give you a company to take down to Alameddine?"

"I don't expect many real Bruglioni to be involved. Except my man, Polo. He's Uncle Divino's spy. He's obvious and inept. We've worked things out. He pretends he's just my batman. I pretend I don't know he's watching me. Appropriate greetings to Bo and Joe. And see that Pig Iron gets a turnip from me. I have to get going. I can't be late."

Ghort grunted.

Else was right. He could not be late. Because he was not expected at any specific time. The summons from the Castella had not mentioned a time to show up.

In addition to working with that painter, Else was being wooed by the Brotherhood. He had, twice, turned down the chance to join. Which, according to Redfearn Bechter, actually pleased Grade Drocker.

Drocker did not consider Piper Hecht Brotherhood material. A blind man could see that Piper Hecht was not devoted to God.

Irony in the extreme, Else thought. *Irony worthy of a divine chuckle.*

The Brotherhood had been having trouble recruiting for decades. Modern Chaldareans were not prepared to endure the austerity and poverty expected of God's Soldiers.

Lamenting the headed-to-Hell-in-a-hand-basket state of the Chaldarean world, Divino Bruglioni claimed, "What this century needs is a good plague to revive the old values."

REDFEARN BECHTER WAITED AT THE BLUE POSTERN. THAT was not remarkable. A lookout on the Castella ramparts would have seen Else coming.

"You're later than we'd hoped."

"The letter said the morning."

"I understand."

"It's like a mausoleum in here." The halls and rooms and corridors were empty and still. The day-to-day austerity of the Brotherhood was intimidating in itself. Else found them every bit as committed and determined as the best Sha-lug.

"Those Brothers who were able went to Alameddine with the Emperor's scouts. Those of us who stayed are too old, too sick, too injured, or too involved in the planning to go." Bechter added, in a whisper, "I'd rather be out there myself. Not that I like fighting."

"Not enough men left to dilute Grade Drocker's venom, eh?"

Bechter chuckled. "You said it. I didn't. But I won't have to gut it out much longer. The convoy from Runch should show up before the end of the week. Hawley Quirke will be back. The sorcerer can stew in his own juice."

That made Else uncomfortable. He was not sure why. "Who else is coming? Anyone I know?"

"How would I know? Hell. How would *you* know any of them?"

"By reputation, I mean. I wouldn't know any of them personally. Unless they shared those happy days in the Connec with us."

"Those men are either all dead, here, or down south scouting out the best ways to stomp Calzir."

They entered a room where, to Else's surprise, nearly fifty men sat quietly while Ferris Renfrow employed a long wand to point out areas of interest on a map of mainland Calzir painted on a blank wall that had been plastered, then whitewashed beforehand. The map had south toward the top, as the foot of the Firaldian peninsula appeared from Brothe. Artists continued painting the map while Renfrow talked about the Calziran kingdom. The painters wore Imperial livery. The major stuff, coastlines, cities, passes, rivers, and fortresses, were on the wall already. The artists were adding finer details.

Else was impressed.

He was more impressed by the gathering. He was late, yes, but not very. The audience had not yet begun to show the inevitable signs of boredom. Several major personalities, including Johannes Blackboots himself and numerous members of the Collegium, were there. He saw Grade Drocker, of course, and some of the most senior commanders of the Patriarchal States and of the Grail Empire. Representatives of the Five Families were present as well, including Rogoz Sayag.

Else did not see Pinkus Ghort. Of course. He had left Ghort on the street, as unaware of this gathering as he had been himself. But if Piper Hecht belonged here, so did Pinkus Ghort. Ghort would be closer to what was going on.

Bechter led him to a seat on the left side of the room. So. His presence was not exalted.

A servant brought tea, a luxury Else had enjoyed only a few times before, long ago in al-Qarn.

Ferris Renfrow watched, apparently amused. But the man did not interrupt his monologue.

Renfrow talked about Calzir as though he had been there.

This was a dangerous man. How well did he know Dreanger? How much time had he spent in the Holy Lands, amongst the Wells of Ihrian?

Ferris Renfrow was a compelling speaker. He brought Calzir to life. He made it sound like a desert in the making, except for scattered olive groves, orange groves, and vineyards. The rest of the country supported sheep and goats. And fishing villages wherever there was an excuse for a harbor.

"A handful of noble and wealthy families control the best land. Which reflects a reality that obtains throughout Firaldia. The political landscape is similar, too. Calzir consists of a dozen principalities, none of which acknowledge the Mafti al-Araj el-Arak, and some more names, at al-Khazen. The Mafti is about as relevant as Immaculate II at Viscesment. Depending on factors involving conflicts between different visions of the Praman faith, the principalities recognize either the Kaif of Qasr al-Zed or the Kaif of al-Minphet as their proper spiritual leader. In practical terms, the kaifates have no more control than el-Arak. Neither kaif receives any revenue. This large island part of Calzir, Shippen, has silver and copper mines that have been in production since before men started keeping histories. Wheat is the island's great agricultural product. It's been an exporter forever. It also produces fruits, olives, and sheep. Fishing is important, but not the way it is on the mainland.

"The inland parts of the island are wild. Nor have the population all gone over to the Unbeliever. A third of the populace are still Chaldarean, even in the main towns—though mainly Eastern Rite. In the deep wilderness, there're still some practicing pagans."

Never saying so, Ferris Renfrow made it plain that Hansel had had his eye on Calzir for a long time.

That made Else wonder if Johannes had engineered the Calziran piracy, through Starkden and Masant el-Seyhan.

Hours later, after hearing more than he ever wanted to know about the topography, geography, economy, and people of Calzir, Else finally found out why he had been brought in.

He got the news during the afternoon meal break.

He started out eating alone. He did not want to attract attention by pushing into one of the circles of his betters. Redfearn Bechter approached him. "Drocker needs to see you, Captain."

Else lifted an eyebrow. "What's up?"

"He figures you're probably curious about why you're here."

"Other than just because I was told to show up? The man is smarter than he looks."

"Bring your chow. This'll be a working lunch."

"All right." Else gathered his food and drink.

"Need a hand? Looks like you took some of everything, then went back for more."

"I got while the getting was good. You'd understand if you ate where I usually do."

Bechter guided Else into a small room. A dozen men had their heads together there. Else recognized Grade Drocker, Ferris Renfrow, Divino Bruglioni, and Bronte Doneto. He pulled himself together. This could be bad.

Principaté Doneto said, "You don't need to feel like a cornered stag, Hecht. It's good news."

"Your Grace?"

"You've impressed quite a few people this past year. These folks all have good things to say about you." Chuckle. "There's that look again. I'll just get to it. We've decided to make you commander of the city regiment for the upcoming campaign."

"Huh!" That was an unexpected blow. "I . . . Really?"

"Somebody has to do it. Brothe being Brothe, we couldn't possibly agree on any native candidate. These men either know you or have heard of you. You're the only candidate the majority didn't reject."

It made sense—in a Brothen sort of way. Partly because so many of them thought they had a claim on Piper Hecht.

"You'll have people looking over your shoulder all the time, nagging you. The Five Families, the Brotherhood, the Collegium, the Colors, even His Holiness himself. Ignore them all, do a good job, and you'll be fine."

"I have no experience commanding large forces. Wait. First, let's talk about how large a force this will be." He would not refuse this opportunity, even if it cost him his chance to get closer to the Collegium.

Bronte Doneto said, "We're looking at two thousand to twenty-five hundred. The same squatters and immigrants you used against the pirates, armed and equipped from city arsenals. But, possibly, more. Recruiting and finance won't be your worry. You handle the training and leadership."

Else did not express an opinion of the weaponry and equipment stored in Brothe's armories. The best had come out during the Calziran incursion. That had been old and poorly kept. Maintenance money found its way into the purses of corrupt officials rather than being wasted on armorers.

In Dreanger Else had commanded no force larger than a

company. Gordimer did not tolerate large commands for popular officers. Else Tage was a missions specialist, meant to lead small bands of highly motivated and thoroughly trained soldiers who enjoyed facing special challenges.

"That many? Really? There's that much money around?" Paludan Bruglioni was willing to finance a basic infantry company of two hundred men. Reluctantly, and only after Divino bullied some country cousins into coming home. And because he hoped the Bruglioni could seize new holdings in Calzir.

Family added that piquant extra spice to Firaldian politics. A family could have holdings in a dozen different principalities.

Principaté Doneto asked, "Are you possessed of strong feelings about Deves, Captain Hecht?"

"I have no feelings, Your Grace. I had no experience of that race before I came to Firaldia."

"Good, then."

Grade Drocker muttered something both venomous and vicious.

Doneto observed, "Our brother militant doesn't share your indifference. He had the misfortune to be in the wrong place at the wrong time during the Devedian insurrection in Sonsa."

"So I've heard. I was lucky enough to reach Firaldia after the riots ended."

"The Devedians will support the Holy Father in the Calziran matter. In return for concessions and guarantees, of course. The Patriarch will grant the concessions. The Deves have more to offer than he'll have to give them in return. This once."

Grade Drocker's opinion of the arrangement was bitter but he remained a good soldier. He kept that opinion to himself. Those slinking, slimy Deves would . . .

"What do they want?" Else asked.

"An end to legal restrictions on Devedians just for being Devedian. They promise not to celebrate their heathen rites outside their homes."

So. The Devedians wanted nothing more than official recognition of the *status quo ante*. Unlike Chaldareans or Pramans, Devedians did not evangelize or try to win converts. Theirs was a tribal religion.

Else said, "There must be more."

"Of course. They want the Calziran Deves and Dainshaus spared when we invade. Their Calziran cousins won't resist. They'll help by providing intelligence. They've begun doing that already."

Else flicked a glance at Ferris Renfrow. "I accept. I like the challenge. And it's a chance to make history."

"Good," Divino Bruglioni said.

"How much discretion will I have? Can I recruit my own officers?"

"You'll have considerable freedom, Captain Hecht. While the rest of us all think that we have a right to interfere. Can you handle the job?"

"Of course." He was Sha-lug. He had trained for it all his life. Though he always assumed that he would lead God's champions, not those of God's enemies.

Principaté Bruglioni said, "Enjoy your meal, Captain Hecht. Relax. Think. This afternoon we'll decide what to *do* with a city regiment."

ELSE SLIPPED INSIDE AS ANNA MOZILLA HELD THE DOOR. SHE said, "It's about time. You're making me jealous, you know."

Her teasing left Else disconcerted. He was never sure that she was joking.

"I spend as much time with you as I can."

"I know that. I don't like it. I don't have to like it. But I do know that. Shall I make dinner? I have a wonderful, fat hen half roasted already."

"You shall. If you will. Perhaps in an hour? Or two?"

"Oh! So you're finally going to make the first move? I thought I'd be all gray and you'd be all bald before you . . . Why are you peeking through the shutters?"

"I was followed."

"Again? I thought they'd given up on that."

"The Bruglioni have. But now some more serious people are interested. I'll tell you later. Right now, though, I have to get the world out of my head. And you're the woman who can empty my brain."

* * *

Anna had the chicken roasting. She listened while Else filled her in. "That's hard to believe, Piper." She was an excellent listener. She did not interrupt. She did not ask stupid questions. She did not let emotion obscure her view of reality. "They're going to make you a general?"

"I find it hard to believe, too. But I was in the right places at the right times."

"You had something to do with what happened to that Brotherhood of War sorcerer in Sonsa, didn't you?"

"He killed my friends. He meant to kill me. But he didn't know who I was."

"Aren't you afraid they'll check your story a little closer?"

"Terrified. But I can't walk away because there's a risk."

"What about the sorcerer? He doesn't suspect you?"

"I'm sure. There was evidence that the man he was after died in the fighting. He never actually saw me, anyway. So he's even more angry at Deves. I'm more concerned about Ferris Renfrow, the Emperor's spymaster. He thinks he knows who I am. He wants to use that to control me."

"Maybe you should go away."

"No. This is what I do. This is what I chose to do. Did your husband have connections with anyone besides my people?"

"What do you mean?"

"Bluntly, that intelligence gatherers sometimes market their harvest to more than one buyer. I'm wondering if he served more than one master."

Anna eyed him doubtfully. "Where are you headed?"

"I'm trying to figure out if anyone besides me would know that you were his wife. Other than the people whose tools we are. Our lives could get uncomfortable if anyone tied us together before . . ." Not good. He had told too many people that he had known Anna elsewhere. Anyone who developed an abiding interest ought to be able to discover Anna's origins.

"He never mentioned working for anyone else. He did what he did for personal reasons. He never explained what those were."

"I wish I could help you there. But I didn't even know he was gone. I didn't know his name."

"He was too clever for his own good."

"I see. Look. I don't know who you pass my information to.

I don't want to know. But a lot is happening. The people at the other end need to know. They need to let me know what they want me to do. And I don't want to talk about it anymore. That hen smells ready to eat."

GERVASE ASKED, "DID YOU ENJOY YOURSELF, CAPTAIN?"

"Yes, Mr. Saluda. I did. Including the rare pleasure of a good night's sleep. I have an idea. Suppose we have Dugo and the boys study leadership skills from the bottom up? If they went through the training company they might face life armed with one small clue about what it's like for the people who actually have to do the work and suffer the bloody noses."

Gervase did not like that idea. But he said nothing negative. He never crossed Else. Else might cause certain documents to fall into the hands of Paludan Bruglioni. Gervase had little faith in his friend's ability to forgive.

Gervase said, "That Deve you brought in wants to see you. He's in the accounting office. He brought some of his cousins along."

"Stop feeling sorry for yourself, Gervase. You're a better man than you think."

Saluda wanted to argue, but realized that by doing so he could only belittle himself.

Else grinned. "Would you like to be captain of the Bruglioni company in the city regiment?"

"Don't start that stuff with me, Hecht."

"Stuff? I never took you for a coward, Gervase. Only for spoiled and ignorant."

"I'm no coward!" No man, however craven in fact, would confess cowardice. Most would fight to keep their terror secret.

"Maybe not. Where is Titus Consent?"

"The accounting office. Going through the business records. And I never had anything to do with any of that."

"Gervase, you worry too much."

TITUS CONSENT, THE DEVEDIAN ACCOUNTANT PROVIDED ELSE by Gledius Stewpo's cohorts, was nineteen years old. And looked younger. And was, without doubt, a dedicated Devedian spy. Numbers were his passion. Though he was married. He had a new son named Sharone he worked into every conversation.

Titus's "cousins" turned out to be more like uncles. One was Gledius Stewpo. Else had seen the other man before, briefly, in the Devedian underground, but could not recall his name. He was one of those quiet, dark-haired Deves who stayed in the background but wielded immense influence in their councils.

Else took a quick look round to make sure there were no eavesdroppers. "What's up?"

Stewpo said, "This seemed like the best way to see you. Now that you're one of the movers and shakers you're up to your ears in Imperial and Collegium toadies all the time."

"I'm glad you thought of it."

Stewpo frowned. "They're watching you?"

"Every minute."

"Who?"

"Ferris Renfrow. He has it in his head that he knows me. I don't know what his game is. Who he thinks I am is who he wants me to be."

"This isn't good," Stewpo said. "He shouldn't know that I'm here."

"Does he know you? Are you somebody he wants to know?"

Stewpo shrugged.

"You could be too late already, Uncle. You haven't been staying out of sight. If Renfrow has eyes in the quarter, he knows. Assuming you're somebody who interests him. Would you be?"

"I shouldn't be."

"So explain what's going on with you and Calzir. Why're your people willing to help Sublime?"

"I'd hoped we wouldn't butt heads over that."

"We haven't. We won't. I just want to understand why you're changing sides."

"There's the flaw in your thinking, Sha-lug. My friends and I are on the side we're always on. The Devedian side. This invasion is going to happen. Calzir can't repel it this time. So we'll try to save our people the customary pain and despair by joining the winners before the fighting."

"The customary pain and despair?"

"In all wars in this end of the world both sides always take the opportunity to punish and plunder their local Deves and Dainshaus."

"Ah." That happened in the Realm of Peace as well, despite a religious law enjoining the protection of unbelievers who submitted to God's law. But it happened less frequently there than in the barbarous west.

"I understand."

Stewpo was surprised. "Not going to argue?"

"No point. You're right. You have to look out for your own. The problem I have isn't with that, Uncle. While I command the city regiment they won't harm your people."

"That problem would be?"

"It's a what-if at the moment. I'm concerned that the Brotherhood reinforcements from Runch might include someone who would remember me visiting Staklirhod under a different name."

After hearing a brief account of Else's stay in Runch, Titus Consent asked, "What would your problem have to do with Deves?"

Stewpo waved that aside. "Sounds like you'd better hope your god outhustles theirs, Sha-lug. Though I wonder why they'd remember your particular incident. It was trivial. Why should they watch for some itinerant crusader to turn up in Brothe? Keep your hair short, run a strong bluff, and be a good soldier."

Else, Stewpo, and Titus Consent talked for an hour, mainly about the execrable state of the Bruglioni accounts, due to incompetent manipulation.

Consent suspected somebody had been bribed to cover up a large debt owed the Bruglioni.

Consent added, "There is an obvious, clumsy scheme meant to disguise the fact that the rural family aren't paying the central treasury as much as they should."

"Really? Do you have anything I can take to Paludan?"

Titus Consent handed Else a sheaf of papers. "Four copies. I know you consider me just a kid. Listen to me, anyway. There's a *lot* of money involved in these swindles. That report will be dangerous to somebody. That's why you get multiple copies. That's why I'm telling you to watch your back."

Polo barged in, startling everyone. He paid no attention to the Deves. "Sir. Captain. There's a messenger. They want you at the Castella. Something's happened."

"Any idea what?"

"No. But the messenger was sure it isn't good news."

"All right." Else told Consent, "Thank you, Titus. Stay in touch. I'll have another job for you soon. It'll pay better."

SERGEANT BECHTER HAD BECOME ELSE'S GUIDE TO THE Castella dollas Pontellas. "You didn't have to run, Captain. The others will take their time."

"What's happening? I got the message secondhand. Polo made it sound earthshaking."

"That may be. I don't know. The way it's being handled suggests there's been a serious defeat somewhere, though."

"Does that make sense? Where is any fighting going on? In Direcia?"

"You'll just have to wait. Like the rest of us."

"But I'm a special guy," Else protested, borrowing from Pinkus Ghort's manual of personal style.

"Blood and turnips, Brother Hecht. I couldn't tell you if I loved you. Nobody told me."

"Probably because they can't trust you to keep marginal types like me in the dark with the mushrooms."

"Sergeant Unreliable. That's what they call me. Go ahead. Take advantage."

"Huh?"

"Isn't the food the real reason you charged right over? Because the first arrivals get all the best?"

Else laughed, but confessed, "I came in a hurry because I thought it would be expected of me."

"The men involved here take a relaxed attitude toward things professional soldiers hold dear. Notably, punctuality and discipline."

No startling revelation, that. The local nonprofessionals tended to think of war as a sport. Despite evidence left by the late pirate raid.

Else's respect for the masters of the Five Families and Collegium, was failing. Paludan Bruglioni was not unique in his mental and moral malaise.

He did fill up on the best food.

A NEW FACE ACCOMPANIED GRADE DROCKER WHEN THE SORcerer arrived, limping. Drocker seated himself, straining against his pain. His companion faced the assembly. "I'm Voltor Wilbe. From the Special Office at the Father House. Will you all please stand?"

Else was not surprised. Chaldareans prayed before, during, and after everything they did collectively.

Wilbe said, "Follow me in the Rite of Abjuration."

Startled murmurs.

Else worried. What was a Rite of Abjuration?

One of the Emperor's generals demanded, "What the hell is that?"

Irked, Wilbe explained, "The Rite of Abjuration. Created by the Special Office. It lets good Chaldareans formally renounce the Great Adversary and the Tyranny of the Night."

The general snorted his contempt.

The Rite of Abjuration was a responsorial. Voltor Wilbe chanted. His audience repeated his chant, renouncing everything to do with the Adversary and all things of the Night.

When Wilbe chanted, "I renounce the Tyranny of the Night. I renounce the Instrumentalities of the Night," responses were almost nonexistent. The clerics said nothing at all. Wilbe was nonplussed.

Wrong crowd, Else thought. Even Grade Drocker failed to participate. By common standards God Himself was an Instrumentality of the Night.

"Pardon me," Wilbe said. "I got carried away. I just want to banish any dark spirits."

"They're gone," Drocker growled. "Get on with it."

"Yes, sir. Gentlemen, there's been a sea battle. It took place in the strait between Penalt and Dole Hemoc." Wilbe seemed to expect his audience to know the geography. "It involved the fleet bound here from Staklirhod. It was an accidental encounter that became a running battle that lasted several days and involved ships from Sonsa, Dateon, Vantrad, Triamolin, the Eastern Empire, and our own warships at the end. Initially, the enemy was a Lucidian fleet carrying troops to Calzir."

"Silence!" Grade Drocker bellowed into chatter beginning to interfere with Wilbe's report. "This will affect our planning." Drocker's outburst had a potent impact. Even members of the Collegium shut up.

Voltor Wilbe detailed a battle that had been a long time in the making.

Naval commanders in the Eastern Empire and Crusader states of Vantrad and Triamolin began to suspect the Lucidians of preparing a naval adventure over a year ago. Ships, troops, and supplies were collecting in several ports. There was speculation about an attempt to invade Staklirhod. Scout ships prowled the Lucidian coast. Sea skirmishes ensued. The Lucidians wanted their intentions kept veiled.

The mercantile republics sent warships to protect their merchantmen and properties when the Calzirans started raiding. Which remained untouched by Calzirans, who focused on the Church.

But Pramans on the scores of small islands in the eastern Mother Sea tried to take advantage of the confusion farther west. They began attacking Chaldarean shipping. The mercantile republics objected.

Else understood before Wilbe explained. There was an inevitability at work. The Lucidian fleet, once it sailed, carried five thousand veteran soldiers, with horses and equipment, weapons and supplies, all destined for al-Healta in Calzir.

So. Lucidia started getting ready to help Calzir long before the Calziran rabble began assaulting the Episcopal Church.

Principaté Donel Madisetti ran out of patience. "What does that have to do with us? Where does the Brotherhood come in?"

"Your Grace, the Brotherhood fleet became involved because it turned up in the wrong place at the wrong time."

A pickup gang of Chaldarean warships, mostly small but fast, began harassing the Lucidians as soon as they put to sea. The Brotherhood fleet got involved because the mess outbound from Lucidia got in their way when they were trying to sneak through to Brothe without being noticed. The Lucidians were trying to sneak, too.

The circus sounded like insanity under oars—coupled with the kind of coincidence the Instrumentalities of the Night conjured for their own amusement.

The appearance of the Brotherhood force doomed the Lucidians. Tide and current carried their older, weaker, smaller ships toward the Chaldareans.

But tide and current carried the Chaldareans as well, around the cape of Dole Hemoc, into the path of a Dreangerean fleet also intent on sneaking through those islands. It, too, was carrying aid to Calzir.

The Instrumentalities of the Night just kept compounding the joke.

Only two Brotherhood ships escaped. Brother Wilbe was aboard one of those. The Praman survivors sailed on to Calzir. Wilbe said, "We shadowed them. They made landfall near al-Stikla, on the east coast of Calzir. The Lucidians disembarked there. The Dreangereans and some Lucidians went on to al-Healta. We couldn't determine how strong they still were. The Dreangereans' seamanship was awful."

Else offered a silent prayer on behalf of those Sha-lug who had perished. Gordimer built his fleet too fast. Its sailors hadn't had time to learn. Dreanger was last a naval power before the rise of the Old Empire.

Wilbe said, "There was a powerful sorcerer with their fleet. His presence made the difference."

This got uglier by the second.

He had to lead a major force against er-Rashal al-Dhulquarnen?

He would fight Lucidians and Calzirans only. Weakening the Lucidians would benefit the kaifate of al-Minphet.

At some point, unannounced, the Emperor drifted in. He remained in the background, small, silent, unnoticed until he declared, "This isn't a disaster. Unless you didn't get away. Adjust your thinking to the new reality." He indicated the wall map that showed only Calzir, Alameddine's cantonments, and the marches of several small principalities bordering those two. "We block the passes through the Vaillarentiglia Mountains. Here. Here. Here. We blockade their harbors. Their crops are going to come in short. Fishing will stop because their fishermen and boats didn't come back. Prefamine conditions will obtain by winter's start. Burdening Calzir with thousands of unproductive soldiers and animals will hasten the bad times. The Lucidians and Dreangereans won't be able to import food."

"Why?" one of the Principatés asked.

"Brother Wilbe said they offended Sonsa, Dateon, the Eastern Empire, Vantrad, Triamolin, and Staklirhod. All those sovereignties will be watching for a chance to even scores."

Else studied the big map intently. And saw a potential Praman disaster much bigger than that festering in the Emperor's mind. Johannes was not looking at Calzir as a whole.

Someone, with the stink of er-Rashal al-Dhulquarnen on him, had plotted and schemed, pulled strings and machinated, until he was sure he had engineered a situation where Sublime and his Episcopal brethren would become bogged down in their own quarter of the world, unable to make themselves obnoxious in Dreanger or the Holy Lands.

But—

Er-Rashal's dream was about to become a nightmare. That chance meeting of fleets had killed any chance that Patriarchal and Imperial forces could be lured into a huge ambush. The Praman allies, despite their victory at sea, were caught in a bottle. And Else suspected that they would not realize that before the hunger started.

Else glared at the map. He saw nothing but disaster for the Faithful. Hansel was too pessimistic.

Unless er-Rashal did have some deep, unfathomable scheme proceeding, he had clevered himself into the loss of two fleets and two armies of seasoned soldiers. Unless defeat was part of the plan.

Else still had no idea why er-Rashal had wanted the mummies from Andesqueluz.

Was er-Rashal as uncomfortable with him as Gordimer was? Gordimer issued orders. Er-Rashal instigated them. Gordimer would not be interested in mummies. But he would not be heartbroken if a potential rival failed while trying to bring in a collection of old bones.

"Captain Hecht?"

"Your Grace? I'm sorry." Principaté Divino had closed in on Else. "That map is trying to tell me something. But I'm not hearing what it has to say. It's something bone obvious."

"Nobody else is spewing ideas like a holiday firework."

"Of course, Your Grace. If it was obvious everybody would see it."

"Tell me what you see. When you see it. And what you think. Because I don't see this new situation benefiting the Bruglioni. Or anyone underwriting the city regiment."

"I disagree. Nobody's contributing anything but money. It isn't like an actual member of one of the Five Families might actually find himself face-to-face with the actual possibility of actually getting hurt."

"Your cynicism is worthy of a born Brothen, Captain Hecht. But."

"Your Grace?"

"Are we in a bad way? Regarding Sublime's grand adventure?"

"I can't give you the answer you lust after in your heart of hearts. We're at the mercy of what the top people decide. The Unbeliever have behaved stupidly. They should've conserved their forces. They should've turned back and let Calzir fend for itself."

Principaté Doneto eyed Else uncertainly. "Explain."

"The Lucidians and Dreangereans wasted a big part of their naval power. They wanted to be able to challenge the western fleets. Or that of the Eastern Empire. Worse than them losing their ships, though, is them losing their best soldiers and sailors when we have a Patriarch who wants another Crusade."

"I guess I don't have a military mind. All I see is how those troops will make it tougher for us in Calzir."

"Of course. That's their mission. But we'll destroy them, ships and men. The time and treasure invested in them will have been wasted. They won't be there when the crusaders arrive. Unless Sublime or Hansel make some boneheaded decisions of their own."

There was a stir. Principaté Doneto said, "Excuse me. I have to go. The Patriarch is here."

Sublime did make a surprise appearance. He contributed nothing. He went away twenty minutes later. Else was disappointed. For years he had heard the Patriarch built up as a great horned and hoofed demon. This was a half-bald, squinty, pinch-mouthed pudgeball who looked more like a dull shopkeeper than a powerful, lunatic religious warlord. He did not seem able to understand what was going on here.

Well, he had been a compromise candidate. Which was why the Church could not now afford his overseas ambitions.

Later, Principaté Divino Bruglioni insisted that what the Patriarch showed publicly was a persona meant to disarm those who did not know him.

Else fixed the man's appearance in mind. Perhaps Honario Benedocto, like Rodrigo Cologni, slipped away to appraise the tenders of the Adversary in person, in disguise. The bodyguards would give him away.

He had no idea why the idea seemed obvious to him but no one else. Everything was right there, in the great map. Everything you needed to know to destroy Calzir and those good soldiers sent to defend that barren realm.

Else asked around. Hardly anyone could name the Mafti al-Araj el-Arak, or any prince or warlord of Calzir. The few who had visited it said Calzir was a realm of chaos, mostly small states run by petty warlords. Much like the Chaldarean stretches of Firaldia.

LYING WITH ANNA TRAPPED IN HIS ARMS, SATED, ELSE WHISpered, "You put new charms and fetishes on the doors and windows."

"Something kept trying to get in. The charm maker didn't believe it could happen here. But she took my money."

"Can't happen in Brothe?"

"Exactly."

"They're fools."

"You'd think it doesn't get dark at night."

"Are the charms any good?"

"I picked a woman with good references."

"Who doesn't take her clients' fears seriously."

"I wasn't born yesterday. Sonsa was no den of virtue, darling."

"Good."

"You think it's because of you? Does somebody want to spy on me in order to spy on you?"

He could not assure her otherwise.

"Oh, my! The serpent is still alive." She reached back and squeezed him. "Well, woman's work is never done. But I'll tame the monster yet."

Else had known just one woman before Anna Mozilla. His wife. She submitted. She endured because that was her lot and duty. She did not become involved.

Anna was always involved, absolutely and completely. Frequently more so than he was. She claimed, "I would've made a great whore. If I could do it with men I don't know. Because I'd go twenty times a day if you could keep up."

Else protested, "I'm not as young as I used to be."

"You were never that young, mister. Quit talking. Start doing."

ELSE SUPPOSED THAT FERRIS RENFROW WOULD WATCH THE widow Mozilla, who had led her neighbors to believe that she was an immigrant from Aparion. Which they thought a lie. They thought she hailed from farther north, somewhere in the southern marches of the Grail Empire. It was at Anna's house that Else always shed those who followed him. Or left them afraid that he had.

He went nowhere that night. Nowhere that Anna Mozilla did not take him.

He began his rounds immediately after returning to the Bruglioni citadel. After dealing with several minor annoyances, he snapped, "You have to figure these things out for yourself, Mr. Phone. I won't be here to think for you forever."

Madam Ristoti would not be cowed. "Mr. Hecht. What about my request for more help? I have too many mouths to fill and too few hands to do the filling."

"You're allowed three new people. You know what you need. You hire them. Don't thank me. Thank my Deve accountant. He can talk Paludan into anything. Paludan thinks numbers are magic. You also get a sixty percent increase in your purchasing budget. So serve something besides turnip stew."

Madam Ristoti grinned. "They liked that, did they?"

"Exactly as much as you expected."

"A rare show of sympathy, then."

"Sympathy had nothing to do with it. Uncle Divino told

Paludan that he was going to lose staff if he fed them that slop. The city is getting ready to go to war. There are alternate opportunities for the working classes."

"There you are, sir."

"Polo. I wondered how long it would take."

"Sir?" Polo did not understand that his allegiance to Principaté Bruglioni was obvious.

"It's all right," Else said.

"Uh . . . Paludan wants to see you. He isn't happy. But I don't think it's your fault."

"Guess we'd better see what he wants, then."

The citadel had changed. Cleaning was nearly complete. Cosmetic restoration was well underway. Halls that had been gloomy and barren of human enterprise swarmed with rustic Bruglioni returnees.

Polo led the way to Paludan's personal suite. He whispered, "His mistress might be there. Pretend not to see her."

"He has a mistress?" Else had discounted the rumors because he thought there would have been more talk if they were true.

"Everybody gets a mistress once he reaches a certain station. It's one of the ornaments of status. The higher your status, the finer your mistress. When you get real big, you have two mistresses. The Patriarch has *three!* They've given him four or five children. But the cognoscenti think he prefers boys."

"Aren't priests supposed to be celibate?"

"That's a rule that'll be honored only in the breech until the Carillon of Judgment."

"Really? Where do the women come from?" Why did Rodrigo Cologni not take himself a few mistresses? He would be alive today.

Polo shrugged. "Wherever a man finds them. Principaté Doneto sleeps with Carmella Dometia, the wife of his man Gondolfo. He's been doing that since Carmella was twelve. He arranged her marriage. He fathered both of her children. He makes sure that Gondolfo's life is good, though Gondolfo spends most of it as the Benedocto factor in the Eastern Empire. Where, no doubt, he has a mistress of his own."

Polo added, "And, like soldiers, women also come to Brothe seeking their fortunes."

"So there's no shortage of exploitable workers, soldiers, or sluts."

Polo felt no empathy. "Men sell their muscle. Women sell their sex. If they're beautiful, personable, and can please a man, they'll do well." He rapped on Paludan's door. "Polo, sir. With Captain Hecht." Hearing an invitation that Else did not, Polo opened the door.

If Paludan had a woman with him he had disguised her cleverly. "Captain Hecht. Thanks for coming." Like Else had a choice.

Paludan had begun accumulating people skills, despite himself.

"Sir."

"The sad day has come. The one I wasn't looking forward to but which I can't prevent."

"Sir?"

"Divino says it's time to move you. So you can concentrate on getting ready for the war. I don't want you to go. That'll leave me out of excuses. Uncle Divino will throw your name in my face every time I let something slide."

"All I ever did was what you hired me to do."

"Sure. And it's all turned out for the best."

"I hope so."

Paludan pulled himself together. What he had to say was difficult. "We'll miss you, Captain. I never found your presence comfortable but it was always positive. You injected hope and ambition into the family. That was a precious gift. Go to the Collegium confident that I'll behave like a grown-up with real responsibilities."

Else nodded. "Of course."

"And thank you for not creating a situation that would've cost me my only real friend. You had him in your power."

Well. Paludan could strike the occasional spark of surprise.

"I did what seemed best. I've enjoyed my stay here. The challenges were tough but not insurmountable."

"Your new job will present challenges you're better suited to handle."

"It's the work I was raised and trained to do, sir. Just between us, though, I don't enjoy it. Though I am good at it."

"You'll make your mark. Here. Take this. A mark of my

gratitude for awakening this house." Paludan handed him a doeskin bag. "Myself, in particular."

"Thank you, sir. Though I'm not sure it's deserved."

Paludan shrugged. "Be that as it may. Polo! Come here."

"Sir?"

"Get ready to move. There's a major planning meeting this afternoon. Uncle Divino wants Captain Hecht settled in beforehand."

Else was not surprised that Polo would accompany him. That colorless little man would be within a stone's throw as long as Piper Hecht was involved with Principaté Bruglioni and the Collegium.

ELSE CONSIDERED THE DOESKIN PURSE WHILE POLO FINISHED loading their possessions. He eased off the drawstrings carefully.

"How much did he give you?" Polo asked.

"There's some of those tiny little gold pieces, like fish scales. And a handful of silver. All of it foreign."

Polo grinned. "He didn't change all his stripes, did he?"

Else offered Polo two silver coins and one little gold piece no more substantial than a scale off a carp. Polo made them vanish instantly. He said, "Paludan doesn't know but I've been working on this since yesterday. That's when the Principaté told me we'd be moving."

"Which would be where?"

"The Chiaro Palace. Isn't it amazing?" Polo babbled about the Chiaro Palace: vast, rich, labyrinthine, a city curled up inside the Mother City. A holy city well and truly saturated with everything unholy.

Else dug out the one item the purse must have been intended to convey.

That was a plain gold ring. Or, not so plain, he discovered as he turned it in the available light.

Characters were engraved on the ring. They could be seen only when the light struck it at certain angles. When held just right those characters stood out boldly, in black, as though in calligraphy.

A magic ring?

Certainly. But what kind of magic ring? It came without instructions. Maybe he was not supposed to notice.

Its ultimate source must be Divino Bruglioni. But why so obscure a means of delivery?

Perhaps Principaté Divino was worried that someone inappropriate would notice if the ring changed hands another way. Though Else was pretty sure that he was not supposed to notice the engraving. Maybe nobody who lacked a special wrist amulet would. Or maybe the ring was just another lump of gold and the engraving had to do with plighted troth five hundred years ago.

"What's so fascinating about that ring, sir?"

"I'm not sure. It's relaxing, fiddling with it."

"Oh. Clemency III used one of those big purple freshwater pearls. And my father had a smooth round stone from the Holy Lands. So maybe it makes sense."

"It's well worn. I'm not the first to play with it." He started to drop it into a pocket. And got the distinct impression that it did not want that.

He slid it onto the ring finger of his left hand, which seemed to satisfy it.

THE CHIARO PALACE WAS VAST, A SMALL CITY IN ITSELF. ELSE'S new suite was a dozen times the size of what he had enjoyed in the Bruglioni citadel.

"These rooms are huge, Polo! Nomad tribes could camp in here." It was too big. It made him uncomfortable.

He did like being so close to the wellspring of western power, just a stone's throw from the mad Patriarch.

He was where Gordimer and er-Rashal could have hoped he would be only in their wildest imaginings.

He wandered the apartment in search of obvious wrongness. He found nothing. But he had expected to find nothing. These people would be subtle.

"Polo, see about stocking our larder. I'm going to lie down till I have to go show the Patriarch how to conquer the world."

Polo suggested, "We could have your woman friend come in to cook. She could live in."

"I don't think so."

"There're baths. If you want to use them." Polo leered.

The Chiaro Palace baths were legendary.

"Really?" Else suspected that, like most things ordinary people never saw, the Chiaro baths were much less wicked than imagined. "You'll have to show me later."

"I'm only saying. I don't know my way around. I've only been here once, when Principaté Bruglioni had me come see the apartment."

Else prowled the suite again, paying special attention to the room Polo had designated his work area. He wanted Polo out of the way. "Get busy with the food and supplies situation."

How often would he get to see Anna, now? Success brought its own complications.

ELSE MADE HIMSELF COMFORTABLE IN HIS NEW WORKSPACE. He studied the ring from Paludan's purse. The gift made him nervous. If gift it was. Might Paludan have been unaware of its presence?

Magic rings lurked large in folklore and legend alike. They served no one well.

Rings of power figured in the myths of the pre-Chaldarean cults of the north and of the cold swamps whence Piper Hecht supposedly sprang. Else learned what he could about that far culture whenever he had a chance. Someone asked him about his homeland almost daily, mostly out of curiosity. He dared not be wrong. Someone would notice.

He glared at the gold band. "Are you Grinling, the ring that was forged for the All-Father by the Aelen Kofer?" The Trickster stole that ring and hid it in the belly of the king of the ice bears. The hero Gedanke challenged the king of the ice bears to a battle with the king bear's liver at stake because a soothsayer told Gedanke that only a taste of the liver of the king of the ice bears would save the children of Amberscheldt from a deadly plague. Gedanke found Grinling when he went after the ice bear's liver.

Grinling bore a curse because the All-Father failed to give the Aelen Kofer everything they demanded in payment. The ring always betrayed anyone who wore it. Including Gedanke himself when the All-Father sent the Choosers of the Slain to reclaim Grinling. Arlensul fell in love with Gedanke, bore him a son, and, thus, sealed all their dooms. "If you are Grinling, ring, I don't want you near me."

Grinling's full tale was dark and cruel. It included rape, murder, incest, and a deadly squabble between the Old Gods and the even older gods who came before. Gods so grim they terrified the current Instrumentalities of the Night.

Character by character Else deciphered each word etched into the ring. Careful angle shifts betrayed additional characters etched in almost the same places as others already revealed. Then he discovered more inscriptions on the inside. He recorded everything painstakingly. And sighed with relief after his fabulation of the Grinling myth.

None of the inscriptions were in the northern heathen stick characters.

He did not understand what he transcribed. The writing on the outside could be preclassical Brothen. The interior inscription was in a different language and alphabet, in characters so tiny Else could not imagine them having been etched by hand. Many were too worn to record accurately.

He wished he could escape to the Deve quarter. Gledius Stewpo would know somebody who could tell him what the ring was all about.

THE CHIARO BATHS RESEMBLED SOMETHING FROM THE FANtasies of wicked eastern potentates. Wine and females were plentiful—though the girls were not there for sport, apparently. Else did not see any of that. He did see wrinkled old Principatés being slithered over by litters of hairless, well-oiled youngsters.

A naked youth approached. "I'm Gleu, sir." Gleu had a strong accent. "I'll help with your clothing."

"This is my first visit, Gleu. How does it work?"

"There aren't many rules, sir. You go to the hot baths—or to the cold, if that's your preference—and choose the girls you want to bathe you. Or the boys, if that's your preference. You don't touch. Unless you're invited. If you do you'll be fined. Second time, they'll fine you again and bar you for two weeks. After the third time you'll be banned forever. Your behavior can even bring you under the lash. So says the Holy Father."

"So there was a time when other rules existed."

"Yes, sir."

Service in the baths was a form of social welfare for orphans and abandoned children. Attractive children, of course. They received food and shelter. Their service needed be no more demeaning than they desired. Clearly, though, if their standards were relaxed their tips would be larger.

"Them that save carefully can be well off when they leave." Those who did not earn good tips or take care often graduated to service in the lowest class of brothel. "You will want girls, won't you?"

"Yes."

Gleu took Else to a room where several score girls, from seven to eighteen, of varied race, waited to help the princes of the Church and their associates bathe and relax. Else hesitated.

Gleu whispered, "Would you rather have boys help you?"

"No."

"Then pick two. Which two doesn't matter."

Else indulged. He indicated two older girls, neither a type he recognized. One was a tall, muscular blonde with large, sharply pointed breasts and eyes of ice a thousand years old. The second, also tall, was a flawless mahogany. She had breasts that reminded him of gourds. The blonde's hair was long but braided. The second girl's curly black hair was barely an inch in length. She seemed pleased to have been chosen. Each girl took an arm and led him to the heated main pool. They sat him down and let him do nothing but absorb the warmth. "Don't talk. Close your eyes. Relax."

The girls snuggled up, one to each side.

He let the warmth in, as they said. And as it filled up, his mind emptied of cares.

A girl rested her head on each of his shoulders. He drowsed.

In time, they led him from the main bath to a cleansing pool. They used soaps and scrubs on every inch of him. The cold blonde did not seem particularly interested in winning a large tip.

The dark girl chuckled. She pointed out his physical response. "More impressive than what these sad old men usually show us." Thereafter, she paid it no special notice.

The erection had not yet subsided when the girls decided he was ready to leave the pool.

Almost immediately he found himself face-to-face with an unclad Osa Stile. Osa said, "Oh, my my," and continued shepherding a bony old man toward a cleansing pool.

The dark girl laughed throatily. "You've made a conquest."

Else did not respond. Why was Osa Stile here? How had he become a bath attendant? Did Johannes Blackboots have a Principaté on his payroll?

Of course he did. Several, probably.

The girls took him into a small, fragrant room. They toweled him dry. The blonde told him, "Lie down on the couch. Face down."

She had an accent that was slight but definite. Firaldian was not her native tongue. The dark girl, though, might have been born in Brothe.

Else lay down on the leather couch. The girls began to massage him and rub him with oils.

His worries drifted away once more.

He was almost too loose to roll over when told to do so.

The girls chuckled over the continued proud glory of his manhood.

After more massaging and oiling, the girls slithered onto the couch beside him. Well oiled, their smooth skin moving on his felt better than the massage had. They slowed down gradually and snuggled up.

He dozed off.

PINKUS GHORT WAS WAITING IN ELSE'S QUARTERS WHEN HE returned. "Sorry I'm late."

"It's good to be one of the wheels, eh?"

"What?"

"I've heard about those baths."

"Doubtless exaggerations that turned a lot worse once they had an opportunity to slither around inside your head."

"Sure." Ghort charged that one word with a hundredweight of cynical disbelief. "What did you need?"

"Need?"

"You sent for me, brother. I didn't just drop in."

"Oh. Yes. Sure. I need an adjutant. For the city regiment. You want the job?"

After a stunned silence, Ghort erupted. "Shit, yeah! Aaron's fuzzy balls, Pipe! Why'd you even ask? Hey! Wait a minute. What's the fucking catch?"

"The catch is, you have to leave Principaté Doneto so you can take on more work than you've ever done in your whole damned life."

"Shit. I knew it. Work. Do I get to hang out in the baths?"

"No."

"Worse and worse. Now you're going to ask me to work for free, too, for the experience."

"I'm going to feed you. What more could you want?"

"Give me a minute, Pipe. I'll think of something. Hell. Here's an idea. How about a whole fucking bunch more money than I'm getting from Principaté Doneto? Where, I might point out, I'm not having to do much of anything that even vaguely resembles work? For damned good pay."

"Darn. I figured on keeping your salary for myself."

"So bring me up to date. What're we doing? What do we still have to do?"

"Everything. I'm just getting started. Hacking my way through the politics. The people underwriting the city regiment behave like they're five years old. You're only the second man I've hired myself. They're making me take on dozens of complete idiots without ever consulting me. These Brothens don't understand what you're talking about if you mention merit or competence. A rock can be a general if it knows the right people. So I'm trying to sneak a few men that are predictable and competent under pressure."

"I was second choice, huh? Who did you need more than me?"

"A nineteen-year-old miracle-working Deve accountant who knows how to get the most out of the money I'm given. He also finds thieves who try to rake off some of it for themselves."

"He good?"

"So good he can screw you out of half your pay while you think you're getting rich."

"Uh-oh."

"I have a meeting coming up. I want you there."

"Going to get my feet wet right away?"

"No. I want the Castella crowd and the tenants of this lunatic asylum to get used to you being around."

"Where do I bunk?"

"Right where you're bunking now. It's not that long a walk. Let Principaté Doneto go right on thinking you're loyal to him. And since you might be, we'll let him go on picking up your room and board."

"Eis's hairy ass, you're cheap."

"That's how I plan to build myself an efficient little army."

"By squeezing every ducat?"

"Until the Patriarch on it squeaks."

ELSE REGRETTED BRINGING PINKUS GHORT TEN MINUTES AFter entering the planning room in the Castella. Ghort took one look at the great, inverted map of Calzir and its environs and blurted, "Shit, Pipe! Look at that. We got them assholes by the nuts."

Silence fell. Twenty pairs of eyes concentrated on Pinkus Ghort. One pair belonged to Ferris Renfrow.

The snake had its head out of the egg. Else could see no way to cover up what ought to have been obvious to anyone not trapped inside centuries of traditional strategy, anyway.

"Uhm?" *Did* Ghort see it?

"Did that fleet of King Peter's sail yet? Did the troops from the Connec start marching yet?"

Ghort saw it.

"I don't think so. Why?" He had to ask.

"Yes," Ferris Renfrow said, over Else's left shoulder. "Clue us in, Captain Ghort."

Members of the Collegium and a couple of Hansel's top planners all clumped together, drawn by Ghort's enthusiasm.

"It looks like your plan is just to punch through the mountains and go after the castles and cities. Same as if you were going after any other Firaldian principality. Same as the last four or five times somebody tried."

An imperial staffer pointed out, "Cities and castles are where the wealth and nobility are."

"Sure. But not the food, dear heart. Not the food. Tell him, Pipe."

The son of a dog. "I think I see. Mainland Calzir is heavily dependent on bread. But wheat doesn't grow well there. It does flourish over here, on Shippen. Shippen's fecundity was one reason the ancient Brothens occupied the island."

"Exactly!" Ghort enthused. "Wheat and silver mines."

"Explain more clearly, please," one of the Imperials said.

"Eighty percent of the people live on the mainland. They raise wine grapes, olives, and sheep. Most of the grain is grown on the island. Across the Strait of Rhype. Now, we have a sizable Direcian fleet up here, going to head this way. It can cut off help from the western Pramans. The fleet could pick up the Connecten contingent as it follows the coast. Those troops could land on Shippen. They could stop any grain from getting to the mainland. Which means no bread on the mainland. Where they have lots of extra soldiers, sailors, and animals from Lucidia and Dreanger to feed."

Ghort preened, smug with good reason. "How long can these assholes over here eat grapes and olives and goats? For a while, yeah. But they're used to bread and fish. They don't have no fishing boats left. So eventually they're gonna be eating roots and grass and river mud and, maybe, each other's babies. How long before they don't got strength enough left to fight? Not too long. If we show up down there in time to take their fields away or keep them from putting in any spring crops."

That caused a buzz.

What seemed as obvious as a naked woman in the street at high noon when first Else looked at that map, and which was just as obvious to Pinkus Ghort, was not at all obvious to men heavily vested in a strategy calculated to deliver them personal mastery of some castle or town, following the same strategies that had failed the Chaldarean liberators repeatedly since the Praman Conquest.

Ferris Renfrow asked, "You didn't see this, Captain Hecht?" With slight weight on the patronymic.

"Did you? No? I did sense that something was there. But I'm from a place that's landlocked. We don't think ships. Did anyone here see what Captain Ghort just pointed out?" Softly, Else told Renfrow, "Pinkus wasn't blinded by what he hoped to steal."

"Enjoy it while you can."

The cat was out of the bag. The pig had escaped from its poke. There would be no stuffing them back.

"Excellent thinking, Captain Hecht. Captain Ghort," Bronte Doneto said. "Inspired and inspirational."

Ferris Renfrow eyed Else with abiding suspicion.

There had to be a catch, to Renfrow's way of thinking.

There *was* a catch. Of course.

This time Calzir would not survive. The intervention of Dreanger and Lucidia sealed Calzir's fate. Even Sublime's enemies did not want those vigorous kaifates to establish a bridgehead on the Firaldian peninsula.

Calzir could not be saved. But Else could try to salvage its people. Calzir's Pramans might survive a quick victory, after little fighting.

It had worked that way in the Connec when Volsard overran the Praman towns. That was how it was happening in Direcia right now. Peter of Navaya never persecuted those who did not resist him, whatever their religion. He was a firm ally of Platadura, which, while remaining Praman, supported him in most of his adventures. Which had caused the inflexible Sublime to bark at Peter more than once.

Peter of Navaya was no more impressed by Sublime's displeasure than was the Grail Emperor. The Patriarch needed Peter far more than Peter needed the Patriarch.

Sublime had definite ideas about how Pramans, Devedians, Dainshaus, and other Unbelievers should be used in order to make more room for God's own chosen Episcopal Chaldareans. Sublime's Church was not a Church Evangelical, it was a Church Militant.

King Peter was mostly indifferent to the Patriarch's grand schemes.

The key point, Else thought, was that he might be able to steal the bloody option away from Sublime. But only by being the most steadfast and cunning opponent that the Realm of Peace ever faced.

28. Alameddine, Weary Soultaken

It took ages to slide down the back half of the Firaldian peninsula, into Hoyal, the easternmost cantonment of Alameddine. Shagot could not stay awake. He was dull and uncommunicative. Life grew harsher. Because they moved too slowly to get away from the scene of any major crime, Svavar did not indulge in activities that might attract attention.

The money the brothers carried became a liability. Low-grade, unemployed mercenaries did not carry double-ducat and five-ducat gold pieces. Men of that despicable level ought never to *see* such coins.

Prolonged hunger forced Svavar to betray himself. The venue was a crossroad town named Testoli, famous for nothing in the entire history of the world. Testoli lay a dozen miles north of the Hoyal canton, which was mostly wilderness preserved for hunting by the Grail Emperors and Alameddine's royals.

A dumb response to hunger turned into a stroke of good fortune. The eyes that noted gold in the hands of scum who ought to be strangers to silver belonged to the brigand Rollo Registi, infamous for a league around. Rollo was stupid and unsuccessful in his chosen profession. His band barely managed to survive—by, secretly, herding sheep in the hills over in Hoyal canton. They poached the Emperor's pastures instead of his game.

Rollo hurried off to collect his henchmen. There were just two of them, in bad health, and not the sort who had friends likely to become upset if something happened to them.

This served Svavar and Shagot well when Rollo and friends attacked them. The Grimmssons took enough copper and small silver off the corpses to complete their journey without attracting further attention.

Svavar did not tell Shagot about the warrior woman who backed them up during the encounter. A kraken of fear now held Svavar in its all-smothering embrace. He, who had been raised by truly terrible parents to deny and defy fear, whatever its source or form.

Any respectable Andorayan of Svavar's time faced fear with bludgeon in hand. That was so deeply engrained, and so intimately known, that Svavar understood his unmanning could have no mortal cause.

He might not be the brightest light in the firmament nor the fastest frog in the race but he was intimate with the beliefs of his people. He knew the common myths well. Which left him certain that he knew his guardian angel. But his imagination was not wild enough to discern her motives.

She would be Arlensul, first daughter of the Gray Walker. Chooser of the Slain, banished from the Great Sky Fortress for having dared to love the mortal, Gedanke. Now a sworn enemy of the Walker and her kin. A cruel, traitorous worm slithering amongst the Instrumentalities of the Night, starved for revenge.

Svavar still told Shagot nothing. Possibly he believed Grim too much a tool of those who trod iron-shod upon the back of the northern world. Or, maybe, those who had done so in the once upon a times.

Today the Old Ones were considered gone. Fairy tales. Increasingly ill-recalled myth. Andoray, nominally, was a Chaldarean realm now. It acknowledged a Chaldarean ruler.

Still, there were old folks back in the mountains there who were convinced that the advance of the wall of ice was due entirely to that adoption of the southern God. Those fools. Those fools!

A more disappointing horror for the Grimmssons was that the kings of Freisland had succeeded in annexing Andoray. Erief's efforts had meant nothing in the long run.

Svavar harbored a sour suspicion that history always reduced the works of man to naught, a suspicion that nothing mattered beyond four or five generations.

Grim did not care. Grim was sullen, silent, focused exclusively on his mission when he was awake.

Just guessing, Svavar suspected that Grim's devotion to sleep was necessitated by his connection to the Great Sky Fortress. It was difficult for the Old Ones to maintain contact from far away.

* * *

In time Svavar hooked up with a mercenary band captained by a thug named Ockska Rashaki, a renegade Calziran with illusions that allying himself with Vondera Koterba would let him repay a catalog of personal grievances beyond the Vaillarentiglia Mountains. Rakshaki's band numbered fewer than sixty men, thieves and murderers all. They were the sort who gave all soldiers, and mercenaries in particular, a terrible name.

Svavar felt right at home, except for the language problem. Shagot did, too, when he woke up long enough to see what was going on. Between them the brothers kicked a half-dozen asses and Shagot killed a huge, stupid beast named Renwal who terrorized the rest of the band on Rashaki's behalf.

Rashaki was not pleased by the loss of his enforcer, but he was a realist. He invested no emotion in his followers.

Ockska Rashaki loved no one but Ockska Rashaki. Ockska Rashaki was interested only in what Ockska Rashaki hoped to accomplish.

Svavar and Shagot settled down to await the arrival of the man they were supposed to kill. He would come, Shagot insisted. And Shagot would know when he did.

It was not to be an onerous wait. Ockska Rashaki did not demand much of his followers. And Vondera Koterba did not demand much of Rashaki's band. They had a smugglers' pass to watch. Koterba made sure they were fed so that they did not start raiding the Alameddine countryside.

Shagot was content to eat, sleep most of the time, and take the occasional shit. He, like his masters, was content to wait.

Svavar endured. He had suffered the world long enough to know that every misery eventually ends.

These days, almost every day, Svavar saw Arlensul, unnoticed by anyone else, lurking around this camp of men with dead souls. He and she were joined in an unspoken conspiracy.

29. Connectens at Sea and Ashore

It was a cloudless day near summer's end. Gulls swooped and cursed. Harbor water stank. Brother Candle watched Connecten fighters board a dozen big Plataduran ships, the most that could be accommodated at Sheavenalle's docks. Navayan and Plataduran vessels stood out in the harbor, among coasters and fishermen evicted so the expeditionary fleet could load. Some of those had arrived already engorged with Navayan engineers, sappers, artillerists, and siege specialists.

Brother Candle wondered if King Peter considered this a rehearsal for Sublime's beloved Crusade to the Holy Lands.

Maybe. There was *something* going on. Peter had been doing well in Direcia, often allying himself with a lesser Praman prince to overcome a strong one. Why suddenly shift attention and key resources to fighting overseas? Peter was honorable, and dedicated to his God, but there had to be more to this than honor and love of his Queen's brother.

The Connectens boarded reluctantly. The Unbeliever sailors wore strange garb. They gabbled in a dialect that was a cousin of Connecten but so weird it went over the heads of soldiers taking ship only to avoid having to walk six hundred miles.

No one knew yet where they would debark. Sublime and Johannes Blackboots had not finalized their plans. Or, if they had, word had not been relayed to the troops.

Count Raymone paused beside Brother Candle. "Time to work up your nerve and go aboard, Master. They're already singling up the lines."

Brother Candle sighed. His few possessions were aboard. He was not eager to follow. His reluctance was shared by his companions, each a respected cleric volunteer. Every religion in the Connec was represented in the expeditionary force, including Connecten Praman slingers from Terliaga. Their presence baffled Brother Candle more than did that of several dozen supposedly pacifist Seekers After Light.

The Plataduran Pramans made everyone uneasy. The Chaldareans could not understand why they were allied with Peter against their religious brethren. Though Chaldarean fought Chaldarean every day, across the Chaldarean world.

Brother Candle's companions were the men who had gone to Brothe.

Count Raymone had accomplished marvels in carrying out his orders from the Duke. Although he was in Castreresone when told that he would move his force by sea, he reached Sheavenalle before the Direcian fleet arrived.

THE JOURNEY WAS BROTHER CANDLE'S FIRST ABOARD ANY-thing bigger than a ferryboat and his first on salt water. It was also his first aboard a platform that rolled and bucked and plunged on even the clearest, calmest day. A platform that never stopped creaking and groaning, muttering and moaning, not for a second, nor did it ever fail to make the horizon stand up at strange and terrible angles. The smell was unlike anything he had experienced before, combining barracks, stable, tar and caulk, sea, and frightful cooking, in a mix that ought to revolt the scavenger gulls following the fleet.

The sailors told him he was being too sensitive. *Taro* was a new ship. She had not yet begun to develop real character.

The cooking generated the worst odors.

The ship's cook served no one but the Plataduran crew. Everyone else cooked on the main deck, amidst the mob, the working sailors, and the daring robber gulls. There was no hot food when the seas roughened up. The Platadurans did not trust Connecten landlubbers not to set the ship on fire.

Sailors feared nothing so much as fire at sea.

The journey was more than just physically uncomfortable. Brother Candle was conscious constantly of the proximity and curiosity of lesser elements of the Instrumentalities of the Night. That was unnerving. Life in antiquity must have been equally uncomfortable. Man had come a long way with the slow task of taming the world.

His touch did not yet lie heavy on the sea.

Off the coastal island of Armun, the one-time summer resort of Brothen emperors, Brother Candle gathered the religious spokesmen for the Plataduran crew and the Terliagan slingers. He was distracted. Armun was far south of Brothe, not far north of Shippen. Meaning they were off the coast of Alameddine, approaching that kingdom's frontier with Calzir. And the fleet showed no sign of turning inshore.

The amateur Praman priests remained wary but Brother Candle had worn them down some by insisting that he just wanted to learn.

"I'm wondering where al-Prama stands on the Instrumentalities of the Night. They never cooperate with dogma. They revel in contradicting doctrine."

These Praman chaplains were not inclined toward philosophical discussion. They were practical men interested only in supplying minimal spiritual support to men working far from home. They could perform the basic sacraments of their faith. And that was their limit.

Brother Candle held an abiding interest in the old eternal questions. Did the minds of men create the gods and the lesser things of the night by shaping the power from the Wells of Ihrian and elsewhere? Or did the Instrumentalities of the Night feed upon that power to establish belief in the minds of those who beheld them?

The chicken or the egg riddle, some called it.

The debate often devolved into speculation about what the world would be like if there were no Wells gushing raw magical power.

For Brother Candle that was a question easily answered.

The Wells of Ihrian were not the only wellsprings of power, just the biggest and most concentrated. There were numerous smaller, remote wells where the power leaked into the world, though the flow there was more often a seep than a gush.

The calculations of generations of sorcerers found that 70 percent of the supernatural power entering the world did so within the Holy Lands. It was a big, strange world deeply scarred by the power, habitable because the power kept the ice at bay.

The world grew darker, colder, and stranger as you moved away from the magical leaks, into the bizarre realms of legend.

There were further, more troublesome questions. If human imagination created the gods and the vectors of the night, then who created Man?

Brother Candle could not conceive of a world without sentient beings to appreciate the Instrumentalities of the Night.

The Praman priests were laypeople. They saw sophistry as the work of the Adversary. They had learned the truth when they were young. No preacher who was a heretic within his own false faith would seduce them with Hell-born free thinking.

Brother Candle discovered that these Pramans believed pretty much what most Chaldareans believed. The significant point of conflict was who got to claim responsibility for the glorious revelation. The Holy Founders from Chaldar in the Holy Lands? Or the later Founding Family, from Jezdad in Peqaa?

One Praman observed, "The real contention is idol worship."

"Idol worship?" Brother Candle asked. "I'm a long way separated from my Episcopal childhood but I don't remember any idols."

"Chaldarean churches are filled with them."

"Those aren't idols. They're statues. Images of the Founders and the saints, not the Founders and the saints themselves."

"They're graven images. Isn't that an idol? By definition? Not the god himself but an image of the god that's there to remind everyone that the god is watching?"

"Not being an Episcopal anymore, I can't argue effectively. Maybe Bishop LeCroes can explain the difference."

Brother Candle had lived long enough to be skeptical of dogma. Dogma reflected the human need to believe there was something bigger and more meaningful than the mayfly individual. That there was a cosmic plan.

Horns called across the water.

The Platadurans signaled between ships using a variety of horns where other navies used signal flags or drums. The Navayan navy had adopted the same system.

The admiral of the fleet was Plataduran. The commander of combined armies was King Peter, who had invited himself along because he did not trust Firaldians. Especially not Firaldians from Brothe. And, least of all, any Firaldian who was the latest in a line of false Patriarchs. Despite his support for the Church as an institution.

Peter's great talent was flexibility. He adopted methods and tools that worked. That included a Patriarch who was not legal but who did control the power of the Church.

The Platadurans and Navayans believed Peter would conquer all Direcia in his lifetime. Many of the peoples of Direcia looked forward to his success.

"What's happening?" Brother Candle asked as sailors flew around, taking in sails. *Taro* was a broad-beamed, long bireme, like most of the Plataduran fleet. She could fight if necessary but was intended for commerce. She did not normally put out oars while on the deep water, unless becalmed. Sails were *Taro*'s preferred means of making headway.

A Plataduran told Brother Candle, "The captains have been called to a meeting aboard *Isabeth*."

The great lady of the war fleet was named for Peter's queen. The armada reduced speed and closed in. The ships dropped anchor and launched boats that carried the captains and leading soldiers to the flagship.

THE SHIPPEN COAST WAS LIKE NOTHING BROTHER CANDLE had seen before. Smaller vessels ran inshore to either hand of a fishing village named Tarenti, which possessed a small but deep harbor. Veteran Navayans isolated the town. Transports headed in to unload.

The same happened at other minor ports. Brother Candle was only marginally in the know. The plan seemed to be to deny Shippen's resources to mainland Calzir. Which should not stand up long if Shippen's produce was not available.

King Peter and Count Raymone meant to subdue an island more vast than half the kingdoms in the Chaldarean world. With Connecten and Navayan forces combined numbering fewer than four thousand men. The Platadurans would not fight ashore.

Brother Candle's military experience consisted of having been present at the Black Mountain Massacre. He did not understand that Shippen need not be conquered in its entirety in order to keep its resources from reaching the mainland.

Local resistance ended quickly.

Historically, Shippen never sustained a fight once an invader gained a solid foothold. The working population did not care who was in charge. The arrogations of the ruling classes had no abiding impact on everyday life. As long as the mines produced copper and silver and the fields and orchards yielded surpluses of grain and fruit. The weather was usually favorable and there had been no natural disaster since a series of volcanic eruptions in pre-Brothen antiquity.

The great disasters in Shippen's past were the handiwork of Man, sometimes a war but more often a demonstration of excess by some sorcerer self-deluded into thinking that he could master the Instrumentalities of the Night.

Only the most brilliant minds could convince themselves that they were capable of exempting themselves from the Tyranny of the Night.

BROTHER CANDLE AND *TARO*'S CONNECTENS NEXT WENT ashore at Caltium Cidanta. The town stank of decaying fish entrails. Clouds of shrieking gulls swirled overhead. Caltium Cidanta had no modern significance. In antiquity it was important, though. It was from Caltium Cidanta that the Colpheroen general Eru Itutmu left the Brothen Empire to go defend his homeland, Dreanger—after he and thousands who believed him to be a god spent a generation plaguing the adolescent empire. Eru Itutmu killed a quarter million Brothens but suffered defeat, both in Brothe and at home. Those early Brothens were stubborn. They fought Eru Ututmu for decades, and conquered every ally Dreanger found anywhere around the Mother Sea.

Far memories of Eru Itutmu were all Caltium Cidanta had to recommend it.

Bishop LeCroes grumbled, "This place is like every other damned town on the island. There aren't any boats. There aren't any men younger than sixty or boys older than twelve. And the women come in three types: homely, homelier, and homeliest."

Brother Candle chuckled. "I'm just a simpleminded heretic, Bries, but I picked up the notion somewhere that we're supposed to treat the local females the way we'd want our stout Connecten wives treated. Not to mention that celibacy is part of your job."

"You're a major pain in the fundament, Candle. A total fun-killer."

"I do what I can."

The real point was, there were no women of breeding age, however liberal your outlook.

LeCroes grumbled, "Anything female that might tempt a sinner, including ewes and nannies and sows, is hiding in the mountains."

Occupation of Caltium Cidanta and its environs was anticlimactic. The sole casualty was a Terliagan slinger who broke a finger while showing off to some local boys. Those villagers still in place betrayed no overt resentment. They did demonstrate a healthy wariness.

Brother Candle sensed a high level of resignation.

"It's part of the culture," the Plataduran chaplain assured him. He had come ashore because he was familiar with the Shippen dialect. "Shippen has been invaded a lot. The people know they'll get through it."

"Yet they'll go out pirating." The fact that they would had nothing to do with how they responded to occupation. The piratical inclination existed because of the island's history.

Most invasions had begun with pirate types who came to plunder and found little worth carrying away. But they did find Shippen to be a good place to hide from their enemies.

The Plataduran chaplain indicated a hazy indigo line of teeth. "If the boys get an urge to misbehave they'll have to jog all the way over there. They'll lose the mood by the time they get there."

THE OCCUPATION OF SHIPPEN PROCEEDED WITHOUT FANFARE or much conflict. Nobles of standing had gone over to the mainland to resist the Unbeliever's attack there. They added to and shared in the privation and misery enjoyed by those who served in the armies of God.

On Shippen, natives and occupiers lived comfortably and harmoniously. The Connectens helped bring in the harvest. The women returned from the hills, a few at a time, bringing their livestock. The Connectens were not impressed. The joke went that Calziran women explained why Calziran men had picked a fight with Chaldarean Firaldia.

Brother Candle pitched in. And talked about his own beliefs. Local Pramans found him amusing. Native Chaldareans, a third of the population, thought the Maysalean Heresy might be on to something.

Brothe, the Episcopal Church, and the Patriarchy were not beloved of Shippen's Chaldareans.

Brother Candle wished Bishop LeCroes considerable distress. The Bishop was out of his element, a chaplain without a flock. The Connectens off *Taro* were all Maysaleans, Terliagans, and Episcopal Chaldareans who favored Sublime V over Immaculate II.

"I'm not trying to cause you misery, Bries."

"I know. I dug my own grave when I decided I'd rather sail with a friend. If I had any sense I'd lay down in it and stop whining."

"Buy a donkey and catch up with Count Raymone." It was evening in Caltium Cidanta. Brother Candle was sampling the local vintage, which was surprisingly good. His expedition was turning out to be a vacation from life.

On Shippen the fact that there was a war on, that men were dying as great religions strove to resolve their relative merits in trial by combat, no longer seemed due much interest.

There was a dearth of determined true believers on both sides, on that island. No one demonstrated any special interest in making sure his God would be the sole survivor of the contest.

BROTHER CANDLE ENJOYED HIS TIME ON SHIPPEN THOR- oughly, loafing and debating nonsense with anyone who felt like bothering. Elsewhere, though, if overly dramatic dispatches could be credited, cataclysms were being brewed.

No one on Brother Candle's side of the Strait of Rhype much cared to find out what those might be.

30. Alameddine and Calzir

All things move slower and take longer. In most cases they also cost more. The Grail Emperor hoped to push through the Vaillarentiglia Mountains in time to distress the Calziran harvest. Only a few of Vondera Koterba's companies made it. A handful of Imperial scouts went with them. They were feeble but had little difficulty fending off the few ragged, undisciplined Calzirans they encountered. They encountered none of the dreaded Praman sorceries they had heard about since childhood.

Calzir's political landscape was as chaotic as elsewhere in Firaldia. Several minor warlords offered to change sides if they could retain their holdings. That availed them nothing. Sublime did not want Unbeliever allies.

The Lucidians and Dreangereans dealt harshly with Calzirans they suspected of unstable loyalties.

Forces like Else's Brothen City Regiment, swollen to more than four thousand men, with attendant animals and hangers-on, were much delayed. Practicalities and political infighting hamstrung progress.

Else and his staff performed miracles of organization and training. Their efforts received universal kudos. Even Ferris Renfrow offered the occasional grudging nod during brief respites from spying on Calzir.

No matter how well prepared the City Regiment became, it never marched. The orders to do so never came because of squabbling on high.

Similar petty behavior hampered volunteer formations throughout the Patriarchal States.

The Five Families all wanted more than a fair share of what might be gained in Calzir. On a lesser scale, the Patriarch, the Collegium, the Brotherhood of War, and every city raising forces, were equally driven by greed. There was so much confidence in a Chaldarean victory that none of the players concerned themselves about the cost of impeding progress.

"MY PATIENCE IS EXHAUSTED," ELSE SAID. "WE HAVE TO GET away from these insane, overgrown children."

"And here we go," Pinkus Ghort told him. The occasion was a small, private staff meeting more than a month past the target date Hansel had set for first operations. "We send the ready companies south now. One a day. Titus has the transit stuff set. It's going to fall apart if we don't use it."

"Interesting." Moving single companies was something Else

could do without getting approval from a dozen interfering Brothes. "How long before the bigwigs start squawking?"

"That'll depend on who's paying attention. Renfrow ought to catch on first. But he spends most of his time in Calzir. Spying. The Deves down there have been producing some great intelligence. But they're getting nervous. We're taking too damned long. The Lucidians and Dreangereans have gotten real active, lately. The Deves are scared they'll figure out what's going on and deal harshly with the infidel community."

Else asked, "Titus, what do you think about that?"

"He's right. Calzir's Devedians are scared. Devedians everywhere are scared. It's part of being a Deve."

"I'm in no position to reassure anyone."

"You don't concern them much, sir."

The Devedian community had given him no cause for disappointment. Though their efficiency at pulling things together stirred old, deep suspicions. Was there any truth in those old tales of secret Devedian brotherhoods out to control the world surreptitiously?

Gledius Stewpo always mocked that notion. He could spark off scores of plausible arguments against it, but there were times when one had to wonder. As, say, when one found Deves armed with firepowder weapons capable of bringing down the most powerful sorcerer.

"Don't be silly," Stewpo told Else. "If we had a quarter of the power those stories claim we'd never suffer the kind of crap that happened in Sonsa."

"Uhm?" Else grunted.

"Whenever you bump noses with the notion that Deves are the secret masters, ask yourself why all the Deves you know live the way they do when everybody else lives the way they do."

Else confessed, "I don't care about the religious business. I don't care who believes what as long as the job gets done."

Stewpo grinned. He lacked a front tooth, on top. A bit more hair, Else thought, and the dwarf would bear a striking resemblance to a creature out of a tale where runt folk spun straw into gold.

Stewpo's whole race hailed from a land where fairy tales reigned, though.

"No secret overlords," Stewpo promised. "If every Deve-

THE TYRANNY OF THE NIGHT

dian agreed that that was the best idea since the Creator declared us His Chosen People, it would fall apart as soon as you pulled four Devedians together to make it happen. You think pettiness, vanity, and envy are exclusive to your world? Try being part of the Devedian underclass. Where every carat of status is jealously nurtured—and becomes a target for anybody who thinks he can profit if you lose."

Else nodded. He could pretend to believe anything. "Titus. The companies have to move south. Now. Advise your correspondents. Gledius. I know you don't speak for Brothe's Deves. But you're the big bull Deve who's here right now. Is there going to be a Devedian company or not?" For weeks the Deves had muttered about adding a company of their own to the city regiment. But their leaders never seemed quite sure what they wanted. Nor was Else sure that the Patriarch and his henchmen would permit it. Though it was common knowledge that King Peter's combined Navayan and Connecten force including not only Chaldarean heretics but Devedians and Pramans, with the latter more numerous than right-thinking pro-Brothen Episcopals.

"There will be a small force of specialists. Men with the technical skills to help you solve your special problems."

Else supposed that meant clerks and accountants whose most important function would be to serve as the conscience of the regiment.

THE SUMMONS WAS SO LONG COMING THAT ELSE HOPED HE WAS being overlooked. A dozen companies had gone south, headed for an encampment near the border town Pateni Persus. One of those companies was Bruglioni. Two hundred strong, it included a dozen actual members of the family. The Arniena force, commanded by Rogoz Sayag, was as large. The well-armed Devedian contingent, gone early to blaze the way, numbered more than three hundred. Quite a lot of specialists.

Eight Principatés sat behind a long table. Else recognized them all. One represented each of the Five Families. Principaté Doneto undoubtedly stood in for his cousin. A senile octogenarian did nothing but make strange noises and drool while a thirtyish bishop read his mind and spoke for him. Finally, there was Principaté Barendt from Smoogen in the New Brothen Empire. Hansel's man.

The Madisetti Principaté was blunt. "What do you think you're doing, General Hecht?"

Else stifled impulse. After all, he had just been promoted. In one man's mind. "Could you be specific, Your Grace? I was hired to train and command a regiment that the City would place at the Holy Father's disposal. I've done that. The Holy Father has often said that he wants Calzir's punishment begun. First, it was before the harvest. Now it's before winter. But we're still here, far from Alameddine and the Vaillarentiglia Mountains, while the Five Families squabble over loot that's still in Calziran hands."

To Else's astonishment Grade Drocker made a surprise appearance while he spoke. Drocker interjected, "Presenting this sort with the accomplished fact is the only way things get done, Hecht. Listen up, Your Graces. I have a message." Drocker sounded far stronger than he had in more than a year.

Else considered the Brotherhood sorcerer warily. He had not known that Drocker was in town. The Brotherhood kept its secrets well.

Drocker continued, "I came back to find out why the delays continue. It isn't a journey I fancied. I have little stamina anymore. It's past time to begin, gentlemen. The Connecten and Direcian forces have established themselves on Shippen. Hunger flirts with mainland Calzir already. The strategy originally approved by the Holy Father is working perfectly. He has expressed frustration, though, because the next step continues to be delayed. The key group of soldiers remain tied up here."

Drocker glowered. He dared. The Collegium dreaded him. Everyone feared the Brotherhood of War. Most especially, they feared the displeasure of the Special Office. Not even the Patriarch himself could compel the Brotherhood of War.

"Colonel Hecht, I commend your initiative." There went the promotion. And here came several new enemies. "His Holiness has bid me take control of the City Regiment, heeding advice from none but its appointed commander." Drocker's battered features dared defiance as he surveyed the Principatés.

The Special Office would turn on the Collegium someday.

The extinction of sorcery was the fountainhead mission of the Special Office.

Drocker said, "The Patriarch has decided that all forces raised for the Calziran Crusade will move to Alameddine now. He told me to deal with obstructionism however I see fit."

Someone tried to raise the point that the city regiment was not a Patriarchal force. Contradicting its specific charter.

Grade Drocker said nothing. His ruined face, intense and cold, was sufficient to close debate. That was real power. More power than Else would have guessed that Drocker possessed.

ELSE REACHED THE PATENI PERSUS ENCAMPMENT ON A DAY reported to be unnaturally cold for Alameddine. Snowflakes flashed amongst the drops of misty rain. Snow and ice had begun to accumulate on the peaks of the Vaillarentiglia Mountains for the first time in centuries. Else did not care. He was miserable enough right where he was. He had ridden all day under conditions that had worsened by the minute.

Perhaps what they said about winter in Calzir was no exaggeration.

Else was not eager for a campaign in this, which could only get uglier. But Hansel, Sublime, and Drocker all were eager to follow up on King Peter's successes on Shippen. The weather did not trouble them.

The last few hundred of the city regiment accompanied Else. If Pinkus Ghort had done his job, those in camp already would be ready to move on south.

"They finally ran your ass out of Brothe, eh?" Ghort asked when Else arrived, though he saved the familiarity till they were in private. He had set up the regimental headquarters inside a deserted church.

"Drocker came to town. He made them turn me loose. They're mad as hornets, too. But they're mad at Drocker."

"And that won't do them no fucking good, right?"

"Not even a little. What kind of shape are we in?"

"You won't be unhappy with the troops. Some of the officers, though . . . My heart wouldn't break if some kind of plague came along that only kills incompetents."

"Take it up with God. Because you won't get help from any earthly power. I tried three times, with three different gangs of power brokers. I might as well have been speaking Lindrehr from back home. They don't comprehend merit or competence. . . . Come on. I'm serious. What shape are we in? We're going to move real soon, now."

"They told you any more about what they want us to do?"

"Everything. I mean, we have to do everything. Like overrun everything west of al-Khazen. While keeping the folks in al-Khazen fixed until the rest of the country has been mopped up. Do we have a movement plan?"

"Thanks to the Deves. They're bringing in some great info. You got something on them?"

"I promised them we'd treat them right. And their Calziran cousins, too. That shouldn't be hard. Should it?"

Ghort shifted uneasily. "I don't know."

Ghort's orderly poked his head into the room. "Captain, there're some Deves out here who say they have to see you and the colonel right now."

Ghort grumbled, "Presumptuous assholes. Tell them . . ."

Else said, "Hang on. I was going to send for them, anyway."

"Bring them in, Colón."

Else asked, "How are Bo and Just Plain Joe getting on?"

"Believe it or not, they both turned competent on us. Bo makes a good noncom. Bo knows all the scams and angles and heads them off before they start to smell. And Joe is a wizard with animals. He isn't the guy in charge but he's the one who makes things work. The critters stay healthy and fed."

"Good. I've always thought that everybody has at least one special talent. An officer needs to figure out what, nurture it, and . . . Hello."

There were five Deves. Else knew Gledius Stewpo, Shire Spereo, and Titus Consent. The others wore odd clothing and were damp, dirty, and darker than the Brothen Deves. Titus Consent said, "Our apologies for disturbing you before you've gotten settled, Colonel, but there's important news from al-Khazen."

So the dusky Deves would be Calziran. "How bad is it, Titus?"

"Not bad at all. Since we're now forewarned."

"Well?"

"The sorcerers who ran the pirate campaign have established themselves in al-Khazen. They believe they've done so without being noticed. They're planning a major ambush. They want to lure the Brotherhood into a trap where they can get Grade Drocker. Along with lots of his soldiers."

Else was impressed. Someone must have been present during a planning session.

"Speak not the Name of the Demon," Ghort muttered, retailing an adage known in all lands touched by the Instrumentalities of the Night. Meaning in all the lands of the unfrozen earth.

Ghort muttered with cause.

A voice said, "I hear my name." Drocker oozed into the room, on crutches. No expression shown on the ruin of his face.

Else said, "I've just learned that Starkden and Masant al-Seyhan have moved into al-Khazen. They hope to lure us into a trap." He told Consent, "Go ahead."

"There's more to it than that."

"Of course. Go ahead." He hoped Consent did not think he could play games with Drocker.

"Starkden and Masant al-Seyhan won't be the only Masters of Ghosts involved. There's another. Our people can't get close, though. We know he exists only by implication. Because there are places no one is allowed to enter."

One of the Calziran Deves said something. Else could not penetrate the dialect. Consent interpreted. "The wizard that nobody sees is . . ." Pause. ". . . one of the foreigners from overseas." Pause. "He came disguised as a foreign soldier." Pause. "Mostly Lucidians came to al-Khazen. But also a few engineers and soldiers came from Dreanger."

Drocker demanded, "Do I know you, dwarf?"

Gledius Stewpo had been easing his way into deeper shadow. "I don't think so, sir." Stewpo laid on an accent Else had not heard before. There was nothing of Sonsa in his voice.

"Perhaps. Yet . . . it seems I ought to. Never mind. This is interesting. I'm curious. Why did they think they could keep that a secret?" Drocker eyed the Calziran Deves intently, barely controlling his abiding distrust.

Consent posed a question in dialect. The spies responded. He translated, "The foreign Pramans don't believe any Calziran would betray them to the Patriarch. They made examples of several warlords who offered to acknowledge the Emperor."

That got right up Sublime's nose. Nobody, anywhere, offered allegiance to the Patriarchy. Which was the case in Direcia and parts of the Connec where Pramans accommodated themselves to Chaldarean rulers.

Consent continued to translate. "There is also a sorcery on al-Khazen that conceals most of the foreign Pramans."

Else suspected that there was something missing from that explanation.

Consent added, "But you can't conceal forever that which lashes out unpredictably. Nor that which has to eat, especially in these times."

Drocker asked, "What are these men doing here if this sorcerer is so powerful?"

Else got a glimmer of what was bothering Drocker. This could turn deadly in seconds.

Consent understood. "These two can come and go because they're agents of the Mafti of al-Khazen. The Mafti believes they're gathering information from Devedian communities in Chaldarean Firaldia." Beads of sweat stood out on the young man's brow.

"Ah," Drocker said. "I see."

Drocker controlled his hatred, perhaps because Consent was so direct.

"I see," the sorcerer said again. "And how will you convince me that they're betraying their Mafti to us instead of betraying us to the Mafti?" Everyone understood that lives were at stake.

Titus Consent was little more than a boy but he found the right answer. "It's a matter of racial interest, sir. A blind man—pardon . . ."

"Go ahead. I know about my eye."

"In harsh times Devedians have to make themselves particularly valuable. It's obvious how this war will end. A Chaldarean triumph is coming. We will work to make that happen more quickly and easily in order to lessen the cost to our people."

Drocker nodded. "Good answer." He started to say something else. A coughing spell took hold.

Drocker could not end it. "Hecht!" he managed to gasp, the remnants of his face ferociously red. "Deal with these people.

Look sharp. Don't let them skin you. They'll be singing the same song in the courts of Calzir. And be ready to march." He hacked all the while, and continued to cough after he left.

Gledius Stewpo emerged from the shadows. He was pale. He gasped for breath. He wanted to say something but Ghort was still there, not yet finished trying to be too small for a Special Office sorcerer to notice. Stewpo asked, "Did anyone see any blood? He didn't spit in here, did he?"

"No," Else replied. "Why?"

"There's an ugly new disease that starts with coughing up blood. It came west along the Silk Road."

"Sounded like pneumonia to me," Ghort said.

"You were awful quiet," Else observed.

"I didn't have anything to say."

"That would be a first. You. Dwarf. Drocker got me wondering. Why *should* I believe that you won't lead me into a trap?"

Titus Consent stepped in. "You heard. There's only one possible outcome for this war. The Emperor and Patriarch will win. Our plan has always been to save our people as much pain as we can. That means establishing ourselves as reliable members of the winning team." He made sounds that electrified the Calziran Deves.

They produced maps. Not just one or two but maps by the score. Large-scale maps, small-scale maps, maps reeking intimate detail. Maps that told Else almost everything he wanted to know about the terrain the city regiment had to cross and what it would find as it approached al-Khazen.

"You happy, Pipe?" Ghort asked, surfacing a couple hours later.

"I'm ecstatic. It's my wedding night. Dwarf, this is pure gold. Sorry the paranoia got hold of me, there. Pinkus, we need to get the whole staff onto these. Titus. I understand you have a marching plan for the road south."

"There's a logistical skeleton in place, Colonel. Our circumstances make it hard to do detailed planning."

"That's fine. A skeleton is all we need."

Ghort said, "A skeleton is more than we usually have. Pipe, this kid is fucking awesome. Just fucking awesome."

"You're embarrassing him. And tomorrow he'll ask for more money."

Stewpo interjected, "You plan to stay up all night fiddling with this? Those of us who aren't well known need to get out of sight. Especially these two. There's no reason to believe there aren't other Calziran spies around."

"Pinkus, make these guys disappear. And think up a way to explain them if anybody asks."

"I'll keep track of who asks, too."

"Good thinking. I'll be here making love to these maps." What he wanted desperately, though, was to see if Polo had a bed ready.

Titus Consent stayed when Ghort spirited the other Deves away. "I'm staff. Nobody will wonder about me."

"You're awfully confident and competent for someone so young."

"I'm a special case. They've trained me and brought me along since I was five."

"To be some kind of messiah?"

"Nothing so pretentious. Just somebody who can take charge if Devedian fortunes flop into a cesspool. Which they do with distressing frequency."

"I should make suspicious noises. But I'm too tired." Else wanted no one guessing how abidingly suspicious he was already.

Consent observed, "I'm sure Stewpo explained the fallacy underlying that concept."

"He did?"

"He didn't tell you that Devedians are so ambitious, jealous, petty, and backbiting that the only Deve conspiracy with any hope of success can't involve more than two people?"

"That would mean that three of the five of you who were just in here will put the screws to the rest."

"It's more a parable sort of thing."

"It doesn't matter. I do believe your tribe will help me."

"You have doubts."

"Not doubts, exactly. I know what you're doing. And why. I can't condemn you for it. But now I wonder where you fit with the Emperor added to the mix. He's never shown much animosity toward your people. And he's a devoted enemy of Sublime. Who hasn't lost his hope of seeing your race exterminated."

"That level of policy is beyond a pup like me. My job is to do what I can to make sure the regiment operates successfully."

Pinkus Ghort returned. "All taken care of, Pipe. What do you think? Scheme? Or surrender to the soldier's favorite whore and get some sleep?"

"The whore can wait. I won't pass out for another hour. Why don't we separate the possible from the impossible and eliminate the wishful thinking of the fools who believe in their God-given right to tell us what to do. Maybe we can amaze the world."

"You need to calm your ass down. Titus. Tell him. Three sorcerers at al-Khazen, Pipe. One of them a bigger bugfucker than the assholes who kicked the snot out of you in Brothe."

"Captain Ghort puts it crudely, but he's right. Three sorcerers. Worth consideration, Colonel."

"You're right. We have to take them into account. They'll be waiting for us. Unfortunately, I don't have much experience with that sort of thing. Do you, Pinkus?"

"Zip. I make a point of avoiding that kind of shit. Which ain't so hard 'cause it seems like it's mainly a Praman kind of problem."

Else noted a subtle shift in Consent's stance. Titus knew about Sonsa, then. What else had Stewpo passed along? Too many people knew too much about Else Tage. "The Special Office is a Praman problem?"

Ghort snorted, "Oh, hell yes! I bet you can't find a bigger carbuncle on Hellalawhosis's ass."

"Maybe. But that isn't really the point. We need to figure out what to do about the ones at al-Khazen."

"Not really."

"What?"

"I just realized, we don't need to worry about shit, Pipe. On account of, Grade Drocker is gonna tell us what to do."

Titus Consent said, "A solid point, Colonel. We won't be in charge."

"Wrong. I'll . . ."

Ghort said, "Pipe, stop for a while. Get your ass to sleep. Let's worry about shit after they tell us how much of it they want us to eat."

* * *

THE CITY REGIMENT ENTERED CALZIR ON A DAY CONSIDERED holy by all four religions claiming the Holy Lands as home. A coincidence. The calendars coincided only once each fifty-six years.

Hard little knots of ice whipped around, stinging cheeks. It was winter. Winter in a land with an old reputation for winter cruelty. The land presented a cold and barren face. Otherwise, Calzir's defenses were fantasies. They were the imaginings of adolescents. Despite examples brutally made earlier, every lesser noble or warlord encountered proved willing to swear allegiance to almost any name put before them. Many expressed a willingness to convert if they could retain their livings.

Ghort observed, "They'll change back if things turn to shit down south."

There was little south left. The coast lay just eighty miles beyond Pateni Persus.

Else nodded. "You notice that there aren't many people around?"

"Yep. And I don't think they're all hiding in the hills. They ran off to al-Khazen. They think the sorcerers can protect them."

"Maybe they will."

Else dealt with local chieftains by accepting oaths, taking hostages, and extracting supplies. He took his time. Grade Drocker did not hurry him. Drocker wanted more information about the enemy, too.

Else also hoped to find out what other columns were doing. The Emperor was supposed to get very busy throughout eastern Calzir.

Else asked, "That black crow still with us?" He meant Drocker. A Brotherhood force of four hundred was on the same road, behind the city regiment, but the commander of all Patriarchal crusaders insisted on traveling with the Brothen force.

"I keep hoping. But every time I drop back to check the rear, there he is. With his little flock. You got to give the fucker credit for determination."

Else did. He was glad that there were not many crusaders like the Special Office sorcerer.

"You think he's prescient?"

"He's who? Keep the words small enough for a country boy to handle, Pipe."

"Can he read the future?"

"Like an astrologer, or something?"

"Exactly like that."

"I don't know. Why?"

"I was wondering if that might not be why he's sticking close. Maybe he sees us stumbling into something and wants to be here when it happens."

"Shit. You're getting scary, Pipe. How about you stop thinking so much about all the bad shit that can happen. Think about us finding a hoard of Praman gold we can steal and use to buy us a villa stocked with a troop of eager whores."

"I have a woman."

"You can suck the fricking joy out of any dream, can't you?"

"You may be right. I become overly narrow, practical, and literal sometimes."

"Sometimes. You do tend to be." Sarcastically.

"Bad upbringing."

"Your whole family the same way?"

"Pretty much." There had been no frivolity in the Vibrant Spring School.

Seen through a western eye, all al-Prama took everything too seriously.

THE VEDETTES OUT FRONT MISSED THE CALZIRAN HORSEMEN hidden in a brushy valley to the left of the line of march. The scouts were overconfident and lazy, not to mention disinclined to range afar in the cold. The vanguard behind paid the price.

The van consisted of young horsemen from the Five Families. They were in constant competition. They did not want to embarrass their families in front of their rivals. They did not run. The attackers, no professionals themselves, broke off when help came up from farther back.

Grade Drocker arrived as Else walked over the bloody snow. The sorcerer announced, "They were Calziran horsemen. Inexperienced. But trained and led by Dreangerean Sha-lug."

Else agreed. But not out loud. Piper Hecht would not know that.

"Shit," Ghort said. "Do we know what they had for breakfast?"

Yes, Else thought. Most likely. But he just tried to look eager to learn from a man who had fought Pramans before.

Drocker's health remained fragile. He could not shake that cough, though the blood Gledius Stewpo feared had yet to show in his spittle.

Drocker was not inclined to teach. Nevertheless, he did explain, "The attack was classic Sha-lug. From ambush. On an exposed flank. All out, with saddle bow and javelin. But true Sha-lug would not have fled so soon."

"A useful lesson," Else said. "Pinkus, see to the dead and wounded. I need to have a few words with whoever was in charge of the scouts."

"That would be Stefango Benedocto."

Drocker tagged along behind Else. Stefango Benedocto turned out to be the son of a cousin of Honario Benedocto. He believed the tie would avert his commander's wrath. It did. There were practical limits that Else had to accept.

Grade Drocker killed the man. Without a word. In front of a hundred witnesses, some of them Benedocto. By sorcery, using a spell that made Benedocto's brain leak out through his eyes and ears. Drocker then announced, "The Special Office doesn't care who your uncle is."

"Another valuable lesson, Pipe," Pinkus Ghort said when he heard about the incident. "That should do wonders for morale." This once he was not being sarcastic.

Soon afterward Else learned that Drocker was no longer with the regiment.

Ghort said, "He just hung around until somebody gave him an excuse to make his point."

"That would be my guess."

"It worked. Even the most useless of these assholes are beginning to realize that this business is as serious as a hot poker up the shit chute."

"It won't last."

"Now you got to be the pollyanna and always look on the bright side?"

"You're not going to be happy with me no matter what, are you?"

"Ain't that my job?"

There were more skirmishes. The Calzirans were not caught unprepared again. Else knew what to expect. He prepared accordingly.

ELSE'S NIGHTS WERE NOT HAPPY. HE FELL ASLEEP WRESTLING his conscience. Logic suggested that he ought to get the crusader forces bogged down. But the city regiment was just a fraction of the invasion, and isolated. The Emperor's forces faced the hardest fighting. That was where the overseas troops had landed. The Patriarchy's closest allies were advancing down the west coast of Firaldia, but most had not yet reached Alameddine, let alone Calzir. The city regiment advanced on an inland route, with Brotherhood troops and contingents from minor principalities close behind. Confusion of command was the order.

God was the answer. God was always the answer, whatever the question might be. Else needed only to trust in the Will of God. All would turn out according to His Plan.

Else feared he was not a good Praman. He could not surrender to the will of the night. Each evening, once the regiment went into camp, Else studied maps and intelligence reports, looking for a way to fail Sublime without discrediting himself.

Had he been sent to Firaldia, expected to fail, so that failure would devour him? Which meant that Gordimer wanted . . .

That math did not work out.

Else thought he knew Gordimer. Gordimer was subtle enough to put a potential rival out where death might overtake him. But would he do that to Else Tage? Else could not imagine Gordimer seeing him as that serious a threat.

Else chose to temporize. He would serve Brothe. How better to serve Dreanger than to soar in the councils of Dreanger's foes?

Pinkus Ghort turned up. "The Deves want to see you, Pipe."

"They say why?"

"Nope. I'm not one of their pals." Ghort glanced around, making sure no nearby shadow harbored anything unfriendly. Constant, unconscious examination of the local scene was second nature in the west.

"Not even a hint?"

"No. I assume it's news from al-Khazen. The vedettes found some Deves beside the road, bickering about whether or not to light a fire."

Ghort did a quick pantomime wherein the freezing-our-asses-off party battled the smoke-will-get-us-killed party.

The weather was miserable and getting worse. Today, there were several kinds, all cold. Bitter winds reminded Else that he had spent last winter cozily tucked into prison. Sleet became snow, falling thickly. There seemed to be a thousand ghosts behind the curtains of white, loping parallel to the road south.

The Instrumentalities of the Night became ever more active as the regiment approached al-Khazen.

The regiment had not yet moved five miles that day. But Else was in no hurry. He was out here alone with a mob of un-blooded and poorly trained soldiers likely to panic at their first glimpse of the elephant. It was imperative that they avoid heavy pressure unless the Brotherhood of War joined in.

Else ordered camp to be made at a site less than an hour ahead.

He wanted to visit with the new Deves.

31. Andorayans Far from Home

Svavar hated life. Svavar hated Firaldia. Svavar hated the bandit mercenaries of Ochska Rashaki's company. Most of all, Svavar hated the Instrumentalities of the Night. He was ready to lie down and find peace.

Shagot slept twenty hours at a stretch, now. Or more. Although his spans of awareness and activity now sometimes stretched out, too. He could be furiously active for twenty hours before he collapsed into a sleep deeper than any coma.

The lone spark in the darkness of Svavar's existence was his confidence that Arlensul stalked these cruel foreign hills beside him. Each day she let him glimpse her from the corner of his eye, or slipping into shadow ahead if the band was making one of its rare moves.

The rogue Chooser wanted him to know she was there. Was

she guardian or death sentence? Or just a tool? The Arlensul of myth was obsessed with vengeance.

Svavar felt no empathy for Arlensul. She wanted him filled with nothing but an abiding resentment of his horrid immortality so powerful he would be her ally when her hour came.

Asgrimmur Grimmsson was not a brilliant man. Given time, though, he worked things out. In these mountains, taking the Emperor's shilling while giving little in return, he had time to brood and hatch ideas.

Svavar, the Imperial mercenary, was in no way the Asgrimmur Grimmsson sturlanger who had tagged along after his big brother a few hundred years ago. This Svavar bestrode the boundaries of the Realm of Night, slowly becoming the thing he hated, tiny fry on the verges of the shoals of the Instrumentalities of the Night. As had been the case a million times before, never noticed by those involved, he was drifting toward becoming something more than a man.

And the exiled daughter of the All-Father was easing his path.

Not one man in a million ever learned that mere mortals might become something more. Godhead itself was there for the man who enjoyed the will and the luck.

The one in a million seldom recognized the role of chance. A great sorcerer might devote his life to grasping ascendance and kill himself in the effort. An ignorant barbarian like Svavar might succeed just by not knowing any better. Shagot's enchanted head once graced a shaman determined to become one of the Instrumentalities of the Night. The Instrumentalities already out there used him, manipulating him through his ambition, in an age when a warmer world was sloughing the rule of ice and both gods and men were simpler.

Svavar developed a sense for Arlensul's whereabouts. It worked better than his sense for Shagot. He felt the cold and the empty, the hatred and the despair, that were the essence of Arlensul the Exile. Not normally interested in the feelings of others, Svavar nevertheless wondered what it might be like to swap war stories with the daughter of the Gray Walker.

SHAGOT DEVELOPED A DISCONCERTING HABIT OF MOVING FROM the coma state to full awareness in a blink. Svavar was roasting a slow, stupid hare betrayed to him by Arlensul. Shagot popped up and roared, "What the hell is going on?" as though he had not been in another world completely for the last twenty-six hours. "There's something wrong." He ignored the two feet of snow that had not been there before.

"It's that asshole Ockska," Svavar said. "He don't want to do what he's supposed to. Rabbit will be ready in a bit." Svavar knew Shagot was not thinking about Rashaki.

"Huh?" Shagot took a moment to orient himself. "He isn't watching the pass anymore?"

"It isn't that, Grim. Since you went to sleep we had three messages from Vondera Koterba. The Emperor wants us to move down past al-Citizi and cut the east-west road. Not to block it, just to intercept messengers." Svavar spoke softly so Rashaki's intimates would not hear. "He says he's holding out for a bigger payoff. I think he's afraid to show us what a stupid ass he really is."

"He defied orders from Koterba and the Emperor both?"

Svavar relaxed slightly. Shagot had been diverted from a strangeness surely to do with Arlensul.

Shagot wolfed down more than his share of the hare. As he cleaned his fingers, he said, "I need you to back me up, little brother." He produced the monster head and the enchanted sword forged in the time before time.

Members of the band, scruffy bandit scum rather than real soldiers, gaped as Shagot strode toward Rashaki's hut. Shagot shattered the feeble door. Inside, he removed the head of one lieutenant and the face of another before saying, "You defied the Emperor's command." His tone was soft, gentle. It betrayed no strain. It was the tone of a man disinterestedly asking the price of a sack of turnips. He kicked his surviving victim for bleeding on his leg.

Ockska considered the old head, the bloody sword, and Shagot. "I thought we could get more money."

"The Emperor is an honorable man. He keeps his word. He expects you to do the same. It's time for a leader who will do his job."

"I suppose you're right."

"Good. Good. You're a reasonable man, after all. You won't find me a harsh captain. And my brother and I will move on soon. Little brother, help our lieutenant rise so we can shake hands on the new arrangement."

Rashaki was an average size man who had made himself leader by being more clever and hard than the others, rather than through sheer wicked brawn. "Are you the Emperor's special agents?"

"Something like that," Shagot admitted. He drove the ancient sword into Rashaki's chest. Svavar held Rashaki for the strike. "Though we serve a power higher than any ephemeral lord of the earth."

Ockska heard that before the light went out of his eyes. He believed because he saw what no one else could see.

Rashaki's surviving lieutenants quickly reported the change to the rest of the band.

No one argued. Everyone recognized that agents of the night walked among them.

Svavar knew Rashaki's lieutenants harbored the same thoughts that Rashaki had before the bronze sword relieved him of a need to think. Play along with the mad foreigner. It would be no trouble to murder his brother, then him, once demonic sleep reclaimed him.

Shagot counted on the Old Ones to get him through. If he thought at all. Svavar trusted Arlensul. Arlensul was immediate and real and had a vested interest in sustaining the Grimmssons.

The band moved out. The snowfalls were no less vigorous down there in the warmer foothills. They melted and created mud as though mud was a treat favored by all gods great and small.

The first six days of the new administration produced four coup attempts. The conspirators all died horribly. Some were mutilated and drained of blood *before* they moved against the Andorayans.

The day Shagot killed Ockska Rashaki the band numbered eighty-eight, counting all bodies but those of the sad handful of slatterns who followed the band with their snotty-nosed brats. When the band moved into the position Vondera Koterba desired they numbered sixty-five. Most of the missing had deserted, along with their women and children.

The band disrupted Calziran communications for two

months. Lone riders and small groups just did not get through. Prisoners went to Ferris Renfrow somewhere to the east. He paid excellent bounties. Life was no daydream but neither was it awful. And it showed promise of getting better.

Svavar soon realized that he was running things. Shagot the Bastard was this wild berserker thing he could conjure up at need. Daily administration and decision-making were his. And he did well. He held the band together. He got it through its assignment without another death, and with only four more desertions.

The Emperor's troops, with those of Vondera Koterba, overran the eastern third of Calzir far more easily than either side imagined possible. The Praman defenders were stunned by their own ineffectuality.

Those Calzirans, even inspired by advisers from Lucidia and backboned by cadre from overseas, could not withstand the disciplined Imperial heavy infantry and heavy cavalry. The Lucidians strove valiantly but insisted on fighting the wrong war. Johannes Blackboots was not interested in elegant maneuvers. He trudged from one town, city, port, or castle to the next, ignoring enemy forces unless they attacked—always a disaster for the Pramans. Imperial pikemen held them off while thousands of missiles sleeted down on them. When they ran, horsemen followed and butchered them.

Warships from Dateon and Aparion blockaded the eastern and southern coasts. The heel end of the Firaldian boot fell. Few Praman troops tried to flee west to join the armies there. Svavar dispatched any stupid enough to use his road.

He first saw Johannes Blackboots when the Emperor's own Braunsknechts Guards passed through, headed west in hopes of outgrasping the less vigorous forces fielded by Sublime and the Brothen Church.

"He's a fucking dwarf," Shagot observed.

Not quite, but close.

The Emperor's whole family accompanied Johannes, a measure of his confidence. The brothers did not see the daughters or learn of their existence until later. They occupied a closed coach surrounded by large, alert, scowling, short-tempered Braunsknecht horse guards.

The Imperial heir, Lothar, rode beside his father, as miserable as one child could be, yet persevering with a will suited to much a stronger body. He was determined to make his father proud.

Ferris Renfrow found the brothers after the Emperor had passed. "You've done a great job. Vondera Koterba says you deserve a bonus. I agree. Would you like to continue your service?"

Svavar accepted a sack of coins while Shagot said, "We will go with you. We're looking for a man. He's west of here. He has to die."

"All men die."

"Soon. It's a holy mission."

Svavar sensed that Renfrow knew who they were. He would have had reports from his agents.

"Tell me about the man you're hunting. Maybe I can help."

Svavar, distracted by passing heavy infantry, which he had never encountered before, replied, "All we know is that he's in Calzir and that we'll know him when we find him."

A Patriarchal company passed. They had participated in the Imperial thrust in the east. Svavar glared at black crows from the Brotherhood of War. They unnerved him. Their order would harbor an eternal grudge because of what had happened in Brothe.

Renfrow kept him talking. Svavar knew Renfrow had pegged him as dim and naive. He didn't mind. He might be those things, but not so much that he could not let someone underestimate him.

Once Renfrow left, Svavar told Shagot, "That fellow thinks he knows our man. He knows where he is, too. And he thinks he knows who we are."

"With the Patriarch's armies?"

"I think so."

"Makes sense. Fits my dreams. We'll get him this time."

Svavar nodded. But he had doubts. Arlensul had not been factored into the All-Father's plan.

There would never be a better time to tell Grim about Arlensul. Words would not come.

Svavar paid off the members of the band. "Anybody who

wants to stick can go west with me and Grim. They still want us."

Only a dozen men who had nothing else in their lives stayed on. The rest ran back to their cold, barren mountains with their newly found wealth.

32. Shippen and the Toe

Bishop LeCroes settled beside Brother Candle. Brother Candle was watching the sun set behind a vague hint of distant indigo peaks. He had his back against an almond tree, the vanguard of a grove. Almonds had come to Shippen with the Praman invaders.

The sun's lower limb squashed down on the far hills, a bloated, distorted vermilion egg that the eye could suffer for moments at a time.

Color flew round the sky as though slung from the palette of a mad artiste god. Shippen folk said that was because of a haze vented by a somnolent volcano off to the north.

LeCroes said, "Sorry to bother you. I wanted you to know. The rumors are true. King Peter will cross over to the mainland."

Brother Candle asked, "Is that Sublime's idea?"

"You kidding? Once this war ends Sublime will be as nervous about Peter as he is about the Emperor."

"Maybe the Emperor suggested the move."

"Peter is clever enough to come up with it on his own."

Brother Candle quickly saw why Peter would make this move.

It would give him a foothold on the mainland and enhance his reputation in Firaldia, where he was not yet well known. *And* it would establish forces friendly to the End of Connec behind the Patriarch should Sublime decide to follow a crusade against Calzir with another against the Connec. At little cost in lives and treasure Peter would triple the lands he held and make Navaya the strongest Chaldarean realm in the west.

Brother Candle had to admire King Peter. The man had foreseen vast opportunities before he decided to transport and support the forces Duke Tormond pledged to Sublime. Who might have done so at Isabeth's urging.

Sublime must be in a tight place now, desperately unable to seize and retain those expanded temporal powers that all Brothen Patriarchs coveted.

Brother Candle ascended to Perfection without losing his cynicism and skepticism. The sad truth was, none of the last dozen Brothen Patriarchs had shown much regard for their spiritual mission. And few had shown much competence in the political lists, either.

"I think I see where this will end up."

"And that would be where?"

"Are you firm in your allegiance to Immaculate?"

"Absolutely! He's the only legitimate . . ."

LeCroes's tight tone and evasive eye told Brother Candle that he had been romanced by Sublime's agents and had not yet rejected them.

"Immaculate is likely to be the last Viscesment Patriarch."

"Excuse me?"

"It's simple. Right or wrong, Viscesment no longer claims many hearts. The holdouts have started making deals so they don't suffer when Immaculate goes away. I'll bet there's no election when he does."

Brother Candle would be brokenhearted, too. A Church divided, feuding with itself, had no energy left to persecute those who did not conform to Episcopal doctrine.

LeCroes bowed his head. "It's true. The Brothens outlasted us. The struggle was doomed from the start, though. Worthy VI should've begged the Emperor for help right away."

Would he have received any? There had been little love between Worthy and Voromund or Spinomund, whoever the Emperor was back then.

Worthy had been spineless. History called him Worthy the Coward. But even determined backing by the Brotherhood of War could not have convinced the Brothen mob that their natural rights had not been usurped.

"Lost in my thoughts," Brother Candle said, perhaps to the almond trees, because Bishop LeCroes had gone. Darkness was closing in. "Your Church is founded on a bedrock of corruption. Yet you're baffled when folk seek a purer way."

Brother Candle sighed, calmed himself. Those who chose the Path understood corruption as native to the human condition.

One had to avoid condemnation, which was not constructive. One had to provide an example. One had to demonstrate that corruption was wicked and the product of an evil imagination.

COUNT RAYMONE SPOKE TO A GATHERING OF CONNECTEN officers and hangers-on, including Brother Candle and the chaplains. "King Peter has a solid rapport with his Plataduran allies. They have sources in Calzir. Except for the hardheads at al-Khazen, the Calzirans are ready to quit. They want to get connected with a Chaldarean leader who will respect and tolerate their peculiar beliefs, King Peter. Grand champion of the Chaldarean Reconquest."

Pramans from Platadura and the Terliagan Littoral made polite sounds of approval.

Count Raymone continued, "Emissaries from several towns in the mainland region called the Toe have run the blockade to come beg Peter to accept their surrender before the Patriarch reaches them."

Brother Candle wrestled his natural cynicism. The Patriarch and Church were, indeed, the last people you wanted replacing the tyrants you had always known.

The mainlander envoys did not appeal to Count Raymone. Connectens had become supporting characters in King Peter's passion play.

An excellent eventuation, too, Brother Candle believed. Peter might yet negate Sublime's insanity. He might see the world around the Mother Sea introduced to an era of peace—should Sublime enjoy the great good fortune of being reunited with his creator.

The Shippen adventure had helped Raymone Garete mature. He had ceased to be all rage and mindless action. The lesson Raymone had taken to heart was patience. Because in Shippen, once the invaders had become established, there was nothing to do but wait.

TWENTY-TWO SHIPS, INCLUDING SEVERAL SMALL COASTERS from Shippen, slipped into the Toe ports of Scarlene and Snucco. The former lay farthest west and was a fishing village without boats. The other was a small port accustomed to un-loading agricultural products sent over from Shippen. There was a noteworthy absence of ships in that harbor, too. The col-laborators who had come to Shippen insisted that had nothing to do with the recent unpleasantnesses suffered by the peoples of Chaldarean Firaldia. Only evil coincidence, that was all it was.

There was no resistance. Those who wanted to fight had gone off to the hosting at al-Khazen, where they planned to crush the crusaders once they were sick and starving in the cold and snow.

The Connecten and Direcians from Shippen encountered only those complications of conquest posed by distance and numbers. Towns surrendered as fast as the invaders could hike.

King Peter was restrained only by the fact that he did not have troops sufficient to garrison all the territories willing to throw themselves at his feet. He considered enlisting Calzirans but had no money to pay them.

Moving boldly, King Peter and Count Raymone overran two-thirds of what Patriarchal forces expected to occupy af-ter al-Khazen's fall. Peter's army pushed east along the southern coast until his troops encountered Hansel's coming westward.

For Brother Candle it happened dizzyingly fast. By midwin-ter unconquered mainland Calzir had been reduced to a fifth of its original territory, mostly around al-Khazen. Enclaves ex-isted at al-Healta and al-Stikla, as well. Warships from Dateon and Apareon blockaded both ports. Patriarchal troops were within sight of al-Khazen, on its northern side.

Brother Candle found a place behind the captains and gener-als during a session about strategy for the endgame. He learned that Hansel was outraged by King Peter's opportunism and dramatic, nearly bloodless success.

Sublime was worse.

Al-Khazen showed no inclination to surrender. The occa-sional prisoner taken suggested that the city's commanders did not lack confidence in their ultimate triumph.

Brother Candle observed, ministered to those of his own faith, and kept quiet. He nursed an abiding dread that the cru-saders had been led artfully into an huge ambush. Someday, sooner than later, the Adversary's most intimate and beloved minions would leap forth.

Unexpectedly, never noticing the process, Brother Candle had been seduced into the sin of despair. He abjured it the moment he recognized it. It terrified him. But, for a long time, he could not conquer it. And there was no other Perfect there to guide him through the slough.

He became so uncertain of himself and his faith that he began to contemplate ending all earthly pain.

33. Sublime's War in Calzir

Courtesy of the indefatigable Titus Consent and his Devedian associates, the city regiment enjoyed a comfortable camp behind a ridgeline within sight of al-Khazen. Even the least of the soldiers and animals enjoyed shelter from the weather. Local peasants and woodcutters, denied refuge inside al-Khazen because they represented useless stomachs, were eager to support their families by hauling firewood, helping the invaders build shelters, or doing whatever else they could. The fuel and timber were harvested from olive, citrus, walnut, and almond groves belonging to Calzirans who were inside the city, applauding themselves for having kept all the useless, hungry mouths outside.

Wood, materials, and intelligence got paid for in food. The regiment's supplies now came overland from Postastati, a ghost town of a fishing village on Firaldia's west coast, just twenty miles from the ever-expanding Episcopal encampment. Calziran peasants did most of the hauling. Draconian punishments befell those who stole supplies.

The regiment kept growing, fatter instead of stronger. Every Brothen functionary of standing, every member of the Collegium, seemed determined to be there when the last Firaldian Praman bastion yielded to the Will of God.

Else chose a cottage on the fore slope of the ridge as his main observation point.

The Pramans mounted a vigorous and aggressive defense,

launching probes and sorties daily, always taking advantage of the worst weather. After a few minor disasters early on, Else's captains realized that their upstart foreign colonel might have what it took to keep them alive.

The Imperial forces suffered more setbacks. Hansel did not understand Sha-lug tactics.

The Patriarchal force had Grade Drocker and his Brotherhood veterans. And Else Tage, who continued to suffer the moral pinch.

Else, Pinkus Ghort, and Grade Drocker were in the lookout cottage considering al-Khazen. A light snow fell, hampering visibility. Locals promised the invaders that this was the worst winter in known history.

Also under foot were a dozen bishops, Principatés, and important members of the Five Families. Grade Drocker had a calming effect on folk ordinarily inclined to be obstreperous. Sublime had declared him supreme commander of the Calziran Crusade, though nobody believed King Peter or the Emperor would take Drocker's orders.

Drocker observed, "It should be our turn today."

Else, who knew, agreed. "Their leadership is too predictable."

"Too predictable?"

"From their point of view. Pinkus. The troop mix has been constant so far, hasn't it? One cadre foreigner for fifteen Calzirans?"

"That's what I hear. I can't get them to line up so I can . . ."

"Stop!" Drocker gasped. He did not like Ghort's folksy style. Ghort claimed that Drocker would die of apoplexy trying to figure out what was wrong if somebody made him laugh. "Pay attention." Drocker pointed. His hand shook.

Else did not expect Drocker to survive the campaign. He slipped a little every day. But an immense will drove the man onward.

A wisp of signal smoke became visible thirty degrees to the right of a line of sight to al-Khazen. It was dark. A plan had worked out.

Else learned the full story later. An unexpectedly large Calziran force had taken the bait. The Pramans chased fleeing Brothen horsemen into a trap where more than four hundred of their number fell in a fierce crossfire and subsequent assault from both flanks. Eighty prisoners were taken, too, none Shalug or Lucidian. The action was a disaster for the Pramans.

Else repeated the tactic. The other side seemed unable to imagine their enemies using their own stratagems against them.

PRINCIPATÉ DIVINO BRUGLIONI TOLD ELSE, "THE PATRIARCH wants an assault on al-Khazen. He's gotten behind repaying the money he borrowed to buy votes to get elected. He's talking about finding officers who are more aggressive."

"Anyone point out that he's not in charge?"

"He wouldn't listen. It verges on heresy to say so, but we erred when we compromised on Honario Benedocto."

The occasion was a gathering in the lookout cottage. Else and his staff spent their days there, now. Grade Drocker was a fixture. A continuously changing cast of Principatés wandered through. Discussion concerned the feasibility of building a stockade around the city, then constructing small forts capable of laying fires on the approaches to al-Khazen's gates and sally ports.

Grade Drocker eyed Principaté Bruglioni like he was a lunatic. Ghort suggested, "We ought to talk that over with my boss." He indicated Bronte Doneto. Doneto stared at al-Khazen, dirty gray behind a fall of snow dust, like he wanted to smash it fast so he could get on home.

Drocker, wheezing and gasping as ever, declared, "If the Patriarch wants those walls stormed he can drag his craven carcass down here and lead the charge."

Ghort said, "Of course. Time will deliver al-Khazen. The Patriarch needs money, let him borrow it again."

He stated the plain truth about al-Khazen. The invaders' circle kept tightening. And the city's storehouses did not contain the grain shown by the records. Corrupt officials had sold it over the years.

Foraging parties had no success. Raiding parties failed to capture Chaldarean stores. In areas held by Episcopal troops, every Praman effort encountered disaster.

Drocker agreed with Ghort. "Sublime needs money, let him borrow it from the Deves." Then, "Doneto will hammer some sense into his head."

"And if he can't?"

"We ignore the ignoramus. We took no oath to commit suicide for Honario Benedocto."

Else suspected there was a personal component to Drocker's relations with the Patriarch.

Drocker spoke in spurts punctuated by gasps for breath, but lately the spoken chunks were longer and the interruptions shorter. "You're being too clever with your ambushes, Hecht."

"Sir?"

"You've done well, anticipating the enemy. But he'll get the notion that he needs to try a more sinister tack."

"Sir?" Else spoke humbly. Drocker's stumbling, halting communications lately recalled every teacher he had had. Drocker had decided to become his mentor.

Drocker said, "You've fought them man to man and mind to mind and have had the advantage because of the Calziran Deves." Those people would pay dearly if the Praman leadership found them out.

Drocker said, "There are three major sorcerers in al-Khazen. Plus the Masters of Ghosts that accompany Dreangerean formations. They don't want us to know they're there. But they won't suffer many more failures."

Else responded, "Another outstanding reason for not attacking. They can conjure all the Instrumentalities of the Night."

"They would start small."

Principaté Bruglioni asked, "Is that true, Drocker? About the sorcerers?"

"It is."

"Why wasn't the Collegium made aware?"

Drocker was blunt. "We didn't want you people babbling the news all over Firaldia."

Easy to see why Drocker was not beloved by the Episcopal hierarchy. He smoldered with contempt for the self-serving pettiness of Church politics. "You'll be needed when the Unbeliever summons the Instrumentalities of the Night, however." For Drocker there was only one worthy struggle, the war against the Night.

"You need to know now," Else told Doneto. "Because they'll come after you first."

Drocker clarified his position. "There will be no attack.

Waiting, not wasting, let's us develop a pool of veterans for the future."

Drocker's longer speeches left his audience impatient. But no one tried to hurry him. This was war ground, the Brotherhood's home country. Few members of that Brotherhood were more terrible than Grade Drocker.

Drocker confided, "They think I'm hard." He laughed. That brought on a coughing fit so violent that Else summoned the Brotherhood physician, who got Drocker inhaling exudations of herbs crushed in a leather sack. Redfearn Bechter helped Drocker with the bag. When the sorcerer recovered, he told Else, "I'm an altar boy. Wait till they meet Asher Huggin, Parthen Lorica, Alin Hamlet, or Bugo Armiene. They scare me."

"Then I hope I never meet any of them."

Drocker asked, "Does that worry you?"

"Sure. It would worry anyone who isn't one of you."

Drocker raised a questioning eyebrow.

"If you're an everyday sort who has to scratch for your next meal you find people who're that absolute in their convictions really frightening."

Drocker seemed amused.

Outside, snow fell lightly but steadily. The weather had settled into an unchanging pattern. Would it end with Calzir under a mile of ice, the way it was in the far north?

Else shivered. Even a well-built structure like the lookout cottage could not keep the cold out. The chills, the drafts, all the talk about Praman sorcerers coagulated in Else's mind. He left Drocker, found Ghort. "Pinkus, all the yammer has got me thinking. If those people over there send spooks to aggravate us, and we don't get ready . . ."

"I got ya, Pipe. What do we do to get ready?"

"The stuff every family does when they live where the Night is always at the door. Plug up all the cracks."

"Plug up all the cracks," was, in fact, an old saw from Duarnenia. Variants existed everywhere. Folk wisdom based on common sense. By plugging all the cracks you kept the cold out and you kept the things of the Night out in the cold.

Plug up all the cracks. "Pipe, I've whispered that sweet nothing into every subaltern's ear starting the first night we had to make camp."

"Then I don't need to nag."

Plug up all the cracks. Else could not imagine anyone in a strange land not doing that automatically.

TITUS CONSENT BROUGHT A PAIR OF LOCAL DEVES TO ELSE. He whispered, "These people have risked everything for us, Colonel. They can't go back. But they still have family inside."

"I understand." He wanted to shriek. He was trapped. These Deves wanted to betray his people to his enemies. And he had to protect and reward them. "Set up some kind of show trial. Script it so it looks like we're lying about Calzir's Devedians helping us. Condemn them to be hung, then grant clemency at the request of the Deves of Brothe."

"It's uglier than a dead baby, but I can make it work."

"Have they been noticed yet?"

"No. We're keeping them out of sight. They won't talk to anybody but you."

"Keep on doing that. Bring them in. Why me?"

"They're worried about spies. They've heard that there's at least one highly placed Praman agent over here."

"No doubt true. Human nature being human nature." Else Tage was careful not to remind any Deve that his loyalty might not lie with the enemies of al-Prama.

Life was not going well for the besieged, the spies reported, though al-Khazen was not yet under a complete siege. The slaughter of dray animals had begun. Cavalry mounts remained untouched but there was little feed for them. The granaries were empty. Execution of the officials responsible eased the strain on stores only slightly.

Inhabitants of al-Khazen who did not share the religious enthusiasms of the majority suffered the most. Else listened to the horror stories. He began to glance askance at Consent. "Be patient," Consent urged. "As you're always telling us."

"I do hope to hear *something* that makes my indulgence worthwhile."

The Calzirans were an elderly couple who had been employed in Mafti al-Araj el-Arak's palace, now occupied by the foreign captains.

"They managed the books," Titus explained.

"So they have a special place in your heart."

"They had a special opportunity to be close to important discussions."

The old folks from al-Khazen were no more patient than Else. They were exhausted. They wanted to lay their old bones down and sleep. Though they were worried about their children and grandchildren.

Else tried not to torment himself wondering why the old Deves preferred the mercies of unknown Chaldareans to those of known Pramans.

Their big news was that the sorcerers of al-Khazen would come out of hiding soon.

Else could not shake a conviction that he had missed something once the interview ended. He snapped, "What did I just miss, Titus? You could've sent me a one-sentence note that would've covered all that."

Consent replied, "I wanted to put a human face on the Devedian tragedy. Obviously, I failed."

Else locked gazes with Gledius Stewpo. The dwarf shrugged. "The young only learn directly. But I do think those old people can help."

"How?"

"They worked in the palace. They know the important buildings."

"I see. You're right. I've grown impatient."

"Easy to do, I'd think, having to stand hip to hip with Grade Drocker."

"You have no idea." He and Consent spent an hour discussing logistical problems. The worst being that other Patriarchal forces thought they could become parasites on the city regiment.

EARLY ENCOUNTERS WITH THINGS OF THE NIGHT WERE SUBtle. The sorcerers in al-Khazen were not eager to declare themselves.

The city regiment handled the probes as men always had, with charms, spells, and by plugging all the cracks.

The Emperor's troops tightened the circle in the hills to the east and south. King Peter was less aggressive. His troops wanted to stay out of the weather.

Else, Grade Drocker, several Principatés, and the commanders of contingents from several Episcopal States were studying the feasibility of infiltrating al-Khazen via a wastewater outlet discovered by Collegium sorcerers, employing the same sort of minor entities the Pramans used to scout their besiegers. Else asked, "Are we sure they don't know this drainage system exists?"

Bronte Doneto replied, "Not even your Deve captives knew about it. The engineering is Old Empire. Cassina was a major city of the Old Empire."

Pinkus Ghort interrupted. "Sorry, Pipe. Colonel. Principaté. Word just came. The foreign Pramans have started rounding up all the non-Pramans in the city."

Else exchanged glances with Doneto. "Does that mean they've figured out that the Deves are helping us?"

Ghort volunteered, "Deves brought the news."

Else asked, "Have there been executions? Have . . . ? Sorry, Pinkus. I won't learn anything with my mouth open, will I?"

"You might. You're special. But that's all the news there is. Nobody knows what they'll do with the prisoners. There's been fighting."

Bronte Doneto observed, "Too bad we aren't set to exploit that drainage system. We could hit them while they're distracted."

Would the Calziran Pramans tolerate the abuse of their minorities?

Probably.

Grade Drocker invited himself in. "That's interesting. But is it germane? Let's focus on the problem at hand. Can we get men inside to seize the gates or murder the Praman leadership?"

Else told Ghort, "Make up a team of our Deves and some refugees to track the situation." He told the others, "Something bigger may be going on. Where do we get out of the wastewater system?"

The Deves of al-Khazen had provided excellent maps, some so detailed they included the number of steps up to the door of an important building.

"Not sure," Ghort said.

Drocker asked Bronte Doneto and Divino Bruglioni, "Are you really sure the Pramans don't know about this? I'd use it as a trap."

Drocker was so weak now that he had to be carried. But he was able to speak almost normally. Else did not expect him to last till spring. And had mixed feelings about that. Because Drocker had become his patron. And Drocker might get him next to Honario Benedocto himself.

THE MOTIVE BEHIND THE ROUNDUP AND SUPPRESSION OF minorities made itself evident immediately. Most were driven out, intended to become a burden on the besiegers. Criminals, prostitutes, old people unrelated to anyone important—anyone who could not materially contribute to the city's defense—were ejected along with the minorities.

Before the next day's end the Dreangereans and Lucidians began ejecting fight-worthy Pramans they did not trust, too.

Else had patrols round up a representative sample of disgruntled ejectees and offered them the opportunity to get even.

Grade Drocker cautioned, "Be careful, Hecht. I've seen this in the Holy Lands. Some of these refugees will be enemy agents."

"I'll keep that in mind."

"NO. I HAVEN'T FORGOTTEN MY PROMISE," ELSE TOLD ROGOZ Sayag. They were walking in darkness, between the observation house and the regimental camp.

"I ask only because Salny tells me the Don is fading."

"The thing weighs on my mind. A commitment is a commitment."

"But."

"Absolutely."

"I understand. You've become one of the key men in the crusade."

"I don't know. I was born in the wrong place and time. No doubt if I was amoral enough to murder my father and sell my sisters into prostitution." One of the heroes of Brothen antiquity had done just that.

Rogoz chuckled wickedly. "Brothens aren't nastier than other people. You just hear about the ones who do the nastiest shit."

"I suppose."

"I'm just asking. Like I said, the Don is failing."

"Which one of the Bruglioni do you suppose the Don admires the most?"

"The Principaté. Divino was almost as close to Draco as Freido was."

"That makes sense. But we are in a war here." Meaning that a senior member of the Collegium was not an asset to be wasted while Brothe's enemies remained standing.

"I understand. I'm just seeing if you remember my father and the Don."

"You have no worries. I won't forget their generosity."

A sentry challenged them. Else gave the countersign.

"Hey! Pipe? Is that you, you old pudthumper?"

"Bo Biogna. Bo, this is Captain Sayag of House Arniena. Bo went into the Connec with us when Captain Ghort and I were trudging around behind Grade Drocker. Bo is a good man. I hear he's even shown flashes of having what it takes to be a good soldier."

Bo had grown since last Else had seen him. "Thank you, Pipe. Uh, Colonel."

Before Else could get inside the little wine-pressing building Polo had turned into comfortable quarters, Bronte Doneto and several Collegium allies swooped down.

"Principaté," Else said, "however much I owe you, and however important you are to the faith, I can't help right now. I'm exhausted. I need sleep. Now."

Doneto said, "I'm sorry. But there may be an important new angle. We've only begun to see it this past hour. There may be something deeper than the old war between faiths at work."

Else refrained from informing the Principaté that he was a major repository for camel dung. "You need to be more specific."

"Bluntly, Hecht, to the east of us somewhere, in or around the Emperor's camp, there's an interested power that could be a fully fledged Instrumentality of the Night."

"You have the advantage of me, Principaté. I don't understand."

"Recall the thing in the Ownvidian Knot. The one we survived because you thought fast enough to wake me up."

"Yes?"

"There's a power out there, perhaps following the Emperor, that makes that bogon look as dangerous as a pet weasel."

Else stared at Doneto, wondering if the man's sanity had become suspect.

Doneto said, "Times like this strain the faith of God's most devout Children, Colonel. This thing out there—Primitive peoples might consider it a lesser god."

Else nodded and shrugged and twitched. "And you're telling me about this because?"

"Because, like it or not, we'll have to deal with it. You and me. If it has an interest in this struggle."

Else indulged in several seconds of deeply felt wishing that the nonsense would go away. "Say you're right. Why is this awful godling here? If it isn't Praman or Chaldarean, why does it care?"

"You'd have to take that up with it. It's one more symptom of the agitation among the Instrumentalities of the Night."

"Maybe I should be glad I'm not sensitive to that."

"Most people drift through life indifferent to the Night until the Night reaches out and smacks them."

"Like that thing in the Ownvidian Knot."

"Like that. I still don't know what that was about. I have no enemies who'd go to that much trouble. Far easier to have me murdered in the Emperor's prison."

"Maybe you offended the Adversary Himself."

"Hardly. There was a human agency behind that bogon."

"What's that noise?" He knew what it was, though. The racket raised by men unexpectedly attacked.

Doneto went pale. "That can't be . . . We'd know ahead of time if they sent troops out."

THE PRAMAN SORCERERS WERE ATTACKING THE BROTHERhood. Which suggested lapses in their intelligence in both senses of that word. The Brotherhood contingent was no major threat to al-Khazen.

The uproar ended before Else reached the scene. Something like the monster from Esther's Wood had been driven off by the Principatés. Three Brothers fell to the thing's fury. None died. Plainly not what those who sent it intended.

Else spotted several key Devedians watching. Was it coincidence that the first blow fell on those who had done the Deves so much hurt? They controlled what both sides knew. Or thought they knew.

The foe tried again, launching point attacks meant to spread terror.

Else asked Doneto, "Is this the thing you warned me about?"

"No. It's a lesser bogon. Entirely foreign."

"Foreign?"

"The overseas Pramans must have brought it. There's nothing like it in Calzir anymore."

"So. Is it the point? Or a diversion?"

"Diversion?"

"What else is going on while we're watching the loud show?" That would be traditional Sha-lug strategy. A fireworks display here while the critical attack went in elsewhere.

"Good thinking, Hecht. I'll look into it. Meanwhile, you should see to your troops."

The city regiment needed no seeing to. The men were nervous but disciplined. Sitting at the center of the sprawl of Patriarchal forces, the regiment enjoyed a moat of human flesh. The probes never came close.

Nevertheless, fear remained an abiding presence through the night.

GRADE DROCKER OPINED, "LAST NIGHT WAS A SETBACK FOR the Pramans." The Patriarchal commanders had lost the habit of calling their enemies Calzirans. The Calzirans were no longer in charge. "The Night bent to our will instead of theirs."

Else learned that small, cruel things had been sent to still the hearts of Patriarchal commanders. Those deadly clots of shadow had been exterminated. The Principatés had been waiting. Especially clever men like Bronte Doneto turned some back on al-Khazen's native Pramans.

The soldier's life consisted mainly of waiting, or of marching somewhere in order to wait. Siege work meant concentrated waiting. Else found himself growing impatient. But never so impatient that he lost sight of the fact that impatience was the mother of stupid decisions.

Ghort turned up. "You get the casualty report for last night, Pipe?"

"Not yet. I didn't think we had any. Did we?"

"I'm not sure. I've seen a few men who say they were but it looked more like they had too much liberated wine and got hurt running around in a panic. Then there's that guy who runs the Arniena company. Sayag. He's your pal, isn't he?"

"Not really. We worked together. I saw him last night. What happened?"

"I'm not sure. He isn't, either. He thinks something tried to get him. Yet that doesn't seem likely."

No, it did not. Unless Divino Bruglioni had found out that the Arniena had it in for the Bruglioni. "I don't know. It's a world full of cold miseries, Pinkus."

"And getting colder fast. Everywhere. You don't want to go back home. That end of the world will be under the ice in our lifetimes."

"The whole world will be under the ice, Pinkus. In our lifetimes. If half the rumors are true."

From the observation house, later, Else stared across the snowscape at the walls and roofs and towers of al-Khazen. They seemed darker and more dangerous this morning. Those were his people. But he could summon no sympathy. He was sure there was no sympathy for Else Tage stashed behind those walls, either.

Would the whole world go under the ice? Or would the Wells of Ihrian start to flow more strongly, as might have happened in the past?

THE FOLLOWING NIGHT BEGAN THE SAME. THE NIGHT-BORN attacks from al-Khazen sputtered sooner, however. Bronte Doneto and his cohorts turned the attack, with more vigor.

Only al-Seyhan and Starkden were active. Did they think the third sorcerer was still a secret?

The third night they turned to the Imperial forces.

Ghort caught Else when they were free of Brotherhood watchers, Principatés, Polo, Deves, and the other plagues upon their lives. "You going crazy with this latest shit, Pipe? I am. These assholes . . . You think the great old-time conquerors had to put up with the horseshit we get every day?"

"What makes stories from the old days seem so great is that they leave out the pettiness, greed, mean spiritedness, backbiting and infighting."

"Yeah, well. Screw it. You're probably right. People are gonna be people. Which means they're mainly gonna be assholes. I wasn't really wanting to talk about that shit, anyway."

"But you do have something on your mind."

"Oh, yeah. There's always something going on in there. But there's a chance it might not be no more important than what goes on in the heads of all those morons who listen to a story but only hear what they want to hear."

"It's cold out here, Pinkus."

"I do have a point. In the sense that I want you to tell me what you're up to. I don't want to get my ass shredded because I don't know the plan."

Else swung an arm across Ghort's shoulder. "Have you been testing the local spoiled fruit juice?"

"That's one thing these Unbelievers do right, Pipe. They ain't 'sposed to drink nothing that might maybe put them in a good mood. Their god must be one sour son of a bitch. But still they manage to make some fine wine."

"You *have* been sampling."

"Which don't mean shit. What does is, what I want to know is, what're we gonna do?"

"What are you babbling about, Pinkus?"

"You don't even realize, do you?"

"You're right. I'm lost."

Ghort did some verbal exercises to get his tongue under control. "You don't realize that you're the number-one guy, here, now. Top dog, after Grade Drocker. Who plain ain't gonna last much longer."

"You haven't cleared the fog much."

"All right. Look. Here it is. We got what, eleven, twelve thousand men in the Patriarch's army?"

Else grunted. "Twelve thousand, two hundred. And some. Maybe eight thousand able to fight." There was a lot of sickness. But that was worse in the city. "And your point?"

"Haven't you noticed in the big meetings how even assholes like Count Juditch va Geiso shut up when you talk?"

He had not. He had seen that even the Principatés and most senior nobles deferred to Grade Drocker. "No."

"Sainted Eis's Holy Hernia, Pipe! For a guy who's so clever about shit in the field, you're dumb when it comes to where you fit in the camp. Those guys have watched you on the job, Pipe. Some ain't happy but they've seen you run the regiment. They've seen you fight it. They know none of their ruling-class types could do half the job. And none of them want any of the others telling them what to do."

Else had seen that. Plenty. "I don't believe you but I see what you're saying."

"You don't got to believe. But we've done good. Them what don't want to be cold and hungry and maybe dead on account of some idiot who knows jack shit about the war business. . . ."

Else shook his head.

Ghort waved that off. "A lot of people think you're the man who can keep everybody warm and fed and breathing if Drocker kicks the bucket."

"Then this discussion is moot. That nasty old man isn't going away anytime soon." Arguing against his own convictions.

"Play a game of what if with me, Pipe. What next, if you was in charge?"

Else scowled. Was Ghort stupid enough to get involved in a conspiracy? "You're serious? Of course you are. You don't have the imagination not to be. Or so you'd like us to think. If I was in charge, what would I do? Exactly what we've been doing, Pinkus. Digging in, drawing the circle tighter, and not doing anything to get any of us killed stupidly. Maximum results for the least bloodshed. Our side and theirs. So what do you really want, Pinkus?"

"I ain't blowing smoke, Pipe. I'm straight on. I think you're the compromise guy. And I don't agree about Drocker being in good shape."

"Now you've heard it, Pinkus. Tell Doneto I'd go right on doing it Drocker's way. Letting time work. Like making wine.

Though I might do a little more than he has to talk the Pramans into surrendering."

"You could shit a shitter, all right, Pipe. You ain't really told me shit that's worth snot."

"Pinkus, I don't know what more you want to hear."

Ghort growled and pretended to yank out his hair. "How come you can't just give me a straight answer to a straight question?"

"I did."

"I bet the reason you left Duarnenia was, they ran you off on account of you've got a stick up your ass."

"I don't understand what you want."

Ghort demonstrated his characteristic flexibility by shrugging, saying, "Guess I lose. I thought I could get you to give me something. Hey. Guess who—or what—turned up? That nasty little sword swallower that used to polish Bishop Serifs's knob."

Startled, Else blurted, "Osa Stile? The catamite?"

"I thought his name was Armand."

"You're right. Stile. Where did I get that? He's here? How did that happen?"

"He's hooked up with one of them Collegium characters. One of the really quiet, spooky, shadowy old ones." Meaning one of the more powerful Principatés when it came to working the Instrumentalities of the Night. One of those men for whom the Night was a place of romance and adventure, not a realm of terror. Which suited Osa's spy role perfectly.

The Collegium was the stoutest bulwark that Sublime could place between himself and the ambitions of Johannes Blackboots. But his party held only that narrowest of edges there. Ferris Renfrow would want to keep a close eye on the Collegium.

"Watch him, Pinkus. There's more to that boy than meets the eye."

"Yeah. Any chance we'll do anything but sit here?"

Back to that. "Not if I can help it. If you're feeling suicidal, though, I'll give you a note introducing you to Starkden and Masant al-Seyhan."

"Bored is the word. Not suicidal."

"Bored? You don't have enough work to keep you busy?"

"I've got plenty. Don't go getting no silly-ass ideas about piling on. But I am a man of action."

"Pinkus, I've never seen you make the least effort to put yourself in harm's way."

"Yeah. But a guy does get antsy when all he does is sit."

"Sitting pays exactly the same as getting pieces chopped off."

"When you put it that way . . ."

"Bottom line, Pinkus. Final sums. Getting out of all this alive. Staggering under the weight of all the treasure. That's what I want."

"In that order, old buddy. Alive first, then rich."

"And after we're done here?"

"I go back to Brothe and be Doneto's number-one guy. You go be the Collegium's best boy. Maybe in charge of some permanent Patriarchal regiment. We're in, Pipe. Long as we don't fuck up."

"That's true. That is true." He had Drocker as his mentor and champion.

"You sigh, Pipe."

"I sigh. Because we're good soldiers. And nobody will remember that."

THE WEATHER SOFTENED. THE PATRIARCHAL TROOPS LEFT their shelters to resume work on raising a palisade just outside the reach of Praman artillery. Else wanted the circumvallation extended in both directions. King Peter appeared disinclined to come within sight of al-Khazen on his end.

Grade Drocker preferred to ignore the Direcian-Connecten army. Those people had done their part. And then they had snapped up way more than their share of the spoils. "If I had my way, we'd make the Connectens storm al-Khazen so they get used up."

Else did not venture an opinion. Later he enjoyed a tense discussion with Titus Consent. Consent had begun to understand his own value. And that had begun to go to his head.

"This isn't a threat," Else told him. "I don't do that. But the man in charge here does. And he has no love for anything Devedian. And isn't just hard and smart, but deep. He's watching you."

Not humbled, Consent said, "Your leaders have been complaining about us wasting food on the people who got driven out of the city."

"Ignore the whining. Those Deves helped us. A lot."

"As you command, Colonel."

"You don't like the way things are, take it up with the Brotherhood."

Titus Consent went away because Sublime's devoted Principatés had found the commander of the city regiment.

Divino Bruglioni isolated Else. "There's something I've wanted to ask for some time, Hecht."

"Sir?"

"It's about the reward purse Paludan was supposed to give you before you came to the Collegium."

"Yes?" This would be about the ring.

"You know I gave him that to give to you?"

"Thank you, then. A man needs affirmation of his work— even if the only measure is coin."

"True. But . . . How do I phrase this? Straightforward is the only way. Did you find a ring in that purse? It would be plain gold, well worn, rather old. Nothing special. But of sentimental value to me. It came to me from my grandfather, who got it from his. I've been trying to find it for months. I know I had it when I made up that purse. I can't remember seeing it since."

"Ah." Else said, "There *was* a ring. A gold band. And some foreign coins. I sold it all to a money changer who said he'd resell everything to his nephew the goldsmith. He was making something for the Patriarch's mother."

Divino Bruglioni spat a curse. "That damned tiara! . . . I know who . . . How could you? Sainted Founders! The Fates are heartless."

"What did I do, Your Grace?" A Prince of the Church whining about the cruelty of pagan forces?

"Hell, nothing. You couldn't know the ring wasn't part of your reward."

"You've lost me completely, Your Grace."

"No doubt. I fibbed. The ring was special. It was magic, in lay terms."

"Wow! Like in stories?"

"No. Not like in stories. I don't suppose the man you sold it to might be one of our Devedians here?"

"No. He was more exotic. I think he was Dainshau. And at least eighty years old. I needed a translator. He was from the old country."

"Dainshaukin all try to make you think that, Hecht. Their purported inability to speak the language gives them an edge. You'd be stunned at how fast they learn when there's money to be made."

"A magic ring? Really?"

"Really."

"I never believed in them." Else wondered how many times Polo had searched his things.

"Most people don't. Most urbanites have no idea what goes on in the wider world. They'd void their bowels if they were aware of a tenth of what they can't see."

"You're scaring me, Your Grace. What did the ring do?"

"Its main power is that it makes itself and whoever is wearing it hard to notice. By creatures of the Night. If I put it on I could stand amid a pack of Night wolves and they wouldn't notice me. But the ring also affects whoever uses it. You forget about it. Then you lose it."

"That's what happened to you?"

"Exactly."

"I'm sorry, Your Grace. I can see where that would be a handy trinket. I'll take you to see that Dainshau when we get back to Brothe. Just in case the ring didn't get melted down."

"There wouldn't be much point. He'll have forgotten the whole incident, probably."

Excellent. The perfect excuse registered for him, up front. "I'm sorry."

"Stop saying that. Never mind. Tell me. Is there any plan to do anything but sit here and freeze our butts off?"

"The weather should start growing warmer before too much longer."

"I mean, will we do anything about al-Khazen? Besides sit here?"

"Not if I can help it. Time is the best weapon we have. They get weaker every day. A few of them defect every day. Defections will increase once they hear we're letting the common soldiers go home to their farms and families."

"I'm not sure I like that."

"It's something my great uncle taught me. Always show your enemy a Golden Path. A way out that gives him a chance to get away. Because if he's sure you're going to kill him, he's going to make you work real hard to get it done. He's going to hurt you bad."

A runner came, whispered in the Principaté's ear. "I see," Bruglioni said. "Yes. I'll be there right away." Once the messenger was out of earshot, Divino said, "There's an Imperial delegation headed our way. They've been getting hurt by the Praman sorcerers. They want to know how to ease the pain. And get some sleep at night."

Uncle Divino hurried away. Else retreated to his quarters. Why was the Emperor not better prepared? The man had Ferris Renfrow covering his back.

Else decided to nap while the opportunity was there.

Polo wakened him, it seemed only moments later. "They're coming, Colonel."

"Who?"

"The Imperials. They'll pass right by us."

Fine. Drocker would have them led through the camp to impress them. "Let's sneak a look, then."

Polo bounced outside, stood gawking in the bitter wind. Else held back because it *was* cold out there. And he needed Polo's help to get into his heavy winter blouse.

The clatter and rattle of tack and armor, and the rumble of hooves impacting cold mud, moved nearer. Else decided to stay right where he was. Ferris Renfrow would be with this bunch for sure. Else did not want to attract Renfrow's notice.

He opened shutters a crack. And spotted Renfrow immediately, along with several Braunsknechts from last year. The nameless captain rode at Crown Prince Lothar's right hand.

Lothar! Rumor said Johannes had his children with him. Else had not believed it. Why take the risk? But here was the weakest of the three, leading a delegation, getting a chance to show what he could do.

Else was deeply disappointed. Helspeth Ege had not accompanied her little brother. Then he was embarrassed by his disappointment.

"Polo! Get in here!"

"Colonel?"

"Inside. Now. I need you." Else sealed the shutters and hoped the Imperials would not investigate.

"Colonel?" Polo sounded concerned. There were moments when Else suspected him of caring.

"Polo . . . that rabbit . . . I've got stomach cramps. This is bad. Get Captain . . . Ghort back. He'll have to . . . stand in for the regiment. This is going to start . . . coming out the other end soon."

"Sir? Are you sure?"

Else groaned. "Polo, if you don't get Ghort in here in the next . . . three minutes I'm going to find you a . . . Oh! A special assignment with the people who manage the drayage teams." Polo had met Just Plain Joe. "Do . . . Uhn! Do you really want to improve your skills . . . with a shovel?"

That kind of work—and there was a lot of it because this force included more animals than it did men—was handled by Calziran day laborers. Polo did not know that. Polo did not wander around seeing who was doing what.

"I'm on my way, Colonel."

While Polo was away Else thought up an errand the man could handle after he returned with Ghort.

"What's up, Pipe?" Ghort asked, but not until Polo had scampered away.

"Is he gone? For sure?"

"Yeah. Tell me. I ate the same stuff you did."

"There are a couple of nightmares out of my past in that bunch that just rode in. I don't want to run into them until I have time to change my look."

"You already changed a lot since I met you."

"Yes. But by changing back to what I looked like before I headed south. Look. I don't want to talk. I've already told you more than you need to know. Go to the meeting. Stay out of the way. Don't tell anybody anything unless they ask. Nobody but Drocker, Uncle Divino, and Principaté Doneto are likely to miss me. If they do ask, say it looks like food poisoning. Or maybe regular poisoning, since you ate with me."

"Sure." Ghort grinned. "Which ones don't you want to see?"

"You don't need to know that."

"I figured that's what you'd say."

Else pretended to be exasperated. "Just go be the eyes and ears of the regiment."

"I'll put on a show."

"No. Don't be Pinkus Ghort. Be invisible. They might not miss me."

"There's some wishful thinking that maybe turned up in a too-much-wine dream. All right, Pipe. Anybody asks, you're dyin' of the drizzlin' shits. I'll beg them to use their powers to save you. I'll get them to burn Polo at the stake for poisoning you."

"Pinkus."

"I'm calm. Your ass is covered. If anybody notices you're missing."

"There you go. That's what I wanted to hear."

Ghort went off to do his job.

Else did not want to participate in any meeting with a delegation that included men who had shared a meal with Sir Aelford daSkees in the Sonsan factor house in Runch.

THE ENEMY IN AL-KHAZEN COULD SPY ON THE IMPERIAL CAMP, some. The Emperor had failed to enlist any major sorcerers. The Patriarchal forces, though, enjoyed the protection of two dozen members of the Collegium. They kept turning up, determined to grab some of the glory.

The Pramans were intimate with the Instrumentalities of the Night. Their chieftains recognized a huge opportunity when they learned that a delegation had been sent to confer with Sublime's crusader commanders.

Hansel held just a quarter of the siege line. His works were not close to the city. They were not connected with the crusader works, nor were they as well developed. That despite the fact that his troops, with Vondera Koterba's contingent, substantially outnumbered those of the Patriarchy. But Hansel had had to leave numerous garrisons behind. The falls of al-Healta and al-Stikla were too recent for the troops there to break away and join the siege of the last Praman stronghold.

Starkden and Masant al-Seyhan, and the wickedness that

stood behind them, were not discomfited by Johannes Blackboots. They were not worried by the surprisingly professional and competent force fielded by Sublime V. Nor
were they rattled by the dramatic successes of the King of
Navaya.

The sorcerers of al-Khazen struck where they were least
expected.

"PIPE."

It was the middle of the night. Nobody honest had any excuse to be up. "What?" Ghort sounded stressed.

"Bad news from the Imperial side. No details yet but it
sounds like some important folks got themselves ambushed
and captured. Including the Emperor's daughters."

Once that sank in, Else said, "Makes me wish I was a swearing man. How do we know?"

"We seem to have Deves under every bed. I got it from the
dwarf. His people overheard the delegation fussing about it.
Messengers are coming and going. Drocker has demanded an
explanation from the Imperials."

"He hasn't interfered, has he?"

"Not yet."

"That wouldn't be polite."

"The Brotherhood aren't fond of the Empire. The Emperors
won't put up with their crap."

"And *vice versa*. Drocker isn't stupid. He won't anger the
Emperor needlessly. If Hansel got mad enough he might create
his own Patriarch, or bring Immaculate back from Viscesment."

"How's your health?"

"Not getting any better."

"Drocker wanted to come over and heal you himself."

"I'll suffer a miracle recovery once the Imperials go away."
He did not ask how the conference had gone. He had had reports. The Deves did have an ear under every chair. Hansel had
two things on his mind. How to get the Patriarchal troops to do
most of the dying if any fighting took place and how to screw
Peter of Navaya out of his conquests.

"Keep your ear to the ground. Come back when you get
some real details."

Else next wakened to the clatter of the Imperial delegation moving out, Lothar and his advisers grimly serious.

An hour later a groggy Pinkus Ghort reappeared, accompanied by Gledius Stewpo and Titus Consent.

"We been took, Pipe."

"Huh?"

"Well, those guys. Lothar and his bunch. Those messages they got were fakes."

"What?" Else tried to rub the sleep out of his eyes. Somewhere, Polo was rattling pots.

"That business about the daughters. It was a hoax. By the guys in the city over there. Once the Principatés got to work they found out that Johannes and his family are snoring happily in a castle fifteen miles southeast of here. There never was any problem. The messages were all fakes."

"How long since the prince left? Any chance we can get help to him?"

"It's been over an hour. He was in a hurry. I sent riders but I don't think they'll catch him in time."

Else pictured a map, tried to judge the crown prince's location and where the Pramans were likely to attack. "You're right. But the Pramans will have to stray pretty far away from safety. Get the commando company ready. There's a good chance we can get between the bad guys and the city. What are the Brotherhood and the Principatés doing?"

Ghort shrugged. "The Principatés are running in circles and yelling."

"They should be trying to protect Lothar."

"You'd think so, wouldn't you? But they're too busy worrying about how they'll look. As for the Brotherhood, I have no idea."

Consent and Stewpo remained blandly silent.

"All right. Arrange the commando thing. I'll talk to Drocker."

Titus Consent asked, "Are you feeling better, then?"

"No. But this is critical. Polo. Is that coffee ready?" Coffee caches had been discovered in several captured towns.

Fifteen minutes later, still feigning intestinal discomfort, Else joined Grade Drocker. "My Deves tell me there's huge mischief afoot. Coffee?"

"No. Thank you. I don't indulge. That's probably why you've got the stomach problem. Can you do your job?"

"I'll do what has to be done." He explained what he had done already.

Drocker nodded. "Good. But hold off. I've already sent my men to do exactly that. We don't want yours tripping over mine. Plus, yours aren't equipped. Mine are used to operating in environments where the Instrumentalities of the Night are active."

"A good point. I hadn't thought of that."

"I'm not making a grab for the glory."

"I understand. You're right."

"Fear not. Lothar may be in less danger than you think. His party included two Brothers from the Special Office. They'll be an unpleasant surprise for the Unbeliever."

"That's good to hear."

There would be interesting confrontations out there. Given remote help by the Principatés, those Brotherhood operatives might fend off Starkden and Masant el-Seyhan. But the Brothers might be surprised themselves.

The men sent to capture Lothar would be Sha-lug.

Else asked, "Do you have time to tell me about the Imperial delegation?"

"See Bechter. He'll fill you in. And lend you a messenger so you can call off your hounds."

"I brought my man Polo. He can run the message. Where do I find Sergeant Bechter?"

ELSE TOLD POLO, "FIND CAPTAIN GHORT. TELL HIM WE'VE been overruled on the rescue attempt but that I want the commando company ready to go anyway. Can you do that?"

Polo bobbed his head eagerly.

"Get going."

"WHERE HAVE YOU BEEN?" DROCKER ASKED.

"Latrine." And he had been.

"That long? Here. Take this. In ten ounces of warm water. I need you working, not riding the Holey Pine."

Unnerved by Drocker's jest, Else accepted the packet. "I'll

be right back." He went away, made a show of following instructions, rejoined the Brotherhood sorcerer. "Does that stuff cause cramps? Because I had a good case before I took it."

"You may have a wind problem for a while. Unless you're so sick that nothing will save you. Sit. Get comfortable. The old ladies from the Collegium are supposed to let us know what's happening out there."

Else nodded, then said, "Sir . . . I've noticed that you're getting better at speaking. Seemingly at cost to your physical well-being."

"I'm touched by your concern, Hecht. But you're wasting emotion. I know what I'm doing—though that may not serve the survival of this flesh."

"Sir, I . . ."

"This worldly cask doesn't matter, Hecht. I would've shed it ere now had I been able to bring you into the Brotherhood. You don't recognize it but you're exactly the sort of man to see our faith through the worst tribulations, then boldly carry God's standard to the Wells of Ihrian."

"Sir? You . . . I . . ."

"The problem is that your commitment to the faith isn't of a depth equaling your abilities to inspire men to accomplish a common goal."

"Sir . . . Sir, you're straining yourself needlessly. You're fooling yourself, too, I think. I'm just a displaced foreigner who's been lucky. Captain Ghort would've done just as well."

"Perhaps." Drocker began to show the strain. "Think about what I've said. Talk to God. Consult your conscience."

Wishing he could go inside Drocker's head, Else said, "God's Will be done."

"Go. Do what you're thinking of doing. Without straying too far from a latrine."

There were no witnesses to this meeting. Else left it thoroughly puzzled. Clearly, Drocker was trying to manipulate him in several directions.

Worthy of reflection.

"PINKUS. WHERE ARE WE?" FIRST COLORS OF FALSE DAWN were creeping over the eastern hills. Shortly, the advantage

440   GLEN COOK

would no longer rest with those whose loyalties hinged on the
things of the Night. "Ready to go?"

"What did Drocker say?"

"You wouldn't believe me if I told you. He did hint that he'd
be looking some other way if we decided to go into the Imperial rescue business."

"Oh? Meaning?"

"Meaning the guy has a private agenda. And he thinks we
can help him get where he wants to go."

"What do you think?"

"I intend to take advantage. Now, what have you got?"

Ghort laid out a detailed plan for a raid into al-Khazen itself,
through the storm water drain found by the Principatés.

"You put this together in three hours?"

"Hell, no. I been working on this since they found that drain.
Just in case."

"Interesting. I see a lot of Deves on your manpower table.
Especially in your reserve."

"Yeah. Who do you think will fight the hardest when we get
there?"

"We?"

Ghort grinned. "You ain't gonna stay behind, are you?"

"Too many people are getting to know me too well." Else reviewed Ghort's plan. It was sound. It included two strong reserve companies meant to extricate the main force if it got into
trouble. "Only thing missing is the name of the Principaté
who'll be going with us."

"Bronte Doneto. But you knew that."

"I guessed. Besides him being your main guy, he's one of
only about three of them spry enough to make the trip. Will
he go?"

"Even if Grade Drocker vetoes it."

"He's got an angle of his own, then."

"They all have, all the time."

"Only one question left, then. Who do we leave in charge
here?"

"I'm thinking the Deve kid. Titus Consent."

"Nobody will stand for that. Not for long. Not even his own
people."

"Exactly. And he won't be underfoot out there with us."

"How soon can we start?"

"Less than an hour."

"I'll go see if Polo wants to go on an adventure."

POLO'S HUNGER FOR ADVENTURE HAD BEEN SLAKED. HE WAS willing to stay in camp and keep an eye on Titus Consent. Else chuckled as he eased down an icy rock face into a gully that would let the raiders approach al-Khazen unseen by watchers on the wall. Ghort had scouted well. Snow in the gully made for slow going, though.

Ghort walked point. Twenty-six men followed, including Else and Bronte Doneto. Doneto was uncomfortable surrounded by so many Devedian fighters. The reserve force fell behind, slowed by elderly but feisty members of the Collegium. Divino Bruglioni was among them, riding in a sedan chair.

Ghort led the band up out of the gully and ordered a halt. "We need the sun to move a little so we'll have better shadows."

"Why?" Doneto asked.

"We need to cross this ridge and slide down the other side. We'll be visible from the wall. Until we have the cover of those shadows. Or we could wait till dark. When the enemy would have his nighttime eyes."

"I see. Good work, Captain."

Good work indeed, Else thought. Ghort showed unexpected flashes of competence. Given his head in an elite crew he might amount to something. "Pinkus, you could make yourself the next Adolf Black."

"I could cut my own throat here and save the world the trouble, too."

Sensitive. "How long?" Else hoped to get inside the city before the crown prince's captors.

What then? Become Sublime's leading field officer? That would be good. He could do so much. . . . But the risks were rising. Those Brothers from Runch . . . He *had* to stop looking like Sir Aelford daSkees—without arousing curiosity here.

"Now," Ghort said. "One man at a time. Stay in the shadows, against the rocks, and go slow till you can't see the wall anymore."

"What about pickets?" Else asked.

"Patrols haven't run into any lately. The top guys over there are afraid they'll keep on going once they get outside the gates."

Calziran soldiers still succeeded in deserting frequently.

The band assembled at the foot of the slope. Ghort was the last man down. While they gathered, Else asked Principaté Doneto what the Brotherhood company was doing. And how the Emperor was responding to the news. Ferris Renfrow, too.

Doneto told him, "You clearly don't know how things work. I can't just snap my fingers and have some know-all devil tell me whatever I want to know. I wish it did work that way. A man who could find out anything could rule the world."

"You don't know anything, then?"

"I wouldn't say that. Just nothing useful."

"I suppose not." Else watched Ghort get the troops moving again.

The next point of risk lay a hundred yards from the base of the wall. Ghort said, "If they're alert we will have to wait till dark."

Bronte Doneto said, "There isn't anyone there."

"Your Grace?"

"Look. There's nobody on the wall. No. I don't know why. Maybe because it's so damned cold. Maybe because they don't think it's worth the bother. Maybe because they've all gone to see something else."

"You sure?" Ghort demanded.

"At this range? Look. Your eyes are better than mine."

"Not exactly a sure thing, then. Oh, well. Follow me."

The band pushed through brush and clutter into the mouth of the storm drain, enjoying cold, wet feet and plenty of stink. The arched drain was four feet high and five wide. It had been roomier. The floor was deep in muck and detritus washed down from above.

Else crept forward, wondering when the trap would snap. Although that drainage outlet had been hidden by ages of overgrowth, and although most fortresses and cities that were captured were first penetrated by some similar means, Else did not want to believe that Sha-lug could be so sloppy.

There were partial collapses that, however, had not impeded

drainage much. The slope was steep enough to wash most detritus past the choke points. Nevertheless, many hours went into conquering the drain.

Else stayed close to Bronte Doneto, out of Ghort's way. Pinkus seemed to know what to do and did it well. Else asked, "How are we doing, Your Grace?" He croaked his words. The fetor was overwhelming.

"They don't seem to be aware of us yet. But there's a lot of excitement. It's getting dark. I should have a better idea what's going on, soon."

Else went forward to help move fallen stonework. He told Ghort, "I hope I'm in half as good a shape as him when I'm a thousand."

"How old are you, Pipe?"

Else Tage was not sure. He did know that Piper Hecht would have no doubts. "Thirty-three. And six days. Unless my mother was a liar."

"You just worry about making it to thirty-three and seven, not no thousand. You shitting me? You had a birthday the other day and you never told anybody?"

"It's not important." And in Dreanger, amongst Sha-lug, it was not. There, you celebrated the anniversary of your ascension into the full rights and responsibilities of a warrior slave of the Kaif of al-Minphet.

"Shit, Pipe. I don't believe you're real. Hey! Look at this."

"This" was a larger, taller space where half a dozen lesser drains collected. Only one was big enough to let a man through.

Ghort said, "You're a skinny little rat, Zalno. Take a candle and slither up that drain." Then he observed, "This isn't looking so good, now. Unless we find how workmen used to get in and out."

Bronte Doneto announced, "There's a celebration starting up there. The Pramans think that having Lothar will turn everything around."

"Where are they holding him?" Else asked. He knew al-Khazen as well as a man could from maps.

"He isn't here yet. They're in a running fight with the Brotherhood. Have been all day."

Ghort said, "That puts us in better shape than I hoped.

They'll all be focused on that kid and how to use him to confound the work of the Lord."

Even Doneto seemed taken aback by Ghort's sudden passion. He grinned. "Got you going, eh? But am I wrong? Principaté, what we need is a way out of here. When you guys found this, back when, you said there was one."

Zalno came sliding out of the large drain. His candle had gone out. He had a gray cast to him. He did not like being in tight places in the dark. He rasped, "That goes on for maybe a hundred feet, uphill, curves left, goes past these big cistern things. There's ladders in those. It goes on to the downhill end of a dead-end street that looks like it runs through the middle of everything."

Ghort asked, "Can we get out that way?"

Zalno glanced around. "I could. Some of you would have to be greased up, though. All the water from this one long street is supposed to run down to this drain thing that's about ten inches high by three feet wide."

"Say no more," Ghort said. "I've got you. Can we get into the cisterns?"

"Yes, sir."

"Good. We're on our way."

Fifteen minutes later Else peered out the cracked doorway of what his memorized maps labeled Waterhouse Four. By twilight al-Khazen appeared to be an abandoned ruin. Nothing bigger than a rat moved or made a sound.

"Move! Sir," someone said behind him.

There was not much room. People were supposed to come get water and go.

Else slipped outside, followed Ghort. "You know where we are, Pinkus? This is almost too good to be true."

The party moved into a cramped structure that, until recently, had housed Devedian jewelers, letter writers, and moneylenders.

"Pinkus, you've done an incredible job."

"But you're gonna take it away from me now, eh?"

"In part, yes."

"You're the boss, Pipe."

"What were you going to do next?"

"Me?" Ghort grinned. "You want the truth?"

"Yes."

"I figured whoever was tagging along, you or somebody from the Collegium, would take it away from me before this."

"Eis's balls, Pinkus, you're the sorriest, most cynical bastard on the face of the earth."

"Does that make me wrong?"

"No. Principaté. What's the story now? Does it look like we can steal Lothar back and make the Grail Emperor love us?"

"Yes. And no. And yes. And no."

Ghort said, "Women love a man who's confident and knows right where he stands."

Doneto gave Ghort a look that suggested the Principaté was considering rendering him down for fat.

"I take it back if I'm wrong."

Doneto told Else, "We're perfectly positioned. When they bring their captives in they have to pass by here to reach the palace and the citadel. We can jump them, grab Lothar, and run like hell. I'd leave booby traps to slow them down while we escape back to our covering force."

"That sounds just plain totally alluring," Ghort said.

Else scowled. He was in that cleft between Else Tage and Piper Hecht. "Can you tell what the Brotherhood has managed to do?"

"No. Sit down and be quiet."

Time passed. Else napped. A hand shook him. He found Ghort and Doneto looming over him.

Doneto murmured, "The Pramans have shaken the Brotherhood. They kept hold of their prisoners. They'll arrive soon. There's less celebration, now. They got hurt, badly. As you might expect, seeing they had to break through a band hand-picked by Grade Drocker."

Pinkus Ghort asked, "How many people do we need to rescue?"

Doneto ignored him.

Else asked, "How many of them were there?" He recalled seeing about twenty pass the wine-pressing house.

Still, Doneto said nothing. Else prodded. "Is it a secret, Your Grace?"

"I don't know," Doneto snapped. "There should be seven prisoners. Most all wounded."

That made sense. The Braunsknechts would not give up without a fight. "Now we're getting somewhere," Else said. "What else? We're going to be in a fight in a while. What you hold back might get us all killed."

Scowling, dejected at having to share any knowledge with anyone, Doneto replied, "There were nineteen men with Lothar. Two were his servants. Two were priests. Two were Brotherhood of War. Ten were Braunsknechts. The rest were more mysterious. Though we saw them in Plemenza."

"Ferris Renfrow. Of course. The Emperor's head spy. He was under foot a lot when we were getting ready for this squabble."

"Yes. I don't think he's one of the captives."

The Sha-lug who captured Lothar, Else believed, deserved the greatest honor.

Else asked, "Do you know anything that might be useful now?" His tone informed the whole band that he was straining to remain patient. "Reminding you, what you don't say could get you dead with the rest of us."

Doneto said, "They're sending out more of their best men to cover the raiders. For their trouble they're getting Lothar, a priest who made no effort to avoid capture, two half-dead brothers from the cult of war, and several Braunsknechts in equally bad shape, still alive only because those in charge want to interrogate them."

Doneto intoned, "Tell me about that building there. Two up and across the street. It feels empty."

"It should be," Else said. "It was the Dainshau temple and exchange. They abandoned it after the Unbelievers arrived."

"Do you know every building in the city, Hecht?"

"Only the ones that the refugees said were important."

"Suppose some of us occupy that building and the rest stay here. The ones over there hit first. Then those of us here snatch Lothar once the Pramans start to react there. They'll be feeling safe and relaxed. We can hit and get."

Else was not pleased. But he was no Grade Drocker. He could not tell a Principaté to shut up and get out of the way. "Pinkus, you'd better warn the reserves to be ready."

"That's their job, Pipe. They're on it now."

Else asked Doneto, "Can you tell, is that building really

empty? There have been a lot of cold, snowy nights since the Dainshaukin fled."

"Go check," Doneto suggested. "If nobody cuts your throat, it's safe."

Else did exactly that. But alone. He could pass himself off as a Dreangerean for as long as it took to become invisible again.

The Dainshau structure had not remained empty. Soldiers had moved in but were not at home now. But, as Else was about to summon reinforcements, the Pramans with the Imperial prisoners appeared.

Else muttered, "Pinkus, I hope you have smarts enough to manage."

Of course he did. A better question might be, would Doneto refrain from interfering?

The Pramans were not alert. And why should they be, deep inside their own stronghold, when they were now confident of their ultimate victory? They were hurrying, in no formation, cracking the dark jokes men make after they have stuck a thumb in Death's eye and gotten away. The first dozen wore Lucidian helmets and rags that had started out as the uniform clothing of Indala al-Sul Halaladin's home cavalry. Next came the prisoners, in the care of Mafti al-Araj el-Arak's lifeguards. Eight or nine Sha-lug brought up the rear.

Something dark and noisome rose from the cobblestones in front of the Lucidians. The stench made Else want to retch. Then Ghort struck from the downhill side. The Lucidians and Calzirans panicked. The Sha-lug were less affected. Even so, Else was embarrassed by their feeble resistance.

Ghort reclaimed the prisoners with little effort.

Many of the fleeing Pramans ran into the building whence Else was watching.

A second stinking shadow hoisted itself up in the gap between the Pramans and Ghort's raiders.

Else had no opportunity to get away. He dove into a shadowy corner, burrowed into a pile of junk and equipment needing repair, pulled some rags up to cover his face, and fought to control his breathing.

It had been a long time since he had heard his own language spoken. It took several minutes to get back into it.

There were twenty angry men within fifteen feet. Some
cursed. Some threw things. Some wanted to counterattack
right now, never mind that they had no idea what they faced.
Never mind that they were so exhausted that they could barely
stand.

A hand passed through Else's limited field of vision. It
grabbed a broken saddle from near his hidden feet, flipped it
onto its side. A man sat down. He panted, having trouble
breathing. He slumped in defeat and a despair beneath which
lay anger like molten stone. The man believed he had been
misused, wasted, possibly even betrayed.

The twenty were a mixture of Lucidians, Calzirans, and
Sha-lug. They went out again after a few minutes. The man
seated on the saddle did not join them. Those who spoke to
him received only grunts in response.

This was the man in charge, Else realized. And he was hurt.
He did try to follow the others but did not have the strength.

Else slapped a hand across the wounded man's mouth as he
came out of hiding. He would do no harm if he could help it.
Then he gasped. "Bone?"

The wounded man looked at Else like he had met his own
ghost.

Else turned. "Bone? That is you, isn't it?"

"Captain Tage? But you're dead. For more than a year."

"Hunh. I hadn't heard. When did this happen?"

"They said you were killed by an infidel sorcerer the day
you landed in Firaldia."

"They did? Interesting." Inasmuch as he had been sending
reports until the city regiment left Brothe. "Who would that
'they' be?"

"Er-Rashal, Captain. He told everybody. The Marshall was
seriously disappointed, mostly because he didn't get more use
out of you. He wasn't sorry you were dead."

Else's deepest, most secret suspicions seemed confirmed.
"Is that our company out there?"

"What's left. And some Lucidians and natives we've been
working with. Captain, I'm pretty sure we're here to get wiped
out. We get all the worst jobs. We keep losing men. We left Az
out there somewhere this time."

"I don't want anyone to know I survived. Not yet. The third

sorcerer. The mystery man. That would be er-Rashal himself. Right?"

"Uh . . . Yes. But how could you know?"

"You know. And probably shouldn't. Right? Bone, we know almost everything there is to know, over there. We have copies of the pay lists of the Calziran companies."

"The Deves."

"They aren't happy about how they were treated here."

"You said 'we.' Who are you now, Captain?"

"Still Else Tage. Your Captain. I was given an assignment. I'm living it. I've had tremendous success, news of which apparently hasn't gotten back to al-Qarn." Else shielded Bone from details the man might be tempted to pass along.

"Bone, I have no idea what er-Rashal is up to. He's managed to waste Dreanger's fleet and a lot of Sha-lug. He isn't going to win here. He seems blind to the real situation. Do us both a favor. Get out before he gets you killed. Get out and carry the word back to al-Qarn."

Bone looked distinctly uncomfortable. Pained in his heart and flesh. "Can't, Captain. We swore the oath. We all did, back when we thought this would stop the crusaders from coming."

Else did not argue. This kind of commitment might seem foolhardy but it was critical to Sha-lug. "Will his death release you?"

"Yes."

Else rested a hand on his old friend's shoulder. "Don't chase us tonight, Bone. Don't make us kill you when we come back. I'm leaving, now. Forget you saw me."

Else darted out of the temple. There was action around Waterhouse Four but the big racket was somewhere else, off to the east.

Else caught snatches before he clambered down into the cistern of Waterhouse Two. Braunsknechts had seized a gate. Imperial troops were in the city.

Else's escape attempt ended quickly. Scores of Pramans had gotten into the drainage system through Waterhouse Four, chasing the raiders. Else stayed where he was, hoping to go unnoticed, wishing he wore less distinctively Chaldarean clothing.

34. Stalkers' Hour

Only Arlensul's encouragement kept Svavar going. He was ready to put this whole mad world behind. People by the hundred were dying over religious differences he found incomprehensible.

Shagot only added to his misery. Grim seemed incapable of not attracting attention when he was awake. Though that problem did ease once Imperial forces settled east of al-Khazen, content to outwait their remaining enemies.

Shagot was frustrated when he was awake. The Old Ones could not locate or identify the Godslayer, though they were sure he was, probably, in the camp of the Emperor's Episcopal allies.

Shagot was little more than a *draug,* one of the walking dead from the legends of lands now lost beneath the ice. Svavar used his brother as a device to endear his band to Vondera Koterba and the Emperor.

Arlensul always warned Svavar when enemy patrols were nearby. If Shagot was awake, they would go kill some and take prisoners. Eventually, the enemy stayed away. But powerful incursions of another sort began to occur after dark.

The rumors were true. There were powerful sorcerers in the city. And the Emperor had not equipped himself to deal with them.

The Imperials were being lured to their destruction.

Arlensul planted that notion in Svavar's head. He could not keep that to himself. He told Grim and the rest of their dwindling band.

One by one, the men who had come when they followed the Emperor found an excuse to fade away. Soon there would be none left who could not imagine a better life.

Svavar and Shagot had been noticed up and down the Imperial chain of command. They were too strange and too effective to be overlooked.

Neither Svavar nor Shagot had any experience of sedentary

warfare. They did not like it. Shagot wanted to drop everything to go hunt the Godslayer.

"We need to know where he is, first," Svavar argued. "What happens if we're wandering around these hills, hunting him, and you fall asleep? I can't protect you by myself. These soldiers won't help us hunt. They don't care. But we're better off here, where misfortune is less likely to find us, till we know where to find our man."

A MESSENGER FROM VONDERA KOTERBA CAME TO THE Grimmssons' shelter. He asked Svavar, "Is your brother awake? The Emperor may need your special skills. It's possible the crown prince has been captured by the Pramans."

"I'll try to waken him," Svavar promised. "How much time do we have?"

"I'm just alerting you."

Events began to move soon afterward. Another messenger instructed them to join a force assembling outside the castle where the Emperor and his court had come to rest. Shagot was disinclined to respond.

Arlensul appeared in the doorway, bent because she was too tall. "*He* will be there."

Svavar believed her. When a goddess told you something you wanted badly to hear, you believed.

"Come on, Grim. We're there. Our man is going to be at the other end of this. Come on. Get up. It's time."

Shagot responded sluggishly, groggily. He heard but did not believe. He had had no word from the Old Ones.

When they reached the assembly point it seemed the whole army was on the move. A delegation to the Episcopals that included the crown prince had been overrun by Praman commandos during the night. Details were scant. Most of the party were believed dead, with just a handful captured.

A long column filed through the cold morning and snow, following a route marked by pioneers. Svavar and Shagot were assigned to the vanguard. They would not be cowed by the dark.

The lead troops were Hansel's best. Their progress was quieter than seemed possible, but slow. Svavar told Shagot,

"Those people won't be surprised. We're headed for a trap."

Shagot grunted. It seemed likely. It seemed so probable, in fact, that Johannes ought not to be falling for it.

Maybe the Emperor knew something no one else did.

The commanders called a halt during the afternoon. Distant fighting could be heard. The crown prince's captors making a fighting retreat, Svavar presumed. But who was harrying them?

The Emperor's scouts reported. Svavar was near enough to eavesdrop.

The crown prince was alive and unharmed. The same could not be said for most of his party. Johannes seemed more interested in the fate of Ferris Renfrow than in that of his son. But Johannes knew his son was all right.

The summons came to Svavar rather than Shagot. Johannes addressed him directly. "Soultaken, do you understand my situation?"

"I do." He experienced the thing that made Johannes Ege so much more than a little man who had lucked into a great deal of power. Hansel made people feel that they were fellow conspirators.

The Emperor asked, "You understand what they want to do to us? That they hope I'll charge into a trap?"

"I see that. And I see you giving them what they want."

"Not quite."

"There's a huge accumulation of dark power behind those walls. The Tyranny of the Night is complete, though the fighters probably don't know."

"Complete? I doubt that. However. Those forces are unaware of you and your brother."

Svavar waited, calm and fearless. He felt the proximity of Arlensul. She lent him courage and confidence.

"I understand what you are. You serve the Instrumentalities of the Night. You're here to accomplish a particular task. It has little to do with the ambitions of those holding al-Khazen."

Svavar did not respond.

"If you help me here, now, I'll throw the weight of the Empire behind you in your mission."

Svavar felt Arlensul would want him to agree. "We'll help, then. In exchange. We won't tolerate . . ."

"Johannes Ege never. . . . Enough. I need entry into that city. And someone who can distract the powers there while I do what I have to do."

Svavar cocked his head, listening.

Arlensul encouraged him.

"We can do what you want done."

Whatever the denizens of the city planned, whatever engines of despair lurked behind those walls, a Chooser of the Slain was no part of their calculations.

THE DAUGHTER OF THE GRAY WALKER WAS CLEARLY VISIBLE for half a minute. Imperial soldiers saw her. Praman soldiers saw her. Mute wood and stone beheld her. Svavar worried that far powers in the Great Sky Fortress might mark her presence as well. Shagot might see her. But he had to trust her. Over the months he had become her ally completely.

Shagot remained unaware of her.

The event at el-Khazen's eastern portal was so violent that not only did the gates cease to be a barrier, the entire barbican and fifteen yards of wall to either hand collapsed. Imperial troops rushed into al-Khazen, encouraged by the Emperor to obliterate anyone and anything not Crown Prince Lothar.

Svavar and Shagot were first to enter the city, Shagot holding that demon head in front of him. Howling devil faces swarmed them—and fled away, repelled by Arlensul. The fury of the assault increased. Svavar was impressed. The sorcerers here were truly terrible. He was fortunate to have a Chooser of the Slain for a guardian angel.

He nudged Shagot whenever a course change became necessary. He was surprised that they did not need to head for the citadel. Not after they covered the first quarter mile.

The Grimmsson brothers fought inside a bubble of invincibility. That did not extend far. Outside it the battle was harsh. It was dark out there. The onslaught of the Night was terrible. The Imperials remained steadfast only because of the power of the soultaken.

As blood flowed, Shagot became more awake and alert and connected to the Great Sky Fortress. Where, Svavar guessed, the Old Ones were becoming more awake and alert and connected themselves.

Shagot carved up three Pramans in a blur of haunted bronze. Done, he asked, "What's going on, Little Brother?"

"We're helping Johannes get his son back from the Pramans." The Emperor was a short distance away, rising boldly above the chaos on his charger, Warspite. "After which he'll devote all his power to helping us find our man."

Shagot seemed doubtful. But his connection with the Great Sky Fortress was strong, now. "This way. He was here not long ago. He went this way."

Wow, Svavar thought. He looked for Arlensul, did not see her but suspected that she was the force stemming the tide of darkness rolling down from the citadel.

The Praman soldiers fled. Their dark sorcery was less powerful than that attacking them.

Shagot said, "This way. The raiders went this way."

"What raiders, Grim?"

A commando band from the Patriarchal army had ambushed Lothar's captors and claimed their prize.

Johannes flew into a scarlet rage. He sent couriers to hasten the arrival of the rest of his army. He would purge al-Khazen of the Unbeliever, then he would find his son.

Shagot entered a low, square stone building that stood by itself. It had unglazed windows and doorways without doors.

Svavar asked, "What's this?"

"A well house. The women come here to get water." Shagot looked down into the cistern. "They climbed down here." An iron ladder going down into the cistern had had the rust worn away. Blood discolored its rungs.

A face appeared below. A Praman face. It betrayed astonishment and terror. It disappeared, shrieking a warning.

Shagot swung over the lip of the well and jumped down. Svavar cursed and followed more carefully. At first, the Braunsknechts refused to go down into the earth.

The Emperor entered the waterhouse. He grasped the situation immediately. He gave orders for troops to circle west of the city in search of a storm water outlet. Below, the soultaken engaged the hindmost of those Pramans who had chased the Episcopal raiders underground.

Hansel stamped out of the waterhouse. He swung onto Warspite's back. For an instant he stared uphill, toward the citadel. He would aim the soultaken that way next.

As he flexed his wrists to shake the reins to urge Warspite forward, an arrow out of the darkness entered his open mouth. Its head severed his spinal cord as it exited the back of his neck.

35. With the Direcian Combine: Cold Spring

The winter was long and bitter but not inconvenient for the combined forces of Direcia, Platadura, and the Connec. They did little but stay warm and get to know the people of Calzir. They saw no fighting.

Brother Candle did not feel he was part of a real war. He had become part of the court round King Peter, in the castle al-Negesi, atop an eminence from which, on a clear day, the hills where al-Khazen lay could be discerned. Peter felt no need to move closer. The Pramans were unable to overawe the forces already facing them.

Brother Candle understood. Peter had tripled his territories at no cost. He had created—and continued to create—a network of personal relationships with foreign nobles and people like Brother Candle, Bishop LeCroes, Michael Carhart, and Tember Remak. The lack of danger, other than from the passage on winter seas, had lured the curious from Direcia and the End of Connec. Duke Tormond and his sister spent a month on Shippen, she enjoying her husband and he learning more about the world and the men who would stand beside him in the dark times to come. Tormond was impressed by how much Count Raymone Garete had matured.

"We'll go home come spring," Bishop LeCroes predicted. "This war is over. It's just a matter of the Pramans figuring that out and laying down their arms."

If Lucidia and Dreanger did not send reinforcements.

Brother Candle doubted the Praman world would blaze with passion for a countercrusade in Calzir. Not when wealthier and more romantic little kingdoms in Direcia were being devoured by King Peter's Reconquest to resounding indifference across the remainder of the Realm of Peace.

Brother Candle was enjoying a leisurely breakfast. Bishop LeCroes stopped to say, "Loafing season may be over. Something major is happening at al-Khazen." His voice was so strained Brother Candle went looking for a high place.

He used his elbows more than was appropriate for a Perfect. Everyone had gotten there before him, equally curious. When he got a good look in the right direction he saw what looked like a tower of black smoke rising from a huge fire a long way away. Only . . . It looked more like a small but intensely ferocious thunderstorm. "What is it?"

"The Night gone mad. Trying to devour itself. It was much gaudier when it wasn't as light out."

King Peter, Count Raymone, and a few others in a higher turret were engaged in an animated discussion.

Brother Candle had a sense of portent. The world was about to change again. Chances were, the change would not be for the better.

Peter and his cronies sent riders to find out what was happening. And couriers to alert the various garrisons that something was afoot. Inasmuch as nobody to the east was inclined to keep their overseas allies posted.

Brother Candle had little sense of the Instrumentalities of the Night. Those who did, like Michael Carhart, assured him that rural Calzir had been sucked clean of every minor spirit. The forces gathered at al-Khazen had drawn them in. The Calziran sorcerers were a mystery. The Patriarch's forces included numerous members of the Collegium. No one knew what dark forces had been marshaled on behalf of the Grail Empire.

As time fled forward Brother Candle increasingly felt his world growing colder—for any whose philosophies did not match those of they who were convinced that they ought to rule the world.

Brother Candle told Michael Carhart and Tember Remak, "I can feel the ice coming to the Connec."

They understood. Life was about to become less attractive for Maysaleans and pagans, Devedians and Dainshaus, Terliagan Pramans, and even those Episcopals daring enough to favor the Patriarch of Viscesment.

But none of them had an imagination dark enough, bleak enough, pessimistic enough, to guess how dreadful the future could become.

36. Enfolded in the Embrace of the Night

Else crouched in the dark cistern beneath Waterhouse Two, feeling like a cowering rodent, though hiding and abiding were Sha-lug skills equaling any involving sword or lance. A Sha-lug slave warrior was obligated to preserve himself, not to waste himself on heroic gestures.

Terrible fighting was going on in the drainage system. And in the city above, from the sound. Else could not follow its progress but it seemed that Imperial troops had entered the city. The combined efforts of Starkden, Masant al-Seyhan, and er-Rashal el-Dhulquarnen were inadequate to repel them.

There was sorcery afoot, for sure. Else's nearly forgotten amulet hurt more than it had at any time since the encounter in the Ownvidian Knot.

Er-Rashal not being able to do as he pleased, when it pleased him to do so, was nearly beyond the scope of imagination. Er-Rashal el-Dhulquarnen had been a distant, almost godlike presence in the Dreangerean world for as long as Else could remember. Not being able to do as he pleased likely strained the Rascal's imagination, too.

Over twenty-five years of training and wartime stress had gone into building Else Tage, the unflappable. But the unflappable Else made a noise like a startled little girl.

Something—that, initially, wore no shape familiar to the Sha-lug Else Tage . . . *Something* filled the overflow from the collection chamber below Waterhouse Two. Else felt something touch his soul, take cues from hidden recollections. Passing through several repulsive shapes first, it took the form of a woman . . . No. A girl. Heris . . . Sister of the toddler who became the Sha-lug Else Tage . . . But big. So big. Too big to push through the overflow.

That thing, whatever it was, winked. It raised a finger to its lips. Then it went away. A fog formed in the space it had occupied. The entrance became invisible.

Once his mind resumed function Else wondered how that thing fit the rest of the storm-water system if it could not get into this cistern . . . The amulet he wore reminded him that it was still there, this time blistering cold instead of hot and painful. Principaté Bruglioni's ring seemed to weigh twenty pounds.

What the hell?

Hell might have plenty to do with it. That was no woman. That was something vast and potent, far beyond human, though probably designed by human hope and fear. It would be the thing he had been warned about. A something that could brush aside the determined efforts of er-Rashal al-Dhulquarnen. One of the Instrumentalities of the Night. Possibly a goddess to some unbeliever who had not found the True God.

Cautioning Else Tage to remain calm, quiet, and still?

This was a difficult hour. He did not need a caution from the demon. Everywhere else was less safe than here. And there was little he could do to affect the situation, whatever he chose to do.

The thing left long silence in its wake. But only where Else remained hidden, behind the glamour she had cast. There was fighting in the streets above. There was fighting in the drainage system. A lot of widows would be made tonight. And Else Tage remained a blind bystander. He could not imagine becoming involved without feeling guilty. He would have to betray someone.

Eventually, he climbed back out of the cistern and deserted the waterhouse for the madness of al-Khazen's streets. Imperial troops were still arriving. Pramans fought on in hopeless desperation. Their sorcerers had failed them again, as they had at every turn since the Brothen raid.

Being cautious, avoiding confrontation, Else used memorized maps to reach a section of wall overlooking the exit from the storm-water drain. He was alone on the battlements. The rest of existence seemed focused on the struggle behind and below. Except that the thing he had seen back there now was engaged in a ferocious confrontation with al-Khazen's defending sorcerers—rather as an afterthought on her part, like a man swatting at a particularly agile horsefly.

Else stared at the moonlighted hillside below. He picked out landmarks he had seen coming in. He saw no sign of the reserve companies. Which was good. He would have been disappointed if he had.

On reflection, he was surprised that he could see much of anything, even with a moon up.

False dawn had begun to creep in from the east. Already.

How could that much time have passed?

Else was so completely alone on the wall that he considered complaining to God about being lonely. There was no one to stop him doing whatever he wanted.

He began to search for some means of getting down outside. Maybe he could escape without going through that claustrophobic drain again.

Fate conspired.

He found a coil of rope inside a guard station. It was long enough to reach the foot of the wall. It had been reworked for climbing. It was knotted at regular intervals. Someone had used it to go raiding or consorting. Or deserting.

After tying the rope off, though, Else settled down to watch. He would have no part in the events. Fortune had moved him out of the way before the excitement started.

His commandos left the storm-water drain in good order. He had no trouble recognizing Ghort, hustling Crown Prince Lothar ahead of the main party. Else wondered how Bronte Doneto would play the game now. Surely his ransom demands for Lothar would exceed those that Hansel had made for him.

Else could make out some members of the reserve companies, now. A few were too restless, too eager. But they gave nothing away. They could be seen from no other vantage point. Had there been witnesses to discover the trap, still it would have been impossible to warn its prey.

The Praman pursuit tumbled out of the drain in a mix with the slowest Brothens.

The first Pramans out, Sha-lug and Calziran royal lifeguards, showed little interest in the people ahead of them, except to mark what direction they ran before selecting an alternate line of flight.

Something only marginally human came out of the storm drain. A huge man-thing, head lost in masses of tangled, filthy blond hair, hoisted an equally nasty mummified head on high and bellowed a challenge that stilled the morning. With his right hand he brandished a bronze sword that was, even to the uneducated eye, obviously enchanted. It was limned by a nimbus that could be sensed but not visually described.

There was power there, with that strange man, and with another of similar stamp who followed him into the light. Else saw no reason why anyone should run from them, though.

They must be the blond men who had caused the stir in Brothe. The men who had decimated the Brotherhood, who had subjected the Calziran pirates to such slaughter, who had turned up during his encounter with Starkden and Masant el-Seyhan. Principaté Doneto called them soultaken. They were living dead men serving the Instrumentalities of the Night. One of which had shielded him and suggested that he lie low.

Imperial troops raced out of the storm-water drain. Once in the light, though, they became indecisive. The Pramans had scattered. Pinkus Ghort and his cohorts had taken cover.

The two soultaken started toward the Brothen reserves. Then the one carrying the head and bronze sword halted.

Slowly, he turned. His gaze rose to Else Tage. Else felt the elation there. He felt the soultaken's thrill of recognition. The man hoisted head and sword aloft. He screamed at the sky in an unknown tongue.

A dense, dark mist gushed from the storm drain. It coalesced into something huge, ugly, foul, and dark, one moment not unlike a classic harpy, the next a monster mantis. Frightened Braunsknechts followed the example of the fleeing Pramans.

The thing wore a new shape but Else knew this was the demon from beneath Waterhouse Two.

She loomed over the soultaken. The one armed with head and sword was not impressed. He beckoned Else down.

Why?

To kill him. And thereby destroy the knowledge he carried.

What? That made no sense.

It does to him. It does to those who sent him. They do not understand that knowledge discovered cannot be undiscovered. Today they will learn.

Those words were not quite a voice in Else's head. They were knowledge that materialized there. He had been touched directly by the Night.

The harpy became mist again. That shrank, became a large blonde woman. She faced off with the soultaken. Both were confused and irresolute.

The Imperial soldiers knew what they were seeing. And did not want to believe that they were.

Else caught some of the buzz. Here was a legend come to life, a goddess risen from an abandoned faith. An Instrumentality no longer sustained by the world.

She squared off with the soultaken.

Else started to climb down the wall. Soldiers of various allegiances pointed and whispered. Had he made a wrong move?

Circle to your right and rejoin your raiders.

Else's amulet burned and froze his wrist. Uncle Divino's ring weighed a hundred pounds. He slunk like a rat making its getaway, darting from cover to cover.

The soultaken paid no attention. They had lost interest.

Pinkus Ghort and his raiders, though, kept track. Ghort and half a dozen Brothens came out to cover him.

"I appreciate this, Pinkus. But you should know better."

"Not that big a risk. They're totally infatuated over there." Ghort poked a finger. "Chooser of the Slain. The Banished One. Who would've thought it possible?"

"Who indeed?" Grateful for the mythological cue, Else mused, "Arlensul, you really think?"

Ghort shrugged. "It fits. But who wants to find out? How about you talk less and hustle more?" By then, though, they were tumbling in amongst the crusaders, who were captivated by the heathen confrontation. "You know the hairball with the extra head?"

"No. He might be the one they were after in Brothe, though. Why?"

"It looked like he was trying to call you out."

"It did, didn't it? What was that about? What happened to our prizes?"

"Lothar and them? The Principatés sent them back to camp."

"That figures."

"Don't it?"

"We'll still be fighting the Unbeliever and they'll already be trying to blackmail Johannes."

"That's politics. What the hell are they doing now?"

Else and Ghort had just slithered into a position from which they could watch the supernatural confrontation.

Principaté Divino eased up beside Else, opposite Pinkus Ghort. He was a mess, wet and muddy. He was terrified. "The Instrumentality that controls those two souls is about to manifest. What happened in there, Hecht? We lost track of you."

Was the man suspicious? Not obviously. Else told the truth, leaving out little but his exchange with Bone and his encounter with the woman yonder.

The elderly Bruglioni said, "Oh my! I've let curiosity murder me."

"What?"

"I should've gone when I could. We all should have."

The soultaken with the head and sword expanded slowly, till it loomed over the woman. She had acquired a brazen shield and golden spear from somewhere. The soultaken opened his mouth and bellowed, "Traitor!"

The woman responded, "Vengeance! All-Father. All-Evil. It is time to die the Endless Death."

"Oh, for sure, I should've gone," Principaté Divino moaned. "I was such a fool! It's real! It's all real."

Ghort said, "Looks like times might get interesting."

The soultaken spoke two words. While those rattled around they took physical form, as two flapping black towels of darkness that transformed into something like a brace of black vultures. Each screamed one of the words the soultaken had spoken. Their names?

Else felt that the female apparition was pleased.

The flapping black things settled toward the soultaken. Uncle Divino murmured, "It's been said that all religions are true. But how can this be?"

These events rattled the faith of everyone watching.

"For Gedanke," Arlensul said, in response to a question unheard.

The possessed soultaken bellowed again, flung himself at his prodigal daughter.

The fabric of reality creaked. It began to tear.

37. A Loving God, a Loving Father

Svavar's mind was clearer and his thoughts crisper than ever. He watched the Godslayer rappel down the wall, unseen by Shagot. Grim saw nothing but Arlensul. Grim did not understand that Arlensul had been with them from their arrival on that ancient battleground. He was not, in fact, Grimur Grimmsson now. He was the worldly avatar of the Gray Walker, come to finish dealing with a traitorous daughter.

The Godslayer had no place in his thoughts.

The Old Ones mirrored their creature Shagot: crude, thoughtless, violent, ignorant of pity or remorse. And none too smart. What use smart if you were omnipotent and immortal?

The black flapping things came together in the gap between Instrumentalities, chased one another in a whirling mandala of darkness that spun in multiple dimensions. The Instrumentalities screamed at one another, proclaiming senseless rage and hatred. While the mandala grew.

Svavar stared at the thing his brother had become, unable to accept it although he believed it. Arlensul's defiance had conjured the One Who Harkens . . . now armed with the hammer club for which his favorite son was famous. The mandala, shedding a ripping roar, revealed glimpses of horrors beyond. Glimpses of old corpses abiding an opportunity to rise up and serve deities who held them in trivial regard.

Arlensul lashed out with her spear, pleased with her father's response so far. The Walker slid aside. His hammer made a gong of Arlensul's shield.

Words formed deep in Svavar's mind. *Do not forget your dearest wish. Do not forget who has been your most devoted protector.*

Which mainly baffled Svavar.

What could he do besides watch the titans clash?

Father and daughter traded blow for blow. The countryside resounded to their fury. Despite their terror, mortals stopped running, watched enrapt.

Soon, my chosen one.

Svavar began to shake, colder than naked in Andoray's iciest winter, dreading the foulness to come.

Which evil most torments the world?

Within the mandala Arlensul's sisters were wakening the Heroes.

Not good, that. There was Erief. . . . What was left of murdered Erief after centuries in that terrible Hall.

The great god of the north flung his hammer aside. It never fell to the ground. A staff appeared in his hands, in myth carved of ash cut from the great World Tree, a living, sentient tree whose roots reached into every well of knowledge there was. The Walker slammed that staff's iron shod foot into Arlensul's shield. The shield split. Only the smaller fragment remained in the Chooser's control. The staff thrust again. The immortal spear spun out of Arlensul's hand. It did not vanish. It fell at Svavar's feet.

Now you must decide.

38. Another View

Pinkus Ghort murmured, "Oh, shit," so gently and so emotionlessly that Else knew he was deeply frightened.

Principaté Divino Bruglioni said, "I agree wholeheartedly, Captain."

Else asked, "Your Grace, can you do anything to shelter the troops?" To right and left the covering force remained in place. The secondary reserve had come forward to witness a once-in-a-millennium event.

The soldiers were mostly Devedian toughs. But Else got little chance to give that any thought.

Ghort said, "Here we go."

Else grasped the hilt of his tired old sword.

The one Instrumentality split the shield of the other, then knocked its spear away. The night lance fell at the lesser soultaken's feet. Wisps of things began to leak from the dark mandala.

The soultaken rained blows on the remnant of the other's shield.

Whispers raced among the witnesses. To a man, they knew they were witnessing the end of a major myth cycle.

There were Pramans on the city wall, now. They were more spiritually distressed than their Episcopal and Devedian foes. Pramans were so fiercely attached to their faith that they could conceive of no other reality. Even granting diabolic status to the Instrumentalities of the Night was an impossible stretch for some.

The lesser Instrumentality fought strongly and valiantly, holding her own. Her opponent was handicapped by the limits of human flesh.

The lesser soultaken retrieved Arlensul's spear.

More than misty ghosts began leaking through the dark mandala. Armed men shambled out, banging into one another in confusion. Were they blind? No. They had just awakened. And few were in prime condition.

Else knew enough of the myths of the north to understand what was happening. The Hall of Heroes, of the Great Sky Fortress, was spewing its harvest across distance and time. No accident, obviously, but definitely senseless. Why would a clutch of forgotten gods get involved in a squabble between unrelated religious enemies half a thousand miles from anywhere they ever held sway?

39. A Living Brother, a Loving Death

Svavar understood what had to be done. That was as plain as anything he ever knew. He and Grim would shake the Old Ones' control no other way. He gathered Arlensul's spear, forged by the Instrumentalities themselves. It felt remarkably light and agile in his hand.

It struck like an adder's tongue dart, entering Grim's back easily as a dagger into soft cheese. He felt his brother's heartbeat, relayed down the haunted shaft. He screamed as Grim's life flooded otherworldly metal and wood.

He screamed again when the rage and madness of the Gray Walker followed. The pain was beyond imagination. But it lasted only an instant. Then the One was away, sprinting for the dark mandala but missing it and continuing onward in a large, blind arc.

Dead men tripping over dead men continued to pour out of the mandala, driven by Arlensul's sisters. They spread out across the slope.

He had done Arlensul's will. He was supposed to fall on the spear himself, now, he supposed. But that was not going to happen. A fragment of the One had infected him through the Chooser's blade.

The adder's tongue flicked.

Arlensul was surprised. This did not fit her plan. Svavar was surprised himself as a part of the Chooser reached him through the spear.

He screamed some. The pain seemed to go on and on and on but in reality lasted only seconds. Then came a flood of emotion as the warrior Gedanke staggered out of the dark mandala, harried by Arlensul's sisters.

The foulest blow, Arlensul ceased to exist while straining toward her dead lover.

Not even the Instrumentalities of the Night are true immortals. And that, Svavar realized vaguely, was the cause of all his despair.

Stupid, enfeebled gods far from events had heard a snatch of an echo running through the canyons of time and, in their dread of marginalization and extinction, had latched onto that one remote moment as the key to their continued existence.

How could he know these things?

Arlensul's spear leapt in his hands. Her sister Sprenghul shrieked in mortal agony. The Great Sky Fortress was bereft of another sustaining Instrumentality. Svavar felt power and knowledge flood him. That spear was something from darkest legend, a Harvester of Souls. Each Instrumentality it devoured made it easier for him to draw power and knowledge from the next.

Svavar smiled weakly. They had guessed wrong. All of them. Their Godslayer was right here among them, the tool chosen to destroy their expected assassin.

There was a mythic irony here. Or, perhaps, Instrumentalities of a higher plane were dabbling. The gods of the gods might be at play.

Svavar turned on the last of the Choosers, Fastthal, still driving Heroes into the world. Her father jogged past. The Heroes milled. Some drifted toward the soldiers Svavar sensed watching from cover not far away. Some meandered along the foot of the wall. Some climbed.

Fastthal shrieked in rage and fled into the dark mandala. Svavar had no trouble seeing through that, now. He saw the rest of the Old Ones, in all their dreaded forms. They were as confused as the Heroes, and frightened besides. They did not know what to do, now.

In the end they chose withdrawal. They closed the dark mandala, isolating themselves from their monstrous regiment of dead and mutilated killers. Svavar could not stop them, nor could he get through to punish them.

He noted that his brother, Grimur Grimmsson, had died as he had expected throughout his life, far from home and to little point, not even in real despair. He had lived as he believed he should. Strong and predatory.

The tale was told at last. Asgrimmur Grimmsson could lie down and abandon his burdens.

Svavar planted the butt of Arlensul's spear in the snow. This should be almost painless.

He tried. He could not do it. Not because he was a coward, though. The spear refused to accept him. The power and knowledge he had absorbed from the Choosers and the All Father, before he got away, would not let him. Nor did the Asgrimmur Grimmsson core of him really want to do it. There was work to be done, still. There were debts not yet paid.

Svavar was slow but he got there. Asgrimmur Grimmsson was dead. What stood in his boots now was an ascending Instrumentality. He could not slay himself even had he that will. Someone had to do that for him, now.

His universe filled with thunder and lightning, sulfurous stench and yet more incredible pain, first exploding in his left shoulder, then at a dozen points elsewhere in his body.

40. The Fire and the Pain

Ghort told Else, "Pipe, I'm ready to check on out. I have officially seen everything."

"What *did* you see?" Else did not trust his own eyes. Those things out there were among the greatest demons of the Night. Holy men in the Kaifate of al-Minphet would insist that they did not exist. They were folktales, nothing more. Like the fabrications of the professional storytellers of Lucidia.

The soultaken attacked his companions. While countless dead men tramped into the world and, after some confusion, shambled toward the living. Meaning some turned toward the city wall, more headed east to meet the approaching Imperial probe, and most came at Else and his crusaders.

Not once had Else seen Gledius Stewpo among the Devedian-heavy reserve but he heard that dwarf bellow, "Stand to your matches! Now, fire!"

Two hundred firepowder weapons barked during a two-second span. The weapons had remained unseen until the dwarf summoned them forth.

The fusillade tore the approaching heroes apart. Else was aghast at how swiftly firepowder missiles flung the power of the Night into oblivion.

Few of the ferocious dead warriors got close enough to engage the Patriarchal troops. The Deves produced an endless rolling thunder. The smoke became oppressive.

Results were less sanguine where there were no firepowder weapons. The Imperials were not prepared to deal with fighters who were dead already. Their best defense was discipline. Once they formed ranks they managed to fend off wild attackers fighting as individuals.

A tenth of the heroes chose to assault al-Khazen. Else saw no obvious reason why some scarecrow figures chose to clamber up the wall, but they did, easy as insects. When they reached the battlements they murdered everyone in sight.

The firepowder smoke cleared away. Streamers of dark mist came from al-Khazen as the sorcerers within engaged the undead warriors. That resistance attracted the interest of most of the dead still facing the Patriarchal troops.

Else pushed up off the cold, wet ground and eased forward. Ghort followed. He crowded in against Else. "What the hell happened here, Pipe? I sure as fuck don't want it to be what I'm pretty sure it was."

Behind them, the Devedian fusiliers prepared to withdraw. Al-Khazen's garrison would not mount a pursuit.

Firepowder tubes continued to crack occasionally. Sharpshooters plinked the blind, howling thing jogging in its wide circle. That thing no longer looked anything like the man it had possessed.

It was aware of little outside itself. It passed near Else without sensing him. The inverse was not true.

The pain was worse than it had been with the bogon in the Ownvidian Knot, though more sudden and stimulated over a much shorter range. Else collapsed. But he was not alone. He would not have to explain to Pinkus Ghort. Ghort was down himself, clawing at his temples.

Devedian soldiers continued to snipe at the wounded god. Every hit weakened him, slowed him, left him less certain of his form. He did not appear human, now. But he was a god. He would be a long time going. Most likely, he would not go at all. He might even recover if enough live mortals were slain around him.

Else's pain faded as the wounded god stumbled away.

Ghort heaved the contents of his stomach. "Ah, Eis's fucking Holy Piles, Pipe! If there's any way to kill that freak, let's get on with it. Or just stay out of its fucking way. I can't take much of this."

Still recovering from his own pain, Else considered his place in events, both as others intended and as chance had conspired. This morning would not set well with Grade Drocker. Nor with er-Rashal el-Dhulquarnen, who had to be stunned.

Only now did Else grasp the implication of those few minutes in Esther's Wood. That which would slay a bogon could dispatch far more powerful entities.

Else said, "I'm not sure what to do, Pinkus. It's only starting to sink in. But I think we're in the middle of history happening."

A shriek of despair came from the wall. They watched as the dead heroes threw someone down.

Ghort cursed. "Them damned things won't quit." A dead hero with one arm, one leg, and no eyes had hold of his ankle.

"Don't cut yourself. That looked like Starkden that just fell."

Ghort severed the wrist of his assailant, then levered the hand off his ankle. "We need us a big-ass bonfire to roast us some dead men."

"Good idea." Else's pain grew. The blind Instrumentality was headed their way. "A pit might be better."

"So they can't run from the fire. Yeah. Shit. Now what?"

Deves were walking the killing ground, finishing the dead heroes with swords and spearheads of blackened iron with silver-plated tips. They gave the blind god a wide berth. At random moments he sparked off lightning.

"They've figured out a way to battle the Night. From a distance," Else said. "The Brotherhood will be thrilled."

Ghort skipped away from a grabbing hand, frowning. "Something like this happened before, Pipe. On a smaller scale. You mentioning the Brotherhood made me remember. This was in Sonsa, a couple years ago, before we hooked up. That's how Drocker got messed up. By Deves. They said it was some new kind of sorcery but I'm thinking it was maybe the same thing we just saw here."

"Could be. They're devious people. Well, this *is* Starkden."

"She dead?"

"Looks like."

"Be careful."

Else collected an antique spear that had lost its operator. He poked the fallen sorceress. "Let's get her bound and bagged and headed up to Drocker. He'll love us even if she isn't breathing."

"He'll have him a shitload of mixed feelings. Should we do something to help them Imperials?" Things were no longer going well for Lothar's would-be rescuers, though the Braunsknechts from the drain had joined them.

"They're holding their own. We need to get busy here."

"The guys look like they're hot to go, Pipe. They've figured out what these dead guys are. Which tells them there might be valuable antique weapons and grave goods to be had. But I'm on the job."

Ghort strode off to draft work parties. Else considered proceedings atop the wall. He saw Bone and Az observing from relative safety. So Az had found his way back to the company. They saw him but gave no sign. Until Az made a quick, small Sha-lug warning gesture.

Else turned as a body lying deep in mud and dirty snow and parts hacked off dead heroes surged to its feet, the soultaken that had speared the crippled god. He felt the fury, fear, and insanity of the thing. And the power. Here raged a new monster of the Night, pulling itself together by culling fragments from dying Instrumentalities.

The thing recognized Else.

Else decided on a swift tactical relocation. A fresh surge of pain hit. He lost focus on his footing. He slipped on an icy stone, fell, slid twenty feet downhill.

Deves maneuvering against the blinded god fired on the new threat.

The soultaken roared, producing an amazing noise from a human throat. Then it shook like a dog suffering a seizure. It swelled up, changed shape, and began to get the hell out of there.

It turned into something like a mantis of twice human size, with twice too many legs for a bug. Mahogany chitin with scarlet scars and highlights ripped through its fur and rag clothing. It headed north at a high rate of speed, undaunted by the terrain.

Else sat in cold mud and gaped till his wrist told him the blind god was coming.

Else started to get up. His hand brushed something his eyes did not see. When he grasped it with his amulet hand it became visible as the bronze sword of power formerly carried by the soultaken now infested by his supreme deity.

The blind god shifted course, toward his nearest tormentors.

Could that hideous head be far from the sword?

Ah. There.

Else's bowels turned to ice. They came near voiding.

The thing's eyes were open. It lay on its left side, in muddy, trampled grass, eyes alive. Eyes aware. And as mad as could be imagined. What was it? It had no hands, no voice, no means to impose its will. . . . Save the mesmerizing power of those eyes.

Else's wrist blazed with pain. The amulet shielded him again. For that er-Rashal el-Dhulquarnen deserved gratitude.

Else clambered to his feet. He stripped a ragged cloak off an unmoving dead hero and used it to bundle the head.

The pain faded immediately.

TROOPS FROM THE PATRIARCHAL CAMP BEGAN TO ARRIVE. Grade Drocker sensed an opportunity to strike a hammer blow on the cheap. Else sent a party in through the storm drain and another to climb his still-dangling escape rope. Whoever got the chance should open a postern or gate. He directed others to help the Deves finish and collect the dead heroes. Ghort he finally did send to help the Imperials. The men from the Grail Empire faced a deteriorating situation.

Exhausted, Else eventually settled down in the bottom of a brushy gully with Uncle Divino. It looked like it had snowed antique weapons. There were scores scattered in the mud or hanging in the bushes.

"Good place to hide, eh?" The bronze sword had drained him. He set blade and wrapped head aside. "I'm ready for a nap."

Bruglioni grunted. "Best I could do. How's it going up there?"

"I think we're all right. You all alone? Where are your guys?"

"Those assholes ran off as soon as it got exciting. Then I managed to get crippled without doing anything but lay here."

Else grunted.

"All that hardware came raining down. This damned dagger got me through the knee. There's a killing spell on it but it wasn't meant for me. It was intended to kill somebody named Erief Erealsson. Presumably one of our undead visitors."

"I don't know the name. Probably somebody who was important once upon a time. History is fickle."

"Do you have any idea what's happening here, Hecht?"

"I think so. This might be the beginning of the end of the Tyranny of the Night. The weapons the Deves used could make it possible to punish the gods themselves."

Uncle Divino scowled. "You're a doctrinal mess, Hecht. But that's near the mark. The Brotherhood of War and the Special Office will be excited. They'll want to get those weapons into the service of God as soon as they understand them."

"Even if the weapons are tools of the Adversary?"

"What?" The Principaté's eyes widened. Had recent events been orchestrated? Was he a witness to the first bell of the Carillon of Doom? "Damn! You might be right. This needs the attention of a quorum in the whole of the Collegium. Damn again! I can't get up. I can't move my leg."

A deep sense of sorrow overcame Else. But he had to honor his promises. He sighed. They were alone in the gully, overlooked. This opportunity would not come again. "Principaté, years ago Freido Bruglioni and his brother did something black-hearted to Draco Arniena. Don Draco found them out. Don Draco told Don Inigo before he died. He made Don Inigo promise to extract a suitable revenge."

Principaté Bruglioni was confused. "That . . . That . . . I'd nearly forgotten . . . Draco knew?"

"Always."

"Then Inigo sent you?"

"He did, Principaté. I'm sorry. You've lived an exemplary life since."

"Hecht! No!"

"A man is only as good as his word." Else folded Bruglioni's own cloak and forced it down onto the old man's face.

Bruglioni struggled. Else's amulet tortured his left wrist yet again.

God was generous. No witness stumbled onto the crime. Else completed his task, then returned the antique dagger to the wound in Bruglioni's knee. He eliminated signs of his visit. Still unnoticed by men whose attention was focused elsewhere, he moved down the gully, away from Principaté Bruglioni.

He had debated breaking his word. He had grown fond of Divino Bruglioni. But there was little doubt that the loss of the Principaté would create huge problems for Sublime and the Collegium.

Ten minutes passed before Else spoke to anyone. He wandered the battlefield with the monster head under one arm and the bronze sword in the other, wondering what Divino and Freido had done to earn the abiding hatred of the Arniena.

He noted one of Ghort's men edging nearer. "Quintille? What is it?"

"Message from Captain Ghort, sir. Your ears only."

The man was shaking in his boots. Why? "Go ahead."

"The Emperor is dead. Slain in the fighting in the city. Lothar is emperor, now. Johannes's daughters have taken charge. Captain Ghort says we should expect confusion in the Imperial camp."

"No doubt. How's he doing?"

"That's the other message. He needs help. Some thundercasters if you can send them. These things don't get tired and they don't give up until you cut them into pieces."

"They're on the way, soon as I round some up."

Quintille fled, obviously relieved to get away.

Else went looking for Gledius Stewpo. The dwarf was elusive. Nevertheless, Else dug him out.

"I don't recollect putting you in charge, dwarf. Nor anything in Captain Ghort's plan including what happened this morning. But it worked out. So far. Do you have firepowder and shot left? Ghort has a problem over yonder."

Stewpo and his henchmen did not protest though it was plain they wanted to. A couple of firepowder tubes swung Else's way.

"That wouldn't be smart. I'm the best friend you've got on this side of the Mother Sea."

"It's that sword, Colonel. You need to get rid of it. It's already begun to dress you in the same aura as the last man who carried it."

Else glanced at the running blind god, now smaller than he had been, said, "I see." He suspected the head more than the blade, though. "You have anybody trustworthy enough, and strong enough, to watch over the sword without trying to use it?"

"Is there one of us righteous enough to reject the tools of alien gods?" Stewpo asked. "I think so."

"Good. Find this paragon. We'll destroy the sword in the same fire as the undead. It's bronze. It should melt. So. If you'll round me up a relief force, I'll go extricate my overly optimistic number two."

As Else, the dwarf, and twenty Deves headed for the brawl between Imperials and undead, Else asked, "How could you afford that much ammunition? They say you people have hoards to beggar a dragon, but you just shot off more silver than I can imagine."

"You're imagining wrong." Stewpo handed him a rough metal pellet the size of the end joint of his thumb.

"Iron."

"Yes. With a few thin patches of silver laid on."

"Uhm?"

"It doesn't have to be solid silver. The silver at the surface is all that's needed. And iron gives most creatures of the night terrible indigestion. The silver in one small coin is enough for a hundred of these shot."

Amazing. "How can we just be learning this? Why are firepowder weapons effective when traditional weapons aren't?"

"But they are. You saw us finishing the undead with silver-tipped swords. A healthy entity can dodge traditional weapons and missiles. They're too slow. The shot from a firepowder tube, though, moves too fast to see. We're almost there. You might want to hang back a few steps."

"One thing before you go get mauled by the undead. Just my

personal curiosity. Why are you out here, openly directing Devedian forces? Grade Drocker knows your name. Why show your hand here, now? How did you know there'd be an outbreak from the Realm of Night?"

"That's several things, Colonel." Stewpo gestured at his men to deploy. "But it's all gone so well, I feel like crowing. My God is the True God."

"Excuse me?"

"An Angel of the Lord came to me at night many times, to tell me that Hell would open its mouth here. I choose to be seen exactly because the sorcerer will remember my name from Sonsa. If he presses my people, they can honestly blame everything on me. And I've told them that the original information about firepowder weapons came from the Dreangerean provocateur who died during the uprising in Sonsa."

Did a deeply veiled threat lie behind Stewpo's words?

"I don't expect Drocker to last much longer. He doesn't have the strength to give you much trouble. And no one else cares."

"You aren't Devedian, Colonel. You don't see things as all being part of the river of time. You barely see beyond yesterday, today, and tomorrow."

Else disagreed but kept his opinion to himself. Though the dwarf might honestly believe that he had been visited by an angel, not a rogue Chooser of the Slain arranging a cruel ambush for a father who had ripped out her heart.

Stewpo asked, "Is that it? I do have your clumsy associate to salvage."

"Go. Save." Else clambered up a rock outcrop. The hillside fell away from the wall steeply. The slope below was littered with dead and wounded men, along with bits and pieces of northern heroes. Seventy yards away a dozen Braunsknechts swayed in a clump around Elspeth Ege. Else felt that same thrill he had experienced in Plemenza. The girl seemed angry and fearless.

Ghort and his crew had failed to break through. They were surrounded themselves. Neither party had much resistance left to offer.

"Do your stuff, dwarf," Else muttered.

There was no thinking going on amongst the heroes. The

Devedian fire teams fired their first volley from ten feet away. There were no misses. By the time the heroes realized that there was a threat the Deves had fired again. Heroes hit went down. And stayed down. It took only minutes to exterminate them.

"You took your sweet time," Ghort gasped. He was pale, his expression strained. "Ten more minutes and there wouldn't have had been nobody to rescue."

"You're bitching so I'm guessing I got here soon enough."

"Oh, yes. I'm going to make your life miserable for a long time to come. Ow! Easy there, hairboy." A Dainshau physician had begun to examine Ghort.

Else told the Dainshau, "Those others need you more than this one. Let the vitriol leak out before you patch him up." Chuckling, Else headed for the Imperial survivors. Most had collapsed once the need to defend themselves ceased. Only the Emperor's daughter remained upright, beside her fallen mount, with a light sword in one hand and her father's standard in the other, taken over from her fallen standard-bearer. She wore some sort of toy mail, a light breastplate, and no helmet. Her dark hair streamed in the wind.

Else inclined his head. "Princess."

"I remember you. But not your name."

"Piper Hecht, Princess. Of the Brothen city regiment."

"Your circumstances have improved." She flashed a melting smile.

"Indeed. While yours appear to have deteriorated somewhat."

"We had them right where we wanted them."

Else could not help grinning. "What can I do to help?"

"You could give me my brother back."

"I'd love to. But I'm in no position to do that. I'm a soldier. He's already in the hands of men more interested in politics."

"Members of the Collegium."

"Yes."

"Is he all right?"

"I don't know. I haven't seen him. But I think so." Else's gaze remained locked with that of the young woman. Clearly, she felt the electricity, too. "What will you do?"

"We are the children of Hansel Blackboots."

"I wish you luck, Princess. The best possible. I wouldn't want to face what you do, now."

She flashed another melting smile. "I told you. We're the children of Ferocious Hans." Her gaze shifted to something behind him. She gasped, astonished.

Else turned as a gout of darkness stabbed up at the belly of the sky.

The sound arrived. It was the roar of a dozen thunderstorms compressed into one minute of fury.

That could be one thing, only.

"I have to go," Else said.

"I'll see you again," Elspeth mouthed, having read his lips.

Ears ringing, Else had trouble discerning nuance. But that seemed to be a promise.

"Stewpo!" he shouted in the dwarf's ear. "Was that what I think?"

"That was the death of a false god."

ELSE WATCHED PATRIARCHAL TROOPS ENTER AL-KHAZEN through a newly opened postern. Bitter fighting lay ahead. Masant al-Seyhan would not go quietly. Er-Rashal would not go at all. He would vanish and reappear in Dreanger, blaming all the disasters on others, getting up to some new sort of mischief.

Else said, "You'd better go underground, little friend. Drocker is deeper than you think."

"He can be as deep as he wants. The firepowder knowledge is loose. He can't make it go away. Not even your great Dreangerean sorcerer can manage that. He is much less clever as a puppet-master than he thinks."

"Life will go harshly for the Deves of al-Qarn, now."

"Life always goes harshly for the Deves of al-Qarn."

"Do you know what er-Rashal was up to? Why he indulged in schemes that hurt his own side more than Dreanger's enemies?"

"I have a notion. It's most likely wrong. I'll tell you what an old man once told me. In politics and war you don't need to waste time looking for treachery or conspiracy if stupidity or incompetence will explain a disaster."

Else nodded. His own people manufactured complicated, improbable conspiracy theories to explain their embarrassments. Those often referenced the secret schemes of the monolithic Devedian religion.

They neared the tower of black smoke. It was slow to dissipate. "Well," Else said. "That's one hell of a hole in the ground." A cone of earth and stone fifty feet across and sixty deep had vanished. The sides of the pit were glassy and had the droopy look of melted candle wax.

Else had worked hard to teach his soldiers to be innovative. To seize any opportunity. They were doing just that, flinging anything remotely flammable into the pit along with pieces of fallen hero. Else said, "The lazy asses didn't want to dig their own pit." He made sure the demon's head and bronze sword went into the fire.

Else organized the removal of the injured and arranged for the Episcopal dead to be buried in al-Khazen's Chaldarean cemetery. Then he joined the troops inside the city. Most of the Calziran defenders had surrendered or fled. Their morale had collapsed. The remaining resistance was holed up in the citadel, under relentless attack by the dead heroes. Else kept his crusaders away from that.

The Imperials had lost interest. They were headed back to their camps. The nobility would be maneuvering to get control of Hansel's daughters.

Those girls would need to be strong and clever.

Lothar ought to be under special guard. Sublime might have the boy murdered as an expedient means of dulling the Grail Empire's teeth.

That could not be allowed. Sublime must always have the threat of the Emperor behind him.

Al-Khazen was dead except for the excitement at its heart. Sorceries flared there. But the efforts of the denizens of the citadel were ineffective. The Collegium had begun harrying them, leaving them little attention to spare for the dead heroes.

A LAST BAND OF CALZIRAN FUGITIVES ELUDED THE FOREIGN Pramans and dead warriors alike. Mafti al-Araj el-Arak and his courtiers, their families, and certain formerly resolutely stubborn lords of the Calziran kingdom were making their escape. In an exchange of messages they had promised to surrender to King Peter of Navaya at al-Negesi. They had sworn their paroles against the Written. Else thought the weather would keep them honest. They had nowhere else to go if they wanted to be warm and fed.

Else watched them move out, shielded by his troops. He hoped the hint had gotten through, that there would be familiar faces among the refugees.

Ah. There were. Bone and the Master of Ghosts, Az, who needed help from his companions. Looking very Calziran today. Bone had found a loophole in their oath.

Wait! There was another face he knew. Not included in the offer of parole. "Stop that man. Chiotto. Brench. In the gray jebalah, with the hood. Cut him out."

The Mafti's chief chamberlain materialized. He had initiated negotiations originally. "A thousand pardons, Lord!" he gasped at Else. "Forgive the Mafti! This gray rat forced himself upon us. He was desperate to escape the mad Dreangerean. It was not the Mafti's plan to violate our parole."

"I see. You drugged him somehow?"

"Indeed. Yes, Lord." His evasive eye suggested that poison was more likely.

"Is this Masant el-Seyhan?"

"The same, Lord. He is a terrible man. We didn't dare . . ."

"Enough. You lie like a dog. But I have no complaint now. Remind the Mafti that he'll be followed to el-Negesi. I've ordered that no mercy be shown parole breakers."

"Your generosity is heroic, Lord. Worthy of a Believer. Your mercy won't be forgotten."

"Go. I can still be overruled by my superiors." There would be, for sure, an outcry about his having let potential ransoms get away. Foo on how many soldiers' lives the arrangement saved.

There were always more soldiers.

He was improvising, not only to save lives but to give old friends a chance to elude the doom er-Rashal al-Dhulquarnen wanted to call down on the remaining Sha-lug.

Else was angry. The Rascal had betrayed al-Prama and Dreanger on behalf of some obscure ambition of his own. But he would pay, in time. Maybe even here, at the hands of Devedian fusiliers. They would be eager to get off a shot at the man who had invented firepowder weapons. They loved irony as much as gold. Or maybe the payback would come later, after news of his treachery crept back to Gordimer the Lion.

Once the groggy man in gray had been hustled off for an encounter with Grade Drocker, Else settled in for a siege of the citadel. Which did not happen.

Private soldiers not as weary as he, still able to reason, saw an opportunity to penetrate al-Khazen's citadel through the some postern the Mafti had used to get away. The undead paid no attention. They were occupied elsewhere.

Er-Rashal el-Dhulquarnen could not be found. Likewise, the commanders of the Dreangeran and Lucidian expeditions. Nor was much treasure discovered. The few servants left behind were so resolutely ignorant that it was obvious their memories had been bewitched.

"Here's what you do," Else told one of his captains. "Put the servants into a slave coffle. We'll question them again later. Then set the citadel on fire. If they're hiding in some secret place that'll bring them out. You can let them surrender if they offer."

He settled down, then, out of the way, and napped. He had but to crack an eye to see a hundred Brothen soldiers doing the same. He nodded off reflecting on how much of his life he spent alone. He was alone even while he commanded ten thousand men.

He would be with Anna Mozilla again, soon, though.

It began to snow. That respite was over.

EXHAUSTION DOGGED ELSE MERCILESSLY AS HE CLIMBED FROM one trail marker to the next, while the snow fell, after dark, making his way back to camp. He was part of a chaotic stream. Younger men passed him. He passed older men. Polo met him and worried around him like a nervous puppy. "Just feed me and put me to bed," he said. He was too tired to worry about the state of a Patriarchal camp that had suffered several days of Titus Consent's tyranny. The confusion could be sorted out later.

Polo shielded him faithfully till well after sunrise, though everyone wanted a chunk of his time. He pushed them away himself, then, and went to see Grade Drocker.

The Brotherhood sorcerer looked dreadful.

"Glad you came out, Hecht. Dramatic things have been happening. I need to know what you can tell me. I have decisions to make." Drocker needed two minutes to get all that out.

"Ask the questions. I'll do my best to answer."

"First, tell me what happened. I recall discouraging you from rescuing the crown prince."

"We did back off and leave that to the Brotherhood."

"Yet men from the city regiment brought Lothar into camp."

"Your soldiers didn't get the job done. Without my men grabbing him when they did Lothar would've died in captivity."

"Just as well you showed the initiative. We lost the Brothers sent to retrieve Lothar. All of them, sadly."

"They fought well. From the little I saw, they made the Pramans pay a terrible price to keep hold of Lothar."

"I'm pleased. I'm exhausted, Hecht. Nearing the end. I have almost nothing left. Not even my usual little kingdom. I'm alone except for Bechter. I should be in a rage about our losses. The behavior of our Deves, down there, should've made me insanely furious. Weapons of that same sort did this to me. But I'm too weak. There is a passage in the Good Book. One of the Unattributed Prophets. 'I am weary unto death.' I won't last the week, Hecht. I may not witness another sunset. I've borrowed all the time that God will loan me." The long speech, made with few interruptions, left Drocker looking like a corpse.

"Shall I send Polo for a physician, sir?"

"No. My time is short. I've done what needs doing. Sergeant Bechter will become your aide. An unimaginative but steady man, Bechter. He'll have all the information and materials you'll need."

"Sir?"

"You will succeed me as commander of Patriarchal forces. The Principatés have accepted my wishes. They'll encourage the Patriarch to make the appointment permanent."

"I'm not worthy."

"Possibly not. There is much about you that I find disquieting. And more that says there is in you a steadfastness of character more important than lip service religiosity."

Else shifted ground. "Did you get anything out of Starkden or Masant el-Seyhan?"

"The woman was too long dead. I'm no necromancer. Worse luck. We had our grievances. The Principatés are working on the other one. It doesn't look promising. His brain has been damaged by drugs and poison. Only Special Office experts could open him up. But the two we have in camp were with Lothar. They're unlikely to recover from their capture."

"And the other sorcerer? The one who came from overseas?"

"Gone. Vanished. Claimed seriously damaged by the undead warriors before he finished them off. That's enough for now. I must recuperate. If I can. As you leave tell that old woman to come in. I need changing."

Drocker was not speaking in jest. He had a nurse, a Calziran Chaldarean so old they might have built the Vaillarentiglia Mountains around her. She did change him like a baby. He could not get out of bed anymore.

ELSE TOOK UP THE REINS OF THE REGIMENT. THE FIRST TASK he set his company captains was a roll and injury call. They came up just eight men short. Three were Deves who had participated in the firepowder surprise. Four were soldiers who had arrived in time for the scouring of al-Khazen, hoping to find something worth stealing. The eighth was Principaté Divino Bruglioni. No one had any idea what had become of the Principaté. His peers were almost hysterical.

Else sent searchers to look for the missing men.

He made an opportunity for a private moment with Rogoz Sayag. "Inform Don Inigo that the thing is done. The client understood clearly why before the transaction closed. I wish I could've let someone closer handle it."

Later, once Principaté Bruglioni had been found, a victim of the undead heroes, Rogoz told Else, "Don Inigo has held on desperately. I'm sure he'll be pleased. The Arniena will consider themselves forever in your debt."

"Warn them that I expect to collect. In time. I remain ambitious."

An extended exchange with Rogoz was impossible. Everywhere Else went, now, Polo and Redfearn Bechter followed. Bechter was determined to groom him to take over for Drocker. "I'm the only member of the Brotherhood in Firal-

dia still standing, sir. And I'm not qualified to be the new
warlord."

"I'm sure they'll send someone from Staklirhod as soon as
they realize the Castella is empty."

Polo clung because he had nothing else once Principaté
Bruglioni turned up. He did not want to be sent to the Bruglioni
company. "I don't get along with those arrogant pups."

There were a lot of arrogant pups in the city regiment. Else
wished he had been able to put more of them out of Brothe's
misery.

He visited Ghort in the regimental infirmary. Ghort immediately insisted, "Pipe, you got to do something about the food
around here."

The chief physician for the regiment accompanied Else.
Else said, "This one is my number two. See that he gets the
same gourmet meals you provide those injured Deve boys in
the next shelter."

The physician in charge was Devedian. Of course.

Ghort protested, "Pipe, if you wasn't my colonel, I'd call
you an asshole and tell you to kiss me where the sun don't
shine."

"Lucky me for being your colonel, then. You'll make a point
of getting back to work soon?"

"I'm teetering on the edge of the abyss here, Pipe. With
them trying to starve me."

"If you're not available I'll promote somebody else. Bo
Biogna, maybe. He'd make a good commander for the city
regiment."

Else grinned as he moved away. He felt Ghort healing by the
moment.

There were four shelters in the infirmary compound. Two
belonged to the city regiment. Two served everyone else. The
smaller city shelter serving Devedians and Dainshaus was
crowded. Those meant for Episcopal Chaldareans, city regiment and otherwise, were not. The last and smallest shelter
served prisoners and outsiders. Else visited because Crown
Prince Lothar was confined there.

The crown prince had suffered minor injuries and frostbite.
Of his party he was the only one hale enough to resent being
on display. He remembered seeing Else before. With few

words exchanged Else became sure there was a powerful mind inside Lothar's feeble body.

He was his father's son.

"Your situation may not be as desperate as it seems, Majesty." Which earned Else a blank yet calculating look. "Make sure you're too weak to travel, though. Unless you're eager to see Brothe again."

Lothar's companions included several severely injured Praman nobles. Else supposed they were being saved in hopes of ransoming them.

The Brotherhood sorcerers with whom he had shared that table in Runch had been isolated in a dark corner. The chief physician explained, "Heavy tangles of sorcery surround those two. I haven't the skills to deal with that. So I put them where they can't cause much trouble."

"Isolation is best. Unless you have a pit to put them in."

"They'll be buried soon enough."

"Oh?"

"Neither will survive much longer. We haven't been able to feed them. They wouldn't have lasted this long without the sorcery."

"Grade Drocker will be disappointed."

The younger of the black crows, whose name Else could not recall if ever he had known it, opened his eyes. Wild and frightened, they fixed on Else. "DaSkees? What're you doing here? Where are we?" Then he closed his eyes again.

"What was that?" Else asked, hoping the hammering of his heart did not give him away.

"I don't know. He may be reliving something. Men sometimes do in the grip of a fever."

"Oh. I've seen that. Heck, I've been that sick. When I was little. You're doing a good job. If you need more resources, let me know. I can't promise anything, but . . . Spring Captain Ghort as soon as you can. I need him." He wanted to suggest that the Brotherhood sorcerers be strangled, too, but that was just wishful thinking.

"POLO. I HAVE A NEW ASSIGNMENT FOR YOU."

Polo was not pleased. Polo lived in a state of despair, now

that Principaté Bruglioni was gone. He steeled himself for the worst, dramatically.

"Come on. It isn't that awful. You'll be Captain Ghort's man, the way you've been mine. Assuming they do make me the head general."

"Sir? But, sir, who'd take care of you?"

"They've already picked Sergeant Bechter. From the Brotherhood."

"Sir? But, sir, Bechter? He's an old man. And a spy."

Else just smiled at Polo, one eyebrow raised.

"Sir, I'll have trouble getting used to Captain Ghort."

"I'm sure you will. He does take some of that. But he grows on you."

"As does mold, in some circumstances."

"Nevertheless, that's the way it's going to be. For now. You can return to the Bruglioni citadel when we get back to Brothe. If you like."

The news spread that Grade Drocker was fading and had chosen Piper Hecht to succeed him. For reasons never made clear the dying general had developed an abiding fondness for the free soldier from Duarnenia.

Else Tage was content to see the hand of the Almighty there.

The news made him the most popular man in the crusader camp. And they were, now, officially, crusaders. The Patriarch had issued the appropriate bulls.

The proclamation had no practical impact other than to underline the fact that Sublime V was determined to make war on behalf of his God.

Everyone who could get to Else immediately wanted something. Mostly they presented petitions already denied by Grade Drocker.

Else put word out that, assuming he did succeed Drocker, there would be no policy changes whatsoever. Although he was considering easing restrictions on the Deves. They had carried the heavy end of the load so far.

Else no longer had time of his own. When he did steal a moment for reflection he worried about the wounded Brothers from Runch.

* * *

THE SQUABBLE OVER THE BONES OF CALZIR BEGAN. ELSE MADE it clear, time and again, that he did not intend to become involved in adjudicating claims amongst the vultures. Those had to be presented to Sublime. The Calziran Crusade had been the Patriarch's war, though the big winner was Peter of Navaya. There was no practical means of making Peter give up what he had taken. The dust was settling still and already Navaya was a brake on the Patriarchy as huge as the Grail Empire had been.

Lothar remained in the Episcopal camp infirmary, apparently too feeble to travel. There were daily demands from his sisters, none of which got a hearing. The Imperial camp was chaotic. The sisters were having trouble enforcing their will. Though the succession was established nobody had anticipated having to live with it.

Grade Drocker threatened to make a comeback. The absence of stress proved a wondrous tonic. Else got no chance to see him during those two days, however.

SERGEANT BECHTER WAKENED ELSE IN THE HEART OF THE night. "It's done, sir. Master Drocker passed over. It was peaceful. He was smiling. He spoke no last words. He did leave letters and bequests."

"And he was alone. But for you. A whole life, come to that."

"Not exactly. Principaté Delari spent time with him. And he accomplished a great deal, for good and ill, in his life. More than most."

Else nodded. "Don't get philosophical on me, Bechter. I need you. We'll be facing a lot of practical problems, now. I don't want to have to think, too."

"You need to think about what to do with all these soldiers. Our Patriarch is the sort who would abandon them in place now that they've won his war. Also, we're starting to see desertions. There hasn't been much plunder. People have started going off on their own."

"Put this out. Any deserter who attacks or steals from the locals will be treated as a bandit. As long as the regiment sticks together it can stroll back up to Brothe and make sure that Sublime pays his debts."

"As you wish."

"Is the news out about Drocker?"

"Only Principaté Delari and we two know. Right now."

"Don't tell anyone until morning, then. Are there Brother-hood ceremonies that will be necessary?"

"Yes. But it takes more than one man to perform them."

"Can you use the men in the infirmary?"

"Possibly. I'm seldom called upon to innovate."

"You're the number one Brother, now, Sergeant. If you're like every other soldier that ever lived, you've always known how you'd run things if you were in charge."

Bechter chuckled. "You don't got nobody standing in line to bitch about you being a nitwit in them circumstances, Colonel."

"You're the last man standing."

"Uhm."

"I didn't have much use for Drocker, early on. He was too bitter. But I developed a healthy respect for him. Make your arrangements. If you need the two from the infirmary, we'll tie them into chairs while you make up voices for them."

Bechter failed to conceal his offense at Else's disrespect.

"Sorry. But you'd better use them quick if you need them. They aren't expected to last."

OTHER THAN ELSE TAGE AND REDFEARN BECHTER, AND THE critically injured Brothers from Runch, only Bronte Doneto and Principaté Muniero Delari attended the Brotherhood pass-ing over ceremony for Grade Drocker. Who had been the Third of the Thirteen Seniors of the Brotherhood of War. Osa Stile was there, too, smirking in the shadows, untouched by time. Osa had found himself a place under the cassock of the most powerful sorcerer in the Collegium, Principaté Delari.

Else murmured, "Why is Delari here?" to Principaté Doneto. Doneto seemed inclined to treat him as a peer, now. At least till Sublime chose not to honor Drocker's recommenda-tion concerning his successor.

"He's Drocker's natural father."

Else sat on that for a while.

"It isn't common knowledge. Delari was a boy when it hap-pened but already a bishop because of his family. Delari never acknowledged the boy formerly but everybody knew. Delari saw to his education and eased his entry into the Brotherhood. Where he got ahead on his own."

Else said nothing. He let the information simmer. This could be important later. Possibly very important, given that Osa Stile kept smirking at him when no one was looking.

Doneto continued, "The question now, I think, is; will Delari take you up the way his son did? You could do yourself a world of good by getting close to that old man."

Which explained the mocking glint in Osa's eye.

The ritual seemed endless. Afterward, Else could recall little about it. His part was as witness. He had done nothing but watch. In time, though, the thing was over and Sergeant Bechter found himself in an unexpected argument with Principaté Delari. Drocker had left unequivocal instructions concerning the disposal of his corpse. He wanted it cremated. He wanted his ashes scattered widespread so no future sorcerer could use his clay to instigate some wickedness.

Principaté Delari was set against cremation. He offered religious arguments but his emotional need was clear in his reedy old voice. He did not want to turn loose of this son that he had had such a limited chance to know—despite the inarguable force of Grade Drocker's fear about how his cadaver might be used.

Else stepped in with a gentle reminder to the old man that, much as they all did not like the idea of cremation, they had no legal or moral right to ignore the wishes of the deceased. They could only rouse the ire of the Brotherhood by doing so. Then he went out to supervise the return of the injured Brothers to the infirmary.

ELSE TOLD THE CHIEF SURGEON, "HE POPPED UP AND STARTED raving. He wanted to run away. He thought devils were after him. Then he collapsed. I got him here as fast as I could."

The younger brother from Runch was not breathing. The chief did something that changed that. The Brother started ranting about somebody named daSkees. Else had considered ending this risk along the way. But he had not dared. Too many potential witnesses. The camp was crawling with men getting ready to travel. No orders had been issued but rumor was rife.

Grimly disapproving, the chief asked, "And the ceremony?"

"It went well."

"Where will you find the celebrants to see these men off?"

"I don't know, Chief. That would be Sergeant Bechter's problem."

Else returned to his new quarters, tired and ready to put everything into Redfearn Bechter's hands. But he had a visitor who could not be put off.

"FERRIS RENFROW. I HEARD YOU WERE DEAD. FALLEN valiantly protecting the crown prince."

"Wishful thinking, I'm afraid. On your part as well as others."

"That being the case, is there any reason not to make my wish come true now?"

"You do have the advantage of me. I confess. Nonetheless, I think you'll find it in your interest to assist me."

"Should I send for a physician?" It was plain that Renfrow had not fared well in the events surrounding the capture of Crown Prince Lothar and had not recovered.

"Call it bravado if you like, but, no. I've actually suffered worse."

Else shrugged. "I'll honor your choice. Of course."

"I suppose I should congratulate you. You've accomplished wonders."

"I've done my job. Which is what a soldier does."

"Yes. Well. Let's not play games. I don't have that much time. I'm at your mercy."

"I'm eager to hear about that."

"Naturally."

"Well?"

"The boy. Lothar. He's here, still."

"In the infirmary. Guarded by men who'd refuse if I tried to let him go. He's worth too much."

Renfrow confessed, "Our camp is in chaos. No one wants to bend the knee to a pair of teenage girls."

"Sounds like knives in the dark time."

"Some of that may be necessary. But murder alienates people. Persuasion, arm-twisting, creation of mutual objectives work better."

Else raised an eyebrow.

Renfrow said, "That's what I want to work out here."

"I can but listen. I'm without power."

Renfrow sneered. "You're the damn warlord of the Patriarchy. And, God knows why, the fair-haired, shining adopted son of the number-three man in the Brotherhood of War, who was the secret pride and indulgence of his illegitimate father. Who, with Osa Stile whispering in his ear, will probably become your great patron in Brothen politics."

Else said, "You seem flustered. Who's Osa Stile?"

Renfrow glared. After a moment, he said, "You're so damned stubborn, you're beginning to wear me down. Osa Stile would be Principaté Delari's catamite. The one who used to sleep with Bishop Serifs."

"Ah. The boy Armand. You've lost me again."

"You're gaming. I don't want to play. Listen. If Lothar Ege should somehow slip through Sublime's fingers, the Grail Empire would be forever grateful."

"Gratitude has a short shelf life. Did it keep well I'd never have left home. And would be dead now. Fighting in the Grand Marsh will be extremely cruel. Rumor has the ice moving in fast." He could not resist retelling his imaginary history to the one man who was sure it was false.

"Enough. You know what Johannes's word was worth. You're a professional, methodical sort. You pay attention."

Else grunted a positive.

"Johannes is gone but I'm not."

"The people who interest you are in the smallest infirmary hut. There's also several there who wouldn't interest you but whose disappearance would confuse somebody trying to work out what happened."

Renfrow steepled his hands, fingertips to his lips, briefly. "So if a band of Praman commandos snatches everybody some night, the gaggle of Principatés you've got here might be mystified for a while."

"And the Grail Emperor would owe me in a big way."

Renfrow nodded. "The balance would tilt in your favor."

"You'd want to time your move. Some powerful men here have almost unrestricted access to the Night. While Imperial forces don't seem to have anything going there."

Renfrow muttered, "Go teach your grandmother to suck eggs."

"You might also work on people who're making trouble for Hansel's girls."

That startled Renfrow. He eyed Else narrowly, trying to get a handle on what lay behind that remark.

Else suggested, "A diversion might be useful, too."

"Don't get overly enthusiastic about responding."

"I won't. Given a choice."

ELSE WAS CAUGHT NAPPING WHEN THE RAID DID COME. HE had given up anticipating it. Renfrow struck only after the camp was completely chaotic with preparations to head north. At first it seemed to be a desperate Praman attempt to steal food.

Renfrow's agents had done a good job of reconnoitering. Else tucked that knowledge away for future reflection.

Three of the men captured with Lothar Ege could not handle the stress of flight. They died before the raiders cleared the camp. Likewise, two of the Praman nobles. Neither Special Office Brother from Runch survived. The raiders made no effort to see that anyone but Lothar came through still breathing.

Else was pleased with himself. He had managed that quite smoothly.

He began to look ahead, counting the days till the army reached Brothe. He had the regular courier carry a message to Anna Mozilla.

41. Back to the Dark Womb

Svavar ran in an endless blur of mantis legs, only vaguely aware of terrified animals and gaping peasants. Night fell, day came and went, night fell. Rivers and mountains appeared ahead and fell behind. A week passed before hunger and exhaustion overcame him. Only then did reason return.

He returned to his native form: Asgrimmur Grimmsson. Naked. Shivering in the cold that gripped modern Freisland year round. In his Svavar form he was not much more than the

Svavar that always was—though his senses were heightened and his mind was clearer and a little faster. And he understood that he was now vastly more than Asgrimmur Grimmsson, pirate and plunderer. He was a new form of terror entirely.

Freisland had changed. The new religion had turned the people into whimpering old women. Naked and unarmed, he still had little trouble taking food and claiming warmth and less trouble dismaying those who tried to fight him.

He flowed back into the insect shape. Terror spread like ripples in a pond. He enjoyed the fear. Grim would be in heaven in this situation. Grim had been a bully born. Svavar had had to learn to take pleasure in the fear and misery of others.

He moved more slowly as the cold deepened. The insect form was vulnerable to low temperature.

The land grew bleaker and more sparsely inhabited. Farms and whole villages had been abandoned. There was no growing season anymore.

Svavar discovered that the insect form was not the only one he could take. That distracted him for weeks, till he learned to assume a dozen more shapes, mostly useful, some just horrible. The limits of his imagination were his only constraint. Someday, he would learn to become a dragon. A huge black dragon, all fangs and fire and claws.

When he became less amused by shape-shifting play he resumed the mission he had assigned himself.

At Grodnir's Point, now uninhabited, he took the shape of a bull walrus, crossed the ice and slipped into the sea south of Orfland. The channel between the mainland and the island was narrower, now, and was frozen over. Sea level seemed to have dropped a few yards. Svavar wondered how much the Shallow Sea had dwindled.

Waters that once teemed with sea people were now almost barren. Svavar needed three days to find a colony sheltering in a cove on the western coast of a small, rocky island thirty miles out in the south Andorayan Sea. A minuscule leak of power kept the cove more habitable than its surroundings.

The power seepage felt like warm sunshine on a spring morning. Svavar had not known about the gentle pleasure the power could give. Nor how much stronger he might grow, given a chance to bask.

The people of the sea were frightened. He was the greatest power they had known. The Instrumentalities of the Night were seldom seen these days. The lesser entities were gone, fled or buried beneath the ice if they were the sort attached to a particular place.

Svavar tried to be diplomatic. He insisted that he meant no harm. He summoned a school of cod, learning that fish were scarce now, too. Then he explained, "Somewhere out on the water there's an opening into the realm of the gods. To the world of the Old Ones."

The fear of the sea people made for a long silence.

Svavar told them, "The One Who Harkens to the Sound is no more. Arlensul and Sprenghul are no more. Once I reach the Great Sky Fortress, the others will be no more as well."

None of these creatures had known any of the Old Ones. The gods of the north had not been active for centuries. Not since, Svavar surmised, a southbound band of hunters from Andoray disappeared a long, long time ago.

He was the fear the sea people knew now.

A reluctant trio of young males received the task of showing Svavar where legend told them the gateway to the realm of the gods lay. The horror the sea people called the Port of Shadows.

SVAVAR THE WALRUS ENTERED THE HARBOR OF THE GODS. Most of the water there contained the warmth of a power leak. But thin ropes of cold snaked around its surface. Everything ashore seemed soft focused, as though seen through cataracted eyes.

Svavar heaved clumsily ashore, assumed the guise of Asgrimmur Grimmsson. Dwarves surrounded him immediately. They brought clothing. It fit. He did not wonder why. Not then.

He stared up the mountain. The Great Sky Fortress looked like a distant dream lurking behind thin trailers of gossamer. The dwarves were solid enough, though. And they were afraid.

Svavar thought back. He could not recall the dwarves speaking last time. Nor could he recall much about them from the myths. They were the wondrous artisans who crafted the magical artifacts that made the legends go. If treated badly or cheated they could become quite unpleasant.

He who was widest, shaggiest, and grayest asked, "Are you the One Foretold?"

"Huh? What's going on?"

"The End of Time." The old dwarf said no more. He answered no questions. His companions were astonished that he had spoken at all.

Svavar looked inside himself for the anger. He tapped it. He began to climb the mountain. A band of dwarves followed.

The road upward was in poor shape. There were no guardians at the rainbow bridge. The bridge itself was little more than a hint of tangled color. No pure mortal could have walked it. There were no guardians at the gate. The gate was in sad repair.

The interior of the fortress seemed little changed. Gloomier, perhaps, but not insubstantial, which was true of everything outside. Neglected, though, yes. For a long time.

Svavar drew upon stolen memories to find his way around. It took just a thought to move to the hall where the Heroes had waited. Hundreds remained there now, never having gone through the dark mandala. But most were in wretched shape, missing so many parts, that Svavar's disgust fanned the flame of his hatred. He would avenge and release those pathetic cripples.

There was a feasting hall where the northern gods gathered. He could not recall how to get there. How could that be? He had to know the way. He was a god. Well, if not wholly a god, definitely a budding Instrumentality. He could step outside himself, even here. And he had other memories. He should know this fortress to the last dust mote. He had taken recollections from three Old Ones . . . Ah. So. There were a dozen more of them, as yet untouched by the disaster at al-Khazen. They were hiding. While blinding him subtly.

He materialized in the place where the Old Ones cowered. It had no evident bounds, neither ceiling nor floor nor walls. Just dark, smoky distances. None of the gods wore the guises seen in the myths of men. But he knew them.

Only the Trickster showed no fear. He believed he could talk his way out of anything.

Svavar discovered that an abiding anger was no substitute for knowledge and millennia of experience.

The fight was nasty. Not a word passed one way or the

other. Svavar withdrew eventually, godly tail between his remaining legs.

The Old Ones suffered, too. Excepting the Trickster, who stood aside. The divine family survived, barely.

Svavar took some of their knowledge away with him.

Dwarves waited at the rainbow bridge. They had reinforced it. The grizzled one who had spoken to him before advised, "Keep the centipede shape. You're hurt too badly to be human."

TIME PASSED. SVAVAR HEALED, DRAWING POWER FROM THE harbor water. The realm of the gods grew more tenuous. But the gods themselves persevered, holed up inside their hidden place.

When he recovered Svavar climbed the mountain again. He found only eleven surviving Old Ones. They were weaker. The Heroes in their Hall were putrefying. They would not suffer the bidding of the Night again. They had found the freedom of death.

Svavar realized that the Old Ones were trapped inside their Great Sky Fortress. How and why were not clear. It might be the dwarves' doing. They were the architects and artisans of the divine realm. After long ages they saw an opportunity to put paid in full to their indentures.

SVAVAR CLIMBED THE MOUNTAIN FOUR TIMES. THE STRUGGLE never went the way he expected. But he was not dismayed. Life never conformed with wishful thinking.

The Old Ones weakened evermore. Svavar fed on their knowledge. The Trickster tried to work his wiles, but Svavar remained stubbornly disinclined to make deals. There was reason to suspect that his meddling had pushed Arlensul into a position of compromise with the mortal Gedanke. Arlensul remembered. Arlensul remained resident within Svavar, in a spectral fashion, still animated by rage and hatred.

The Great Sky Fortress was a shimmer against a lowering sky. Svavar went up the mountain for the last time, but this time the rainbow bridge would not support him. The Aelen Kofer had abandoned it.

The dwarves knew the heart of the Great Sky Fortress remained real to the surviving Old Ones. But the exterior reality was tenuous. The entire realm would vanish soon. The Old Ones would be locked in an inside without an out. They would spend forever trapped inside a shrinking bubble.

Svavar was satisfied. Though his Arlensul side did crave the pleasure of witnessing their final, screaming madness.

There was no warmth left in the harbor when Svavar swam away. The dwarves had left on the golden barge already.

He had no greater goal than to find himself a warm power leak somewhere in the Andorayan Sea.

42. The End of Connec: The Return

Connecten forces evacuated Shippen after the spring storm season. They disembarked in Sheavenalle after an easy twelve-day passage. Brother Candle and the chaplain corps made the passage aboard *Taro,* the vessel they had ridden southward. Insofar as Brother Candle could determine, ship's company and human cargo were short fewer than a half-dozen men, none of whom had been slain by Calzirans. Accident and illness accounted for most of the expedition's losses.

Big changes were under way in the End of Connec. That was plain before Brother Candle cleared Sheavenalle's waterfront. He saw armed men in leather armor, never alone, going in and out of low places. They spoke harsh foreign dialects. They were employed by the wealthy families who were the real powers in a city that owed fealty directly to the Dukes of Khaurene.

Duke Tormond's vacillation, his perceived weakness, his failure to stand up for his people and the legitimate Patriarch when bullied by Brothe, had begun to yield their fall of poisonous fruit. Those hotheaded nobles and knights who had taken part in the Black Mountain Massacre, those they inspired, and the wealthy bourgeoisie, had been hiring thugs to protect themselves—initially from the predations of the

Brothen Church. But, once they had armed men available, they succumbed to the temptation to settle old scores.

Duke Tormond possessed neither the means nor the will to suppress these abuses of law, ducal rights, and the ancient peace. Not while the horrors could still be smothered in the nest. Bishop Richenau was the worst offender. He had recruited three hundred toughs during Count Raymone's absence. He insisted he needed them to punish the enemies of the Church.

Mathe Richenau was only modestly less corrupt than his predecessor. And at one time had counted himself amongst Anne of Menand's lovers.

HOWEVER MUCH COUNT RAYMONE HAD MATURED WHILE ON crusade, so had he been hardened and his confidence in himself been tempered. He returned to Antieux one afternoon in early summer. Next morning, as the sun cleared the hilltops beyond the Job to the east, he and his veterans attacked the manor house formerly occupied by Bishop Serifs, now the residence of Bishop Richenau. Outnumbered, nevertheless they routed the Bishop's bullies with great slaughter. They then fired the manor house to flush Richenau. Following a ten-minute trial the Bishop was reunited with his god by being buried alive, head down, with his desperately pumping legs exposed.

Count Raymone had not matured to the point where he understood that these kinds of messages are never understood by those for whom they are intended.

Count Raymone ordered all confiscated properties returned to their rightful owners and all Brothen Episcopal priests turned out of Antieux. Some suffered cruelly. Nobody cared. Raymone turned on those who had conspired in, collaborated with, and profited from Bishop Richenau's corruption.

BROTHER CANDLE HAD JUST SETTLED INTO THE BAKER Scarre's home when Khaurene began to buzz with rumors about events in Antieux.

The Perfect Master wept.

The time of despair, which he had foreseen two years earlier, was about to claim the End of Connec, worse than ever he had imagined.

Once he regained his equanimity Brother Candle took up the task begun in St. Jeules ande Neuis, two years ago.

The Seekers After Light, and their neighbors, must prepare for the onslaught of darkness.

43. Brothe: Last Draught of Summer Wine

Else flung himself into an exhausted sprawl on Anna Mozilla's bed. Why had he walked all the way to her place when he could have taken himself to the Castella dollas Pontellas? Where he could be wrapt in the sweet arms of sleep already?

Redfearn Bechter lacked something that Anna Mozilla did not.

"Well?" she asked. When he did not respond, she said, "I can see it was rough. Give me a hint. Did you see the Patriarch?"

"I did."

"So what's he like? Up close."

"Not what you'd expect. Shorter than he seems from a distance. He looks like a shopkeeper. Who drinks a lot. And eats too much food overspiced with garlic. And doesn't seem interested in the workaday chores of his office. There'll be a lot of corruption around his court."

"That's not hot news, sweetheart. Corruption's been the hallmark of the Patriarchy for eight hundred years. You're messing with me. Tell me."

"I got the job. I'm the new Captain-General of the Patriarchal armies. Pinkus is thrilled. Bronte Doneto and Paludan Bruglioni are thrilled. The Sayags and the Arniena are excited. Principaté Delari is ecstatic. I'm the only one who has reservations."

"That's because you think too much. Take a nap. I'll cook something special. We'll celebrate."

Else did not listen. "I've gotten too important. Too many people will be looking at me too closely. People from Duarnenia won't remember me."

Anna kissed him on the forehead. "You think too much. So real Duarnenians won't know you. Every adventurer in Brothe lies about his past. Nobody cares as long as you don't screw up here."

True. But that did not temper his unease. "And I'm worried about Principaté Delari. He's way too interested in me." That disturbed him the most. He could not work out why Delari wanted to be his patron.

"So maybe he wants to replace his little boy with a real man."

"No! It's more of what was going on with Grade Drocker, there at the end. Only more so. People have noticed. They're beginning to wonder."

"You just can't stand it when things go well, can you?"

Else let a silence grow before he replied, "They aren't going that well."

"Uh-oh. I've got a bad feeling about this."

"Yes. The Patriarch only needed two minutes to appoint me Captain-General. Then he wanted to talk about the End of Connec. Endlessly."

"He's not still? . . ."

"He is."

"People are still screaming for him to pay off his loans from the Calziran Crusade."

"That may be all that keeps him from doing what he wants. The fools who live in the Connec have given him all the excuse he needs. They murdered the Bishop of Antieux."

"That's the second one." Anna joked, "Antieux must be a very corrupting place."

Else recalled the city. "No. The problem is the men Sublime sends there. They're corrupt already. Hoping to get rich. The local count came back from Calzir and found Richenau trying to steal anything that survived our visit two years ago. So he killed him. I hear Richenau was just as ugly in his last post."

"Then this count did the world a favor."

"No doubt. But the bishop was an old crony of Honario Benedocto. With ties to the Arnhander court. Which means

Arnhand will want to punish the Connec. And the more so because this count engineered the Black Mountain Massacre."

"So Sublime hopes."

Else was surprised by her tone. "I expect." He could not focus. But he did not want to fall asleep.

"Would he appoint this felon *because* of his character? Counting on this fire-breathing count to serve up an excuse for a crusade?"

Sleepily, Else said, "I hadn't thought of that. He could do it." His eyelids had lead weights riding them.

Anna said, "Go ahead and nap. I'll fix something. . . ."

He heard no more.

ANNA POKED ELSE. HARD. "WAKE UP!"

Else sprang up, momentarily disoriented and confused and on the verge of panic.

"What?"

"You were moaning and talking. Even yelling."

"I was having a dream."

"Must've been ugly."

"Uh . . . I don't know. For sure. It had to do with when I was little. My mother . . . my sister . . ." He did not admit that he had been having these bad dreams occasionally since witnessing the destruction of those Instrumentalities beneath the wall of al-Khazen.

Nor were the nightmares unique. Others who had been there were suffering similar night troubles. Gledius Stewpo had committed suicide.

He hoped time would work its cure and the awful, agonizing memories would subside into the darkness where they had lain quiescent for decades.

He did not want those memories back. Not for a moment. There was too much pain back in the deepest depths of the past. Much better to square up to the future, work to exhaustion, and forget all that.

"Are you all right now?"

"I'm fine. I don't know why my mind started throwing this stuff up. Not much scares me. This does."

Anna reflected for a moment. "Maybe it's coming back because you're afraid you're losing your family again."

"Huh?"

"It must be awful to be kidnapped and sold when you're practically still a baby." Anna knew most of his story now. "You really attached yourself to your training school family. And now you're afraid your surrogate father and Sha-lug family have rejected you."

Else stared at her, trying to follow her thinking, hating it, wanting to counterattack, and, yet, feeling that her bolt had struck near the bull's-eye. "I'd rather not talk about it anymore. Is supper ready?"

"That's why I woke you up. It's on the table. Getting cold."

"Let's go, then. I'm famished."

THE DREAMS WERE THERE AGAIN. ELSE WAS WITHIN MOMENTS of getting a direct look at the faces of his mother and sister. Heris? No father ever entered these harsh dreams.

Anna interrupted again. Again, he came up out of sleep confused and uncertain of his whereabouts. He clutched the covers as though they would shield him from an internal bridgehead of the Night.

"There's a man on the stoop who insists that he has to see you right now."

"Who?"

"I don't know. He won't say. In a heavy accent. He claims it's important. He won't go away. So you go decide. And get rid of him fast. You've still got work to do here." She punctuated with a brazen pelvic thrust.

STILL SHAKING THE COBWEBS OUT, ELSE OPENED THE FRONT door. He expected a messenger from the Castella driven by yet another nonemergency that nobody wanted to risk making a decision concerning. Instead, the visitor was someone he did not know. "Yes? You are? And how can I help you?"

The visitor had escaped his teens not long ago, yet possessed the wary eyes of a veteran. He was handsome in a blue-eyed, Nordic way. Else noted small scars beneath his right eye and on the back of his left hand. He clicked his heels and bowed his head minutely, a noble acknowledging the accomplishments of a warlord who had risen from an inferior station.

"Ritter fon Greigor, at your service, Captain-General."

Interesting. That news had not yet been made public. Greigor had inside connections. The name and accent said Grail Empire. The inside knowledge suggested a connection with Ferris Renfrow.

"Ritter fon Greigor. How can I be of service at this time of night?"

Greigor betrayed a flash of irritation. "I've brought a packet of communications. By command." He produced a fat leather wallet bearing the Imperial seal.

Else accepted it warily.

Greigor waited briefly, as though expecting Else to read any letters and offer an immediate response. Else asked, "Is there something more?"

Again, Greigor seemed piqued. He had a superior opinion of himself. A veteran, true, but of what? Those scars might have been caused by dueling, not a war.

With obvious reluctance, the Imperial presented a second wallet. This was slim, old, worn, and bore a barely discernible crest of the House of Fracht und Thurnen, creators and operators of postal concessions throughout the Empire and much of the Chaldarean west.

Else accepted the second wallet.

Greigor said, "Responses can be presented at the Penital any time during the next three days. Then I'll return to Plemenza." He clicked heels, nodded, turned to indicate that his visit was over.

Else let him out. A coach and bodyguards awaited him.

"What was it?" Anna asked as Else locked up.

Else was sure she had eavesdropped. "Imperial mail. Not something that couldn't have waited." And maybe have been noticed by day. "That letter carrier had an exaggerated notion of his own importance."

"The sea routes from Dreanger are open again. I picked up some coffee this morning. Should I brew some?"

"That would be marvelous." He settled into a comfortable chair, stared at the two mail wallets. Nervously. Reluctant to open them because of what might lie within.

The fatter, official packet proved to contain letters from Emperor Lothar and Ferris Renfrow, the latter not surprising. That the boy was inclined to write, though, was.

The second wallet contained what Else truly dreaded. A letter from Helspeth Ege. A missive in a clear, confident hand that, he was certain, had been opened—an eventuality anticipated by Helspeth. There was little of substance in the text. An expression of abiding gratitude for his timely assistance at al-Khazen. A few words of concern about her brother's health. Gratitude for his return. Then shallow meanderings of a sort to be expected of a girl of privilege who was unaware that the rest of the world might not be privileged. The real message lay beneath the text. Its author was lonely and frightened.

The writing of the letter was a powerful message in itself.

Else cautioned himself. This was just a spurt of romantic nonsense from a spoiled child. Helspeth had heard too many Connecten jongleurs sing their ballads of love. True love was the tale of Gedanke and Arlensul. But he could not quite stifle the excitement the letter caused.

Anna returned with coffee. "What's all that about?"

"The head imperial spy trying to recruit me again. The new emperor thanking me for helping him escape. His sister thanking me for rescuing her band from the undead warriors that attacked them."

"I thought you were saving Pinkus."

"Sure. But I don't have to tell her that, do I? Anyway, none of it was anything that had to be dealt with right away." There was, of course, Helspeth's brief and indirect mention of her brother's illness. That suggested a potential for major future dangers.

"Then he had some other motive for bothering you here."

"Almost certainly."

"Because he wanted to see me? Or because he wanted to find out how vulnerable you might be here?"

"I don't know. I'm sure we'll find out. Let me finish seeing what Renfrow says, then I'll see about finishing that special task you had for me."

"Ooh! Read fast, then, lover."

Else read fast. And did not like what he read.

Lothar meant to continue the Imperial alliance with Sublime V. In exchange for Sublime remaining solidly behind the established Ege succession.

"Finished?"

He told Anna what she wanted to hear. "I've only just begun, darling." Thinking about Helspeth Ege.

FROM GLEN COOK

♦

LORD

OF THE

SILENT

KINGDOM

(0-765-30685-9)

Available February 2007 in Hardcover!

Turn the page for a preview

1. Caron ande Lette, in the End of Connec

The enemy came out of the forest on the Ellow Hills, sudden as a spring squall. There had been no rumor of their coming. Brock Rault, the Seuir ande Lette, thought they were bandits when the first handful appeared. Then his conscience threw up the fear that they might represent Tormond of Khaurene. The Duke of the End of Connec had forbidden the construction of new fortifications except under ducal charter. Unfinished Lette was just the sort of fastness that Tormond had proscribed.

Fortifications were appearing throughout the End of Connec. And caused more despair than comfort. The universal inclination seemed to be, once a man was confident of his own defenses, to hire mercenaries and become a plague upon his neighbors.

The Seuir ande Lette was an exception. Barely twenty-one, nevertheless, he had been with Count Raymone Garette at the Black Mountain Massacre and was a veteran of the Calziran Crusade. He had smelled the cruel beast War's foul breath. He had tasted blood. He loathed his family enemies but never so much that he felt compelled to gift them with terror, death, or pain.

Peace was the root of his faith, though he was a warrior born and consecrated.

Brock Rault was Maysalean, a Seeker After Light. Peaceable by belief and a heretic by declaration of the Brothen Episcopal Church. He did not hide his beliefs.

The enemy drew closer, too quickly for some peasants to get safely inside Caron ande Lette. The seuir realized that the invaders were no brigands. But neither were they much more, except in numbers. A banner identified them as followers of the Grolsacher mercenary captain, Haiden Backe. Backe operated under letters of marque from Patriarch Sublime V. He roamed the northeastern marches of the Connec, supposedly punishing heretics. In actuality, he plundered anyone who would not buy an exemption.

For his troubles, Haiden Backe received a third of the plunder, which he had to share with his troops. The rest went to the Church.

The Church was desperate for funds. Sublime had to repay loans taken during the Calziran Crusade. Any default meant there would be no loans in future. Nor had he yet finished paying for votes he had bought during the Patriarchal election. *And* he wanted to raise new armies to launch another crusade against the Pramans occupying much of the Holy Lands.

Past crusades had established Brothen Episcopal footholds amongst the Wells of Ihrian, as Crusader principalities and kingdoms. During the last decade, though, those states had been under severe pressure from the Kaifate of Qasr al-Zed and its great champion, Indala al-Sul Halaladin. Sublime desperately wanted history to acclaim him the Patriarch who wrested the Holy Lands from the Unbeliever forever. His extermination of heresy at home would finance the glorious mission overseas.

Honario Benedocto, who had schemed and bribed his way into the Patriarchy, was loathed with enthusiasm by millions.

The Seuir ande Lette turned to his nearest companion, a gray man in his early sixties. "What say you, Perfect Master? It seems the hour of despair has arrived sooner than you forethought."

The Perfect Master of the Path, Brother Candle from Khaurene, bowed his head. "I'm tempted to declare my shame. As though my coming conjured this pestilence. As to advice, I can only repeat the admonition of the Synod of St. Jeules. Let no Seeker After Light be first to raise his hand against another man. But let no Seeker strengthen evil through any failure to resist it."

Brother Candle had argued against that stance. He was a pacifist at heart. But once the synod reached its decision he set out to prepare his Seeker brethren to defend themselves. Some would destroy them rather than recognize their special relationship with the Divine.

The young knight told Brother Candle, "He'll talk first. His men won't want a real fight or a long siege. Get away from

Lette while you can."

Brother Candle stared out at the raiders. Few of them were driven by their devotion to the Episcopal faith. They were mercenaries because they could do nothing else. Without this marginally religious pretense they would be simple brigands.

More than one darkness stalks the earth.

"No stain of cowardice would attach to you, Master," Brock Rault promised. "We'd all rather that one so rare as you be removed from harm's way. Haiden Backe will offer you no respect." Rault's brothers and cousins nodded as they prepared to fight. "And you can carry our plea for help to Count Raymone."

Brother Candle went to stand alone, to meditate. To seek the best path. To discover how he could best serve. To let the Light move him.

The flesh was loath to go. The flesh dreaded what secret thoughts others might entertain if he chose flight. Yet he would do no one any good, ever, if he let himself be butchered at Caron ande Lette. The Church would crow because one of the Adversary's most favored had fallen—while insisting that it had nothing to do with Haiden Backe's campaign. Slipping the Grolsacher a bonus for having disposed of one of those pesky Maysalean Perfects.

Rault said, "I'll have a fast horse brought to the water postern."

"I arrived on foot," the holy man replied. "So shall I depart."

No one argued. A man afoot, in tattered clothing, would be ignored. The outlanders did not understand Maysalean vows of poverty.

Brock Rault engaged the Grolsacher warlord in pointless discourse. He hinted that, offered the right terms, Caron ande Lette might yield without an exchange of blows. Haiden Backe would not find negotiations unusual. Connectens seldom chose to fight in the face of superior numbers. Then Brock's youngest brother, Thurm, reported, "The Perfect Master is out of sight."

Rault grunted, gave the signal. The result would stain his

soul indelibly. But he knew that soul would return for another turn around the wheel. He did not hesitate to greet evil with unexpected evil. He had learned that from Count Raymone Garete.

Archers sprang up and let fly. Backe's standard bearer and herald fell from their horses, as did two priests in dun cassocks. A third priest, of substance because he wore armor, survived the hail but had to extricate himself from his wounded mount.

Haiden Backe flung a hand into the path of an arrow streaking toward his face. Which exposed the gap in armor under his arm. An arrow found it, broke as its head hit a rib and turned. It failed to reach his heart.

A companion snatched the reins of Backe's horse. The remaining raiders galloped away, pursued by missiles. A ballista shaft slammed through one, deep into the neck of his mount.

Only the armored priest escaped unscathed.

Brock's sister Socia, just sixteen, observed, "Sublime will use this against us."

"Of course he will. But these men, who don't work for the Patriarch, were here already, without just cause. They mean to steal our lives, our fortunes, and our good names. What else can their not-employer take away?"

Thurm sneered, "He could always excommunicate us."

Everyone in earshot laughed.

Brock said, "None of those people appear to have perished. Let's help them get to this heaven they're determined to force upon us."

Even the fallen priests were disinclined to meet their God today. One volunteered to renounce Sublime V in favor of the antiPatriarch, Immaculate II.

Brock let that one inscribe a letter confessing the Brothen Church's Grolsacher connections. He had the rest bound to stakes and left to the mercy of their deity. Within easy bowshot. Should their fellows be overwhelmed by an impulse to rescue them.

The mercenary force surrounded Caron ande Lette.

"Wow!" Socia said. Fearfully. "There's a lot of them."

"But in disarray," Brock replied. "They don't know what to do now. And Haiden Backe can't tell them."

That situation persisted for three days. Backe's underlings launched several clumsy attacks. Each failed.

Haiden Backe lost his struggle with fever and sepsis. The Bishop of Strang, the Grolsacher priest who could afford armor, declared himself Backe's successor. The mercenaries quickly expressed their confidence in the Bishop and the aims of the Brothen Patriarch. That night more than thirty resigned under cover of darkness.

Morcant Farfog, Bishop of Strang, was one of countless corrupt, incompetent bishops associated with the Brothen Patriarchy. Sublime had found that he could ease his fiscal woes by selling new bishoprics.

A rudimentary bureaucracy meant to raise funds through sales of livings, pardons, bequests, and indulgences was in its formative stage.

Sublime needed the money.

The Anti-Patriarch, Immaculate, at Viscesment, moaned and carried on but never really seized the moral opportunity. He was close to abandoning the struggle against the Usurpers of the Mother City.

The mercenaries besieging Caron ande Lette had little to recommend them. But most were not stupid. Few failed to see through Bishop Farfog's bluster. He was supremely incompetent, completely self-involved, and certain to cause fatalities amongst those dim enough to remain in his vicinity.

Desertions continued apace.

About the Author

The author of many novels of fantasy and science fiction, including the bestselling Annals of the Black Company series, Glen Cook lives in St. Louis, Missouri.

TOR BOOKS BY GLEN COOK

An Ill Fate Marshalling
Reap the East Wind
The Swordbearer
The Tower of Fear

The Black Company
The Black Company (The First Chronicle)
Shadows Linger (The Second Chronicle)
The White Rose (The Third Chronicle)
Shadow Games (The First Book of the South)
Dreams of Steel (The Second Book of the South)
Bleak Seasons (Book One of Glittering Stone)
She Is the Darkness (Book Two of Glittering Stone)
Water Sleeps (Book Three of Glittering Stone)
Soldiers Live (Book Four of Glittering Stone)

The Silver Spike
The Tyranny of the Night